Carol Townend was born and brought up in York-shire before moving to London to study history at university. She is married with one daughter and began writing full time in 1987. In 1989 she won the Romantic Novelists' Association Netta Muskett Award for new writers.

The Stone Rose

Carol Townend

KNIGHT

First published in 1992
by HEADLINE BOOK PUBLISHING PLC

First published in paperback in 1993
by HEADLINE BOOK PUBLISHING PLC

This edition published 1997 by
Knight an imprint of Brockhampton Press

10 9 8 7 6 5 4 3 2 1

ISBN 1 86019 6292

Printed and bound in Great Britain

Brockhampton Press
20 Bloomsbury Street
London
WC1B 3QA

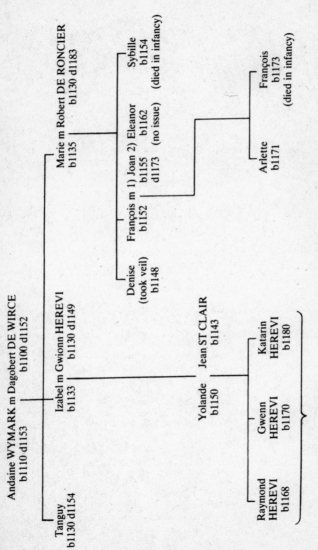

Andaine WYMARK m Dagobert DE WIRCE
b1110 d1153   b1100 d1152

Tanguy
b1130 d1154

Izabel m Gwionn HEREVI
b1133   b1130 d1149

Marie m Robert DE RONCIER
b1135   b1130 d183

Denise
(took veil)
b1148

François m 1) Joan 2) Eleanor
b1152   b1155   b1162
            d1173   (no issue)

Sybille
b1154
(died in infancy)

Arlette
b1171

François
b1173
(died in infancy)

Yolande m Jean ST CLAIR
b1150   b1143

Raymond HEREVI
b1168

Gwenn HEREVI
b1170

Katarin HEREVI
b1180

(Out of wedlock)

PART ONE

The Concubine's Daughter

A garden enclosed is my sister, my spouse;
A spring shut up, a fountain sealed.

Song of Solomon 4:12.

Chapter One

Lady Day, Spring 1183. The Port of Vannes, South Brittany.

The nightmare began on the day thirteen-year-old Gwenn Herevi disobeyed her grandmother. It was the first day of the New Year and she was going out, unaccompanied, to listen to the preaching of the Black Monk at the cathedral.

The moment Gwenn stepped onto the threshold, a dirty bundle of rags, hunched against the weathered boarding of another wooden dwelling opposite, shifted and took on the solid shape of a man. The man's name was Conan, and he was a pedlar when nothing more lucrative offered itself. Today, although he carried his huckster's tray, he was not peddling. He was spying on the Herevi household on behalf of no less a person than Count François de Roncier. He had been paid to inform the Count's mercenary captain when one of the Herevi women next went out on their own, and his wares were his cover.

Conan adjusted the leather strap which held his tray of goods in place, small eyes peering past bushy brows. Conan was not usually a man to be troubled by conscience, but the girl's appearance had caught him off guard. Seen across the narrow street, at such close quarters, she looked fresh and innocent – too fresh and innocent to be a concubine's daughter. She was tiny, a dainty creature with delicate bones. Her long gown, however, matched Conan's expectations; it was of a rich blue fabric and girdled with a plaited silk belt, both in

3

mint condition. But her face was all wrong. It did not match the sumptuous, decadent clothes.

The girl was not wearing a veil, and a glossy, nut-brown rope of hair hung over one shoulder as far as her waist. She had a veil with her, but she had scrunched the blue cloth up with scant regard for its delicate quality and had stuffed it into her belt. Conan watched as she tossed her hair over her shoulder. He crept furtively out of the shadows cast by the noonday sun, and into the narrow street. So St Clair's bastard was abroad without that watchdog of a grandmother, was she? That was most unusual.

The spring sunlight made the girl blink. Conan saw her glance back at the closed shutters and, for a moment or two, the clear light played over dusky, childish features which were as easy to read as the finest illuminated manuscript. The girl's brown eyes were warm and alive, shining with a mixture of excitement and anticipation. The pedlar watched his quarry closely. Captain le Bret must be told the girl was out and about, though Conan would rather it had been her grandmother . . .

'Hell,' Conan muttered. His tray was heavy, the straps were cutting through to his bones. With a grimace he flexed his shoulder muscles. She had no right to look so young. How queer, that the daughter of Yolande Herevi, the town's most notorious concubine, and Jean St Clair, knight, should have the face of a babe. Surprised to recognise the stirring inside him as pity, Conan squashed it ruthlessly. Pity would not give him his fee. He should leave thinking to the clerics. Pain stabbed in his guts. All he ever gained from thinking was indigestion.

Letting out a belch, Conan slid a grimy hand behind his tray and massaged his belly. The ache persisted. Perhaps he had drunk a drop too much last eve – that new wine must have unsettled him. He lifted his thick brows, and his sharp huckster's eyes gleamed. At least he could do something about that; Mikael's imported

4

burgundy cured most ailments. He would reward himself with a liberal dose.

Firmly resolved to wash all thoughts from his head, and bad wine from his system, Conan straightened his shoulders and trailed after the girl. Best to obey his orders, however indigestible. It was not for him to judge. He was being paid to keep the mercenary captain informed when the next woman left that house on her own, nothing more. How Captain le Bret and his lord chose to use that information was no business of his.

Inside the Herevi house, in the simply furnished bedchamber that Gwenn shared with her grandmother, that elderly lady had woken from her mid-morning nap. Izabel Herevi was wide awake and spoiling for an argument with her daughter, Yolande. Neither woman realised that Gwenn had slipped out and was currently scurrying to St Peter's with a dark shadow at her heels.

'Have you no shame, Yolande?' the older woman demanded, in the fluent French which betrayed her noble Breton blood. She flung her hairbrush onto her polished oak coffer with a clatter, and sank onto the stool in front of the mirror. Yolande was standing directly behind her. Izabel sent a look of calculated entreaty at her daughter's reflection which hung beside hers in the silvered glass. A treasured wedding gift from her long-dead husband, the costly leaded mirror, with its scrolled and gilded frame, was worthy of a princess; and it sat oddly in this plain cell of a bedchamber. 'Keep it from your girl. Gwenn has no need to know – knowing about your reputation, what respectable people think of you, can only hurt her. Keep it from her as long as you can. Have you no sense?'

Her daughter's green eyes were very cool. Like Gwenn, Yolande Herevi was small in stature. Everything about her was composed, and in its place. Since she was at home, Yolande wore no veil, but she was no slattern, Izabel would grant her that. Her brown hair had been loosely wound into soft, elegant coils

5

which on any other woman would have unravelled themselves into a disorderly mess, but not on Yolande. After the birth of each of her three children, Yolande had wrestled to keep plumpness at bay, and she had won. She had kept her high cheekbones, and her waist was trim. Though she was over thirty, the skin on Yolande's cheeks was as fresh and clear as a fifteen-year-old's, which was remarkable in an age where hunger or disease or overwork carried most people off before they saw forty. She used a charcoal pencil to darken her eyelashes and eyelids, and was not above using lip-balm to moisten her lips; but she looked well enough to scorn the pastes and other cosmetics which some women used. As far as looks went, Izabel was proud of her daughter. She had a direct gaze, an honest gaze which gave the lie to her notoriety.

'I did what I had to,' Yolande spoke coldly. 'It ensured our survival.'

The two women glared at each other in the cloudy glass.

In the street below, a street hawker with a trumpet of a voice was selling fish. The densely packed houses channelled the man's patter through the window and projected it into the centre of the bedchamber. Izabel listened, hauled in a deep breath and tried another line. 'Raymond had to know. I see that. He hears the townsfolk tattling. You can't conceal anything from a lad his age. But not Gwenn. I pray you, Yolande, don't tell Gwenn. Please, listen to me. She's only thirteen.'

'*Only* thirteen,' Yolande murmured.

There was profound bitterness in her daughter's voice, and Izabel knew what Yolande was alluding to. She had been thirteen when she first met Jean, but then, many were married at twelve. Out of the corner of her eye, Izabel glimpsed her own reflection and, with something akin to surprise, saw that her features seemed to have collapsed. She was showing every one of her fifty years. Her eyes had been as bright a brown as Gwenn's when she had first stared into this mirror.

Now they were faded and circled with a white rim of age. The black widow's homespun that she had worn for years was a washed-out grey. Drab it looked against the fresh green of Yolande's silken gown with its fashionable pendant sleeves. Izabel clutched at the silver cross which hung at her breast with fingers bent like crabs' claws. She looked more like an ancient nun than a widow. On one thin claw a wedding ring gleamed, but the golden band was scratched and worn, and it shone feebly. 'I wonder which of us will wear out first?' Izabel muttered, staring at her ring. She had not meant to speak aloud.

'Maman!' Her daughter's green eyes flew wide. 'What a dreadful thing to say!'

'I was referring to my ring, not to you,' Izabel laughed. 'Look, there's naught but a thread of it left. I was wondering if it would wear out before me . . .'

'It won't work, Maman,' Yolane said flatly.

'Work? What won't work?' Izabel raised a sparse brow.

'You won't deflect me from my decision by distracting me with black thoughts. I know your tactics after all these years.'

'Black thoughts?' Izabel snorted, and waved at her image in the mirror. 'Look at me, Yolande. I'm being realistic. I can't have much time left.'

'Maman, don't—'

'How did the girl called Izabel Herevi turn into that faded fool we see in the glass?' Izabel put her hands to her head and smoothed a wisp of grey hair into place, noting that Yolande had caught her lower lip between her teeth. Hiding a triumphant smile, Izabel rummaged in the coffer. 'Have you seen my wimple, Yolande? I seem to have mislaid it. I'm glad they're in fashion. They hide grey hairs so well.' And in another tone. 'Jean loves you, and it's my belief he always has. Why did he never marry you?'

Yolande set her jaw, took hold of her mother's shoulders and shook them gently. 'Maman, look at me.

7

You know he cannot because of your land.'

Izabel's head sagged. 'My land. Land I never had possession of, and never will, not while my nephew has breath in his body.'

'De Roncier. Oh, how I hate that name. Jean hopes to secure it for you, Maman. But he cannot declare his interests openly, and if he marries me that would be tantamount to a declaration of war.'

Izabel gave a weary sigh. 'You said that before.'

'Aye, and obviously it bears repeating, for you will harp on about my being an outcast, and marriage—'

'I hate to see you shamed. I want you to be able to walk about with your head held high. And now you're thinking of telling Gwenn that you're a . . . a . . .'

'A concubine, Maman? A kept woman, her union unblessed by Holy Church?'

Izabel flinched. 'You can't Yolande. You mustn't.'

'Gwenn has to face it sometime, Maman,' Yolande said, quietly ruthless. 'Time is running out.'

'And what of the babe? Have you thought of that? If you tell Gwenn—'

'Maman,' Yolande sighed, 'Katarin has almost reached her third birthday. She's a child, no babe, but still too young for it to make any difference to her. And as far as Gwenn is concerned, why it's my belief she knows already. My girl's no fool. She knows what the townsfolk call her moth—'

'Ah! Here it is!' Izabel drew out the length of coarse bleached fabric that served as her wimple, and set about covering her head. Dragging on her veil, she meticulously tucked the grey strands out of sight.

'Maman, you can't hide everything behind a veil.'

'What do you mean?'

Yolande ran a hand over her smooth, high brow. She had no proof, but instinct warned her that Father Jerome, the so-called 'Black Monk' and a consecrated priest, was connected with Count François de Roncier. 'Mother, do think. You went to Mass this morning. You must have heard the people chattering about the monk.'

'Monk?'

'The Black Monk.' Yolande set her teeth. 'The new preacher who is urging everyone to "Repent!" ' Izabel was pretending to adjust her headgear, but Yolande knew she was listening. 'De Roncier is spinning a web to trap us in. Our past is catching up with us.'

'*Our* past? Don't you mean *your* past?'

'No, ma mère, I mean *our* past.'

Izabel's cheeks reddened. 'I wish you hadn't chosen that road.'

'What other road was there?' Yolande snapped. 'You were glad enough to take the coin I brought you! If it wasn't for me you'd have rotted in a gutter long since!' No sooner had she spoken than Yolande regretted her momentary loss of control. Had guilt made her mother flush? She doubted it. Guilt was not an affliction Izabel was ever stricken with. Her mother clung to her self-righteousness as though it were a shield; and if self-righteousness was her mother's protection in this corrupt world, who was Yolande to snatch it from her? Izabel had known little enough joy in the span of years allotted her.

Izabel was gazing past her prie-dieu at that wretched pink statue of Our Lady, her lips moving in prayer. Yolande repressed a sigh. Once her mother started on her intercessions, there was no stopping her.

Yolande looked at the statue standing primly in its niche. No one would ever guess it concealed a secret . . .

The statue was not much bigger than Yolande's hand. Crudely carved from a chunk of rose granite, it was mounted on a cedarwood plinth. Izabel had placed it in the larger of the alcoves set in the wattle wall of the bedchamber. She had turned the alcove into a shrine, and unfailingly referred to her icon as the Mystic Rose. Father Mark, she said, called Our Lady by that name. Yolande thought Izabel's Virgin had an expressionless face. It did not speak to her at all, and blasphemy though it was, there were times when she wanted to smash it. It seemed to wield an unhealthy influence over her mother. It seemed . . . evil, but that must be nonsense, for how could a statue of Our Saviour's Mother possibly be evil?

The dead, granite features looked blank and empty, hideously vacant, not secretive as they should. The Virgin's sculptor could not have been representing a real woman, for the figurine did not bear the expression of a woman who had lived; instead it had the countenance of a woman who had wandered through life and escaped being touched by it. Her mother's Virgin was pure, but it was a cold purity that had no place on God's living earth. Izabel's Lady had never loved, she had never hated, or laughed, or cried. For the Blessed Virgin to have any value, Yolande thought scornfully, she had to have lived. She had to have *suffered* – as Our Lord's real mother had suffered.

Like Izabel, the statue kept the world at a distance. Yolande's lip curled. 'Mystic Rose' indeed. She'd always thought that 'Stone Rose' was more apt, particularly in view of the figurine's hidden purpose. The secret was one which Yolande shared only with her mother. For years she had kept her lover from ferreting it out. It was ironic really, how Jean never failed to mock at her mother's piety. If only he knew what Izabel's piety hid from him, and right under his nose.

It was not that Izabel was irreligious. Her piety was genuine, but piety was not the only reason she guarded the Stone Rose so jealously. Within the statue's granite heart was lodged a valuable, clear gemstone. It was not a large one, but its worth was such that it would see Yolande and her children to a safe harbour if needs be. Yolande did not want to sell the gem, for once it had gone she had nothing else to fall back on. Prudence had warned her to keep knowledge of it from her lover. It was not that she mistrusted Jean, but the fewer the people who knew about such a thing, the better. It was a secret for the women of the family, so they could protect themselves and their own. Didn't the men always see to themselves? Women had a right to look to their safety too.

A draught from the window sent a superstitious shiver racing down Yolande's neck. Instinctively, she made the sign of the cross.

In the next chamber, Katarin, her youngest, began to cry. Yolande's face softened. Katarin must come first. She'd deal with her mother later. She moved towards the door.

'If only I'd known,' Izabel whispered, 'if only I could have foreseen . . .'

Yolande froze mid-stride. 'I'm surprised you stayed with me, Maman, if it stuck in your gullet so. I always wondered why you never went back to the convent. You would have liked it there. No one forced you to stay with me.'

The veiled head jerked, Izabel's faded eyes flashed with hurt and indignation. 'You're my daughter!'

Yolande smiled her sweetest smile. 'And Gwenn is mine, or had you forgotten?'

'She's *my* granddaughter. She'll think badly of you, and of me. I pray you, don't tell her.'

'Whining doesn't suit you, Maman. And I flatter myself that Gwenn would try to understand.'

Katarin had stopped wailing. The chamber door rattled, and the child began a new chant. 'Mama. Mama. Mama . . .'

Yolande reached for the latch.

'Please, Yolande. Promise me.' Izabel's fingers clutched at the silk of Yolande's elongated sleeve.

Yolande had spent years protecting her mother from hardship and hurt, and the habit was hard to break. She compromised. 'I'll do my best to avoid telling her.'

'Swear it.'

Katarin's litany increased in volume. 'Mama. Mama. Mama . . .'

'I'll try. Ma mère, allow me to see to Katarin.' Suffocated, Yolande prised Izabel's fingers from the material of her gown, and opened the door. She seemed to have spent a lifetime failing to satisfy her mother. She was glad that her children's wants were more easily met.

In the dusty street, Gwenn noticed that the pedlar who had recently taken up a position outside her house was staring at her. She had no money, but nonetheless she glanced briefly at his merchandise. It was tawdry stuff, cheap ribbons and stale-looking honey cakes, and of no interest to her.

A half-starved mongrel cur, whose wiry white fur was worn away with the mange so you could see his ribs, sidled towards the pedlar, and sat down in the earth. His eyes were riveted on the pedlar's tray. The dog's black nose twitched, and his stumpy tail wagged, hopefully. The animal could smell the huckster's sweetmeats.

'Piss off!' the pedlar hissed, aiming a worn boot at the dog, but whether by accident or design, the animal sat just outside his reach.

Gwenn grinned. Having satisfied herself that her unauthorised departure had not been noticed, she remembered that her grandmother had drummed into her that a lady should never, never walk abroad unveiled. She twitched the blue silk veil from her belt and fastened it on. She'd be in enough trouble if they discovered she'd gone out alone, there was no point in making matters worse.

The street was busy. A peel of bells rang out the hour, and a fluster of pigeons hurtled skywards. Gwenn did not want to be late. She threaded her way through the growing crowd of people in the direction of St Peter's. The pigeons fluttered down again.

Someone grasped her arm. The pedlar. He was waving fistfuls of his garish ribbons under her nose. 'You buy, pretty lady?' the man whined in the local Breton dialect. His fingernails were filthy, and even over the stink of fish and rotting debris which carpeted the cramped thoroughfare, Gwenn could smell him, a sour, unwashed smell.

12

'I've no money,' Gwenn answered, peeping through the veil as her grandmother had taught her. She read disbelief in the pedlar's eyes and knew her clothes proclaimed her a liar. The silk her gown was fashioned from had come from Constantinople. She had a real gold ring on her finger. Only last week her mother's friend, Jean St Clair, had given it to her. Gwenn liked Sir Jean, and wondered if he was her father. But any questions she posed on that score were invariably parried. Eventually Gwenn had learned not to ask. And because she suspected Sir Jean was her father, she had worn the ring ever since. But it was true that she had no money. Up till now she'd only managed to escape once or twice on her own. Her grandmother who usually accompanied her carried the money. The pedlar's eyes were cold, they made Gwenn shiver. His clothes were threadbare and shiny with grease, and his hose had need of a darning needle. The sour stench of him was overpowering. Cursing the vanity and thoughtlessness that had made her pick out this particularly opulent dress, Gwenn shook free of the roughened hands and carried on.

Conan stared after the concubine's daughter, guilt gnawing at his innards. Why did the wench have to be so young? She could not possibly have hurt anyone. The mongrel was back, its optimistic whine a triumph of hope over experience. 'Damn you, le Bret,' Conan muttered, 'and damn your paymaster.' The freshness of the girl seemed to cling to Conan's fingers, but he was too old to start nurturing a tender conscience. His face contorted. Wiping his fingers on breeches that had not seen water since the previous spring, Conan lashed out at the mongrel. This time his boot connected with the dog's rump, and with a whimper it hopped out of range. Conan spat into the dirt, counted to ten, and then, with his eyes pinned on the girl's back, followed at a discreet distance.

Walking quickly, and happily oblivious of her shadow, Gwenn noticed the housemartins were back.

13

Last year's nests had waited out the winter, strung out under the eaves along the whole length of her route like clumsy grey beads on a string. The birds even nested on St Peter's Cathedral – known as St Per's to the local Bretons. The nests faced west, so that the martins' young, when they hatched, could bask in the glow of the evening sun. The birds' high-pitched twitterings overrode the hum of human voices below them in the street, a sure sign that more clement weather was on the way.

Ahead of her, St Peter's bell tower loomed over the untidy rows of houses. The martins were there too, high in the sky, tiny black and white arrows diving and darting over Vannes. They would be able to see the whole of the port from up there.

Once, before the stiffness had crept into her bones, Izabel had taken Gwenn to the top of the wooden bell tower. The view it gave out over the town was extraordinary, and Gwenn would never forget it. To the south, the shadow of the tower pointed towards the port. She had seen the harbour, a long, dark finger of water which shone in the sunlight and teemed with boats reduced by the distance to a child's toy flotilla. And beyond the harbour was the glimmer of the Small Sea. Nearer to hand – to north, and west, and east – Gwenn had looked down on line after wiggly line of ramshackle wooden houses hugging the Cathedral Close.

Vannes was a beehive of a town. From the vantage point of the tower, it looked as though a giant hand had reached down from heaven and squashed them together, but the hand had done its work badly, for there was not a straight line or angle in the whole town. Many of the dwellings were little more than decaying hovels, and many needed rethatching. Doors swung at improbable angles, and the sea breeze rattled shutters dangling precariously on rust-eaten hinges. All the buildings, shabby and otherwise, buzzed with activity. Most of the streets were narrow, cramped, and crooked, an unplanned cluster of alleys reeking with the stench of fish, but a few were marginally broader and grander; these radiated out from the cathedral. La rue de la Monnaie, on which Gwenn lived, was one of these more prosperous streets. She did not have far to go to reach St Peter's, there to await the preaching of Father Jerome, the Black Monk.

Chapter Two

Duke's Tavern sat across the square from St Peter's Cathedral, and trade was so brisk that the innkeeper, Mikael Brasher, was beginning to worry. His inn was bursting at the seams with unruly strangers, wine was being quaffed as though it were water, and violence of some sort seemed inevitable.

Uneasy, he scratched the back of his neck, and blinked through the smoke haze which spiralled out from the cooking fire. Over the years, Mikael had developed an instinct for trouble, and he recognised that itch as a warning signal. A bench crashed to the ground. It was not the first that morning. Someone let out a bellow worthy of a prize bull.

'More wine!' Mikael cried, grabbing a flagon and donning his most genial smile. In spite of his broad girth, the innkeeper could be as nimble as a dancer when he chose. Double chins wobbling, he slid swiftly between the rough-hewn tables to the source of the noise, and signalled to the potboy, Tristan, to set the bench to rights. If anyone in Vannes could stop a riot it was Mikael Brasher. The trick was to sniff out the troublemakers before they had time to brew up a riot. Sniff 'em out and disarm 'em.

Two men, red-faced with wine and anger, confronted each other across a table. Mikael waved the wine flask like a flag of truce between them. They were ugly customers these, their calloused hands already clawing out their daggers. They looked like mercenaries. Professional killers. Professional swillers. French mostly.

17

Scum. They drove away good, honest Breton locals.

'It's on the house!' he bawled over the din. The bellowing subsided, and an astonished silence gripped his audience. Four drink-hazed eyes locked onto the flask as though it was the Holy Grail itself. Mikael's lips twitched. His supposition had been correct. They *were* mercenaries. And the mercenary had not been born who would turn down an offer of free wine. Daggers clicked back into sheaths, the flagon vanished from his hand, and the two mercenaries flopped back onto their benches. The regular hum of conversation resumed. Mikael rolled his eyes to the rafters, and suppressed a satisfied grin. The free wine trick worked every time. It was like pouring oil on troubled waters. Jesus, but it was busier than market day, Mikael thought, squinting at the ungovernable crew filling his benches.

Tristan was at his elbow, a worried crease wrinkling his forehead. 'It's noisy, sir,' Tristan commented.

Mikael nodded brusquely. 'Aye. And hot.' He waited for Tristan to go about his business, but the lad fixed him with a peculiarly intense stare and didn't budge. 'Tristan?'

'Shall I fetch help? We . . . we're a bit short of it this morning, I think.' Again that intense, meaningful stare.

Mikael grinned and gave the boy a playful punch in the stomach. 'A kind thought, but there's no need. I'm not in my dotage yet. We can handle 'em. Go and tap that new barrel in the yard.'

Tristan gazed at his employer a moment longer, then he nodded and turned away.

The boy was right about the noise. It was reaching unbearable levels. And the lack of air was stifling. Using the cloth wrapped round his waist, Mikael scrubbed the sweat from his brow. It was not the first time that the advent of a preacher at the cathedral had doubled his business overnight, but these foreigners – Mikael grimaced – were not the usual sort. He'd take

18

his oath that they'd not a spiritual bone in their bodies. Their kind would sooner die than see the inside of a church. As for their coming to hear the Black Monk, it simply did not tally.

He edged through the door for a breather. It was curious how his regulars had given his inn a miss this morning; he hardly recognised a soul. Perhaps they had itches at the backs of their necks, too. Hardly a Breton in sight. The sweat-beaded brow furrowed, as the inn-keeper scowled up at his upstairs window. That Frenchman closeted up there had to be paymaster for the rabble below. He racked his brains for the foreigner's name. Ah! He had it now. François de Roncier. A French count.

The innkeeper cocked a weather eye at the sun. He made it to be after noon. A crowd was gathering round the cathedral porch. Now *there* were the folk he knew. He caught sight of his daughter, Irene, in her pink bliaud, her over-gown, with a basket hanging on each arm. If Irene was waiting, the monk would be spouting soon. Irene never wasted time. She was a good girl, was his Irene.

Irene had seen him standing in the doorway. She crossed the square. 'Why so glum, Father? Custom looks good today.'

Mikael smiled resignedly. 'Too good, my sweet. Too good. I'd wish them in hell if I thought it would get rid of them.'

'Father?'

'Don't trouble your head over it, daughter.'

Irene's red lips curved. 'I begin to comprehend. Your customers must be French.'

Mikael spared her a startled look. She understood more than he gave her credit for. 'They are. And I can't help wondering what devil's draught they're brewing.'

'Why do you dislike the French so, Father? I've always wondered.'

Mikael swiftly ran his mind over the countless border disputes and wrangles that had disrupted the peace in recent years and gave as honest an answer as he could. 'It's not just the French. It's foreigners in general. They're all greedy and quarrelsome. Look at the French king and English king; they fight over Brittany like two dogs scrapping over a bone. Whenever foreigners appear, Irene, you can bet your last denier that trouble isn't far behind them.'

Irene digested this. 'Why are they here this time?'

'Christ knows. Nothing springs to mind, it's been quiet of late. The two foreign kings must have been snarling over other bones.' The innkeeper shot another glance of acute dislike at the upstairs window. 'I can think of no reason for a French count to be skulking in our private chamber with his pack of hell-hounds straining at the leash.' Seeing his daughter's brows twitch together, the innkeeper hastened to reassure her. 'It's probably some petty personal feud, my sweet. Though why in God's name the nobility don't learn to keep their quarrels to themselves, I don't know. They've no cause to bring chaos to Brittany as well as their own lands.'

'What will you do?'

Mikael shrugged philosophically. 'There's nothing I can do, Irene, except put up with them, fill their bladders with wine, and pray they'll be on their way soon. Don't you fret. Run along and listen to the monk. All I want you to worry about is fetching those eggs from Stefan after the sermon.'

Irene's cheeks went the colour of a wild rose. 'I'm not likely to forget.'

Mikael grinned. His daughter had a liking for young Stefan.

'But, Father—'

'The eggs, my girl. Just remember those eggs.'

'Aye, Father.'

Fondly, the innkeeper watched his daughter walk back to the crowd filing through the cathedral porch. Like locusts, routiers never stayed long in one place. He grimaced, and wished he'd chosen a more appropriate simile. Locusts only moved on when they'd stripped a place bare.

Mikael didn't hold with fanciful notions. There was nothing for these men in Vannes. He should find it in his heart to pity them. Mercenaries were only men, flesh and blood like anyone else. Lost souls. A name sprang unbidden to the forefront of his brain. 'Alan le Bret,' he muttered. One of de Roncier's captains had answered to that name. The man must be of Breton origin. 'Alan le Bret,' he repeated, shaking his head in disgust. The man was doubly damned in Mikael's eyes; a Breton hiring himself to a Frenchman – obviously he didn't have a grain of decency left in him.

He was halfway through the inn door when, out of the tail of his eye, he saw a flash of blue. He stiffened, recognising the concubine's daughter, in her silken plumage. The girl danced up to the porch. Only last week she had attempted to befriend his Irene. Mikael did not want his daughter to mix with St Clair's by-blow, even though it was rumoured her father doted on her. Hesitating, he chewed the inside of his cheek. The maid *looked* harmless, and he was busy. The girl's veil had slipped and Mikael caught a glimpse of lively, sparkling eyes and an open, honest face. If truth be told, she looked more like a wealthy merchant's daughter than a concubine's bastard; pretty, spoilt, over-fond of silks and satins, full of mischief, but perfectly respectable. The irony of it never ceased to amaze him.

Dubiously, he eyed the girl smiling at Irene. He took a step towards them. Then he stopped. Nay. As an innkeeper he had learnt the value of tolerance, and though the child's birth caused her to be shunned by most reputable folk, Mikael would take his oath there was no wickedness in her. She went to St Peter's with her stiff-necked grandmother often enough. Let her make friends where she could.

A roar from inside the tavern drew Mikael's gaze. He sighed. He had some real riffraff to worry about this morning. At least the concubine's daughter had

Breton blood in her veins, not like most of the dregs that had drifted into his tavern. With luck it would not be long before his inn was clear of them. Mikael prayed that his stocks of wine and cider would last. He did not want to be the one to have to tell this lawless pack of thieves their fun was over.

A down-at-heel pedlar slid past Mikael, silent as a wraith, while a crusty voice bawled from within. 'Hey! Landlord! More wine!'

Regretfully, Mikael exchanged the cool air of the street for the stuffy atmosphere of his tavern, and left his musings for a less fraught day.

In the upper chamber of the tavern, Count François de Roncier was conferring in his native tongue with his two mercenary captains. His bulky frame was sprawled untidily over the only chair. A table stood before him. Le Bret and Malait, the captains in question, were perched opposite the Frenchman, on three-legged stools designed to stand firm however uneven the floor.

Captain Malait bore the clear stamp of his Nordic ancestors; a handsome, bearded giant in his third decade, he had straggling corn-coloured hair tied back with a length of sheepskin ribbon. Almost beautiful, he was far from effete, with bulging biceps that his short-sleeved tunic was unable to cover. Otto Malait was larger even than his lord, and valued because the power built into his sinews looked ready to burst out at any moment; and as the Norseman was short-tempered, it often did. This had a most salutary effect even on the more hardened routiers in his troop.

By contrast, Captain Alan le Bret – who must have inherited his dark colouring from his Breton forebears – was neat and compact, for all that he was judged exceptionally tall for one of the Breton race. Le Bret's slender strength would never have the driving force of the Viking's, but a glance at his cool grey eyes told one that here was a man who had learnt the value of total self-control. Half a dozen years younger than Captain

22

Malait, and of a more thoughtful cast of mind, le Bret was not one to mindlessly squander resources – his own, or anyone else's. Taciturn by nature, he kept his thoughts to himself, yet gave the impression that he was a man with a steel will, with hidden talents held in reserve. For these albeit very different reasons, Alan le Bret's value to the Count equalled that of the burly Norseman's. Each was a foil for the other.

The trestle table was cluttered with wineskins and goblets, and the air was thick with wine fumes. Standing at the end of the table, confronting the seated men, was a young English trooper, Ned Fletcher.

Fair of face and colouring, and taller than le Bret, the trooper had his feet planted slightly apart in an attitude of defiance. He was very young, and his cheeks were stripped of their usual bright colour, for all that he held himself as stiff as a post. About eighteen, the youth's skin did not bear scars or marks of dissipation as did the others in that room. He had the fresh-faced innocence of a healthy peasant farm lad, but his youthfulness was not the only thing that set him apart from his officers; the clarity of his blue eyes hinted that his soul had miraculously escaped contamination by his profession. Ned Fletcher was cousin to Captain le Bret, but he was defying his master, and he knew this would not weigh in his favour.

Alan le Bret glanced at his liege lord. As usual, François de Roncier's ruined hazel eyes were boring into a wineskin, but then the Count leaned forward and his florid features twisted into an expression of intense, almost petulant, irritation. Alan knew de Roncier to be a dangerous man, and the petulance increased rather than diminished the sense of danger. Alan was looking at a man to whom a whim was reason enough to kill, and the pallor on his cousin's cheeks confirmed that Ned knew this, and that he was afraid.

'Repeat that, Fletcher,' the Count asked with deceptive mildness. 'I think I must have misheard you.'

'I . . . I like not . . .' Ned cleared his throat,

'. . . the sound of this commission, mon seigneur.'

When Ned had left England two years ago with Alan, his gift for languages had guaranteed him work far from his homeland. Like most men, Ned could neither read nor write, but he spoke two languages well: his native English, and the French that nobles were wont to use whether in England or on the Continent. He was still coming to grips with the Breton tongue, which Alan, naturally, had learnt from his father.

Alan saw the Count's freckled fingers reach for the wineskin and toy with its stopper. An ugly silence fell. De Roncier let it drag on deliberately, doubtless to unnerve Ned. He succeeded. Ned's pallor grew more marked. Alan held his peace. It was not for him to interfere unless he had to. Ned had put his head in this particular noose himself. He would have to get himself out of it on his own.

At length, the Count broke the hush by tapping his fingers sharply on the edge of the table. 'You interrupt our discussion to tell us you mislike this commission, Fletcher?' The Frenchman shifted, his chair squealed a protest, and the bloodshot eyes flickered at Alan. 'One of yours, le Bret?'

Alan tossed back his blue-black fringe. 'Aye, mon seigneur. I'll have him disciplined. Fletcher, get back below. I'll see to you later.'

Alan's cousin opened his mouth to protest, but when the soft, cornflower-blue eyes clashed with Alan's, he had the sense to falter. Alan gave an almost imperceptible headshake, Ned's mouth snapped shut, he turned on his heel, and to Alan's relief his cousin's feet carried him to the door.

Captain Malait was taking no interest in the proceedings; indeed, he appeared to be sinking into sleep, blond head pillowed on his strong arms.

De Roncier teased the stopper from the wineskin and, disdaining the goblets, raised the flask. 'Malait's had a skinful,' he observed, though all of them knew that the Norseman was no more out of commission than

24

the Count himself was, for even when reeling drunk there was not a man in Malait's troop would dare disobey him.

Otto Malait's pale eyes opened. He stretched, and glanced towards the door. 'Moralisers always send me to sleep.'

To Alan's dismay his cousin was hovering on the threshold. Biting back a groan, he spoke coldly: 'Fletcher?'

Ned started, and large, haunted eyes looked pleadingly across at him. Alan tightened his jaw, and kept his face expressionless. Devil take the young fool. Not for the first time, Alan regretted bringing Ned with him to Brittany. He should have stayed home on the farm in Richmond, he was not adapted to this life. If Ned were going to succeed in de Roncier's company, he should try using his brains instead of diving into something he knew nothing about with woolly, half-formed objections. It was time he learnt to accept realities. They were mercenaries now, not peasant farmers. 'Get someone to bring up some of the local cider, will you, Fletcher?' Alan ordered, in English, with a steely edge to his voice. 'I mislike this wine.'

'Aye, sir.'

His cousin whisked out of the chamber.

François de Roncier leaned back in his chair and grinned at his captains. He was pleased they were in his employ. The Count had never known them to lose either their heads or control of the rabble below, even when they had downed a hogshead of wine apiece. They were as reliable as any routier ever was and, given that their world was one of ever-changing alliances and shifting allegiances, they had proved themselves loyal. Malait had been with him for three years, le Bret for two, and the Count was confident they would not cavil at the job in hand.

De Roncier considered his captains through a haze of drink fumes. As soldiers, he did not think there was much to choose between them; they were a different as chalk and cheese, yet they worked in harness well enough. He knew little that was personal about either man. All that mattered was that they should follow his orders.

The door gaped, and Ned Fletcher marched in, a brimming pitcher in his hand. He set it carefully on the table. 'Mon siegneur . . .'

The Count's eyes kindled.

Reading determination on his cousin's young face, Alan's heart dropped to his boots. Oh Jesus, not again. There was something, a hint only, in Ned's eyes that reminded Alan of his brother William. He too had the suicidal tenacity of the idealist.

'Fletcher,' Alan invested his voice with menace, 'get below.' Ned was a reckless fool. The ones with a conscience were always the first to the wall. Had the boy learnt nothing since leaving Richmond?

'I . . . I'm sorry, Captain,' Ned lifted his chin and continued with a baldness that made Alan close his eyes, 'but I must have my say. I . . . I do not like the sound of this commission, and I do not wish to take part in it.'

The Norseman emerged briefly from his pitcher. 'Insubordinate,' he muttered. 'Begging to be flogged . . .'

De Roncier's hazel eyes narrowed, became slits.

Alan held his breath. Ned had gall, he'd give him that, but God help him. Did he realise the enormity of his folly?

Ned stood his ground. 'Mon seigneur, I've never used my sword against women, and I don't plan on starting—'

'Use your sword against women? Who told you that?'

'The . . . the men below.'

The Count lifted a tawny brow. 'Le Bret, is this the trooper you're kin to?'

'Aye, mon seigneur.'

'Did you betray my plans to him?'

'No, mon seigneur.'

26

'You disappoint me, Fletcher,' de Roncier flicked his eyes open, a trick Alan knew had disconcerted many a more seasoned man than the one now in front of the Frenchman, 'listening to idle gossip.'

'I'm . . . I'm sorry, mon seigneur, if I misunderstood,' Ned stammered doggedly on. 'But I want it noted that I will not attack women.'

'Christ on the Cross! We're only going to frighten a couple of thieving whores named Yolande and . . .' de Roncier frowned, 'I forget the other name. Whores don't count, surely? You pick a fine time to tell me you've got *principles*!' Uttering the last word with blistering scorn, he turned his gaze on Alan. 'Do you have scruples, le Bret? Is this a family failing?'

'I've never been able to afford them, my lord.' Ned's fists, Alan noticed, were clenched white at his sides, so he must realise that the whipping post was the most likely reward for his dissent.

The Count linked his fingers, flexed them till the joints cracked, and took time to examine his fingernails. 'Can you afford scruples, Fletcher? How much back pay do I owe you?'

'Four months, mon seigneur.' Alan's cousin went red and white in quick succession as the implications of what de Roncier was saying went home. 'No, mon seigneur! Whip me if you must, but you can't withhold my money. I've earned it! I need it. My mother is ailing . . .'

Malait's hand went to his chest. 'Our hearts are breaking, Fletcher,' he drawled, eyes as round as pennies. The Viking continued to stare at the young trooper, and a disturbing light flared in the pale eyes.

Ned stuttered. 'M . . . mon seigneur, I . . . I beg you—'

'I never withhold payment from those who serve me well.' De Roncier smiled pleasantly. 'And you will serve me well, won't you, Fletcher?'

Ned's sturdy, peasant's jaw jutted. His lips parted. Alan concealed a sigh. His cousin was about to add insult to injury, and it was rather like seeing a child thrust its hands into a fire, hard to stand by and let it happen.

Alan climbed to his feet and, clicking his tongue in disgust, he clapped Ned on the shoulder. 'The way to get noticed is by proving yourself indispensible, not by threatening to withdraw your services, Fletcher. My lord has seen through your bluff.'

Ned choked, 'B . . . b—'

Alan's hand bit into his cousin's neck. Ned subsided, scowling. 'Let me advise you,' Alan went on. 'There are surer routes to promotion, and if that's your aim, I'm willing to instruct you. I could use a good sergeant.'

'But—'

'Take heed of le Bret, lad,' Captain Malait intervened, unexpectedly. Then, as though ashamed that he had broken out of his usual mould by speaking on another's behalf, the Viking flushed and beat a hasty retreat behind the flagon of cider.

Alan blinked, he had not expected assistance from that quarter. He hoped it did not mean what he thought it meant. He shot his cousin a startled glance, but Ned's innocence had in this instance kept him from noticing the Norseman's interest. Ned was not even looking at Malait.

Just then, the cathedral bells began to peal and the chamber was flooded with sound, a welcome diversion. 'The sermon's about to start,' Alan said.

De Roncier shot to his feet. 'Aye. No time for this now. Deal with your half-wit cousin later, le Bret. And keep an eye on him, will you? I want a report on his conduct. I'll support no slackers in your troop. The men are ready? They know what to do?'

'Aye, mon seigneur.'

'Very well. Get on with it. Go and mingle with the crowd in the cathedral.'

Chapter Three

The nave of St Peter's was a dim and draughty place, even when crammed to capacity. As was the custom, the people stood on the bare earth floor. There were no pews or benches.

A bony elbow dug Gwenn in the ribs. A pair of unfriendly black eyes leered out of an unshaven face, and a pungent, sweaty odour wrinkled Gwenn's nostrils. There were some rough characters in the cathedral today, with cold, hard faces. Belatedly remembering her modesty, Gwenn pulled her veil close about her as her grandmother had taught her, and shuffled towards Irene Brasher. She shivered. If only she had been more sensible about her choice of clothing. She should have worn a woollen dress instead of the flimsy blue silk. A series of frosts and thaws, damp mists and winds during the winter had caused the wooden walls of the ancient church to warp even more; draughts whipped through the cracks and whistled over the heads of the assembled townsfolk.

High in the shadows of the lofty roof, sparrows hopped along crossbeams with twigs and straw fast in their beaks, like tiny tumblers carrying balancing poles. The sparrows' nests were clustered among cobwebs that hung thick and black with the dust of ages. The sparrows, like the martins, were rebuilding for spring with a single-minded determination that no Lady Day sermon would stop. A spatter of bird dropping plummeted earthwards, and landed slap in the centre of a merchant's cap.

Gwenn nudged Irene's foot. 'A hit,' she hissed. Irene giggled. Giggles in church were invariably infectious, and Gwenn felt laughter rise within her for all that she bit her lips to contain it.

'Hush!' Jammed next to Gwenn was an elderly woman swathed in widow's garb from head to toe. She lived near the Close but was not on speaking terms with Gwenn's family. The woman was wagging a censorious finger under Gwenn's nose, and all at once she looked startled as she recognised Gwenn. 'I didn't expect to see *you* here today, girl. Get out, if you've sense.'

'Shhh! Shhh!' someone quieted the woman and a coarse, male voice barked out a word Gwenn had never encountered before, not even from her brother Raymond, but instinctively she knew it was more suited to a tavern than a holy place. The widow went the colour of ripe strawberries and her snowy wimple shook with fury. She shot Gwenn one final, warning look and sealed her lips.

Gwenn was wondering if the woman's agitation at her presence was due to her being out without Izabel, when a movement in the choir caught her attention. 'Look, Irene.' She pointed, and Father Jerome, it could be no other, stalked through the vestry door and into the transept. His dome of a head was held high, his eyes shone with conviction, and his countenance alone was fierce enough to put the fear of God into all who looked upon him. Gwenn exchanged glances with Irene, and the woman's strange warning went right out of her head. She was used to the comfortable friendliness of Father Mark, the local priest. Father Jerome did not look comfortable, nor did he look friendly. He exuded power. He looked more powerful even than the bishop, and he was not at all what Gwenn had been expecting. The Black Monk looked – she searched for the word – warlike.

Like most of the throng in the nave, Gwenn had been drawn to the church because the monk's reputation had preceded him. A member of the Benedictine Order, and addressed as Father rather than Brother because of his position as a consecrated priest, Father Jerome was famed for his powers of oratory. Today, as part of the Lady Day celebrations, he was condescending to speak in the Breton tongue, so all would be able to understand him. It was a rare privilege to be permitted to understand a man of the Church. Most services were held in Latin, God's special language. Churchmen spoke, and wrote, in that exclusive tongue, and the simple folk were not expected to understand it. Gwenn was reasonably familiar with Latin because she had sat in on Raymond's lessons, but she and her brother were very unusual in this. Normally, understanding was reserved for the highest orders. People attended church for fear of God, or because it was expected of them, or because it was a good place to meet their friends. In Vannes the townsfolk were drawn to the cathedral because they loved Father Mark.

When it became known that Father Jerome was prepared to spread God's word in the language of the people, the townsfolk had been intrigued. It did not matter that he was reputed to be uncompromising and hard on sinners. He was going to speak in Breton – in their own dialect. Gwenn had been looking forward to hearing what the Benedictine had to say, but now that she had seen him, and noticed the unfriendly looks on the faces of some of the congregation, doubt stirred within her.

Tall and stately as a king's champion, Father Jerome gathered his habit into his hand and strode onto the platform. It was odd seeing him in Father Mark's place, odd seeing his fierce eyes glare at the assembly when Father Mark and their own bishop usually smiled gentle blessings on everyone. Father Jerome did not look like a man who would understand the common failings of the congregation. He did not look like a man who would understand the meaning of the word mercy, or, for that matter, like a man who would forgive people their sins. Gwenn felt depressed, and though it was ridiculous, she felt as though Father Jerome had stolen the joy out of the day. He looked like a man who would steal the joy from everything.

No one in the crowd was moving. Would they dare? No one so much as coughed. Father Jerome's eyes shone like lamps over the people of Vannes. A sparrow chirped from its vantage point on a crossbeam, and a spasm crossed the monk's severe features. Despite Gwenn's growing sense of unease, an irreverent thought bubbled up. Rather than blessing the birds of the air, Father Jerome would have that sparrow in a pot for daring to spoil his performance.

'Brothers and sisters,' he began, 'we are gathered here on the day that Our Lady received the glad tidings from the Angel of the Lord . . .'

Gwenn did not like the monk's voice any more than his face. It was high for a man of his build and stature, high and scratchy; but she had to acknowledge it was penetrating, which for a preacher was no doubt a good thing. And with those beacons instead of eyes . . . Doubtless Father Jerome had chosen the right vocation, but Gwenn did not want to waste a promising spring morning listening to him. And the air, there was not enough air in the nave for all these people.

Gwenn looked at Irene, who ignored her. Her friend was already in the monk's thrall.

'Blessed art thou among women . . .' Father Jerome intoned.

Craning her neck, Gwenn tried to see how far the crowd had jostled her from the door. There was nothing new in what the monk was saying. She'd known the Hail Mary by heart since she was small; her pious grandmother insisted she recite it several times a day.

The door was wedged open, and bright, spring sunshine was lighting up the disgruntled expressions of several latecomers who were pressing into the nave. Why was everyone looking so dour this morning? It was almost as though they were frowning at *her*, so many of them seemed to be looking in her direction. With a sinking feeling, Gwenn scrutinised her neighbours' faces. With the exception of Irene, and the wimpled widow who was studiously ignoring her, they *were* frowning at her. Feeling stifled, Gwenn took a deep gulp of the rank, sweat-laden air. She caught sight of the same cold, dark eyes she had seen when she had first entered the nave, and a wave of nausea swept through her. She would have to get out, into the fresh air of the Close.

The strident tones resounded from the pulpit, 'I have come to you today, brothers and sisters, because it has been brought to my attention that here, residing in your town, are women whose presence brings shame on you all. Women whose very existence is an insult to that most blessed of women, Our Saviour's Lady Mother, whom it is our duty to honour on this her feast – Lady Day.' Father Jerome leaned on the lectern and paused, for effect.

Gwenn began pushing to the door. She did not like the sound of that. She would not listen to another word. She would wait out in the sun and speak to Irene after his sermon was over. She'd not have her new friend being gulled by a man like that. Quietly, she left the church.

Leaning her back against the south wall of the cathedral, Gwenn closed her eyes. The sun was warm on her skin, the air blessedly fresh. The house martins twittered in the eaves, and Father Jerome's scratchy voice was muffled to just a low, distant drone. Gwenn focused her mind on the martins, and drifted into a pleasant daydream.

A sharp cry jerked her back to reality. She strained her ears and heard the sound again. 'Get 'em out!' Gwenn frowned. That cry came from within the cathedral. Surely even Father Jerome would not permit . . . ?

'Out! Out! Out!' The chorus of harsh voices came

from the vicinity of the choir. A strange sermon, this.

'Purge!' someone screeched.

'Purify!' cried another.

The shouts floated out via the west door, the one Gwenn had left by. She ran her hand – it was trembling – along the rough grain of the wood until she found a knot-hole in the wall. Applying her ear to it, she could hear the congregation shuffling and mumbling inside. It was sounding more nasty by the minute.

A man's screech overrode the general mutterings. 'They're naught but leeches.'

'Aye!' A woman's dissonant howl took up the cry. 'Leeches! Get rid of 'em. They prey on our men. They seduce them onto the Devil's path, and rob them of hard-won silver. What does that leave for *honest* women?'

'Kill! Kill! Kill!'

'Brothers! Sisters!' Father Jerome shrilled over the swelling clamour. The hole in the planking did not permit Gwenn to see the monk, but she could visualise him, holding his thin white hands up for silence. 'The Church cannot condone murder. We must endeavour to turn our erring sisters back onto the True Path. We must purge them of their sins.'

'Nay, Father. Get rid of them!'

'Cast them out!'

'Aye. God cast Adam and Eve out of Eden.'

'Out! Out! Out!' An ugly chanting began. Where was kind Father Mark?

The hairs lifted on the back of Gwenn's neck, and her senses sharpened. She was being watched. Straightening slowly, she backed from the wall. The air in the Close seemed to pulse with menace.

One of the youths who had been squeezing into the porch had come back into the square. He was tall, with shining flaxen hair grown below his ears. He was slender, and perhaps a couple of years older than her brother, Raymond. He wore a sword. A sword? Surely he should not have been wearing his sword in God's house? As Gwenn stared at him, her mouth went dry. Was he the source of the evil she felt? He did not look evil. His leather military tunic looked wrong on him. He was surely a handsome young farmer wearing borrowed attire. A sheep in wolf's clothing? She hesitated.

'Get away, girl! Run!' the young man hissed, in heavily accented French. He waved his arms frantically in her direction.

He could not be talking to her . . . Astonishment pinned Gwenn to the spot.

'Get away!' he repeated, and his blue eyes seemed to be pleading with her.

He had kind eyes. He was not evil, Gwenn decided, not with eyes like that. Definitely a sheep in wolf's clothing. But with his soldier's gambeson, and his sword, he must be a mercenary. If the sense of threat had not emanated from him, from whom had it come?

The fair youth glanced over his shoulder into the porch, and when he looked back at her, his face registered desperation. He meant her no harm, but the air was thick with evil, Gwenn could all but see it.

'Run!' the young man begged. 'Run!'

The urgency in his eyes communicated itself to Gwenn, but before she had time to move, someone else stepped out, and this man also wore a padded military gambeson. 'What is it, Fletcher? Found something interesting?' the newcomer asked in a bored voice.

'N . . . no, Al . . . I mean, Captain le Bret. Only a girl.'

'A girl, eh?'

The man named le Bret looked at Gwenn, and the heat went out of the sun. His hair was thick and dark, long for a soldier like his companion's, and swept back to one side. His skin was swarthy. He had steely grey eyes, and the sardonic lines etched into his face told Gwenn that here was a man who looked at the world and found nothing in it that was pleasing. He was unshaven and in need of a wash. He terrified her.

Alan found himself scowling at a small doll of a girl,

35

dressed up in a blue gown that the Duchess Constance would have been proud to call her own. 'Fletcher,' he rubbed his chin, 'it's the one. She answers the pedlar's description.'

'Let her go, Al . . . Captain!' Ned gabbled. 'Look at her – a child. She can't be involved.'

Alan felt a stir in the porch behind him. The zealots were about to break out, and the girl did not seem to be aware of the danger she was in. With an oblique smile, Alan bent to pick up a stone. Ned grabbed his sleeve. 'You're impertinent, Fletcher.' Coldly, Alan shook his cousin off, his tone a reminder of the differences in their status. 'As it happens, I agree with you. That's why this,' Alan took careful aim, 'will see her on her way and out of danger.' The stone flew across the square, and hit the girl square in her stomach. Alan heard her whimper, but his stone had served its purpose and goaded her out of that perilous immobility, for she picked up her skirts and turned tail, running like a doe in the chase.

The stone had been flung none too soon, for no sooner was she darting towards the maze of streets than the vast oak doors burst outwards.

'Here come the hounds,' Alan murmured as the townsfolk charged out of the cathedral. 'Good, honest men all.' His lips curled. His men had done their work. He waved them to one side. There was no need for them to waste wind chasing the girl. The good people of Vannes, whipped up by Father Jerome, would see the task completed.

It had been one of the easiest commissions he'd taken on. Who would have thought that it would take so little to stir peace-loving townsfolk into a frenzy? All he'd done was station a man here and there in the crowd and have them call out the odd phrase or two of encouragement. A shout here, a shout there, and their work was done. Naturally, as excommunicate mercenaries, none of them should have put a toe past the threshold of the church, but the congregation had been so taken

36

with Father Jerome that not one of them had noticed. And if they had – his scorn grew – none of them would have had the backbone to object.

He propped a strong shoulder against a painted angel on a carved porch pillar. 'Look, Fletcher, all we have to do is sit back and watch. The God-fearing townsfolk will finish the job. It couldn't be better. De Roncier won't be implicated. He'll be delighted. And to think they miscall us—'

'I'm disgusted.'

Alan had never seen Ned look so miserable. Smiling, he shook his head. 'That's humanity for you, my lad,' he said, not unkindly. 'We're all rotten when it comes down to it. We all have our price.'

But his cousin stood dumb at his side, staring after the girl. Alan saw him swallow. There was a flash of blue, brief as a glimpse of a kingfisher, and the girl disappeared round the corner.

A howl went up from the mob that had lately been a pious congregation. 'There! Did you see?' A man pointed.

'What? Where?'

'That's Herevi's daughter! The whore's daughter!' The crowd surged down the street, trawling for missiles as they went.

Ned understood that guttural Breton all too well, and his hand inched to his sword hilt.

Alan sighed and moved to block his way.

'But the girl, Alan!' In his anxiety, Ned had forgotten his cousin was his commander. 'They'll tear her to shreds!'

'I think not. She looked fleet, and she had a head start.'

'I want to make sure she's safe.'

'You make one move after her, Edward, my lad, and I'll see to it you forfeit every penny de Roncier owes you.'

Alan took Ned's slack-jawed look of disbelief without flinching. 'You b . . . bastard!' Ned got out, tripping over his tongue. 'You bastard!'

Alan shrugged. The more enraged Ned became, the easier it was for him to maintain his distance. Long ago, Alan had discovered that an ability to remain unmoved in the face of other people's anger was a great strength. 'Aye,' he agreed blandly, 'and you'd do best to remember that.'

The anger was slow to fade from Ned's face. 'My mother told me you were like this,' he said when he had calmed enough to speak coherently, 'before we left England. She was against my going with you. But I admired my clever older cousin; I was envious of the skills your father had taught you, and longed to be as deft with the sword. God help me, I longed for your sang-froid. I looked up to you, and I thought my mother was wrong. I took your coldness for a mask which you chose to hide behind. But my mother was not wrong, was she, Alan? It's more than a mask. It goes right through.'

Alan simply looked at Ned.

'Jesu, Alan! You've a heart of stone!'

Alan let a corner of his mouth twitch upwards. 'But I survive, Ned. And that's the beginning and the end of it.'

Ned snorted.

Alan turned on his heel. 'It's time we left, before St Clair hears of this. De Roncier doesn't want a full-blown war on his hands. For God's sake, pull yourself together, Ned. You've the makings of a good soldier if you don't let your emotions master you.'

Though Alan would never confess it, he was relieved this distasteful business was concluded. With luck the townsfolk would scare the women witless, and they would fly Vannes. He wondered what they had done to incur de Roncier's wrath; but when a few moments' thought did not throw up a satisfactory answer, Alan fell to wondering what his next commission would entail. He hoped it would be a good, straight fight. He'd do anything as long as he was paid for it – he

38

was a professional – but affairs like this left him with a sour taste in his mouth for all that he affected otherwise. Privately, he agreed with Ned, it *was* a shabby affair. They had been setting a mob on a defenceless girl. She'd be bound to outrun them, but whatever angle you viewed it from, it remained a dirty business. He rubbed the bridge of his nose. A good, straight fight, that's what he wanted. There was nothing quite like pitting yourself against an equal and winning.

A happy thought came to him. 'Fletcher?'

'Sir?'

'Didn't the good monk say today was Lady Day?'

'He did. What of it?'

'Lady Day is a quarter day.' Alan signalled to his men to fall in behind him.

'Pay day!'

'Quite so. Remind me to have a word in my Lord's ear. We can't have de Roncier neglecting his obligations when we're so efficient, eh?'

'N . . . no, sir.'

With Ned toeing the line again, Alan turned his mind to de Roncier. De Roncier had a bad name when it came to paying his dues, and when Alan had enlisted with Ned, he knew there was a chance they might never get paid. But work for inexperienced soldiers was hard to find, and when they'd *both* been accepted, he'd jumped at the chance, being unwilling at that stage to leave young Ned to fend for himself. Alan might well have become a cold-blooded mercenary, as his cousin claimed, but of all de Roncier's officers he prided himself on the fact that he saw his men got paid first. Impatiently, Alan pushed Ned's disapproval to one side. Ned could do a lot worse, and he knew it.

Gwenn pelted down the full length of la rue des Vierges in an attempt to shake off the mob, but she could still hear them and knew that she had failed.

It was the worst of nightmares.

Burned into her brain was the image of the dark

mercenary bending to scoop up the stone. Over and over in her mind's eye she saw his cold eyes narrow as he took aim. The bruise on her stomach throbbed in time with the thumping of her heart; but despite this proof that this was no nightmare but grim reality, Gwenn's disbelieving mind was frozen with shock. She could not believe that this was happening to her. Why should someone she had never seen before set a mob on her? Why? The question echoed back and forth in her head.

Fortunately, her legs worked independently of her stunned brain, and Gwenn flew to the crossroads where la rue des Vierges and la rue de la Monnaie met. Her veil slipped from her head. She left it behind. She ran on up the street towards safety. She slipped in some mud, lost a shoe, and staggered on without it. Never had the street seemed so long before.

Clutching her chest to keep her heart from bursting, Gwenn skidded to a halt and dragged in a lungful of air. Ten dwellings away, her mother's house beckoned. Safety. Gwenn balked. Safety? Frozen no longer, her thoughts whirled. What was she to do? Lead the mob to the doorstep of her home? What would they do if they followed her there?

It made no sense. None of this made any sense. There had been people she knew in St Peter's, people who yesterday, while they had not been friendly, had at least exchanged the time of day with her and her grandmother. Why was this happening? Why? If Father Jerome's words had wrought this change in the townsfolk, then his words must issue from the mouth of the Devil. This was not the work of God.

Gwenn sucked in another lungful of air, and glanced back the way she had come. 'Sweet Mary, let them not have seen me come down this street.' And then her heart leaped into her throat, for her veil was fluttering from a nail on a post, as bright and brash as a knight's pennant at a joust. Her blue silk slipper betrayed her too; it sat glowing like a jewel in a dark muddy patch.

She couldn't have left a more obvious track if she'd tried. She must retrieve her possessions before they were seen.

Two people hurtled into view. There was no sign of the soldier who had thrown the first stone, but an exultant howl rose on the warm spring air. 'The whore's bastard! Get her!'

More people appeared, and more. They stopped at the head of the street. They looked at her. They seemed to be waiting, and all the time more of them came, and more, like floodwater building up behind a beaver's dam that must give way at any moment.

Gwenn let out a whimper and was off again. No time to retrieve either veil or shoe. It was too late anyway, they'd seen her. No time to think what they'd do when she got home. She must run, run, run. Something stung the back of her head. She ignored it. Something struck her shoulder. She missed her footing. All but blind with panic, Gwenn found her feet and charged on.

'Run, Gwenn! Run!' Her brother's voice! It came from somewhere in front of her. She raced towards it, sobbing with relief. 'Run, Gwenn!' Raymond was at her side. She could not see him clearly for a dark mist clouded her vision.

It was raining missiles. One of them smacked her cheek. Raymond must have been hit too, for the blood was streaked across his temple, and his wavy brown hair was plastered with mud. Two years her senior, Raymond had long legs. She would never keep pace with him. But Raymond had her by the arm, was dragging, pushing, shoving.

'Raymond!' Gwenn managed to screech. 'They're on us!'

'Save your breath! Inside!' Wrenching the door wide, Raymond bundled her inside. The door crashed. Three heavy bolts rammed home. Gwenn's legs gave beneath her and she fell gasping onto the floorboards. The dark mist was thicker, and starred with white dots.

Izabel had been setting pleats in a chainse – a shirt – in the light inside the doorway. 'Whatever is it? Gwenn, where have you been? What's amiss?' she demanded querulously, throwing the snowy linen aside.

Gwenn looked up as her grandmother floated towards her through wave after wave of starry blackness. The starry blackness began to drift up and down in front of Gwenn's eyes, like a curtain waving in the breeze. 'Blessed Mother—'

'No swearing, Gwenn.'

Gwenn choked down a bitter laugh. Did Izabel not realise? Something heavy smashed against the door, bowing the planks inwards. Yelping like a scolded cat, Raymond jumped backwards.

'The shutters!' Gwenn scambled onto legs of jelly. She lurched for the window. Wrenching the shutters to, she dropped the bar in place, and plunged them into a shadow world.

'What's the matter?' Izabel demanded. 'What's happening?' And on another note, 'Just look at the state of you!'

'Oh, Grandmama . . .' The hinges rattled, freezing the words on Gwenn's tongue.

A white-lipped Raymond was wrestling with the linen press, which he dragged in front of the door. 'That should hold them, for a while.' He attempted a smile, but the green eyes that were his legacy from his mother were not warmed by it.

'What have I done?' Gwenn groaned, as the reality of their plight dawned on her. Was the mob out at the back too? If so, they were caught like rats in a trap. 'Sweet heaven! I led them here! I've brought them home!'

A missile crashed against a shutter. A rock? A stave?

Izabel's face was still, her eyes bulged, as she watched the shutter bounce under the impact of another blow. 'Who, dear? Who have you brought home? Gwenn, what have you done?'

'Done! Blood of Christ, Grandmère, Gwenn's done

nothing!' Raymond exploded. 'It's that prattling priest who's to blame!'

'I brought them here!'

Stiffly, for her bones ached liked the plague, Izabel went to put her arm round her granddaughter. 'Oh Gwenn, why did you go out alone? I told you – why, you're shaking.'

Gulping down a sob, Gwenn did her best to explain.

Izabel listened, and the blood drained steadily from her withered cheeks as Gwenn's tale drew to its appalling conclusion.

'But why should anyone want you stoned?'

'They want to frighten me, Maman,' Yolande declared, coming down the stairs. Katarin was balanced on one hip.

'You, Mama?' This from Raymond.

Nodding, Yolande set her youngest down and put a gentle forefinger to the congealed blood on her son's temple. She looked immeasurably sad.

'But why, Mama?'

A man had followed Yolande downstairs. He stood in the doorway listening. The man was upstanding. He had a young-looking body, fit and strong, but the lines round his eyes and the grey strands which threaded through both hair and moustache betrayed him to be in his early forties. 'Your kinsman Count François de Roncier's been sowing seeds, if I judge it aright,' he said tersely.

Gwenn's head shot up, and she stared into dark brown eyes that mirrored her own. The eyes were angry, burning eyes, like a banked-down fire which was likely to flare up at the slightest draught. 'Sir Jean!' Climbing to her feet, Gwenn made a valiant attempt to curtsy, her legs wobbling. 'I'm sorry, sir. I . . . I didn't mean to bring them here.'

Jean St Clair put his hands on his daughter's shoulders and smiled gently at her. 'Don't apologise, Gwenn. Where else would you come but to your home?'

43

Gwenn realised his fury was not directed at her but at those who might have harmed her, and at himself for not foreseeing this. It had gone ominously quiet in the street.

'Shouldn't they have got in by now, sir? I thought they would have had the door down in no time, they were baying for blood. What's keeping them?'

The knight took Gwenn's elbow and steered her to the window. When he reached for the shutter, she flinched and strained back. 'All's well, Gwenn,' he soothed, and flung back the shutter. 'I have men out there. Look. No one's going to break in.'

Four men-at-arms wearing St Clair's red and green colours ranged across the street. Their tunics might be shamefully moth-eaten, the dyes might be faded, but the March sunlight sparkled on carefully polished steel. Facing them, at a distance of not more than two yards, was the crowd. They were silent, and now that they had been robbed of their prey, they looked sullen. The heat had run out of them, like water from a sieve. Some stood awkwardly, guilt etched into their features, while others sneaked away, shamefaced.

'See, Gwenn, how four can hold back an army,' St Clair boasted with a tight little smile.

Yolande came across and took her daughter in her arms. 'It's over. Over and done with.'

'Is it, ma mère?' Raymond murmured, with meaning.

Yolande eyed Izabel. 'Maman, please take the children upstairs. There's water in the ewer. They've mud in their hair, and Raymond's cheek needs attending.'

'It's not mud, Mama,' Raymond said. 'Can't you smell it? It's fish entrails and horse-sh—'

Izabel's age-spotted fingers stopped his mouth. 'Hush, Raymond. Your mother's right. You look like a pair of beggars. Upstairs with you both.' She held her hand to Katarin, and the toddler scurried towards her.

Raymond thrust out a lip above which a fuzz of

adolescent hair was evident. 'I'm not a child. I'm fifteen.' But nonetheless he permitted his grandmother to shepherd him towards the stairs. Gwenn followed.

Yolande kept up the calm pretence until her mother and children were out of earshot. 'How could you, Jean? How could you? You keep your ears to the ground. You must have got wind of what de Roncier was planning. You know what Gwenn's like. Why did you not warn me to keep a particularly sharp eye on her?'

Jean flushed. 'Father Jerome keeps a sword where other men keep their tongues. I did warn you—'

'Warn me?' Yolande's voice cracked. 'All you said was that if you were me you wouldn't let her fill her ears with the monk's nonsense. You didn't tell me our daughter would be risking her *life* if she ventured onto the streets!'

Jean moved towards Yolande, hand outstretched. 'Yolande, I'm sorry. I swear I didn't realise the extent—'

Yolande batted the hand away. 'Liar! You knew. You suspected something was going to happen. Why else bring your men today?' She read her lover's silence as guilt. 'Holy Mother, you *did* know!'

'No. No. I misread the signs.'

Yolande took a pace or two round the chamber while she fought for calm. 'We shall have to leave.'

'Eh?'

'Leave.'

'But Yolande—'

She spun round, green skirts swirling. 'I insist, Jean. The sooner the better. I won't stay in a town where the people terrorise thirteen-year-old girls!' Glaring at the knight, and gripped with a clear, cold fury, Yolande wondered whether she could persuade him to take them to his manor at Kermaria, a small hamlet to the west of Vannes. She had put up with the little town house while her family had been safe, but now that the Benedictine had infected all Vannes with virtue, that had

45

changed. She swallowed down her bile, wise enough to realise that she did not want Jean on the defensive. An enraged man never gave a woman anything. 'I've had enough of this life,' she said, testing the waters. 'You have to choose.'

'Choose?'

Yolande ground her teeth. Those innocent brown eyes looked warm as melted honey, but they didn't blind her for a moment. Her lover was playing for time. 'You know what I mean. If you don't decide soon, by the Rood I'll decide for you!' She had always been generous with her love, never withholding it from Jean despite the fact that he had not married her as he had promised. It was not that Yolande questioned his love for her. No, she was certain of that, but she suspected that his love was out-ranked by his ambition. It was vaulting ambition that had kept him from marrying her all these years. She must play the concubine while he affected to chase after a Frenchwoman. He had it all planned out. He had maintained that he never intended to marry Louise Foucard and Yolande had believed him. He would not marry the Foucard woman, not while marrying Yolande Herevi might bring him better gains. If Izabel's old claim to the family lands were ever ratified, Yolande would be worth her weight in gold. As ever, Jean kept his feet in two camps.

He jerked his grizzled head towards the ceiling. 'Do the children know?'

'Know what? That they're yours? That they're bastards,' her lover flinched, 'and that, though you swore you'd marry me years ago you've not honoured that promise? You made me what I am, Jean, and now . . . now I begin to think you're ashamed of me.'

Jean reached out a finger and gently touched her cheek. 'Not ashamed, love, never that. Politics have dictated my actions. The time has not been ripe.' He lowered his eyes and twisted at the ring which adorned the little finger of his left hand. 'If only Waldin would retire from the lists.'

46

'Your brother?' Yolande snorted. 'The moon will turn green before that happens. Everyone knows how the great tourney champion Waldin St Clair is married to the lists. He'll not leave the circuit till age or infirmity drive him away.'

Mournfully, Jean agreed, 'I know,' he brightened, 'but when he does retire we could use his name to drum up support. Men might not like to ally themselves with a poor knight, but with Waldin at our side . . .'

'Sometimes,' Yolande murmured softly, 'I wonder if you are afraid.'

Jean shot her a sharp look, bridling, but her smile disarmed him, as she hoped it would. To Yolande, and Yolande alone, Jean St Clair could confess to fear. His shoulders drooped. 'Who would not be afraid? As a mere knight I've never had the manpower to uphold your mother's claim to her inheritance. De Roncier would have wiped us out before we had begun. No, love, I believed it to be safer for you and the children if he thought you were no threat. As my mistress you pose no threat. As a wife who could provide me with a legitimate male heir, an heir to those lands of your mother's, it becomes altogether a different kettle of fish.'

'So I believed, until today.' Yolande drifted away from him. 'Have you heard the latest gossip concerning your Frenchwoman?'

'La belle Louise?' He grinned, and smoothed his greying moustache. 'You're not jealous? I thought you understood I've been ingratiating myself with her family in order to lull de Roncier's suspicions. If he believes I am considering an alliance with the French, he'll not harm you. Come, sweet. Don't be angry. You know I'll never marry her.' He directed a smile she recognised as one of his best at her.

'Why do you think he took it into his head to loose his dogs on Gwenn?' Yolande asked, eyeing him closely.

'I'm blessed if I know.'

'Perhaps he heard that Louise has got tired of waiting and has married another.' That was the rumour that was flying round the town.

He stared, moustache drooping, face ludicrous with dismay.

Yolande had to laugh. 'It never occurred to you, did it? You never stopped to think that your French flower might not wait for ever. You've been dangling her on a string for years. Of course, it might not be true, but my source was good.'

'Source?'

'Father Mark, who married her.'

Jean's eyes looked cloudy and confused. 'Christ, I go away for a week's hunting and look what happens. She kept that dark. I thought she'd wait.'

'Such arrogance needs humbling, my love.'

'So that's why he moved today,' Jean murmured.

'Don't test *my* loyalty to the limit,' Yolande warned. 'Don't be certain I'll wait for ever. I, too, may get tired of waiting.'

He ran a hand through his hair. 'Nay, love. What of our ambitions?'

'*Our* ambitions?' Yolande knew her laugh was brittle. 'The only ambition I have ever had is to be able to tell my children, and my mother, that I am your lawful wife. With all my heart I wish that our children were legitimate, but it would take a Papal decree to accomplish that.'

'Do they know I'm their father?'

'No. Aye. Oh, I don't know. Jean, my life is becoming a tangle of lies and deceit. Raymond heard the townsfolk tattling – you can't keep a fifteen-year-old boy in the dark – and I had to admit the truth to the lad.'

Jean's eyes were bleak. 'What do you want me to do?'

'There must be an end to the lies. Take us to Kermaria.'

'Kermaria?' Yolande's lover shook his head. 'I've

neglected it sadly. Kermaria's a backwater.'

'I'd live in hell if it meant my children would be safe! And my mother longs to leave Vannes. Izabel is conscious of great shame here. She has always hated it.'

'I doubt she minds,' Jean said with a flash of dark humour. 'Shame is a cross your mother likes to bear. There's something of the martyr in her.'

'Jean!'

'Believe me, she enjoys it.'

'You say that because it suits you. You say that because you don't want to take us.'

'It's no use your turning those green eyes on me,' Jean said stiffly. 'It's not a time of my choosing.'

'Not a time of your choosing!' Yolande lost grip of her temper. 'I've been waiting sixteen years for the time to be right! When will it be right, that's what I want to know? When?'

'It could spoil every—'

'It could *kill* our children if that thieving vulture strikes again!' She saw Jean's jaw harden.

'Be reasonable, woman,' he said, striking a fist against his thigh. 'It's for the best. Think of our children's future.'

'Our children's future?' Yolande spoke so quietly that Jean had to bend his head to hear her. 'If you sacrifice any more of the present, they'll have no future left.'

Sighing, Jean draped an arm round his mistress. 'It won't be for much longer. I'll write to Waldin—'

'Waldin! Pah! You've not been in touch for years!'

'I'll write,' Jean insisted, 'and enlist his aid. We were close before he left to fight his way through the tourneys. He may be a champion, but I don't think he will resist a call to arms from his brother. Waldin will come home, and you, my love, will be forced to eat your scornful words. Soon we'll be in a position to strike. Soon.'

'And you'll take us to Kermaria?' If Jean refused her, she would be forced to sell the gem and flee.

He stared at her, brown eyes shielded, and Yolande stared back at him, balling her hands so that the nails dug into her palms. 'Sometimes Jean,' she muttered, 'I think that I hate you.' She had come to the end of her tether.

He capitulated. 'Of course, my love, we'll go to Kermaria.'

Yolande closed her eyes, unaware that the intensity of her relief made her face haggard. 'Thank the Lord.' She let her head rest on Jean's familiar shoulder. 'I pray this tangle can be unravelled soon. I'm tired of living in fear. Our children have a right to be safe.' Moving out of her lover's arms, she crossed to the shutter and fastened it with a snap. She glanced up at the rafters; she could hear movement upstairs. 'Jean, when shall I tell them we're going?'

He shrugged. 'Whenever you like.'

Yolande smiled.

That evening, without consulting Izabel, Yolande decided to remove the diamond from its resting place in the cedarwood base of the Virgin.

Gwenn's ordeal had been a poignant reminder of the vulnerability of their position; and until her family was safely housed at Kermaria, Yolande was taking no chances. The gem was all the security she had, and she wanted it safely in her personal keeping. The jewel had once belonged to François de Roncier's grandmother, Andaine, and he might know of it. He might strike again.

Waiting till her mother's bedchamber was empty, Yolande crept in and twisted the wooden plinth from the statue. A leather pouch fell from the secret cavity. Opening the pouch, Yolande removed the gemstone and dropped it into her own purse which hung from her belt.

There was a danger that Izabel might decide to look at the diamond, but Yolande had thought of that. She had a substitute in the pocket of her gown. It was a

50

sunstone, or sailor's stone, so named because pieces of quartz like it were once used in navigation. Its shape roughly resembled the gem's. It would not bear close inspection, for the sunstone was cloudy and chipped, and had none of the sharp brilliance of the valuable jewel. But if her mother were to make an inspection, she would most likely to do so at night, when there was less chance of Raymond or Gwenn discovering her. Weighing the sunstone in her hands, Yolande smiled with satisfaction. Its weight matched that of the real gem. Carefully, she put the sunstone in the pouch and tightened the strings. As long as Izabel didn't look too closely, she might not remark on the difference. The exchange would give Yolande a little time, and would save her from lengthy and tedious explanations. There was little to be gained in alarming her mother with her fears. Once they reached Kermaria, Yolande would replace the real gem.

Pushing the pouch into its neat hollow, Yolande re-fixed the base and returned the statue to the shelf in front of Izabel's prie-dieu. Then she tiptoed from the chamber.

Chapter Four

Five miles outside Vannes, Count François de Roncier's favourite residence glowed in the moonlight like a monstrous egg nestling on a wooded hilltop whose crown had been shorn of trees. Once part of the de Wirce patrimony, the castle was known as the Château Ivoire to the French-speaking section of the population. The name derived from the fact that an earlier lord, Dagobert de Wirce, had whitewashed every wall of his castle, inside and out. Keep, bailey wall, curtain wall – everything down to the last pebble had been painted white. 'My château,' Dagobert had declared, 'will shine bright as a beacon. It will be visible for miles, and all who look upon it will be reminded of my authority. No one will dare to challenge me.'

And now, though the ancient paint was cracked and peeling, and the wash was more grey than white and needed renewing, Château Ivoire still clung to its ancient name. A different lord was master now, but when the moon floated full and bright in a clear, cloudless sky, the old grey walls continued to blaze their defiant challenge into the encircling darkness.

The native Bretons had another, less romantic, name for the Count's château; to them it was simply Huelgastel, or High Castle.

In the solar of the fortress, four flaring cressets lit the room. It was close on midnight, but the Dowager Countess, Marie de Roncier, had not retired. She sat before the stone fireplace in the loose black garment she considered suitable for her newly widowed status.

A tapestry warmed her knees. The mother of François, Marie had seen the old Count, her adored husband Robert, buried less than a month ago.

Marie de Roncier was tired. She longed for the comfort and privacy of her bed, but she had a bone to pick with her son and was waiting up for him. Her vigil was a lonely one, for her daughter-in-law, Eleanor, and her granddaughter by her son's first marriage, Arlette, had said their goodnights hours ago and she had only a tongue-tied young maid for company.

The Countess was making a poor pretence at working on the tapestry. Always a slender woman, grief had wasted away what little flesh she had had, and the hands that rested on the tapestry were skeleton thin. Notwithstanding, she kept her back as straight as a spear, and her head was as high and haughty as a queen's. Marie de Roncier gazed at the world past a splendid beak of a nose, and her jet-black eyes glared with a habitual defiance that the years had done nothing to diminish. Only the red circles faintly rimming her eyes betrayed human weakness. She had been weeping, but the set of eyes and head were fierce enough to keep sympathy at bay. Sagging folds of skin covered her cheekbones; they had a bruised look to them, which even the wavering cresset lights could not obscure. Bitter lines were firmly etched about a pale, thin mouth. Marie de Roncier had the air of a woman who had not laughed in a century.

Two iron firedogs held the burning logs in place in the great stone fireplace, preventing them from rolling onto the rush-covered floorboards. At the Countess's side, her maid Lena crouched on a stool; the girl was genuinely working on the tapestry, despite the gloom. Being newly promoted from the laundry, she was in awe of her mistress. The tapestry, several yards long, was half worked. It depicted a hunting scene and bore the family coat of arms, of cinquefoils on argent in a circlet of black thorns. It had originally been destined for Marie's bedchamber, but now that her husband was gone, both bedchamber and tapestry must of course devolve to her son – and his Countess, Eleanor.

Marie sighed, something she invariably did when she thought about her current daughter-in-law. She did not believe for a moment that François' useless second wife had gone to bed. 'It's more likely the woman's wearing out her knees in the chapel praying that God might grant her a son,' she muttered.

'Countess?'

'Nothing, girl.' Marie answered in Breton, for the benefit of her maid, who mangled French like the washerwoman she was. 'I'm thinking aloud, and I'll thank you to close your ears.'

'Aye, madame.' Diligently, Lena bent over her work, leaving Marie to muse in peace.

Eleanor had married François seven years ago, and in all that time there had been no sign of her quickening. It was becoming increasingly obvious that the woman was barren. The fault must lie at Eleanor's door, not at her son's, for had not François already got twelve-year-old Arlette out of his first wife, Joan? And later Joan had produced a boy child, a sickly infant who had not lived three days. Joan had not been barren. Would that Joan had lived, but she had caught an infection and had out-lived her son by only a day. Joan and her babe had been buried together. And two years after Joan's death, François had married Eleanor. After that there had been no more babies, not even girls.

A rustling in a corner brought a grimace to Marie's thin lips. Mice again. She would have to remind young Arlette that she was doing the household no favours by over-feeding the cats. Wielding her needle like a dagger, Marie jabbed it into the wall-hanging. Then, holding her work at arm's length the better to inspect it, she flung her section of the tapestry into the rushes. 'It's little more than a bird's nest,' she declared disgustedly. 'My son will think I've gone senile on him. I used to set a fine stitch, Lena. I don't know why I bother. I think I'll let you finish it. You have a neat hand.'

'It is very dark, my lady,' Lena said soothingly, 'and the torches give an unsteady light. I could fetch a lantern, or more candles.' She sprang to her feet with a litheness the older woman envied, and retrieved the dropped section of needlework. Grasses from the rush carpet clung to the fabric. Lena shook it, folded it, and set it neatly on a bench. This done, she looked to her mistress. 'My lady?'

The embittered mouth eased when Marie saw the girl waiting meekly for her agreement. A tactful maid – that was rare. This Lena showed promise, she clearly had more sense than most her age. 'Never mind, Lena,' Marie relaxed enough to yawn. 'My fingers are too stiff to sew any more. I've been waiting in vain. I'll prepare myself for bed. The Count cannot be coming home tonight.'

'As you wish, my lady.'

'Pass me my stick and give me your arm. My legs have seized up with too much idling about.' A distant door slammed, and a series of crashes and thuds floated up the stairwell. 'Who the devil disturbs the peace at this hour?'

Lena flushed. 'It . . . I think it is your son, Countess. He . . . the Count must have returned.'

In confirmation of the maid's words, François de Roncier erupted into the solar, spurs a-jangle and thick riding boots thumping across the wooden floorboards. Windblown, his jowls had a brazier's glow to them.

Marie drew herself up and raised a disapproving brow. With her son she invariably spoke in French. 'You're wearing your sword in the solar, François.'

Mail gauntlets chinked like bags of money as the Count removed them and tossed them onto the table, where they skidded along the boards till they came to rest against a wooden puzzle box Marie had asked Arlette to tidy away earlier. 'Too busy feeding the cats,' Marie muttered, clicking her tongue in irritation. It was plain her granddaughter needed a talking to.

Meek as a lamb, her son was unbuckling his sword belt. 'Here, girl,' he threw his belt at Lena, 'drop this on the windowseat, will you?'

The maid's flush deepened, and Marie drew her own conclusions. She made no comment, for it was beneath her dignity to comment on her son's philanderings with the lower orders. What a pity, she thought, reassessing her maid. The girl is just another common trollop. But she's probably fertile, an unwelcome voice nagged inside her; she might be only a mindless peasant, but it is possible that she will be carrying your bastard grandchild in a couple of months while delicate, high-bred Eleanor . . .

But this night, Marie had other matters on her mind. 'Well, François? Have you got rid of them?'

'They'll be gone soon.' François' grin was that of a contented man. 'Father Jerome created quite a storm.'

'I feared he might,' Marie acknowledged, adding a crease to her brow. 'I mislike him, but there's no doubting his genius with words.'

'He's dangerous.' François shook his head, reflectively. 'You should have heard him. He's headier than any wine I've ever tasted. He had the townsfolk in the palm of his hand, itching to cleanse every alley in the place. And men who had lain with a whore not an hour before were fighting among themselves to be the first to serve his will.'

'But did they frighten *them*?' Marie was half afraid of what the answer might be. Izabel Herevi was her sister, and mad though she was . . . 'It was *them* you were set on frightening.'

'We had a stroke of luck. The girl was in the church.'

'With Iz—' Marie broke off, recollecting in time the presence of her maid. The girl's French was virtually nonexistent, but it was better to say no names out loud lest they were repeated to Eleanor or Arlette who had been kept in ignorance of their lost relations. 'With the old woman?'

'No, she was alone.'

57

Marie hissed on an indrawn breath. 'And?'

François tramped to the fire and spread his hands before the blaze. 'She led the mob straight to the house. It couldn't have gone better.'

Marie clenched her stick. 'They were not hurt?'

Her son's russet brows came together. 'Mother, we've been through all this. Who are they to threaten me? Would you have me play the woman's role? I'll not wait upon events.'

'Robert never lifted a finger against her.'

'No, and you know why that was, don't you?'

Marie reeled back as though she'd been struck in the face. 'François, how could you?'

'I'm sorry, ma mère, but it's the truth. Father never lifted a finger against Izabel Herevi because he loved her. She jilted him, but still he loved her.' Callously, François rubbed salt into a wound that he knew had never healed in over thirty years. 'Face it, Maman. Your Robert is dead, and I am Count now. I'm not a man to leave loose ends lying about. That land is mine, and I will be rid of them, whatever the cost.'

Marie sank onto a bench and rested her back against the table. '*Whatever* the cost?'

'Aye. I never trusted St Clair for all that he was courting the Foucard woman. He's a jumped-up knight with eyes on my rights. I'll teach him to covet the possessions of his betters.'

'But they're family, François.' Marie thought the years had turned her to rock, but her son's ruthlessness made her shrink. 'Izabel's your aunt!'

'Enough, madame.'

Gripping her stick, Marie jerked her head furiously in Lena's direction. She'd not be belittled before a peasant trollop, language barrier or no. 'Lena!'

'My lady?'

'Go and prepare me a posset, will you?'

'Aye, my lady. Would you like cinnamon or cl—'

'Anything, anything.' An imperious wave sent the girl scurrying to the door. 'Just see that it's hot. Take it to my chamber and wait for me there.'

'Aye, my lady.' Lena curtsied and went out.

'Now, ma mère, where were we?'

'I think you were talking murder.'

The red-bristled chin lifted. 'Not murder, politics. I'll have them out of Vannes.'

'And if they won't go?'

'They'll go.'

Marie impaled her son with her eyes. 'I want no killing.'

'And if St Clair marries his slut?'

Marie gave a strained, incredulous laugh. 'Knights don't marry their mistresses. St Clair isn't witless. It would be social suicide. Think of the potential allies he'd lose.'

François stumped across the room to the side-board where red wine from Poitou was glowing in a costly glass decanter imported from the East. Beside it, on a pewter tray, waited a set of matching goblets. François lifted a glass and poured himself a measure. Cupping the bowl of the glass in his hands, he swirled the liquid round. The wine was better warmed.

Turning round to rest her arms on the table, Marie gazed at the saints carved round the sides of her grand-daughter's puzzle box, lost in her memories. 'Who would have thought that my sister's infatuation with a squire would have led to this.'

'Forget Izabel, ma mère, she's mad. She must be to have married a squire when she should have married a count.'

Marie swallowed and idly drew Arlette's puzzle box towards her. 'It was a dreadful time. Robert was betrothed to Izabel, but it was I who loved him. And all along Izabel had eyes for one man – Gwionn Herevi.' Drawing a shaky breath, the dark eyes lifted to meet her son's. They were steady eyes, proud eyes. 'Do you think it was easy living with your father all those years, knowing I was never more than second best?'

'Father loved you,' said François, wishing now to

make amends for his earlier wounding statement.

Marie made a negative gesture. 'No, François, what you said was no less than the truth. Robert loved Izabel.'

'Oh Christ, Mother, I'm sorry for what I said. I did not mean . . . I was angry. I don't like being questioned.'

Slowly Marie shook her head. 'I was never any more than a clause in a contract Robert felt bound to honour. He could not have my elder sister, but he had made an agreement with my family and, being an honourable man, he kept it. He married me in Izabel's place. And I loved him so much. I was glad to be his wife, for I'd always adored him. I wanted him to profit by his alliance with me. When our brother died and Izabel as the eldest daughter should have inherited . . .' She hesitated. 'I thought it fitting that Robert should have her lands when she never claimed them. I didn't want him to have married me for nothing.'

'No, not for nothing. I'm certain he—'

'Came to love me for my own sweet self?'

François stared hard at the thin line that was his mother's mouth. 'As it happens, yes. I'm sure Father did come to love you. Besides, you did not go to him empty-handed. You brought your own dowry.'

Marie's harsh laugh cut in. 'Aye, but next to the de Wirce patrimony, my dowry was a paltry thing. I wanted to give Robert more. And now that your father is gone, those lands—'

'Are mine. And I aim to keep them.'

Marie sighed, tapping her fingers on Arlette's box. She had mixed feelings about her sister, but she did not want Izabel and her family murdered. Jealousy had twisted her emotions, and more than once in the past she had wished Izabel dead, but she had never meant it. 'You know, François,' she leaned her chin on her hand, 'you're wasting effort on what in reality is a minor matter. They're small game.'

A scowl scored deep furrows in François' forehead.

'Small? I want the matter settled, so when Eleanor bears me a son—'

'Naturally,' Marie agreed. Now was not the time to dispute Eleanor's depressing lack of fertility. She picked up the puzzle box. When it was new it had kept Arlette amused for hours. It had come from the Lebanon, part of a crusader's booty; and it had probably been designed to be a reliquary box. It opened only when three of the saints' haloes were depressed at the same time. 'But consider, François, if we wait and consult a lawyer, we might find we have the law on our side. Izabel was in default, and we . . . you are in possession.' A peek at her son's disgruntled face told her that he was not won over. A man of action, words never counted for much with him.

'Mother, don't think I'll balk at acting without your support.'

'I don't,' Marie admitted tersely. 'I don't want a whelp of St Clair's lording it over us on our holdings any more than you do.'

The hazel eyes gleamed. 'Today was calculated to scare them off, once and for all.'

Marie bent her head and applied pressure to three of the carved haloes. Nothing happened. It was a clever toy. She tried another combination. 'What will you do next?'

'Watch them run.'

'And if they do not?'

'They'll run,' François said with conviction. 'I'm sending my men there again tomorrow at noon.'

Marie threw her son a sharp look. Worry gnawed at her insides, as for the first time it struck her that she might not be able to control her son now his father had gone to God. François' nostrils were flaring. He was losing patience, and the hot embers were glowing in his cheeks. She must step warily. 'Izabel's foolish marriage caused bloodshed once,' she said softly. 'I don't want anyone else to die over this.'

'Bloodshed, ma mère?'

61

Bending over the Lebanese box, Marie murmured, 'Gwionn was killed, or had you forgotten?'

He had not forgotten. 'Your brother, Tanguy, challenged him to a duel.'

'Aye. Tanguy refused to believe Izabel de Wirce had married a landless squire. He killed Gwionn, and Izabel fled. Mama caught her leaving, and though it broke her heart, she did not prevent her going. Mama gave Izabel her statue of Our Lady. Mama loved that statue.'

François could see his mother's eyes were full of ghosts.

'Mama should have given the statue to me,' she continued, 'for I stayed and tried to put right what Izabel had put wrong.'

Forbearing to point out that it had suited his mother to stay and 'put things right' as she had designs on Count Robert de Roncier, François tossed back another glassful of wine.

Marie was silent, thinking about the statue. There had been something unusual about it . . . At that moment Arlette's box slid open. 'Aha! Done it!' she exclaimed delightedly, and peered inside. The box was empty but for the spicy scent of cedar of Lebanon. 'Oh, that smell, it takes me back years. The base of Mother's statue held that same tangy perfume, it must have been made from the same wood.' And, like Arlette's box, the base of the statue had opened. Picking her brains, Marie extracted a vague child's recollection of her mother conjuring a gem as if from the heart of the Virgin. The child that she had been had thought it magic. Magic. Lurching to her feet, leaning heavily on her cane, Marie hobbled to her son. If she did but know it, for a second her black eyes shone with the cunning of a fox scenting its prey.

'Mother?'

Marie blinked the look away, but her eyes remained bright. 'There's a secret compartment in the base of the statue, François! A gemstone is concealed there.'

'In the Blessed Virgin?' François stroked the tawny

62

stubble on his chin. 'Your imagination is running away with you. Izabel's piety is legendary in Vannes. She would not mock Our Lady in such a way.'

The thin lips smiled, confidently. 'No, François. It was my mother's device, not Izabel's. My mother, Andaine, had the gem put there to keep it from Father. Arlette's toy has put me in mind of it. That fragrance, that distinctive fragrance . . .'

François was wondering if his father's death had unhinged his mother. Her eyes were as sharp as her bodkin, she *appeared* to be in sound mind . . .

'I'd forgotten about the jewel,' Marie continued. As a child I did not know its worth. At the time I thought it simply a pretty toy, but it's big, François, big as a blackbird's egg. It should have been mine. Why should Izabel have had that *and* Robert's love? She had it all.'

'Ma mère, the house she lives in, though adequate, hardly speaks of a life of luxury.'

'Good.' This with spite.

Wearily, François poured another goblet of wine and wished that skirmishing with his mother was less debilitating.

The fire crackled, and a log shifted, sending up a small tower of sparks. 'I'd wager they've not sold it,' Marie added.

'What, after all these years?' François scoffed. 'Mother, if Izabel ever had such a jewel, which I doubt, it's long gone.'

Marie lifted her chin. 'There was a gem, and Izabel would have kept it. I know her miserly nature. She'd not part with anything unless she had to. First she and Yolande were in that convent, and no sooner had they left, than Yolande took up with St Clair. They still have the gem. I feel it in my bones.'

'Dear Lord, spare me from women's instincts.' François stared at the ruby liquid glinting in the delicate glass and fought to keep his temper.

'I want that statue,' Marie announced. And so that she would not be fobbed off, she placed herself directly before him. 'You must – how shall I put it? You must reappropriate it before my sister and her family leave Vannes.'

Her son knuckled bleary hazel eyes and did not respond.

'François?' Marie cracked her cane on the floor. 'Show some grit, will you?'

Jerkily, he crashed the priceless, fragile goblet onto the table but by some miracle it remained whole. 'Grit? Grit? Blood of Christ, madame, you wrong me! I'm the one who wants to make a clean sweep of things. It is you who is ever yapping caution, caution. All I want is to keep my father's lands.'

Unmoved, Marie shook her cane at him. 'You *have* your father's lands. Sweet Jesus, if it weren't for the fact that I birthed you myself, I'd wonder sometimes whose son you were. You've less brains than a sheep. I've told you, François, you'll never have to defer to St Clair on the de Wirce lands. They don't have a case to answer. We've held uncontested title for thirty years. All I'm asking you to do is not to harm Izabel's family. And I want that statue.'

'I'd prefer to cut my way out of this mess cleanly. Getting the statue will slow things down, it will cause unnecessary complications.'

'So? Let it.' Marie's thin lips curved. 'Counts can afford complications.'

Reluctantly, François capitulated, realising there would be no peace in his castle till his mother had Andaine's statue. 'Very well. If it pleases you, you shall have it. But I still intend pushing them out of Vannes.'

'My thanks.' The black eyes that stared past the proud nose were unwavering. 'If you feel you must push the Herevis out, then I'll not try to sway you, but I want your sworn oath they'll come to no harm.'

'Very well, ma mère. I'll not touch a hair on their heads. I'll swear it on Father's tomb if necessary, but if the day ever dawns when St Clair *marries* Yolande Herevi, I shall consider that vow void.'

Marie allowed a complacent smile to soften the lines on her face. 'There's not the remotest possibility of St Clair marrying Yolande Herevi. I told you, knights don't marry their concubines. Even St Clair wouldn't stoop so low. Will you get the statue tomorrow?'

François held down a sigh. 'Don't bleat. If the gem is there, it's as good as in your grasp.'

The thin mouth was prim again. 'It's my mother's statue of Our Lady that I want, François. The jewel is incidental.'

François was not deceived, though he knew better than to admit it. His mother was evening up old scores.

Someone tapped on the door which led via the stairwell to the main hall below. Mother and son exchanged conspiratorial glances. The door was ajar, and the flickering torchlight illuminated the padded leather gambeson of a mercenary captain. Alan le Bret was waiting to see his lord.

'Damn! How much has he heard?' François muttered. He had never found le Bret an easy man to read. He raised his voice. 'What is it, Captain?'

'A word only, mon seigneur, no more.' On entering, Alan le Bret sketched a graceful bow in the Dowager Countess's direction. 'My apologies, madame, for interrupting you.'

The man has removed his sword, François noted resentfully. He was astonished to see his mother respond to the mercenary's careless courtesy, even going so far as to hold out her hand to him. 'Get on with it, le Bret,' he snapped.

Serene now that she had got her way, Marie tapped slowly across the boards. 'I'll take my leave, François, I'm fatigued. Good night to you both.'

François, not wishing his manners to be put in the shade by an ignorant mercenary, bowed grudgingly in his mother's direction. 'Good night, madame.'

Chapter Five

Gwenn woke abruptly. Her linen nightgown was drenched with sweat, for in her dreams she had been reliving the nightmare chase through the street. She lifted her thick plait of hair from the back of her neck, grateful that her grandmother had kept a candle lighted in their bedchamber, a luxury she usually denied them on the grounds of expense.

Gwenn shifted in her narrow cot, half afraid to recapture sleep, for that way lay terror. Even now her heart was pumping. She pressed hot, tear-stained cheeks into her bolster to try and cool them, moving as little as possible in the hope that her grandmother would think she was asleep. Gwenn knew Izabel had been upset by her weeping, and did not want her to know she was wakeful. Once, with a rare flash of humour, her grandmother had said that Gwenn slept so soundly she would sleep through the Last Judgment. But not tonight.

There had not been a precise moment when Gwenn had realised that her mother's relationship with Sir Jean was unorthodox. Realisation had come in slow stages. Izabel had guarded her closely, almost jealously, not permitting her to mix with other girls in the town, and this, Gwenn now realised, had kept her unaware of the townfolk's hostility for much longer than would otherwise have been the case. At the time, Gwenn had assumed that Izabel disapproved of the other girls, had thought them not worthy friends for her. Then had dawned the day when, like today, she had escaped for a couple of hours on her own. She had befriended

Lucia. Lucia lived in the house opposite, and they had played happily until Lucia's mother had appeared and dragged her daughter away. And the next time Gwenn had seen her playmate, and had smiled at her, Lucia had looked at her with glassy eyes and turned her face aside. There had been other, similar, incidents, which Gwenn had never liked to examine too closely, but the violence that had flared up today and the consequent chase through the streets forced her to face it squarely. Gwenn had spoken to her mother, and Yolande had at last admitted that she was St Clair's mistress. She had admitted that she and her family were outcasts. They were undesirable, and were reviled more than the lepers that begged for alms at the town gates, for the lepers were given pity at least. Gwenn had not seen much pity in the eyes of the mob that had hounded her and Raymond through the streets. The tears welled again.

Izabel thought her granddaughter was safely asleep. Hoisting herself out of bed, the old woman set the candle in the middle of the floor and crept to the stool in front of her mirror. A gigantic, misshapen shadow travelled with her across the limewashed plaster walls. The candle flame, nudged by draughts drifting in through chinks round window and door, made the shadow jerk and twitch, as though it was palsied. Izabel cocked her head to one side and listened. All was silent, both inside the house and out.

On hearing Izabel rise from her pallet, Gwenn stayed silent, unconsciously waiting for the familiar grating sound which would signify that the chamber pot was being pulled out from under Izabel's bed. Moments later, when the scraping sound did not come, Gwenn peered across the room. What was her grandmother doing?

Izabel was quietly clearing her brush and hairpins from the top of her coffer. With both hands on the lid of the chest, she took a deep breath and heaved. The trunk opened reluctantly, for Izabel's arms were losing their strength and the coffer had been hewn from solid oak. The old woman was short of wind by the time the lid was resting back against the wall. She fished about inside, and drew out some cloth. She began to hum, softly, and then ceased abruptly, seeming to wink at the dusk-shrouded figure that was her reflection in the mirror. 'I'm putting my house in order,' Izabel murmured and smoothed out the cloth.

What *was* her grandmother doing?

The piece of fabric was sailcloth, which Izabel had obtained from a fisherman on one of the quays. Pushing stiffly to her feet, Izabel hobbled to the alcove and picked up her icon.

Gwenn kept very still.

'This,' her grandmother muttered with a sidelong glance at Gwenn's pallet, 'will be my legacy to you, Gwenn. This will keep you safe. Raymond does not need it. Boys are tough. They look after themselves. It's the girls who are defenceless, left to suffer . . .' The old woman blinked away a remorseless tear. 'If only I'd told your mother about the gemstone sooner. She need never have become St Clair's mistress, need never have sold her soul. I failed her, but I shall put it right, I shall not fail *you*.' She wrapped the statue in the sailcloth.

Miserable but burning with curiosity, Gwenn could contain herself no longer. She pushed back her covers and sat up. 'Grandmama, what are you mumbling about?'

'Gwenn! You're awake!'

Gwenn rubbed eyes that were hot and puffy with too much crying. 'Aye. What is it, Grandmama? Are you unwell?'

'My thanks, Gwenn, but I am quite well.' Dropping her burden in the coffer, Izabel closed the lid. She crossed the chamber and levered herself onto the edge of Gwenn's mattress. Gwenn heard her joints creak. 'It is you I'm concerned about. Do you feel better?'

Dipping her head, Gwenn lied. 'Yes. I'm sorry I cried. I hope I didn't upset you, Grandmama.'

Izabel patted her hand. 'It was an unnerving experience.'

'Grandmama, you don't understand. Of course I was frightened by the mob – actually, I was terrified out of my wits – but it was the hatred in their voices when they cursed Mama that shook me most. I had my suspicions we lived under some sort of a cloud, but I had no idea that most of Vannes disliked us so intensely. Father Mark had always been kind to us, and I know Mikael Brasher likes Raymond. Raymond is always talking about Duke's Tavern.'

'But you did have suspicions?'

'Aye. I've read about liaisons like Mother's and Sir Jean's with Raymond. Our tutor explained—'

'I knew Yolande was making a mistake to have you sit in on Raymond's lessons!' Izabel said, scandalised. 'No good ever came of a girl learning to read and write. I shall have it stopped at once. I should have thought Father Mark of all people would know better than to corrupt a young girl. Holy Mother, what have you been reading?'

Under cover of darkness, Gwenn smiled, and took her grandmother's hand. She loved her grandmother deeply, but she could not resist teasing her. 'The Bible, Grandmama.'

'The *Bible*? You can read Latin?'

'Father Mark says I'm a better student than Raymond—'

'Is the Bible all you have read?' Izabel demanded, frowning. In her mind it was neither necessary nor sensible to teach a girl to read. Few enough men had that skill, and she feared that outlandish ideas might warp her impressionable granddaughter's mind. The scandal of Heloise and her teacher Abelard loomed like a dreadful warning in the old woman's mind.

'I've read other writings too, Grandmama,' Gwenn said. Izabel made a clucking sound with her tongue. Swallowing down a giggle, Gwenn could not resist adding, 'But it was the Bible that taught me about fornication and adultery.'

70

'That's enough, Gwenn!' Izabel clapped her hands over her ears. 'Enough!'

'My apologies, Grandmama. What I'm trying to tell you is that I suspected that mother was a concub—'

'Don't say that word.' The old woman stopped Gwenn's mouth with her palm. 'We must pray that God in His infinite mercy will forgive your mother.'

'You sound as though you doubt that, Grandmama.'

Silence.

'Grandmama?' Conscious of a disrespectful desire to shake her grandmother, Gwenn laced her fingers tightly together and lowered her voice to a whisper, for she did not want her mother disturbed. 'Grandmama, I would like to understand something.'

'Mmm?'

'Why is it us they turn on?'

'Us?'

'The women of the family.'

'They were after Raymond, too,' Izabel pointed out.

'Aye, but only because he came to my aid. It was me they were really after. I've noticed this before, Grandmama. People tolerate Raymond far more than they do Mama or me. And they seem to like Sir Jean. But when it's you or me, or Mama . . .'

'Your mother is a grievous sinner and will not repent.'

'And she deserves to be reviled? Along with you and me, and no doubt Katarin too when she's grown? No, Grandmama, I refuse to accept that. We're all sinners. Mama hasn't done more wrong than anyone else. Mama's no more wicked than Sir Jean. All anyone has to do is look at the way she and my f . . . Sir Jean care about each other. They love each other. They are faithful to each other. I don't see what difference there is between them and all the other married people in Vannes. It's sheer hypocrisy.'

'But, Gwenn—'

'In fact, Grandmama,' Gwenn ploughed on, 'my parents are better than most. They are honest sinners. Did you know, for example, that Pierre, the herbalist down the street, is having a clandestine affair, and his wife, poor love, knows nothing?'

'I never pay any heed to the doings of the common townsfolk,' Izabel said loftily. 'Honest sinners, indeed. What will you think of next? Clearly, this tutoring will have to stop.'

'Pierre is an adulterer, Grandmama. Would you call him discreet, or dishonest? I can't see *him* being lynched for his sins.'

'It has been known,' Izabel murmured.

'Grandmama, I'm trying to understand. Why do they want us out of Vannes? Why do they hate us so? They condone Pierre's adultery – can't they see the good in Mama's relationship with Sir Jean?'

Izabel pressed her granddaughter's hand, but held to her litany. 'She's a sinner, a sinner in the eyes of Holy Church. And I am to blame.'

'No, Grandmama.'

'Do you mind what your mother has made you?' Izabel demanded, disconcertingly.

Gwenn jerked her head aside and stared mutely at the flickering candle.

For Izabel that was response enough. 'Do you care that every day Yolande stays with St Clair she puts her immortal soul at risk?'

'I wish . . .' Gwenn hesitated. 'I wish you and Mama had trusted me enough to confide in me.'

'Yolande wanted to tell you, but I thought you too young.'

Gwenn shoved a thick skein of hair from her face. 'But not too young to lie to?'

'Lie? I thought only to protect you, child.'

'Too much protection can be dangerous,' Gwenn said, astutely. 'I wish you hadn't protected me. I'd far rather have been trusted with the truth.' She hung her head, and plucked at her bedcover. 'Grandmama?'

'Mmm?'

'There's something I've never been clear about. And I'm curious. I . . . I'd like you to explain it.'

72

'I'll try.'

'How is it that a woman of your . . . er . . . strong religious principles elected to remain with Mother after . . . after . . . she had become St Clair's mistress? I would have thought you'd have left her, perhaps have become a nun. Didn't you want to become a nun?'

An ominous silence fell, giving Gwenn time to regret her curiosity. 'I'm sorry, Grandmama. Forget I ever asked. It was impertinent of me.'

'It was,' her grandmother agreed. 'But since you have asked, I'll try and answer you. Naturally, I never approved of your mother's relations with St Clair. And she was so young when it started. She was your age, you know.'

'She was thirteen?' Girls were often wed at that age, but Gwenn let that pass.

Her grandmother nodded sadly. Gwenn's hair had flopped forwards again and tenderly her grandmother looped it behind her ear. 'Thirteen. We had taken refuge in St Anne's Convent, but when Yolande was thirteen, we were cast out into the world. Yolande thought we'd not a clipped penny between us.'

'A convent cast you out? Why, Grandmama? Why were you in need of refuge anyway? What about your husband?'

'He died, before Yolande was born.'

Something in her grandmother's voice warned Gwenn not to pursue that line of questioning. In the past, whenever Gwenn had asked about her mother's childhood, she had come up against a wall of silence. But tonight, Izabel seemed disposed to talk. Greedy for anything which would reveal more about both her mother and her grandmother's background, Gwenn felt her way step by tentative step. 'What about your parents?'

No answer. Her grandmother was as motionless as a menhir. Gwenn tried again. 'Where were they? Were they dead that you were lodged in a convent?'

'I never think of those times, Gwenn.'

Gwenn grimaced; that solid wall again.

'It's too painful,' Izabel went on. 'Besides, I was ill. I . . . I had a fever, as I recall, and was out of my mind. Yolande went to beg for food. She met St Clair, and the rest you know.'

'They fell in love.' Gwenn sighed, wondering how to wheedle more out of her grandmother. 'He lifted her out of the gutter. It must have been very romantic!'

'Romantic?' Izabel laughed harshly. 'It was nothing of the kind. Your mother sacrificed herself so she could look after me. When I recovered and realised what she had done, it was too late. She was a fallen woman. If only I had told Yolande about the jewel, if only . . .'

'You said Mama did it for you,' Gwenn reminded her.

'Aye. She did it for me. She's immoral, but she *is* my daughter, and that's a strong bond, as you might discover if you ever have a daughter of your own. I love her, whatever I might think of her morals. Sometimes I can see my Gwionn shining through her expression. She's all I have of him, and . . .' Izabel gave her shoulders a little shake and smiled through the darkness. 'And I confess she's been lucky with her chevalier. Jean St Clair may not be the wealthiest of men, but he does care for us in his way. He bought us this house. Yolande did what she could when she thought us destitute, but the price was high – her immortal soul.'

'Grandmama, you can't believe that.' Gwenn brought her brows together.

'I love Yolande.'

It did not escape Gwenn that Izabel had avoided her question. 'I know. Grandmama—'

The latch clicked, and a tall, slight figure squeezed past the door and crept towards Gwenn's pallet.

'Raymond?'

The figure, cloaked in shadows, went down on its haunches. 'The same,' her brother's voice confirmed. 'I could hear you from the landing. What are you two whispering about?'

'We haven't woken Yolande, have we?' Izabel worried.

'She's not asleep,' Raymond said. 'St Clair's with her. They're talking.'

Izabel held out an arm to her grandson. 'Help me up, Raymond.' She heaved herself upright. 'My thanks. I'm glad you've come in, because I've an errand you can run in the morning.'

'Oh, aye?' Raymond answered equably, seating himself on the bed. 'All right, little Gwenn?' he asked, tweaking a lock of his sister's hair.

'Aye.'

Izabel reached her coffer. The hinges creaked as she grasped the lid.

'Here, Grandmère, let me help you.' Belatedly, Raymond sprang to his feet.

The lid fell back with a crack. 'I've done it.' Izabel was panting but triumphant, and holding a package.

'You should have let me.'

'Never mind, never mind. Raymond, listen. I'm going to give Our Lady to Gwenn. It's for her and Katarin – for the girls. You don't mind, do you?'

'Why in heaven's name should I mind?'

Izabel looked momentarily nonplussed, as though her grandson's question had put her off her stride. 'No reason, no reason. Raymond, I want you to take this statue and hide it. Take it some miles from here, somewhere no one will think of searching.'

Raymond stared blankly at the parcel. 'Why can't you simply hand it over to Gwenn and have done, Grandmère? Why do I have to hide it?'

'Because . . . because I want it out of here. As long as we have it with us, they'll come looking for us. We'd not be left in peace. Without it, there's a chance—'

'They?' Gwenn wondered. 'Do you mean this Count de Roncier? I heard Sir Jean mention him, he's behind this violence, isn't he?'

Izabel ignored her, murmuring, 'We're in danger while it's here . . .'

'Danger? What danger?' Raymond demanded. 'What haven't you told us, Grandmama?'

Izabel sank back into the pallet and fumbled for her granddaughter's hand. 'I can't explain,' she said with a sharp glance at Raymond.

'Grandmère, this is ridiculous. For Christ's sake, what—?'

'Raymond, I'll thank you not to swear,' Izabel said primly. 'Will you help me or not?'

'It must be some silly women's secret,' Raymond said, patronisingly, and when the young man saw a guilty spasm twist his grandmother's face, he laughed. 'I knew it!'

'Raymond . . .' Izabel's voice was choked.

'Oh, keep your secrets,' he said carelessly. 'Calm down, Grandmère, I'll do as you ask. But I don't see—'

Izabel waved both her arms at him. 'You're not expected to see. Just take it, and hide it, and be sure you tell Gwenn where to find it. Remember, I'm giving it to her, not to you. It belongs to her. You'll do that for me? At first light, mind?'

Raymond had intended going out before dawn in any case, for he had clandestine pleasures to pursue. He would not have to go out of his way to please his grandmother. 'Yes, yes.'

'Bless you, Raymond.' Izabel yawned ostentatiously. 'It is very late, my lad. I suggest we get what sleep we can, there's not much of this night left.'

The young man recognised finality when he heard it in his grandmother's voice. He padded softly to the door. 'Good night, Grandmère, Gwenn.'

The latch rattled and he was gone.

'Men!' Izabel muttered softly. 'They're all the same. We've aroused his curiosity now, my girl.'

'Have we?'

'He'll be back in the morning, pestering us with questions. Never mind. He's not as bad as most of them.'

'You don't like men much, do you, Grandmama?'

Izabel chucked Gwenn under the chin. 'I don't hate them all. There was one once,' her voice went soft and dreamy, 'but now I can't even see his face.' She caught her breath, and finished briskly, 'That was long before you were born. Past history, my dear.'

'Tell me about him,' Gwenn urged, not feeling at all sleepy. 'Was it Gwionn, the man you married?' Izabel tensed, and Gwenn knew by her grandmother's posture that the barriers were in place again.

'No. Some wounds never heal.' A firm hand was placed on Gwenn's chest, and she was pushed onto her pillow. 'Go to sleep, my dear. You need your rest.'

'But, Grandmama—'

'Sleep,' Izabel insisted. 'But remember, the Virgin is my legacy to you.'

'Thank you, Grandmama,' Gwenn said, aware that the statue was her grandmother's most treasured possession. 'Mama calls it the Stone Rose.'

'I know. We'll talk further on the morrow. Remember, the statue has been my strength and security for many a long year. Now it can be yours. I want to know you're provided for. I know you'll take care of Katarin.' Lovingly, Izabel smoothed Gwenn's coverlet into place.

'Yes, Grandmama.'

'You'll have cause to thank me for it one day.' Izabel said, smothering a yawn.

'Thank you, Grandmama. I do love you.' And then Gwenn shut her eyes lest she was treated to one of Izabel's lectures.

'God bless you, my dear.'

François de Roncier stood before the dying fire in the solar at Huelgastel and ran an exasperated hand through his cropped copper hair. He regarded his Breton captain guardedly. 'What is it, le Bret?'

Having bearded the lion in his den, Alan saw no reason to beat about the bush. 'Mon seigneur, I come on behalf of my company. The quarter day is here. I take it you'll be honouring your debts?'

'Naturally. The money's in the vaults.' The Count rubbed the side of his nose. 'I'll dispense it on the morrow, as soon as you have executed your commission.'

Alan stared. 'Mon seigneur, we have already executed our commission.'

'Not quite, Captain.' Count François gave a cold smile. 'They remain in Vannes, do they not?'

'I'll warrant it won't be for long. They'll be gone within the week.' A brief glance told Alan that this private family solar was more exotically furnished than the communal hall below. The lower half of the walls was decorated with a frieze of life-size herons. Above the frieze, the stonework was painted and the pointing picked out in red. Tapestries adorned the upper walls, framed by an intricate array of roof beams, with bold multi-coloured chevrons drawing the eye the length of the beams from corbels to apex. Alan noticed the delicate goblet in the Count's hand, the rich, ruby wine he was sipping. His lord lived well.

'A week is too long,' the Count said. 'Captain, you're to return to Vannes and see them off. I want you to *execute*,' he put heavy emphasis on the word execute, 'your commission as thoroughly as you are able. There's not to be the slightest chance they'll come back.' He glanced over his shoulder at the door by which the Dowager Countess had left. 'And I do not wish to be implicated. Understand?'

'I'm not certain I do understand you, mon seigneur.'

'You've wits, le Bret. Use 'em. I speak plainly.'

Alan's grey eyes bored into the Count's. François waited, hoping his captain was not going to be difficult. He considered this a trifling matter to be finished with swiftly. He could not afford any marks on his slate when he approached the King of France with his proposals. An aspiring duke must have no family skeletons lurking in closets.

'Well, Captain?'

'If I understand you correctly, mon seigneur, I'm bound to say I like it not.'

'You're not paid to like it!' First his mother put obstacles in his path, and now this presumptuous mercenary was pitching in with his pennyworth. 'Mon Dieu, you're paid to obey!'

'I'm not paid at all,' le Bret said, dry as dust. 'Mon seigneur, you know very well that my men are paid by the quarter, not by the commission. And the quarter day has passed. Our money is due *now*.'

There was a short silence, and the two men eyed each other, wary dogs with their hackles raised.

François decided he would not like to confront this man in open combat, when his true nature would be unleashed. Le Bret was a determined, ruthless man. A calculating man. Could he be bought? he wondered.

His captain broke the silence. 'So Count François de Roncier does not deal honourably with hired men.'

François looked down his nose. 'Honour? What would a peasant like you know of honour? You hire yourself out to the highest bidder. You care for nothing but money.'

Le Bret's lips curved in a mocking travesty of a smile. 'Money is reliable, mon seigneur. You know where you are with money. Money does not break its bond.'

'Insolence!' The Count's heavy jowls purpled with rage.

'I have already reminded you, mon seigneur,' Alan went on inexorably 'that payment is due by the quarter, not by the commission. As an honourable nobleman, I'm sure you will appreciate the necessity of settling your debts. You wouldn't want to lose a good company to another employer, would you?'

The veins in de Roncier's neck stood out like dark cords. 'How dare you threaten me! I'll teach you respect for your betters.' He dived for his sword which lay where Lena had placed it on the windowseat and snatched it free of its scabbard.

Standing his ground, Alan spread his arms wide. 'Here I am, mon seigneur, at your mercy. This will be the only chance you get. Make the most of it.'

The two men glared at each other, the one apoplectic with rage, the other infuriatingly, insufferably cool.

The Count's sword quivered. '*Merde!* Your death solves nothing.' Dropping his eyes to the tapestry his mother had been working on, he resheathed his weapon. 'For my mother's sake, I'll not shed blood in her solar.'

Alan swallowed down a scathing reply. He had taken a risk with de Roncier's temper, but he had been fairly confident that he would not have the stomach to kill an unarmed man. The Count hired others to do his dirty work.

'Look here, le Bret,' de Roncier had recovered his composure, 'you're a good soldier. I know the rank and file respect you, and I don't want trouble with the men. I'm willing to add half a pound of purest English silver to your pay if you finish the job. You can have it tomorrow.'

'Half a pound?' Alan looked deep into his lord's hazel eyes. If de Roncier was trying bribery, he must be desperate. In Duke's Tavern, a sergeant had revealed that the Herevis were distant kin to de Roncier. It must be some ancient quarrel over birthright for it to matter so much.

'Ten English shillings,' the Count confirmed with a confident grin.

The form of a young girl in a vivid blue dress sprang into Alan's mind. Ned was not the only one to dislike this commission. 'I'm uneasy about this, mon seigneur. It's a women's household.'

'There's a lad—'

'That one!' Alan dismissed Raymond Herevi with a scornful wave of his hand. 'He'd be no more use in combat than a lute plucker. I'll wager he's never wielded a knife on anything more lively than the meat on his trencher.'

'Don't you turn womanish on me, le Bret.' The Count thudded a heavy fist on the table, and the costly Eastern wine glasses shivered and tinkled. 'You are beginning to sound like your lily-livered kinsman, Fletcher. What's his problem? Is he a coward?'

Alan recalled the gangling colt of a boy who had trailed faithfully after him when he had been forced to leave England looking for work, because mercenaries were banned in England. Ned had been all eyes and legs, and it could not have been easy for the lad to leave everything he held dear to follow his older cousin. 'No, mon seigneur, Ned Fletcher's no coward.'

'I'll have his tongue nailed to the whipping post so he can't infect any more of the troop with his high-minded tattle. I'm surprised at you, le Bret. I'd have thought you would have been immune.'

'It is nothing to do with Fletcher,' Alan said, though privately he wondered if there was a germ of truth in what de Roncier was saying. He did feel torn. He needed the money – who didn't? – and normally never thought twice about what he did to get it. But when Ned had spoken out, Alan had taken a long, hard look at his lord. And if he had summed up the position truly, the man was no more than a blustering coward out to steal someone else's birthright.

Alan was no saint that he could sit in judgment over others. He had smothered his conscience years ago in the need for coin. How much lower than that could you sink? That he needed the money was irrelevant. Did his need justify the shedding of blood, the killing of women and children? Alan was tired of dancing to de Roncier's tune. He wanted out, and here was de Roncier offering to increase his pay. He wished his conscience had remained dormant a little while longer. Perhaps he'd take the extra money and push on to greener pastures . . .

'What about St Clair?' Alan asked. 'Don't you antici-pate a fight while he protects his woman and children?'

De Roncier's hair gleamed like fire in the cresset

lights. 'St Clair hasn't got enough guards to keep the house under surveillance all the time,' he said. 'Besides, he won't be expecting an outright attack on the house.'

Alan brought his brows together. 'Mon seigneur, I don't think I'd recommend an outright attack. It's too obvious. Someone's bound to recognise—'

The Count swung round, picked up a solid, brass-topped poker and stirred the fire into life. 'Point taken.'

'And afterwards, mon seigneur,' Alan pressed on, 'don't you think St Clair will retaliate? Yolande Herevi means much to him. I've heard he's faithful to her.'

Dropping the poker against the iron firedogs with a clang, Count François let out an ugly laugh. 'The woman's his harlot, le Bret, his harlot. What man would risk starting a war – and that's what it would amount to – over a whore?'

Alan looked unconvinced.

'Remember the half pound of silver, Captain. Can you think of an easier way of earning it?'

Alan couldn't.

'All you have to do is see them off.' The Count raised a russet brow and slapped Alan on the back with a false bonhomie that jarred more than the gesture. 'Think of it, Captain. Think of the girls—'

'I've better uses for money than to waste it on whores,' Alan declared flatly. 'But your offer is tempting.' Half a pound of silver, plus his pay, was a fortune to a mercenary. He could live off the coined silver for a long time, but what counted most was that de Roncier's money would give him the freedom to choose a better master. Two years ago, when he had joined the Count's troop, he and Ned had been desperate. He'd have signed his soul to anyone. But with English minted pennies swelling his purse, he'd be rich enough to pick and choose.

'You'll do it?' de Roncier asked. 'I'll pay you tomorrow, when it's over. I'm taking a strongbox to the tavern. I'll dole out there, when I hear they've . . . gone.'

82

'And my troop?'

'Aye, fry your eyes, I'll pay your troop too.'

'I'll do it.' And, saluting the man who would be his lord only until the sun set the following night, Alan marched briskly from the solar.

François let his breath go on a sigh. Captain le Bret was an awkward man, and he seemed to have misjudged him. At times the fellow was as hard as tempered steel, but at other times . . .

Absently François refilled his glass. Le Bret was an enigma. But one thing was clear, he was single-minded; he had come in to get his back pay, and he had left with exactly what he came for – and more. 'He's an opportunist,' François murmured, 'and as tough as they come.'

He sipped his wine and, grimacing, deposited the glass on the pewter tray. The bottle had been open to the air too long; the contents had soured, and set his teeth on edge. Heading for his bed, and his wife, he wondered how long Alan le Bret had been stationed outside the solar door. How much had he heard? There was no telling, but perhaps it would be prudent to despatch Malait with him on the morrow. François nodded to himself. He would charge the Norseman with finding the statue his mother coveted. He need make no mention of the gem. One could not trust routiers. The less they knew, the better.

Wondering if Eleanor would be asleep, François mounted the spiral stairs to his turret bedchamber.

Chapter Six

The bottom of the fishing boat was wet with a combination of dew and sea water that soaked through cloak and breeches to Raymond's bones. He had counted on being able to sleep on the pre-dawn trip across the bay, but his clothes were too damp, he felt cold, and to add to his miseries the Small Sea was choppy and the rocking motion of the boat gave him *mal de mer*.

'How much longer, Edouarz?' Raymond groaned, lying back so he could try counting stars and forget his nausea.

There was a closed lantern attached to the mast, which let out a few shreds of light – barely enough to reach the face of the man at the tiller, the boat's owner. Edouarz glanced briefly at his passenger, bit back a grin on seeing the boy's tight lips and greenish tinge, and tipped his head back to examine the sail of his tiny vessel. The patched canvas bellied out with the wind. 'Half an hour, maybe longer.'

Raymond moaned. The stars danced dizzily. The lights of other fishing vessels returning home with their catch danced too. His stomach heaved.

'Seems a long time, does it, young sir?' Edouarz teased. Another groan. The fisherman jerked his thumb at a dark, low-lying mass on their left. 'That's Monk's Island', he announced. 'With this wind, we'll be at Locmariaquer in no time.'

An hour later, Raymond's feet were planted firmly on *terra firma*, his stomach was calmer, and he was in a better state of mind, having persuaded a carter to give him a ride as far as the dolmen. That's where his rendezvous with the girl was.

The carter was heading inland to the market with what he thought was last night's catch of mackerel, a basket of crabs, and some shellfish. But the fish smelt high. The waggon rattled over the dirt road. Poised on the edge of the tailboard, with his long legs dangling, Raymond pressed one hand tightly over his nose, but the stink was persistent, and to his dismay his stomach began churning all over again. His brown tunic would never be quite the same again. How long would the reek cling to his person? Anna, the girl he was intent on meeting, might not be so ardent if he stank of rotting fish.

'This stuff is crawling!' Raymond yelled over the clatter of wheels.

'Eh?' The carter had a solid back.

'Edouarz has pulled the wool over your eyes with this lot,' Raymond said. 'Last night's catch could not possibly smell like this.'

The carter lifted lumpy shoulders and stolidly kept eyes and face towards the road in front. His monotone voice floated back to Raymond, 'A bargain's a bargain.'

'No one will buy 'em,' Raymond predicted with the arrogant confidence of one who has never been reduced to eating second-rate food.

'They will. They're cheap, see.'

The crack of the carter's whip was loud in the dawn hush. 'They might pay more if they were fresh,' Raymond said, pegging his nose.

'Can't afford it, young sir.'

Raymond shrugged, and kept his smile to himself. The fellow's mind was closed, and Raymond found his narrow, peasant doggedness amusing. The carter had probably never changed his views since birth, and would cling to them, blindly, till Doomsday.

The waggon lurched on over a causeway whose surface was scarred with deep ruts. The sky was lightening fast, and one or two trees stood out, stark, black silhouettes against the dawn grey.

'Have we passed the crossroads?'

'Aye, 'bout a mile back. We're a stone's throw from the farm. I'll let you down there. The pathway to the dolmen runs off to the west.'

'That's a mercy. I'm bruised all over.' Raymond winced, and tried to cushion his buttocks with more of his woollen cloak. The package his grandmother had palmed off on him rolled out and clunked against the side of the cart. Raymond wedged the statue between two baskets of fish. It was fortunate that he'd made the assignment with the girl, for his grandmother's odd request and his own plans had dove-tailed neatly. What better place to stow her statue than in one of the ancient temples of the Old Ones? It was the perfect hiding place, people seldom visited them, being superstitious and frightened of rousing the old god's anger.

Raymond had never tried to understand his grandmother, he simply accepted her for what she was, a pious woman of venerable years. But jolting along on the waggon, he found himself wondering why Izabel wanted to hide her icon. It must be connected with the business yesterday, but he could not fathom it. 'I must be mad,' he muttered, 'to fall in with her whim.'

The carter turned his head and eyed him over his shoulder. He had greasy, lank hair, and his skin was pitted with pox marks. 'Pretty, is she?' he asked slyly.

Raymond flushed to his ears, and despite himself an image of smiling dark eyes and a warm, red mouth sprang into his mind. Anna *was* pretty. But all he said was, 'Who?'

'Now who's trying to pull the wool over my eyes?' the carter grinned. 'I'm talking about the maid you're meeting in the temple.' He made an obscene gesture.

Raymond's eyes widened. He was amazed that the man should have known, and furious that he had been so obvious. 'By St Guirec, how—?'

The man cackled. 'Why else would a soft young man like you be sneaking out in my cart at the crack of dawn?'

'I'm not soft!' Raymond cried, much stung. The man

had the most infuriating grin, he itched to slap it from his face.

'No?' Another cackle. 'You're not the first to use that temple as a trysting place.'

'I've gone far enough.' Raymond jumped off the waggon as though the rough wood bit him. 'My thanks for the ride.' He dug a coin from his purse and flung it towards the carter.

The carter's hand snaked out and snatched the coin from the air. His tongue clicked, the whip snapped, and the mule put on a turn of speed. 'Haven't you forgotten something?' the toneless voice asked sweetly, pitted face split in two with that spiteful grin.

'Hell! The statue! Slow down, will you?' Raymond ran after the waggon. A burst of wheezy laughter drifted back from the driver's seat. 'Jesu! Stop! Stop!' Hurling himself at the edge of the cart, Raymond grabbed the sailcloth bundle and tumbled into the road, arms and legs flailing. 'My thanks,' he spat bitterly at the fast-disappearing waggon.

'Any time,' the mocking monotone was carried to him on the early morning breeze. 'It was a real pleasure.'

Raymond picked himself out of a pothole and eyed his soiled clothes ruefully. What wench would look twice at him now, covered in mud and smelling riper than the midden? He did not think Anna was that sweet on him – she'd probably get one whiff and run a mile. He scowled at the brow of the hill. Curse the peasant. Anna was delectable, but girls were unpredictable, mysterious creatures, and there was no telling how she would react.

Stuffing his grandmother's bundle into his tunic, Raymond turned hopefully towards the track that led to the dolmen. Even if the wench deserted him, he'd not have made a wasted journey. He could see Grandmère's wish fulfilled. The temple was not visited as often as the carter had implied. The Virgin would be perfectly safe there.

The hedgerows were wreathed in a light mist. The sun was breaking through it from the east, shining like a lamp viewed through a veil. The sweet, fresh morning air was a benison from heaven. Raymond drew in a lungful, lips curving with youthful optimism. Anna would *not* run a mile. He would be lucky. He could feel it. Despite the unpromising start, he was certain today was going to be quite beautiful.

About to go downstairs to break her fast, Gwenn was tidying her pallet when she looked up to see Yolande step into her bedchamber, her travelling cloak flung about her shoulders. Fatigue had drawn and pinched her mother's delicate features into the mould of an older woman.

'Where's Raymond?' Yolande asked, fastening her cloak with a silver filigree brooch in the shape of a butterfly.

'We've no idea,' Izabel responded. 'We know what he's doing, but not where. He'll be back later this morning.'

The floorboards creaked and Jean St Clair walked slowly in; slowly because Katarin had attached herself to one of his hands and was trying out her paces at her father's side. Gwenn's mouth fell open. This was the first time that she had known him to have spent the whole night with her mother. Normally he slept elsewhere, for form's sake, a shallow pretence Gwenn had long suspected he kept up for her sake. Such a departure from his carefully established habit could only mean that he was profoundly concerned for them, and that he intended to protect them.

'Good morning, ladies.' He smiled, and released his daughter's hands. Katarin sat down with a bump. 'Where's the boy?'

Yolande answered. 'Not here.'

'Devil blast him!'

'I'll thank you to remember the company you're in, Sir Jean,' Izabel said, throwing a meaningful look at

Gwenn. 'You're not in an alehouse.'

'My apologies,' unrepentantly, Jean stroked his trim moustache, 'but the lad would have to choose this morning of all mornings to go gallivanting. Are you sure neither of you knows where he has gone?'

Izabel folded her hands primly under her bosom. 'He's running an errand for me.'

Gwenn had a pretty shrewd idea where her brother had gone, for he had confided to her his infatuation with the farmer's daughter, and he had once let fall that they met in a dolmen near Locmariaquer. Providently, Katarin crawled into Gwenn's line of vision, giving her something to pin her gaze on. She had never been any good at lying, and if her parents had the slightest suspicion that she knew of Raymond's whereabouts, they would be bound to winkle it out of her.

Sinking to Katarin's level, she offered her sister a supporting hand. 'Good morning, sweetheart.' Katarin grabbed her fingers and clung like a limpet. The unformalised nature of the relationship between her mother and father did not mean that Raymond's affair with a farmer's daughter would be taken lightly. Yolande had taken pains to instil into her son that love was not a game, and Gwenn was in no doubt that her brother would be severely reprimanded if his secret were discovered. Her father's views on the subject, like Raymond's, were ambivalent – typically male. While Gwenn did not condemn either her brother or her father for their opinions, her own views were, by virtue of her female sex, closer to her mother's. What sensible woman could afford to think otherwise? It was women who were ultimately responsible for the consequences of casual affairs. Gwenn had always been puzzled that her mother should have turned to St Clair in the first place. She must have been desperate to help Izabel. Or deeply in love. Or both.

But it was not her mother's history that was at issue here. Should Raymond's secret come out, he would be in trouble, and whatever Gwenn might think of his dalliance with the farmer's daughter, it was his affair, he must not suffer because she was a poor liar.

Jean spoke briskly. 'We're leaving Vannes today.'

'Leaving?' Gwenn gasped. 'Today?'

'Aye. I suspect de Roncier was behind yesterday's incident, but as none of his men were seen here, we cannot prove anything. Personally, I doubt he's audacious enough to move openly against us, but to put everyone's mind at rest, we'll be leaving this morning.'

'This *morning*?' Gwenn echoed.

'Where are we going?' her grandmother demanded.

'My manor at Kermaria.'

Gwenn's grandmother blinked, and sank onto her bed, expression dazed. 'Kermaria? In truth, you're taking us there?'

Jean smiled. 'Aye.'

Izabel's mouth worked. 'Oh, Jean,' her voice was weak. 'You're acknowledging the children? Openly?'

He inclined his head. 'It won't affect their legitimate status I'm afraid, but—'

'But for them to have a father,' Izabel's aged eyes were moist with tears. 'Oh, Jean, how I have prayed for this day.' She was so overcome, she made an attempt at humour. 'We . . . we'll almost be respectable.'

'When are we leaving?' Gwenn stared at her father, unable to believe in this new turn of events. She only had one friend in Vannes, Irene Brasher, it was not as if she would be leaving anyone behind. But, for all that her family had been outcasts, Vannes was all she knew. She had only been outside the town walls twice as far as she remembered, and Vannes was her world. Was her father really acknowledging her? Could they really be going to his manor? Gwenn had only a vague notion of what a manor was like. Was it a large house? A *very* large house? Was it made of wood, like this one? Or stone?

'The sooner we leave the better,' Yolande said firmly. 'I'm ready. Gwenn, I want you to help your grandmother pack her things.'

Izabel did not have much in the way of personal possessions, none of them did; the packing would not take long. 'What about all our pots and cooking things?' Gwenn asked.

'Forget them,' Jean said. 'There's a cookhouse at Kermaria. And a cook. You won't have to cook again. Though you'll have to learn to keep the cook in order! I had planned for us all to leave shortly,' he went on. 'But as that young scoundrel Raymond is absent, your mother and I will go on ahead. You can follow later, and tell Raymond, when he appears.' He reached out and enfolded Gwenn's hands in his. 'I'll detail a couple of men to act as your escort. They'll be here at midday. I want you to arrive in state.' And in one piece, he added mentally. 'Do you think you can manage, my dear?'

'Yes, of course. We'll bring Katarin.'

Jean's brown eyes twinkled. 'Would you? That would be kind. Your mother and I have matters to discuss en route, and much as we love the little one,' he bent and gave Katarin's rounded cheek an affectionate pinch, 'Yolande's mind works best when not centred on the child.'

'Raymond will be back soon, I'm sure,' Izabel said agreeably, waving her daughter and Jean from the chamber. 'You go on ahead.'

'God speed, sir,' Gwenn said. Though her father was apparently acknowledging her as his, she would continue to address him as 'sir' until such time as she was commanded otherwise.

When Yolande and Jean left the house, the pedlar was back on the patch that he had occupied the morning before. A mangy white cur sat a couple of paces away from him, tongue lolling.

Yolande walked vigorously. Much as she might regret being driven from Vannes like the town pariah, she was not sorry to be moving out of la rue de la Monnaie. She was glad to be leaving the old life behind her. This would be a fresh start, the one she had longed for, and she would not look back.

The bright beacon of the sun warmed her head through her veil. Jean's arm was under her hand, strong and firm. She had been right to trust him. Wasn't he taking them to Kermaria, where they would be safe? Keeping her head firmly to the front, she fastened her eyes on the horses Jean's squire, young Roger de Herion, was holding for them at the end of the street. Who knows, she thought, one day he might marry me. She did not mind about her unmarried state for herself, she and Jean were already bound together and no priest's mumblings could strengthen that bond. It was the children that worried her. Of its own accord, her head turned. One last glance wouldn't hurt.

Her eyes lit on the pedlar. The shiftless fellow was already deserting his place, kicking that poor dog out of his path. Yolande watched him shuffle towards the square and guessed that he was heading for Duke's Tavern. How could he hope to make any money when he didn't have the sense to stick to his patch for more than five minutes at a stretch?

'Taking a farewell look?' Jean asked.

Yolande nodded, throat suddenly too constricted for speech, and blinked rapidly. She had lived in that small wooden building for sixteen years. She had borne all her children in it. Jean's hand covered hers.

'A new life,' he murmured.

From a distance the house was unremarkable. It was just one of the many thatched wooden houses in Vannes. Yolande swallowed. 'A new life,' she managed. And slowly, sedately, the town's most innocent, most notorious concubine left la rue de la Monnaie for the last time. She had no idea that by the time the midday Angelus rang out, not a trace of that street would remain.

Otto Malait sauntered into Duke's Tavern with as much bravado as he could muster, fine hair hanging in rats' tails about his shoulders, beard uncombed. Mornings were not a good time for the Norseman, but he invariably felt stronger when he'd downed a potful or two. He saw Alan le Bret at once, half hidden by a smoke-blackened beam in a corner to the left of the fire. Ned Fletcher, the lad Otto was interested in, and the pedlar, Conan, were at le Bret's table, bread and ale set before them, and a lousy hound was shaking fleas into the rushes. The yawning potboy was removing last night's spent torches from the wall sconces and replacing them with fresh ones which would be lit that evening. Otto caught the potboy's eyes and, signalling for service, went to join his colleagues.

'An unholy trinity,' he observed. His mind was fixed on religious concerns as well as Ned Fletcher, for that morning Count de Roncier had asked him to obtain a statue of the Holy Virgin from the concubine's house. The Holy Virgin? In a harlot's house? Shaking his head to clear it of last evening's wine fogs, Malait recalled that de Roncier wanted the statue's existence kept dark. Now why should that be?

Alan kicked a stool out for him. 'If we're the unholy trinity, Malait, what does that make you? A fallen angel?'

Ned Fletcher smothered a laugh, but the potboy, Tristan, waiting at Otto's elbow for his order, was foolish enough to snigger aloud.

'Get me wine, boy,' Otto growled. 'Or mead. Anything but ale. *Move.*' Otto's calloused hand descended to the potboy's shoulder to twist him round.

'You're late, Malait,' Alan observed. 'The Count beat you to your post this morning.'

'Oh?' That's what le Bret thought. Count François had had him roused before sunrise to confer with him, which was one reason he felt so rough. As to the other reason – the Norseman glanced briefly at the Saxon lad, whose innocent blue eyes were watching him – the boy hadn't the first idea that he was the reason Otto had dipped too deeply in the barrel last night. This morning Otto's head felt as though it was compressed in too tight a helmet, but another drink would soon mend that.

Alan's grey eyes were trained on the soot-blackened ceiling. 'The Count's up there,' he said. 'Counting his coin. He's sworn to pay up, and he's had the strongbox carried up.'

'And a woman too, I'll be bound.' Otto scowled. 'It's fortunate for the Count that there are men like us prepared to do his work for him while he plays.'

The potboy stumbled up, bearing a tray with an assortment of vessels, variously filled, and all slopping over to make a muddy brown lake on the tray.

Alan passed the Viking the largest vessel. 'Here's a drinking horn worthy of Odin himself. You can souse yourself in this today, Malait. You need sweetening. *Washeil!*'

Rolling a jaundiced eye at his companion-in-arms, Otto thrust the goblet to his mouth.

'Sweetening?' Ned asked. 'What is it?'

'Mead,' his cousin informed him as the Viking drained the cup dry. 'He's a bear without it.'

Tristan unloaded his swimming tray and shuffled off.

Emerging from his goblet, with mead spreading warmth along his veins, Otto scanned the inn. 'Tavern's a morgue today,' he said, sleeving golden liquid from his beard.

The pedlar, glimpsing his opening, lurched into speech. Conan calculated that if he was especially helpful a large *pourboire* might be forthcoming. 'Aye, Captain. It's like this most mornings, early on. It was only yesterday because of the Black Monk . . .' The pedlar became aware that the three pairs of eyes watching him were bored, and his voice trailed off to finish lamely, 'But of course you know that.'

Alan nodded. 'Awake now, Malait?'

Otto grunted.

'Good. Conan informs me that Yolande Herevi and Jean St Clair left Vannes half an hour ago. They had horses waiting, and rode out via the postern gate.'

Otto's pale eyes bulged as he digested this information. 'God rot them, don't tell me the old crone has turned tail too?' The Count had been most explicit about wanting the statue, which apparently belonged to Izabel Herevi; now Otto would have to chase after them and retrieve the statue – not that he relished the idea of an ambush in broad daylight. He eyed Ned Fletcher and the cups on the table with regret. He could think of far pleasanter ways of spending a morning, but his orders had been most specific. Reluctantly, he rose.

'Where are you off to?' Alan demanded. 'If they've gone, our task is done.'

The Viking combed blunt fingers through his beard. De Roncier had been most insistent that Alan le Bret was not to be in on this. 'Er . . . best to tail them, make sure that they're off for good.'

'They are,' the pedlar assured him. 'I kept my ears pinned to the shutters; St Clair told his woman he was sending someone back for her travelling chests. I heard one being pulled down the stairs. Made a hell of a row. Thump, thump, th—'

'Thank you, Conan,' Alan cut in, 'we get the drift.'

'What about the old woman?' Otto demanded.

The pedlar's protruding belly rumbled; he scratched it and helped himself to some bread. On the floor, the dirty white cur pricked up its ears and shuffled closer. 'As I heard it, she's to follow later, with St Clair's bastards.'

'Relax, Malait,' Alan said. 'Vannes will be clear of them by sunset. Sit down and have another drink.' He slid a cup towards the fair giant. 'You've a problem?'

'No. It's nothing,' Otto said swiftly. 'I . . . wanted to make sure we'd carried out our orders.'

'Exceptional diligence.'

'Eh?'

The English mercenary smiled thinly and, to Otto's relief, fell silent.

'I've a confession, Captain Malait.' Ned Fletcher leaned forward, blue eyes bright and confiding. 'I'm glad they're going without us having a hand in it.'

'Are you, lad?' Reseating himself, Otto smiled with

what Alan realised was uncommon tolerance. Though the Viking's teeth were even, they were discoloured with wine, and this spoilt the effect.

Alan did not like the way Otto Malait was regarding his cousin, not that he cared how his fellow captain and his cousin took their pleasures. However, he knew his conventional cousin well enough to realise that he would consider an advance from the Viking an abomination. Ned might be one of the softer members of his troop, he might well crave affection, but his cornflower-coloured eyes only ever strayed to the lasses.

'To tell you the truth, Malait, I'm relieved myself,' Alan admitted. 'I intend resigning this day. De Roncier will have to find another captain for my troop.'

'Resign your commission?' Ned blurted, and his artless eyes went round and filled with hurt. 'You never mentioned it to me.'

'I'm mentioning it now. I intend pitching my tent elsewhere.' His cousin looked thunderstruck, and Alan felt bound to elaborate. 'I intended resigning yesterday. You will recall, Ned, we signed on till this quarter day; but as de Roncier seemed disinclined to pay the men until the job was done, I thought I'd see it through.' Alan saw no reason to mention the additional silver he had been promised.

'Does the Count know your plans?'

Otto snorted. 'If I know our captain, he won't inform de Roncier that he's not going to renew his contract until he's got his grimy paws on his pay. Am I correct?'

A dark brow lifted. 'I trust the noble Count about as much as I would trust you, Malait.'

Mellowed by his mead, the Viking looked delighted. 'I'll take that as a compliment.'

Ned butted in. 'Alan—'

'Don't fret yourself over your pay, Ned. I won't leave until you've got yours.'

'It's not that, Alan, but . . . but . . .' Ned stuttered to a halt, scarlet flags flying in his cheeks.

'Your kinsman's going to miss you, le Bret,' Otto

drawled, amused. 'Never mind, I'll be here to hold his hand.'

The flush deepened on Ned's cheeks but the innuendo escaped him. 'But why, Alan? Why leave? You told me yourself that the Count always pays in the end.'

'I've stayed with de Roncier long enough.' Alan lifted his shoulders. 'Let's just say I'm going in search of greener pastures.'

Ned jerked his flaxen head at the ceiling. 'You don't like him.'

Alan looked blank. '*Like* de Roncier? What's liking got to do with it? You don't have to like a man to work for him.'

'Don't you?'

Ned's gaze could be very penetrating. Exasperated, Alan shook his head, but he held his peace. If his cousin wanted to think he was resigning for moral reasons, then who was he to disabuse him? Wearily, he reached for his ale, and as he did so he became aware that a hush had fallen over the thin company. Looking up, he was shocked to see the concubine's daughter brazenly threading her way through the tables. She was swathed in another of those filmy veils which were more fitted to a Saracen's harem than a tavern in Vannes. This one was sea-green.

The pedlar had seen the girl too, and he was choking on his drink. 'Look, Captain!'

Alan shrank back to conceal himself, partly behind Otto Malait's substantial bulk, and partly behind a wooden beam. 'I've seen her,' he muttered. 'No. Don't turn round, Malait. The concubine's daughter has just flown in.'

'What? Here?' Malait turned and looked her up and down.

'Christ, Malait,' Alan groaned.

'Simmer down, Captain, the wench doesn't know me from Adam. It was you set the mob on her.' Otto's straw-like beard concealed a malicious grin. The Viking knew he was speaking too loudly for Alan's peace of mind, but he enjoyed needling him. He took everything so seriously, did Captain le Bret. Above the straw the pale eyes narrowed. 'I wonder if she's left the old witch on her own?'

Alan deemed it wiser not to respond. With the inn being all but empty, there was a real danger she might recognise them. Ned had turned his face away, half covering it by resting his cheek on a hand. Duke's Tavern was the last place Alan had expected to see St Clair's bastard after yesterday. He strained his ears to hear what we she was saying.

'Is Irene about?' She addressed the yawning potboy who was clearing a nearby trestle of wine slops and crumbs with a filthy, discoloured cloth that Alan's mother would have burnt a year ago.

'Eh?' Tristan flicked a piece of gristle into the rushes. A furry white streak flashed across the floor. Jaws snapped. Amiably, Tristan kicked the dog towards the routiers and continued his ineffectual wiping.

'Irene, is she about?'

Heaving himself to his feet, Otto adjusted his sword belt and lifted one of the fresh, unlit torches down from its wall stand. 'I'm off,' he said. If the girl was in the inn, the old woman had to be alone, for the pedlar had informed them the boy was elsewhere. This was a God-given opportunity to get de Roncier's statue. One weak old woman wouldn't be able to offer much resistance.

'Malait,' Alan glared, 'what the hell are you playing at?'

'I'm going to stretch my legs, le Bret,' Otto answered, belligerently waving the torch. 'Any objections?'

'Keep your voice down. I don't object. But what the hell are you doing with that torch?'

'I've a use for it,' came the cryptic reply.

'And your pay?'

'I'll collect that later.' Otto's gaze rested briefly on Ned Fletcher, as he realised, with regret, it was most

99

likely the lad would accompany his cousin. 'We'll meet again?'

'Perhaps.'

Swinging stiffly back to the table, Otto shoved a scarred fist under Alan's nose. 'In case I don't see you, I wish you good luck. I hope you find your Valhalla.'

'My thanks.' Solemnly the two mercenaries shook hands.

'I trust we'll never find ourselves fighting on opposite sides in anyone's war, le Bret.'

'Amen to that, Malait. I'd have to kill you.'

'Not a hope this side of the underworld.' Otto's mouth split in a gaping grin. 'You'd be mincemeat before you knew what hit you. Au revoir, le Bret.'

Meanwhile the concubine's daughter was persisting with her quest. 'I . . . I'd like to see Irene.' Her eyes darted nervously to the Viking as he shouldered past her and left the inn.

'Irene's not here,' Tristan answered.

The concubine's daughter placed herself in the potboy's path, and when he went to move to the next trestle, she was there, waiting for him. Her fingers were crumpling the edges of her veil. There was something different about her, and it puzzled Alan. Yesterday, when he had seen her for the first time, her face had been full of confusion and not a little fear, but he had sensed hidden reserves in her. She had at first refused to accept what was happening to her – she'd not begun to flee until his missile had actually struck her. Alan had put that down to natural arrogance. But watching her now, he realised his assessment had been inaccurate.

Today, though the girl was insistent that Tristan take notice of her, her confidence had gone, and with it that touch of pride. She had lost that blind faith in human nature that only the truly innocent possess. Well, that would do her no harm, the sooner she learnt the harsh realities of life, the better. However, it was surprising to discover that a concubine's daughter could have been so innocent. Alan rubbed his chin. She must have been fenced off from hurt, and blind prejudice and hate – until yesterday, when all those things had come hurtling towards her in the shape of the good citizens of Vannes.

The girl must be wondering whether she was safe in Mikael Brasher's tavern. She was wondering whether the people sitting at the table were the same people who had chased her yesterday. Her eyes travelled inevitably to their table, and hastily Alan ducked his head.

'Not gone yet?' Tristan asked with lazy insolence.

'As you see.' The girl's cheeks were white as snow. She gave the lad a shaky smile. 'Would you give Irene a message for me?' Fine-boned hands were clasped in front of her small breasts. 'Please?'

'Very well.' Grudgingly, the potboy put his hands on his hips. 'What's your message?'

'I . . . I want you to say au revoir to Irene for me.'

'Au revoir? You're coming back?'

'N . . . no. No. I mean adieu.' Her pale cheeks coloured, and pitilessly Alan suppressed an unasked for pang of fellow-feeling. The boy drummed rude fingers on the trestle. 'Say farewell, and please give Irene this.' She held out a narrow strip of parchment, which Tristan looked at with the wary eyes of a man to whom reading was a deep mystery.

'What is it?' he demanded suspiciously.

'It's only my direction. If Irene needs a friend, tell her she can find Gwenn there.'

Gwenn, thought Alan. Her name was Gwenn. And she could read and write. Alan shook his head in amazement. Her mother must be quite mad. What use was that to a girl?'

Tristan stared at the creamy ribbon of vellum. 'Irene can't read,' he announced with gloomy triumph.

The girl looked nonplussed. 'No. How stupid of me. I suppose not. Of course she can't.'

Tristan appeared to relent. 'She could ask Father Mark to make it out.'

The girl's face cleared and she thrust the scrap of parchment at Tristan who, with uncommon fastidiousness, wiped thumb and forefinger on his breeches before touching it. 'Many thanks. Farewell.' She scuttled into the street, and the potboy tucked the parchment into his sleeve.

At the trestle in the corner, Alan, Ned, and Conan the pedlar all breathed again. Ned spoke for all of them. 'I thought she'd be bound to see us.'

'Gwenn,' Alan muttered. 'It's very apt.'

'What was that?'

Alan's eyes focused on his young kinsman's. 'The girl's name is Gwenn.'

'So I heard. But I don't—'

'You ought to polish up your Breton, cousin, but I'll translate for you. Gwenn means white. It's the Breton equivalent of Blanche.'

'White?' Ned echoed. 'You've lost me.'

'Think about it. White. It also means fair.'

'She *is* pretty . . .' his cousin responded, gazing admiringly through the door.

'Is she?' Alan picked up his tankard and swirled the dregs of his ale round the bottom. 'White, symbol of purity and innocence. But the mud's beginning to cling, wouldn't you say?'

'What?'

'Don't worry about it, Ned.' Alan tossed back the last of his ale and met his cousin's cornflower gaze straight on. 'Permit me to give you one last piece of advice.'

'Aye?'

'If you intend to stay in this business, it's advisable not to get to know your enemies too well before you start a campaign. You can end up feeling sorry for them, and that only leads to disaster.' Alan pushed back his stool.

'I'll bear that in mind,' Ned said agreeably. 'Are you leaving at once?'

'When I've collected what's owed me.'

'Where are you going?'

'That, Ned, my lad, is no one's business but my own.'

Ned hauled in a breath. 'I know. But as you pointed out, I was only committed to serving Count de Roncier to this quarter day too, and I hate the man. I want to leave his service. I'd like to go with you.' He flushed self-consciously.

'You're no longer a beardless boy that you need a mentor.'

'But I'd like to go with you.' One of Ned's square hands ran through his flaxen hair. 'Damn it, Alan. I *like* your company. Does our friendship mean nothing to you?'

Deliberately Alan turned his eyes from his cousin's eloquent blue gaze. 'I travel alone this time, Ned. Nothing personal, but I need to travel alone.' He extended a hand, which his cousin blinked at. 'Fare you well.'

Ned's stool scraped back and the young trooper got stiffly to his feet. 'I understand.' He gave Alan a last, searching look. 'I'll accompany you upstairs, Alan. I still intend to quit, but I'll make my own way after.'

'Captain,' the pedlar snatched at Alan's leather gambeson, '*I've* not been paid.'

Peeling the grasping, wiry fingers from the hem of his jerkin, Alan groped in his pouch for a silver penny and dropped it on the pedlar's palm. 'Thanks for the information, Conan.'

'You'll commend me to Count de Roncier?'

'I will.' Mentally, Alan added the pedlar's coin to his tally of what de Roncier owed him. He headed for the stairs, Ned hard on his heels.

Conan noticed the stray dog lying by his feet as faithfully as if he were his master. He threw it the heel of the loaf, which vanished in one hungry bite. Rising slowly, Conan picked up his tray of goods and prepared to leave. He kicked the dog in passing.

Chapter Seven

Standing with the well between her and the entrance to la rue de la Monnaie, Gwenn tried to calm herself. The two routiers who had been outside the cathedral yesterday were slumped over a trestle in Duke's Tavern; and the Viking who had pushed past her with a torch had been sitting with them. They had to be de Roncier men. Gwenn was almost certain she had concealed her dismay from them, and that they had no inkling that she had recognised them; but her mind was a bubbling brew-tub of questions.

Why were they in the tavern? Were they planning more trouble? And what did that giant of a Norseman want with a torch on a clear day? If only she could believe their presence that morning was an unlucky coincidence, and that they were merely quenching their thirst.

Conscious that her hands were trembling, Gwenn curled her fingers into her palms. She had believed her mother and grandmother had been exaggerating when they attributed the trouble to the French noble. All this talk of ancient grudges stemming from those long-distant days before her mother had even been born had seemed most unlikely, but now . . .

She tried to still the ferment inside her. She told herself that mercenaries were men of violence. What had been a stomach-churning nightmare to her, to them was more than likely only a mildly exciting romp through the streets. And de Roncier's men had not chased her home, the townsfolk had done that. And now, in the square, in broad daylight, with the citizens going placidly about their daily business, it was hard to believe that they meant her any lasting hurt. The mercenaries were only drinking in the tavern, as they did every morning, no doubt. It meant nothing. The cathedral was behind her. The sun was shining down la rue de la Monnaie as it did every morning.

A brisk wind raised goosebumps on her arms, its gusts buffeting the martins, screeching and scissoring after insects in the sky above. A dark canopy of clouds hung over the thatched roofs in the western quarter. Gwenn drew her veil over her head. The martins would have to hurry, or the coming rainstorm would put paid to their meal. She hoped the rain would pass quickly, for her grandmother could not have ridden in a decade and it would make a penance of the journey to Kermaria.

Casting her glance past the well to her house at the far end of la rue de la Monnaie, Gwenn pulled up sharply. A restless crowd had gathered outside. Gwenn's blood ran cold, and her brief feeling of calm vanished. St Gildas save us, she prayed. Don't let this happen again. Yesterday had been a bad dream, but Jean St Clair had been there, and his men had fended off the crowd. Today he had gone to Kermaria with her mother, and the promised escort had not yet arrived.

More citizens were joining the crowd milling about at the other end of the street. They were like ants when their nest is disturbed, running back and forth with distracted, disorderly movements. There were shouts of confusion. Some people started to run; they were charging towards *her*. Gwenn's heart shifted in her breast.

'Sweet Jesus, no!' She stumbled back a pace. 'Not again. Sweet Jesus . . .'

Several townsfolk roared up to the well, blocking her way to the house. Poised for flight, Gwenn edged backwards. 'Mother of God, help me . . .'

Outside her house, the crowd was still growing. More desperate questions bubbled up. Was Raymond back or were Izabel and Katarin alone in there? Would the mob break in? What would they do to them? Her limbs locked and, like yesterday, she couldn't run. Grandmama! Katarin! And then she realised that it did not matter that she could not move, for she could no more abandon her family than fly up with the martins. 'No,' she said, firmly, to brace herself.

One of the men at the well looked across at her. He was, to her astonishment, hauling on the well rope. It was Pierre, the herbalist. She waited for the onslaught that was sure to follow his sight of her.

'Gwenn! It's Gwenn!' Pierre screeched, and irrationally he grinned at her. 'She's not in the house!'

Why was Pierre pulling up the well bucket? A new terror broke on the roiling surface of her mind. Surely they were not intending to throw her down the well? Of all the crimes that could be committed in a town, polluting the water supply was one of the most heinous. The laws protecting wells were upheld by people in every walk of life. Everyone from rich merchant to poor beggar, from Breton to Frenchman, from nun to cutpurse, all sang out with one voice against anyone low enough to contaminate the well. Gwenn conquered a violent compulsion to scream.

Pierre was shouting at her. 'Gwenn! Gwenn! Is anyone in there?'

'What?' Fear hampered her thoughts, and understanding was slow. 'What?'

'Your house!' Pierre shrieked, pouring water from one bucket to another. Handing the overflowing vessel to another man, he cast the well bucket down the shaft again and hauled on the handle without pause. 'Is anyone in there?'

Peculiarly divorced from the scene unfolding before her, Gwenn watched the bucket Pierre had filled being passed hand over hand down a long line of townsfolk which stretched to the bottom end of la rue de la Monnaie. That torch. The Viking had taken a *torch* with him . . .

The light dawned. Gwenn lurched to the well-head, white fingers clinging to the cold, mortared rim. 'Why are you doing that, Pierre? Which house is burning?'

Pierre's honest face was creased with concern, and he was sweating profusely. How could she have thought him malevolent, even for a moment? She should have known better, Pierre was a healer, and anyone could see that he was frantic with fear.

'Is anyone in your house?' The herbalist secured the well-handle and shook her by the arm. 'Think, Gwenn!'

'Grandmama and Katarin.'

Pierre went the colour of goat's cheese. A woman down the line drew a hasty sign of the cross on her breast, caught Gwenn's disbelieving eyes on her and flinched. 'Sorry, love.' The woman shook her head with brief sympathy before turning back to the herbalist. 'Hurry, Pierre, other houses are smoking like the devil's pit.'

'For God's sake, move!' A neighbour, a tanner by trade, nudged Pierre, work-stained hands outstretched for the pail. Too practical a man to waste time on Gwenn, he did not even look at her. 'The whole street's about to go! Pierre!'

Gwenn choked down a sob.

'Steady, girl,' Pierre said, and compassion filled his eyes.

Gwenn bolted. She ran so fast that she reached her house before the first bucket of water. The woman had exaggerated. There wasn't that much smoke, and what there was seeped through the closed shutters to float in the street as innocently as a sea-fret on an April morning before the sun chased it away. Perhaps Izabel had spilled fat on their cooking fire in the tiny yard at the back of the house where her mother grew herbs. It couldn't be anything sinister. But Izabel was not cooking today . . . That torch, what had that giant done with that torch?

She aimed for the door. Hands tugged at her skirts. Voices tried to capture her attention.

'No, Gwenn, don't!'

'You can't go in there!'

'Come back, girl!'

She shut her ears to the voices, fought through the hands, saw an opening and dived through it. All light and sound faded. A solid pall of smoke hung in the downstairs chamber. Peering through it, Gwenn saw the torch. It lay against the back wall of the house. Both torch and wall were smouldering. Along the planked floor the flames had caught hold in places, someone had flung a wet blanket on them in an attempt to douse them, and the blanket was the source of the smoke. The fire had been set, deliberately, and she knew by whom.

The rounded water cauldron was off its hook. It lay on its side, rolling gently on the boards, as though it had fallen only moments before. A distant but persistent wailing reached Gwenn's ears. Katarin was very much alive.

Coughing, for smoke filled her lungs, Gwenn thrust her veil in the small puddle of water washing about in the iron pot and wound the damp cloth round her mouth. She groped towards the stairs, following the sound of her sister's crying. 'Grandmama!' She tried to call again, but there wasn't the air. Gaining the door at the top of the stairs, she pushed it aside and stumbled through. The door had kept the smoke out, for the pall hung thinner and higher in the bedchamber and breathing came easier.

Izabel stood by the window, baby Katarin fast in one arm, while the other was held up to protect her face for, towering menacingly over her, was the form of a giant. It had to be the Viking, though his features were masked by trails of unkempt blond hair. Gwenn watched in disbelief as he lifted one ham of a hand and delivered a vicious blow to her grandmother's head. 'Where is it, witch?' he said.

Gwenn dashed forwards. 'Grandmama!' The man turned, and she stared directly into the bearded face of the Norseman whom she had seen not ten minutes earlier in Duke's Tavern with the other routiers. The smoke was thickening. Izabel sagged against a wall.

Katarin ceased wailing long enough to draw breath, and loosed another high-pitched assault on their ears. 'Mama! Mama! Mama!' she cried, a steady stream of sound. Burning wood crackled. The house was firing fast.

Izabel's free hand scuttled sideways to fumble with the shutter catch. Her grey headdress had been torn off. Her mouth was bleeding. The blow that Gwenn had witnessed had not been the first. Making a missile of her body, Gwenn hurled herself at the Viking. 'Leave them alone!' she yelled, and struck out with both hands.

The Viking bared a dreadful row of teeth. A thick, muscled arm snaked out, and Gwenn was tossed head first to the floor as though she were no more than a bundle of rags. 'Keep out of it, wench.' He turned back to Izabel.

Izabel had managed to open the shutter. She thrust her head through the opening. 'Help! Help!'

Her tormenter gave a warped grin. One stride carried him to her and he snatched her from the window. 'They'll not come in here, witch,' he said, with terrifying confidence. 'The blaze is upon us.'

He spoke the truth, for butter-coloured flames were climbing the stairs. He whirled Izabel round, holding her in a hideous parody of a lover's embrace. She strained to twist her head away from the Viking's, but his skewed smile only widened, and he pushed fingers as punishing as steel claws into her grey hair.

'Where is it?' he repeated, hoarsely, because even the untamed men of the north were affected by smoke.

White as chalk, Izabel made a choking sound. Katarin stumbled through the curling smoke and fell into Gwenn's arms. Her plump cheeks were stained with tear tracks, and she was coughing, her small lungs unable to cope with the dense, suffocating smoke.

Helpless to do anything for her grandmother, Gwenn clung to her little sister and shielded Katarin's eyes from the nightmare scene that was being played out before them. She shrieked through black, billowing clouds at the brute who was manhandling her grandmother. 'Stop it! Stop it!'

'Where is it?' The Viking gave Izabel a teeth-rattling shake. Izabel spluttered, and her mouth shut tight as a clam. 'Answer me, bitch. Where is it?'

The air was painfully thin. Gwenn's lungs burned and a singing noise began in her ears. Katarin had stopped crying; the little girl's breathing was so shallow that it was all but non-existent, and her moon of a face was turning blue. 'Katarin!' Gwenn tried to drag her dampened veil across her sister's mouth, hoping it would filter out the worst of the smoke, but the child's starfish-shaped hand came up and pushed it away. Gwenn let her be. Katarin was probably right. They were beyond that remedy. The darkness was closing in on them. Her lungs were a tight, painful mass in her chest. When a strangled whimper emerged from her sister's blue lips, Gwenn was goaded into action.

She must get air into Katarin's lungs. She had to get air herself. They were suffocating in smoke. More grey clouds wafted through the door. Amber flames flickered. The stairs were out of the question, that route was closed. She looked at the window. Light poured through it – light and fresh air. She must get to it. Hauling herself upright and ignoring the figures swaying about in a deadly embrace in the centre of the room, Gwenn swam through the clouds to the window. The clean air hit her like a slap in the face. Gasping and sobbing with relief, Gwenn fell on her knees. With the last of her strength she lifted Katarin up so she too could breathe. Katarin took half a dozen shuddering breaths, went pink, and recommenced her wailing. Panting, Gwenn rested her head against the wooden sill. If Katarin could cry, she was all right.

'Give her to me!'

Gwenn's head jerked up. Someone was shouting, but she could not make out the direction.

'Give the baby to me!'

It was not her grandmother. Where the two figures had been locked together, there was nothing, only spiralling black smoke. It must be someone in the street. Gwenn stuck her head through the narrow window, towards light and hope. 'Pierre . . . ?' The crowd of anxious people had grown. The breeze had fanned the fire, and the building next door was smouldering. For the townsfolk, a house blaze spelled disaster; the wooden dwellings packed tightly together caught fire more quickly than kindling. Yesterday's antipathy was forgotten. In such an emergency, everyone dropped what they were doing and rushed to assist. The line of fire-fighters was lengthening by the second. Some were flinging water at the houses, but not all of them were actively helping. A circle of faces was upturned towards her; some strained, some anxious, and others merely curious. A bitter condemnation flashed across Gwenn's consciousness. Some of them were looking on as though this were an entertainment devised solely for their pleasure.

One of the upturned faces was shouting. 'Throw the baby down! I'll catch her!'

Katarin squeaked and hid her face on her sister's shoulder. 'Wh . . . what?' Gwenn must have misheard.

'Throw her down!'

Gwenn gripped her sister hard. Her brain wouldn't work. Throw Katarin out of the window? Was the man mad? 'I . . . I can't!'

'For the love of God, girl!' His voice was urgent, compelling. 'You must!'

He was familiar, she had seen him before. Young, with startling blue eyes, and a tangle of fair hair like a Saxon's. He wore a soldier's leather jerkin . . . Her stomach cramped.

'Come on, girl! You've no time to think! Throw her down! It's not so high. Hurry.' He gestured to the man next to him. 'Your cloak, Alan. It's stronger than mine.

112

Stretch it out.' Strong hands grabbed a thick, fur-lined cloak, stretched it out and made a hammock of it. 'Throw her down! She hasn't got far to fall. This cloak will be as safe as her cradle!'

In the inferno behind her, Izabel cried out. The soldier was right. She had to do it. It was better than Katarin suffocating to death. Dropping a swift kiss on her sister's forehead, she leaned out of the window. 'I'll see you in a minute, darling.' Katarin's wail became an ear-splitting screech. Gwenn extended her arms as far as she was able.

'Now!' The young man's shout drew her gaze. 'She'll be safe with me. Now, Gwenn!' Steady blue eyes held hers, honest eyes. Gwenn's mind raced. How had he come by her name? No matter. He had a sensitive, open face for all that it clashed with his mercenary's attire. She could trust his eyes, if not his profession.

The young man's neighbour moved impatiently, and she saw the top of his dark head turning to the gawpers clustered below the window. 'Help us.' He held out the hem of his cloak, and people jumped to take it. Incongruously, she noticed a ring on his middle finger, for she caught the flash of gold as the sun bounced off it. He had bitten fingers, but they clutched the edge of the cloak securely. Both men looked fit and capable. Reassured that her sister would have a soft landing, Gwenn screwed her eyes shut and let go. When she opened them again, Katarin lay motionless in the valley of the cloak. 'Katarin!'

Katarin blinked and moved her arms. 'Gwenn?' the child's voice bleated. Katarin pointed at her, and smiled. 'Gwenn?'

A ragged cheer went up. A strong hand reached out, plucked the infant from the cloak, and Katarin was pressed against the broad leather-clad chest of the blue-eyed soldier. He smiled at the infant, ruffled her hair, and placed her in the outstretched arms of a woman behind him. His flaxen head tipped back. 'Your turn now.'

'Jump, Gwenn! Jump!' Mikael Brasher had joined

113

the knot of people round the cloak.

The dark-haired man glanced up, and Gwenn's heart jolted. It was the mercenary who had set the mob on her. 'You! You threw the first stone . . .' Horrified, she stared accusingly at the young Saxon. 'And you . . . Why are you always with him?' Biting her lip, Gwenn shook her head. They had both been in the Duke's with the Norseman, that monster who had set fire to their house. What had he done with her grandmother?

Filling her lungs with untainted air, Gwenn wound her veil back round her nose and forced herself to go back. Her eyes smarted. In the swirling, choking black-ness she was all but blind. Praying her grandmother was close, Gwenn felt her way inch by lung-burning inch. Her foot nudged against something soft. Heart thumping, she went down on all fours, but the softness was the softness of fabric, not of a body. Her grand-mother's wimple. She cast it aside.

'Grandmama?'

Her lungs were bursting. The oak floorboards felt warm. Gwenn whimpered and tried to swallow, but her throat was dry as parchment. The crackling grew, was all but a roar, and the gaps between the floorboards shone yellow like the sun. The flames from the chamber below must burst through any second. The floor groaned a warning and shifted under her hands and knees. Gwenn gulped. Cold sweat trickled down her back. She was hot and cold all at once. Gritting her teeth, she crawled forwards another inch, and another, until eventually her hands encountered what felt like a corpse.

'G . . . Grandmama?' The body moved. It coughed. 'Thank God! You're alive!'

'Gwenn . . . ?' The old woman's breathing was harsh, laboured. 'Get out, Gwenn.'

'Grandmama!'

'Out,' Izabel whispered hoarsely. 'I'm finished.'

'No!'

'Finished.' Izabel was shaken by coughing. 'Divine retribution . . .'

That Viking animal had deranged her grandmother's mind. 'No.' Gwenn heaved on Izabel's arm, to little avail. She heard a roar as the back wall of the chamber became a curtain of fire. Great tongues of flame licked up it. The cracks in the floor glowed brighter, bright as molten gold in a goldsmith's crucible. 'Grandmama! Don't give up!'

'Tell . . . Yolande . . . I am sorry,' Izabel breathed, in distant, dreamy tones.

'Grandmother . . .' Gwenn sobbed. Izabel's mind must have gone; she seemed heedless of the danger.

'Though Yolande sinned . . .' Izabel choked weakly '. . . I see that my narrowness, my bitterness . . . was a far greater wrong. Tell her . . . ask her . . . forgive me?' Her voice faded; she blinked through the swirling drifts of smoke, seeming to rouse herself as she strained to raise her head. Rheumy eyes fell on Gwenn, and looked stricken. 'Why, Gwenn. Why have you not gone? *Your* time is far off. You must go . . .'

Roughly, Gwenn gripped her grandmother's arm. 'Grandmama, you're not even trying!'

Izabel twisted her head towards Gwenn's. 'It's my time, my dear. The Lord has spoken.' Her old eyes glistened with moisture. 'But you should not be here. Go. Say a Mass for my soul. Obey my last wish, and get out.'

It was hopeless. Dry, gulping sobs ripped through Gwenn. A loud crash informed her that part of the staircase had collapsed. She heard a drumming in her ears.

'Out!' Her grandmother's head thudded on the boards.

The drumming was louder, nearer; it sounded like footsteps. Gwenn screwed up her smarting eyes to squint through the smoke and went rigid. Someone was kneeling on the other side of her grandmother. Her senses deserted her.

She had been consigned to a furnace in Hell, and the Devil had sent one of his minions to torment her, for the flickering flames illumed swarthy features that were dirty with soot and streaked with sweat. Night-black brows arched over frenzied grey eyes. It was the face of a demon, and he had come to choose between her and her grandmother. Gwenn screamed, and reached for Izabel.

Her grandmother's hand fluttered to meet hers. 'Go,' Izabel gasped. 'And remember, Our Lady is yours. The Stone Rose is yours.' Izabel let her breath out, on a rattling sigh, and was still.

The demon was making his choice. Sick to her core, Gwenn watched as his fierce eyes passed briefly over her grandmother, seemed to find her lacking, and came to rest on Gwenn. The demon smiled.

'No!' Gwenn's lips were stiff with fear. He took her by the wrist and, as fiends do, he had the grip of ten men. Gwenn knew it would be useless to fight him.

'Come, girl.' Unceremoniously, he dragged her to her feet and shoved her towards the window and daylight.

Mercifully, with the clear, sweet air easing the pain in her chest, the panic receded, and with a flash of insight Gwenn knew that he was no demon. It was the routier, the one who had thrown the first stone, and for some reason he was trying to save her. He must be intending to throw her out of the window, after Katarin. But Gwenn was bigger than Katarin . . .

'Hell's teeth!' The mercenary's mind and hers ran the same course. 'The window's too small!' Jerking Gwenn to one side, he aimed his boot at the frame and sent it spinning into the street. Another moment and he had her on the ledge, facing inwards.

She found herself looking directly into his eyes. 'I'm too big,' she protested, clinging to his arms, as though his strength alone could save her.

His dark head shook. 'A tiny thing like you? Never. Bonne *chance*, my Blanche.'

The flash of white teeth as he grinned was the last thing she saw from the sill. He hooked his arm under her knees and sent her tumbling backwards out of the window and out into the fresh air of la rue de la Monnaie. The impact of her body striking the cloak forced that life-giving air from her lungs, and for a second or two it was all she could do to catch her breath. But she was not allowed any respite. The townsfolk muttered. The cloak was lowered. Helping hands rolled her out, onto the ground, where she lay gasping like a fish out of water.

'Gwenn! Gwenn!' Katarin cried. Blindly, Gwenn held out her arms to her sister, and then the tears came.

The cloak was stretched out over her head. It blacked out the sun. 'Hold it steady there!'

'Ready, Ned?' a new voice asked, coughing, from further off.

Silence gripped the crowd. All Gwenn could hear was the crackle of burning wood and the hiss of water on fire.

'Ready, Alan. Jump!'

There was a crack like thunder, a sickening thud, and someone gave a gasp similar to the one Gwenn had made when the air had been knocked from her lungs. A bulging purse, with its strings snapped, landed with a clunk at Gwenn's side. No doubt it belonged to her rescuer. Hugging Katarin, Gwenn retrieved it, climbing unsteadily to her knees, and peered over Katarin's brown mop of hair into the dip of the cloak. It had split, she saw, under the man's heavier body. The cloak was lowered to the ground, and the mercenary's grey eyes went straight to her.

'You all right?' he asked. Sweat beaded his brow.

'Aye.' Gwenn held up the purse. 'Yours?' He nodded. Lips curling, she chucked his no doubt ill-gotten gains onto his chest.

'My thanks,' he gasped, white about the face, but he made no move to pocket his coins.

'What's the matter?'

Her dark saviour stretched taut lips into a grin. He was a stranger to Gwenn but she would recognise excruciating pain on the face of the Devil himself. 'You're hurt!' she exclaimed, dashing away a hot tear.

'Aye. It was me who was too big,' he gasped, and winced. 'I think my leg has broken.'

Because the mercenary had saved her, and she did not like to see even a devil in pain, Gwenn moved towards him. Her grandmother was beyond help, but this man was not.

Chapter Eight

The hamlet of Kermaria perched on the eastern bank of a marshy river tributary which wandered lazily through vast uncharted tracts of forest to the north, and flowed south through the wetlands, eventually seeping into the Small Sea. To the south the village was bounded by a flat, boggy area; the western approaches were protected by the river, and the woodlands screened it to the north. From a military point of view Kermaria needed little to make it defensible, it could be reached easily only from the east – the route to Vannes.

Its population was small. Neglected by their lord this past two years, a few stalwart villagers managed to scrape a meagre living from the marsh. They either cut wainloads of rushes and sedge for thatch and carted them to Vannes, or they netted fish and eel as well as the wildfowl which gathered in flocks on the reed-edged waters.

Riding into Kermaria along the main trackway, her clothes sodden from the steady drizzle, Yolande tried to appreciate the forethought that had gone into the siting of this isolated manor. Her children would be secure here. But nonetheless her heart sank. It was a desolate, unlovely spot, and her first sight of it, with the landscape reflecting back the oppressive, unremitting grey of the clouds, was enough to depress the spirits of the hardiest soul. A spine-chilling shriek, like that of a wild pig, whipped through the damp air. 'What was that?' she demanded.

'Water rail.' Jean's smile mocked foolish fears. 'An insignificant, timid bird.'

'With a large voice.' Shivering, Yolande drew her cloak about her shoulders though the dripping garment could not possibly warm her. 'It almost had me out of the saddle.'

'I'd forgotten what a townswoman you are, Yolande. You'll become accustomed to the birds, there is an abundance of them here.' Jean's eyes wandered along the approach road, and Yolande followed his gaze.

The avenue was protected on either hand by a stone wall two yards high. Ahead of them, at the end of the avenue, loomed three storeys of squat, drab building. Jean's manor was a dumpy tower. Built on a square base, it was solid, grey and ugly. Green-grey lichen clung to the walls. Several window slits were visible, but only one of them, the larger central opening, would allow more than the slenderest spear of light into the interior. Pigeons nested in the sagging roof. All grey. Ivy-hung walls skirted an unkempt yard, in the midst of which a tumble of stones marked the spot where once there might have been a well. There was no well rope, the iron mechanism having rusted to dust. The outbuildings were in a similar state of disrepair and spoke of a lifetime of neglect. Rooks swirled on the horizon above the edge of the forest, black shapes against leaden clouds. Grey. Grey. Nothing but grey.

'What do you think?' Jean asked, a half-smile playing about his lips.

Yolande dredged her mind for a positive comment. 'It . . . it looks very . . . safe-looking, Jean, very . . . sturdy.' She eased her damp veil from the skin at the back of her neck.

'You don't like it,' he observed, lips twitching.

Yolande blinked through wet eyelashes at the pile of weathered stone. What could she say?

As they drew nearer, the dilapidation grew more apparent. The stones of the manor were broken and eroded; the mortar was gone in places; the stairway leading to the door had subsided, and some steps were missing. There was a gap between the top step and the door. A garden of weeds and moss was flourishing on the flat roof. If the building was left untended much longer, it would crumble back into the ground completely. Yolande knew her lover had rarely even visited the place since he had inherited two years ago, but to give him his due, the neglect was not all his; his father before him had let the place go to seed after Jean's mother, Lady Anne St Clair, had died. God only knew what horrors lurked inside.

'It has . . . possibilities,' Yoland got out, hardly daring to look Jean in the eye. 'But there's much to be done.'

'Aye.' His dark eyes were smiling, teasing. 'Go on, say it, my love. Admit that it could hardly be worse, and then we can laugh and have done. I'm lord of a bog. Do you understand now why I was loathe to bring you here?'

Yolande's mare picked her way along the walled trackway towards the manor, and suddenly a woman materialised as if out of nowhere, work-reddened hands wrapped firmly round a sedge scythe. Yolande's mare skipped sideways. Thin as the reeds in the riverbed, the woman stared at Yolande in unsmiling silence, hostile eyes lingering scornfully on Yolande's soaked finery. She clutched her scythe to her scrawny breasts as though it were a talisman to ward off evil. The scythe moved, fractionally.

Biting her lip, Yolande reined back. There was no doubting the challenge in the woman's mien. 'Jean?'

His mount brushed past her. 'It's only Madalen, my love. They are unused to strangers, but I think she'll remember me.' He nodded at the woman, who stared sullenly at him before a reluctant smile tugged the disapproving features into a semblance of friendliness. Madalen returned Jean's gesture, bobbed him a curtsy, and melted back into the wall.

Recovering her composure, Yolande straightened her

back and spurred both her mare and her own flagging humour. 'I hope there's nothing else skulking in the stonework, Jean.' She wagged a finger at him. 'I think you'd best tell me the worst—' She broke off, for her horse had drawn level with the spot where the woman had been, and the wall was pierced by a door. Further down she saw another. 'By my faith, are all their houses built out of the wall? Look, there's a window.'

'The wall was begun in my grandfather's time, as a defence,' Jean said. 'But it was never finished, and when it fell into disrepair, some of the villagers propped their cottages against it. You'll see them more clearly from the window in the solar. They're lined up on the other side, wooden shacks leaning against the wall, nothing but hovels really.' Jean drew in a deep breath, and grimaced ruefully. 'I've let my holding fall apart at the seams. When my father died, I was daunted by what needed doing, and by the lack of funds. My name will be mud when I make a start. The cottages will have to be resited, and the doors bricked up – they're a liability where they are.' Jean trotted briskly over a small bridge spanning an overgrown ditch.

The moat would have to be cleared. A portcullis should be erected by the courtyard entrance. It would all cost a pretty penny, but his first task must be to arrange for a steward to set down how many bondmen he had at his disposal, and whether any freemen had remained in the village. More used to hawking and hunting and dining in comfort with the Foucard household while he 'courted' Louise, Jean was aware that he would not find it easy to shoulder his responsibilities.

'I hear Brittany's in the area,' Yolande said.

'Aye. My father was sworn to the old Duke, but since he died I've not renewed the oath. Perhaps if I swear fealty to Brittany and apply for further revenues, he may grant a sum to tide me over until I knock this place into shape.'

'I thought you favoured France, not Brittany?'

'De Roncier favours France.'

'I see.' Having completed her inspection of the village, Yolande's eyes returned to the main dwelling. Cheek by jowl with it, at its eastern base, she noticed a smaller edifice, also in stone.

'The chapel,' Jean informed her, and their horses came to a halt at the steps of his abandoned home, 'dedicated to Our Lady. The village, Kermaria, takes its name from Her.'

'I had best visit the priest and pay him my respects,' Yolande said, wondering whether the local incumbent would be as understanding towards her and her dubious position as kind Father Mark had been.

'No need,' Jean relieved her mind of that burden, 'there is no resident priest. The prior from St Félix's Monastery ministers to the village on Sunday.'

'Monastery? Where's that?'

Jean pointed his crop at the forest. 'There's a small community of monks in there. I came across them while hunting as a young lad and was horrified. Sometimes I think holiness borders on insanity. Why, at least one of their number had the others wall him up in a cell – for life.'

'An anchorite!' Yolande shuddered.

'Exactly my reaction. The other monks put his food and water through a tiny slot in the wall. There's no light, and not much air. The hermit swears the most sacred of vows to spend the rest of his life in there. The poor wretch rarely speaks. They have to be mad, but they're quite harmless. I expect the old boy who was walled up has died by now. The others were not so . . . zealous.' Jean dismounted, and offered his hand to help her climb down.

'I mistrust zealots.'

He lifted Yolande to the ground, and squeezed her waist reassuringly. 'Don't worry, my love. They live in sickening squalor, but there's no malice in them. And as I said, one of their number comes visiting on Sunday.'

Satisfied, Yolande nodded. 'Well, until the Sabbath,

123

I'll content myself with a swift prayer in the chapel. But before that, you must show me what needs doing inside.'

Jean linked arms with his mistress. 'Yolande, I love you.'

'And I love you, Jean. Come on. Show me our new home.'

The solar at Kermaria was on the first floor. Yolande stood in the window embrasure, leaning against the open shutters. For all that she'd had a large fire built and had dried out, she was cold. Hugging a woollen wrap to her, she stared out of the window. The rain had ceased, and night was drawing in. Worn to the bone, she would be glad to see this day done.

She had met most of the women, and for the most part she thought she would soon have them yoked ready to resurrect Kermaria. She sighed. One or two, it had to be said, had not viewed her arrival with the greatest of delight, being set in the old, slothful ways that Jean's long absence had let them fall into. But the younger ones seemed actively pleased to see her. One especially, a fresh-faced girl called Klara who had a bloom in her cheeks and a shining sheaf of light brown hair, had leapt to help sweep the festering rushes from the solar. Klara had been sent out for fresh ones, and had strewn them liberally before the fire to dry, together with a clump of fragrant thyme which had survived the winter beneath a tangle of weeds in its overgrown plot. Mattresses were being aired. Bread was being baked. Meats were roasting in what passed for the cookhouse.

Progress had been made, but it had been slow and wearisome, and the musty bed which Yolande had unearthed in an alcove off the solar looked more and more attractive by the minute.

Long, thin slivers of mist were inching in from the marsh. Cautiously, delicately, they drifted up the walled lane, piling one on top of the other until they formed a white pool in the middle of the yard and made an island of the tumble of stones which had once been a well. They had been drawing water from the river, but on the morrow, Yolande resolved, the well must be cleaned out and its housing rebuilt. She shivered, and conscious that the chill she felt was more than merely physical, frowned. Her children and their escort were late. She could hear a bell tolling in the distance, but no hoofbeats. The ringing did not appear to come from any particular quarter. It glided in on the mist; it was everywhere and yet nowhere. The sound, like the white fingers of mist, hung suspended. It was eerie.

Jean strode into the solar, and Yolande jerked her wrap close about her shoulders. 'Listen, Jean.' She tipped her head at the window and Jean came to wind an arm about her. She rested against him, glad of his warmth and his solidity.

'I don't hear anything.'

Yolande could see that Jean was preoccupied with his duties. His villeins had been used to going on as freemen, and it was years since his freemen had been called upon to work out their rents. Bondmen and freemen alike were fearful that Jean's return heralded a loss of privilege. Yolande understood their resentment at being dragged out of their comfortable ruts by a lord they had not learnt to trust. They could not see the advantages that would come to them if life was breathed into Kermaria. No words of complaint had been uttered thus far, Yolande had learned all this from their eyes, but in time there would be complaints enough. There was nothing for it but to give Jean's retainers time to adjust. He must prove he meant to deal justly with them. If they refused to adapt, the freemen could go and make their livelihoods elsewhere, while the bondmen would have to be sold. 'There, a bell. Jean, you must hear it,' she said, worrying at her lower lip.

'Your ears must be sharper than mine. But it's the hour for Vespers.'

'The brethren in the forest, of course!'

'What did you think the bell signified?'

Yolande avoided his eyes. 'Nothing. You will think me most odd, Jean, but now I've stopped running about, I feel like death. It's like . . . It's like . . .' She struggled to find words for her sense of disquiet; but her fears drifted just beyond expression, formless and elusive, and as impossible to grasp as the mist. 'It's as though an evil spirit is hovering round the corner. Where are they, Jean?'

'You distress yourself unnecessarily.' Soothingly, he rubbed the small of her back in a way that normally calmed her. 'You put me in mind of a mother hen who has lost her chicks.'

A smile trembled, doubtfully, on the corners of her mouth. 'I do feel rather like that.' She vented her worries. 'But I wish they'd come. Where are they? It's only a couple of hours' journey. They should have arrived long since. Do you think something's happened?' Restlessly, she turned back to the window. 'I'm very concerned. Where can they have got to?'

Three strides took Jean to the door and he beckoned for her to follow. 'Come, Yolande, let's go up to the roof. You can see the whole road from there. We'll watch them ride up.'

'There!' Yolande pointed into the half light, where, seeming to float on a cushion of snowy mist, a small cavalcade was drawing nearer. 'I can see them!'

'I told you they'd be all right.' Jean screwed up his eyes. 'That's odd.'

'What? What have you seen?'

'I sent two men with the pack horses. But there are three now. See, there's another on one of the mules, and—' Jean gasped. 'Holy Christ! I can see what looks like a litter.'

Yolande clutched her throat. 'Someone's been hurt! Not Raymond, I can see him on that pack horse. And there's Gwenn, riding with Katarin before her.' She shaded her eyes. 'Jean, I can't see Izabel anywhere. Or any of their baggage.'

Jean swallowed. He had seen the coffin; a simple, ungilded box such as the common folk used in Vannes. But of Izabel Herevi there was no sign. Even when he squinted, the cavalcade was too distant for him to make out who was reclining in the litter, but he did not think it was a female form. He cleared his throat. Yolande was white as milk, and she had not yet marked that plain, unpainted box. 'I think we had better go down, my dear,' he said.

When they reached the top of the uneven flight of steps leading into the yard, Jean threaded a steadying arm through Yolande's. Shreds of unearthly mist clung to the ground. A bedraggled cockerel moved through the pale, vaporous pools with his hens, scratching for seed in the rain-soft earth while there was yet daylight. The air was dank and smelt of river. A pig squealed. In the walled lane, the doors gaped like greedy mouths; and as the procession drew nearer, figures gathered in the open portals, eyes blinking. Rooks circled overhead. The bell ceased tolling; the silence was doleful, and more tangible than the wispy evening mist.

'They take for ever.' Yolande forced the words through her teeth. 'Why don't they hurry?'

'The litter slows them down.' Jean observed that his eldest daughter was in a desperate state. She wore a travelling cloak that must be borrowed, for it swamped her. The hem of her dress was ripped, her hair was unkempt and plastered to her cheeks by wind and rain. She wore no veil, and her face was scratched and black with dirt which the storm had not washed away . . . Black?

'Jesu, Jean! Look at Gwenn!' Yolande pulled free and stumbled down the broken steps. 'Gwenn!'

'Mama!' Katarin responded, wriggling in her sister's arms and reaching towards her mother. 'Mama!'

Yolande lifted her youngest from Gwenn's lap and all but squeezed the breath out of her. 'Come here, darling. Give Mama a kiss. That's better.' Scrutinising Katarin, Yolande discovered the child did not seem unduly distressed. Relaxing, she transferred Katarin to her hip. A glance at the litter relieved her mind further, for it did not contain Izabel, only a stranger. The man's coal-black hair was streaked with sweat, and like her eldest daughter his features were obscured by a mask of what looked like soot. Under the filth, severe pain cut lines in his face. One of his legs was in a crude splint. 'Where's Izabel? Where's my mother?'

A huge tear rolled down Gwenn's grubby cheek and, lips trembling, she looked appealingly at her brother. Raymond dismounted, a look of bewilderment blurring the handsome lines of his face. His bright green eyes were glassy with shock.

Yolande felt as if she had been plunged into a trough of icy water.

'Mama . . .' Her son ran a hand – a shaking hand – round the back of his neck. 'Mama . . .'

'Raymond, why won't you look at me?' Following the direction of her son's gaze, Yolande saw the coffin.

'Mama, I'm sorry.' Raymond's voice shook. 'There was a fire. The house is gone. And Grandmère . . .'

Clutching Katarin to her breast, Yolande's knees buckled. One of Jean's arms curled round her waist, and Katarin was eased into the crook of his other.

'No. No!' Yolande backed away. 'I don't believe it! I won't believe it!'

Someone stepped into the unhappy circle in the middle of the yard, a hardy young man with a shock of fair hair and pleasant, open features which were easy to read. Sympathy filled his blue eyes. 'Madame,' the young man said, and his accent was strange to Yolande, 'I am very sorry. We did all we could, but we could not get her out. We got your daughters out, but the roof caved in.'

'Roof? Caved in?' Yolande did not like the compassion in those blue, blue eyes. It told Yolande that Izabel was truly gone. 'No,' she muttered fiercely. 'Not now, when we have finally come here.' In Kermaria, Izabel could have lived free of the shame that had shadowed most of her unhappy life. Desperately, Yolande willed the young man to vanish back into the mist, but he remained large as life, feet planted firmly on the ground, and his beautiful eyes were round with fellow-feeling. She would never be able to look at anyone with blue eyes again without remembering this day. She lifted a hand to block out the sight of those eyes, and gripped her daughter's bridle for support.

'Face it,' someone rasped from the ground by her feet.

It was the stranger in the litter. There was no compassion anywhere on that dark visage. Yolande looked at his eyes which were grey and dark with pain, but pitiless. Strangely, she found it easier to regard this man, who gave no quarter, than the other, compassionate one. 'I . . . I . . . I . . . beg your pardon?'

'Ned's telling the truth.' His voice lacked the foreign ring of the younger man's. 'Face it. The whole street was a mass of fire. The old woman's gone. Be thankful we got your daughters out.'

Jean surveyed the man on the litter. 'Your name?'

'Alan le Bret.'

'Master?'

The man paused before replying. 'None, at present.'

'Is it true, Alan le Bret, that Izabel Herevi is dead?'

Alan, whose skin was ashen under his black mask, grunted assent. 'Aye. Izabel Herevi sleeps her last sleep in yonder box.'

Yolande gave a soft moan and stepped blindly towards the coffin.

Jean thrust Katarin at his son. 'Raymond, take your sisters inside, and see that that man's hurts are seen to, will you? I shall look to your mother.'

Having settled Katarin with Klara in the relative comfort of one of the alcoves off the solar, Gwenn elected to tend to the routier herself. His litter had been dragged into the hall downstairs, and she was examining a willow basket the serving woman had told her was stocked with bandages and salves, while Raymond nosed around the solar.

'God, this is a midden of a place we've come to,' he said.

Gwenn looked up. Her brother was picking flakes of limewash from the damp-stained walls. Gwenn had been so full of grief for her grandmother that she hadn't had eyes for Kermaria. 'I expect the walls will dry out when the fire's been going awhile,' she said.

'For two pins I'd return to Vannes,' Raymond continued. 'I have friends there. I can't see that there's going to be much going on here. The nearest tavern must be three miles away.'

'You can't return, Raymond. None of us can, not now.'

The shock was back on Raymond's face, and for a moment Gwenn thought he was about to break down. 'I know.' Her brother's voice cracked. 'It's not something that's easily forgotten, is it?' His voice strengthened. 'I know de Roncier's to blame. One day, I'll make him pay, Gwenn, I swear it.'

Gwenn's eyes filled. 'Revenge won't bring Grandmama back.'

Her brother strode over the rushes and gave her a rough hug. 'Don't cry, Gwenn. That snake'll pay, I'll make certain of that, if it's the last thing I do.'

Her brother was offering her the only comfort he could, and Gwenn nodded, folding a linen cloth which she added to the basket of medicaments.

'Why are you soiling your hands tending to that villain downstairs?' Raymond demanded abruptly. 'Let someone else do it. Let that wench, Klara, see to him.'

'No. I want to help him. If it wasn't for him, I'd be dead.'

'I don't trust him. He could be working for de Roncier.'

'I don't trust him either, but he did save me, and I

confess I'm curious. That day we were chased, I saw him.'

'What? In the mob?'

Gwenn nodded. 'He was the first to throw a stone.'

'Mother of God!' A dark flush mottled Raymond's cheeks. 'And you want to bind his wounds as though he were some unsung hero! I'd steer well clear of him if I were you. That man's a bucket of trouble. I shall mention that you saw him in the mob to Mama.'

Gwenn grimaced in the direction of the spiral stairs. 'He couldn't hurt a fly at the moment.'

Making an impatient sound, Raymond swung away. 'And what about when he's healed? What then? Believe me, there lies a wolf that's not to be tamed.'

She dug in her heels. 'I don't want to tame him, I only want to heal him. It's a debt I owe him, for my life.'

Her brother flapped her out with a weary hand. 'Oh, go and tend your wounded wolf, Gwenn. But don't come crying if he bites.'

She picked up the basket. 'I won't.'

'The sooner he's better, the sooner we'll be rid of him,' Raymond observed sourly.

Gwenn smiled back from the doorway. 'There is that. Raymond?'

'What now?'

'Father Mark said the man has not been born who cannot be redeemed.' Basket tucked securely under her arm, she stepped quietly onto the winding stairs.

'Christ on the Cross!' Raymond exploded. 'Women! Will they never learn?'

Alan was stretched out on a pallet close to the fire in the hall, thinking that a drink would ease the throbbing in his leg. Someone was walking down the stairs, and he glanced up to assess his chances of persuading whoever it was to see to his needs. It was the girl, Gwenn Herevi.

'I've come to look at your leg,' she announced,

131

clutching a basket close to her breast.

That sounded hopeful. She had obviously decided to play at being an angel of mercy. Her eyes were wary, but brimming with good intent. At the moment nothing could suit Alan better. 'I could murder a drink,' he admitted.

'M . . . murder?'

He had forgotten how young she was. 'I'm thirsty.'

'I'll find water.' Gwenn Herevi set her basket on the edge of his pallet.

Alan put out a hand. 'Wine would be better. It kills pain.'

Having poured a generous measure from a pottery bottle into an earthenware cup, St Clair's daughter handed it to him. Alan noticed she was careful to avoid contact with his fingers. Ignoring this, he drank deep. It was a coarse red wine, flavoured with herbs. It warmed his stomach. Alan had never appreciated how much it meant to have a healthy pain-free body until this moment. His pain dulled. She watched him. The girl, Gwenn, made him feel self-conscious, though he was damned if he knew why this should be. 'My thanks, Mistress Gwenn.' He looked pointedly at the bottle.

The girl took the hint and thrust the bottle into his hands. 'Here, you'd better have charge of this.' Kneeling at his side, she unwrapped his makeshift bandages.

Pain knifed through him. 'I hope to God you know what you're doing.'

'I do. Grandmama taught me.' Her face clouded, but though her grief was fresh she did not give in to it. Head high, she waved at two yokels who were lurking in the doorway. 'If you must watch, you can make yourselves useful. This man must be held down.'

'I can hardly run away,' Alan said dryly.

She flashed him a look. 'Nonetheless, you must be restrained, or you'll wreck the bone-setting.'

The two boys took hold.

'Are you ready?'

Alan assented and gritted his teeth. Black pain swallowed him up and wrenched him out of the hall, and he was master of himself no more. He gave himself up to the agony and rode it out. After an eternity in a dark vortex with nothing to cling on to, the girl's soft voice hooked him back. 'There. You can relax now, Alan le Bret. It's over.'

He came back slowly. He'd spilt the wine. He was sweating like a pig and could hardly see for the perspiration running into his eyes. He could taste blood in his mouth. Lifting his fingers to his lips, he discovered he'd all but bitten them through. 'My thanks,' he managed to croak.

The two serfs had gone. His leg was neatly bandaged. He had new splints. 'It doesn't feel as though its mine.'

'It will.' Her eyes were steady. Candid, truthful eyes.

'Will it set straight?' An important question, that. Lame mercenaries didn't have a prayer.

'Like a lance,' she assured him, dipping a cloth into a bowl of water. She began wiping his face, as tenderly as though he were a babe.

'Don't do that.' He tried to bat her hands away.

'You're all sooty, and you're in no fit state to do it yourself.'

It unmanned Alan to have a maid like Gwenn Herevi washing him. 'No amount of polishing will make me shine, mistress. I'm tarnished to the heart.' Her steady brown eyes flickered, but that was the only sign she gave of having heard him, for the gentle, inexorable washing continued. Alan wanted to jerk his head away, but to his shame he found that she was in the right, he hadn't strength even for that. Fighting the pain had used up all his reserves, and the hall was rocking from side to side as though an enormous crowbar had been placed underneath it and a giant was levering it up and down. He endured in stoic silence while the room tilted.

'You were very brave,' the girl said, conversationally. 'I should have screamed.'

Talking was the last thing Alan wanted to do, but he reminded himself that it might be useful to win the girl's friendship. At Huelgastel, Alan had overheard de Roncier and the Dowager Countess discussing a statue and a gemstone; and in the fire, Izabel Herevi had babbled about Our Lady. She had said that she had given it to Gwenn. Was it the same statue? And what about the gem? Alan forced his bitten lips to smile. 'I'm a soldier, I'm meant to be . . . brave.'

The cloth was withdrawn. The large brown eyes were thoughtful. 'You're a mercenary. I've never talked to a mercenary before.'

Alan sighed.

She stared at his purse which he had restrung about his neck. 'And you make your daily bread by killing people.'

Alan fastened the neck of his tunic and watched her tip back on her heels. With a faint feeling of alarm he recognised the light dawning in her eyes as a missionary one. Useful though her friendship might be, he'd not stand for that.

'How many people would you say you have killed?'

Transferring his gaze to the fire, Alan refused to answer, hoping she'd change her tactics, or grow bored as children do. She was very young.

'How many people have you killed?' She rinsed out the cloth and started on his face again.

Alan smothered an oath. Gwenn Herevi was persistent in more ways than one. 'I provide a service, little Blanche,' he said, and having disconcerted her with the French version of her name, he succeeded in pushing her hand away. 'I help people fight their battles.'

'Blanche?' She wrinkled her nose.

'Your name.' Pain made his response more curt than he had intended. 'Gwenn is Breton for Blanche, is it not?'

'Yes, only no one ever calls me by the French version.'

He shrugged.

134

'The Church condemns mercenaries,' St Clair's daughter went on without rancour.

'Do you condemn me as a murderer?' he asked softly.

'You . . . you make your money by killing people, don't you?'

He flung back his head and gave a creditable laugh. 'Pot calling the kettle black, is it?'

'I . . . I beg your pardon?'

Lunging for a slender wrist, Alan pulled Gwenn Herevi so close that her face all but touched his. Beneath the grime from the fire, her skin was smooth as marble. Her breath was sweet, and stirred his hair. 'Who are you,' he whispered in her ear, 'to call me a murderer? You've been brought up on the proceeds of whoredom, when all's said and done.'

The girl gave an inarticulate cry and wrenched herself free. 'You . . . You . . .' Poppy-red, she stammered to a halt.

'Bastard?' Alan only mouthed the word, but he could see from the way her face grew pinched that she understood him at once. To be quite certain, he rammed his message home with a callous smile, murmuring, 'That name belongs to you also, sweet Blanche.'

The girl pokered up, leapt to her feet, and flung the cloths and bandages into her basket. Her mouth was set and her hands were trembling. She was speechless with hurt, and fury, and wounded pride. Alan's conscience stabbed him, and he found himself wondering how low it was possible for a man to sink. He felt no triumph. It was as though he had kicked a puppy who had come running up tail a-wag. Not a pleasant feeling. It was disturbing, too, to find he was not yet able to put guilt behind him.

She snatched up her basket and twisted away, taking a second to dart a malevolent look at his broken limb. 'I could kick it,' she hissed through clenched teeth.

Alan looked straight at her. 'I wouldn't advise it,' he said, smooth as silk. 'It would undo all your good work.' It was only after she had stormed up the stairs that it occurred to him that in wanting to kick his leg, she had mirrored his own guilty thoughts with accuracy.

In answer to her mother's summons, Gwenn pushed past the faded, rotting rag that a generation ago might have been a creditable door-hanging, and entered the sleeping-alcove that Yolande was to share with her father. Her grandmother's bier had been placed in the chapel, and Jean was organising a vigil for her. Gwenn would attend the vigil, as would her mother; none of them would rest that night. 'Mama?' Her mother was reclining on a moth-eaten mattress, a hand shielding her face.

The hand was removed and red-circled eyes met hers. 'Come in, Gwenn.'

Gwenn sat down by her mother. A musty odour filled the small chamber, and by it Gwenn knew that the mattress was filled with chopped straw and that it was damp. 'I wouldn't lie on that, Mama. It will make your joints creak.' She reached for her mother's hand, which gripped hers hard.

'It's only for a moment,' Yolande answered distantly. 'Tomorrow, you can help me organise new ones for us all.' She hesitated. 'Gwenn, I . . . I'm sorry to have to ask you this, I've asked Raymond, but as he wasn't there at the time, he couldn't tell me.'

'Tell you what, Mama?'

Her mother's breast heaved. 'Was . . . was it a swift end for her, do you think? I . . . I cannot bear to think of her suffering.'

Gwenn's throat closed up. 'Oh, Mama. It . . . it was the smoke. I was with her at the end. She charged me with asking for your forgiveness—'

A sob. 'She wanted *my* forgiveness?'

'She loved you, Mama.' Gwenn said.

This was not the moment to inform Yolande that the Norseman had set the fire. Had he escaped? Was he in de Roncier's pay? It seemed likely. And what had he wanted from her grandmother?

'Grandmama did not suffer long.'

Yolande closed her eyes and turned her head away. After a few moments' silence, she lifted swollen eyelids. 'Raymond told me that you've seen Alan le Bret before?'

'Aye. He was by the cathedral when the Black Monk—'

'He could be a de Roncier man. I won't have him lodged here.'

Gwenn remembered how Ned Fletcher had tried to wave her away from the cathedral and the mob inside. While she was not certain of Alan le Bret, she would trust Ned Fletcher with her life. And if Ned Fletcher was Alan le Bret's friend, le Bret could not be all bad . . .

Aloud she said, 'But he saved me, Mama. He broke his leg saving me.'

'He's got to go.'

'Let him stay till his leg is healed, Mama. We owe him that.'

Yolande sighed wearily. 'I don't trust him.'

'Please, Mama.'

'I shall consider it. Now, will you lend me your arm as far as the chapel? I . . . I don't think I could make it alone.'

Chapter Nine

Later that evening, with his belly filled, Alan took stock of his surroundings. As halls went, this one was small. Damp torches smoked in cobwebby wall sconces. The trestle tables – so recently scrubbed they had eaten from them before the water had dried – had been cleared and pushed to the walls. The wine had been stowed under lock and key in vaults below the hall. He smothered a sneer. The St Clair family had fled to this rundown pigsty of a manor, and despite the tragedy that had struck them, they were already managing to run it as though it were a full-sized castle. De Roncier was obviously no fool to fear St Clair's ambitions, for the man had pretensions that soared way above the station of a lowly knight. The St Clair family them-selves had not eaten a morsel, spending most of the time in the chapel, watching over the body of the con-cubine's mother.

Not surprisingly, Alan's leg was aching. Wearily, he sank back into his pillow and chastised himself again for antagonising the Herevi girl. He hoped he hadn't ruined his chances; if what he had overheard Marie de Roncier say about the statue was correct and it did indeed contain a jewel, Alan intended to have it.

His cousin entered the hall via the solar stairway. Dragging a stool to Alan's pallet, he sat down beside him. 'Feeling better, Captain?' he asked, in English.

Alan glanced round the hall, but no one was paying them any attention. 'Don't call me Captain, Ned. Alan will do. Although it's unlikely that anyone can understand us, I for one don't wish to cry it about that we were signed with de Roncier. And I'm no longer your captain.'

'Aye. I'm sorry. It's become a habit, Alan.'

A companionable silence fell over the two men. The combination of too much wine and the warmth of the fire made Alan sleepy. He closed his eyes and allowed himself to drift.

Ned dragged him back to reality. 'Cousin?'

'Mmm?' Alan opened one eye.

'St Clair's asked me to stay.'

Alan opened his other eye. 'He has? In what capacity?'

'Man-at-arms, initially.'

'You've accepted?'

'Yes. Alan?'

'Mmm?'

'He's offered you a place. He needs more freemen and said to tell you that he'll employ you, when your leg is healed. He's grateful to us.'

Perhaps there was a God in heaven after all. It appeared he had not ruined his chances of easing his way into the household. He may yet find the gem, and carry it away with him. Alan tried not to look too enthusiastic. Dimly he recalled telling Ned he had greener pastures to go to. If he accepted St Clair's offer immediately, Ned would know if he was up to something. He yawned. 'He did, did he?'

'Go on, Alan. It won't kill you to stop here. Sir Jean seems a reasonable man. We may find ourselves crossing swords with de Roncier, but if you're afraid—'

'Have you marked how many men St Clair has? What would the odds be if it came to a straight fight between St Clair and our old friends?'

'Not good,' Ned admitted soberly. 'They are in great disarray, with not above half a dozen men, and two of them are no more than babes. One is in his dotage.'

'Pitiful. I think I'll stay,' Alan added, illogically.

'Good, I'm glad. But tell me why. The odds are

140

appalling, and I know you only take calculated risks.'

Alan grinned, and thought of the gem. What would it be worth? 'Every now and then, Edward, my boy, I relish a challenge. Besides, St Clair's brought a palatable wine with him. Did you not notice?'

Pleased but none the wiser, Ned gave his invalid cousin a bemused smile. He was fond of Alan and had always admired him, but he had never understood him. Despite his surname, Alan had been born in England, in Yorkshire. It was Alan's father who was the true Breton born and bred. As well as being his kinsman, Alan was the only other person in Kermaria who could speak fluent English. Ned's French was acceptable, and his Breton was improving daily, but it meant something to be able to converse with his cousin in his native tongue. The link between them may have become tenuous over the years, but Ned was pleased he'd not be stranded with foreigners.

'How long do you think till you'll be up and about?'

His cousin spread his hands. 'Who knows? A month if they feed us right and I heal quickly. Six weeks otherwise.'

The flaxen head nodded. 'Lucky for the lass that we were heading up her street.'

'Luck?' Alan was examining his bitten nails and the suggestion of a smile flickered across his lips. It had been the thought of the mysterious statue and what it might contain that had prompted Alan to suggest they take that route. Only when they had reached the well and Alan had seen the smoke had he realised that Otto Malait had beaten him to it. 'I wouldn't call it luck exactly,' he murmured.

Ned dragged his fair brows together. 'What? Oh. I see what you mean. Not lucky for you with that leg. But you must agree, Alan, that destiny had a hand in today's events.' The younger man intercepted a quizzical look from his companion and was moved to enlarge. 'What else could it be but destiny when we'd finished our service with de Roncier? We needed employment, and now,' a wave of his hand included the hall, 'thanks to your bravery, we find ourselves neatly settled.'

'Destiny had nothing to do with it,' Alan said shortly. He found his cousin's irrepressible faith wearing at times.

'God then.'

Alan rolled his grey eyes at the rafters. Not another. He had had his fill with the girl. One dose of an innocent in search of meaning was more than enough for one day. 'Shut up, Ned,' he said irritably, and settled himself down into his blankets. 'I'm for sleeping. Shouldn't you be on guard duty?'

Izabel Herevi had been laid to rest, and in the hall the funeral breakfast was over.

Seated at the board, Yolande turned lacklustre eyes on her lover and tried to be practical. 'Jean, I'd like to see the undercroft cleared today and have an inventory of the stores taken so we can send for supplies from Vannes. Gwenn knows what needs to be done, but she'll need help.'

Jean nodded, realising that it would be good for all of them to work hard today. It would take their minds off their grief. 'She can have Raymond.'

Raymond was idly carving a piece of wheat bread into a ball. He groaned, and flung down his eating knife. 'Cleaning? Me? But that's woman's work.'

Jean's brows snapped together. 'You'll do as you're bidden, my boy. There are heavy barrels down there. You don't expect your sister to move them on her own, do you?'

'No, sir.' Raymond picked up his knife, stuck it in his belt, and rose reluctantly.

'You can take that new lad, Ned Fletcher. He'll lend a hand.'

'Thank you, sir.' Raymond beckoned Ned Fletcher over.

Yolande watched the young Saxon that Jean had sworn in the night before and wondered about him, and his companion, Alan le Bret. This fair one looked as though he could be trusted. Yolande watched him spring to her daughter's side, ready and eager to lift the trapdoor for her. There was no deviousness in that young man's nature, she was sure of that. She would raise no objections to his being part of Jean's company. But she could not say the same of Alan le Bret in view of what Raymond had told her of his involvement with the mob.

Alan's pallet was pulled up before the fire, and at the moment he was watching Gwenn as she held a taper to a candle lantern. Yolande did not feel competent to assess his character. She was grateful to him for saving her daughter, but there was something about him that made her uneasy. However, he could not do much harm in his present condition. He could stay while he mended, but she would watch him like a hawk, and at the first sign of trouble she would have Jean remove him.

The wick of the candle Gwenn was lighting was damp, and it was a moment before it sputtered into life. Ned held out his square, blunt-fingered hand. 'Let me take that, mistress,' he said. 'I'll go first. You never know what might lurk below.' He took the lantern and peered down the steps.

'I expect there'll be rats,' Gwenn answered matter-of-factly as Ned began descending, 'but I'm not afraid of rats.' Tucking up her skirts, she picked her way after him with care, for the stone steps were coated with a slippery film of damp moss and masked by shadows. Raymond dragged his heels.

Halfway into the shadowy depths Ned stopped and rolled large eyes at Gwenn. He lowered his voice as though he were afraid. 'There might be worse than rats in here . . .'

Gwenn laughed, rather to her surprise. That morning, when they had buried her grandmother, she could not have imagined laughing in a hundred years. 'Worse than rats?' she said, and feigned fear.

'There might be evil spirits from the past,' Ned made his voice hollow and it echoed round the vaults, 'waiting for a young maiden, ready to put her under some terrible enchantment.'

Gwenn let out a mock shriek.

'But I'll save you, mistress, never fear.'

Ned leapt lightly down the last of the steps, and as he turned to see her safely down, Gwenn's heart warmed to him.

Raymond joined them. He had brought another lantern and cast disparaging eyes around the undercroft. It was a cool, rectangular room, divided into two by a row of heavy round pillars. It had barrelled vaulting. Along the walls, rows of storage jars were buried under tangles of cobwebs and a dusting of grit that had fallen from the ceiling. In the corners, where the lantern light could not reach, there was a scuffling sound. There really were rats down here, and mice. They would have to be ferreted out.

Raymond's nose wrinkled in a lordly sneer. 'Phew, it stinks down here! A fellow can hardly breathe.'

Gwenn found herself exchanging amused glances with Ned. 'It's been closed up for years, Raymond. What do you expect? Now the trapdoor's open, it will soon freshen up.'

'It might be an idea to have some air vents made,' Ned suggested, examining the storeroom walls. 'I should think here,' he shouldered a disintegrating casket aside and indicated a spot near the top of the wall where the vaulting began, 'and here.'

'That sounds a very good idea,' Gwenn said, smiling. 'We can mention it to Sir Jean.'

Ned smiled back at her. Raymond, Gwenn noticed, was moodily tapping a wine barrel. 'Empty,' he pronounced in gloomy accents. He moved on to the next, and tapped that. 'This is empty too.'

Gwenn and Ned grinned at each other, and Gwenn's heart lightened. It would be so good to have someone near her age to talk to apart from Raymond.

'Where do we start, mistress?' Ned asked.

'More lanterns, I think, and brooms. Then we must sort out—'

'Hell,' Raymond cut in, 'there's no wine here at all, save what Sir Jean brought with him.'

'Isn't there?' Gwenn said sweetly. 'Then hadn't you better lift those empty caskets out of here for scalding and repair? They can be refilled then.'

Reluctant to take orders from his sister, Raymond moved slowly. Ned was there before him, a casket under each arm as he headed up the stairs. 'I'll fetch more light, mistress,' he said cheerfully. Raymond would not be much help that day, Gwenn realised, but Ned Fletcher would, and willingly too. She liked him, very much.

One fine morning about two weeks later, Gwenn was leaving the hall to lay fresh flowers on her grandmother's grave when Alan addressed her from his place by the fire. 'Mistress Gwenn?'

'Yes?' Curious, for the routier never spoke to her except when she was tending his leg, Gwenn drifted over.

'I was wondering if you could spare a moment or two,' he said courteously.

'Is your leg troubling you? The bandages chafe?'

'No, not at all.' He raised his smoky eyes to hers. 'Would you mind if I talked to you about your grandmother, mistress, or would it upset you?'

'It wouldn't upset me.'

'Good. I have been thinking.' His lips curved wryly. 'Lying here all day, I have little else to occupy my time, and there's something I've been itching to ask you.'

'Yes?' Gwenn felt shy and gawky when Alan smiled at her.

'In Vannes, on the day of the fire, your grandmother made mention of a stone rose. What is it, mistress?'

'A statue of Our Lady.'

Alan let his breath out in a soft sigh. He had thought as much. He threw another smile at the girl, who seemed to like them, and watched a delightful flush steal across her cheeks. 'Was it precious to her?'

'I suppose so.' Gwenn's voice went croaky. She would have liked to ask why her grandmother's statue fascinated him so, but she seemed to have lost control of her tongue. When Alan le Bret smiled, his eyes were as clear as a mountain brook dancing over grey stones, yet disturbing, too.

'You are sorry that a keepsake of your grandmother's was destroyed in the fire?'

'It wasn't destroyed. But what does that matter? Grandmama's dead. What good did the Stone Rose do her?'

Alan clicked his tongue. 'Careful, sweet Blanche, that borders on blasphemy. Your mother's entered the hall and she must have heard you, because she's frowning.'

Yolande beckoned her daughter. 'Gwenn, come upstairs.'

'Here.' Yolande waved Gwenn onto her bed and drew the dingy curtain across the alcove's entrance. 'Sit down. It's high time you and I had a little talk.'

Thinking that she must have committed some sin and was about to be rebuked for it, Gwenn scoured her mind for her misdeed. 'My apologies, Mama. Should I not have been talking to Alan le Bret?'

Yolande touched her daughter's arm. 'Naturally you must converse with the man seeing as you have taken him under your wing.'

'I felt obliged, Mama, because he saved me, and it would be churlish to refuse to speak to him.'

Accepting this, Yolande inclined her head. 'I know. You are a girl who likes to honour her debts, but I trust you are not blind to that man's nature.'

'He's a mercenary. As is his kinsman, Ned Fletcher.'

Yolande moved her face to within a handspan of her daughter's. 'Aye. Just so. But I do not think that Alan le Bret is cast in the same mould as Ned Fletcher, and I'd be grateful if you would tell me what you were talking about when I stumbled across you just now.'

Gwenn lifted finely structured hands. 'Nothing much, Mama. He was asking about the Stone Rose.'

Her mother's green gaze sharpened. 'Was he, indeed? How interesting.' Yolande rose, and drawing back the curtain screen, peered into the solar. It was empty. 'Listen attentively, Gwenn, I've something to discuss with you, and I want you to swear to me, on your honour, which I know means much to you, that you'll never breathe a word of this to anyone, not even to your father or brother.'

Round-eyed, Gwenn stared at her mother.

'This secret is not one for men,' Yolande murmured. 'Do I have your promise?'

'Yes, Mama.'

'Good. Now hear me out, and afterwards I'll tell you my plan for ridding this house of the vermin that has slunk into it unasked.'

Later, Gwenn escaped to tend her grandmother's grave.

On the glebeland, sparrows were quarrelling in an old yew tree, and in one of the apple trees which edged the graveyard a blackbird was singing. Gwenn plucked the faded primroses and cowslips from their pot and arranged fresh blossoms, turning her mother's words over in her mind. All at once, a prickling at the back of her neck warned her that she was being observed. Out of the tail of her eye she saw someone slip out of the chapel to crouch in the shadows of the porch. She caught sight of long, straggling hair as yellow as the cowslips in her grandmother's vase, and gained an impression of muscle-bound bulk. Her stomach knotted. Imprinted in her mind was the face and form of the Norseman, and though Gwenn had not seen this prowler's features, she knew him to be male, and that glimpse, brief as it had been, had reminded her of him.

'Who's there?' Her voice was sharp with alarm.

The figure shrank back. With slow deliberation, Gwenn climbed to her feet and shook out the skirts of her gown. Ned Fletcher had hair as bright as that when the sun was on it, she reminded herself. But the man in the doorway had been standing in the shade, and Ned Fletcher did not wear his hair so long.

The blackbird stopped singing.

As fast as her feet would carry her, Gwenn sped across the grass and through the arch in the graveyard wall. The iron gate clanged behind her and she did not pause for breath until she had scrambled up the steps and catapulted into the hall.

At that hour, it was filled with people. Her mother was addressing Joel, the cook. Her father and her brother were deep in conversation at one end of the trestle, and at the other sat Alan le Bret. He had been given employment teaching one of the village freemen recently drafted into Jean's service how to keep an edge on a sword. A whetstone had been brought up from the vault, and a pair of crutches were handy at his elbow.

'Where's Fletcher?' Gwenn demanded of the room at large.

'Here, Mistress Gwenn.' Ned Fletcher detached himself from the knot of men by the fireplace. 'What's amiss?'

'If . . . if you're here,' she stretched her eyes wide, 'who's sneaking around the chapel?'

Jean and Raymond jumped up, and Jean barked out a series of commands. 'Raymond, take Fletcher and search the chapel. Take your arms and bring any loiterer here. At the double. Move!'

Raymond and Ned clattered out.

Yolande had assumed Alan le Bret's interest in the Stone Rose was proof he was in league with de Roncier, but she was suddenly assailed by doubts. Hand smoothing her high forehead, she thought rapidly. Was le Bret working for himself, or was he feeding information to de Roncier's scavengers piece by piece? For an instant the mercenary's swarthy features had registered surprise – he had been as startled as any by Gwenn's announcement. Now he was sitting stiffly at the board, head cocked to one side, listening. How slow I have been, Yolande chastised herself. It was plain as a pikestaff that he would only be working for himself. Aye, that glove fitted him more closely. Alan le Bret would own no man his master for long. 'Count de Roncier is having us watched,' Yolande said, voicing the words which hung on everyone's lips. And for the routier's benefit she added a plaintive, 'Oh, Jean, will this nightmare never end?'

'Peace, woman.' Jean turned to his daughter, who was gazing at her mother in the oddest manner. 'What precisely did you see, Gwenn?'

'Someone lurking in the chapel porch.'

'Could you describe him?'

'No . . . at least . . . I couldn't be sure. He was a big man, with hanks of straw-coloured hair. I . . . I got the impression he'd been there for some time. I hoped it was Ned Fletcher. But—'

'Fletcher's been here this past half-hour.'

'Sir,' Gwenn's voice came out shrill, and catching the mercenary's gaze on her, she toned it down, 'I pray I'm mistaken, but I'm afraid it might have been the Norseman I saw on the day of the fire. Remember? I told you about him.'

Yolande gasped and crossed herself. 'I knew it,' she said in accents of doom. 'De Roncier will be content with nothing less than our blood.'

Raymond charged through the door. 'Nothing,' he announced, with a studied glance in Gwenn's direction. 'The bird, if there was one, has flown.'

'There was someone!' Gwenn burst out. 'There was!'

Jean strode to the door. 'I'll have a look myself. Fletcher, accompany me.'

Gwenn's brown eyes burned as she looked at her brother. 'Why don't you believe me, Raymond?'

Raymond did not disbelieve his sister; in fact he

believed her only too well. But he loved Gwenn, and had observed the invisible scars the fire had left on her. Her confidence wavered whenever she left the hall. She walked Kermaria with fear perched on her shoulders. Raymond wanted to free her from her terrors, even if that meant lying to her. 'I'm sure you *think* you saw someone, Gwenn.'

'Don't take me for a birdbrain, Raymond,' Gwenn snapped. 'You were there when the mob went wild; you know I saw someone threatening Grandmama in the blaze; and you know as well as I that de Roncier is at the root of our trouble.' And then she clamped her mouth shut, for she could say no more without breaking her promise to her mother.

Alan had been taking a keen interest in the conversation, but at this point Raymond steered his sister aside.

'Hell and damnation,' Alan muttered, frustrated. He'd give a week's pay for more information. Diligently polishing the blade of his sword, he stretched his ears. If Malait was scouting around, then he must make his move soon, lest he was beaten to the prize.

'Sorry, Gwenn,' he heard Raymond apologising. 'I only wanted to reassure you.' With a flourish, the boy gave his sister a charming bow that Alan recognised was a copy of his father's. 'Can I make amends? I'm going for a ride. Would you like to come? You could do with a few hours in the saddle, you've the most appalling seat.'

'Don't be rude,' Gwenn answered. 'You've had more practice than I. The only ride I've had in years was when we came here. And how would you be with Katarin wriggling about in your arms?'

'Pax. Pax. Forget I ever spoke. Can you come?'

Gwenn pulled a face of regret. 'I'm sorry. I promised Mama I'd help her mend the linen. Most of it's in ribbons. Where are you going?'

'I thought I might explore the forest.'

Gwenn positioned herself so she had an unobstructed

view of Alan. 'When are you going to retrieve Grandmama's statue, Raymond?' she asked innocently. The mercenary's head was bent over his sword, guiding it to the whetstone, but as she spoke his fingers went white on hilt and blade. Gwenn smiled.

'Oh, Jesu, I'd forgotten all about that cursed thing,' Raymond said.

'I know it's worthless,' Gwenn saw a pulse beating in Alan's neck, 'but I would like it. Where is it?' The grindstone creaked to a halt.

'Locmariaquer. In one of the temples.'

Gwenn caught her brother's arm. 'Go that way today, Raymond. Please. I'd love to have it back. It means even more to me now Grandmama is gone.'

'I'll see. I've a mind to explore the forest.' Raymond didn't want to commit himself, but observing his sister's crestfallen expression, he relented. 'If I don't fetch it today, I'll fetch it soon. Agreed?'

'You're a beast,' she said with a grin.

Raymond grinned back, unrepentant. 'I know.'

A month slipped by. Alan's leg was all but healed, and his splints were removed. Yolande and Gwenn decided that the time was ripe for them to set the wheels in motion.

It had rained all night, and ragged, wind-bitten clouds chased across the sky, but Gwenn was determined that this was the day she would ride to Locmariaquer and reclaim her statue. A few paltry raindrops were not going to stop her.

Despite Raymond promising that he would collect the Stone Rose, he had not yet done so, nor had he taken her riding. Today, he was going to be made to fulfil all his obligations. Gwenn began wheedling as the family were eating their early morning crust. The men-at-arms were at a separate table, nearer the door. 'Raymond, may I ride with you today?'

'No,' Raymond mumbled, through a mouthful of bread.

Prepared for this response, Gwenn edged along the bench till her shoulder touched his and dimpled up at him. 'What excuse have you today, Raymond? Yesterday you were too busy hunting; the day before that you'd a wager with Denis; the day before that you were writing for Sir Jean . . .' She let her voice trail off, noticing the pebble-grey eyes of Alan le Bret resting on her. Turning her back on the mercenary, she smiled at her brother and wondered what excuse he'd produce today.

'My apologies, Gwenn.' Raymond flashed her a smile that she recognised was as charming and meaningless as hers for him. 'I have been busy. Sir Jean lacks a clerk, and I've been helping out. I'll take you tomorrow, I swear it.'

'Always tomorrow,' Gwenn muttered.

'What's wrong with today?' Yolande said, entering the conversation.

'I'm to help Sir Jean with plans for the guardhouse,' Raymond informed them importantly. 'It's much more to my taste than the clerk's task I've been lost in, and I want to prove my worth, else Sir Jean will have me play the clerk for ever.'

Jean set his cup down. 'I do need Raymond, Gwenn,' he confirmed, wiping droplets of wine from his moustache with his sleeve. 'I'm planning radical alterations to the fortifications. He will assist.'

Gwenn let slip a groan of disappointment, reached for a loaf, and broke off a large chunk. She wanted action, and today. 'He promised *me* he'd fetch Grandmama's statue nigh on a month ago.' Her dark brows formed a discontented line. 'The men in this household only honour their promises when they are made to other men. Women don't count, do they?'

Jean's eyes filled with reproach. 'Don't be ungrateful. You are allowed your say far more than most young ladies.'

Gwenn bristled until she read affection in her father's expression, and then she grinned. 'I'm a nuisance, I

152

know. But I would like the Stone Rose back. Raymond swore to Grandmother that he'd see it in my hands, and that was six weeks ago.'

'She has a point, my love,' Yolande said, taking her part.

'I don't know what all the fuss is about,' Raymond threw in. 'Not only is it worthless, but it's a dreadful, ugly carving.'

'I agree' – Alan le Bret's eyes were boring holes in Gwenn's shoulder-blades – 'but since it belonged to Grandmama, I would like it.'

'It's a small thing Gwenn asks, my love, and it means so much to her.'

'Where is the damned thing, Raymond?' Jean demanded.

'Locmariaquer.'

Gwenn sat very straight.

'Not too far,' Jean observed. 'But no, Gwenn, I cannot spare Raymond.' His daughter's spine sagged, and he winked indulgently at her. 'But if mademoiselle has set her heart on it, one of the grooms can take her.'

In a flash, Alan hoisted himself upright and limped across. 'I'll accompany your daughter, Sir Jean. I'm not much use as a soldier yet, but the exercise will put some strength back into my leg.'

'No, Jean!' Yolande grasped her lover's hand. It was no part of her design that Gwenn should ride off alone with the routier.

Jean tugged doubtfully at his moustache.

'If your son furnishes me with the direction, I shall be pleased to escort your daughter,' Alan pressed, pleasantly.

Gwenn turned a blind eye to the frantic looks Yolande was firing across at her. 'Oh, please, sir, let me go. I'm longing for a ride.'

'She's not that good on a horse, Papa,' Raymond said, dampeningly. He could see that his mother was concerned, and he did not trust the fellow either.

'I doubt that I'd be that skilled a horseman myself at the moment,' Alan admitted, ruefully. 'I'll take it quietly, Sir Jean. I'll look after your daughter.'

'Oh, let me go with him, sir.' Gwenn smiled at Yolande. 'It will be all right, Mama. I can manage.'

'But Gwenn . . .' Yolande lifted a despairing hand, and words failed her. She was not prepared for this contingency. It had never occurred to her that her daughter might ride off with Alan le Bret, but without betraying the whole, she could say nothing. And Gwenn, dreadful child, knew that.

'Please, sir.'

Jean did not want to spend the whole morning discussing trifles. Time was pressing. He relented. 'Very well, Gwenn. Be back before sunset.'

'My thanks, sir!' Gwenn skipped round the table and hugged her father. 'My thanks!'

Yolande said nothing. Her headstrong daughter was too sure of herself for her own good. Sweet Jesus, look after her, Yolande prayed, for my hands are tied.

For Alan, the ride to Locmariaquer was purgatory.

Surprisingly, the girl was not a thorn in his side. She did not assault his ears with ceaseless chattering; on the contrary, she rode placidly at his side, only occasionally throwing him a comment. Nor did she seem to expect any response from him. For these small mercies Alan was grateful. His leg, however, was another matter. For the first half-hour he was able to persuade himself that it was back to normal; in the next half-hour it had begun to throb; and by the time they were into the second hour of the ride, he was gritting his teeth and could barely keep his mind on their route. As they progressed, his pain intensified. Like a snail retreating into the shell that protects it, he shrank deeper and deeper into his capuchon and kept his face from the girl.

Her saddle creaked as she turned to him. 'I can smell the sea. Do you think we're almost there?' Her father, probably with her welfare in mind, had mounted her on a lazy nag that needed some encouragement to make it move at all, and she had snapped off a birch stick for a goad.

Alan emerged unwillingly from his hood. 'This path hugs the coast. We should be very close. Your brother mentioned a stone farmhouse.'

'We passed one half a mile back.'

Alan swore. 'Did we? I confess my mind was wandering.'

The look she gave him was understanding. 'Mine wasn't, my leg isn't sore. Raymond described a lane which runs to the left between two hawthorn hedges.' She used her birch whip to point. 'Do you think that's it?'

'Could be.' Alan guided his horse to where road and lane met. The ground was soft and speckled with fallen blossom that great hoofs had pounded into the mud. A wind had sprung up, and a stormcock was singing its heart out from its perch among the flowering hawthorn. Wondering what they were wandering into, Alan eyed first the ground and then the sky. One way or another, a storm was brewing.

'What's the matter?'

She was an observant girl. 'The mud's all churned up.'

'It probably rained here this morning,' she suggested. 'It did at home, early—'

Alan cut her off with an impatient wave of his hand. 'I'm sure that it rained, but look at those tracks. Many horses have passed this way.'

'So?'

He lifted his head, unaware that the grey of his eyes matched the pewter-coloured clouds massing on the horizon. 'The weather's the least of our problems, mistress. Doesn't it strike you as strange that so many horses should have come this way this morning?'

Gwenn Herevi gave the much-furrowed ground her full attention. 'I thought the path led only to the Old

Ones' temples. Raymond said no one ever came here.'

'Exactly.' Alan grasped her horse's bridle.

'What are you doing?'

Alan swung stiffly from his saddle and led their horses into the hawthorn-edged lane, favouring his good leg.

Gwenn wondered what he was planning, and when he would show his true colours.

'I advise a careful approach,' he said. He found a gap in the hedge and dived through it, dragging the animals after him.

The blossom-laden branch of a wild pear drooped over the hawthorn, and Gwenn doubled over to avoid being scratched. They found themselves on the edge of a series of peasants' strips. The spring planting had been done and already the young shoots were sprouting, fresh and green.

'Get down, mistress. I'm leaving the horses here and going on on foot. I can't afford to take any risks. Your father would have my hide if you got hurt.'

'Why should anything happen?' Le Bret had not struck Gwenn as a man to sound the alarm unnecessarily, and his caution frightened her. Was his wary attitude genuine, or was it a blind to mask some darker design? She had decided to risk riding with the mercenary on impulse and now she wished she had been less rash. Would he hurt her? She did not think so, not when she had mended his leg. She looked at him, but as ever the swarthy face was closed. Her best course was to go along with him and make sure she did not rouse his suspicions. She lowered her voice to a whisper. 'Who do you think is up there?'

His brows bunched together. 'God knows. But you can be sure it's no meeting of peasant farmers. You can see from the prints that these animals have been shod; and judging from the size of the hoofs, a fair number are warhorses.'

Gwenn slid from her mare's back, and the animal began nosing about in the hedge for the palest, most tender hawthorn shoots. 'Perhaps we should wait until they have gone?'

'No.' Alan was set on discovering what was going on. The knowledge might have a commercial value. The concubine's daughter would think the worst of him soon enough, when he relieved her of the jewel, but illogically he felt uneasy confessing to those great brown eyes that he couldn't afford not to pick up any information that might prove a source of income in the future. A gust of wind slapped him in the face. In different circumstances, a man could grow fond of a girl like her. 'I'm for going on now, mistress,' he said curtly, 'before the storm blows us away. Your brother told me where to look.' He turned on his heel.

She clutched the hem of his cotte, or over-tunic. 'What about me?'

'You'd best stay here.'

'You'll come back? You'd not leave me here?'

'You've got the horses.' He smiled lopsidedly. 'Don't you trust me, mistress?'

The foliage rustled, and Gwenn was alone. She did not believe he had the slightest intention of returning for her. Once he had his hands on the statue, he'd be off faster than the wind – or perhaps not quite that fast, she amended, remembering his stiff leg. But then, as he himself had pointed out, she did have the horses. Maybe he would be back.

Pondering her next move, Gwenn ducked behind the hawthorn. The minutes crawled by. The wind piled up more clouds, and the thin strips of blue sky shrank. Someone sneezed. Someone sneezed? The sound must have come from the direction of the dolmen, but with the wind whistling round her ears, it was hard to be certain. A second sneeze made her jump out of her skin. It came from the other side of the hedge. Dropping the horses' reins, Gwenn peered through the leafy screen.

Another rider was approaching the dolmen. He was bound to see Alan le Bret. She strained to see who it was, and a cold shiver shot down to her toes. It was the Norseman. He was wiping his nose with the back of his hand, and his pale, deathly eyes were fixed on the waves of mud on the path, as though they were a knotty puzzle he'd like to unravel. Had he been trailing her and le Bret? The Viking reined in level with her.

Her mother wanted le Bret convinced that the gem had been sold, and Gwenn had been confident that she could achieve this safely. He might be motivated by self-interest, he might be after easy pickings, but he was no murderer, she was sure. He was not as base as he pretended. But *this* character, she sensed, would be capable of anything.

The Viking's mount, a scrawny grey, sniffed the wind. Gwenn froze, realising with a sick shock that the animal could in all probability smell her horses. Her mare's nostrils flared. 'St Gildas, no!' Gwenn lunged for her mare's mouth, but she was too late. Her mare's whinny of welcome coincided with the first crack of thunder and the first drops of rain. The Viking's light eyes slowly traversed the ruts in the lane. The thunder had drowned out her mare's neigh. He cast a puzzled look up the lane, and pulled on his beard. He *had* been following their tracks.

Thankful the jumble of hoofprints prevented him from seeing they had gone through the hedge, Gwenn did not stop to consider whether she could trust Alan le Bret, but hared up the field. Another deep rumble rolled across the heavens. Gwenn struggled on. She was following the line of a new-ploughed strip and her course was parallel to the one le Bret had taken but concealed by the scrubby hedge. The wind drove the raindrops into her face so hard they felt like hailstones. The crops were protected from the livestock which grazed on the common land by a fence of crude willow hurdles. Gwenn's eyes skimmed its length, but there was no opening. She must get through and find le Bret. The corner then, where hedge married fence. Oblivious of scratching briars, Gwenn forced her way through.

Her feet skated on wet grass. A green mound rose before her and, feet slipping and sliding, she scrambled up it. She saw stone steps, a stone lintel, a muddy entrance passage. 'Sweet Mary help me. Let it be the right one.' And she tumbled into the Old Ones' temple.

Chapter Ten

She found herself in a dank chamber that was as quiet
and as cold as a grave. The lump in her throat was as
big as a gull's egg. 'Alan . . . Alan le Bret? Are you
there?' Outside, the storm whirled, but inside, there
was only a thick, black, ominous quiet. 'Le Bret?' She
was alone. She bit her lip. She had picked the wrong
dolmen and was caught like a rat in a trap. If the
Viking had seen her, and followed her . . .

Perhaps there was another way out. Her eyes were
adjusting to the gloom. There was only one source of
light, and that was where she had entered. Feeling her
way along wet, rocky walls for another exit, Gwenn
skirted the dolmen. She had come full circle when a
change in the atmosphere told her she was no longer
the only person in this tomb of a place. A shadow fell
over her and something light brushed her arm.

'Mistress?'

Alan le Bret's voice. Gwenn closed her eyes and made
a hasty sign of the cross. 'Thank God, it's only you.'

'*Only* me?' There was definite laughter in his voice.
'Why did you follow me, Mistress Blanche? I thought
you were minding the horses.'

'I . . . I was afraid. Your friend—'

Steel fingers clamped round her arm. 'My friend?'

'Aye. One of your old cronies is . . . is following us,'
Gwenn informed him, trying to prise his hand off her
arm.

'Old crony?' His tone was as hard as his hold on her
flesh.

161

'You're hurting—'

The grip eased. '*Old* crony? Not Fletcher?'

'No. Another one. I saw him at Duke's Tavern, and again at the fire. He's built like an ox, and blond – a Norseman's looks. And the other day, by Kermaria chapel—'

'Hell! It has to be Malait.'

He released her, and she massaged the bruise that he'd made. 'I don't know him by name,' Gwenn said, throwing a worried glance at the yawning entrance.

'What was he riding?'

'What? Oh, a grey.'

'Thin and bony? Long in the leg? Looks barely able to hold him up.'

'That's the one.' The entrance was still clear.

'Hell. De Roncier has such a stallion, and for some reason Malait favours him.' His voice was low and fuelled Gwenn's fear. 'Otto Malait is as hard as nails, mistress. A dangerous enemy.'

'He's not *my* enemy,' she squeaked.

'You'd best pray you're right.' Striding over, he thrust a soggy bundle of rags at her. 'Here, I tripped over this. Is this what you're after?'

Gwenn accepted the bundle with a cautious lifting of her heart. Perhaps le Bret was not after the jewel . . .

'Hurry.' The wind and thunder were reaching a peak. 'If it is Malait out there, we may not have much time.'

Unwrapping the sodden bundle, Gwenn felt the familiar shape of her grandmother's statue chill in her hand. 'This is it,' she confirmed, smiling. 'We can go.'

Alan le Bret shook his head. He loomed over her, standing so close that his breath fanned her cheek. 'Open it,' he demanded in clipped tones.

Her heart sank. Holding the statue tight to her breast, she retreated.

Le Bret took another step towards her. 'Open it, girl, or by God you'll regret it.'

'You . . . devil! You mercenary—'

162

'Do it.'

She thought quickly. There was little to be gained from antagonising him over the sunstone. She gave what she hoped was a casual shrug and held it out to him. 'You do it. It's too stiff for me.'

He was startled that she should give it up so easily; the brief hesitation before he lifted the statue from her hands betrayed that. 'How?'

Her mother had told her what to do. 'Twist the statue in this direction,' Gwenn mimed the movement, 'and the wooden plinth in the other.'

He drew in a breath and pulled. There was a slight resistance, and then the two sections came apart with a creak. A small object plummeted into the earth. Dropping both statue and cedarwood base, Alan fell to his knees, and groped – a beast in the mire.

'Got it!' he exulted, plucking impatiently at the strings of the leather pouch. The crystal rolled into his palm, hard and cold as steel. It captured the pale light and drew it into its heart, where it was muted before being thrown out again. It glowed dully, like flawed lake-ice on a sunny January day. 'Got it!'

Gwenn gazed at the diamond-shaped stone on Alan le Bret's palm. Yolande had warned her that the sunstone did not shine brightly. Le Bret, who would not meet her eyes, apparently had not noticed. But then the light was weak, and he had not known what to expect. He saw what he wanted to see.

'Do you want to keep that, Alan le Bret?'

Strong, bitten, soldier's fingers snapped over the stone, and the feeble glow was snuffed out. He climbed to his full height and turned his head towards her, but would only look at her shoulder.

'If you want it,' Gwenn continued softly, 'I'll give it to you.'

'Give?' The darkness shielded his expression.

'I'm not prepared to die for a rock.'

The sudden stillness of his body told her she had shocked him. A hand came up and a finger feathered across her cheek. Gwenn drew back, and his hand fell. 'I wouldn't have killed you for the gem, little Blanche,' he said reproachfully.

She caught his elusive gaze. 'I would like to believe that, Alan le Bret, but then I would have liked to believe that you were an honest man.'

He swung on his heel. 'Don't fix those big brown eyes on me like that, curse you.'

'Like what?' she asked, sweetly.

He flung her a withering look. 'You know, mistress. You may be a child, but you know very well. I've told you before, you're wasting your time preaching to me. I'm a lost soul.'

Outside, the wind howled and whistled. There was thunder too, much muffled by the roof of heaped earth and stones.

'I wonder if you are as much of a devil as you would like to think. Like it or not, you have a conscience.'

He waved a closed fist under her nose. 'You forget, I have the stone.'

'Aye, you have it. But what do you have? What is that stone's true worth?'

'What do you mean?'

'The stone is pretty, Alan le Bret, but it belongs to the past. Your friend out there,' she jerked her head towards the mouth of the cave, 'his ancestors would have valued it. Today, it's worthless – a lump of crystal, no diamond.'

Alan stared into the girl's large eyes, but they were as soft and open and honest as always. A hard hand clenched in his stomach, and he was horribly certain that Gwenn Herevi was telling the truth. Slowly he uncurled his fingers. 'Worthless?'

She lifted it from his palm, and nodded. 'It's a sunstone.'

'A sunstone?' He let out an oath that burned Gwenn's ears. 'What the hell is a sunstone?'

'A sunstone tells you where the sun is on a cloudy day. You hold it up to the clouds and when you have

164

it pointed at the spot where the sun is hiding, you can see a rainbow in it.'

'Rainbow? Jesu! What children's tale is this? What of the diamond?' he demanded, roughly. '*Is* there a diamond?'

He had backed her into a place where the only road open was a liar's one. Boldly, Gwenn stepped into it, fighting to keep her features from betraying her. 'There was, once. But you've seen my father's manor. You have remarked on the poor quality of his horses. My father is not a rich man. The jewel was—'

'Sold?'

She nodded, obscurely relieved that she had not had to speak the false words aloud.

'Well, isn't that lovely?' he drawled with ponderous sarcasm. 'We could have done with a sunstone to light our way this morning. Come, Mistress Blanche, let's get out of this stinking tomb. I'll take you home.'

'You will? I . . . I thought you'd abandon me for fear I would betray your intentions.'

'It had occurred to me. But I won't escort you the whole way. I'm bound . . . elsewhere, but it's no burden to take you to the crossroads just east of Kermaria. My road goes that way.'

'My thanks,' Gwenn murmured. Her assessment of him was not so wide of the mark. A man who had completely lost his soul would have tossed her in a ditch and run off with her father's horses, worn-out nags though they were. 'You don't want to come back with me? My father did offer you work.'

'No.' He gave her one of his oblique smiles. 'I've burnt my bridges as far as your family is concerned, mistress.'

'If . . .' she hesitated, 'if you wanted to stay, I'd not say a word against you.'

For a heartbeat he stood stock-still, and then he bowed over her hand with perfect, heartrending gallantry. 'My thanks, sweet Blanche. But I have other plans.'

'You don't trust me. You think I will betray you.'

'No.' His tone was curt. 'I do trust you, mistress, and there's not many I could say that to. But I'll not stay. Here,' he stooped for the statue, 'take your blasted rock and we can be on our way.' Impatiently he rubbed his bad leg while Gwenn replaced the sunstone in its compartment. He led her to the entrance. 'Up you go.'

A stream of water was pouring down the steps, making them slippery. Gwenn went a couple of paces and drew up, like a balky horse.

'What now?' Alan groaned. She was flattened against the entrance wall, shaking her head. Screwing his eyes against the cutting rain, Alan saw a horned metal helmet and broad shoulders shift against the tempestuous sky. 'Malait!' he exclaimed. 'So it *was* you she saw!'

Otto gave his former colleague a shadow of a smile. 'Grazing on your green pastures, le Bret?' Water trickled down the point of a dagger in the Viking's left hand, and an axe as heavy as Thor's hammer swung on a thong from his waist. His right hand rested casually on its ivory haft.

Alan's sword hissed free of its sheath.

Gwenn screamed. 'No!' A jagged javelin of lightning flew across the sky. Above them, a cloud burst and counterfeit tears streamed down the Norseman's implacable face. 'No!' Gwenn's second cry was lost as the wind worried the branches of a nearby oak.

Roughly, Alan pushed Gwenn behind him and heard her scuttle back into the dolmen. 'What do you want, Malait?'

Blocking the entrance with his brawn, Otto didn't mince his words. 'Where's the statue?'

Alan laughed. 'Show him, mistress.'

She moved slowly. 'Here.'

The Norseman grabbed the carving. 'De Roncier kept me in the dark. I was commanded to look for a holy statue. Enlighten me.'

'Twist the base from the stone,' Alan said, obligingly. There was a splintering noise. 'No need to break it.'

But he spoke too late. Tossing both statue and wooden shards aside, Otto weighed the sunstone in his hand. 'Is this it? I'm keeping it.' He tucked the stone into his pouch, concluding that it had to be what Marie de Roncier was panting for, not the holy icon. It must be worth a king's ransom. Otto made slits of his eyes. 'No objections, le Bret? It's not like you to surrender easily. Is there more you're hiding?'

Alan resisted the temptation to exchange glances with the girl. 'More? I only wish there were,' he said, hoping he sounded convincing. He lifted his shoulders and, keeping his eyes on his former comrade, sheathed his sword. Limping to where the statue lay embedded in the mud, he pulled it out and handed it to her. Her fingers were like icicles. 'My leg's too painful for a fight, Malait,' he continued candidly. 'I'm not fool enough to let you make dogmeat of me. I'll be content with escorting Mistress Gwenn home. Do we have your permission to leave?'

The Norseman glowered past thick brows at his former associate. He flattered himself that he knew Alan le Bret as well as any man, for they had diced away many a long evening together. Le Bret always wore that look when he was certain he was winning. But he had relinquished the stone without so much as a murmur. Otto patted his pouch; he had the jewel the Dowager Countess craved. He had won this round. So why did he have a nagging suspicion that he was being played for an ass? 'Come here, wench,' he said.

Gwenn planted her feet firmly in the mud and stared a refusal.

'Come here, I say.' Otto took a threatening step towards her, but Alan barred his way.

'Leave the maid alone, Malait.'

'What ails you, le Bret? Turning into the white crusader?'

167

'She's only a child. Leave her alone.'

Otto rolled a contemptuous eye. 'Becoming quite the nursemaid in your dotage, aren't you, le Bret? Where's the pretty boy, Fletcher? Where's your other charge?'

Alan's jaw tightened. 'Shut your filthy mouth.'

A blinding explosion of lightning bleached their faces. There came an almighty crack, an awesome tearing sound, and the ground quaked like Judgement Day. A scatter of pebbles tumbled down the entrance passage and came to rest in a puddle at the bottom. More rainwater trickled down the steps, and with each passing second, the pool grew.

Paddling to the entrance, Alan peered up the stairs. 'An oak has fallen across the steps,' he announced. Gwenn waded after him, and Alan felt an icy hand slip into his.

'What are we going to do?'

He barely caught her low whisper and threw her a sideways glance. 'Afraid of the storm, Mistress Blanche?'

Her head was bowed. 'My name is Gwenn. And no, storms don't frighten me. But devils do.'

Alan let his fingers curl round hers; such tiny, delicate icicles. 'Didn't you say *I* was a devil?' he murmured. Her head came up and a shy smile caught him offguard, warming his belly.

'You know what they say, Alan le Bret. Better the devil you know . . .' She flung an expressive look in the Viking's direction.

'You flatter me,' Alan declared with a snort of appreciative laughter. Keeping a wary eye on Otto, he loosed Gwenn's hand while he twisted his injured leg safely out of the bone-chilling draught. Gwenn wrapped her arms round her middle and kept close. 'Decided you like me?' Alan couldn't resist enquiring.

'Aye . . . I mean . . . No. Th . . . that is . . .'

Laughing, he reclaimed her hand. 'You're only a baby, aren't you?'

Gwenn considered snatching her hand away, but her

fear of Malait prevented her.

The cold and damp were playing havoc with Alan's leg. Ignoring the Norseman who seemed to be lost in thought at the bottom of the steps, Alan dropped his cloak onto a relatively dry spot. 'We'll sit here and wait out the tempest.' Pulling Gwenn down with him, he eased his leg.

Otto glowered half-heartedly at them, a seed of an idea germinating in his mind. He resented the fact that his lord had misled him by not mentioning the jewel. He fell to speculating how much it was worth. He knew a goldsmith in Vannes with a loose enough tongue if it was oiled with liberal quantities of wine . . .

'I'm going,' he announced, though a weak thread of suspicion held him back. 'Why is it that I feel as though you've stolen a march on me, le Bret?'

The grey eyes opened wide.

Otto placed a capacious boot on the bottom step. 'I never forget a slight, le Bret. I'll come looking for you if I find you've bested me.' He threw Alan a look that would have frozen the blood of Lancelot himself and tramped up the steps into the teeth of the worsening storm, grunting as he forced his bear-like bulk past the fallen tree. Then he was gone.

Gwenn sighed, and kept her hand tucked in Alan's. He found no reason to disengage himself. The concubine's daughter was only a child. No threat. After some time, the child lifted her head and spoke.

'Did you learn what you wanted to learn?'

'Eh?' Alan had been in another world, a world where he never had to worry where the next coin was coming from. He had been dreaming.

'The people whose tracks you followed.'

'Oh.' She had caught him unawares, she seemed to make a habit of that. Alan thought swiftly; he had indeed learned something, but he did not want to inform this chit of a girl. He had seen riders with their cloaks fastened down, and had known instantly that they were more intent on concealing the colours emblazoned on their surcoats than of escaping the icy wind. The angels had sided with him; as he had taken cover behind a lichen-encrusted boulder, a helpful gust had lifted one of the riders' cloaks high over his head. The flapping material caused a squire to lose control of his mount, the animal had reared up, and in the ensuing tangle Alan was granted a clear sight of their colours. The unfortunate squire had a chastening whip slashed across his face for his sins.

'Ermine,' Alan mused, 'that's Geoffrey, Duke of Brittany. And the Count of Toulouse – Toulouse, here?' What had he stumbled upon? The high rank of the participants in this clandestine rendezvous warned of deadly secrets. There was a third lord in the group, whose coat of arms had remained covered. Surprisingly, given their high rank, the other noblemen seemed to defer to him. He wore heavy rings over richly embroidered gauntlets. His cloak was lined with priceless sables, and fastened securely with golden clasps. His face was muffled. Not a glimpse of a colour peeped out, but in all probability the man was too important to wear colours himself. Then a stray finger of wind lifted the mantle of the squire at the nobleman's elbow. There was a brief flash of gold and crimson. On seeing the colours, Alan's innards dissolved and he jerked himself out of sight behind his rock. What he had seen was the royal lion of England. The other participant in this furtive meeting was none other than His Grace, Henry, the Young King of England, who was Duke Geoffrey's elder brother.

Gwenn shifted restlessly beside him, her face turned expectantly to his. 'Who were those people?'

Alan hunted for a plausible lie. 'It was nothing out of the way,' he said. 'The local nobility out hawking.'

Gwenn lost interest. Pushing back her hood, she tugged off her veil. 'The wretched thing's soaking.' Against all the odds, her voice was sleepy. A diminutive hand came up to hide a yawn, and her dark head drooped against his shoulder. 'Wake me when it's time to go home,' she said. And, child that she was, a heart-beat later she was asleep.

Alan resigned himself to a long wait. After a spell he was forced to flex his leg, for it burned like fire. No doubt he would have cause to regret offering to escort the girl back. He winced. As far as he was concerned, this past month had been one tedious chronicle of disaster. First he had broken his leg; but he'd managed to discount that, thinking of the profit he'd make when he took the jewel. And now he had discovered that he had broken his leg in vain. He'd gained nothing from the whole business, not so much as a clipped farthing.

Gwenn stirred in her sleep. Her hair was glossy even in this feeble light. Her head hung at an awkward angle. Gently, Alan eased his hand free of hers and draped his arm round her shoulders, turning her so that her face rested more comfortably against his chest. She gave a contented sigh. Such faith. He found himself wondering whether she would grow up to be pretty. He thought so.

Alan turned his mind to the royal brothers who had met in this place: Duke Geoffrey of Brittany and Young King Henry of England. What were they planning? The Plantagenets were not noted for their unity. He had heard – who in Christendom had not heard? – how the Young King and Duke Geoffrey were constantly in rebellion against their father. In order to safeguard the succession, Henry of England had had his eldest son, who confusingly was also christened Henry, crowned during his lifetime. But the royal house of England was a house divided, and the Young King was not a loyal son. Aided by his mother, the redoubtable Eleanor of Aquitaine, the Young King had stirred up rebellion after rebellion against his father. What was he up to now? Another quarrel over land? Now if Alan could only ally himself with men like those, that would be a challenge. Those men held the future in the palm of their hands; men like Jean St Clair did not. St Clair was poor; the royal brothers must have money, fresh-

171

minted silver to purchase new recruits. Alan wondered how he might approach them.

A strand of silky hair had twined round his fingers, and Alan realised he had been caressing Gwenn's head. He snatched his hand away, and in doing so woke her.

Dark, trusting eyes met his. 'Is it time to go, Alan le Bret?'

Alan looked at her. She smiled again. And before he could think about it, Alan had put his hand under her chin and brought her mouth round. He kissed her. Her lips were soft and trembled under his. Alan's eyes closed, and slowly he deepened the kiss, taking her startled gasp into his mouth. He did not think she had been kissed properly before, for at first she resisted opening to him. A small hand came to rest on his shoulder, and he was absurdly pleased when she did not push him away. All at once she seemed to understand what he was about, and her mouth opened. Her innocence enchanted him – she was quite the sweetest thing he had ever kissed . . .

Before he was utterly disarmed, Alan pulled free of her and pushed himself upright. He had to clear his throat, and force himself not to look at those dark, trusting eyes, which by now would be full of bewilderment. 'Aye, come on. It's time to go.'

'Have a drink, Tomaz.' Otto indicated a brimming pitcher of wine, recently shipped in from Bordeaux. 'I've something to show you.'

The goldsmith's eyes gleamed bright as the lamps which swung in the onshore breeze floating through the door of the Ship Inn. 'Bless you,' he said and, giving a resounding belch in appreciation of the routier's generosity, he poured the blood-red liquid into his leather tankard.

The Ship Inn was perched on the edge of the quayside in the fishermen's quarter of Vannes, and in its rare, quiet moments it was possible to hear the gentle lapping of the sea against the harbour wall and the creaking hawsers of vessels tied up for the night. Tonight's quiet moment was far off though, for the night fishermen were busy filling their bellies with the various brews that they swore kept out the cold. It would be an hour before they were gone; an hour before the Ship Inn would fall silent enough for someone with sharp ears to hear either slapping wavelets or groaning ropes.

The goldsmith drank lustily. 'Ah, that's good.' He scrubbed his mouth with his hairy hand. 'Out with it, Malait. Have you more ill-gotten gains for sale? You must have taken to robbing the dead, you bring me more than anyone else.'

Accepting this tribute as no less than his due, a brief grin flashed across Otto's lips. The two men often met, for Tomaz bought whatever Otto offered without asking questions, and they did a roaring trade in stolen goods. 'Here.' Otto dropped the stone into the goldsmith's waiting palm. 'What is it?'

Unhooking the lantern which dangled overhead, Tomaz placed it on the table. As he stared at the diamond-shaped crystal, his dark brows twitched.

'Is it a diamond?'

'A diamond?' The goldsmith's shoulders began to shake, and he dissolved into barely smothered laughter. 'Fancy you bringing me one of these, and not knowing . . .'

Malait clenched his fist.

Holding the crystal between finger and thumb, the goldsmith prudently swallowed his amusement and held the stone to the light. He did not want to offend the hot-headed Norseman, or lose a good source of income. 'See how cloudy it is? There are countless flaws. And look, here's a chip.'

'Aye. But what's it *worth*?'

'It's a sunstone. I could smash it with my heel.'

'Its *worth*, Tomaz.'

'Paol could answer that.' Tomaz tossed the sunstone into the lap of a fisherman whose ancient back was as bent as a bow, and whose skin was as brown and tough as the leather of Otto's boots. 'What value would you give this, Paol?'

Paol picked up the sunstone, glanced at it, and his mouth split in a gummy smile. 'Wouldn't give you an oyster for it.'

'What!' Otto shot to his feet.

'It's a sunstone, Malait,' Tomaz said. 'Your ancestors would have fought tooth and nail for one, for their ships.'

'Ships?' Otto repeated, dazedly. Bitter anger flared in his breast. Alan le Bret had taken him for a half-wit.

'Aye. Might be useful out of sight of land. Round the coast? Worthless.'

'Worthless?' Here he was, thinking he'd never have to work again, and all the while Alan le Bret must have known the damned thing's true value. Why else would he have relinquished it so tamely? One question remained. Had there been anything else in the statue, or had le Bret made a fool of him on that score too?

Tomaz smirked. 'Imagine a Viking not knowing a sunstone when he sees one.' Then, seeing Otto's visage grow black as a smith's, he curbed his mirth.

'God rot you, le Bret,' Otto spat through gritted teeth. 'I'll spill your guts.' He focused on the goldsmith whose mouth was curving despite himself. 'What are you laughing at, Tomaz?'

'Nothing. Have another drink, my friend.'

'Give me that thing, old man.' Otto held out his hand. He would have to return to de Roncier; the sunstone was some sort of proof that there was no jewel. And by the bones of Christ, Otto thought, it had better be the gem that the Countess had been hot for, and not the statue. If de Roncier's mother coveted the statue, he'd be lucky if he was put to cleaning the castle midden.

Tomaz stared pointedly at the pitcher of Bordeaux. 'What about the wine?'

'You drink it, and I hope it chokes you,' Otto said

uncharitably. He rose and stalked into the dark.

At that moment, Alan was travelling on horseback along the rue Richemont in the company of Ned. It was a broad highway, wide enough for several knights to ride abreast, and it was easy to follow because the moonlight made rocks and road shimmer.

'Where are you bound, Alan?'

'East gate.'

'Won't it be secure at this hour?'

'They'll let me in.'

'Oh.' Ned looked puzzled. 'Alan?'

'Yes?'

'If you're so set on getting a fortune, why didn't you desert Mistress Gwenn and take off with her mare? You would have got yourself two horses that way. This way you get nothing, for I'm to take yours back to St Clair's stables.'

Alan couldn't answer Ned's question. All he knew was that when he and the girl had arrived at the crossroads, he found himself spurring on to the manor alongside her. And when they had got there, she had kept faith with him. She had not tattled about his attempt to steal the nonexistent gemstone, or his kissing her. He shrugged. 'By the Rood, I don't know. It must have been a momentary lapse. You'll not hold it against me, surely?'

Ned was accustomed to Alan's warped humour, and he greeted this with a laugh. 'No. But it made me think, that's all. There might be some hope for you. Alan?'

'Stop prattling, will you, Ned? You make my head ache. You're worse than any maid.'

Smiling, Ned obliged.

Alan could see a pale flickering of lights in front of them. Below the lights was a long, thin, winding darkness which he knew was the wooden wall encircling the port. After riding some way in silence, he said, 'Our ways will part at the gate.'

'Aye, so you mentioned before. Where will you go?'

'I've a mind to seek out our noble Duke.'

'What? Brittany himself? I understood he was in Rennes.'

'You were misinformed,' Alan said, his mind on the black and white of Duke Geoffrey's ermine that he had seen that morning in Locmariaquer. He'd wasted enough of his life on the intrigues of petty lordlings. He wanted to move on to higher things.

'Alan, why don't you reconsider—'

'Don't sing that old ballad, Ned,' Alan said wearily, rubbing the thigh of his mended leg. 'The melody sickens me.'

'You'll regret it.'

Alan laughed shortly. 'I've fatter fish to fry.'

'You're a heartless dog,' Ned murmured, without heat.

'Not quite, else I'd have been long gone. Here.' Alan came to a halt and swung himself out of the saddle, tossed his mount's reins at Ned, and heaved his pack from the animal's back. 'You can lead this bag of bones back to the shack that St Clair calls his stable. I'll walk the rest of the way. Fare you well, Ned. I should think you'll do well with Sir Jean.'

Ned clutched his cousin's reins and gulped down a constriction in his windpipe. 'God speed, Alan. Will I see you again?'

'I should think so,' Alan answered carelessly. 'I know where to find you.'

'Yes.'

Alan shouldered his pack, sketched Ned a mocking bow, and turned his face towards the wooden palisade.

Marie de Roncier was breaking her fast in the hall of Huelgastel. Seated at the head of the table, beside her son, she tipped the sunstone from one dry palm to the other as though it scorched her. A silver-topped cane lay within reach on the trestle.

Weeks earlier, when news had reached her of her sister's death, the Dowager Countess had been overcome with guilt. If she had stayed her son's impetuous hand, if she had not demanded the statue, her crazed sister Izabel would yet be alive. However, in the days that had followed, Marie had stopped chastising herself. Life was easier when she turned her back on her uneasy conscience. She flung the sunstone on the table with a crack. 'My thanks, Malait, for bringing us this relic from the past, but I asked for the Virgin.' Had Izabel died to protect a glass pebble? It looked as though her informants had been right, her sister's wits must have gone at the end.

'You see, Maman,' the Count said. 'The diamond only had form in old wives' minds.'

'You are insolent, François,' Marie said frostily.

'No, Maman, practical.' He smiled. 'Honestly, accepting there was a jewel, which I doubt, is it likely they would have retained it all these years?'

Relieved to find the wind in this quarter, Otto took a pace towards the Dowager Countess. 'If there had been anything of value, madame, I'm sure Alan le Bret would have known.'

Regally, Marie waved him out. 'You may leave us.'

François booted the door shut after his captain. 'Well, ma mère? You advocate that I do nothing, I expect.'

Marie did not want any more blood on her hands. 'Do St Clair and his brood of bastards threaten you?' she asked, investing her voice with as much scorn as she could.

'Advise me.'

Marie's dark face lighted. 'With pleasure, François.' Her Robert, God rest him, had often asked her advice, she liked being consulted by her menfolk. 'Stay your hand and let matters rest. If you act, you acknowledge St Clair as a threat. And that would be tantamount to admitting you occupy shaky ground – it would be a tactical error. The man is weak, François; weak-minded, and weak in manpower. He'll never be a real danger.'

'Suppose he marries Yolande Herevi?'

'He won't. I've told you before, even that man wouldn't stoop to marry his concubine. Don't thrust a stick in a wasp's nest.'

François rubbed his red cheeks and looked dubious. 'I'd be happier if the nest was completely burned out.'

Marie grew pale. 'No, François.' It was not easy for her to plead, but she reached a hand towards her son. 'Enough is enough. Please.'

François held his mother's gaze for a heartbeat or two. 'If it pleases you, Maman,' he answered off-handedly, 'I'll play it your way, unless circumstances should change.'

Marie's hand fell. 'My thanks, François. I knew you'd see reason.'

PART TWO

Champions and Heroes

O God, the sea is so wide and my boat so small:
Be good to me.

Prayer of a Breton fisherman.

Chapter Eleven

Kermaria, two years later. Spring 1185.

Jean St Clair and his family gathered for supper in the hall, together with the men-at-arms, serving women and other members of the household. The whiff of mildew and decay had long been banished, and the scents of lavendar and beeswax mingled in the air. The rushes were changed regularly, the whitewash was renewed annually. A large wall-hanging brightened the gloomy north wall; and as last year's harvest had been good and Jean had money in his coffers, terracotta tiles had been carted in from Vannes, and the hearth and fire-surround had been relaid in bold chevrons of terracotta and gold.

'The duck smells good,' Raymond said, hooking a stool from under the trestle with his boot. Raymond's thick brown hair lay in tousled waves on his well-modelled head, for not only had he inherited his mother's fine emerald eyes, he also had her beautiful bone structure. His muscles had filled out, and he had the ungovernable appetite of any active young man. Without waiting for his parents to choose their birds, Raymond took his knife from his belt, wiped it perfunctorily on his breeches, and speared himself a fowl. It thudded on his trencher, and an onion rolled across the table leaving a glistening trail like that of a snail.

'Raymond, your manners!' Yolande chastised him, smiling.

Her son flashed her an incorrigible grin and flung

himself on his stool. His charm he had from his father. 'Apologies, Mama, but I'm famished! Where's Gwenn?' Gwenn was his dinner partner, and she was supposed to share the food on his trencher, after the fashion of nobles in larger households. Raymond never understood why they had to affect these ridiculous manners, but to save family argument he was prepared to pay lip-service to the odd caprice of his mother's.

'Here I am.' At fifteen, Gwenn remained petite and darkly pretty.

'Hurry up, sister. Or there'll be none left.'

Gwenn took her place at her brother's side while Raymond lunged at the sauce jug.

'This bird suit you, Gwenn?'

'Aye.'

'And wine sauce?'

Already he was drowning the bird, and a dark pool of sauce seeped out under the edge of their trencher. 'It would be too bad if it didn't,' Gwenn observed wryly.

Raymond stared at the jug as though it were bewitched and had leapt into his hand on its own. 'Sorry, Gwenn.'

'That's all right. I like the sauce.' Gwenn noticed that Ned Fletcher was watching her from the other trestle. Goaded by some inner demon, she lowered her head and peeped experimentally at him. Recently, she had discovered that Ned went bright pink when she did that. A tide of crimson swept up the Englishman's neck and surged into his cheeks, and he swiftly transferred his attention to a flagon of wine. Gwenn smiled.

Yolande's clear brow – she had marked this exchange – clouded.

Everyone, with the exception of Raymond who was already carving his bird, was looking to the master of the house for the signal to begin. The door opened, and Denis the Red, so called because of his fiery crest of hair, tramped in. One of Ned's peers, Denis had been posted at the bridge on the avenue. A travel-stained stranger dogged his heels. Someone groaned. This would mean a delay in eating.

'Aye? What is it, man?' Jean asked irritably, for he was as eager for his meat as were the rest of them.

The stranger, a courier, stepped forward and proferred a scroll. 'I've a despatch for you, sir.' He lowered his voice. 'It's from your brother, Sir Waldin.'

Jean raised startled brows. The St Clair brothers wrote only rarely to each other, and the last time Jean had heard from Waldin had been two years earlier, after Jean requested Waldin's support. Waldin's reply had been curt and to the point. He had sent his regrets, but it was not convenient for him to comply with his brother's wishes. He had promised to join Jean later. Jean had not taken Waldin's promise seriously.

While his household waited, knives suspended over trenchers, Jean broke the seal on the parchment and ran his eyes slowly over the script. He was a novice where reading was concerned, but this hand was bold and clear, and easy on the eye. Waldin must have done well in the last tournament to be able to afford so neat a scribe. Jean looked up. 'Waldin is coming home,' he announced with a smile. He turned to the messenger. 'Is my brother in good health?'

The man started. He had been staring at the heaped trenchers; he had not eaten in hours, and the smell of the braised fowl was making him giddy. 'Aye, sir.' Swallowing down a mouthful of saliva, the courier mustered a smile. 'He's been Champion of Champions this past two years.'

'Has he, by God? So that's why he wouldn't come when I beckoned. I thought you were going to tell me he'd been injured, and was coming home to lick his wounds.'

The rush-strewn floor was shifting under the courier's feet. 'No, sir. Sir Waldin is as sound of wind and limb as he has ever been.'

'Thank the Lord.' Jean grubbed in his pouch for a coin, and tossed it at the messenger. 'Sit you down, man. On my soul, you look half famished. Eat,' he said, addressing his household as well as the messenger.

'My thanks, sir.' The envoy stumbled to the soldiers' board and fell upon the food.

Denis the Red watched in envy. His stomach growled. Tonight, he would have to be content with cold fare by the bridge. He stumped sullenly for the door and wondered what they'd be getting tomorrow. He wouldn't be on look-out at suppertime tomorrow.

'So we're to meet the great tourney champion at last,' Raymond said.

'Yes, if he doesn't change his mind.' Waldin was notoriously unreliable, and tourneys were his life.

Gwenn saw that Ned Fletcher's gaze was once more trained on the top table and she tried another smile. This one failed to bring the slightest flush to the young trooper's cheeks, and Gwenn thought she knew why. Ned knew all about Sir Waldin, and he had his ears stretched to catch every last word about the champion knight-at-arms. She herself had met her father's younger brother when she was only seven, and she longed to see him again.

Waldin St Clair was, in his way, a rebel. He had refused the expected career in the Church and had gone off to make his fortune at the tournaments. Gwenn's memory of him was hazy. All she could remember was that he had appeared out of nowhere, but she had vivid recollections of the tournament that he had taken her to with Raymond on the outskirts of Vannes. Of course, Gwenn was older and wiser now, and she realised that, for Waldin, that small local tournament must have been an insignificant affair, but it had given her a taste of the excitement they offered. She had seen the silken pennants flying, and the gaily caparisoned horses. She had heard the thundering of great hoofs and the squealing of the horses. She had smelt the excitement.

Waldin had not taken part that day; instead he had devoted himself to answering Raymond's questions and plying Gwenn with scoopful after scoopful of honeyed almonds and raisins. For months afterwards Gwenn had relished their sweetness and had carried in her mind the brightness and colour of the tourney. After the tournament, Waldin had vanished out of her life as inexplicably as he had appeared; but that day with her uncle had stood out among other, duller days as one filled with magic and wonder.

Gwenn could not now call Waldin's face to mind, but she was sure she knew what he would look like. He would be tall and strong and brave. He would ride a white charger like the hero of a troubadour's song. She conjured up an image of him, and it was clear as day.

'Why should Sir Waldin change his mind, Papa?' she asked. Since bringing his family to Kermaria, Jean had given his children permission to name him 'father', explicitly acknowledging them as his. He had not, however, kept his promise to marry his mistress.

Jean smiled. 'The reasons why Waldin could be delayed are legion.'

'From what I've learned of life on the tourney circuit, I should think they're most likely female,' Raymond cut in with a man-of-the-world snigger. He looked more than happy to expand on this theme, but Jean silenced him with a look.

'My brother's a law unto himself, and always has been,' Jean said. 'But judging from his missive, it would seem he's retiring from the lists.'

'Thank God for that mercy,' Yolande said softly.

Gwenn clapped her hands. 'I can't wait to see him! Think of it, Raymond. The tales he must have to tell. Why, he will have met the King.'

'Which King are you talking about?' Raymond asked dampeningly. 'France or England?' He seized a decanter of wine and upended it into his cup.

'Does it matter? To have met a king, *any* king! Oh, Raymond, aren't you excited?'

He was, but at seventeen Raymond felt conscious

that he was a man full grown, and he'd die rather than admit it. 'I should think Sir Waldin will have better things to do than gossip with maids,' Raymond retorted.

Yolande intervened. 'It will be lovely to see your brother again,' she declared. 'I'm glad he's retiring from the circuit. Perhaps we might persuade him to stay.'

'I pray so. I can always use a good man.'

'Why is Waldin retiring, Papa?' Raymond asked. 'I thought tourney champions made sackfuls of money.'

'They do. When they win. As you know, they take all the loser's accoutrements – his horse, his arms, everything. But each time they fight they risk their lives and their goods. And they cannot always win. The life of a champion often ends in penury, if it is not cut short. Waldin's had a good, long run. Only God is infallible, and Waldin knows his time as a champion is limited.'

Raymond toyed with a piece of meat he had impaled on the point of his dagger. 'He's running away.'

'He's using his brain.' Jean set his stoneware cup down smartly. 'But don't ask me. You can ask the champion himself in a couple of weeks. He plans to be here around Ascensiontide.'

'So soon?' Yolande murmured, under her breath. Her hands were at her girdle, tightening it, and her eyes were turned down to their trencher. 'That's not long at all. I'll have to have done it by then.'

'What are you muttering about?' Jean demanded, noticing for the first time that Yolande had lost her sparkle. 'Whatever's the matter?'

But she declined to meet his gaze; instead, her eyes wandered to the fire flaming in the newly tiled hearth. She sat straight as a nun, folded her hands neatly over her stomach, and replied absently, 'We'll be needing new linen sheets if Waldin is to come. The spare ones are fit for nothing but dish clouts.' Then she turned her head and met her lover's eyes straight on, though

186

her own were remote. Her face was set like rock, and her wide forehead was furrowed. Jean's heart lurched. That look; it was as though she did not like him, had never liked him, and was sure she never would like him. Bemused, he ran his hand over his moustache, and then Yolande was smiling warmly at him, and her hand had come to cover his.

Having picked at her evening meal, Yolande retired early to the solar, taking a rush-light with her. At Kermaria, peace was almost as rare a commodity as privacy, and Yolande needed peace desperately tonight. She had some thinking to do. Pressing her hand to her belly, she paced the boards. A tiny fluttering made itself felt, as though there were a butterfly inside her. But it was no butterfly. Yolande had known that fluttering sensation before, and recognised it. Each time she had noticed it, a babe had followed some months later.

She was pregnant. Yolande had misgivings about this baby. She did not want another child; or, more precisely, she did not want another bastard.

The Stone Rose stared proudly down from a new walnut plinth on a shelf Jafrez the carpenter had fixed to the east wall. Kneeling before it, Yolande offered an Ave Maria before murmuring a more personal prayer. The Virgin watched with cold, granite eyes. 'Holy Mother, help me. Advise me. I had thought the time had passed that I could bear a child. Why else should my courses have stopped when Katarin was three? What purpose do you have in giving me another child? I count it no blessing. Why?'

It seemed to Yolande that the hard, almond-shaped eyes judged her; judged, and found her guilty. 'I know I have sinned,' she bowed her head, 'but I love him. I would have married him if I could. Before each child was born, I prayed that it would not have to bear the taint of bastardy. Three times I did that. I pray that same prayer today. Holy Mother—'

The shadows shifted, light danced and skittered over

187

the limewashed walls. Someone had entered the solar, carrying a lantern. Yolande's moment of private contemplation was ended.

'Mama?' Gwenn set the lantern on a coffer, and opened its door, so that the light strengthened. 'Is anything amiss?'

Stiffly, Yolande got to her feet and forced a smile.

'You look so sad. What is it, Mama?'

Yolande longed to confide in someone. Why not Gwenn? Her daughter was fifteen now, old enough. 'I'm enceinte,' Yolande announced bluntly.

Gwenn looked delighted. 'But Mama, that's wonderful! I love babies. There will be someone else for Katarin to play with.' She kissed Yolande on the cheek. 'Don't be sad about that, Mama. That's lovely news.'

'Is it?' Yolande murmured, bleakly. 'That will make four of you. Four.'

'So?'

Yolande swung away. 'Four illegitimate children, Gwenn. I think three is more than enough for any woman to bear a man, don't you?'

Some of the shining joy left her daughter's expression. 'No one minds that out here, Mama.'

'Don't they? Don't *you* mind, Gwenn?'

Her daughter's eyes slid to the newly worked arras hanging across the chamber door. 'No.' Her chin inched up. 'It was only in Vannes that people minded. Here, on Father's land, it is different.'

'Is it? I'm not so sure.' Another matter had been preying on Yolande's mind, and dimly she perceived that the two worries were linked. 'Lately, I have noticed that your relationship with Ned Fletcher is over-familiar – no, Gwenn, it is no use your scowling like that. It won't do. I worry about you. If your father and I were married, Ned Fletcher wouldn't dare let his eyes stray.'

'Ned Fletcher is good to me,' Gwenn said stubbornly. 'I won't hear a word against him.'

Yolande kept her voice cool. 'I'm sure he is, dear.

But you must remember, he's from common stock.'

'Common stock!' Gwenn spluttered. 'What do you mean?'

So Gwenn did mind . . . Yolande sighed. 'Oh, my dear, if I were married to your father, you would understand immediately what I mean. My life of sin has blinded you to the truth.'

'That's hogwash and you know it.'

'Gwenn! Such language!'

Higher went that defiant chin. 'Well, it is hogwash, Mama. If you're trying to say that the common folk lack the finer qualities, then I must disagree with you. Ned is kind.'

Ned. Yolande suppressed a groan. She called him Ned. Worse and worse.

In full spate, Gwenn rushed on. 'Ned listens to me. Ned doesn't patronise me like Papa. And unlike my dear brother, Ned Fletcher keeps his promises. It seems to me that Ned Fletcher is more honourable than both my father and my brother put together! Remember that it was Ned . . .' Gwenn caught the spark in her mother's eyes, '. . . I mean Fletcher and his cousin, Alan le Bret, who saved me. That took courage. If that doesn't put the case for those of *common* stock, I don't know what does.'

'Oh dear,' Yolande said weakly, trying, and failing, to put her objections into a reasoned argument. She was too old to be carrying, and wished she was not so fatigued. 'I never did like Fletcher's kinsman.'

'But he did save me.'

There was no answer to that. 'I was misguided,' Yolande murmured, 'to let you sit in on Raymond's lessons. It's enabled you to talk the hind leg off a donkey, and it's not becoming in a girl. You've grown so clever, you could argue wrong into right. We've spoiled you. God knows if we'll ever find a husband to take you.'

'Oh, Mama,' Gwenn tossed an impatient head, 'it's your thinking that is crooked.' But then she saw how tired her mother was, and relented. She led Yolande to her bed in the curtained recess. 'I'm sorry, Mama. You should be resting. You've the babe to consider.'

Meekly, Yolande permitted Gwenn to direct her to her couch. As Gwenn pointed out, she had the babe to consider. Since de Roncier had loosed his fiends and set that terrible fire, Yolande had dismissed all thought of marriage from her mind. Marriage to Jean would not legitimise the children they already had, and a wedding might provoke the Count to further outrages against her family.

But if there was to be another child . . .

After Gwenn had crept out, leaving her with the lantern, Yolande settled under her downy coverlet and laid a hand over her womb. The babe was growing within her; and growing with it was the resolve that by hook or by crook this child would be legitimate. She accepted that in many respects Jean had been criminally irresponsible. He had neglected his inheritance for years, claiming he had not the funds to manage it when a more far-sighted man would have put his shoulder to the plough and husbanded his land to make it fruitful. Latterly, Jean had seen the light and had mended his ways, and these two years past had seen him wearing his fingers to the bone. Kermaria was improved beyond recognition. A disloyal voice chimed in, suggesting Yolande consider how much more improved Kermaria would have been if he had begun his stewardship of his estate when he had first inherited it.

No matter. Jean was . . . Jean. He may have been irresponsible, but he was reformed, and even in his earlier, feckless days he had always been able to win her over with his charm. She loved him.

A yearning sigh fell from her lips. It was all very well for her to feel inside her that their unsanctified relationship was blessed by God, but latterly she had come to the conclusion that it mattered little what one thought if one was out of step with the world. It was the world, after all, that named her children bastards, and it was the world that thought the worst of them for it.

If only Jean could be persuaded to marry her. Yolande hoarded another, more telling wish close to her heart. She did not wish for gold, or for power or influence. Her wish was simple, and it astonished her, for she liked to think of herself as a free spirit. Yolande wished that one day she might be able to present Jean with a babe and say to him, 'This, my love, is your heir, your legitimate heir.'

A flagon of Rhenish later, Jean tiptoed past the sleeping women of his household, heading for bed. The women's pallets, neat as a row of beans, ranged across the floor of the solar, a hazard to the unwary. Of the four recesses built into the walls of the solar, three had beds in them. Jean glanced at the one Gwenn and Katarin shared. All was quiet there. Katarin must be sound asleep. Releasing a thankful sigh, for his youngest could raise hell if she did not feel like sleeping, he picked his way across the shadowy room. The third niche, which Raymond had appropriated for his sole use, was empty, for Raymond was drinking below. The fourth and last recess stank. No one slept there. One day, Jean vowed, he would have the mason fit another privy. The need for it was dire.

Above his bed a lantern burned. 'Are you awake, my love?' he whispered, as was necessary if he did not want to be overheard by his household. Jean unbuckled his sword and, as was his habit, placed it within arm's reach by his bed. His mistress stirred and yawned. 'What ails you? You looked as though you were miles away at dinnertime.'

Yolande propped herself up on her pillows. 'Perhaps I was.'

'Eh?' Jean couldn't find her meaning easily, and was too full of wine to try very hard. Sinking onto the edge of the mattress, he unlaced his knee-high boots and flung his tunic aside. In a corner, a bowl of water waited on a stand. He splashed his face perfunctorily with it; it was as chilly as a March sea. 'Hell.' He shivered, and cracked his elbow against the wall. 'This bedchamber is too cramped,' he observed, not for the first time.

'It grants us some privacy.'

'You have something there.' Jean grinned and, leaving both chausses and linen chainse on, he clambered into bed. He slid a hand over a warm, rounded breast, and nuzzled her arm. 'You have something here.' But instead of the response that he hoped for, he was greeted with a soft sigh. He shifted his hand to her waist and lifted his head. His lover looked pensive. He resigned himself to a lengthy and probably tedious conversation, and valiantly tried to rally wits that were more than ready for rest. 'What is it?'

Under the sheets her breasts rose as she inhaled deeply. 'I had thought to keep it from you, Jean. I had thought to cope with it on my own. But then I realised that that would never do. I have never liked keeping secrets from you, and to do so in this instance would be very wrong.'

Linking his hands behind his head, Jean waited for her to come to the substance of the matter, and watched the rise and fall of her bosom under her chemise. It must be no trifling concern, that she went about telling him in such a circuitous way. He'd picked a good woman, he thought complacently, admiring her breasts – they were still firm, still beautiful, even after three children and more years than he cared to count.

Yolande sat up abruptly and leaned across him; one long brown plait tickled his neck. She tugged one of his hands from under his head and pressed it to a soft breast. 'Go on, Jean. Touch me. You want to, I can see it. Touch me, and tell me if you notice anything different about me.'

In a flash, Jean understood. So that was it. That was what he had, without realising it, noticed. Her breasts were fuller because she was breeding. 'You're with child!'

'Aye.' She sank into her pillows and folded her hands over her belly in that prim nun's manner that Jean was

192

learning to suspect. Her eyes were cold, green ice. 'Are you pleased?'

'Pleased? Naturally I'm pleased.'

'I thought at first to keep it from you' – Jean noticed her voice lacked colour – 'I thought it best to try and . . . lose it.'

'Lose it?'

'There are women who know what to do. Why even here in Kermaria, I'm told Berthe—'

'Blessed Jesu!' Jean grapsed her shoulders. 'I forbid it! I forbid it! Do you hear me?' He felt hollow with fear.

Throwing a pointed glance at the curtain screen, Yolande said mildly, 'I should think all Kermaria can hear.'

He shook her, hissing, 'I'll not have you going to those old crones. Will you swear it? Besides, it's a mortal sin.' Bewilderingly, Yolande's shoulders began to shake. The ice in her eyes had melted. She was laughing. 'Yolande?'

'Jean, you are wrong if you think that fear for my soul will keep me from visiting Dame Berthe. I've been your leman for a score of years. I doubt that one more sin will tip the balance over much – I'm already bound for the devil's pit.'

He stared intently at her. 'Don't listen to the priests, love, or you'll end up twisted, like your poor mother. You're an honest woman, and God would not—'

'Honest? Your mistress, and honest? There are those who would gainsay you on that, my love.'

'Nevertheless, it's true. You're honest, and steadfast – the best mate a man could have.'

Yolande was not seeking praise. 'Jean, I think this one's a boy.'

The knight didn't move a muscle, but Yolande knew where his thoughts were winging. Jean was thinking that if he married her now, and the child was male, he would have a legitimate heir, and he would have good reason to resurrect their tenuous claim to Izabel's lands.

193

And now that Waldin was coming home, to reinforce their hand . . .

He took Yolande's chin and tipped her face to his. 'I thought it was impossible to tell?'

Yolande crossed her fingers under the bedcover. 'So it is. But I sense it strongly, Jean. This one will be a boy.'

'An heir,' he murmured. 'An heir.

Wisely, Yolande let his thoughts run on. If Jean believed the babe was a boy, he might yet marry her. He had something worth passing on to his heirs these days. Was it wrong for her to use the unborn child as a weapon, if that was the only weapon she had? She was only trying to ensure that the child was born legitimate.

'Waldin has such a reputation, Yolande. With him home, every soldier in Brittany will flock to our standard.' Jean's face glowed as in his mind's eye, ambitious dreams were fulfilled.

'Only if God wills it, Jean.' Yolande touched his arm. 'Don't tell me you're going to use the arrival of that wastrel of a brother as an excuse to make an honest woman of me after all these years?'

'Nay, love,' he had the grace to look ashamed, 'you know I would have married you years ago, except that—'

'It was not politic. I know. Do you remember that Frenchwoman you pretended to woo?' She clucked her tongue, gently mocking. 'No, don't start apologising. You explained it years ago. I understood your wish to better yourself.'

Jean looked at her past jutting brows. 'Aye. And then that fire – on my soul, I feared to provoke the Count.'

'The fire is one event I'm not likely to forget. My poor mother . . . But let's turn our minds to the future. Waldin—'

'Waldin will be here before we know it,' he mused. 'He will strengthen our position immeasurably.' He picked up her hand. 'Let's marry when Waldin gets here, Yolande.'

'What?' Triumph disarmed her.

Jean tweaked a braid, and his mouth turned up at the corners. 'You heard. Waldin can witness our wedding. Let's have one legitimate child.'

Yolande gulped and gazed wordlessly at her lover through a rush of tears. Her child was saved. One at least was saved.

'Can you wait?' He eyed her belly as though confused.

'What, till Waldin gets here? Of course.' Then she caught his meaning. He must be stupid with fatigue. 'Oh, I see. The babe. That's not a problem, the babe's not due till after Lammas.'

'Good.' Relaxing back onto the mattress, Jean shut his eyes. 'Now that we've raked that one over good and proper, can we go to sleep, please?'

Yolande remembered Gwenn. 'Not yet, I'm afraid.'

He groaned and lifted weary lids. 'Can't it wait?'

'No. It concerns Gwenn. I don't think you realise that she's a young lady, Jean. We ought to plan her future.'

Airily, Jean waved that worry aside. 'Plenty of time for that. Let's see ourselves wed first.'

Yolande studied her lover, trying to assess whether she was pushing him too far. She didn't want to lose what ground she had gained. It might be no bad thing to leave settling Gwenn's affairs till after her own wedding. Her belated marriage might not confer legitimacy on Gwenn, but it would make her a more attractive proposition.

Yolande nestled against Jean's side, resting her head on his shoulder while one hand pushed open the neck of his chainse and drew circles among the hairs on his chest. There was grey intermixed with the brown, they were neither of them growing any younger. 'I pray you are right,' she said softly, 'but I'm not sure that we do have plenty of time.'

'God's bones, of course there's time. We've years of living left to do.'

Yolande spread her fingers on his chest. 'I daresay

I'm wrong, indeed I hope I am, but I have noticed that Gwenn seems to spend a large portion of her day with one of the men-at-arms. It would be dreadful, would it not, if she were to get herself,' a deprecating smile touched the corners of her mouth, 'into the same state that I find myself.'

Jean caught her hand and stilled the circling movements. 'I've noticed nothing. You must be mistaken. None of them would presume . . .' Jean watched Yolande arch an immaculate brow. 'Who is it?' he snapped.

'Ned Fletcher.'

'Fletcher? I trust Fletcher. I let him take her riding.'

'Exactly. Think of the opportunities that presents.'

'Ned Fletcher?' Jean drummed his fingers on the back of Yolande's hand. 'I own you've surprised me. I'd not have thought it of that lad. He's one of my best, he's responsible, and hard-working.' Impatiently, he thrust back his hair. 'Damn it all, Yolande, I *like* the boy. I'd hoped to make him sergeant.'

'I like him too, Jean. But don't you see, that makes him even more dangerous.'

'You don't think he's had her already? No one will want her if she's lost her virtue.'

'No. I'm prepared to take my oath that they are both innocents. You should have seen the way he blushed when she fluttered her eyelashes at him this evening.'

'The hussy. It would be damned inconvenient if she fancied herself in love with him. Does she?'

'I think not. But you know what a baggage Gwenn can be. She has discovered the effect she has on the boy and cannot help but try out her wiles on him. The result is that the poor lad is being teased mercilessly. I'm sure Gwenn doesn't mean to be cruel, but you know Gwenn, she has to test everything to the limits.'

'Something will have to be done, I agree. I'll keep an eye on them. I won't have my Gwenn wasting herself on some peasant boy who couldn't keep her in clogs. I had it in mind for her to marry a wine merchant in Vannes, Maurice by name.'

'No, Jean! Not Vannes! Gwenn hates Vannes.'

Jean looked down his nose at her. 'The whim of my daughter does not come into this.'

'It's more than any whim, Jean.'

Her objection went unheeded, and the sensuous lips tightened. 'Marriage is a matter of politics,' Jean said, mouthing the beliefs of his class. 'Daughters marry to suit their parents, and if it suits me to make an alliance with one of the richest men in Vannes, she'll obey me. However,' the muscles round his mouth relaxed, 'as *we* are to be married soon, I think I'll commence negotiations in another quarter. Since our household is to turn respectable, and Gwenn's brother,' he placed tender fingers on Yolande's belly, 'will claim your mother's lands, we'll want more than a vintner for our eldest daughter.' He rubbed his eyes with the back of his hand. 'By St Patern, I'm worn out. If I promise to look into this, will you let me get some sleep?'

Yolande smiled. 'I will. Good night, Jean.'

He reached for the lantern and snuffed out the flame. 'Good night, my love.'

Chapter Twelve

At dawn two days later, Gwenn went to the stables to meet Ned for their early morning ride as had become their custom. The day was bright and clear, so clear it seemed to shine.

When Gwenn entered, Ned was securing the girth on Yolande's brown mare. He greeted her with a warm smile, and hoped he was managing to conceal the effect she always had on his heartbeat. 'Good morning, mistress. Here is Dancer all saddled up.' Yolande had asked Gwenn to exercise Dancer while she was carrying.

'My thanks, Ned. Where are we going today?'

'I thought we could aim for Locmariaquer.'

'Locmariaquer? But won't that take too long? Can you spare me so much time?'

Ned grinned, and answered as lightly as he could. 'I'd give you all the time in the world, mistress, if it was mine to give.' He led Dancer and the grey gelding that he was to ride out into the yard.

'But your duties?'

'I don't have to report for duty till this afternoon.'

'So we have the whole morning?'

'We have the whole morning.' Ned linked his hands and squired Gwenn onto Dancer. 'I wanted to show the old earthworks to you. There's a curious temple that some say was used for human sacrifice by monsters from the past.' He contorted his face into a hideous grimace and brought it as near to hers as he dared.

Smiling, Gwenn pushed him away. 'Why is it that

199

you're always trying to scare me out of my wits, Ned?'

'I don't know. I must like it when you scream.' Ned turned away. 'But if you've seen them before . . .'

'You can still show them to me. I've not been there since your cousin left, and when I saw them I was . . . somewhat distracted. I'd love to see them with you.'

'Good. And on the way you can tell me all about your Uncle Waldin. And tournaments, and jousting, and—'

'I don't know much!'

'Tell me what you do know.'

They were all but out of the yard when Raymond hailed them from the top of the manor steps.

'Hey! Hold on you two! I'm to come with you.' Rubbing bleary eyes, Raymond stumbled into the stables, and thereafter a series of bumps and scuffles and muted swearing drifted out on the dawn breeze.

Gwenn groaned. 'I was afraid of this.'

'Mistress?'

'It's nothing, Ned. Just some stupid idea that has lodged in Mama's head. Raymond's been sent to keep an eye on us.'

Ned looked sharply at Gwenn and felt his colour rise. 'You mean . . . b . . . but Mistress Gwenn, I'd never . . .'

'I know, Ned,' Gwenn sighed. 'We're *friends*. But others, apparently have other ideas.'

That afternoon, Ned took his turn on guard at the top of the tower. Cooing white doves roosted in nesting boxes all round the rooftop. Ned was bored. His scalp itched. Removing his helmet, he ran a hand through his fair thatch of hair, which he wore shorter these days, like a veteran. Since Alan had gone his own way, Ned had discovered within himself an untapped well of personal ambition. He wanted to succeed here. He wanted to win promotion. He crammed his helmet back on and diligently scanned the well-ordered village laid out below.

The road to St Clair's holding was empty, with not even a drover in sight. The weather was warm for April, and the air still. From the village, Ned could hear the clanging of the blacksmith at his forge. Geese honked on the marsh. Mechanically, Ned ran his eyes over Kermaria's defences. The manor had been transformed in the two years since he had ridden in with his cousin on that litter. Kermaria's ditch was free of lilies and weeds. The well-shaft had been cleared and repaired, and a trough stood hard by. The cookhouse had been reroofed. The road had been widened. The perimeter wall had been strengthened, but the houses which clung like barnacles to the wall had remained, on condition that they were buttressed. The cottage roofs had been reinforced and doubled as a walkway for St Clair's sentries.

Most notable of all were the alterations to the manor itself. Mortar been reapplied to the crumbling stonework. The entrance steps had been reconstructed. The village carpenter, the well-fleshed Jafrez, had made stout new doors for every archway in the building, even fixing them at the top and bottom of the spiral stairs leading from the common hall to the more private family solar on the first floor. Many had muttered at the rank waste, but Ned looked at the solid iron-studded doors with a soldier's eye and he could see that if ever Kermaria were attacked, behind those doors would be a final refuge, a place from which one could make a last, desperate stand.

St Clair's crowning achievement had been to slap an entire floor on top of the solar, transforming his squat, vulnerable manor into a properly defended tower. This upper floor boasted a shelter for the guards; and, absurdly, Mistress Yolande had been permitted to turf the old grey pigeons off the raised roofline and replace them with snowy doves. They nestled happily in roosts set in the stonework.

Jean St Clair took his responsibilities seriously. The man might be a knight, with people to protect, but what lord in his right mind would lay siege to this place? St Clair's domain, though improved, remained little more than marshland and mud. What could anyone want with that?

Ned sighed. Nothing ever happened here. Thankfully, it appeared de Roncier had forgotten St Clair existed. The last Ned had heard of his former lord was rumour of him betrothing his daughter to some doddering lord in the Aquitaine. Thank God that Waldin St Clair was due to arrive soon. That should prove interesting. Perhaps, if Ned could prove his worth, the champion might give him the odd piece of advice.

A door slammed. Someone was leaving the tower. Ned craned his head to see through the machicolations, and a girl walked into his line of vision. Ned's gaze sharpened. 'Gwenn,' he murmured to himself, savouring the sound of her name on his lips. 'Gwenn.' Knowing himself unobserved, save for the cooing white doves, he blew her a furtive kiss.

Ned was hopelessly in love. But his love was a sad and secret thing, never to be brought out into the open. He had hidden it from Gwenn; and till today he had hoped he had hidden it from everyone. Love tied him to Kermaria, when otherwise boredom would have driven him to follow his cousin. Ned knew his love was doomed. Mistress Gwenn might only be the natural daughter of a knight, but she was as far out of his reach as the moon. She might as well be the daughter of an earl. A lad from peasant stock must keep his eyes from straying to a knight's daughter.

Normally, Ned denied himself the pleasure of watching her. He did not want to shame her with his love, he did not want her disparaged by it. But now, alone on guard duty at the top of the tower, he could indulge himself. He knew Gwenn liked him. But that, if anything, made his situation more impossible. Ever since she'd set her heart on improving her riding, St Clair had permitted her to ask for him. And until today they had invariably ridden out alone.

Ned had to admit that teaching Gwenn had been as much a torture as it had been a pleasure. He lived for their rides, yet when he was alone with her things were worse. His fair skin flushed easily, and whenever she was near, his face burned. He was painfully, agonisingly, conscious of her every move. And all the time he must strive to appear unaffected. He had considered leaving, for there were times when the touch of her hand on his as he helped her to her horse were almost more than he could bear. Even when he was not looking at her he could see her bright, teasing eyes; her shining fall of hair, her slender hands on the reins.

When they were alone, Gwenn was never the aloof daughter of the master of the house. She was warm and friendly. And to compound matters, she would tease him. 'What are you thinking about, Ned Fletcher?' she would ask, laughing. In vain he would strive to keep the hot blood from rushing to his cheeks. Had she divined that he loved her? She may like him, but what did that signify? Mistress Gwenn had been blessed with an open, friendly nature. She liked everyone. Ned knew he should leave, nay, *must* leave. This half-life he lived was a barren, futile one. But now Waldin St Clair was arriving, and he had another reason to stay. If he could persuade the champion to teach him swordsmanship, if he could really master that skill, he would be able to find a place for himself anywhere he chose.

Gwenn disappeared round a corner and Ned stepped back from the crenellations onto the parapet walkway. Conscientiously, he reminded himself of his duty. Perhaps another turn about the watchtower would serve to push Gwenn Herevi to the back of his mind. He had inspected the masonry on the roof last week, but he could do it again. Like that of the lower walls, the pointing was in good repair. Moss and leaves were regularly cleared from the gullies on the ramparts; nests were ruthlessly expelled from the guttering. The only birds permitted on the tower were Yolande's fluttering doves, which she insisted would make a welcome addition to the household's diet, though Ned could not recall dove ever being served.

The door of the guardhouse creaked open, and Denis the Red stuck his fiery head out. 'St Clair wants a word with you.' Denis jerked his thumb at the stairs. 'Down in the hall.'

'Oh? Any idea what it's about?'

Denis's freckled face did not show much interest. He hitched up the belt girdling his protruding belly and scrubbed his red crest of hair. 'Beats me. Joel said St Clair told Captain Warr to pull himself together.'

'Warr can be sloppy,' Ned said. 'He left the targets out last week, and they got rained on.'

'Aye. Well, you know how the man can't stomach the slightest criticism. He and St Clair exchanged pointed words, and the upshot is, he's leaving. Says he's got a woman waiting for him in Vannes, but no one believes that one. I don't think St Clair thinks much of him for leaving at such short notice. Perhaps he heard you mumbling about going and all. You did mention it at table last week.'

An image of Gwenn, laughing, filled Ned's consciousness. 'Yes,' he said rather quietly. 'I remember.'

'Best go and tell him.'

'You're to take my place on guard?'

'Aye, worst luck.'

'Don't forget your helm,' Ned reminded him. St Clair was a stickler for that.

'I won't.' Denis shook his head grumpily. 'It's in the guardhouse. I thought I'd escape sentry duty today, having done my stint yesterday, but I happened to be in the hall at the wrong time.'

'Foraging for food, were you?' Ned asked astutely and, grinning, he ran lightly down the four twists of stairs.

Sir Jean sat at the head of the board, feet stretched out before the fire. A roll of parchment curled on the table, next to an inkhorn and quill. Though Ned could not read, he recognised the parchment as being the one he had put his mark on when swearing loyalty to St Clair.

The knight was flanked on the one hand by the lanky Captain Warr, and on the other by his firstborn, Raymond Herevi. Mistress Yolande and two of her women were also in the hall, spinning. Katarin, the baby of the family, who was now a sturdy five-year-old, had stolen one of the spindles and was playing with it. Behind Ned, the main door slammed, and without turning round he sensed that Gwenn had come back. She pushed past him, her skirts swishing and her arms full of newly carded fleece, and the smoky atmosphere of the hall was for an instant sweetened with fragrance of rosemary. Ned stared stolidly at the scroll and struggled to keep the damnable colour from his face.

'You called for me, sir?' He saluted his master.

'Aye.' St Clair indicated Nicholas Warr – an indifferent archer whom the knight had been forced to promote to captain two years ago due to a paucity of seasoned soldiers willing to work for the meagre coins which were all he could then scrape together. 'Warr's of a mind to leave, and I'd like to know your mind, Fletcher. Will you be following him?'

Ned could feel Gwenn's gaze boring into his shoulder blades. Now that it came to it, he could not bear to go. It might be hell living near her, but without her . . . Besides, if he left, he'd never meet Waldin St Clair.

'I . . . I've no plans to leave,' he heard himself say. A soft sigh emanated from the direction of the fireplace.

Jean St Clair leaned forward and rested his chin on his hand, watching Ned sombrely from under grey-streaked brows. 'Good. What say you, Fletcher, to a promotion?'

'P . . . promotion, sir?' Ned was temporarily tongue-tied, and he knew those wretched crimson flags were flying in his cheeks. He heard a throaty giggle.

St Clair tossed him a smile. 'I regret Warr leaving

us, but if you will accept the position of sergeant, that will ameliorate the loss. Who knows, one day you might step into his boots.'

Ned was so astounded, he forgot his discomfiture.

'And, Fletcher?'

'Sir?'

'I feel confident that you will not abuse this new position.'

Ned was trying to come to terms with his astonishing change of fortune. This was the answer to his prayers. 'N . . . no, sir,' he blurted, stammering like a dolt.

Sir Jean's lean face warmed. 'You show promise, my lad. You're hard-working, diligent, I trust you' – an audible chuckle from the fireside brought the jutting brows down – 'in almost every respect. Besides, I have the feeling you've been under-employed of late. You've had a restive look about you. What say you?'

Ned pulled his scattered wits together. 'I'd be honoured, sir.'

'Good man.' St Clair jabbed a finger at the parchment. 'Put your mark there. Warr and Raymond will witness it.'

Scarcely able to credit this was truly happening, Ned picked up the goose quill. Gwenn drifted to her father's elbow and every nerve in Ned's body reacted to her nearness. It was the most exquisite agony. Was love always so painful? he wondered miserably.

Bright, brown eyes smiled boldly at Ned. 'Well done, Ned,' she said.

The knight glowered at Gwenn. 'Back to the women, daughter,' he said, tight-lipped, and he plucked his riding switch from the trestle. 'And by St Patern, what do you think you are about, addressing him,' he sounded as though he was talking about the dirt beneath his feet, 'as Ned?'

Gwenn cast her eyes to the floor, but Ned was not deceived by this apparent humility. Her pretty mouth was sullen. If her father noticed that look – and how could he fail to? – his wrath would be fearful. Would she never learn? St Clair doted on her, as he did all his children, but such looks never failed to wake a demon in him. The knight sucked in a breath.

'Are you listening to me, girl?'

'Aye, Papa.'

Sir Jean put his crop under Gwenn's chin to force it up. Ned winced. 'Have the courtesy to look at me when you're talking to me, daughter. And wipe that defiance from your face.'

'Aye, Pa . . . sir. My apologies, sir.'

'His name,' Sir Jean jerked his head at Ned, 'is Fletcher to you, or Sergeant. Do you hear?'

'Aye, sir.'

'Fletcher,' Sir Jean repeated.

'I'm not deaf.'

The knight's moustache bristled.

Quickly, Gwenn gave a bob of a curtsy. 'I'm sorry, Papa, but knowing N—' swiftly she corrected herself, 'Fletcher so well, I forgot—'

'He's a hired man,' Sir Jean said in clipped tones.

Grimly, Ned stared at the oak table, and wished himself back in England.

'A free man.' Gwenn said this lightly, but with an edge that was not lost on her father.

'He hires himself out for pay,' her father said scathingly as though that were the most damning condemnation one man could level at another. And in his knight's eyes, perhaps it was.

'Raymond calls him Ned.'

'Over-familiar of him, I'd say, but a different case entirely. And don't ask me why, because you know very well. Raymond's a man.'

Raymond smirked.

St Clair flexed his riding switch. 'I'd use this on you, mademoiselle, if I thought it would do any good, but no doubt your hide is as tough as a donkey's.' And to Ned's inexpressible relief he smiled and cast his whip onto the board. 'Pick up that spindle, girl.'

Meekly, Gwenn turned on her heel, but her eyes flashed.

'If I hear you call him Ned again, it will mean a

birching.' Something about his daughter's posture gave Sir Jean pause. He stared keenly at her slight back for a moment or two, stroked his moustache into place, before turning his attention back to the young Englishman.

'Now, Sergeant Fletcher.' His master smiled with charming formality. 'About your remuneration . . .'

Three weeks later, a leggy stranger whose limbs looked as though they had been flung together swaggered across the drawbridge of François de Roncier's main residence, Huelgastel. Bow and quiver were slung over one bony shoulder, and his left forearm was bound with the leather guard of an archer.

Though the castle's drawbridge was lowered, the gatehouse was shut, and the spy-hole in the central door was closed to all comers. The man, who was in his late thirties, rattled the door, and when that failed to gain any response, pounded on it with his fist. 'Hey! Wake up sluggards! I've information for Captain Malait.'

Nicholas Warr, archer, had been furious when Jean St Clair had criticised him for slackness. The knight had complained when Warr had asked for a couple of men to spare some time to make more targets. St Clair had had the cheek to infer that it was Warr's fault they were damaged, when everyone at Kermaria knew the man's penny-pinching, miserly ways were to blame. The targets had not been replaced since St Clair's father's time, and it was only thanks to Warr's good management that they had given as much service as they had. Not content with that, St Clair had criticised the condition of the spare bows and arrows, not to mention Warr's method of training the villagers . . .

Nicholas Warr never stayed anywhere his talents were not appreciated. He had wasted no time in informing Jean St Clair that he had a woman waiting for him and that he was to be married. This had been no lie, but he had not seen the woman for some months, and when the archer reached his lady-love, he found himself turned down for a cooper. A cooper! The faithless woman had said she wanted someone who paid her more attention. She wanted someone who wasn't about to go and get himself killed. Storming off, Warr had drunk his pay away, and then, too proud to go back to St Clair and admit that his woman had deserted him, and that he had been in the wrong, he had decided to head for Huelgastel. Warr was bent on refilling his purse, and he had done Otto Malait a good turn once. He hoped the Viking would not have forgotten it, for Malait was to help him gain admittance.

The archer was betting that the Count, St Clair's old adversary, would be anxious to learn that Waldin St Clair was coming home to roost. Warr could also tell him about Sir Jean's forthcoming marriage. He had been quick to see the possibilities. Here was an easy way to feather his nest, for the Count would doubtless pay handsomely for the information. Warr had intended coming here three weeks ago, direct from Kermaria, but after being jilted as well, the prospect of a few weeks' indulgence after being mewed up at Kermaria had been more temptation than he could stand.

But now, with his wings clipped by a depressingly light purse, Warr wished he had come earlier. His idiotic fling was over, and he felt desperate. Perhaps they would ignore him. Or perhaps they would listen and then throw him out. Perhaps he should have stayed put at Kermaria. Admittedly the money was poor, but one could always fill one's belly at St Clair's tower.

The peep-hole squeaked open and a blue, bloodshot eye with a mean gleam peered out. 'State your name and business,' the owner of the eye said.

'Nicholas Warr, archer.'

'We've a full complement of archers.' The peep-hole slid back with a click, and Warr was left contemplating a blank oak door.

'Jesus wept.' Warr reapplied his fist to the door.

The peep-hole slid open. The bloodshot eye came

back into view. 'You deaf?' The gatekeeper's snarl was muffled by thick oak. 'Or merely brainless? Go and plague some other soul.'

Warr had to grab the guard's attention fast, before that loophole was sealed. He took his purse from his belt and shook what he had left of his pay. Being all but empty after three weeks' dedicated riotous living, the purse didn't make a very convincing noise. Undaunted, Warr ploughed on, 'I fought with Otto Malait in seventy-three—'

'They all say that.' The eye rolled disparagingly at Warr's slender purse.

Losing heart, he tried to make his last coins chink more loudly. 'It would be worth your while.'

'And who'll pay me? You?' the porter sneered. 'That wallet sounds more like a baby's rattle than anything else. What will you pay me with, seashells?'

'It would be worth your while,' Warr repeated, tucking his purse back into his belt and speaking fast while the window yet gaped. 'It's true I haven't got much, but you will be rewarded. I must speak to Captain Malait. I've valuable information to pass on to the Count.' The eye blinked. Warr hoped its owner was listening. 'It would be worth your—'

'It will mean a flogging if you're lying.'

In despair, the archer resorted to the truth. 'Do I look as though I'm lying? Christ on the Cross, you noticed for yourself that my purse is as hungry for coin as I am for food. I need money. Is it likely that I'd be wasting my time and yours if I didn't think that what I had to say was worth something? Let me in. Please.'

The peep-hole snapped shut. Warr's nostrils dilated. There was a hollow thud, a grating of bolts which set his teeth on edge. As he heard the heavy iron bars being slowly drawn back in their sockets, he felt the first drops of rain.

Warr spread his hands and blinked gratefully up at a dull sky. 'My thanks,' he said. It was not that the archer believed in the Almighty, but he felt a need to express his gratitude. And just in case, he added, 'I owe you one.'

Slumped in a kingly high-backed chair with padded seat and backrest, de Roncier heard Malait and the archer out with ever-darkening brow.

'So you see, mon seigneur,' Warr summed, up, 'Jean St Clair is planning to marry Yolande Herevi.'

'And you say she's carrying?' the Count demanded.

'So her maid, Klara, maintained.'

François rubbed the bridge of his nose, and as his fury rose, so did his already high colour.

Having shot his bolt, Nicholas Warr felt sweat break out on his brow. He chewed the inside of his mouth and hoped his bringing this news would not misfire on him; de Roncier looked to be taking it extremely ill. Was the Count a man to punish the bearer of bad tidings? Warr wished he had thought of that earlier instead waiting till he was so hard-pressed.

'I'm sorry, mon seigneur, if this news distresses you,' Warr said, as coolly as he could, 'but I thought it in your best interests that you should know, so that you could make plans. I thought—'

De Roncier levelled callous hazel eyes at him, and Warr's blood went cold. 'You thought you saw your way to making a profit.'

'I . . . I assure you, mon seigneur . . .'

The Count stood up. 'See he's paid, Malait, and boot him out.'

'Come on, Warr.'

Warr hung back. 'Mon seigneur?'

'What now?'

'I'd be grateful for a position,' the archer blurted, stammering to a halt when he saw a cunning, feral gleam enter the Frenchman's eyes.

'I'm not convinced I would benefit by employing a loose-tongued serf,' de Roncier murmured.

Warr was a free man, but he let that one glide past him. 'L . . . loose-tongued?'

211

'You betray your former master very easily.'

Only a lie would serve Warr now. 'May I burn in sulphur, but St Clair never paid. Do I give a man my loyalty if he never shells out?'

François hesitated. He could well believe that St Clair hadn't settled up. What man did if he could get away with it? Why, he himself often delayed doling out for as long as he could – it was only prudent. And St Clair's estate could not yield much. He subjected the archer to a thorough scrutiny. 'And if I employ you – and pay you, naturally . . .'

'You . . . you'd not regret it. I'm one of the best archers in the duchy.'

'Do we need another archer, Captain?'

Otto exchanged a brief look with Warr. He had not forgotten the skirmish when Warr had saved his life. A brace of Englishmen had had him at a disadvantage, when suddenly blue and white feathers had sprouted from one assailant's chest. Warr's quiver was full of arrows fletched like that. 'We can always use a good man,' he said. He did not like to be beholden to anyone, and this, an easy thing, would set the tally straight.

'Very well. See he's tested at the butts. If he hits the spot, add his name to the roll.'

'Aye, mon seigneur.'

Returning from the butts with rain-dampened clothes, Otto Malait and Nicholas Warr strode into a vast hall which was abuzz with talk. The fire gushed forth an acrid blue smoke which caught in the back of the throat and lay across the room like fenland fog. Supper was on the trestles, and the rich smell of roast boar filled their nostrils. Stools creaked. Goblets clattered. Knives flashed over piled trenchers. Hounds snarled and fought over scraps in the marsh – the soiled rushes under the tables. Cats with thievery in mind streaked between dogs' legs.

'Come, Warr, don't look so down at mouth.' Otto

headed for a vacant space on the soldiers' table near the door. 'I'll enrol you, though I've seen you do better.'

'My thanks, Captain Malait. I'm grateful,' Warr said, eyeing what was left of the pig with apparent misgivings.

The men who had got to the roast ahead of them had taken the best cuts, and all that was left was a massacre of gristle and bone, to which scarcely a strand of flesh clung. The meat had been charred almost to a cinder, so it must at one time have been hot, but it was now cold, congealed, and frankly unappetising.

'You don't look it,' Otto said.

'No, I *am* grateful,' Warr assured him, and sat down.

'What was it like at Kermaria?' Otto probed, and hewing a gobbet from the burnt offering, he thrust what was left at the archer. The hands that took the platter from him were long. Nicholas Warr had surprisingly thin bones for a military man. Broad-shouldered though, he got that from his archery, but otherwise too lanky for Otto's taste. Now Warr had enlisted with de Roncier, he would be given the chance to prove his loyalty by telling them all he could.

The archer cut what he could from the ill-fated boar, and resigned himself to a night's indigestion. 'It was warm at Kermaria,' he said, dryly.

Otto, whose wits were never at their sharpest when he was intent on bagging a wine jar, frowned. 'Warm? That damp bog of a place?'

'You misunderstand, Captain. It was the food I was referring to.' Warr looked round the ring of gobbling, hard-faced men-at-arms. 'And the people.'

Otto let his eyes wash coldly over the archer. 'The people? You've gone soft, Warr, since I knew you. Wasn't it you who once boasted that you never allowed affection to come into your working relationships?'

'Did I say that?'

Otto laughed, and choked as some pork went down the wrong way. 'Bones of St Olaf! You're showing your years.'

'We're all showing our years, Malait,' Warr said soberly.

'There was someone else who lived by your old precepts, Warr, Alan le Bret.'

'Le Bret?' The archer nodded. 'I knew him, briefly. He left St Clair. Must have been two years back.'

'That fits. At least he showed sense. Thank God you can rely on some folk. Your change of heart shakes my faith in human nature. Warmth, indeed,' Otto snorted. 'Tell me, what happened to the stripling with an unruly conscience – Ned . . . Fletcher, I think it was. Is he at Kermaria?' Now there was a handsome lad. Otto had never met a better-looking boy than Ned Fletcher. Though he had found a friend at Huelgastel and was fond of him, he could not touch Ned Fletcher on looks. A sturdy lad, with rosy cheeks . . . Otto sighed, he had always regretted not being able to get closer to young Fletcher.

'Ned Fletcher's still there.'

Mouth full, stained teeth grinding his meat like a mill, Otto grunted with satisfaction. 'Aye. That fits too.'

'Maman?' Groping his way through the half-light on the landing outside the Dowager Countess's bedchamber, François pushed the heavy door-curtain aside with a shove that set the curtain rings rattling.

'Who's that?' Marie de Roncier's voice came querulously from the bed. She had slipped on the worn flags in the bailey a month ago and damaged her hip, and had been carried up to the round tower room she'd converted to her private use. She was a truculent patient, and she had gone unwillingly, fighting every step of the way and invoking curses on anyone within range. She did not know it, but she was not likely to leave her chamber on her own feet again.

'It's me, Maman.' François' foot caught on something on the floor. A leather mug. 'God's blood! Why doesn't that maid of yours light more torches? It's blacker than Hades in here.' He bent for the mug, setting it on the stone ledge which ran partway round the wall.

'Hades is the right word for it,' came his mother's bitter response.

'Nay, Maman, don't be like that.' His mother's tireless complaining was one of the reasons François had been avoiding her company of late. He knew it was hard for her, a vigorous woman, to be so cooped up, but if she sweetened her tongue, he might beat a path to her chamber more frequently.

'You should come to see me more often,' she said, unaware that her plaintive echoing of her son's guilty conscience merely served to alienate him further. He would not be visiting her now if it were not for the tidings from Kermaria. 'My hip aches. I'm bored. No one comes to talk to me.'

'You've got Lena,' François pointed out. His mother recited complaints as lovingly as a priest mouthed the Creed.

'Lena! That girl's got a skull made of wood. How would you like to be laid up in bed with only a foolish chit of a girl for company?'

A grin flickered across François' dissolute mouth, and was quickly repressed, but not before his needle-eyed mother had spotted it. A reluctant light gleamed in her black eyes.

'Ever the ladies' man, eh? I should have thought getting that whey-faced Countess of yours with child was enough to keep you fully employed.'

'Maman, please,' her son replied, in pained tones. For all that Eleanor was barren and he must have a son, he had a fondness for his Countess, which bade him take her part. 'You should not speak of Eleanor in so disparaging a manner.'

Marie laughed. She wanted her son to have a male heir as much as he did, but there was a perverse pleasure to be derived from his discomfiture. 'Don't bother to deny it, François. Do you think I don't know why Lena never answers my calls in the long, dark hours? She never answers because she can't hear me, not being in her own bed but warming another's.'

A look of remorse flitted across her son's face. 'I'm sorry, Maman. I never thought you'd have need of her in the night.'

'I do have need of her in the night. It's not that I mind your copulating with my maid—'

'Maman!' The florid cheeks brightened with colour. François found his mother's coarseness a constant embarrassment. It was not seemly that a dowager countess should use such language.

'But will you at least ensure that someone else is put in Lena's place, so my calls don't go unheeded?' François' coppery head dipped in brusque agreement and, feeling that she had emerged from the exchange the victor, Marie was able to regard her son with a degree more warmth. 'What brings you to my lonely tower today, François?' She was unable to resist one final dig – it made her feel so much better. 'Missing me, were you?'

'I received word from Kermaria.'

'And?'

'Waldin St Clair is coming home.'

Marie furrowed her brow. 'Why should that worry you? Waldin is but one man. What can one man do?'

François shifted impatiently. 'From a military point of view it could be disastrous. Waldin is bound to attract recruits.'

'So?' Marie shrugged eloquently. 'You weren't thinking of laying a siege? We agreed to let St Clair and his hatchlings moulder away in their stinking bog. They cannot topple you from your perch.'

'I wouldn't stake my life on that, Maman.'

Marie examined her son's expression. 'You've learned more. Don't spare me, I can shoulder it. It's my hip that's weak, not my spine.'

'He's going to marry Yolande Herevi.'

'That strumpet!' she responded scornfully, unable to

perceive why her son's hazel eyes were so strained. 'I don't know who your informant is, François, but he must be mistaken.'

'I have every confidence the man was telling the truth. And God's teeth, Maman, you know the blood that flows through Yolande Herevi's veins also flows through ours. It's not as though she crawled out of the gutter.'

Marie bridled, and her dark eyes snapped. 'My sister threw herself in the gutter when she married below her station!'

'Gwionn Herevi was a squire and bound for higher things, if I heard the story right. He was no nameless beggar.'

'I will not discuss my sister's marriage.' Marie's damaged hip twinged, and delicately she kneaded her side. 'Oh, let St Clair marry his whore, the matter's beneath contempt and we should ignore it.'

François was galled by his mother's indifference, but he had saved the juiciest morsel till last. Casually, he threw it at her. 'My informant tells me she's breeding.'

His mother's body jerked convulsively. 'What?'

'Another case entirely, eh, Maman?'

The pallid lips worked. 'That bitch could not be in pup – she must be turned forty!'

The vulgar turn of phrase made François flinch. 'She's thirty-five,' he said mildly.

'Saint Félix protect us!' Age-spotted fingers clenched on the bed furs. 'What if she produces another boy?'

'Exactly. If Yolande Herevi becomes Yolande St Clair and has a son, that son would have a claim to half my lands, would he not?'

Marie lay motionless. Her face was glazed, her eyes burned. Her pupils were tiny, hard and shiny as jet beads on a rosary. Down in the inner bailey, François could hear the drumming of many feet as the castle guard drilled in the yard. Rooks cawed on the battlements. But in his mother's chamber, there was only a stifling, oppressive silence. The window slits were too

217

slim to allow much sunlight in, and in the eternal twilight of the room, his mother could easily be mistaken for a corpse . . .

François repressed a shudder, and blaming the suffocating sickroom atmosphere for his dark imaginings, he went to the window splay to breathe in fresh air. An unlit torch was propped against the log basket by the fire. Dipping the flambeau into the fire, he jammed it in a wrought-iron wall sconce. His hair brightened to flame in the light. 'Maman, what do you advise?'

'Nothing. We should do nothing.'

The heavy jaw sagged. 'Nothing? But we cannot allow them to marry!'

The bedridden woman gave a slender smile. 'Yes, we can. And we will. There is nothing else we can do. We have no cause to take action against St Clair, and it might prove to be needless.'

'No cause! Needless?'

'Let me finish, François. She might produce a boy, but who's to say she will? She's had two daughters already, and may produce another. No court in the land would uphold the claim of a girl against you, my son.'

'I agree St Clair's mistress could produce a girl, but what's to prevent her having a boy later on? If that happened, we'd have to go through this all over again.'

She tutted. 'Ever eager to ford streams before you've reached them. Learn to wait. The woman may contract a fever, St Clair could drop dead – anything might happen. Don't get in a lather until events are come upon you.'

'Very well, I'll hang back till the bitch births. And if it's a girl, I'll follow your woman's plan. But if it's a boy, I'm for adopting my own strategy. I'll not stand by and let some whelp of St Clair's filch my birthright.'

Marie withdrew into her pillows, satisfied. 'I'd like to rest now, François.'

'Very well, Maman.' He strode to the door. 'You should come down to the hall. I'll have someone knock up some crutches for you, we can't let you fester up here for ever.'

'Crutches?' Marie hauled herself up on one elbow, black eyes flashing contemptuously. 'Crutches?'

'Be reasonable, Maman. It would do you good to get out and about.'

'I'll have you know I'd rather be seen in my winding sheets than hopping about on crutches!' The milk-white cheeks were mottled with anger.

'As you wish.' François bowed. 'I was only trying to help.'

Muttering, Marie subsided. 'Go away, François. Crutches? I don't need any damned crutches. What I need is some peace, so I can sleep and recover properly.'

'Very well, Maman. I'm going. And I'll stay my hand as far as Kermaria is concerned, at least until the babe is born. After that, we shall have to see.'

Chapter Thirteen

One morning not long after Easter, His Grace Geoffrey, Duke of Brittany, was twitching and fretting outside the King of France's pavilion in a cleared area in the woods outside Paris. Tents belonging to both entourages sprouted like brightly coloured mushrooms all over the stubbly field.

Duke Geoffrey frowned at the blue silk tent flap which was tied down despite the lateness of the hour, and spoke to the captain of his hand-picked bodyguard, one Alan le Bret. 'It lacks but two hours to noon,' he complained, foot tapping a tent peg. 'Our young King sleeps late.' The Duke was in his mid-twenties, a full half-decade older than the King of France. Under a red damask tunic encrusted with embroidered leaves, the Duke wore a chainse of best Reims linen. Bored, he folded the cuffs of his shirt over his tunic sleeves, admired the effect, and turned to face his captain; a dour but efficient fellow who had risen high enough in his favour to be clad not in the Duke's heraldic colours – black and white – but in his own choice, in this instance the delicate green of good quality homespun that had been dyed with birch. The captain wore his gambeson over his tunic. He was, the Duke had been pleased to discover, a man with a sense of humour if one troubled to dig for it. 'Methinks our royal host delights in delaying us,' Duke Geoffrey went on. 'Philip knows I have to visit my duchy.'

'King Philip had visitors last eve,' le Bret informed him, 'and they did not leave till late, past the third hour.'

'Did you manage to glean who it was?'

'Messengers from Flanders.'

Duke Geoffrey's interest waned. 'Marriage troubles, I should think. And how did you discover that titbit, Captain?'

Alan folded his lips together and glanced briefly at the royal tent.

'It couldn't be,' amusement lifted the Duke's lips, 'that you were visiting the daughter of King Philip's cook?'

'Sir?' Keeping his face as blank as a stone slate, Alan stared past his liege lord at a silver fleur-de-lys flying high on a standard on the top of the French King's pavilion.

'You don't answer, le Bret.' Duke Geoffrey's voice took on a warning note, but his eyes were smiling. 'I think you tell but half your tale. While we wait, I'd have you entertain me with the whole, if you please.'

Alan raised grey eyes to his noble lord's. 'Your Grace, you may have bought the strength of my arms, but I can't think you own all of me.'

'I always knew you were half-hearted in your loyalties.'

'My liege?'

'You're holding out on me. You reserve your strongest member for your private use.'

'I did but go for a walk, and happened to pass this way.'

'Walk!' The Duke hooted. 'I've heard it called many things, but walking's not one of them.'

There was a stir in the royal tent, the flap opened, a girl emerged and ran off, giggling. Her features were shrouded in her veil, but the men outside the tent got a clear sight of a blushing, boyish face and laughing eyes.

'So help me, Church and Mass, that was the cook's daughter, was it not?' The Duke eyed his captain with malicious delight.

Alan shrugged. 'I believe the wench is daughter of King Philip's cook, aye.'

Geoffrey of Brittany gave a bellow of delighted laughter. 'Snatched from under your nose by no less than a king, eh, le Bret?'

'Kings can pay more than captains.'

'So she's a whore?'

'Aren't they all?'

Duke Geoffrey's face grew sombre while he thought of his neglected wife, the Duchess Constance. 'I wouldn't know, le Bret. It always seems to be too much trouble to find that out.'

Alan smiled. 'Just so, my liege.'

The tent flap yawned and Philip of France's dark, tousled head emerged. The King rubbed his eyes. 'Good morrow, Brittany. You're up with the larks.'

The Duke bowed. 'My apologies, sire. But I'm leaving for Brittany—'

'Short of funds again?' the King probed. He was always probing, always trying to stir up conflict between his friend the Duke of Brittany and the Duke's father, Henry of England, in the firm belief that it might give him the advantage in the ceaseless jostling for power that went on in Henry's Continental dominions.

'Funds? No, sire. I thought I would pay my respects at my brother's tomb in Rouen, and continue on into Brittany.'

The Young King Henry of England, Duke Geoffrey's elder brother, had died of dysentery in 1183, a few months after Alan had sighted him at Locmariaquer. Although the Young King had been crowned in his father's lifetime, he had predeceased his father and never come into his inheritance. The Young King had been a king without a kingdom, and Alan was coming to see that wealth was relative. The Young King's need for money had been a key factor in the rebellions he had mounted against his father.

Duke Geoffrey, Alan's liege lord, was Henry Plantagenet's third son, and never likely to wear the crown. His father favoured the youngest of his four sons, John, while his mother Eleanor, favoured Richard. Alan had chosen the Duke of Brittany for his master over Henry for purely sentimental reasons; the Duke's Duchess, Constance, had family connections in Richmond, where Alan's home was.

The Duke continued, 'My wife has an estate on the Morbihan gulf I've not yet visited.'

The rivalry which existed between the King of France and the Duke of Brittany, though friendly, was such that Duke Geoffrey would not dream of admitting any weakness, however insignificant, to the French King.

'Refusing to pay their dues, are they?' King Philip continued to probe.

'Certainly not. But it's time I showed my face.'

'I understand.' A calculating look entered the King's eyes. 'Pity you'll miss the tournament though, Geoffrey.'

Geoffrey of Brittany bowed. 'I am desolate, sire. But there will be other tournaments.'

'There will be others. You'll attend my Christmas court?'

Duke Geoffrey refused to be committed. 'My thanks. I'll certainly bear it in mind.'

The King waved him away. 'Go on with you. And may God watch over you.'

'And you, sire.'

Philip of France ducked back into the blue silk pavilion.

'Shall I see our tents packed away, Your Grace?' Alan asked.

'Do that. I've had my fill of pomp and ceremony.'

After two years in the Duke's service, Alan knew what he meant. Every day, he thanked God he didn't have the Duke's responsibilities, but he nevertheless felt that if he had power, he would spend less time feasting and jousting, and more time taking his duties seriously. Until he had joined the Duke, he had had no idea that people in such high office could be so devil-may-care. But he did have a liking for his lord.

'We're to travel light, Your Grace?'

'Aye. Choose a handful of like-minded men to ride with us, le Bret, and the baggage can follow at its own pace. I'm not of a mind to trail along.'

It was the first of May, and Gwenn woke before dawn. She was excited. Lent being over, today was her parents' wedding day.

Not wishing to disturb Katarin, she contained herself until the first grey strips of light crept over the broad windowsill. Then she eased herself out of bed, dived into her robe, fumbled for her shoes, and grabbed her cloak from the peg on the door. She padded downstairs. Early as she was, she was not the first to rise, for in the hall the fire had been kicked into life, and the men were stirring and mumbling in their blankets, preparing to rise.

Gently, she let herself out, pausing for a moment on the top step to draw in a lungful of fresh air and assess the promise of the day. The sky was wearing its palest colours that morning, mostly blue, but strung out in the east were long, feathery clouds fringed with the gentlest pink. Wood-smoke drifted lazily out of the cookhouse and curled about the yard. She could smell bread baking. Pleased her parents should be granted such a beautiful day, Gwenn smiled and stretched.

Absorbed as she was in the quiet glory of the morning sky, she was slow to notice that her uncle, Waldin St Clair, and Ned Fletcher were in the yard. Waldin was leaning against the trough by the whetstone, and Ned – disobediently, Gwenn persisted in calling her father's sergeant Ned in her mind – was beside him. They had been shaving, and Ned was firing questions at Waldin. Of late Ned had become her uncle's second shadow, ceaselessly picking his brains on matters military. It was becoming quite an obsession with him.

'And you, sir?' Ned was asking. 'Which type of helm would you recommend?'

'What, in a tourney? If it's safety you're after, I'd

go for the closed pot, Fletcher. It's more likely to stay in place, but it's very restricting in terms of vision, and my personal preference is for one of the lighter ones.'

'And the disadvantages?' Ned wanted to know it all, but at that moment Gwenn's uncle became aware of her presence.

'Good morrow, niece!'

Blushing slightly, for Ned's bright blue eyes transferred immediately to her, Gwenn flung her cloak about her shoulders and said cheerfully, 'Good morrow, Sir Waldin. Sergeant Fletcher.'

'Fine day for the wedding,' the champion said in a friendly manner.

'It is indeed.' Gwenn was curious about her uncle. He had not shown himself to be the greatest conversationalist, except with Ned, when it seemed he never stopped, but this had only fuelled her determination to find out more about him.

At thirty-two, Waldin St Clair was ten years younger than his brother, and in his looks he was far from the courtly champion of Gwenn's romantic imaginings. She was not, she told herself firmly, disappointed, but he was not at all as she remembered him. Her father maintained an air of easy elegance, and Gwenn had assumed that his brother, the famous victor of many a joust, would have his share of that quality. This was not the case. The two brothers were quite unalike.

This morning, her uncle was scantly clad in linen chainse and breeches. He had rolled up his sleeves to reveal brawny arms thickly covered with dark hairs. The veins on his hands stood out like corded rope. His shirt hung open to the waist, and Gwenn averted her eyes from the mat of vigorous hair covering his broad chest. Waldin's neck was thick and sinewy. His eyes, like his brother's, were brown; but his brows were blacker, and thicker, and quirked upwards. His nose was squat and, having been broken more than once, sat slightly askew, giving his face the comical mien of a jester. Most of his front teeth were chipped or cracked. No one, however partial, could call Waldin handsome, but as the champion had never had any pretensions to vanity, this had never concerned him. There did not appear to be the least subtlety about either Waldin's person or his manner.

He winked at his niece and, plunging his head into the trough, re-emerged scattering bright droplets. He squatted down on his haunches before Ned. 'Get on with it, Fletcher,' he said.

Ned grasped Waldin's head and began shaving the crown.

'What are you doing?' Gwenn demanded as handfuls of thick brown hair dropped to the ground.

Waldin squinted up at her. 'What does it look like?'

'Keep your head braced, sir,' Ned advised, 'or my hand might slip.'

'What are you doing?' Gwenn repeated.

Ned's hands stopped their work and ardent blue eyes met hers. Gwenn felt her cheeks grow warm. He ought not to look at her like that in front of her uncle, especially after what her father had said.

'I'm shaving his hair off,' Ned said, and his burning eyes came to rest on her mouth.

His naked longing was too much for Gwenn. She looked away. 'I . . . I can see that. But why?'

'It's an old habit of mine,' Waldin explained as Ned reapplied himself to his task. 'I let it grow to see how I liked it, but I prefer it shaved. I found it convenient when on the tourney circuit, and I see no reason for changing my habits because I have retired. In high summer, when you spend most of your waking hours crowned with a metal pot, you work up a fair sweat. It's easier to wash a bald pate.'

'It looks odd. It's all white,' Gwenn observed, intrigued.

Her uncle's lips twitched. 'You'd be surprised how quickly it browns.'

'Even when crowned with your helmet?'

'I don't spend every second in a helm.'

Ned had worked round to the back of Waldin's skull, and as the hair there fell away, Gwenn gasped. 'You've cut him, Ned!'

Dismayed, Ned snatched back his hands. 'Cut him? No, I'm sure I have not.' But, staring at the jagged red mark which was emerging from under the champion's hair, Ned felt a twinge of doubt. 'Sir?'

Waldin ran his hand over the back of his head. 'You're all right, lad. It's nought but an old scar you are uncovering. The consequences of my preference for a lighter helm. Pray continue.'

Ned resumed shaving, and when he had done, the full extent of the scar was revealed. Purple in places, the skin was shiny and puckered.

Waldin stood up, flexed his knees, and ran an appraising hand over Ned Fletcher's handiwork. 'Not bad,' he commented.

'It will need doing again,' Ned said, rinsing the razor in a bucket.

Waldin gave a gap-toothed grin. 'Aye. I reckon on once a month.' A bushy brow rose. 'You volunteering, lad?'

'If you're content to trust me, I'd be glad to do it for you, sir.'

'Good lad. I'd rather you than that dozy bunch in the hall.' Waldin nodded his thanks, and Ned, with one last glance in Gwenn's direction, saluted and walked off. The tourney champion hadn't missed the way his niece had recoiled on first seeing his scar. Dismay? Or disgust? 'I'm told it's not pretty,' he said. He had not made up his mind what to think of his niece, but he felt duty bound to try and like her. Waldin had the feeling she had been disappointed in him though she had never said as much.

Gwenn stared a moment longer at the mark on his skull and then said in a very matter-of-fact manner, 'It is quite repellant. I hope, sir, that it no longer pains you.'

Her blunt honesty warmed him, and he laughed. 'I

don't feel a thing.' His clothes were lying in an untidy jumble by the side of the trough. He picked them up, shrugged himself into his tunic, and in doing so noticed Ned Fletcher's fair hair shining in the strengthening sun as the young sergeant looked down from the battlements. A silver-helmed guard came to stand at his side and then Ned clapped his own helmet on, and Waldin could not mark the difference between them. Poor lad, Waldin thought sympathetically. He's got it badly. He could ruin himself over her. Waldin had heard his brother and Yolande speaking in disparaging terms of their English sergeant's infatuation with their daughter. Apparently the lad had been warned off, and if something were not done soon, he was heading for dismissal. A shame, Waldin reckoned, when of the dozen men currently manning his brother's tower, the sergeant showed most promise. The two men withdrew from his sight, gone into the guardhouse, no doubt.

Waldin considered Gwenn. He had seen spoilt knights' daughters by the waggonload on his travels, and most of them had their heads stuffed so full of their own consequence that they only counted the hearts they had broken. Had his brother bred another of these? He wanted to think there was more to his pretty niece than that.

Waldin did not view Ned's lowly birth as being an impediment in the way his brother did. Waldin was no snob, far from it; he had seen many a low-born lad start life as a servant and work his way up to squire. A select few attained the dizzy heights of knighthood, and Waldin saw nothing wrong in that. Tested men often made better knights than those born to it. However, it was becoming clear that Ned Fletcher was unsuitable for his niece, although it was for none of the reasons Yolande and Jean had put forward.

'I don't believe in hiding things, you see,' he declared, rubbing his disfigurement as though it were a badge of honour. 'I like them out in the open.'

A frown nicked Gwenn's brow. 'What do you mean,

Uncle? You sound as though you're trying to score a hit. Are you?'

Waldin grinned. He liked people who were quick off the mark. A swift glance assured him that Ned Fletcher had not reappeared on the battlements, and he plunged straight in. 'What do you intend to do with Sergeant Fletcher?'

'Do? Do I have to *do* anything?'

'Aye. I think so.'

She looked puzzled.

'I'm taking the liberty of telling you this, my dear, because I like you. But the way you have that young man on a leading rein is nothing less than a scandal.'

'L . . . leading rein?' Her mouth fell open. 'But Uncle, I've done nothing!'

Waldin impaled her with his hard gaze. 'That's not quite true, my dear, and if you give it but a moment's thought, I think you'll agree.' Gwenn spluttered, but Waldin took no heed and thrust his point home. 'I know you are young, and I know you are innocent. But unlike your parents, whose love blinds them to your faults, I see you clearly.' Once more he ran his hand over the back of his head and gave her a wry grin. 'As I said, I like things out in the open. And fortunately God blessed me with a few brains as well as brawn. That's why I survived so long on the circuit. That's why I see you so clearly. It's no use your using your youth as a shield and hiding behind it.'

'But Uncle!' Gwenn's small bosom heaved, indignantly. 'I am innocent, I swear—'

'Not so innocent that you don't know what you're doing. You're playing with that lad. Leave Sergeant Fletcher alone. He's not for you.'

Her eyes smouldered. Her lips formed a resentful pout. 'You're beginning to sound like my father.'

'I've not done, my girl. When I've had my say, you can have yours.'

She subsided, simmering.

'Sergeant Fletcher's not for you,' Waldin allowed an

understanding smile to lift one side of his mouth, 'and the reason has nothing to do with his birth, and everything to do with the fact that you would swallow him up in one bite. Forget your pride, Gwenn. Let the lad go. Let him find someone more suited.'

'Hell's teeth!' Gwenn borrowed one of her brother's curses. 'What has pride to do with it?'

The smile reached the champion's brown eyes, warming them to a rich mahogany. 'Don't swear, Gwenn. It doesn't look pretty on you.'

'Because I'm a girl,' she said, nettled, 'and girls mustn't swear.'

Waldin was not tempted to go skirmishing down that blind alley. 'It doesn't look pretty on you. Think, Gwenn. Pride has a lot to do with it. Admit it. You love Ned Fletcher—'

She choked. 'What?'

'Hold your horses. You love Ned Fletcher's being in love with you. You don't love Fletcher himself, I'm well aware of that. It's play to you.' He leaned closer, took her arm, eyes serious. 'But it's not play to the Saxon. The lad truly loves you. Don't hurt him. Find someone more like yourself to flirt with, someone who sees it as you do, as a game. Ned Fletcher doesn't know the rules. You, however,' the smile was back and with something approaching real affection Waldin flicked her nose, 'were born knowing them.'

Gwenn swallowed, and Waldin had to hold down a laugh. He could see the struggle going on within her while she debated whether or not to be offended. He grinned. 'And if you toss your head at me, I swear I'll have you in that trough.'

She beat a hasty retreat. 'Uncle, you wouldn't!'

He raised an impudent brow. 'Try me.' Her shoulders began to shake. Her hand came up and hid a smile. She would do, he decided; a sterling girl.

'Wretch!' The sterling girl let out a throaty giggle. 'And to think I expected my famous uncle to be the perfect, chivalrous knight.'

Waldin sighed hugely. 'Life can be disappointing.'

'It can. But your criticism is just,' she admitted with admirable candour, and groped to express exactly how she felt. 'I like Sergeant Fletcher, but as for loving him . . .'

'There's something missing, isn't there?' Waldin supplied gently. The look in her eyes told him he had hit the target.

'Aye. I like his looks, his manners, his . . . everything, but . . .' she spread slim hands, 'perhaps the bit that's missing doesn't exist, except in my mind?' She looked to him for an answer, but Waldin did not have one to give her. She must find her own answers. 'I'll let Ned alone. You've helped me see how wrong I have been.' Her eyes twinkled. 'But life will be tedious, Uncle.'

'No it won't. Pick someone else to play with.'

She made an impatient noise. 'Who else is there? Ned is the only man around here who's half way personable.'

Her uncle looked pained and struck his deep barrel chest. 'What about me? Ah, Gwenn, your insult cuts me to the quick. I'm standing before you, and you don't even see me.' He kept a straight face. 'Look at *me*, Gwenn. I won't make the cardinal sin of taking it to heart. I know it's a game. I'm your uncle. You'd be safe with me.'

'But you're so . . .' She flushed.

'Ugly?'

Gwenn's colour deepened, and she lowered her eyes. 'My pardon, Uncle,' she muttered.

Unperturbed, Waldin went down on one knee. 'Fair lady,' he said with a splendid flourish. 'I beg you to grant me the honour of being your chevalier.' He rolled his eyes in idiotic longing.

Gwenn felt a bubble of laughter rise within her.

'I dream,' Waldin was warming to his role, 'of your long, dark tresses; of your eyes, dark and deep as pools in the wood . . .'

This last was too much. Frantically, she bit her lips, but a giggle escaped. 'This is ridiculous.'

Waldin got up and dusted his knee. 'But amusing? Not boring?'

'Not in the least.'

'So, my niece. You see how it can be fun, even with an ugly old bear like myself. And now that we have that settled, I want you to tie your favour round my arm, and I'll take you, my lady,' he bowed so low his forehead almost touched the ground, 'for a ride.'

Obediently, Gwenn pulled a ribbon from one of her plaits and wound it round a well-muscled arm. 'About the ride, Uncle. I had other plans.' Gwenn had no liking for Waldin's brutish warhorse, Emperor. He was a big devil whose coat shone like polished ebony. He terrorised the other horses in the stable, and broke his fast by taking chunks out of the grooms. Gwenn valued her skin enough to stay clear of him.

'Surely a brave girl like you is not afraid of a horse?' Waldin asked innocently.

'Afraid?' About to deny his accusation, Gwenn caught the knowing gleam in her uncle's eyes. 'I'm not afraid of horses in general, but aye, I'm afraid of Emperor. That one is more dragon than horse, and I'd not go near him if I was offered all the gold in the duchy.' Her chin inched up, daring him to mock her, but instead saw approval in his eyes.

'It takes courage to admit to fear,' he said. 'And I would far rather have a courageous girl as my niece than some prissy little mademoiselle who lies through her teeth.' He buckled on his sword. 'You're a saucy baggage. I like you, but you're a saucy baggage.' And chucking her with rough, ungallant affection under the chin, he marched to the stables and ducked through the door.

Gwenn rubbed her chin and grimaced. Waldin did not know his own strength. Remembering what she had come out to do, she crossed to the iron gateway which led into the churchyard. She was going to the wood to gather flowers for her mother. The bluebells were out, and the great yellow buttercups; and in the hidden, secret places, sweet violets, with purple, velvety petals, and lightly veined wood anemonies. There was hawthorn and blackthorn too, but she would not pick those for her mother's posy, since they were unlucky.

Jean had reclaimed some of the land the trees had engulfed since his father's time, cutting back the undergrowth on the northernmost margin of the glebeland and turning it into an apple orchard. The saplings were young and spindly, but the sap was rising and they had burst into blossom. Gwenn loved the forest, but was not permitted beyond St Félix's Monastery without an escort. Her father had warned her about the dangers both from outlaws hiding out in the woods and from wolves and wild boar that were known in the area.

As she walked through the churchyard towards the apple trees, a woodpecker drummed from deep in the forbidden reaches of the forest. Nearer to hand, two squabbling sparrows flew tight circles round each other on the reed-thatched church, tumbling over each other as they somersaulted down the sloping roof, furious, chirping balls of flying feathers and pecking beaks.

Dew-drenched grass tugged Gwenn's skirts. The cool, woody fragrance of the apple trees soothed her senses. Leaving the orchard behind her, another, more pungent smell wrinkled her nostrils. The wild garlic was out, too. A faint smile flickered across her lips. 'No garlic for Mama either,' she thought aloud. 'I want only sweet-smelling lucky flowers. My mother deserves the best that there is, for today is her day.'

Chapter Fourteen

The wedding took place at noon. Being a brief ceremony performed at the church gate by Prior Hubert who had been winkled out of his sylvan retreat, it was over almost as soon as it had begun. The prior was invited to the celebration afterwards but, a hermit at heart, he was unused to worldly folk and had a strong dislike of crowds and noise. Politely, he declined the honour. Yolande pressed him into taking a gift of food to share with his brothers, and after some gentle persuasion the prior accepted her bounty. And no sooner had his duty as priest been discharged than the holy man sketched a cross over the heads of the assembly and scuttled back into the safety of the cool, slow-moving shadows in the forest.

It was expected that the feasting would stretch on well into the night. Everyone was welcome; and because it was not only the lord of the manor's wedding but May Day also, it promised to be an uproarious event. After the austerities of Lent, the household had been looking forward to it, and none doubted that it would be remembered for years to come.

The St Clair family processed from churchyard to hall. The first to follow them was Denis the Red, who pushed his way to the front of the retainers. He drew up in the doorway, greedy eyes popping like a horse that had chanced on a field of pink clover. The trestles were clothed in spotless linen. Swags of shiny green ivy decked the cloths, and tucked into the ivy were dainty bouquets of bluebells and sprigs of apple blossom. It was not the foliage, however, that caught the soldier's eye; it was the sheer quantity of food. It quite took his breath away. There was roast beef steaming gently from the fire; a suckling pig with an apple in its mouth; a showy dressed peacock which being chewy Denis knew looked better than it tasted. There were duck and geese by the score. There were jellied eels, loaves by the dozen, large round cheeses, saladings, custards, sweet-meats. A grin of delight spread slowly across the plump freckled face. Denis's hand crept to his belt and deftly he undid it a notch or two.

'When you've quite finished drooling,' Ned said in his ear, 'you might move along.'

Eyes glazed, Denis the Red stumbled to a bench. It was Paradise, and he hardly knew where to begin. A tower of trenchers was stacked at one end of the table. He took the top one.

Ned, as Red's sergeant, should by rights have taken the upper crust, but no slight had been intended and Ned let it pass. Settling beside Red, he reached for a wine jar and poured himself a measure. 'You must find Lent an ordeal,' he said, glancing at the festoons of flowers which he knew to be Gwenn and Katarin's handiwork, for he'd seen the girls at work that morning.

Pained folds creased the plump cheeks. 'Don't men-tion Lent,' Red groaned. 'You'll give me indigestion. Lent's hell on earth.' He stuck his fingers in the waist of his braies, which since he had undone his belt hung in loose, baggy folds. 'Look, I'm a shadow of the man I was. That's what Lent does for me. My breeches are falling off.'

Sir Jean had given the signal for everyone to begin. Ned tasted the wine. Since leaving England, he had learned a thing or two about wine. This one was a good Burgundy, rich and mellow. St Clair was generous with his men. Ned glanced towards the knight, sitting on the special high dais that had been made expressly for today's festivities. Sir Jean happened to be looking in his direction. Smiling, and careful to keep his eyes from Gwenn, Ned raised his cup in acknowledgement of the wine and the compliment St Clair paid his men that day. It was an open-handed gesture that not many men in his position would have bothered to make, especially when one considered that there was not likely to be a sober head among them in half an hour's time, not sober enough at any rate to tell the difference between good wine and vinegar. 'Aye,' Ned murmured softly, 'Lent's over for another year.' Casually, he twitched a cluster of the apple blossom from the ivy and tucked it into his sleeve.

Later, when bellies were full – most of them over-full – Ned judged that enough wine had been downed for no one to care where his eyes wandered. Inevitably his gaze was pulled to the top table. Lady St Clair, as Yolande Herevi must now be called, sat between her husband and his brother. Her gown was of cream silk brocade trimmed with gold braid. She was laughing, her face alight with happiness. Ned had never seen her looking so well. As was the custom, Gwenn, in the bright blue she favoured, was further down the board, sharing her meats with her brother. Her cheeks were flushed with the good Burgundy wine, and her head was flung back. She was laughing too, at something Sir Waldin had said. Her veil, held in place by a slim circlet of flowers, was slipping. The champion leaned across the trestle and gave one of her thick, brown plaits an affectionate tweak. Favouring her uncle with a slow smile, Gwenn twitched her hair out of his hand and tucked it demurely beneath her veil. Ned felt his stomach twist and gulped down another mouthful of wine. What he wouldn't give for the right to sit at her side.

'Pretty, isn't she, Ned?' Red nudged him in the ribs, a knowing expression in his eyes.

Ned coloured to the roots of his hair, but he drew himself up. Ignoring Red's snatching the top trencher was one thing, but he could not let this pass. 'Sergeant

Fletcher to you, Red,' he said, more sharply than he had intended.

Red raised a russet brow. The wine had made him careless of the fact that he was Ned's subordinate. 'Hark at you.' He grinned familiarly. 'You'll be trying for a knighthood next.'

Ned ground his teeth. Red was impertinent, but it was all the more galling because there was a grain of truth in his quip. Ned did dream that perhaps, if he won favour, he might better himself. It flashed across his mind that his cousin Alan le Bret would not stand for such insolence. Alan would have had a man flogged for less. Aware that he had supped a drop more wine than was wise, and that his command of his temper was slipping, Ned sucked in a breath and counted to ten. Today was meant to be a celebration, and he was not about to sour it. He moderated his tone. 'In any case, you're wrong.' A white lie might put Red off the scent. 'I was looking at Lady St Clair. She looks about sixteen.' This last was no less than the truth. She did look sixteen, her eyes were sparkling every bit as brightly as her daughter's.

Red crowed. 'I'm not the clod you take me for, Ned . . . Sergeant,' he amended, with the understanding but insensitive smile of a drunk unable to recognise when he was going too far. 'Come on, we're none of us blind moles. No one need follow the direction of your eyes when you wear that dreamy expression. Every man in the guard knows who holds your heart in her keeping.'

Feeling his temper heat up, Ned flung Red a look that was all daggers.

A temperate man would have heeded the warning. But Red was not temperate, the wine was flowing freely in his veins, and it had driven caution from his head. 'It *is* May Day . . .' He made a lewd gesture.

Ned could not stomach this. He'd not sit around listening to bawdy suggestions about Mistress Gwenn. Standing precipitately, his bench rocked, and one of his neighbours pitched into the rushes. A chorus of slurred complaints reached his ears, but Ned ignored them. 'Your tongue wags too freely, soldier,' he said, using a voice that was a cold copy of one he'd heard his cousin employ. 'Take care lest it wags once too often.' Turning on his heels, he stalked out.

Denis the Red's jaw sagged, and he twisted his head to watch Ned slam out of the hall. 'Well, well. I must really have touched him on the raw for him to storm off like that.' His gaze still towards the door, he blinked in astonishment, and his mouth sagged further. Ned was not the only one to be leaving the hall. Others were drifting about, among them Mistress Gwenn, Red noticed. She was sailing serenely towards the door. He leered. 'The dice have finally rolled in Sergeant Fletcher's favour.'

Ned was not in the yard when Gwenn reached it. All that morning, she had meditated on the conversation she had had with her uncle, and she saw that it would be wicked to let matters drift as they had been doing. She must tell Ned that though she liked him, her liking did not match his.

The churchyard gate was open; concluding that Ned must have gone that way, Gwenn went through the glebeland towards the wood. Her supposition was correct; a few minutes later she came across him sitting on a tree stump in a pool of sunlight a little way from the main path. His head was bowed, he was staring at the ground, a sprig of apple blossom in his hands. 'Ned?'

Ned started, and the blossom fell to the ground. 'Mistress Gwenn! I thought you were at the feast.' He stood up clumsily, and while the too-ready colour flooded his cheeks, the wine Ned had drunk made it easier for him to speak to her. 'Will you sit and talk with me?' he asked, halfway between a request and a command.

Gwenn seated herself on the bole of the tree and shook out her sapphire skirts. The sun's rays streamed

239

through a gap in the leafy canopy. Ned's cornflower-blue eyes blazed with love. He moved closer. Gwenn held her back stiff as a post. Ned was never devious, but he was not usually so bold. This was going to be more awkward than she had anticipated. She hauled in a breath and launched in. 'I'm glad I found you, Ned. I wanted to speak to you.'

'You did?'

Ned's voice was breathless and so full of hope that Gwenn's heart contracted. Waldin had made her see that sometimes one had to be cruel to be kind. So, because she realised she must, Gwenn hardened her heart to the pain her words would bring to Ned. And in order that he might be spared some dignity, she turned her head away from him, so the sun played on her cheeks. She did not want him to think she was willing to witness the hope dying on his face.

'Ned, I must tell you—' He took her hand. She tried to pull free. 'No, Ned. No.' He held her hand gently, but firmly, and without an unseemly struggle, which Gwenn was not prepared for, she was unable to free herself. A cloud threw a chilly shadow over her shoulders. Strange, one part of her mind found time to think, she never would have guessed that so fine a day would turn dull.

'Gwenn . . . May I call you that?' Ned blurted. 'Gwenn . . .'

To add to Gwenn's confusion, he dropped to his knees, and for the second time that day she had a man kneeling at her feet. Only this time it was no jest. This time she did not laugh.

'No, Ned. Please. Listen to me.' But Ned shook his head and gripped her fingers more tightly. He touched her cheek. His hand was trembling. Gwenn felt tears prick behind her eyes. 'Oh, Ned,' she said, despairingly. 'I'm so sorry.'

The shadow was growing longer. Everywhere as far as she could see the dappled sunspots winked out one by one. She shivered. The birds fell silent. The leaves stopped rustling. It was eerie. It was as though all life in the wood was suspended, and everything – birds, animals, trees, shrubs – had stopped breathing. The hairs rose on the back of her neck. 'Ned,' she whispered, urgently. 'Ned, something's wrong.'

Reluctantly, Ned tore his eyes from her face. The bright colour ebbed from his face. 'You're right.' He jumped up, pulling Gwenn to her feet. 'Something is wrong.'

The light had taken on a dusk-like quality, and it was growing darker and more like night by the second.

'A storm?' Gwenn asked optimistically, though in her heart she knew it was no such thing.

'No. Not a storm.' Ned's hand crept to the reassuring solidity of his sword hilt.

The darkness was still thickening, it hung like a pitchy awning over the glade.

Vainly Gwenn tried to pierce the twilight gloom which had gathered in the gaps between the trees. 'Ned, I'm scared. I've never heard such a silence in the forest.'

Ned was scared, too, but he wasn't going to admit it. He should protect Gwenn, but he was damned if he knew what he was meant to be protecting her from. Valiantly trying for lightness, he threw a swift grin over his shoulder. 'You can't hear silence, Gwenn.' His witticism was ignored. He heard Gwenn move closer, felt her fingers, clammy with fear, curl round his belt. Her breath fanned the back of his neck. He shut his eyes and steeled himself from turning and taking her in his arms.

'Ned?' Her fingers clung to his as though he were a lifeline. 'Holy Mother, Ned! It's the end of the world!'

He whirled about. Gwenn's head was tipped upwards, her eyes so dilated with terror they were solid black. She was staring through a gap in the leaves.

'Look!' She pointed. 'Look at the sun!'

Ned looked, and wished he hadn't. One moment he could see its brightness, and the next he could not.

The sun was snuffed out. Gwenn's panic fuelled Ned's, and the boundaries of his world tilted. God and His Angels must be at war with the Devil and his minions. Order was fighting chaos, and chaos had triumphed. They were enclosed in a dark, quiet world, and the only sound was the sound of their heartbeats and their flurried, frightened breathing. Then, because Gwenn's slight body pressed trembling to his, and because Ned had pledged himself to her and wanted to comfort her, he pulled her into his arms. It felt the way it did in his dreams. She was warm, and soft, and clinging to him. His hands cradled her tenderly, as though she might break, for Ned knew this was not real. It could not be real. The darkness at noontide, Mistress Gwenn in his arms – how could any of this be real? If he held her too tightly, she would melt into the air as she did in his dreams.

'Ned?' Brown eyes looked at him, and they were no longer afraid. 'Don't worry, Ned. It's an eclipse.'

'Eclipse? Will the sun come back?' His voice shook, but whether from fear or emotion Ned could not have said.

'It will come back quite soon.'

Ned rested his cheek against Gwenn's head and wondered how long eclipses lasted. How soft her hair was. How slim her waist. However long it lasted, it would not be long enough for him. Marshalling his dazed senses, he reminded himself that he came of peasant stock while the blood which coursed through her veins was finer, purer stuff.

She was watching the sun, angling her head towards that dark slash in the leaves. Ned was not interested in the eclipse, he was too busy observing the play of expression on Gwenn's face. He wanted to watch her while he could still hold her. He might have a minute or two longer. He let his eyes drink their fill. He loved the delicate line of her nose, and the freckles which the spring sunshine had scattered across her cheekbones. He loved the curve of her cheeks, the shape of her mouth, the small, white, even teeth. Hoping she was too absorbed to notice, he pressed a swift kiss on her temple. He loved the scent of her. A heady mixture of rosemary and Gwenn.

'Gwenn.' He bit his lip, foolishly he'd spoken aloud. She stirred in his arms and instinctively, for he wanted to prolong the moment, Ned tightened his hold.

Fortunately, Gwenn was oblivious of him and conscious only of the wonder she was witnessing. 'It's getting brighter. Look, Ned, it's as though God's drawing back a curtain. Ned?'

He would have a second or two . . .

'You're not looking,' she chided, and understanding that his taste of heaven was over, Ned slackened his hold and obediently tipped his head back to follow her pointing finger.

The first shaft of sunlight slanted through the trees, and as the rays strengthened, the spots of light jumped back into place. A breeze rattled the leaves, and the sunspots shimmered and twirled about the clearing. A blackbird flung back its head, opened its orange bill, and a phrase of song floated out. The bird hesitated, but only for an instant, and the song was completed on a confident ripple of sound. A bluetit flew to a perch on an overhanging branch and blinked at them with eyes like shiny glass beads.

'It's over,' Ned said regretfully.

Gwenn's eyes were as bright as the bluetit's. 'It was incredible, Ned. I've never seen an eclipse before.'

'Incredible . . .' Ned swallowed. It was all he could manage. He wondered miserably if he'd ever have Gwenn in his arms again. She was looking down the path to Kermaria.

'Ned, you don't think it was an ill omen, do you?'

'An ill omen?'

Pearly teeth worried an almond-shaped nail. 'You don't think God is angry with my father?'

'Why should God be angry?'

'Because . . . because of the wedding.'

'I should think God would be pleased, wouldn't you?'

'I don't know. Perhaps it's too late to make amends. Perhaps He does not approve of Mama . . .'

Gwenn's expression was unhappy, and Ned's arms ached to hold her, for her comfort and for his. 'I don't believe that,' he declared stoutly. 'Your mother's a fine lady.'

'I agree with you. But does God? Remember what happened in Vannes?' Recalling his involvement in that, Ned felt sick. 'Remember what the townsfolk said about her? Perhaps God will not forgive someone like my mother. Do you think God forgives great sins?'

'He must.' Ned moved closer, pinning his arms to his sides to prevent himself from taking her hands. 'Gw . . . Mistress Gwenn,' now the eclipse was over he must remember to address her formally, 'we cannot be the only people who witnessed the eclipse. Why should such a phenomenon be directed solely at your parents? If God had a message for your parents, wouldn't He find a more personal way of delivering it? And now, Mistress Gwenn, we should be getting back. Your parents will be wondering where you are.' He waved her ahead of him.

She proceeded ten paces and then, halted. 'Ned, I . . . I . . . There's something I've been wanting to tell you.'

'Mistress?'

Gwenn twisted her hands together, and her cheeks went the colour of a dark rose. 'Ned, I . . . I wanted to tell you how much I like you, and how much I value your friendship, b . . . but . . .' She stammered to a halt, and her brown eyes gazed helplessly up at him. Her flush deepened.

She was embarrassed, and Ned thought he knew why. He swallowed, and tried to ease her mind. 'It's all right, mistress. You don't need to worry. I know I shouldn't have held you. It won't happen again. I know my place.'

'No. No, Ned, it's nothing to do with place. It's just that I don't feel that way about you. Do you understand?'

The hollow feeling in the pit of Ned's stomach told him he understood only too well. 'I do understand,' he said. But that didn't mean he would have to stop dreaming. Perhaps, one day . . .

She smiled her bright smile. 'Thank you, Ned. I knew you'd not make difficulties.' She straightened her veil and circlet of flowers and walked on.

'Mistress Gwenn?'

'Yes?'

'You won't forget your father's orders, will you?'

'Orders?'

'Concerning your mode of addressing me.'

'I won't forget, *Sergeant* Fletcher.'

Ned intercepted her smile and sent her one from his heart. He could smell apple blossom. They had reached the orchard.

'Gwenn! Gwenn!' Raymond was striding towards them. 'Did you see it?'

Gwenn hastened towards her brother, while Ned turned towards the iron gateway which led to the yard.

'The eclipse?' Gwenn said. 'Yes, we saw it.'

Raymond took his sister's arm in a purposeful grip and marched her into the chapel porch, and out of Ned's sight.

'Gwenn, come with me, will you?' Raymond said. 'I want your views on something.'

'You want my views, Raymond?' Gwenn asked, once they were in the cool of Kermaria chapel. 'It must be serious, you never normally ask my opinions on anything. What is it?'

'It's Mama,' Raymond said abruptly. 'And dear Father, of course.'

'You sound cross, Raymond,' Gwenn observed. 'What's the problem?'

'The problem is our parents' wedding.'

'That's a problem? I rejoice for them.'

'You might well. I don't,' Raymond said baldly. 'Why do they have to marry?'

'Mama's having a baby, you know that.'

'Aye. I do know. But she's had babies before and they never saw fit to marry.'

Gwenn bent her head. 'They think to legitimise the child, Raymond, so it will not have to bear the burden we do.'

'Quite.' Raymond's green eyes glittered with a fierce anger. 'The child will be legitimate, but we, dear sister, will remain bastards.'

'Don't be bitter, Raymond. They can't undo the past. But they can help this babe.'

'Holy Christ!' Raymond bit out. 'You haven't seen it, have you? You haven't thought about the implications.'

'Implications?'

'For years our dear father wouldn't acknowledge us openly, and then we come here and he does acknowledge us. At last, poor Raymond thinks he has a chance of an inheritance. Then this sham of a wedding ruins everything. If the child Mama is carrying is a boy, Gwenn, I'll lose all I've gained since coming here. I'll be of no account, and I'll have to bow down to some snivelling little brat who's no better than me but who happens to be born in wedlock.'

'Oh, Raymond. I'm sorry.' She had not considered the wedding from his point of view. Being a girl, with no inheritance to worry about, she had not thought what would happen to her brother if the baby was male. 'Do you remember how lovely Katarin was when she was a babe?' she said.

To her relief, Raymond's face softened slightly. 'Aye, but she's a girl.'

'This new baby could well be a girl. And then you will have got yourself stewed up over nothing.' She gave him a straight look. 'Don't spoil today, Raymond. Mother has longed for this for years.' She took his hand. 'Think. You'll gain nothing but Father's anger. Try to calm down, Raymond, please. For Mama's sake.'

'I've put a lot into Kermaria,' he said, but Gwenn sensed he was weakening.

'You have. I know that, and don't you think Papa appreciates your efforts? He's a fair man, Raymond, he'll see you're looked after. Don't spoil the wedding, please.'

A dubious smile lifted a corner of his mouth.

'Come on, Raymond, let that smile break through. And then we can go in and dance at our parents' wedding.'

The smile broadened. 'You're a witch, Gwenn, but you're right. I'll try and smile today, and I'll bite my tongue.'

Gwenn looked warmly at him. 'And pray for a girl?'

He shot her a sharp look. 'And pray for a girl.'

Chapter Fifteen

By the time August was almost over in that same year of 1185, three months of strong sunshine had baked the earth as hard as fired clay. The sun's harsh rays had been beating relentlessly on the marshy waters around Kermaria so that the pools dwindled, shrinking almost out of existence; and the waterfowl who lived in the wetlands were forced to congregate on increasingly smaller and more crowded patches of water. Fish swam sluggishly in the stagnant waters, easy prey for the herons and divers, who gorged themselves till their bloated bodies could hardly take off from the water. Against all predictions, the heatwave continued. The lakelets began to smell, and the time came when the gasping fish could no longer survive in the murky shallows. When this happened the herons and divers left.

It had been the hottest summer that Yolande could remember.

In a rare moment of idleness, she was sitting in the window seat on the first-floor solar, gazing dreamily at the bridge and marsh beyond the village. One hand rested on her burgeoning belly, and with the other she shaded her eyes. She rocked her body to comfort herself, for the heat was distressing her. A pile of sheets sat on the window seat opposite. However hard she worked, there was always more to do. Yolande threw the linen a half-hearted scowl – she was too tired to be more than half-hearted about anything in this heat – and leaning heavily on the stone window ledge, she succumbed to the feeling of lassitude that she had been wrestling against all day. It was well into the afternoon, and she'd done enough to warrant a brief respite.

This pregnancy had not been easy, and she still had a month to go. Yolande knew she had nothing to worry about, but she wished she did not feel quite so huge. It was five long years since Katarin had been born, and it was strange how easily one forgot the discomforts a pregnancy could bring. She had no recollection of feeling so swollen with her other pregnancies. A ridiculous idea came to her, that if this baby should grow any more, she must surely burst. The idea took root in her mind and, shaking her head to dislodge it, Yolande pushed the shutter wide. She *must* increase the draught through the solar. In winter she spent all her time keeping out the draughts, but at this moment she'd exchange her eye teeth for a whisper of wind. The incessant heat was making her breath come in short, shallow, inadequate gasps, but she knew the babe was well. And, as if the child in her womb could read her thoughts, it moved vigorously. Yolande smiled. There was nothing wrong with this one. If only it would not push so hard against her ribs and lungs.

'You're not helping,' she gently admonished the child in her womb. 'You should leave room for me. You can't manage without me, remember?' Another twinge – a kick? – was all the answer she got, but it satisfied Yolande.

A blow-fly, huge and drunk with the heat, buzzed in through the window. Yolande followed its flight, too drowsy to attempt to swat the nuisance. The fly lurched out again, and Yolande's gaze wandered out over the landscape. The flies had hatched in their thousands that summer. Great swarms of mosquitoes hung in the air. She could see shadowy drifts of them floating over what was left of the marsh, twisting slowly in the fetid air like fragments of a gossamer veil hung out to dry. Shimmering dragonflies hovered over lily pads. Everything had slowed its pace. The abundance of insects made even the swallows lazy, and they skimmed across the patchy pools so slowly it was miraculous they stayed airborne.

The dark, holly green of the tunic her husband was wearing caught Yolande's gaze. Jean was with her brother-in-law on the bridge, presumably inspecting the tower's defences. The natural protection of the moat, formed by marsh and stream, had gone, dried up along with the rest of the water, and this was causing Jean no little concern. What they all needed was rain. The water in the well had turned cloudy that morning; the privy stank, and she couldn't spare the water to have it swilled out lest the well went completely dry.

A tightening sensation in Yolande's belly drew her attention momentarily back to herself. The sensation was not unpleasant. She had noticed it many times before in her earlier pregnancies, and knew she did not have to call anyone. Her labour was a month off, more's the pity. She waited for the sensation to pass before resuming her perusal of her husband's parched domain.

They needed a deluge. The peasants, too, were panting for rain. The little that had fallen on the strips they farmed had done no more than wet the surface, leaving thirsty crops unsatisfied. The few raindrops had run over the surface of the parched earth, and evaporated almost at once. Yolande did not need to consult the sky to know that no rain was on its way. It was a solid blue dome, as it had been for weeks. They needed a downpour, something like the one which had sent Noah scrambling to his ark. Anything less didn't stand a chance of penetrating the cracked topsoil. A shower in this heat would scorch the already withered leaves, and shrivel them to nothing. Down in the yard, there were deep fissures in the ground, visible even from this height. The sun had wrought terrible changes in the landscape of Kermaria. The sun had scarred the earth. The peasants would harvest early, and there would be hardship this winter. Jean's store of coin, carefully hoarded from the plenty reaped last harvest, would be eaten into in the dark months of this lean year.

Sighing, Yolande eyed the tower of darning which cried out for her needle. 'I've been slothful long enough,' she spoke to the babe inside her. 'Come along, we'd best get started.' She bent forward, reaching for needle and thread, but noticed the tightening sensation was back. She relaxed back into the seat, holding her body still, to allow it to pass. Except that it did not pass. A sudden tug on the muscles of her womb drove the breath from her lungs. And then the window seat no longer felt comfortable. She dropped to her knees, leaned her head on the seat opposite, and waited.

'Mama! What is it?'

Was that Gwenn's voice? Turning her head, and trying to see past the pain which threatened to fill every fibre of her being, Yolande saw Gwenn and Katarin entering the solar. Releasing her sister's hand, Gwenn ran towards her. Disoriented by her unexpected precipitation from the wide world beyond her body into a narrow one which contained only herself, the babe in her womb, and the pain, Yolande found words difficult. It was as though Gwenn and Katarin were separated from her by a thick curtain.

Pale but composed, Gwenn took the situation in at a glance. Like most girls her age, she had seen all this before. She had assisted at Katarin's birthing. In a world where boys were made guards at eight years of age and fought with armies at twelve, girls were involved early in every aspect of domestic life. Life was short, and many girls were married at twelve, with their own households to run. They had to learn young, if they had sense. 'Katarin,' Gwenn said, 'go and tell Klara to fetch the midwife, and ask her to boil some water.'

'Too soon,' Yolande jerked out. Gwenn knelt beside her. Relieved to relinquish command of herself into Gwenn's capable hands, Yolande let her daughter remove her veil.

'Can you walk, Mama?'

'A moment . . . give me . . . a moment.' Yolande

rested her head against the cool stone seat while the first fury of the spasm passed. Gwenn – Yolande blessed her for her understanding – did not fuss her, but waited patiently until it had gone. At length Yolande directed a weak smile at her. 'I'll try now. But it's too early. If I rest . . .' she dragged in a lungful of stale, unrefreshing air '. . . perhaps it will go away . . . till the babe is fully grown.'

Gwenn sent her an unreadable look, but all she said was, 'Lean on me, Mama. Save your strength.'

Never had the solar seemed so large. They had to stop twice to let the contractions pass; and each time Yolande was more drained, each time they felt fiercer than the time before. Finally, they gained the haven of the bed and Yolande sank onto it with an exhausted sigh. 'My thanks, Gwenn.' Her daughter looked so worried that she added, 'I'll rest, and it will pass.'

'No, Mama.' Gwenn shook her head, tugged off her own veil and cast it into the corner by the washstand. 'You can't rest.'

Yolande could not accept that. She was hot, and wanted to sleep. She struggled onto an elbow. 'But Gwenn, I want to rest. Later I can cope with it . . . Later, but not now.'

Her capable daughter rolled up her sleeves and washed her hands, though her hands must have been trembling, because water splashed from the ewer. 'Sorry, Mama,' Gwenn repeated, heartlessly. 'You can't rest.'

'But, Gwenn . . . it can't—' And then her muscles contracted so viciously that Yolande gasped and fell back. Gwenn twisted round, and it was the concern darkening her daughter's brown eyes to black that forced Yolande to accept the truth of what her body was doing. She was in labour.

A series of thumps heralded Klara's entrance into the stuffy chamber. 'My lady!' her tirewoman wailed, wringing her hands. 'I've not actually attended a birthing afore. What do I do?'

That was all they needed, an ignorant assistant. Lost in another wave of pain, Yolande forced the words past her teeth. 'Look to my daughter. She . . . watched Katarin . . . being born.' Then a sharp convulsion engulfed all rational thought.

Gwenn was brisk. She had to be. 'You've sent for the midwife, Klara?'

'Aye. Berthe's coming, and they're dredging the well for water to boil.'

Gwenn took her mother's hand. It was hot. 'Good. My mother's waters have broken.'

Have they? Yolande thought distractedly. So that's why she insisted that I could not rest. Odd that I should not have noticed . . .

'The babe will be born early,' Gwenn continued, 'and my mother needs all the help we can give her. First, help me remove her gown.' Gwenn fumbled with the lacings. 'Has Sir Jean been informed?'

'Aye, mistress.' Klara's hands were shaking more than Gwenn's. 'Master Raymond's gone to tell him. But I didn't let on how grave things would be—'

A furious glance cut off the rest of Klara's thoughtless tattle. How could the woman be so dense as to say such a thing within her mother's hearing? Fortunately, Yolande was focused on the inner workings of her body and had not heard. Grabbing Klara's wrist, Gwenn hauled her into the solar. 'Don't let me catch you saying that again in Mama's hearing,' she hissed.

'But it is grave, mistress.' Klara might not have attended a birth before, but she had heard the midwives chattering. It was the lot of women to die in such a way, and if God willed it that the Lady Yolande should die bringing forth her only legitimate child, then that was His judgment, and no one should fight it. Lady Yolande had survived more than most women – three bastards she'd borne. Fatalistically, Klara met the determined gaze of one of the bastards in question and went on, 'And you'd best face it. At her age, and with it being so early,' the maid sucked in a breath, finishing kindly, 'we'll be lucky if we save the infant.'

'Don't say another word, Klara. You're wishing her dead!'

'Not I.' Genuinely shocked, Klara fixed Gwenn with an earnest look. 'But there's little chance, mistress. Do you recall that eclipse?'

Gwenn did recall it.

'That was a portent, that was.'

Tongue-tied with a numbing combination of anger and dread, Gwenn gritted her teeth. Klara was revelling in this, and her blind acceptance of a disaster which had not yet come upon them sickened her.

'I told my father at the time,' Klara intoned dolefully, 'it was a sign—'

A low groan issued from behind the curtain, and immediately Gwenn moved towards it. She brushed the curtain aside, inwardly racked by the doubt that showed so clearly in Klara's eyes and the seed of latent superstition which she knew dwelt in her own heart. Outwardly, she'd not show her fear. 'No more heathen-ish babblings. Understand?'

Klara's dolorous eyes travelled to Yolande. Slowly, she nodded.

'And one thing further. Don't look at her as though she were breathing her last.'

Another nod.

From some hidden store, Gwenn found a ragged smile and pinned it to her face. 'Good,' she said briskly. 'Now, Klara, wash your hands. We have a baby to deliver.'

A month ago, the stream had turned into a trickle. Now it had dried up altogether, and the bridge spanned an empty ditch instead of a brook. Jean and Waldin were standing on top of the bridge, peering into a moat that was covered with burned grass instead of green duckweed.

'Not good, is it, Waldin?' Jean frowned.

'I can't say I'm surprised.' Waldin rested a heavy

boot on the low parapet wall and wiped his forehead with his sleeve. Tied to his arm was one of Gwenn's red ribbons, and with no wind to lift it, the silk fluttered only when the knight moved. 'Jesu, I've never known it so hot.' Waldin's head needed shaving again and, fingering his scar through the stubble growing on his skull, he grinned as he recalled the first conversation he'd had with his niece. He had grown fond of Gwenn.

'There's no need to grin about the drought,' Jean said irritably. 'It's not amusing. For Christ's sake, what are we going to do? With the river dried up, we're vulnerable to attack, and I've only a dozen guards, not counting us and our squires, and not even a captain to order them.' And if the heat wave doesn't let up, Jean thought bitterly, I'll not be able to afford a captain's pay. He needed to replace the captain he'd lost. With Yolande's time drawing near, he was increasingly concerned that Kermaria should be well fortified and well manned. He'd have to take on another dozen men. Financial considerations had delayed him. With a month to go, he had time in hand, but with the likelihood of this drought sapping his resources, he had wanted to stave off any expenditure as long as he could. Since Waldin's arrival they'd not had a shortage of volunteers, but the harvest would be poor that year, and he had had to take that into account.

Waldin directed his gaze to the crop of sun-ripened weeds sprouting in the waterless moat. He found it hard to take Jean's worries to heart. He had not survived fifteen years on the circuit to die in a petty squabble over this dessicated bog. 'I can see rye growing down there,' he observed before he could check himself.

Anger flashed briefly in his brother's eyes. 'I'm being serious, Waldin,' Jean snapped, for the heat was getting to him too. 'If you've no sensible suggestions to make, you can go back to Raymond. Crossing swords with boys seems to be all you're fit for these days.'

'Someone's got to teach your lad,' Waldin said equably. 'He's got the finesse of a butcher. Why, that Saxon lad shows more promise than your son.'

'Ned Fletcher? I thought he'd shape up.'

'Aye. He's been exercising hard. A strong lad, and keen. And the questions he asks! You could do worse than make him your captain. I find Fletcher useful when demonstrating the passes to Raymond. I don't know who taught your son before me, Jean, but—'

'It was difficult in Vannes,' Jean put in stiffly, guiltily aware that he had only supplied priests to see his son was literate, and that he had himself to blame for Raymond's military deficiencies.

'Aye, well, I came home none too soon. Fortunately, Raymond has a natural aptitude with horses, but as for his swordplay,' Waldin clucked in disgust and then shut his mouth abruptly, for Raymond was racing towards them, raising a cloud of dust.

'Papa! Papa!' Raymond skidded to a halt amid a hail of pebbles. 'It's Mama! The baby! You'd best come at once!'

The brothers exchanged glances. 'Early, isn't it?' Waldin asked.

'Yes, but my wife's done this before. She knows what to do. Is the midwife called, Raymond?'

'Aye. Come quickly, Papa!' Raymond plucked his father's sleeve.

Shaking his head at his son's impetuousness, Jean gave him a complacent smile. 'No need to hurry, my boy. Babies take their time.'

'But, Papa—'

'I'm coming.' Jean draped his arm companionably round his son's shoulders and steered him down the road. 'We'll wait in the hall, then we can be the first to know whether the child's a boy or a girl.'

'I hope it's a girl,' Raymond muttered at the dusty ground, and the tension in his body reached his father through the arm about his shoulders.

'Raymond? What's the matter?' When Raymond stared blindly at a magpie's feather lying by the road,

Jean gave him a friendly hug. 'You're not sulking, are you?'

Raymond raised hard green eyes. 'I hope the brat's a girl.'

'These thoughts are unworthy of you.' Jean spoke gently. 'If you are jealous, you have no need to be. If the child is a boy it will not affect my relationship with you. You are my firstborn. No one can take that away from you. This new child, boy or girl, cannot affect that.'

'You hope for a boy,' Raymond said, mouth one sulky line.

Jean saw no advantage in lying to his son. 'Aye, but boy or girl, I will love the child.' He gave his son an affectionate squeeze. 'I do need an heir.'

'An heir!' Raymond flung off his father's arm and thumped his chest. 'What's so wrong with me? Why can't *I* be your heir?'

Jean drew in a sharp breath. A portion of him could sympathise with Raymond, but he could not excuse him. It was the way of the world that legitimate children should inherit. Raymond knew that. Even legitimacy was no security, for estates could not be broken up, and it was common for the eldest legitimate son to take all, while younger legitimate children must fend for themselves. That was why Waldin had chosen to carve his way through the lists. Waldin had not let the fact that he had been a penniless second son sour his nature. It had been the making of him. He had understood that a small estate could not be sliced up like so much bread.

'There's nothing wrong with you, Raymond. You know the reason.'

'Aye! I do. It's on account of my birth, and the fault's not mine! The fault is yours, Papa. Yours! Why didn't you marry Mother before I was born?' He groaned his frustration. 'Why did you leave it so late?'

A heart-wrenching cry of pain floated out on the hot, motionless air. The three men froze mid-stride.

Waldin laid a blunt hand on his nephew's back. 'Have a care for your lady mother, will you?' Another harrowing cry had the hoary, unvanquished champion of many a battle wincing like a green page. 'Where the hell is that midwife?'

In the yard, Ned Fletcher and Roger de Herion, Jean's squire, had been fencing in their shirtsleeves. The two were at rest now, still breathing heavily, eyes trained on the high solar window. Waldin was unable to prevent himself running critical eyes over the pair of them. Fletcher, as usual, had his stance right, but Waldin grimaced when his eyes reached his brother's squire. 'De Herion,' he barked, 'what did I tell you about keeping your fingers *behind* the guard?'

Roger started. 'But, sir, we've finished. We're at ease.'

'If your sword's unsheathed, hold it properly. God's blood, it's a weapon, not a walking stick! You could learn by watching Fletcher. He's at ease, but he's ready for anything that might come to him. You should be, too.'

Jean had reached the steps. Tight-lipped, he indicated that his son should precede him into the hall.

But Raymond was still angry. 'I shall pray for a girl, Father. And you'd best do the same, because if it's a boy, I'll not let it take precedence over me. Burn me to ashes, but I'll make its life hell. If this babe is a boy, sir, he'll never succeed to your—'

'Enough!' Jean barked. 'We'll talk later, you and I.' He leaped the steps, two at a time.

Raymond glowered after him, but he was aware of his uncle's lowered brows.

'You can thank the saint that guards you,' Waldin said, 'that your father is too preoccupied to heed you, Raymond. I'd think twice before I'd voice such a threat again, if I were you.'

Raymond scowled and barged into the hall.

'Mama's crying,' Katarin said, rushing towards her father almost before he had lifted his boot over the top step. There was a hush in the hall, for everyone was listening to the scurrying feet, thumps and groans in the bedchamber. Katarin knew something mysterious was going on, something secret. She was used to being present at most important events in the household, and after she had summoned Klara she had run back to her mother. But Gwenn had waved her away as though she had no more business in her mother's chamber than a fly on a butcher's slab. 'Is it a secret, Papa?' she asked. Katarin liked secrets, but only if they were hers to share. Her father stared at the door at the foot of the stairs and did not respond. As he often kept his distance, Katarin was unperturbed. She jammed her thumb into her mouth and kept her eyes hooked onto her father's face. She longed for a cuddle, but the most she could hope for was not to be sent away. Instinct told her that today, if she was quiet as a mouse, her father might welcome her presence.

Hesitantly, for Katarin's keen eyes observed that the skin was drawn tightly across her father's features as it did when he was angry, the little girl touched her father's hand. She removed her thumb from her mouth. 'Papa?' Her father inclined his head, and his lips shaped a smile that her child's eyes could see was counterfeit. 'Papa? Aren't you going to see if Mama is getting better?'

Jean's expression softened, and to Katarin's delight he scooped her up in his arms and hugged her. 'No, my little blossom, I am not.'

Pleased with this contact, Katarin beamed, and when her father went to the trestle and sat down with her on his knee, her joy was complete. 'Why not, Papa?' she asked, wriggling with pleasure.

'Because, sweet girl, we have to wait.'

'It *is* a secret!' The smile on her father's face was more like a proper smile now.

'In a way it is,' he agreed.

Raymond stumped up to a bench, accompanied by Waldin. Ned and Roger de Herion came in, shrugging on their tunics. They made straight for the ale jugs.

Katarin put her mouth to her father's ear. 'Do you know what the secret is?'

Her father rolled his eyes mysteriously. 'I do.'

'Tell me, Papa,' Katarin begged. 'Tell me the secret.'

Emulating his daughter, Jean put his lips to her tiny, pink ear. 'Your mother is having a baby.'

Katarin gave another excited wriggle, her unformed child's features composed themselves, and her question flew straight as an arrow to the nub of the matter. 'Will it be a boy or a girl, Papa?'

Jean shot his firstborn a look, but Raymond was glooming into a wine cup. 'That, my flower, is the biggest secret of all. Only God knows the answer to that question. We will know soon.'

'How soon?' Katarin was wondering what her father's moustache felt like, and whether she dared to stroke it. From the solar there came a strangled shriek that was more animal than human. 'Mama!'

Jean squeezed his youngest daughter, and as her arms twined round his neck, he wondered bleakly who was comforting whom.

'It won't take long, will it?' Katarin asked. Her father's moustache tickled her cheek.

'Let's pray not, for your mother's sake.' And observing that his daughter's eyes were more green than brown, he asked, 'How old are you, Katarin?'

'Five, Papa,' she said, proudly.

'Five, eh?' Katarin was five years old, and he had only just noticed what a pretty colour her eyes were. He resolved to try and spend more time with her. 'You'll be able to help with the baby now you're so big.'

Ned was breaking a crust on the lower trestle with an expression of studied neutrality on his face.

'Fletcher!' Raymond bawled. 'Throw that wine jar over, will you?'

Ned looked startled to receive such a peremptory order, as well he might, for he was no manservant, but good-naturedly he did as he was requested.

'Here, Fletcher,' pointedly ignoring his elders, Raymond kicked out a bench for Ned, 'do the honours for me, would you, and pour one for yourself? I like drinking in *congenial* company.'

Ned looked at Jean, who tiredly indicated that he could take a place at their board.

'I know a prayer,' Katarin chirped up.

'Do you, sweet?' Pressing a kiss on Katarin's downy cheek, Jean disposed the child more comfortably in his arms. 'You say it quietly to yourself while I talk to Uncle Waldin. Your prayer will help Mama.'

The hazel eyes filled with pleasure and, thumb in mouth, Katarin began mumbling the Paternoster.

'Obliging child,' Jean murmured, realising from his daughter's glazed expression that she would be asleep in a few minutes.

'You've another lovely maid in the making there, Jean,' Waldin commented.

'Aye.' Jean steered the conversation away from children. 'I hear that France is planning a grand tourney the like of which has never been seen.'

Depositing brawny arms on the table, Waldin leaned forward. 'When's it to be?' he demanded.

'Next year, after Lammastide.'

The wide shoulders drooped. 'I'd hoped it would be sooner than that. Where will it be?'

'I'm not sure. Paris, I think.'

'Paris,' Waldin murmured.

'I thought you'd retired, Waldin,' Jean teased.

The champion gave a self-deprecating smile. 'So did I. I thought I was being very clever saving my skin before I got too old, but I confess I miss the circuit. You've no idea what it can be like, Jean. The noise. The excitement. The horses feel it too. They know, Jean.'

'Do they like it?' Ned cut in.

'What? The horses? Oh, aye. They like it all right. You should see them champing at their bits before the baton falls . . .' Waldin flushed, the force of his enthusiasm embarrassed him. 'It's hard to convey how I feel.'

'It's in your blood,' his brother observed.

'Aye. It's a fever that's got into my blood. And now I'm home. I'm old enough to know better, I've enough money in my scrip to last several lifetimes, and good lads to pass my knowledge on to,' he jerked his head at his nephew and Ned, 'I should be content.'

'Will you attend the tournament?' Ned's blue eyes were bright with interest.

Waldin hoisted heavy shoulders. 'Who knows? A year's a long time, Fletcher. Maybe I will go, but I'm sadly out of practice.'

'I'd love to go,' Ned declared.

Waldin smiled a smile of complete understanding. 'Perhaps I'll ask my brother to give you leave, and you could act as my squire.'

'Would you?' Delight shone from every line on Ned's face.

'I might, if you continue to improve the way you're doing at the moment.'

'Thank you, sir. Sir Waldin, I've been wanting to ask you . . . it's about swords . . .'

'Go on, lad.'

'I was hoping you'd explain why Damascened swords are prized so.'

'Damascened swords, eh? Excellent in single combat, but they're of no use in a mêlée. I don't recall mentioning Damascened swords to you, Fletcher.'

'You didn't, sir. But last time I ran an errand to the armourer, I overheard his conversation with another customer. They were extolling the virtues of Damascened blades.'

'Damascened swords first came over from the East,' Waldin was happy to explain. 'There's no denying they will carry an edge no other sword can take, and they have a flexibility I've yet to see in another sword. But they're too light for the tourney. A knight needs a sword with more clout in a mêlée.'

'How are they made, sir?'

'In simple terms, the swordsmith beats out the steel over and over, before folding it back on itself. Then he starts the process all over again. It's a very skilled and lengthy business.'

'Expensive, I should think,' Ned commented.

'It is that.' Waldin grinned. 'Only princes and dukes can afford them.'

'Could the heavier swords be made to take a similar edge?'

'Here, Fletcher,' Raymond plucked peevishly at Ned's tunic, 'you're supposed to be talking to me.'

The excitement vanished from Ned's face as swiftly as though someone had snuffed a candle out. 'My apologies, Master Raymond.'

'Pour me more wine.'

Lifting the flagon, Ned looked across it at Waldin. 'I'll hold you to your promise, sir,' he said earnestly. 'I'll keep my nose to the grindstone in order to be your squire.'

'You ought to try and forget the tournaments, Waldin,' Jean said. 'You were courting disaster to go on as long as you did, and at your ripe old age you'd be begging for it.'

'It's a form of madness, I cannot deny that,' Waldin agreed. 'But there's glory in it.'

Jean looked tenderly at the sleeping child in his arms. 'I've never understood your fascination with glory. When it comes down to it, you end up spilling a gallon of blood and it seems to me it's largely a matter of chance whether it's your blood or someone else's.'

'I understand,' Ned put in.

'Heaven help us,' Jean said in a resigned voice. 'Your prating about glory is unsettling my men, Waldin.' He glanced warmly at Ned. 'I want to keep my sergeant. I don't want to lose him to the jousts.'

'Oh, I'd come back, sir, but it's good to dream.'

Raymond felt it was time he stuck his oars in.

'Dream!' He snorted. 'All you ever do is dream.' Predictably, Ned flushed. Raymond turned his fire on his uncle. 'And as for wasting yourself for glory's sake, Uncle, I agree with my father. You're mad. I would only risk myself for something . . . tangible.'

Waldin's brown eyes narrowed. 'Like an inheritance, perhaps?' he suggested softly. He was hoping his nephew was merely stirring the pot to see what was in it.

Raymond took his time answering. 'Aye. I'd say an inheritance was worth fighting for. Father, do you not agree?' But his father's attention was fixed on the sounds filtering down the solar stairs. 'Father?'

'What's that you said, Raymond?'

'I was telling my uncle that I wouldn't risk my neck for glory alone.'

'No.' Jean's eyes were glued to the rafters. One of his hands stroked his daughter's hair. 'I've always needed something to fight for myself.'

Lurching for the wine, Raymond forged on, making what he thought was a winning point. 'Being the eldest son, Papa, you had something to fight for. Whereas Waldin, being the poor, younger son, had to make do with glory.'

'I've been content, lad,' Waldin put in quickly.

'You might have been. I—'

A muffled shriek leeched the colour from Jean's cheeks. 'Sweet Jesus, does she have to suffer so?'

'Here, Jean, have a drink,' Waldin suggested. 'It will help you forget—'

'Forget! Forget? God's teeth, Waldin! How the bloody hell do you think I can forget that she is suffering?'

'It will help you relax.' Firmly, Waldin pressed an earthenware cup into his brother's hand. 'Take it. You look like a death's-head.'

Jean caught Ned's sympathetic glance on him and knew he must set an example. An excess of sympathy never made for efficient fighting men, and Ned Fletcher was not the only one of his troop in the hall. Denis the Red and some others had drifted in for their evening meal. The mistress of the household might be fighting for her life, but the evening meals must still be served. Now why had he picked on that unfortunate phrase? God grant that Yolande was *not* fighting for her life . . .

Jean cleared his throat. 'Sergeant Fletcher.' He was pleased how curt his voice came out.

Ned sat up. 'Sir?'

'Do you recall when the armourer said that he'd have the links mended on my spare coat of mail?'

'Aye, sir. He promised it for the first of the month.'

'So you could collect it on the morrow?'

'If you wish, sir.'

'Leave at first light, will you, Sergeant? That way you should be there and back by sunset.'

'Very well, sir.'

An agonised groan floated into the hall, and though it was muted and cut off sharply, it succeeded in killing conversation. Jean clenched his fingers round his wine cup and stared blankly at the trencher someone had set before him. Desperately he tried to order his thoughts. If it was a boy, he must put his house in order. He didn't trust de Roncier to let well alone if it was a boy. If the infant was a girl . . .

Another muffled shriek had him burying his face in his daughter's soft hair. He felt a tentative touch on his shoulder and looked up. The turnspit was standing beside him, a question in his eyes. 'Roast beef, sir?'

A platter of beef swimming in red juices was waved under his nose. Jean's gorge rose. Sickened, he waved the meat away. 'Not for me. I've no appetite this evening.' He lifted resigned eyes to his brother. 'It would appear that it is going to be a long night, Waldin.'

Waldin dipped his head in acknowledgement. What they needed was something to speed the passage of time. 'Mulled wine might help,' he tried again.

Jean knew it wouldn't, but he dragged on the best

smile he had. 'My thanks, Waldin.'

Chapter Sixteen

Duke Geoffrey of Brittany had a hunting lodge at Suscinio on the remote Rhuys peninsula. This long arm of land curved round the Small Sea, or Morbihan Gulf, at its southern end, and acted as a vast windbreak, holding the unruly weather from the larger ocean – the Morbraz – at bay. Miles from the town of Vannes, the peninsula was a wild, windswept place, where the trees were bent by a relentless wind. The Duke's lodge was an unpretentious wattle and daub building with a beaten earth floor, mean as any villein's hovel. No lady would set foot in the place, which was one of the reasons Duke Geoffrey chose it for his bolt-hole. There were times when he felt the need to escape the restrictions his responsibilities imposed on him, and his lodge at least provided adequate protection from the elements.

That August night, while Yolande St Clair laboured to give birth to her fourth child, Alan le Bret lay on his cloak at his Duke's side at Suscinio, listening to the wind whistling through the thatch. 'Makes you shiver to listen to it,' he commented, hands linked behind his head, 'and everywhere else your people are sweating the fat off their ribs in the heat.'

'Aye,' Duke Geoffrey answered, lazily paring his nails with his dagger. 'It's always cool here. I hope you don't resent me dragging you from Rennes, le Bret. Did you have a sweetheart there?'

'No sweetheart,' Alan said. 'And I'm glad you brought me, Your Grace, because I've a brother at a monastery on this peninsula, very close by, and a visit's long overdue.'

'I didn't know you had a brother, let alone one in holy orders.'

'He's a novice and his name is William.'

'You want leave to see him?'

'Please. He's at the monastery of St Gildas and—'

The Duke cut him off with a gracious wave of his hand and reached for the lantern. 'Granted. But not on the morrow, le Bret. My forester tells me there's a wolf on the prowl, and I've a mind to nail its head on that beam. We'll be up before dawn and in the saddle all day.' The Duke stuck his dagger into the beaten earth floor and closed the lantern, throwing them into inky darkness. His languid voice floated gently through the murk, 'You may visit your brother the next day, le Bret.'

'My thanks, Your Grace.'

The following morning, in the grey hour before sunrise, the Kermaria cockerel stirred, blinked once, twice, gave his head a comb-waggling shake, and tipped his head sideways to listen to the slow, warm, sighing exhalations of the sleeping horses. His black eyes winked up at the sky. It was a cloudless one as it had been these several months past, and the light would be faint for another half hour. It was not quite time for him to crow, not quite time for him to wake the world and announce that morning had come.

A whisper of sound sent the cockerel's head swivelling in the direction of the tower. Up there, riding on the soft morning breeze, so weak that it was almost inaudible, was the thin, reedy cry of a newborn infant. Another noise was adrift on the breeze . . . someone was sobbing, and a phrase was being repeated over and over again. 'Don't go, Mama! Don't go! *Mama!*' The voice faded. More exhausted sobbing. But the cockerel had stopped listening, the sounds had no meaning for him. He flung back his head and crowed the new day in.

270

'I'll take the baby down. Papa must be . . . told,' Gwenn volunteered, as soon as they'd made her mother's body decent.

'Are you sure you want to do it?' the midwife asked, handing the infant to the dead woman's daughter with ill-concealed relief.

'Aye. It will be best if he hears it from me.' Gwenn read concern in Berthe's eyes, and tried to smile. 'I'm well enough,' she declared. Didn't duty decree it? 'In any event, I can't bear to bide here for another moment.'

'I understand,' the midwife said. The commingled smells of birth and death were overpowering for those not inured to them. 'You tell Sir Jean. I'll . . . tidy up.'

Do you understand? Do you really? Gwenn thought bleakly as she stumbled on legs made of wood towards the twisting turn of stairs. Her eyes were sore with lack of sleep and the few tears she had shed, but aside from that she felt quite dead. She was cold inside, a numb coldness, as though all the feeling had gone out of her and she had truly turned to wood. It would have been a relief to have been able to indulge in a fit of shaking and sobbing and screaming.

At the bottom of the stairs, Gwenn snapped off the thread of her thoughts. Cradling the newest member of the family against her breast, she lifted the latch.

Outside, the cock was crowing. A solitary candle, burned to its last inch, guttered in the draught. Her eyes swept the room, seeking her father. Jean had borrowed a pallet and pulled it up to the fire. He was asleep, Katarin beside him. Gwenn's heart went out to him – to both of them. She must tell him at once. She stepped into the hall.

'Good morning, mistress,' Ned said, moving towards Gwenn, smiling. 'Mistress Gwenn?' His smile disappeared. 'What's amiss? Is the child . . . ?'

On hearing his sergeant's voice, Jean sat up abruptly, dislodging Katarin. He was at Gwenn's side before she had time to blink. Lightly, he touched at the bundle in Gwenn's arm. 'The child?'

Gwenn strove to keep her features in order. 'Aye.' Her windpipe closed up.

Her father plucked at the baby's wrappings. 'It looks small. Is it healthy?' Almost afraid, he stared at his child. A boy, or a girl?

Around them everyone was surfacing. Raymond groaned and groped for a flagon. Waldin yawned and stretched. And all the while Ned's blue eyes were nailed to Gwenn's face. So much compassion flowed from him, it was almost her undoing. Ned had guessed. Gwenn felt tears prick behind her eyes and tried to gulp down the lump that was stuck in the base of throat. She must tell her father – and this instant. 'Aye, the babe is healthy. Papa—'

'Boy or girl?' Raymond demanded, knuckling sleep from his eyes.

'A boy. The boy Papa so wanted.' Gwenn tried to infuse some joy into her voice, very much aware that it should be Yolande who was presenting the child to her family. Her mother had so wanted to give Jean his legitimate heir. 'We have a brother, Raymond.'

'A boy.' Raymond looked appalled. He hawked and spat into the rushes. 'Naturally, it would be.' Twisting round on his heel, he stormed out without waiting to hear the other, more dreadful part of Gwenn's news.

Jean strode to the stair door and looked back with his hand on the latch. Gwenn flinched to see his face so wreathed with smiles. 'I'm going upstairs,' he announced with quiet pride. 'I'm going to see my wife.'

'No! Blessed Mother, no!'

Her father tossed her an indulgent smile. 'I know she'll be tired, Gwenn. I won't stay long. I won't exhaust her.'

Thrusting her new brother at Ned, Gwenn launched herself at her father. 'No. Papa!' Warm tears welled up and spilled down her cheeks. 'Please don't. Not yet.'

Jean's smile faded painfully slowly. Stone-still, he drew in a harsh breath and stared at his daughter in a puzzled, incomprehending way. 'Gwenn?' His voice came loud in the gruesome quiet, and there was no escaping his eyes, or the hollow despair growing in them. 'What are you trying to tell me?'

Gwenn choked down a sob. It was a little like watching someone die from the inside out. 'Mama has gone to God, Papa.'

Her father's eyes released hers and travelled to the ceiling, halting at the place above which his bed should lie. He aged twenty years in a moment. White-faced, he stared at the rafters as though his eyes would pierce solid oak and see through them to where his wife's body lay.

'No. No.' His voice broke. What evil curse hung over him that now, when his star was in the ascendant, his plans should turn to ashes? He had taken it for granted that Yolande would be at his side. Without her, there was . . . nothing. 'How could you let her go?' His accusation tore at Gwenn's heartstrings.

'It . . . it was a difficult birth. We did our best.'

'Jesu, Gwenn,' Jean said quickly, shocked by his hasty words, 'you don't have to tell me that. Accept my . . . my . . . I'm sorry . . .' He waved at the heir who had cost him his beloved wife. 'But how could it have happend? That puny child . . . he's so small, how could he . . . ?'

'Papa, your son came early. And with the heat, Mama was not well. He was in the breech position.'

'A breech,' Jean muttered, unable to accept what his daughter was telling him. This could not be happening. Conscious that every eye in the hall was fastened on him, he squared his shoulders. He ought to say something which would demonstrate to the people in his hall that he remained in control of himself. A man who could not master his emotions was not, in his mind, fit to master others. He caught sight of Ned Fletcher awkwardly juggling his newborn son from arm to arm. 'What are you doing here, Sergeant?' he demanded. 'It's well past cockcrow. Don't you have duties in Vannes?'

'Sir?' Ned responded, clearly startled. 'Oh, the coat

273

of mail. Aye, sir. Sorry, sir.'

Jean looked coldly at the bundle in Ned's arms. 'And while you're about it, Fletcher, see if you can find a wet nurse for that.'

'Aye, sir.'

Jean faced Gwenn. 'I shall go up now,' he said, and his tone brooked no argument.

Gwenn bent her head in acceptance. Her father had withdrawn his feelings behind a protective shield of authority while his dazed mind absorbed the shock. In time, she prayed, he would heal.

Ned deposited the babe in Gwenn's arms and went to take his sword from the rack at the other end of the hall. The last thing he saw as he left was Katarin shoving her thumb into her mouth and Gwenn, head bowed to hide her tears, holding the babe in one arm and her sister in the other.

Wondering miserably which of St Clair's mounts would best suit a wet nurse, Ned blinked, wiped his nose with the back of his hand and went to choose a couple of horses.

His commission with the armourer completed, Ned found himself within a stone's throw of la rue de la Monnaie. Curiosity drove him on. He wanted to see what had happened to Mistress Gwenn's old home, and he guided his horse towards St Peter's Cathedral, which he knew was being rebuilt. He heard the mason's hammers before he reached the square. Rounding a corner, he drew rein. There was not a trace of the old wooden building, instead the outline of a monumental stone cathedral met his eyes. Its contours were blurred beneath a mesh of scaffolding, and dozens of men were crawling and balancing all along the mesh, like fleas on a dog's back. Wondering at the scale of the activity, he hailed a passerby. 'When is the cathedral due to be completed?'

'Stranger, are you?' the fellow asked, eyeing him warily.

'From Kermaria,' Ned hoped that the man had heard of the place. Kermaria was ten miles off, but ten miles was further than most men journeyed in a lifetime, even the worldly townsfolk.

The man was obviously well travelled and talkative, for his expression softened, and he chose to answer Ned's question. 'God knows, but I shouldn't think I'll live to see it finished. I preferred the old cathedral myself, but a fire started in one of the streets nearby.' He scratched a hairy ear. 'It would have been . . . let me think now, some—'

'Two years back,' Ned supplied thoughtlessly, and could have bitten his tongue out, for suspicion fired immediately in the man's dark, Breton eyes.

'Aye. It were two years back. It gobbled the guts of the area, and the cathedral was damaged beyond repair. They're rebuilding in stone. What's your interest?'

Ned shrugged. 'None really. I remember the wooden cathedral, from way back. And although I've had business in Vannes since then, it has never brought me here. This place has changed.'

'Oh, aye.' The man grunted, about to move on.

'Tell me one thing.' The Breton stopped but did not look back. Ned knew he was listening. 'Was Duke's Tavern burnt out?'

'Nay. The devil keeps his eyes on that place. The wind changed. The fire didn't touch the tavern.'

Ned couldn't resist riding round to the inn. He wondered whether de Roncier's men frequented the place these days. Now that de Roncier's business in the area had been concluded, there was no reason why they should be there, but nevertheless Ned felt an uneasy tingle in his spine. He had no plans to go in, intending only to amble past; but when he arrived, he took one look at the dun gelding tethered outside, swore, and swung out of the saddle.

He tossed his reins and those of the mare he'd brought for the wet nurse to the urchin guarding the door. 'Is that animal's rider inside?'

The child, a grimy boy of about seven years of age who had lost his front teeth and whose replacements had not yet grown, jerked his thumb at the gloomy interior. 'Aye. But I should think he's past riding. He's roaring drunk, by now.'

Ned sighed and showed the lad a coin. 'This is yours if you keep an eye on these horses and my gear,' he said, indicating the rolled-up bundle that was Sir Jean's valuable hauberk. He hoped the boy was wrong and the gelding's owner was not inside. Above all he hoped he would not find himself confronting old friends.

Moving reluctantly into the tavern, Ned found that the boy had not lied. The horse's rider was in the tavern, and he was drunk, not roaring drunk but drunk enough to give Ned trouble. Raymond Herevi, for the gelding was his, was slumped over one of the trestles close to the door. And Ned's old comrades-in-arms? Ned's eyes made a quick tour of the room. Thank God, trade was slow, he saw no one he wanted to avoid. One table away from Raymond's, a man was enveloped in a shabby cloak, dozing and lost to the world. A filthy mongrel slept at his feet, whimpering fitfully. There were a couple of greybeards dicing by the fire, and there was the potboy, Tristan. He had not changed, except that he'd shot up like a beanshoot and was even lankier. Mikael Brasher was not about, and neither were de Roncier's men. Ned's conscience was clear, there was no reason he should not meet up with his former comrades – he had not betrayed anyone in sign-ing up with St Clair because his old commission had run its course. Nonetheless, he was relieved not to run into them, and he was especially relieved not to run into Captain Malait, whose interest in young men, and himself in particular, Ned had noticed.

Raymond had been supping alone. Green, drink-dimmed eyes gazed morosely at a capacious glass bottle. Only the best wine was bottled in expensive glass. Ray-mond was not stinting himself. When Ned's shadow fell over him, he looked up.

'Hello, Fletscher,' he said, too far gone to remark upon his presence. 'We never did finish our drinksh last eve.' He waved inaccurately at the bottle which still held enough to put four men with stronger heads than Raymond's under the table. 'Help yourshelf.'

'My thanks.' Ned pulled up a stool but didn't touch the wine. He preferred to drink ale in the day, and in any case he had yet to find a wet nurse for Raymond's new brother.

Raymond noticed Ned's abstemiousness at once and pounced on the Englishman with the missionary zeal of a drunk who cannot bear to see a companion sober. 'Why aren't you drinking, Fletscher?' he demanded, so soused his tongue tripped over almost all the words. 'Don't you want to shelebrate my new brother's birthday?' Temptingly, he waggled the wine under Ned's nose. 'Washamatter, Sergeant? Don't you want to shelebrate the birth of my father's legitimate heir? If I can shelebrate it, surely you can?'

Wine sloshed from the mouth of the bottle, pooling like blood on the table. Firmly removing the vessel from Raymond's unco-ordinated grasp, Ned set it to one side. 'No thank you, Master Raymond.' He must somehow get Raymond out of here and take him home. And he had that wet nurse to find.

'Master Raymond—'

'You can go to hell, Fletscher, if you've come to root me out of here. Didn't my father give you an errand to run?'

'Aye. I've to find a wet nurse for your brother.'

'A wet nurse for the heir, naturally. *I* can fend for myself.'

Ned was not about to argue with Raymond. When drunk, he was impossible. 'I know that, Master Raymond,' Ned said mildly. 'But your father needs you . . .' He broke off, recalling with dismay that Raymond had ridden off without being informed of his mother's untimely death. He struggled to keep his features from betraying the evil news. He could not tell

Raymond now, not here, when he was in this state. But how otherwise to convince Raymond he must go home? Ned was Raymond's senior by three years, but his position as a hireling negated any advantage he might wrest from his superior age.

Raymond missed Ned's fleeting change of expression. His finely cut mouth twisted sourly. 'Father needs me? Like hell he does. My father has a new son to play with. Hey! Boy! Get me a fresh bottle, will you?'

Coming reluctantly to the conclusion that only strong-arm tactics would work, Ned countermanded Raymond's order. 'No, Tristan. Forget the wine,' he said firmly. 'We're leaving.' And before Raymond could muster an objection, Ned stood up, hooked an arm through one of Raymond's and heaved him upright. 'Come on, Master Raymond. It's time we headed for la rue Richemont and the road to Kermaria.'

Ruthlessly, Ned hauled Raymond towards the sun-bleached street. In the tussle, he failed to notice the strings of the young man's purse had caught on a nail protruding from the bench. The ties resisted the pressure and then snapped, and Raymond's purse fell like a ripe peach into the rushes.

The cloaked figure stirred, a furtive eye blinked. A hood flopped forwards, obscuring shifty features; and out of sight beneath the worn cloak, long fingers were flexed. There was a rattling, chesty cough, and a heart-beat later the purse was gone.

Hoping that his charge would not get violent, Ned steered Raymond inexorably towards his horse. Feebly, the young man tried to shake him off, but to Ned's relief he had drunk too much to be effective. 'Do you think you can ride, Master Raymond?'

Raymond scowled, the street was waving up and down in front of his eyes like the Small Sea. 'Of course I can ride,' he said, staggering, but when Ned steadied him he flung off his arm. 'I can always ride. I may not be able to walk, but I can always ride.'

Ned responded with a smile and watched him climb groggily into his saddle.

Raymond belched. 'Who in blazes do you think you are, Fletcher? What gives you the right to lord it over me and fetch me home like a runaway serf with my tail between my legs?'

Raymond's tone had sobered considerably, and Ned risked a grin. 'Someone's got to keep an eye on you, Master Raymond.'

Raymond struggled into an upright position and took stock of his surroundings. 'We used to live near here, Ned.' He stabbed a finger at la rue de la Monnaie. 'Down there. I liked it better when we lived there.'

'Did you, Master Raymond?' Ned kept his face as blank as he could, and mounted. The urchin held out a dirty hand and grinned hopefully.

'Master Raymond!' Tristan was loping towards them.

Raymond slewed round in the saddle, clutching his pommel for balance.

'Master Raymond, one of my customers found your purse.'

Raymond reached for it, swaying so much that Ned grimaced. Raymond weighed his purse in his palm to make sure it wasn't any lighter. He didn't have much, but he didn't want to lose what little he did have.

Tristan hovered. 'Excuse me, sir . . .' Realising he would not get much sense out of Raymond, the potboy turned to Ned. 'I . . . I could not help overhearing what you were saying inside, about the wet nurse . . .'

'Go on,' Ned said. 'Have you someone in mind?'

Tristan seemed to pick his words. 'Aye. I don't know her personally, sir, but I'm told there's a young maid been delivered of a stillborn child. Would . . . would you like to meet her?'

Ned leaned his elbow on his saddle horn. 'Where does she live?'

'Live?' The question seemed to discompose Tristan, who lifted a vague hand and said, 'Oh, nearby.'

'She could be here soon?'

'If someone fetched her, she'd be here in a flash.'

'The work's outside the town,' Ned told him. 'Won't

her husband object to her living in Kermaria for a few months?'

'Husband?' Tristan went red and shuffled big feet. 'She doesn't have a husband, sir. Does that matter?'

It did not matter as far as Ned was concerned, but he couldn't vouch for St Clair's reaction. Then he remembered that the knight had not always been married to Lady Yolande. He shot a sideways look at Raymond and said, 'Matter? No of course not. As long as the wench is healthy and her milk is good.'

Tristan hesitated, thinking of the money he'd been offered by the maid's brother for getting the girl honest work. 'I'm no expert, sir,' Tristan said, the thought of the coins inspiring him, 'but I should think that if the maid has not got her own babe to feed, her milk will be the richer.'

Not one to look a gift horse in the mouth, Ned swung down from the saddle.

'What's up Fletcher?' Raymond demanded.

Ned grinned. 'I've changed my mind. I've decided to have that drink with you after all, Master Raymond.'

Raymond's brain felt as though it was stuffed with clouds, but he rolled off his horse and showed his teeth. 'Good. I'll finish that bottle of wine I bespoke earlier.'

With a wry smile Ned flung the horse's reins at the confused urchin. 'You've to work for your coin today, my lad.'

In the tavern, Tristan was exchanging words with the man who, despite the warmth of the day, was drowned in that unseasonal wool cloak.

On the counter, a wasp wound a wavering path through a pool of spilled mead. Spotting the insect, Tristan took a grey rag from his belt and flicked it aside. The insect spiralled to the floor. Not two feet from where the wasp landed, tucked out of the way behind an upturned barrel, a pedlar's tray sat on the beaten earth. It was half full of tawdry ribbons and sticky sweetmeats. The wasp, scenting a heaven of sweet delight, staggered like a toper, rose uncertainly into the air, and landed amid the sweetmeats. Some ants had beaten the wasp to it but the wasp was full of mead and not inclined to fight them off; there was enough on the tray to satisfy every wasp in his nest, and the ants too.

The fellow in the mantle, the owner of the tray, left the inn. The decrepit hound cocked a ragged grey ear, whined, and trailed faithfully after him. Having taken the unprecedented step of handing in a purse which rattled with coins, the pedlar had his sister to find; and that being done, he had information to sell. He had a buyer all lined up, for Conan the pedlar had no doubt that a certain French count would pay handsomely to learn what he had overheard in Mikael Brasher's tavern. Add to that the likely reward for having taken the initiative in installing his sister at Kermaria . . .

Conan smirked. Not only was his luck in that morning, for once it was paying him to be honest. His handing back of that purse, though it had gone very much against the grain, had been a masterstroke, and he would yet see a profit from it. He had done a good day's work without even trying.

Tristan put the broached bottle back on a tray with two goblets.

'Ale for me, if you please,' Ned said. 'Wine's too rich at this time of the day.' He wanted a clear head when he met the wet nurse.

'I've a strong stomach,' Raymond declared.

'Mmm.' Ned was not going to dispute the obvious.

Grasping firm hold of the bottle, Raymond took refuge in mockery. 'Ale,' he sneered. 'You're only a beginner, aren't you, Sergeant Fletcher?'

Suppressing a resigned sigh, Ned reached for his watery ale and hoped the wench would come soon, before the level in that bottle sunk much lower.

Outside his hunting lodge, Duke Geoffrey was examining the rough wolf pelt his huntsman had brought him. 'A princely beast, eh, Gilbert?' he commented, running his hands over the soft fur.

'Aye, Your Grace. Quite remarkable. I've not skin-ned a larger one, and he led us a merry dance.'

The Duke's eyes lit up. 'He did that. It was fine sport. Three days he eluded us, and—' The Duke broke off, head cocked to one side. A horseman was approaching. 'Who's that?' he demanded, ready to dive into his lodge. 'I'm not expecting anyone, and I don't want to be run to earth for a few days yet.'

The huntsman screwed up his eyes. 'The horse is yours, Your Grace. Captain Le Bret is returning.'

'Already? It must have been a very brief reunion.' The Duke emerged from the shadows and directed a jibe at his captain. 'Don't tell me, le Bret, you lost your way and couldn't find the monastery.' Alan was the best scout Duke Geoffrey had and they both knew it.

Dismounting, Alan wound his reins round a nearby shrub. 'My brother wasn't there, Your Grace.'

'I've heard it's a harsh regime.' The Duke hesitated. 'He's not . . .'

'Dead?' Alan smiled. 'No, William's not dead. Though I daresay he would be if he'd had to stay there much longer. I can see why Pierre Abelard – infamous old philosopher and abbott he was – took against the place all those years ago. No, my brother's very much alive. Apparently the monks have unearthed a rare talent in him. William's an artist. He's become renowned for his wall-paintings, and it seems his talents must be spread around. Another house has borrowed him – he's repainting their chapel.'

'So you missed him?'

Alan pulled a rueful face. 'Aye. And by only a week. But it's of no moment. I'd not seen him in years.'

'Pity though. Do you know where he went?'

'They sent him to an obscure cell tucked away in the forest west of Vannes, before you come to the megaliths. It's dedicated to St Félix.'

'You could visit your brother later, in a month or two. I can't spare you just yet,' Duke Geoffrey said. Losing interest in his captain's affairs, the Duke looked proudly at the animal skin spread out on the ground.

Taking the hint, Alan followed his Duke's gaze. 'You've had the head removed,' he remarked.

'Aye. I'm having that on the beam, remember?' Alan nodded. 'But I don't need another pelt. Do you want it, le Bret?'

'I'd be honoured, Your Grace.'

The Duke waved a generous hand. 'I'll have it tanned and stretched for you then, to compensate for your missing your brother.'

Alan bowed.

Chapter Seventeen

Mid-April 1186

Johanna the wet nurse was a stranger to modesty, like most nursing mothers. She saw no reason to blush when she unlaced her gown, and often fed baby Philippe in the bustle of the hall. Johanna liked feeding him there for two reasons.

The first was that her brother, Conan, expected her to keep him informed of events at Kermaria, and as the hall was the centre of activity, it was the ideal place for her to sit and sift the wheat from the chaff. All she had to do was find a seat, latch St Clair's heir onto her breast, and keep her eyes peeled and her ears open. She could talk if she wanted to, but generally she found this not worth the candle, for the people most likely to bother with her were the other women. And they, Johanna thought scornfully, never knew anything. So most days she would sit quietly in the hall, stroking Philippe's head and pretending to look down at him in a loving way. She hoped she looked as pretty as Our Lady did on the mural in the chapel. Jean paid Johanna well for the pains she took with his son, and she did take pains. Eventually Johanna did not even have to pretend to look lovingly at Philippe; she came to love him in truth, and her look betrayed her.

Philippe St Clair was almost eight months old. He had taken to his nurse, and had lost his wizened, premature face. The child Johanna fed now could almost be weaned were it not the fashion to keep children on the breast for as long as possible. His cheeks had filled out and were as rosy as apples. He was plump, and always smiling. He had strong, sturdy fists which he waved in the air. Johanna did not like to think that soon he would no longer need her, and not just because she was being paid twice. Sir Jean paid her. Her brother paid her. She'd never known work could be so easy, so enjoyable; and she dreaded its ending.

The second reason Johanna liked sitting in the hall was connected with her desire to look pretty. Johanna had no sooner spied Ned Fletcher in Duke's Tavern than she wanted him – him and no other. She was no simpering virgin to be taken in by a handsome face, as the fact that she was able to give suck to the knight's child proved. But that day when her brother had wrenched a comb through her hair and shoved her all unwilling into Duke's Tavern had changed her life. Conan had warned her to talk pretty because they'd not take a slattern; having seen Ned Fletcher, Johanna had obeyed him, and she had been taken to Kermaria.

Up until that fateful August morning, Johanna had lived from hand to mouth, drifting aimlessly, content to grab as much as she could for herself. However, once she had set eyes on Ned Fletcher, that changed. Suddenly, she had a mission in life, and she was willing to try anything to get him, including sitting in St Clair's hall for hours longer than was necessary in the hope of seeing the foreign captain. Ned Fletcher had been a sergeant when he had brought her here, but the very next day Johanna had witnessed his promotion to captain, apparently on the recommendation of Jean St Clair's brother, Sir Waldin. A squat red-headed man called Denis had been made sergeant in his place.

Ned was unlike any man Johanna had ever met. He did not seem to realise how those golden looks of his turned ladies' heads, or if he did, he failed to make the most of it, a fact which was extraordinary to Johanna. Life was tough. Nothing came easily, and her view was that you must make the most of the meanest of God's blessings. God had gifted her with some charms. She was plump, and generally men admired her full figure. Johanna would reckon herself simple-minded, and not deserving of God's favour, if she did not put her charms to use.

She tried baring her generous breasts in front of Ned, even if baby Philippe had already sucked himself into a stupor. But though the other men gawped at her, the Saxon never did. And she spent time considering how best to sit in order that her full bosom would be better displayed before his eyes. His subordinates ogled her, their gazes fastened as greedily as a hungry babe's on her breasts every time she sat by the fire, but Ned Fletcher might as well have been walking about blind-fold for all the notice he took. His lack of interest fuelled Johanna's desire. Why didn't he look her way?

It took Johanna a day or two to work out that his interest was fixed elsewhere, but this did not daunt her. Gwenn Herevi – for the girl was illegitimate and as such had no right to her father's name – posed no threat to Johanna. She had a skinny, childish body. What man could possibly see Johanna and still want Gwenn Herevi? Confident that her moment would come, Johanna bided her time. But the days turned into weeks, the weeks into months, and Ned Fletcher had yet to do more than nod at her.

One day when baby Philippe got the gripe, Johanna came to the reluctant decision that she would have to feed the child in the solar, for he was so distracted by the goings on in the hall that he began to carp and would not feed properly. Settling the baby on her broad hip, she carried him upstairs. His cradle had been placed alongside his sisters' bed. Johanna would learn nothing this morning, thanks to the babe. Nor would she see the handsome captain. Scowling at her charge, Johanna dragged the curtain across the opening lest a chance visitor to the solar should disturb the already unsettled infant.

'You're a nuisance, you are.' She wagged her finger

at him but, being genuinely fond of the baby, she bore him no illwill. Philippe gurgled, and stopped grizzling. He smiled, and waved a chubby fist at her. Johanna gave him a loving shake. 'You're a charmer, and all. All smiles now you've got your own way.'

She plumped down on the bed, stretched out her legs and unlaced her gown. Philippe responded well to the peace and quiet, and was soon sucking vigorously. The bed was bulging with feathers; it was soft, and baby Philippe warm. After a minute or so, Johanna's eyelids became heavy. The conversation down in the hall was no more than a distant buzz. Now and then one voice or another would rise above the others, but gently like waves breaking on a distant shore. Half asleep, Johanna's mind wandered. She visualised herself walking the length of a beach and, striding at her side, was Ned Fletcher. His hair was bleached by a summer sun. He turned and looked at her. His eyes were as blue as the sky, and he was smiling . . .

Philippe's head lolled heavily to one side, the milk dribbling from his tiny rosebud mouth. He was sated, and his eyes were closed.

In a minute I'll lace myself up and put him in his cradle, Johanna thought lazily. She was too comfortable to rouse herself, and surely no one would object if she took a short nap. She folded her arms securely round the sleeping babe, exhaled softly, and joined Philippe St Clair in sleep.

Half an hour later, Johanna jerked suddenly awake, wondering what had disturbed her. Instinctively she looked at the infant, but Philippe's small body lay tranquil against her breast, fast asleep. A nippy draught was blowing through the window slit; that must have been the cause of her abrupt awakening.

Easing the baby from her breast, Johanna pulled the edges of her gown together, moving slowly so she did not joggle him. She did not want to rise from this downy couch, but she couldn't lie on Gwenn Herevi's bed all day. Baby Philippe might have the colic, but her brother would be avid for news. Conan had bribed the carter who brought in Kermaria's supplies from Vannes, and usually Johanna left verbal messages with him. More rarely Conan himself would ride in on the carter's wagon and arrange to meet Johanna in the stables. If caught he would say he was peddling. Johanna failed to see why Conan was so interested in life at Kermaria. Her plump red lips pursed. She must ask him why he needed to know so much; she didn't want to help him if it meant harm might come to Captain Fletcher. Thoughtfully, Johanna ran grubby hands over the fine coverlet. It was silk, imported from Nicaea in the Holy Land. Johanna did not know what silk felt like, nor had she heard of Nicaea, but she recognised quality when she came across it. She hoped Mistress Gwenn and Katarin appreciated how fortunate they were to slumber in such a bed.

She heard a soft footfall in the solar. Someone was moving about out there. It must have been the creaking of the solar door that had woken her, not the chilly spring breeze. Tenderly, Johanna wiped Philippe's mouth with her sleeve and put him in his cradle. Philippe didn't so much as murmur. Babies were so trusting.

The breeze lifted the curtain of the sleeping-alcove and Johanna saw Gwenn Herevi. She sucked in a breath, and the tender expression vanished. Full lips thinning, she drew back. She hadn't made a sound, nor would she; she would snatch at this heaven-sent chance of observing her rival unseen.

Gwenn was standing by the shelf where the statue of the Virgin was housed. She had her back to Johanna. Then, as she turned, Johanna saw that she was holding the carving. She seemed to be talking to it. The girl must be mad, Johanna thought hopefully. And salting that idea away in the back of her mind, where it would stay until she found a use for it – perhaps in her bid to win Ned Fletcher – Johanna squatted down on her haunches to watch what St Clair's bastard was doing.

★　★　★

'What do you mean, the wench refuses to do it?' the Dowager Countess snapped. 'We've been generous enough, haven't we?'

Since her fall, Marie de Roncier's legs were shaky, and as she continued to spurn crutches, she had had to submit to being carried down to the hall of Huelgastel. She had consented reluctantly to this indignity, but her son had sweetened the draught by ordering her a chair similar in construction to his own. Throne-like, it had armrests at the side, and Marie had discovered that there was nothing she liked better than to sit in state in her cushioned chair and queen it over her son's kingdom. The Countess Eleanor, who spent more and more time in the chapel, made no objection. Enthroned in her chair, a rug draped across her useless legs, Marie glared at the pedlar from Vannes.

'You've been more than generous, madame,' Conan answered, and, seeing danger in his patroness's flashing black eyes, he fell on his knees. The granite flags were hard and cold through the scant rush covering, but the pedlar had learned early on in life that the nobility liked respect enough to pay for it, and he didn't mind a bit of boot-licking – or, in the Countess's case, slipper-licking – if it meant the noble lady would keep him in her employ.

'Why won't she do it?' Marie demanded testily.

The woman was as tenacious as a terrier with a rat to shake, Conan thought. Then, because this thought set in motion an impolitic smile he had difficulty suppressing, he hastily looked at the floor. Let her think me subservient. Stammering, he tried to explain the unexplainable. 'I . . . I think Johanna has a f . . . fondness for the child.'

'Fondness!' Marie trumpeted, eyes hard with disbelief. 'Fondness! Don't fob me off with lies! You can't tell me that all these months we've been paying your sister to keep her ears to the ground, she's been nursing a fondness for St Clair's brat!'

'I'm sorry, madame, but it's the truth,' Conan mumbled, bowing his head so low he could have kissed the flags at the Countess's feet. He wished his belly did not ache. This bending double did not help his delicate constitution. A drop of that wine on the side trestle would put some fire in his insides . . . Out of the corner of his eye Conan saw the Countess's red satin slippers tap – there was life left in those feet then – and the next moment he felt the sting of her cane as she flicked his temple.

'Oh, stop grovelling, do,' she clucked impatiently. 'I can't make out what you're saying when you mumble at the ground.'

Conan tried to hold the Dowager's gaze, but her coalblack eyes were bolder than any whore in Vannes and, finding himself out-stared, his eyes slipped and came to rest on her bosom.

Marie made a choking sound in her throat. 'It's not good enough,' she said.

'My apologies, madame,' Conan mumbled, uncertain whether she was referring to the disobedience of his sister or his looking at her sagging breasts. To be safe, he shifted his eyes to the wimple covering her throat. Was it a scraggy throat under the spotless linen? The throat of an old bird who had lived too long?

'You're certain she can't be persuaded? Have you offered her more?'

'Aye, madame. I only had to hint at poison, and she went all tragic on me. Saying as how did I think she could harm a child who'd sucked the nourishment from her own p—'

Marie flourished her cane for silence. 'Spare me the sordid details.'

Her bold eyes fastened on something behind Conan and, turning, the pedlar saw Count François de Roncier stalking up the hall. With a sigh, he bent his creaking spine even lower. His stomach gurgled a protest. 'Good evening, mon seigneur.'

'You may go,' Marie said, dismissing him. Conan hesitated, and she glared past her hook of a nose, restively tapping her cane on her chair leg.

'You . . . you will employ me again, won't you, madame?'

Thin, bloodless lips were stretched into what might have been intended as a smile. 'Naturally I'll employ you. I can't rely on your sister, but so far I've not been able to fault you.'

'I . . . I assure you, madame, I am yours to command,' Conan said eagerly, and because he knew it was expected of him, he ignored his griping belly and gave another ingratiating bow. 'My thanks, madame.' Thankful that his sister's mutiny had not lost him a good source of income, Conan bowed himself out.

Marie smiled apologetically at her son. 'I have to admit, Francois, that the plan I discussed with you earlier has failed.'

'The brat's wet nurse refuses to "spice" his gruel?'

'That's it in a nutshell. I'd hoped the wench could be persuaded, and we could have solved your problem with the minimum of bloodshed, and without arousing suspicion. After all, infancy is fraught with dangers; why, your own sister Sybille died when she was barely six months old. It would have been the lesser of the two evils.' Marie sighed. 'However, apparently the pedlar's sister has feelings for St Clair's heir. I regret her attitude, but the girl's brother says she won't budge on this.' Her thin mouth drooped. 'I don't want you to lose ground to St Clair any more than you do, Francois. Perhaps the time has come for firmer measures.'

Francois smiled. 'You've come round to my way of thinking, Mother?'

'Aye, my son. I think that I have.'

Jean was in the stables. He had dismissed the groom and was brushing his dead wife's horse, Dancer, himself. The mare's coat was brown, she had liquid eyes and white stockings on three of her legs. A pretty creature, Jean had bought her for Yolande soon after she and the children had been evicted from Vannes. Yolande had not ridden Dancer since she had first realised that she was pregnant, but Jean knew that she had loved the animal. After Yolande's death, Jean had lifted responsibility for the grooming of the horse from the stable boy's shoulders and taken it upon his own. He had not missed a day since his wife's death. The grooming of Yolande's mare had become in some inexplicable way a ritual whereby he imagined he maintained a link with his wife. No one came running to him with day-to-day concerns while he was in the stable, and he indulged in flights of fancy that a year ago he would have dismissed as unrealistic, maudlin, self-indulgent foolery.

He would, for example, pretend that he was grooming Yolande's mare prior to their taking a ride together. Any moment now, he would think, Yolande will walk smiling through that open door, and I will link my hands together to form a step for her, and she will mount, and we will be off, trotting sedately out of the yard and . . .

'Ned? Ned?'

Recognising his eldest daughter's voice, Jean came out of his daydream with a jolt. He moved to the door and leaned out. Gwenn was tearing across the yard towards the too young and too handsome captain. Jean sighed wearily and his brows jutted, for Gwenn was barefoot and her skirts were bunched up round her knees. She was running so fast she looked certain to run into the Englishman. Momentarily forgetting his bereavement, Jean slipped into an older, happier, mode of thinking and resolved to remind Yolande to have a word with the girl. Then, remembrance shivered cold through his veins. Yolande would not speak to Gwenn, or anyone, not in this life. Yolande was dead. It was up to him to sort his daughter out . . .

'Ned?' Gwenn panted. To add insult to injury, as his daughter slithered to a halt in front of the captain, Jean saw her grasp his arms to steady herself.

'Mistress?' Ned responded warily, and disengaged

himself as soon as he was able, for he had seen Jean hovering hawk-eyed in the stable doorway.

Gwenn tossed a shining but dishevelled rope of hair over one shoulder. 'Ned, can we ride—'

'Gwenn, what are you about?' Jean interrupted as forcefully as he could. It was a task these days, finding energy to be forceful about anything. A month ago he had finally taken his heir's case to the justiciary to establish his claim to the de Wirce lands. He had made his hold reasonably secure; he had promoted Fletcher to captain, taken on more men-at-arms. He knew he ought to do more, but lately Jean left everything to Waldin. He had lost heart.

'P . . . Papa?'

'If you could see yourself,' Jean strode over, 'pelting across the yard with your skirts hitched up. You're a disgrace, Gwenn, a disgrace.'

'I'm sorry, Papa, but I'm bursting for a ride, and I thought Ned—'

Jean made a hook of one brow. 'Ned?'

'My apologies, Papa. I forgot . . .' Gwenn trailed off. Her father's face was set harder than the Israelites' stone tablets. She lifted speaking eyes to her father's, but was prudent enough to keep her tongue wedged between her teeth and any rebellious comments locked inside her. Her father looked so tired.

'Get inside, Gwenn,' Jean said coldly.

'Aye, sir.' She bobbed him a curtsy.

'And do something about your hair, will you? It looks like a haystack this morning. What would your Mama have said?'

A hand flew to her hair. 'I'm sorry, Papa.' Head up, she walked back to the hall.

'And as for you, Captain,' Jean roused himself to speak severely, 'leave my daughter alone, will you? By Christ, if I catch you speaking familiarly to Mistress Gwenn . . .'

The threat was left hanging in the air, but Ned understood. He would lose his captaincy and would have to go elsewhere for his daily bread.

'I'll try, sir,' Ned answered, 'but sometimes I find it a trial, because your daughter . . .'

Jean found a smile. 'I know, lad,' he said, with complete understanding. 'She forgets the difference in your stations. I should have found her a husband long since, but now that Lady Yolande is gone, she is a great comfort, and I am loth to lose her.'

'Aye, sir.' Ned sympathised with that. He did not want to lose Gwenn either, not that she would ever be his, of course, but the idea of her marrying and leaving Kermaria left him sick inside.

'But,' Jean's voice took on a hard edge, 'it is up to you, Captain Fletcher, to keep her at a proper distance. It is up to you to remind her.'

'Aye, sir.'

Nodding gruffly at Ned, Jean returned to Dancer, and picked up the curry comb. He knew he ought to resume enquiries and choose a husband for Gwenn. He had a couple of candidates in mind, but after a few minutes' miserable contemplation, he abandoned his line of thought. It didn't cheer him at all.

Pensively, he stroked Dancer's immaculate coat. He didn't want to lose his daughter. The loss of Yolande was enough for one lifetime. Apart from his children, Jean had nothing left worth losing. Another, twisted, smile surfaced. The one positive thing to come out of Yolande's death was that he had become immune to fear. Nothing on this earth could intimidate him. Having lost his darling, he was beyond anyone's reach. And as for title to the land that he had coveted for so long, he had his heir now, and doubtless the lawcourts would decide in Philippe's favour. It was up to Philippe to pursue that when he was grown. Jean no longer cared.

Alan shortened his reins and, waving Duke Geoffrey's mounted guard to one side, he looked about the port of Vannes with interest. It was high tide, and the sky was overcast. Cloud-grey water lapped near the top of the jetties. In the mouth of the harbour a fishing boat had been moored, and a lone cormorant stood on its bow, wings outstretched. It had been diving. Alan smiled as the bird shook its wings in the breeze to dry them. The smells of a thriving quayside, of salt and oysters, of crabs and fishes' entrails were inescapable.

It was almost a year since the Duke's business had last brought Alan to Vannes, and it hadn't altered in that time. It was true that work had progressed well on the cathedral. The walls were soaring up, and it was rumoured the bishop was bringing glaziers all the way from Paris to install some of the new coloured glass that had been so admired in Nôtre Dame. But St Peter's aside, Vannes was unchanged.

Alan looked towards the Duke. He was riding Firebrand, a chestnut courser Alan had always admired, and he was surrounded by his vast, glittering retinue. Alan grimaced. This was one aspect of life with the Duke that he could do without, the hangers-on. There were always hangers-on, except when the Duke made a rare escape to one of his bolt-holes. And look at them. Knights in their court finery, lords wearing heavy velvets, embroidered hats, great plumes, and gauntlets encrusted with seed pearls, riding horses with ribbons plaited through shiny well-groomed manes as if the poor animals were lovesick girls. Why, half of those pretty, plumed knights didn't know one end of a sword from the other. There on the quayside was all the noise and brashness of a ducal court used to moving around the country wherever its duke went. It was a pageant, staged to impress. But did it? Alan noted a handful of fishermen watching the show, but they appeared unmoved, their eyes cynical as they took in the Phrygian caps, the bright flowing capes, and the gilded harnesses. The fisherfolk were unimpressed. Alan felt he understood. What had the Duke's court to do with the grinding poverty of their lives?

The court was on the quayside to meet a ship from

Nantes carrying a new warhorse for the Duke. He hoped to have a few months' drilling with his latest acquisition before trying his luck at the King of France's tournament in Paris. They would shortly be leaving the Morbihan Gulf, riding north for Rennes and the practise lists there. Alan looked forward to it; the tourney and war games were one aspect of his service that he enjoyed. But before they departed, Alan intended to ask for leave to visit his brother William, at St Félix's Monastery, situated in the forest about ten miles west of Vannes. He only hoped that William was still at the monastery and that his talents as a painter had not been required elsewhere.

Alan kneed his mount through the crowd of courtiers. 'What's the name of the vessel, Your Grace?' he asked. He had seen François de Roncier's colours flying from a number of ships, and concluded the Count must yet be a force in the area.

'Name? Oh. *Sea Serpent*.'

'It's in. There.' Alan pointed past a wide-brimmed hat at a slender ship with a green painted snake curving along its prow, squeezed between two hulks flying de Roncier's flag.

'Out of my way, Martell,' the Duke said. 'And try and keep this lot out of it, will you?'

'Yes, Your Grace,' replied a handsome young knight clad simply in brown, a pheasant among the peacocks.

'Come on, le Bret.' Duke Geoffrey spurred through his courtiers towards the ship. Even as the Duke and Alan trotted up, the charger was being led off. He was vast, with heavy bones and crushing hoofs the size of trenchers. Every time he put a hoof down, the gangplank creaked and shuddered. His coat was dark as a moonless night. The Duke's Master of the Horse was no runt, being a long stick of a man who topped Alan by over a head, but the Duke's new warhorse dwarfed him.

'Jesu!' Alan let out an appreciative whistle. 'I hardly reach his shoulders!'

Duke Geoffrey grinned. 'He'll even the odds for me, eh, le Bret?'

'Fit for a king,' Alan said, sincerely.

The Duke's grin enlarged. 'That's what I hoped you'd say. Philip will be green.'

'And the stallion will bear your colours well, Your Grace. His midnight coat will be handsome against the black and white.'

'That had occurred to me.' The Duke dismounted, his eyes fixed on the warhorse.

Alan decided that now would be as good a time as any to put in his request for leave. 'Your Grace?'

'Mmm?' The Duke dropped Firebrand's reins and moved forward.

Jumping down to the quayside, Alan stooped for the abandoned courser's reins. 'About my leave—'

'Not now, le Bret.' Duke Geoffrey put his hand to the coal-black withers which rippled under his touch. The stallion stood firm, and blew out through his nose.

'Your Grace, at Suscinio last August you said I could take my leave in a month or two. It's April now.'

The Duke sent him a preoccupied look, and turned back to his stallion. 'Is he ready, Brian?'

'As ready as he'll ever be, Your Grace,' the Master of the Horse declared.

'Fetch his saddle.'

Brian looked concerned. 'But Your Grace . . . in town?'

'In town,' the Duke insisted.

Alan patted Firebrand's silken neck. 'We're forgotten, my friend,' he said. Firebrand's ears twitched. Alan raised his voice. 'Your Grace?'

The Duke frowned, he was anxious to try out his steed's paces. 'Christ's wounds, le Bret, I thought you'd gone back to your troop.' Brian was returning with the saddle. Grabbing it, the Duke threw it over the war-horse's broad back himself. 'Go on then, le Bret. Where did you say you wanted to go?'

'St Félix-in-the-Wood.'

'Never heard of it.'

'It's near Kermaria, Your Grace.'

The Duke straightened. 'Kermaria. That name's familiar. Who holds it, do you know?'

'Sir Jean St Clair.'

The Duke rubbed his chin. 'A tenant of mine, a small one, but nevertheless . . . Has he sworn fealty?'

'Not to my knowledge, Your Grace.'

The Duke grunted. 'You may have a week's leave, le Bret, on condition that you visit Kermaria on my behalf. I want a full report on this Sir Jean, and the state of his manor, number of serfs, freemen, soldiers, and so on. The place was derelict, but that may have changed. It may even be useful these days. Sort it out with your men, and ask my chaplain for a letter of introduction to take with you. I'm to meet Duchess Constance, and if I'm gone when you return, make your way to Rennes. I'll need you there.'

'My thanks,' Alan said, well content to have a legitimate excuse to visit his cousin. He had often wondered how the boy was faring. A lot could have happened to young Ned in the two years sice Alan had seen him. And apparently St Félix's cell was a stone's throw from Kermaria. Alan was owed rather more than a week's leave, but at this moment a week was all he wanted. He gestured to the chestnut courser whose reins he still held. 'Shall I have Firebrand stabled, Your Grace?'

The Duke tightened his warhorse's girth. 'No, you can take him, le Bret. I know you'll enjoy riding him. Brian here can take your mount.'

'Thank you, Your Grace.' Alan tossed his own mount's reins to the Master of the Horse, switched his gear to Firebrand, and mounted him swiftly, lest the Duke should change his mind. He nudged the shining chestnut flanks with his heels and trotted briskly towards his men.

The larks that were carolling over the fields to the east could be heard clear over Kermaria marsh. But the larks were the first creatures to waken, and as their song was the only sign of life, it went largely unheard. Dawn was an hour away. The whispering sedge and rushes, which a sharp frost had coated with a delicate film of ice, stood dumb, unmoved by wind or wildfowl. The coots and moorhens, snug in nests in the reeds, slept on. The stillness was absolute. It radiated from the marsh, a web of silence spun so large, it cloaked not only mere and reeds but also the bridge, the peasants' cots, the stables, and all of St Clair's tower right up to the sentry who sat behind a merlon with his red head nodding over his spear. Everything was snared, gently but firmly, in that web.

The disturbance was small at first. Hardly more than a shiver in the chill, dusky air, an imperceptible ripple of movement which shook the strands of the web, and then faded. The silence seemed to grow heavier. Then the movement came again, only this time it was stronger. There was an insignificant sucking noise, as though someone had been marching through the marsh and had inadvertently put their foot into a boggy patch and was pulling it free.

'Hell!' A harsh whisper rattled the reeds. A lantern flap opened a crack, and as a yellow wedge of light streamed forth, it lit up a fenland bristling with men who stood taller than the fresh willow shoots pushing their way to the sky. The men's spears were more pointed than the frost-tipped reeds, and in the light of the lantern they flashed more brightly.

The big man holding the lantern clenched his fist and controlled an urge to strike the fool who had broken the silence. 'Quiet, dog,' Otto Malait mouthed.

'Damn sedge,' the trooper muttered, licking blood from his palm. He displayed a vivid slash running across his hand. 'Edge is sharper than m'sword.'

Otto's hand rose and he delivered a swingeing clout to the fellow's ears. 'Be silent,' he hissed, and flicked the horn lantern cover, extinguishing the light.

A sedge warbler gave a warning cry as Otto pushed

forwards. The web of silence trembled. A moorhen shot out from under his boots, echoing the warbler's note of alarm. Resigned that the silence was lost, Otto ploughed on. He knew his orders, and his men must cover as much ground as possible if they were to be in position before the sun melted the frost on the silver-tipped, shivering reeds.

Count de Roncier planned to lead his attack from the north, while Otto had been commanded to direct his men via the marsh to the village. From there they were to force their way into the courtyard. Otto wondered if de Roncier was in position. If this raid was to be effective, they must strike before first light.

Katarin's whimpering disturbed Gwenn. 'What is it, little one?' She yawned, turning in bed so she could embrace her sister.

'Thunder,' Katarin muttered, burying her head in Gwenn's shoulder. 'Katarin doesn't like thunder.'

Gwenn listened. 'But that's not thunder, Katarin. That sounds like someone trying to get in.' She pushed her sister's clinging hands to one side and strained her ears. 'No, it most certainly is not thunder. Someone's forcing the—' Gwenn broke off. This was no casual visitor seeking shelter.

Wondering what had happened to the guard and why the alarm bell was not ringing, Gwenn swung out of bed and groped for an unlit candle stub. 'Stay there, Katarin. Watch Philippe. Papa! Papa!' she called, running to the solar hearth and shoving the wick of the candle into the faintly glowing embers. The candle sputtered reluctantly into life, and, belatedly, the tocsin began to peal.

Jean emerged from his bedchamber half clothed and buckling on his sword. 'Get dressed,' he ordered. Snatching up his shield, he dived for the twisting stairs. 'Keep Katarin and Philippe up here. If necessary, don't hesitate to bar this door.'

'Aye, Papa.' Barring the door would be a last, hopeless measure, for it would mean that all her father's men were . . . Fear tied a knot in Gwenn's belly, and her mind shied away from the gruesome images her imagination conjured up. Her father could not have meant that. Gwenn wondered what he had meant, and how she was to judge when locking the door was necessary. A thousand other questions milled round in her sleep-dazed mind, but they too must go unanswered.

Holding her candle high, Gwenn's gaze swept the solar. The glazed eyes of half a dozen women blinked up at her. There was no sign of panic yet, only confusion. The thundering assault on the hall door had settled into a rhythm so regular it was almost soothing.

'You heard my father,' Gwenn was pleased her voice was steady, for she did not want to set them screeching, 'we must get dressed. Mary, light the candles, if you please. And Johanna, I'd be grateful if you could come and see to Philippe.' Candle aloft, she led Johanna back to her niche, trying to remember if there were any weapons up here. They all had their eating knives, naturally, and there was a dagger at the bottom of Izabel's ancient chest.

A tearing crack, which could be nothing else but a solid oak door being hewed apart, made her miss a step. A roar from below, and she felt herself grow pale. She heard the clash of steel on steel. A man howled like a wolf and fell silent, and the silence was worse than the howl. Hot wax spilled on her hand, burned her. She gasped.

'Mistress?' Johanna's dark eyes were watchful.

The wet nurse was commendably cool. Gwenn found this surprising, but had no time to ponder on the vagaries of Johanna's character. Directing her mind to the seemingly impossible task of keeping her candle steady, Gwenn went to rouse her sister. 'Come on, Katarin,' she said brightly. It was a miracle her tongue worked at all, for her throat was dry as dust. 'We're rising early today.'

Katarin had her thumb in her mouth. She removed

it long enough to ask, 'Why?'

Gwenn wrenched her lips into a smile. 'We are going to pray.' The thumb came out again, and Gwenn's heart lurched. Please God, she prayed, don't let Katarin start asking questions, not now.

'What's all that crashing, Gwenn?'

'The men are practising,' Gwenn answered briskly. It was a feeble answer, for Katarin was no idiot child and knew well enough that the men never practised in the small hours. But it was the only explanation her beleaguered mind tossed up, and if she kept her voice firm enough, perhaps Katarin would believe her. 'Come along, Katarin. Prayers.'

The thumb went in, and obediently Katarin climbed from the bed. Blood-curdling noises were being channelled up the stairwell. Gwenn shut her ears, and found her sister's clothes. The child was old enough to dress unaided, so, having handed her sister her dress, Gwenn rooted in the coffer for the dagger. Digging it out, she looked disparagingly at it. It wasn't much of a dagger; the blade was dull, the whalebone haft yellow and cracked with age; it couldn't have seen a whetstone in years. She ran a finger down one edge, and grimaced, it was blunt. However, it looked stronger than her eating knife . . .

She shook her head. What use was one dagger when it appeared they'd been invaded by an army?

The solar brightened. Mary was holding a couple of reed dips to the cressets. Klara whimpered. Bella the dairymaid began to sob. Gwenn clenched her teeth. Like frightened sheep, the other women clustered round Bella, making sympathetic noises. Gwenn stalked to the centre of the chamber. 'Think of the child, Bella,' she said sternly.

'But, mistress—'

'Will someone lead us in prayer?' Gwenn forestalled her. Mary wore a calmer face than the rest of the flock. 'Mary?'

'Aye, mistress. As you will.'

As Gwenn waved the women into place round the Virgin, the flaring cresset light fell on a mason's hammer and chisel that had been kicked into a cobwebby corner. A week ago her father had set a mason to work on a new privy, and the man must have left his tools out, handy for finishing his work.

'Hail Mary,' Mary began to intone.

Gwenn shivered, and was for an instant whirled back to Lady Day two years ago. She was in St Peter's Cathedral, listening to the Black Monk preaching. She could see two mercenaries leaning against the cathedral porch. She was fleeing them, running, running . . .

'. . . Full of grace. Blessed art thou amongst women . . .'

Gwenn took a grip on herself. It was Mary taking the prayers, not Father Jerome. And the two mercenaries were no longer callous strangers, but Ned Fletcher, her friend, and Alan le Bret who, while he was no friend, had saved her life. Dragging her mind to the present, Gwenn moved to the corner where the mason's tools lay. They might make weapons.

'. . . Blessed is the fruit of thy womb, Jesus . . .' Mary dropped to her knees and the other women followed her lead.

The hammer was old, its handle worn, but it was solid. The chisel needed sharpening, but – Gwenn's mouth twisted – it was no blunter than her dagger. She'd hate to have to use them, but if she must . . . She flexed her shoulders. They had three possible weapons between them. Three weapons, seven women, and two children. She shot a furtive glance at the door. Exactly what were they up against? Women and children would be safe, wouldn't they?

A chilling screech rang in their ears. Klara moaned. 'Enough of that,' Gwenn said, tightly. Klara ignored her, rocking to and fro as she knelt. Her moaning rose, became a wail.

Mary chanted more loudly. 'Save us now and at the hour of our death.'

Katarin emerged from their sleeping alcove and looked at them with a child's wide-eyed curiosity. Gwenn dredged up a smile and held out her hand. 'Good girl, you're dressed. Come here, sweetheart.' And wrapping her sister's cold hand securely in hers, Gwenn knelt to pray.

Chapter Eighteen

Waldin St Clair, champion-at-arms, was in his element. Glad to be in harness again after his recent life of ease, his sword whirled before him, clearing a route directly to the centre of the maelstrom in the hall. Surrounded by his brother's enemies and cutting them down as though they were no more than stalks of corn and his sword a reaper's scythe, he was outnumbered but undaunted. He bared his teeth in a fierce grin and welcomed the frantic pounding of his heart. The blood rushed invigoratingly through his veins. He felt alive as he hadn't for weeks.

The clamour was deafening. It was like the mêlée in a tournament, with one notable difference. In the mêlée, Waldin's inbuilt sense of chivalry made him temper the blows he had delivered. Chivalry did not shackle his hands today. There was no need for him to take care to avoid giving a death-dealing blow or a crippling strike. These lousy assassins had crept up on Kermaria like thieves in the night and deserved as bad a death as he could give them. They were allied to a lord whose quarrel with Jean ranked them lower than the meanest outlaw. In Waldin's eyes, they had signed their own death warrants.

François de Roncier was fighting by the great fire, and though mailed and helmeted so his shock of copper hair was concealed, his round, ruddy visage was plain for anyone to see. He had stepped outside the law in loosing his cutthroats on Kermaria. Barely a month ago Jean had taken his claim to the de Wirce lands to the lawcourts. The judgment had not been given, and it might well be made in the Count's favour, for his family had held the land for years and possession was nine-tenths of the law. If the courts found in favour of de Roncier, this mindless slaughter would be for nothing.

And it was slaughter. One keen, professional glance told Waldin that the couple of dozen men who guarded his brother's manor were outnumbered four to one. Though Waldin's own dexterity and the tactics he had passed on to Jean's guard tipped the scales a little in Kermaria's favour, most of the St Clair men would probably meet their maker before the sun rose. Against so large a force, they did not have a chance. Waldin was not afraid to die – not this way. For this would be a glorious death. He would go with his sword in his hand. He would go cleanly, fighting a just cause.

The winter of 1184/5 had brought him the odd twinge of rheumatism, his first. It had been a depressing warning of what was in store. Reluctantly, Waldin had resigned himself to a slow diminishing of that vitality by which he had lived. If his fate was to grow old slowly and painfully, growing less mobile and more feeble with each passing season, then so be it. He had managed to convince himself that he was resigned to his fate. But now, with his blood running hot and fierce, he acknowledged he had been deluding himself. He did not want to die a slow, lingering death with his faculties diminishing year by year. And all at once he was presented with the opportunity to go the way he would have chosen – the warrior's way. And for his brother's sake, Waldin vowed to give a good account of himself before his soul was hewn from his body.

Waldin saw Jean's squire, young Roger de Herion, go down squealing, a spear through his belly, and winced. He repaid the man who'd skewered Roger with a clean thrust. 'More than you deserve,' he muttered, pulling his sword clear. There was no time to wipe his sword clean on his victim's leather breeches before another of the Count's men stood before him. Buoyed up, exhilarated, Waldin parried thrust after thrust. Another de Roncier heathen threw down the gage. Waldin ran him through with cold efficiency, but instantly another sprang up to take his place. The odds were stacked against them, and knowing that his end must come soon, Waldin's mind worked feverishly, as though it could squeeze several years' thinking into one minute. Jean, Waldin recalled, scorned his love of glory. Jean would not appreciate the honour in dying outnumbered. Jean would not want his lifeblood to drain away on the floor of his hall. He scanned the room for his brother. Jean had engaged de Roncier himself and, like most of the St Clair men, he had not had time to don his hauberk.

'You won't get away with this,' Jean gasped, making a pass at the Count.

François side-stepped nimbly and lifted his lips in a snarl. 'You think not?'

Jean made another stroke. 'They'll know who did this.' François lunged, aiming for the knight's heart. Jean turned his opponent's blade aside with a grace that brought a smile to Waldin's lips.

'Neatly done, brother,' Waldin breathed approvingly, and started clearing a path towards them.

'The Duke will suspect,' Jean ground out, 'when it comes to light we're at odds in the courts.'

François shook his head.

'Who else would dare break the Duke's peace? This land is his, and his writ is absolute here.'

François held up a mailed hand. 'If you'll hold off a moment?'

Jean nodded, and shifted his sword to one side, eyes wary, but listening.

'Misplaced chivalry. That stinking cur does not deserve it. Make him eat steel,' Waldin growled, but there was too much din for him to be heard.

A wolfish gleam fired in the ruined hazel eyes. 'You must know that a band of pirates have taken to mooring their ships in the Small Sea,' François said. 'They've been working their way inland, up the estuaries, of which yours is but one. They take cover in the forest. I think you'll find it's the pirates who shoulder the blame for this, not I.'

A blond hulk blocked Waldin's view, and made a pass. Waldin turned it aside without conscious thought and tried to forge towards his brother and the Count, but the hulk had a long reach and barred his way. Waldin swore, for his mind was set on purging the world of the parasite that was de Roncier.

His brother and the Count re-engaged. Little by little de Roncier was driving Jean back to the tiled hearth. Waldin frowned. Another step and Jean would be dancing on hot ashes. He saw his brother's sword sweep wide of the mark, and his frown deepened. That was not Jean's style, a four-year-old could have done better. What was he up to?

But almost before that question had finished forming, Waldin's febrile mind threw up an answer. Jean was not even trying. Staring at his brother, it dawned on Waldin that for months they'd been gazing at the face of a man who had already suffered a mortal blow and was scarcely keeping body and soul together. Behind the front, his brother had crumbled to dust. Jean had relinquished responsibility for all military matters, and he had not merely been providing a bored brother with something to stop him twiddling his thumbs. The delegation had been total. Jean had had the stuffing knocked out of him. He had lost interest in life, he had given up. He remembered the moves – witness that brilliant warding pass he had made a few moments ago – but he was not choosing to use them. He was fighting feebly. He was already dead. Jean had lost his soul; bonded with Yolande's, when her spirit had flown to the skies, Jean's had accompanied her. Since the day his wife had died, Jean had been a shell of a man.

Waldin flicked his wrist, and severed an artery in the neck of a de Roncier trooper. Petrified, the soldier stared at Waldin with the eyes of a man who knew that he had been dealt a mortal blow. He toppled slowly, soundlessly, his blood pumping into the rushes. Jean was practically in the fireplace. Stepping over the fallen man and forcing his way through the scrimmage, Waldin went to give him aid. It was far better to go on your own home ground, he thought with a queer kind of relish. Far better to go fighting for a brother you loved than to die on a stranger's land for a cause you had no share in. He would have his warrior's death, and it would be a burning, glorious, defiant death. He'd fight to the bitter end, and if he couldn't take François de Roncier with him, he'd have to trust in God to see that that swine's felonies did not go unrewarded.

Crouching in the doorway, Gwenn stared at a scene from the mouth of Hell.

Gone was the well-ordered hall she had sat and sewed in with her mother. Pallets still strewed the floor, mute testimony to the unexpectedness of the attack. Lying across the bedrolls were bodies; but the bodies were broken, bloodied bodies, and the sleep those men were sleeping was not one from which they would ever awaken. Men were screaming. Men were groaning. Men were chillingly silent. Transfixed by the scene in her father's hall, Gwenn was unaware that her sister had left the women and was climbing down the winding stairs after her.

Catching sight of Roger, her father's squire, for one moment Gwenn fancied him festooned with red silk ribbons. Then she realised the lad was beribboned with his own guts. Her gorge rose, and she reeled back, till her shoulder hit the solid stone wall. She forced her gaze back to the conflict. She was rigid with fear for her father. And where was Waldin, and her brother, Raymond? Were all the men she loved dead already? What of Ned? At first she could not mark any of them among the seething mass of fighting, living men. Her eyes were skimming the lifeless forms sprawled over pallets and rushes, when the fray cleared in front of her and she was granted a clear view of her father.

Jean and Waldin were standing hip to hip, measuring swords with a man whom Gwenn did not recognise. She had picked up enough knowledge of arms to know at a glance that the man's hauberk and helm were out of the ordinary. This must be the detested Count de Roncier. He shouted hoarsely, and in an instant four soldiers were at their lord's side, their swords directed at the St Clair brothers.

Gwenn's breath was coming in fast, uneven gasps. She tried to swallow and couldn't. Though it was unnecessary, for the brothers had seen de Roncier, she tried to shout a warning. The words lodged in her throat. Her legs were unable to support her, and she sank to her knees.

A shadow fell over her. A blood-smeared face stared wildly into hers and her heart dropped and thumped about in her stomach. Under the red streaks, the face was pale, and one that she knew. 'Ned!' she blurted, giddy with relief, for she had feared that her last moments had come.

'Get upstairs!' Ned gasped, pointing with his sword.

Without his gambeson he looked alarmingly vulnerable. He had a helmet, but it was dented. His tunic was torn and hanging off one shoulder. His knuckles were scraped raw.

'Ned . . .' Sick with fear, Gwenn pinned her eyes on his face, for bloody and changed as her father's captain was, he was at least recognisable. Nothing else in that hell of a hall was the least bit familiar.

'Move, Gwenn.' He was so concerned for her safety, that not only did he forget the title that was her due, he reinforced his command by giving her a bruising kick on the thigh. 'Get upstairs,' he said, and groaned in frustration when she didn't obey him.

'Papa!' White as bone, Gwenn looked past Ned at the figures grouped round the fireplace. Ned's fist clenched. 'Papa!' Gwenn repeated, on a rising note. She shot Ned a look of agony. 'Where's the glory in this, Ned?'

'Gwenn, you *must*—'

'This is butchery, not glory. Look! Five against two!' Ned whirled round. 'Give them aid, Ned. Please.'

It was then that Katarin reached the comfort of her sister's skirts.

'Katarin!' Gwenn exclaimed, and her hands came up to shield Katarin's eyes.

'I'll help them,' Ned promised. 'But you *must* go up. For your sister if not for yourself.'

Gwenn nodded and, sword up, Ned dived back into the mêlée.

If Gwenn was rigid with fear, Katarin had slipped into another world altogether. The little girl's sixth sense had informed her that today was going to be worse than the day her mother had died. Afraid that Gwenn might be stolen from her too, she had crept after her sister. The women upstairs had tried to restrain her, but Katarin had wanted Gwenn, no other would do. Katarin wound her arms tight as bindweed about her sister's narrow waist.

Ned fought his way to the fire. 'Sir Jean! I'm with you!'

Jean grunted acknowledgement. Both he and his brother had a crimson-tipped sword in one hand and a dagger in the other. They were fighting like Saracens, but it was only a matter of time before one of them went down.

'Get out, Ned!' Jean gasped between strokes.

'Sir?' Ned shouldered an iron candlestand onto one of de Roncier's company, and found himself smiling when the man backed onto Denis the Red's blade.

Jean jerked his head at the stairwell. 'Gwenn . . .'

Ned's heart missed a beat, for Gwenn had not gone up as she had promised. She and her sister were kneeling, and Gwenn's eyes were staring straight at them, watching them like a frightened rabbit watches the hound that is about to tear it limb from limb.

'Get her out!' Jean yelled. Sweat poured down his forehead and into his brown eyes. 'Get them upstairs!'

De Roncier lunged, and a thin ruby line sprang across Jean's lean cheek. The blood mingled with his perspiration.

Clashing swords with a de Roncier henchman, Ned saw another drop to his knees. Waldin was giving a good account of himself.

'To me!' François de Roncier bellowed. 'To me!' And two more of his company sprang out of nowhere like dragon's teeth in the ancient fable. Both were confident enough to be grinning, and one of them had been causing havoc with an axe. He was no stranger to Ned.

Ned gulped. 'Malait!'

Recognition flared in the cool Nordic eyes and, astonishingly, the flailing axe paused. 'Greetings – Fletcher, isn't it? You switched horses once. I take it you're not of a mind to do it again?'

The only response was a deft twist of Ned's wrist, a trick Waldin had taught him. It sent Ned's blade slicing through the air and wiped the smirk from the Viking's lips. To save his nose, Otto leapt backwards and, slipping in some blood, went sprawling.

'Fletcher!' Jean roared. 'Run, damn you!' Breathing hard, he punctuated his words with wide, sweeping sword strokes. 'God curse you . . . I'm commanding you . . . Run! Take Gwenn, and run.'

'Wh . . . where?'

'The woods, Christ's wounds! Anywhere but here! Do what you have to, but keep Gwenn and the children safe.' Never had Ned received an order more to his liking, but he hesitated, and a razor-sharp blade whistled past his ear. 'Well? Do you obey me?'

Ned put on a ragged smile, remembering how St Clair warned him off his daughter. 'Aye, sir. I'd die for Mistress Gwenn.'

'I hope . . .' Jean was tiring '. . . it won't come to that. If . . . If it comes to the worst . . . take them north . . . Relatives . . . north . . .'

'Where?'

'Gwenn knows.' Jean gasped, and his cheeks went grey. The blade of his opponent dripped scarlet. Drop-

314

ping his dagger, Jean clapped a hand to his ribs.

Ned started forwards. 'Sir Jean!'

But Waldin caught Ned's left hand and thrust something at him. 'Go, lad! Take this. Don't let her look back.' And the champion booted Ned in the small of the back, leaving him no choice but to race for the stairs.

Ned thrust whatever it was that Waldin had given him down the front of his tunic.

Jean flung a dazzling smile at his foes and made a dreadful pass that a limbless leper could have evaded. François de Roncier's men closed in for the kill. The final blow, when it came, was greeted with another of those extraordinary smiles.

Blackness. Tumult. Screaming. Pressed to her sister's side, Katarin's mind was spinning faster than a wheel. Her sister had made a blindfold of her hands and had covered her eyes, so she could see nothing. She felt Gwenn's body jerk, as though she'd been hit. Someone screeched. To the child, the screaming sounded like the end of the world. Who was it? Not Gwenn? Not Papa? There was no comfort in the blinkered dark behind Gwenn's hands. Katarin felt smothered. Was not death dark? A war had broken out in her father's hall, and she had to see.

Impulsively, she shoved at Gwenn's hands. They fell at the first push. Her hazel eyes blinked into flaring torchlight which made monsters of the men upon whom she gazed. Katarin's heart banged louder than a drum and seemed to add to the uproar.

One of the monsters was tearing towards her. His eyes shone like blue lamps and his helmet was askew. His cheek was streaked with red paint, and there was more of it daubed on his hair. It was a moment before Katarin realised that the monster was Captain Fletcher. She whimpered. And because his expression was more frightening than the darkness beneath Gwenn's blanketing hands, she looked beyond him, and saw what no child should ever see.

She saw her father as the cold steel of his enemy's

sword was buried in his chest. Katarin saw everything: the sudden gush of bubbling blood on her father's lips, the gloating triumph which lit the eyes of the shining metal man towering over her father, and the impotent rage which distorted her uncle's face. She even saw her father's final, serene smile.

How peaceful Papa looks, Katarin thought, in all this horror. Death sits well on him. And with a pang, she wondered if Papa would be able to talk to Mama now he had joined her. Katarin would like to be peaceful too . . .

Ned hauled on Gwenn's arm, trying to lift her. Terrified that she and her sister were to be torn asunder, Katarin squeaked, buried her face in the warmth of Gwenn's breast, and clung like fury. She'd seen enough.

Blackness. Tumult. Screaming.

'Come, Gwenn. Come with me,' Ned said urgently. Katarin felt herself lifted. She shuddered. Was there no peace left on the earth? She only wanted to be quiet and peaceful.

'Take Katarin.' That was Gwenn's voice. Katarin screwed up her eyes in case they should open without her willing it. Didn't Gwenn want to be with her? Releasing her sister, Katarin slapped her hands over her ears. She'd heard enough. Outside her own, small self, there was nothing. With eyes and ears closed, Katarin began stumbling about in her mind for a quiet place where she could hide from the ravening monsters. And while Ned carried Katarin up the twisting stairs, the child found what she was searching for. It was a refuge, a haven, deep in a secret part of her she had not visited before. It was heaven, for no one could touch her when she was there. She was safe. Her eyes remained closed. The rosebud mouth relaxed. Her private retreat was all brightness and calm. There were no dark shadows which might shroud the Devil. God was not there either, because since last August when her mother had died, Katarin had stopped believing in

God. But there was peace in abundance, peace and quiet. And because peace was all Katarin wanted, she resolved never to leave her sanctuary; never, ever again.

Casting a final look round her father's devastated hall, Gwenn noted, with the cold detachment of one who has taken more than she can stomach, that Raymond had fallen. Her brother lay on his belly in the rushes, still as death. His sword had been knocked from his hand, and his head was twisted to one side, brown hair half concealing a gaping wound across temple and ear, which even at this distance Gwenn could see glistened with congealing blood. The rest of him was pale as alabaster. The Archangel Gabriel could not help Raymond.

With a resolution that yesterday she would have condemned as callousness, Gwenn slammed the door at the bottom of the stairs, threw the heavy bolts home, and darted after Ned and Katarin. At the top of the spiral, she rammed the second door shut and barred that too.

'Thank God your father built these doors,' Ned said, frantically calculating how long they would hold out against a sustained assault. And more as reassurance for himself, he added. 'The twists of the spiral favour me.'

Stooping to pick up her sister, Gwenn frowned. 'I don't see—'

'The stairs were constructed to favour the defenders – the turns favour a right-handed swordsman at the top,' Ned explained briefly, while he sized up the solar with a military eye. This was the first time he had entered the women's quarters and private family rooms. They were smaller than he had imagined, barely large enough to hold the beds. He saw nothing that he could put to use in this crisis, not even another door to barricade the children behind.

Feet thudded overhead. Looking up at the rafters, Ned swallowed a curse. His worst fears had not included de Roncier's company scaling the tower walls. If the Count's wolves were prowling the ramparts . . .

Most of the women were weeping, save two. Of these braver souls, one – he recognised Mary – was crouched before an ugly pink statue of Our Lady, praying. The other, the wet nurse Johanna, was cradling St Clair's heir. Seeing that Johanna's dark eyes were pinned on him, Ned addressed her. 'Did anyone think to bolt the door to the parapet walk?'

The wet nurse started, and blushed like a coy virgin. 'No. No. I don't think—'

'Christ save us!' Ned tried to distinguish the thumps and scurryings overhead, but with the uproar from below, it was impossible.

'What is it, Ned?' Gwenn's touch on his arm made him start.

He did his best to smile. 'We're bottled up. They've got to the roof, and they'll be coming at that door from above and below. When I defend you from the landing—'

'No, Ned!' She saw immediately what he was driving at. 'It would be suicide! You must stay in here.'

Crazily, Ned's spirits lifted. So she did care, a little. Then he remembered he was the only protection she had. 'But mistress, I must—'

'Defend us from here. I want you in here.'

It made little difference, Ned thought wretchedly, whether he fought in or out of the solar. In the end, the outcome would be the same. So much for St Clair's carefully constructed stairs. He spread his hands.

'Very well,' he said. 'You'd best prepare yourself.'

Juggling her sister in her arms, Gwenn drew a battered dagger from her sleeve. It was rusty enough to have belonged to one of the knights of the Round Table. 'They'll not get me.'

'No, mistress,' Ned said as reassuringly as he could. 'They'll not harm a woman.'

The wet nurse gave a distressed murmur and clutched the baby to her breast. 'They'll hurt my little lamb though, won't they, Captain?'

Ned bit his lip and placed a bruised hand on the baby's fluffy hair. He couldn't find it in his heart to lie to the woman, whose dark melting eyes were brimming with great love for the infant. There was no doubt that de Roncier had come for the babe, and it was beginning to look as though God had decreed that Philippe St Clair's lifespan would be short. If only Sir Jean's much-vaunted improvements had included building another way out of the solar . . .

'They'll not harm Philippe! I'll not permit it!' Gwenn declared, eyes glowing with a martial light.

Swamped by the turn of events, Ned felt desperate enough to clutch at straws. He scoured the solar for inspiration. St Clair had entrusted him with his children's lives, and though there had not been time to confer with him, Ned had the distinct impression that he assumed they could escape. 'Take Gwenn and run,' he had said. Run. But they were trapped. How could they run?

He spoke aloud, 'There *must* be a way out.' If Jean St Clair thought they could escape, then escape they could. There was a window seat below a couple of narrow window slits, piled high with hastily tidied bed linen. No inspiration there. There were a couple of sleeping chambers, a privy, a pile of rubble left by the mason.

'I think,' Ned announced cautiously, 'we might have a chance. Gwenn, grab some warm clothing and those sheets.'

Brown eyes blinked. 'We're going?' Gwenn turned to see what Ned had been looking at and her eyes opened wide. 'Ned! You don't think—?'

'Hurry!' There was no knowing how long they had. While Gwenn scrambled to her alcove, Ned snatched up a candle and took it to the privy. He tore back the tapestry hanging. The wet nurse was keeping closer than his shadow, he could feel her breath on the back of his neck. Together they peered down a shaft that was darker and smelt viler than any pit in Satan's lair. The candlelight did not shine to the bottom, but this was probably a mercy.

'Stinks a bit.' Johanna screwed up her nose and set

a hand on Ned's broad shoulders, almost caressingly. 'And it will be a tight squeeze. You don't really intend to drop Mistress Gwenn down that, do you, Captain?'

'I do.'

She drew her head back, revolted, and shook it decisively. '*I* wouldn't go. What makes you think *she* will?' Johanna's jealousy had set Gwenn down as a vain, over-indulged knight's daughter who'd not sully her clothes for anything.

'She'll go if I have to throw her,' Ned said uncompromisingly, 'but I doubt I'll have to resort to force.'

'And you? Do you go too?'

'Aye. I will protect her. And the children. Gwenn is my life,' Ned declared with painful clarity.

A sharp cry and the pounding of a multitude of booted feet had his head twisting round.

Johanna swallowed down a rush of bile. Confronted so blatantly with Ned Fletcher's blind devotion to Gwenn Herevi, she had no option but to acknowledge it and concede defeat. Sourly, she reflected that from the beginning she had not had a hope of winning his affection. But while Johanna was able, albeit reluctantly, to dismiss her dreams of winning Ned Fletcher's heart, she could not find it in her to like her rival. And she continued to love him. The privy shaft yawned, a hell of an escape route, but the only one he had. François de Roncier's reputation being what it was, Johanna had little doubt that he would give no quarter to St Clair's English captain. De Roncier would have Ned Fletcher spitted on a sword sooner than he'd blink.

Holding Philippe fast in one arm, Johanna took Ned's hand. Blue eyes met hers, and the fair brows lifted in faint surprise. Johanna shivered. She'd like to remember Ned's eyes shining and bright, not clouded in death. Gently, for his hand was hurt, and she was savouring the warmth of his skin, Johanna guided the candle he was holding towards the unfinished privy shaft.

'This privy's a mite wider, Captain,' she informed

him, huskily, 'on account of it not being finished. The carpenter has yet to fix the wooden seat. But I fear it is doubtful whether you would fit down even this one.' Her eyes lingered on his face and shoulders as though she would brand an image of him in her brain for all time.

'And as this one has not been christened, it's clean,' Ned pointed out with a wry grin.

'I'm ready,' Gwenn announced from the door arch. She had a bundle and some sheets under one arm, and her sister was attached to the other. Releasing Katarin, she removed an object from the wall shelf.

'What's that?' Ned demanded. They could only take what was absolutely necessary.

A stubborn chin inched up. 'Grandmama's statue.'

'Jesu, Gwenn! We're running for your brother's life and you'd weigh us down with that millstone?'

'The Stone Rose is coming.'

'Jesu!'

Gwenn wrapped the statue in a torn sheet, stalked to the privy and without another word lobbed both bundles down the half-constructed shaft.

Johanna's jaw dropped. 'You don't balk at going down, mistress?'

'To save him,' Gwenn nodded at the babe nestling in Johanna's arms, 'I'd spit in the Devil's eye. But I'll go down the new one, if you don't mind, Johanna.'

'Mistress?'

'Stand aside, will you? You're blocking my way. See, Katarin?' Gwenn addressed her sister gently, and began winding a sheet about her. Ned helped, tying the knots as securely as he could. 'We're going to climb—'

'What about the rest of us?' Klara wailed from the archway. 'You're not leaving the rest of us to be carved up, are you?' The other women crowded up behind Klara.

'Don't leave us,' Bella pleaded over Klara's shoulder.

Ned looked impatient. 'De Roncier's not interested in you. It's St Clair's heir he's after.'

'But he's murdering them all downstairs!'

Gwenn stepped forward. 'He's trying to get to my brother, don't you see? It's vital we get Philippe out of here.'

'Take us!'

'I want to go!'

'Damn,' Ned muttered in an undertone. 'They'd never keep up.'

'Listen, Klara,' Gwenn said. 'I can't stop you following us, if you want to try and escape. But I swear de Roncier won't harm you. And it would help if you'd stay and put him off the scent.' Deliberately, she turned her back on the archway and the muttering women, and held out her hand to her sister.

Katarin stood dumb, thumb filling her mouth.

'She seems to have lost her tongue,' Gwenn sighed. 'Send her after me would you, Ned?'

'Perhaps I should go first,' Ned offered. He had estimated the drop to be fifteen, perhaps twenty feet at most. 'Then I could catch her.'

A frenzied pounding heralded the beginning of the assault on the solar door. 'No, Ned. Me first. Then Philippe, I know I can catch him. Then you, and Katarin last. It will reassure her to see her brother go down before her.'

'Aye. I trust the Count would spare her if he broke in before we got her away.' Ned shot an agonised glance at the beleaguered door.

Johanna watched as Gwenn lifted her skirts and swung slim legs over the rim of the shaft. She would never understand why Ned Fletcher had taken a fancy to such a skinny girl. A woman's thighs should be soft, not firm and muscled like a boy's. It must be something to do with all that riding the girl did.

Ned stretched his long length on the floor beside the opening. He grasped Gwenn's hands. 'I'll lower you as far as I can, Gwenn, before I let you go.'

His brow was puckered with worry for her. He had called her Gwenn. Johanna's heart ached. And because she couldn't bear to see the pain on Ned's face, she occupied herself with swaddling the infant as securely as she could in a coverlet she had taken from his cradle.

'See you in a minute, Katarin,' Gwenn said brightly. 'Goodbye, Johanna.'

Johanna looked up. 'God speed, mistress.'

And then Gwenn's head ducked out of Johanna's view, and so, for a moment, did Ned's. There was a pause while he released Gwenn, and he strained his eyes after his love. Johanna stared longingly at his back.

'Hell, I can't see her. Where's that light?' he demanded harshly. Johanna slid it across with her foot. Ned cupped his hands to his mouth. 'Gwenn! Gwenn!'

A groan. Scuffling. It occurred to Johanna that in all likelihood she would never see Gwenn Herevi again. 'Sounds like rats,' she said.

'Gwenn!' Ned repeated, desperately. 'Gwenn!'

'I'm down safe.' Distorted by twenty feet of rock, Gwenn's answer was hollow, but firm.

Ned's brow cleared. 'She's safe,' he said, and smiled at Johanna, expecting her to share his pleasure.

She might never see him again, either. 'Aye,' she said with a wan smile and bent her head over Philippe. She had left a small portion of the infant's face showing. Feeling as though her chest would burst, Johanna dropped a farewell kiss on the tiny nose before folding the last corner of the coverlet over his face. He was wrapped as neatly as a butterfly in its cocoon.

'Hand me the babe.'

Philippe began to squall. Johanna hesitated.

'Hand me the babe.'

'He feels suffocated.'

'It's only for a moment. Here.' Striding over, Ned relieved Johanna of her precious burden and set him in the hollow of a looped sheet. He leaned over the shaft. 'Ready, Gwenn?'

Back came the hollow answer. 'Ready.'

And then Philippe was gone. Johanna's vision swam. 'Johanna!' Ned was bending over her, gripping her arm.

She wiped her face, sniffed. 'Aye?'

The battering continued. Ned flung a harried look across the solar. 'Holy Mother! They're almost through. Listen, Johanna. It's my turn. I'm relying on you to send the child after me.' He was at the head of the shaft.

'I will. No sheet for you, Captain?'

'No time. Besides, you couldn't bear my weight.'

Ah, would that I could . . . He was going. Johanna knew they would never meet again.

'Farewell,' Ned said over his shoulder, and peered down the pit. 'All's well, Gwenn?'

'Aye.' Her voice was faint.

'Stand aside, I'm coming down!'

Johanna's hand fluttered out. 'Ned?' He paused, suspended by strong arms over the gap the mason had cut into the stone. He hung like a man halfway between Heaven and Hell. 'Good luck, Captain.' And Johanna could not prevent herself from moving towards him. She planted a kiss full on his mouth and received a preoccupied smile of acknowledgement; a crumb that she would have to treasure for the rest of her life. Ned lowered himself into the unfinished shaft. Johanna could see the metal rivets on the top of his helmet, and his bloodied hands gripping the mouth of the well. His fingers moved, and he vanished from Johanna's life. She sagged against the wall and put her fingers to her lips where they had touched his.

He had gone, and not a moment too soon. The solar door was giving way. In a trance, Johanna listened to the wood splintering apart and the rasping male voices which were getting louder. Her throat ached as though she'd been throttled. Sucking in a lungful of air, Johanna became aware of something moving at the boundary of her vision.

'Katarin!' He had asked her to send the child down. The child, all eyes, made no answer. Wiping her sleeve across her eyes, Johanna held out her hand. 'Come along, Katarin.' The child was sucking her thumb so hard her cheeks were hollow. Johanna hoped she was not going to kick up a fuss. 'Katarin, Mistress Gwenn's waiting for you.'

Meekly, the child stepped forward and offered Johanna the hand that was not in her mouth.

'Good girl,' Johanna said, much relieved. 'I'll have you with your sister in an instant.' And securing the sheet Gwenn had tied round her sister, Johanna guided the child to the privy and eased her through the gap. She lowered her down. And during the whole proceeding Katarin said not a single word, not even whimpering when the sheet was stretched to its full length and Johanna released it, so Ned could catch her at the bottom.

In the solar the air was heavy with sobbing and Holy Mary's tireless chanting. Holy Mary was Johanna's private name for the serving woman. Mary knelt, dutiful to the last, with her head bowed before the vacant shelf where the statue of Our Lady had rested minutes earlier. The other women knelt in groups around her, clinging to each other as they wept.

Behind the tapestry screening the privy, Johanna felt stifled. She was not afraid, as the other women were, for she had good reason to believe that she would not be harmed. She did not want to join either the wailers or the God-botherer, but there was something she ought to do . . .

Taking up the candle, Johanna kicked the other incriminating sheets out of sight down the shaft, and stepped confidently out. The solar door would not withstand that relentless hammering many seconds longer. The gap between hinges and wall was widening, the door curving inwards.

Swift as an arrow, Johanna sped for Philippe's walnut cot. She stripped what was left of the bedding from it and stuffed the baby's mattress under Gwenn's bed. Collecting all the infant's linen and blankets, she rolled them into a ball and ran to the hearth. Raking the ashes into life, she cast the ball of cloth onto the embers and poked it till a warm, golden glow was thrown over the room.

When the glow fell on Holy Mary's pallid face, the flow of petitions faltered. 'What are you doing, Johanna?' she asked in a strained voice. Mary had always struck Johanna as a jumpy, nervous woman. It was a wonder she wasn't wailing with the other ninnies.

'Covering up stray tracks,' Johanna said. Someone had to be practical. She didn't think praying would do much good. Satisfied that Philippe's belongings would be unrecognisable charred fragments in a matter of seconds, Johanna scooped up a handful of ashes and ran back to the crib. Booting it into the darkest corner, she smeared its polished surface with the ashes, and stood back to admire her handiwork. She wiped her hands on her skirts, and walked back into the solar.

At that moment, the door hinges came out of the wall and the door crashed flat, raising a small cloud of dust. For a few seconds there was a grim silence. A nail rolled loudly across the wooden boards. A woman gasped, and muffled it. Klara gave a shaky wail. And a heartbeat later Otto Malait, puce in the face and eyes because his blood was up, bore down upon the kneeling women, brandishing a crimson-tipped axe. He was wearing a horned helmet. Bella screamed.

Otto quartered the chamber for resistance; encountering none, he regretfully lowered his axe. Throwing a scornful glance at the quaking women, he strode past them, raised his frightful axe, and let it bite deep into the window shutters. 'It's black as pitch in here,' he growled.

Outside the despoiled manor, darkness was retreating; and as wooden splinters darted in all directions, the rising sun shot orange spears of light into the solar. More de Roncier mercenaries poured over the wreckage in the doorway. Nicholas Warr, archer, was among them, his face carrying the uneasy expression of a man wearing a tunic that did not quite fit. He was carrying a blooded shortsword instead of his bow.

Mary saw him, and her jaw sagged. She drew a shaky cross on her breast. 'Save us, Sweet Mother.'

Johanna regarded Otto with dull eyes. This was the Count's righthand man. 'Captain Malait, isn't it?'

He had gore in his beard. 'Aye. And who might you be?' He took off the barbaric helmet, but was no less terrible.

'My name is Johanna.'

Otto's eyes narrowed. This was Conan's spy of a sister. 'I hardly recognise you, you're gowned so grandly. Where's the brat? And where did Fletcher fly to?'

Johanna's heart began beating with thick, slow, heavy strokes. She did not care a scrap about Gwenn Herevi, but this man must not reach Ned Fletcher, or her Philippe.

'Spit it out, slut.'

'You're too late, Captain Malait.'

'Too late? Where are they, girl?'

'The babe caught a marsh fever,' Johanna improvised. She knew a peasant's baby had died a few days ago. 'They buried him a week ago. Jean St Clair has no legitimate heir.'

The Viking's eyes bored into her. 'You're lying! You would have sent word. Why did you not send word?'

It was a struggle to hold the pale, disbelieving gaze. 'I would have, if Conan had come. Only my brother has not been here this past fortnight.'

Otto came to stand in front of her, and Johanna felt as though his merciless eyes could see through her flesh to the marrow of her bones. 'You're lying,' he repeated, and lifted his grisly axe. 'And I want the truth, my pretty.'

Johanna discovered that she was prepared to die to protect Ned and the infant. She steeled herself not to cry out. She was dead anyway now *he* had gone.

'She speaks truly!' Mary burst out. Johanna watched, bemused, as the God-botherer surged up from the hearth, poker in hand, and corroborated her hastily spun web of lies. A flake of ash drifted from the tip of Mary's poker. 'Master Philippe died the Sabbath before last, and the little mite sleeps in the graveyard yonder.' Using her poker, Mary pointed at the wall beyond which lay the hallowed ground of the graveyard.

Not in a thousand years would Johanna have guessed that Holy Mary had it in her to lie so convincingly. Finding that she was glad to have kept all her limbs in one piece, Johanna fired a grateful look at Mary before squinting surreptitiously at the fire. Not a shred of the baby's linen remained. Relief – which she never thought to feel again – flooded through her. Perhaps, with Mary's assistance, she might secure Ned's escape . . .

'Look, Captain,' Johanna said, 'look at the cradle. You can see for yourself it's not been used lately.'

Stalking to the empty wooden crib, Otto peered in. 'It's soiled.'

'Aye,' brave, saintly Mary backed her up, 'it's not been used in over a week.'

Otto drew off his gauntlets and ran a calloused finger the length of the crib. It came away coated in grime. He rubbed finger and thumb together and lifted them to his nose. He sniffed. 'Too soiled, perhaps?'

Johanna looked innocent.

'You're lying.'

'No,' Johanna said, too shrilly. 'No.'

'Here, Warr.' Otto addressed a man whom Johanna had not seen before. 'Take this wench and get someone to disarm the one with the poker.'

'Aye, Captain.'

Otto did a tour of the chamber. Johanna held her breath. When he reached the privy he ripped the screen aside. The curtain rings jingled and danced on their pole. Johanna saw a muscle clench in the furred, blood-spattered cheek, and closed her eyes. She wished she had more courage, not for herself, but so she could help Ned Fletcher. Mary's lips were moving in silent prayer. Was it the praying that had imbued Mary with this startling new courage? Perhaps Johanna had mis-judged this praying lark. If it worked for Mary . . . For the first time in her life, Johanna started to pray.

'Keep these two in custody till I get back, Warr,' Otto ordered tersely. 'I don't want them slinking into the shrubbery.'

'Aye, Captain.' The man was bruising Johanna's arm. 'Where are you going?'

'I've a mind to play tag with the concubine's daughter.'

Johanna held the muscles of her face in as neutral a pose as she could. 'The babe is dead,' she declared, in a voice as clear as a bell. 'You're wasting your time.'

The Norseman's smile was repellent. 'I'll learn the truth of that when I catch them, won't I? You can't keep a baby stowed away for long – a live one, that is. And when I get back, you and I, my girl, will have a little chat. I shall look forward to it.' Roughly he pin-ched Johanna's chin and strode to the stairwell.

'Captain?'

'What is it, Warr?'

'What about the other women?'

Otto hoisted heavy shoulders. 'Let them go,' he said contemptuously. 'Spineless jelly-fish, every one. They're no use to us.'

'They might know something.'

In the thick beard, Otto's lips curled. 'If we set to work on that lot, we'd get nothing but screams.' Bella let out a howl. Otto raised an eloquent brow and exchanged looks with Warr. 'See what I mean?'

'Aye, sir.'

'The jelly-fish may go, but I want these ladies,' he jabbed a thumb at Johanna and Mary, 'kept safe for me. If you lose them, I'll have your liver roasted for my dinner.'

Warr gave a thin smile. 'They'll be safe, sir. There's a vault under the hall. I'll lock them in there.'

'Judas!' Mary screeched. And to her own surprise as much as Johanna's, she spat in his face.

Chapter Nineteen

Firebrand was full of the joys of spring and too many
oats, Alan reflected, as he concentrated on keeping the
courser on a short rein. They were passing the huddle
of stalls and booths which had been set up by enterpris-
ing traders inside Vannes' West Gate. Alan did not
want the Duke's highly strung horse to cause an accident. A proud, showy creature, Firebrand drew all
eyes. Alan felt like a knight.

A whore with lips painted red as ripe cherries gave
Alan a hopeful look. She was up early. Alan returned
the harlot's smile, shook his head, and rode past her.
Ribbons which matched the girl's lips were threaded
through a mass of curly dark hair. She was youthful,
and pretty if one did not look too closely at her eyes –
they were hard as flint. Alan intended to visit Kermaria
first, before going on to find his brother.

Firebrand resented the restraining hand on the reins,
and sensing Alan was momentarily distracted, bucked
experimentally. The whore hopped briskly out of the
way. 'Poxy knight!' she shrieked with the rancour of
someone who saw a fat profit slipping through her fingers. Her breasts heaved. 'Trampling over poor, simple
folk.'

'Easy, boy,' Alan steadied Firebrand. If the whore
had looked at Alan and not the courser, she would have
seen that his spurs were plain steel and not gilded like
a knight's. Alan was relieved to see the gate ahead of
them, with la rue Richemont running away from
Vannes. Firebrand pranced under the teeth of the port-

cullis and no sooner had his hoofs hit the open road than he was fighting to be given his head. Alan kept the reins close to his chest until the road was clear. Then he slackened his grip, and with a whinny of delight Firebrand lengthened his stride.

Taking a handful of men with him, Otto prowled round St Clair's tower till he found the cesspits. One of them stank, and needed clearing. The other was empty.

'This is the one, Captain,' one of the mercenaries said, holding up some muddied linen. A zealous lad, he had a cast in one eye but his other was bright. 'Those prints were made recently.'

'I have two perfectly good eyes of my own,' Otto murmured cruelly, for he had a private and quite illogical aversion to physical deformities. His trooper's sharp eye clouded.

Two sets of footprints, clear as noonday, travelled in a straight line across the dew-drenched grass to a gate in the boundary wall. As Otto had anticipated, they were widely spaced, indicating that his quarry had been running. The gate led to the woods, and its lock had been smashed, either by the Count when breaking in or by Fletcher when leaving.

'Get horses,' he demanded of another soldier.

'Horses, sir? From where?'

Their mounts had been tethered half a mile away, the better to approach St Clair's guards unheard.

'From St Clair's stables, dolt, and move your legs.'

The mercenary bit his lip. 'One of St Clair's grooms was sleeping in the stable, Captain. He loosed the horses before anyone marked his presence.'

Behind the corn-coloured beard, the red blood surged. 'By St Olaf—'

'The groom's been dealt with, Captain.'

'Captain?' The trooper with the cast in his eye edged forward.

Otto drummed his fingers on the ivory haft of his axe. 'Yes?' he snapped.

'It will be no bad thing to trail them on foot, sir.'

'How do you work that one out?'

'I know this forest, it's pretty dense in places.'

'Local man, are you?' Otto's interest in the boss-eyed soldier rekindled.

'Aye.'

'Odin be praised. You can be of use.'

The mercenary's eye picked up some of the brightness which it had lost earlier. 'Aye, Captain. And I think I know where they might take refuge.'

'Why are you standing about jawing, then? Lead on.' Otto gave a brusque signal, and his troop moved towards the gate.

In the compound of Kermaria manor, which had been so abruptly and rudely aroused, the dust was settling. And though it was broad day, a thick, midnight quiet had fallen over the tower. The cockerel, who had taken refuge on a cross-beam in the empty stable, flapped down from his perch, pecked indignantly at the body of the stable boy, and hopped into the courtyard. It was not the time for sleeping. The groom might have lost his senses, but the cockerel knew day from night. And to prove it, he lifted his head and crowed as loudly as he ever had. The sound floated out over the tranquil marsh where the climbing sun had melted the frost from the reeds and shimmered on mayflies' wings. Frogs croaked. Wildfowl padded placidly across lily pads.

Brother Dominig was whistling happily as he made his way down the narrow boar-run in the Bois des Soupirs, the Forest of Sighs.

As Brother Dominig was a novice and had yet to take his vows, the title Brother was an honorary one. The young man was confident that none of his fellow monks could hear him. It had been said to him on more than one occasion that a novice on the point of taking his vows should take life seriously, and Brother Dominig could not pick holes in this argument, although at times he caught himself thinking that God might love some of his more serious-minded brethren a little more if they learnt to laugh. He strode energetically to the river which ran past the edge of the monastery. A large shovel was slung over one shoulder, and a hazel basket swung from the other. Nearby a mule was braying.

That morning, the novice's rota had come full circle, and Brother Dominig had been given his favourite chore. Today he must empty the eel traps and clear the fishponds of weeds and silt. It was a chore which his superiors in their wisdom had decided required only one pair of hands, and as Brother Dominig loved the river and was of a solitary disposition, this was the job he looked forward to most. He enjoyed outdoor work, and was determined to make hay while the sun shone, for the prior had ordained that his profession, and that of his fellow novice, Marzin, was to be on the Feast of Pentecost tomorrow.

The novice's rota was a means whereby Brother Dominig's superiors gauged where a new brother's talents might lie. Once his vows had been taken, Brother Dominig would be allocated a permanent chore. He doubted that he would be given the privilege of maintaining the traps and fish tanks once he was professed; for while doing his stint in the kitchens, he had miscalculated . . .

During the prior's last fish fast, Dominig had cooked a beaver's tail for him – as beavers spent their lives in water and as their tails were hairless, they were counted by churchmen as fish – and Prior Hubert had enjoyed the dish. So much so that he had sent for Dominig to congratulate him on his cooking of it. Brother Dominig wished now that he had burnt that wretched beaver's tail. His culinary success probably meant that he would be employed in the monastery kitchen rather than by the river.

Feeling a pang of jealousy for his fellow novice, Marzin, Brother Dominig frowned. Marzin, who had been christened William but was adopting the name of that saintly protector of beggars at his profession, was a lucky man. Marzin's talents and his inclinations tallied exactly with those of their superiors. Brother Marzin was an artist of no mean ability, sent to them from the main house of their order to finish a mural in the chapel. Marzin had brought with him a letter from the Abbot of St Gildas on the distant Rhuys peninsula, singing his praises. Prior Hubert had been cautious – Marzin was only a novice, and there was a danger of his head being turned by too much praise. But when Prior Hubert had seen Marzin at work, he had changed his tune and had showered the novice with praise. Brother Marzin's future as an artist was secure.

Dominig shook his muscled shoulders. He did not admire jealousy and was not about to sour today worrying about tomorrow. Sufficient unto the day, he told himself. He smiled. He felt nearer to God by the river, and loved it in all seasons. This May had brought with it a flurry of late rainstorms; the river had been fed by them and was now so gorged its banks were brimming. The swollen waters swept past the fish tanks, a dark, gleaming rush of water heading inexorably for the marshes and finally for the Small Sea. The river was clouded with mud which it had snatched from somewhere deep in the Argoat. It looked as thick as Brother Peter's best bone broth. Noah's flood, Brother Dominig thought, must have started like this.

Drooping willows, planted by an earlier generation of the monks, trailed delicate, greening fingers in the swollen river. Behind the willows, bushy hazels and slender birches reached for the sky. Behind these, rank on rank of giant oaks marched deep into the heart of the forest, shading the woodlands with a spring-fresh canopy of leaves. The brothers still harvested the willows and hazels, and the fish tanks were edged with coppiced trees whose roots held the banks together at times like this when the river was in full spate.

Dominig slipped off his sandals, tucked his habit into

his belt and stooped over the riverbank. With his toes gripping the edge, he hauled on one of the lines. His smile broadened. The net was heavy. He heaved it out. It was gratifyingly full of wet, wriggling eels. A shaft of sunlight slanted through the arching trees, silvering the water which dripped from the eels' slippery bodies.

A kite's alarm call tore through the woodland, fading as the bird winged away. A twig snapped in the shrubbery. Brother Dominig lifted his as yet untonsured head and said cheerfully, 'Good morrow.' Receiving no answer, he sighed. No answer meant that whoever was skulking in the woods was more than likely on the run. He turned without haste, wondering whether he was going to be attacked for the food in the nets.

St Felix's Monastery, whose only stone building was its simple chapel, was protected by God alone. The church's reed-thatched roof was easily fired, and simple to break through. There was no stone wall to keep out predators. There were no fortifications of any sort, and the community was vulnerable to those with no respect for God's Holy Writ. Despite its holy status, Brother Dominig's order had borne the brunt of attacks from outlaws before now. Whoever was watching him was keeping well out of sight in that hazel thicket. Were they outlaws? Poachers? Pirates? All he saw was a wall of lush foliage, but he could hear them. At least two of them, panting hard.

'May God protect me,' Dominig murmured, and though he did not approve of violence, he cast about for his spade. It lay on the grass, a few feet to his left. He dropped the net back into the fast-flowing river, and shuffled casually to his spade. Violence or no, Brother Dominig did not pretend to have martyr's blood in his veins. He pitched his voice louder. 'Good morrow.'

'What shall we do, Ned?'

A young woman's voice that, and it was verging on the edge of panic if Brother Dominig was any judge. He scooped up the spade, and thus emboldened, repeated his greeting. 'Good morrow.'

The hazel shook. Its branches were parted by a young man with untidy flaxen hair who stepped into the clearing. The young man, whose mien was military, was about Brother Dominig's age. Sweat and blood mingled together on a countenance that might be fresh and comely were it not so bruised. The stranger's chest was heaving, and in his arms he carried a small child. A child?

"Ware, Ned!' the girlish voice issued, trembling, from the sprouting hazel. 'He's holding his spade like a spear!'

The battered young man, presumably Ned, deposited his burden – a small girl – on the grass behind him, and placed his hand on his sword hilt. 'Help us,' he said, and his blue eyes blazed like beacons. 'Give us sanctuary, for God's sake. We cannot run for ever.'

'We?' Brother Dominig gripped his spade.

Another twig cracked, the kite mewled overhead, and the young man's hidden companion emerged cautiously from the thicket. 'There's only me and the babe,' a girl said. She wore a simple blue gown, and no veil.

Brother Dominig lowered his spade, disarmed and dumbfounded. When Brother Marzin had first joined them, he had started on a mural which depicted the Virgin Mary. The wary brown eyes of the girl hovering on the edge of the fish pond mirrored Marzin's Virgin with uncanny exactness. 'The flight from Egypt,' Brother Dominig murmured, moving forward to gaze at the child in the young woman's arms. He had taken the infant's crying to be a kite, he realised, while she must have been trying to muffle the sound.

'Yours?' he asked, wondering who was after this youthful pair and what they had done. The prior loved saying that evil came in many guises, but surely so handsome a couple could not have done evil. Were they married? They must be, he decided, for the young soldier's eyes were fiercely protective whenever they lighted on the girl.

'The babe is my brother,' she responded, breathlessly. 'Help us. Please, Brother. They'll kill him if they catch us!'

This was resembling the flight from Egypt more with every passing moment. Brother Dominig was intrigued, and his soft heart was moved. 'Who are you running from?'

The young man, Ned, drew closer, an angry spark kindling in his eyes. 'We don't have time to explain. Do we look like a party of brigands?'

Brother Dominig gazed pointedly at Ned's bloody sword, at his beaten features, and ripped clothing. He spread his hands. 'You tell me.'

'We've done no wrong!' The girl thrust the infant under the monk's nose. 'Help us, or you condemn Philippe to death. If you doubt us, you must see that he can have done no wrong.'

They seemed to care more about the children than themselves. They could not be evil. Uncertain as to the best course, Brother Dominig temporised. 'Our chapel is not secure from attack . . .'

The girl lost colour, clutched the babe to her breast, 'Ned, there must be somewhere else,' she said. 'There has to be.'

The young man ran a hand round the back of his neck. His hand had been hurt, dark blood was congealing on his knuckles. 'I don't know. If the brothers won't help us, we'll have to keep running.'

'Running!' she repeated helplessly, as though she had come up against a lofty stone wall.

Dominig had marked this exchange with some interest. 'I will help you,' he decided, 'if you tell me about your plight. The prior will not take it kindly if I bring trouble to our order.'

The young man named Ned drew his brows together. 'But Brother, you say your church is not secure. If we cannot claim sanctuary, how can you help us?'

Brother Dominig smiled. 'I know nothing about you. You could be murderers for aught I know. I'm taking a risk in trusting to your honesty. Will you not trust me?'

'You've somewhere we may hide, and rest?' the girl asked with heart-rending eagerness.

'Aye.'

The couple exchanged glances. 'Well, mistress?' The young man waited for her answer. 'It's for you to decide.'

Ned's mode of address revealed to the novice that the pair were not wed, and Dominig found himself wondering as to the propriety of what he had in mind. But a moment's reflection brought him to the conclusion that since the infant's life was at stake, the couple's need outweighed any petty moral considerations. He prayed Prior Hubert would see eye to eye with him on this.

Large brown eyes surveyed Brother Dominig from the top of his unshaven crown to his bare toes. The baby wailed fretfully, and a tired smile flickered briefly across the young woman's lips. She looked spent. 'Aye,' she agreed, rocking her brother, 'we had best go with this good monk, Ned. We can explain on the way. I swear I can run no more.'

The anchorite's cell was built into the north wall of the monastery chapel in order to test more severely the vocation of its occupants. As a consequence, it was dank and cold with rising damp. An odour of death clung to the porous stones, and Gwenn faltered as she forced herself through the low break in the wall. 'It smells in here, Ned. I don't like it. Is there nowhere else, Brother?'

Ned turned enquiringly to Brother Dominig. The novice was holding a bucket of mortar he'd lifted from a fellow monk who had been doing some pointing around the piscina. There had not been time to consult Prior Hubert, but he had dispatched Brother Marzin to stand as look-out.

'This cell is the safest place there is,' the novice said. 'You can thank St Félix it's empty. No one has been called to fill it since Brother Biel died.'

'When did he die? Yesterday?' Gwen shuddered. 'I swear I can smell him.'

Brother Dominig smiled. 'Nay, sister. Your imagination plays games with you. Brother Biel died last Christmas. The hermit's cell has been empty since then.'

Swallowing, Gwenn gripped her baby brother and ducked into the cell. Ned pushed Katarin after her and followed himself.

'It's cramped, I know,' Brother Dominig thrust his head through the opening to apologise. 'It was only designed for one person. Here,' he tossed a bundle onto the earthen floor, 'I sent for some blankets for you. And here's bread and cheese, and some milk for the baby.'

As Gwenn's eyes adjusted to the poor light, she perceived a stone ledge running along the back of the cell. She set her brother down and lifted the blankets from the floor before the damp got to them. Katarin pressed close to her skirts, and Gwenn dropped a comforting arm about the child's shoulders. 'We'll need water too,' she put in, 'to drink, and to cleanse Ned's hurts.'

The novice lowered his head in assent. 'Don't worry, mistress, I can give you food and water in the usual manner via the other opening. This is to tide you over.'

'Other opening?'

'Anchorites do drink and eat, sister.' Dominig was mildly shocked at her ignorance. 'There's a slit in the north wall which opens onto the yard. It's shuttered from the outside – that's why you can't see it. Brother Biel took all his food and drink through it.' Dominig smiled at Gwenn. Both she and the little girl were white as chalk, poor things. And no wonder. Brother Dominig might like to be solitary, but he would hate being bricked up in that unnatural hole where sunlight never ventured. 'Never fear, sister,' he said, reassuringly. 'I'll not leave you sealed up any longer than I have to.'

A shout drew the novice's kindly eyes to the church door. 'That's Marzin,' he said and snatched his head out of the cell. 'He must have sighted someone.'

Stone scraped on stone. Brother Dominig grunted as he shifted the first granite block into place. Dipping a trowel into the bucket, he slapped mortar onto the stone and smoothed it down. He had three courses to complete, and though he was no mason, he must do it quicker than a master. He hauled another stone into position.

'That's mortar, isn't it?' Ned said, blue eyes sharp as steel. 'Won't mortar be difficult to break down when they've gone?'

With deft strokes, Brother Dominig smoothed the mixture onto the block, and hoisted another stone. That was the first course done; with another two to go, the entrance was shrinking fast. 'I only wall anchorites with mortar,' Brother Dominig said, discovering that urgency had not blunted his sense of humour. 'With women and babes I use mud.'

'Mud?'

Through the diminishing gap, Ned's countenance was not amused. He was no dissembler, this honest young man. 'My apologies,' Brother Dominig grunted, heaving on another block. 'It is mortar. If I piled the stones on dry, it would look out of place, and your pursuers might be tempted to rip them down to investigate. It's got to look convincing. On my soul, it will be easy to get you out when all is clear.'

Another trowel-load of mortar slapped on stone. Another course completed.

Ned backed into the cell and trod on Gwenn's foot. 'Sorry, mistress.' Her teeth were chattering.

'I don't like confined spaces,' she said.

'Neither do I,' Ned confessed. He took her arm and drew her towards the ledge. Clinging to her sister like ivy, Katarin came too. 'As we have a long wait, I think we should sit down, don't you?'

It was soot-black in the anchorite's cell, save for a couple of feeble splashes of illumination where two small apertures admitted a grey light from the interior of the church. The greater of the apertures, a quatrefoil carved out of the wall, threw the distorted shape of a Greek cross onto the muddy floor. The cross on the ground measured less than a foot, but the quatrefoil itself was smaller, large enough for the anchorite to receive Our Lord's body through it when Mass was being celebrated but with not an inch to spare. The quatrefoil had been carved at an angle, to prevent the hermit from taking a too-worldly interest in the goings-on in the chapel. The other, dimmer, source of light was the squint. As its name implied, this reed-like crack was positioned so as to allow the anchorite to squint through it and glimpse the High Altar. No other portion of the church was visible, but despite this Ned had been standing with his eyes glued to it for most of the half-hour they had been incarcerated in the cell.

'Can you see anyone, Ned?'

'Not a soul.'

'What can be happening? It's some time since the alarm was raised. Perhaps it's another visitor to the monastery. Perhaps it's not – what was the name?'

'Malait.'

'Perhaps it wasn't Malait. It could be anyone. A pilgrim?'

Withdrawing from the squint, Ned groped for the stone bench and wedged himself next to Gwenn. Katarin had her head buried in her sister's lap, and Gwenn was caressing her. 'I wouldn't pin my hopes on it being anyone else,' he said candidly. 'This monastery is too small and too out of the way to attract pilgrims. Besides, it has no relics.'

'Aye, but until last Christmas they had a hermit,' Gwenn pointed out, clutching at the faintest hope. 'You know how people will bring their troubles to holy men.' She shivered, hugging Katarin. 'Ned, I'm cold.'

'So am I.' Ned draped an arm round Gwenn's shoulders and reached for a blanket. She did not draw back. 'Better?'

'A little.' He felt her body sag against his, and when she spoke again, her tone had changed, become hesitant. 'Ned? Do . . . do you think my father was killed outright?'

'Aye. That thrust would have killed anyone,' Ned said firmly.

'I . . . I would not want him to die a lingering death.'

Ned's hold on Gwenn tightened. 'It would have been a swift end.' He slanted his body towards hers. 'Mistress Gwenn—'

'I don't want your pity, Ned,' she declared, stiffening her spine. 'It would weaken me, and I have to be strong, for my sister and my brother's sake.'

'Your father's last thoughts were of you, mistress,' he said quietly. 'He bade me look after you. He said to take you and the children north. He said that you would know where to go. Do you know what he meant, mistress?' He heard her swallow.

'Aye.' Ned could feel her struggling to hold back the tears. 'How like P . . . Papa, to think of us when he was f . . . fighting for his life.'

'He was a good man,' Ned said, and then regretted it for he heard a stifled sob.

'A g . . . good man. Aye. A dead man.'

Ned had no words with which to comfort her, though he hurt with wanting to help her.

'Ned?'

'Mistress Gwenn?'

'Did you see my brother? I saw him lying in the rushes. He was only knocked out, wasn't he? Do you think Raymond will have managed to escape?'

Ned chewed his bottom lip. He had indeed seen Master Raymond, lying on the floor, disarmed, and with the blood drained from his head. He had been as pale as the limestone effigy of St Agatha in the church back home.

'Ned?'

'Mistress . . .' Ned gulped.

'You think Raymond's dead.'

343

He cleared his throat. 'Aye.'

She sagged against him. 'The children are all I have left,' she said, her voice catching in her throat. Katarin lifted her head.

'What is it, my love?'

The little girl reached for the bundle which Gwenn had insisted on bringing and without a word dropped it onto her sister's lap.

Gwenn gazed at the child, uncomprehending. 'There's no one in the chapel. You can whisper, Katarin. What are you trying to tell me?'

'Perhaps she's reminding you that you have your grandmother's statue as well as her and Philippe,' Ned suggested.

'Next to the children, Grandmama's icon is as nothing,' Gwenn said irreligiously. Her voice warmed. 'But you are right to remind me of it, Katarin. I'm glad to have the Stone Rose. It will remind us of home when we are on our travels.'

Katarin made no response.

'Why is she so quiet, Ned?'

Ned shrugged, before he remembered the poor light shrouded him. 'No doubt she loathes it in here. Count it a blessing she's silent. Rather that than she fill the cell with crying.'

'Yes. And thank God Philippe has gone to sleep. He screeched his head off while we ran through the woods, poor lamb. He's worn himself out.' Close to tears, Gwenn set the Stone Rose to one side. It was too soon to be reminded of the past, better by far to concentrate on the future. She was pleased she had her grandmother's statue but, practically, she was more glad of its hidden treasure. She would tell Ned about that later. In all likelihood they would be forced to sell the gem if they were going to survive on the long and hazardous road north. If it bought them their lives and liberty, it would have been sold in a good cause. Izabel would approve of her selling it under these desperate circumstances. 'Ned, if we ever get out of here, will you . . . will you stay with us?'

'I am at your command, mistress,' Ned declared simply.

'Because my father ordered it, and like him, you are a man of honour? I told you, Ned, I don't want your pity.'

'I would never desert you, mistress. It's very simple, I love you.'

Touched by the simplicity of his declaration, Gwenn put her hand on his knee. 'You are a good man, too. What would I do without you?'

'Mistress—'

'Hush!' Gwenn caught his hand. 'Someone's entered the chapel.'

Scrambling to his feet, Ned put an eye to the squint. 'It's Malait,' he hissed. 'I'd know that tone anywhere.'

'Not a word, Katarin,' Gwenn mouthed in her sister's ear. 'Understand?'

Veiled by half-light, Katarin nodded.

The gentle Prior Hubert, having received a garbled and to his mind inadequate briefing from one of his novices, gripped his walking staff and roused himself to stand up to Captain Malait. On sight, he pigeon-holed the Viking as one of the damned – an excommunicate mercenary. He had been reluctant to allow such a heathen to defile the saint's chapel, but Malait's sword won the argument. The prior was not prepared to die to defend that particular tenet of the faith; Saint Félix would understand and forgive him. The wretch had entered without even bothering to remove his devilish helmet.

Otto Malait saw a plain, pathetic barn of a chapel. But it was the only solid building this woodland retreat boasted; and save for a couple of wall-paintings which put the rest in the shade, it was completely unadorned. These monks did not have so much as a brass crucifix; theirs was of varnished beech. One scornful glance told Otto that the chapel could not house his quarry.

'What's behind the altar stone?' he demanded. He was beginning to regret having listened to that local trooper. He should have known better than to heed the advice of a man with an eye like that. Trooper Bernard probably couldn't see past his own nose. Otto pictured Fletcher and the concubine's daughter racing deep into the forest while he rattled about in this place. His feet itched to continue the chase.

'Why nothing, Captain,' Prior Hubert replied blandly. The prior was of a retiring nature, but he could, if pressed, set his shyness aside. He misliked the burly, martial looks of the Norseman, who was of a breed the prior despised. He was a just man, and he did not want to betray the people who had claimed sanctuary in their hermit's cell before he had had a chance to judge the merits of the case for himself. He looked into the mercenary's light eyes; the pupils were mere pinpricks. This blond Goliath was full of hate. Saint Félix would approve of a mild deception in a good cause.

'You have no hidden entrance? No vaults?' Otto swung on his heels, impatient with the churchman's unctuous manner.

The prior's grey, tonsured head shook. 'This is no cathedral, my son.'

'No silver plate tidied away?' In the matted, sweaty nest of a beard, greedy red lips curved.

'As you have doubtless observed, my son, our community prides itself on the simplicity of its rule. But I suggest you look for yourself, then you will have no doubts.' Prior Hubert sucked in a breath, wondering whether it might be in the refugees' best interests to make mention of the anchorite's cell. If the prior omitted to do so, then the Norseman's trooper, who clearly knew the area, would be bound to say something. The prior came to the conclusion that if he drew the Viking's attention to the cell, he would dismiss the information on the grounds that anything freely given was worthless. 'The only item worthy of interest in our chapel is the anchorite's cell,' the prior said.

'Anchorite's cell? Where?'

Prior Hubert pointed with the staff he used as a

walking stick. It was curved at the top so it resembled a bishop's crozier, and the prior fooled no one with his assertion that he needed the staff to hobble about, for he was a slender, sprightly man with a spring in his step.

Following the direction of the prior's staff, Otto found himself scowling at the only plain, undecorated wall in the building. He could see why the other walls had been whitewashed, ready for painting, for the mortar was appallingly botched. 'All I can see is an ordinary wall you've neglected to limewash. Where's the door?'

'My son,' the prior was astonished that even a faithless mercenary should be so ignorant, 'an anchorite abjures everything this world offers. He makes an oath never to leave the cell while he has breath in his body. There is no door.'

'No door?' Otto was fascinated, despite himself. 'I had heard of anchorites, but I never thought a living man would prison himself freely.'

'Not all anchorites attain the same levels of self-denial,' Prior Hubert informed him. 'Our Brother Biel, who went to God last Christmas, was renowned for his asceticism.'

'Careful, Father,' Otto grinned, 'lest the Tempter sows pride in your heart.'

The prior flushed.

'It's a tomb for the living.' Otto was revolted.

'A pathway to Heaven, my son.'

'Don't pontificate. Is anyone in it now?'

'Aye. A young man has taken Brother Biel's place,' Prior Hubert said, trusting that God would forgive him for misleading the mercenary. He was not lying, there *was* a young man in there . . .

Otto stalked to the quatrefoil. 'Can't see a damn thing through this. You've been penny-pinching with your mason. The mortar's done very ill, and he's chiselled this askew.'

Prior Hubert ran a thin finger over the curve of his

crook. 'You're not meant to see in,' he explained pleasantly. 'If you could, it follows that the hermit would be able to see out. He might be distracted by the world he has forsworn. He might be tempted—'

'To break out?' Shifting to the squint, Otto tried to peer through that, but he could see only sable shadows. 'I can hear breathing.'

'It's God's will that the young man lives. I pray he lives longer than Brother Biel.' Prior Hubert lifted his hand and drew a blessing in the air.

'Christ on the Cross, you're insane!' Otto strained his eyes at the squint. 'It's black as sin in there. We laymen treat prisoners better than this!' He wrenched his head back and strode for the door.

'Won't you stay and pray with me, my son?'

Otto paused, ox-like frame filling the doorway, and turned his face to the sun. His shadow spread like a dark stain over the church floor – a man turned demon with a horned head. The horns shook. 'Not I.'

'My son, you have a soul. It needs care.'

'You're the man of prayer, Father. Say one for me. I prefer action.' Otto saluted indifferently, and was gone.

In the cell, Ned unclenched his fingers from his sword hilt. He had been holding it so hard he had driven the blood from his fingers. 'Not that there would have been room for me to wield it in this oubliette of a place,' he muttered to himself.

'Has he gone?'

'He's gone.'

Gwenn sighed. 'We'll have to wait before they release us. The brothers will want to make sure he's not coming back.'

'Aye.'

Time dragged in the dismal cell until it seemed they had been immured for hours. In reality, less than an hour later the shutter on the north wall rattled, and a pale smudge of light appeared. This dimmed almost at once as one of the brethren pressed a fleshy, rotund face to the opening. 'Here. Dominig mentioned you needed water,' the monk said, withdrawing to thrust a goatskin flask through the aperture. 'And here's linen for your hurts, and for the infant.'

Ned knelt on the stone ledge to take them. 'My thanks.' He stared at the soft contours of the countenance framed by the wall. There was something familiar about the monk's eyes. They were light brown, and brimming with dreams, and he was sure he had seen them before. 'What's your name, Brother?'

'I'm known as Brother Marzin, but I've yet to take my vows,' the monk answered scrupulously.

'Marzin,' Ned murmured. 'Doesn't fit . . .'

'Eh?'

'Nothing. I must be mistaken. When will you release us?'

The monk blinked uncertainly while his eyes accustomed themselves to the inky darkness of their prison. 'The prior says—' Brother Marzin broke off and turned aside to speak to someone who must have come up to stand beside him in the chapel yard. After a few moments' murmured consultation, the monk's round cheeks came back into view. 'Prior Hubert is here.'

The prior's clear-cut features replaced the blurred roundness of Brother Marzin's. 'Good day, young man.'

'Good day, Brother.'

'Father,' the prior corrected him, thinning austere lips. 'I am prior here.' This bloody young man looked scarcely more personable than the knave who had just left. Prior Hubert did not like soldiers of any class. If monks were the body of Christ, mercenaries must be Satan's. And because of these men of violence, the routine of St Félix's was in disarray. Prime had been delayed . . .

'My apologies, Father,' Ned said politely.

The prior's taut lips eased. This one appeared to have some conception of courtesy. 'I am sorry that you have been housed so ill, but Brother Dominig stressed the urgency of your plight, and his idea, though unorthodox, has proved sound. Your pursuers have left, and as far as I can ascertain, they have no idea of your presence here.'

'Thank God,' Ned said, with feeling.

'Do you think they'll come back?' Prior Hubert asked.

'Christ's wounds, I hope not.'

The prior rapped on the shutter with his staff. 'I'll not stand for blaspheming in God's house.'

'Sorry, Father.'

'Would you mind telling me your circumstances? Brother Dominig's account was inadequate.'

Gwenn moved into the weak slant of light. 'We're from Kermaria, Father Hubert,' she said. There was no reason to be secretive with the man who had married her parents.

'Kermaria?' The lines on the lean face sharpened. 'Who are you? What happened there?'

'I am Gwenn Herevi, Sir Jean's . . . natural daughter. Father, we were attacked. My father has been butchered by his enemies, and we are fleeing them. I can't tell you how grateful we are that you took us in. They would have murdered my baby brother.'

Prior Hubert frowned. 'Brother? I was under the impression that the infant was your son.'

'No, Father. He's my brother.'

'Is this young man your husband?'

'No, Father.'

'Bear with me, my child, while I get this clear in my mind. You say your father is Sir Jean St Clair?'

'Was. My father has been murdered,' Gwenn said, and bit her lip to stop its trembling.

The prior's voice gentled. 'Forgive me for not realising sooner, mistress, but I could not make out your features in the murk. I am sorry for your loss.'

'Th . . . thank you, Father.'

'If this young man is not your husband, who is he?'

'Ned . . . Ned is . . . was . . . Papa's captain.'

A pause. 'It won't do,' Prior Hubert murmured. Truly God was testing this poor girl more than he tested most. 'It won't do at all.'

'Father?'

The prior met her gaze. 'Thinking you husband and wife, I deemed it safer for you to remain in the cell awhile.'

Katarin whimpered.

'No, Father. My sister is frightened.'

'Your father's enemies might return to Kermaria via the monastery,' the prior pointed out, 'and you cannot outrun them.'

'They might,' Ned agreed. 'It's most likely they'll have hidden their horses nearby, and this is the clearest track.'

'I want Katarin out of here, Ned. It's not healthy, and the poor child hasn't said a word since we left Kermaria.'

Prior Hubert's crook rapped on the shutter. He was determined to find out what God's will was for these two, but the veil seemed unusually thick today. St Clair's captain was obviously a foreigner. Could he be trusted? 'Young man, do you have a . . . ah . . . what is the term? A strategy?'

'Aye, Father. Before Sir Jean died, he instructed me to escort Mistress Gwenn and the children to kinsfolk in the north.'

'And the name of these kinsfolk?'

Helplessly, Ned looked to Gwenn.

'Wymark, Father,' Gwenn supplied. 'They have a manor at Ploumanach.'

'Mmm.' The prior glanced at the length of the shadows to assess the hour. By rights he should have finished reciting the morning office, but the plight of Jean St Clair's offspring was no light matter. Prime would have to wait. He would do a penance for this later. The two faces in the pitchy cell were white like twin moons. Could he allow St Clair's offspring to put their lives in the hands of this young man? Were his intentions good or bad? 'The name Wymark rings a faint bell,' he said. 'Tell me, Mistress Gwenn, how well do you know your father's captain?'

'Very well, Prior Hubert. But what—?'

The prior lifted a silencing hand to the opening.
'Calm, daughter. I seek to help you. Do you have faith
in your father's captain? Is he an honourable man?'
The prior observed how intently the captain awaited
Gwenn Herevi's verdict. He had open blue eyes and
they were filled with the most blatant longing, and a
pinch of fear. Fear of what? Rejection?

'Trust Ned?' Gwenn was indignant. 'Of course I do!
Ned has more honour and nobility in his little finger
than some great lords have in their entire bodies.'

Pleased, Prior Hubert inclined his tonsured head. He
was beginning to see a light at the end of the tunnel,
and tentatively groped towards it. 'You are confident
that . . . er . . . Ned has your best interests at heart,
my daughter?'

'I am.'

'Do you *like* him?' Prior Hubert was a realist. Bastard as Gwenn Herevi was, her chance of finding happiness had been low while her father lived. Now with
Jean St Clair killed, she would have even less to look
forward to. A flush had washed over the captain's
cheeks. He was gnawing his lower lip, and his eyes
were pinned on Gwenn with an adoration Prior Hubert
deemed best reserved for one's patron saint. On second
thoughts, perhaps not. Ned's look of longing was not
particularly chaste. The prior's feeling was that the lad
loved the girl and would see them all safely to their
relatives.

God in his wisdom had directed the young couple's
feet to St Félix-in-the-Wood. If the prior saw them
married, Gwenn Herevi would bear a new name. He
could help her wipe out her parents' sins, and start
afresh. But though the prior was eager for the matter
to be neatly resolved, he would not marry them if
Gwenn Herevi had no liking for the lad. Patiently he
waited for her answer. Her dark brows, he saw, had
lowered. She had pride, considering she was a bastard,

and she resented being manipulated.

'Like Ned, Father?' Her chin tightened. She might be a pretty and dainty maid, but Prior Hubert could see she could be trouble if she put her mind to it. She threw a smile at Ned, whose cheeks were as red as a poppy. 'I like him very much, but when will you let us out of this dismal hole, Father?'

'I apologise for the poor quality of the accommodation,' Prior Hubert responded dryly, 'but I fear it would be incautious to release you sooner than dawn tomorrow.'

'Tomorrow! No, Father! We can't spend a night in here! Have pity on my sister! And what about Philippe?'

'I'll release you now, on one condition.'

'Anything,' Gwenn said, recklessly.

Prior Hubert drew in a breath. 'I'll release you if you'll marry this young man.'

She gaped. 'M . . . marry Ned?'

'Sir Jean would not rest in peace if I permitted you to chase about the duchy with—'

'But Ned told you, Papa commanded him to take us north!'

'I remember. And that merely strengthens my resolve to have you married. He would not have entrusted his children to this young man if he did not think him worth—'

'But, Father,' honesty compelled Ned to butt in at this point, 'Sir Jean did trust me, but he would not countenance an alliance.'

Gwenn was lost in a tangle of emotions too entwined for Solomon to unravel, but she did know she felt strong affection for Ned. Perhaps she did love him. At any rate, she did not want to lose him as she had lost everyone else in her life. After all that had happened that morning, she could barely think, but if she married Ned, she would always have a friend. And she *must* get out of this cell . . .

She thrust Ned aside. 'I agree with you, Prior

Hubert. I'll marry Ned, if he'll have me.'

'But mistress,' Ned objected, 'remember how Sir Jean—'

'Not another word, Ned. I'm happy to marry you.'

'B . . . but—'

'I'm going to my devotions, my children.' The prior could see that Ned's objections might take some time to overrule. 'And while I am gone, consider my proposal.'

'Proposal!' Ned blurted. 'It's rank blackmail! You know Mistress Gwenn wants her sister out of here.'

Prior Hubert's eyes were cool. 'Blackmail? No, my son. Prudence? Perhaps. Consider how Mistress Gwenn might be treated by relatives less tolerant, and . . . er . . . partial than her father.'

'I don't need time to consider,' Gwenn said, with a sidelong glance at the silent Katarin. 'I'll marry Ned this instant. Only, please, get us out of this pit.'

Prior Hubert relented. 'Very well. Brothers Dominig and Marzin will fetch sledgehammers. Stand clear of the wall.'

'We will,' Gwenn smiled. 'Thank you, Father.' Prior Hubert walked off.

'Mistress Gwenn, you cannot marry me.'

'I can.'

'No. It . . . it's disparagement, mistress.'

'Disparagement, pooh.' Gwenn dismissed disparagement with a click of her fingers.

'It *is* disparagement,' Ned insisted doggedly. 'Your father would not be pleased. Don't you recall how angry he was when—?'

'I remember, Ned. But Papa is dead. Circumstances have changed. Besides, he trusted you. He charged you with seeing us to Ploumanach.'

'I'll see you safely there without your having to marry me,' Ned vowed. Such an opportunity would never present itself again, he knew, but he could not take advantage of Gwenn's vulnerability. His skin scorched. 'You know what I feel for you, Mistress Gwenn. But you are safe with me. I'll not touch you.'

'Shut up, Ned. The monks are about to break this cell open. I've said that I'm marrying you, and there's an end to it.'

Ned swallowed. 'You'll hate me . . .'

She laid a hand on his. 'Hate you? Never. I need you to marry me.'

'You . . . *need* me to marry you?' Ned stammered, struck by this original idea.

'Think, Ned. Prior Hubert is right. If you don't marry me, what kind of reception will I have when we reach Ploumanach? When I arrive, a bastard and unwed, tongues will wag.'

'I'll spear the first man who besmirches your honour!'

'In this world, bastard daughters have no honour, Ned,' Gwenn pointed out gently. 'Hear me out. I don't know if my relatives are rich or not. It might be difficult for them when I arrive with Katarin and Philippe both needing support. We'll be the poor relations, for we'll have no money. Do you think my kin will greet us with open arms?'

'They'll take you in,' Ned said, sounding less than sure.

'They'll take the children in. But me?' Gwenn shook her head. 'I'll be an embarrassment. They'll want rid of me. Either they'll compel me to marry some pock-marked merchant I'd have to be grateful to to the end of my days,' she gave a strained laugh, 'or else they'll force me into a nunnery where all unwanted women go. Do you want that for me, Ned?'

Ned stared at her, his heart too full for words.

'So if you don't mind, Ned, I'd rather marry you.'

'You don't love me.'

She hesitated, and paid him the compliment of admitting to the truth. 'I like you very much. I feel more for you than I have for any man. But love . . . I don't know what love is. I admit that I'm marrying you to get us out of this hole. I'm marrying you because apart from the children you're all I've got, and I can't bear the thought of losing you too. Perhaps I'm using you as a prop, I can't say. But I do like you, Ned. I'm very fond of you, and I trust I will learn to love you.'

'I'll care for you, mistress.'

A warm smile lit her eyes. 'I know. And don't you think you should start by calling me by my first name?'

'Gwenn,' Ned breathed. Raising her hand to his lips, he kissed it reverently and pressed his burning cheek to her cool palm.

Chapter Twenty

Alan recognised where he was. The crossroads was a bow-shot ahead of him, round a curve in the road, which meant that Kermaria was less than two miles away. The long run had improved Firebrand's temper; once the courser had worked off his excess energy, he was a delight to ride. It was a beautiful morning, with bright sunshine and not too much wind. Alan could smell the sea. Contentedly he trotted along. In his pouch sat a letter sealed with the Duke's seal authorising him to carry out his survey, but today Alan felt free of his responsibilities. It seemed a long while since he had taken any time for himself, and he was enjoying it. It was good to be away from the court for once, and he was looking forward to seeing his cousin. He could not be certain that Ned would have stayed at Kemaria, but he thought it likely.

Pleased with himself, and the world in general, Alan scanned the hedgerows. They were bursting with life. The sloes were coming into flower, a gnarled old crab-apple had unfurled its leaves, birds were nesting in every branch and bough. Idly, he fell to speculating on what sort of a girl the concubine's daughter would have grown into.

Alan's ears caught the sound of frantic hoofs ripping along the Kermaria road. He frowned, and drew rein. There were deep ruts in the highway left over from last winter's mires, and that rider was doing his mount no service. At that speed the animal was likely to trip and break a leg.

Kicking Firebrand's chestnut flanks, Alan urged him forward in order to have a clear view round the bend. A pretty palfrey thundered towards him. She was riderless.

'Steady, Firebrand,' Alan murmured, and holding the Duke's courser firmly he waited for the lathered mare to reach him. He caught her trailing bridle easily, and dismounted.

The palfrey rolled her eyes. She was frightened and a white froth of foam dripped from her mouth. 'What's happened, girl?' Alan spoke softly. The horse, a lady's mount if ever he saw one, carried no saddle and was haltered for her stall, so she was not being ridden when she was alarmed, Alan concluded. He ran his hand over the mare's quivering withers and felt something sticky. He glanced at his fingers, eyes widening. Blood? Wondering who in his right mind would beat such a gorgeous animal, he bent closer. The mare's coat was undamaged; the blood was not hers then, but someone else's. Alan thought aloud. 'Where have you run from? Kermaria?'

He set his sights on the road which led to St Clair's manor, and his brows formed a black line above his eyes. What was going on? Taking the palfrey's reins firmly in one hand, Alan remounted Firebrand. Suspicions aroused, he decided to proceed cautiously. He did not like the look of this.

Brother Marzin had his habit rolled up to his elbows. A dumpy young man with a pot of a stomach, he was unused to wielding anything more weighty than a paintbrush, and he was sweating from his exertions. Setting hammer and chisel aside, he wiped his hands on his habit and extended them to help Gwenn through the breach he and Dominig had made in the wall of the anchorite's cell. He puffed. To think Dominig had incarcerated them unaided . . .

'My thanks.' Gwenn clambered over the rubble, cradling a bonny baby in the crook of one arm. Her hair was all but loose, her dress was torn, and brambles were hooked onto the hem of her skirts. 'Please help my sister.'

Brother Marzin eased the silent child over the stones. 'Relax,' he said softly. 'You're stiff as a board.' Briefly the girl's hazel eyes met his and the look in them sent an icy shiver racing down Brother Marzin's spine. No child ought to have eyes like that. They were tired, exhausted eyes; the eyes of an old, embittered woman who had too many sorrows to mourn them all. And under those chilling eyes, charcoal smudges bruised olive skin that was otherwise smooth and unblemished. The girl's clothing and person, unlike her sister's, were scarcely disturbed. Brother Marzin was puzzled. Unless cne saw those tragic eyes one would assume that she had escaped entirely unscathed from whatever Armageddon had driven them here. He put the child down, and Gwenn's free arm curled protectively about Katarin's shoulders, like a mother hen hiding her chick under her wing.

The soldier was emerging. He did not need assistance. Brother Marzin caught sight of his profile and stared. With the captain's countenance no longer masked by the funereal gloom, this was the first time the novice had been able to take in the details of his appearance. Stiffening, the monk's brown eyes narrowed as they washed over the dust-dimmed fair hair, the square chin, and the widely set blue eyes.

'Ned?' He mistrusted the testimony of his eyes. 'Ned Fletcher?' The last time Brother Marzin had seen his cousin had been well over four years ago, at Easby, back in England. His playmate had changed. Ned had filled out; he had been a thin, stringy streak of a child but the young man standing in St Félix's chapel was all lean, hard muscle. There were other changes. Ned's jawline was more pronounced, he carried himself with a deal more pride; nonetheless, he was recognisable as the cousin with whom Marzin had played many a game in their brief childhood.

Stepping into the nave, Ned blinked as his eyes adjusted to the comparative brightness of the church. 'Brother?'

'Ned!' Marzin held out hands that were splotched with paint pigments, and his eyes twinkled. 'Don't you recognise me?'

'I . . . I know your face, but your name . . . Marzin?' Ned gave his head a shake, as though that might prompt a faulty memory.

'Ned, you're from my old life. To you, I am William.'

'William!' Ned's face cleared and, striding forward, he shook him vigorously by the hand. 'Cousin William! I should have known you at once if it wasn't for the soupy murk in there. William!' The years rolled away, and Ned prodded the novice's protruding stomach with easy familiarity. 'You're exactly the same, except that this has grown. You're as plump as a partridge.'

'Aye. And you're taller than ever, Longshanks.'

Ned grinned. 'Ah, William, you're a sight for sore eyes, truly you are!' He turned to Gwenn. 'Mistress . . . that is, Gwenn . . .' He flushed, it was hard to remember he had the right to call her by her first name. 'I know this monk.'

'So I see.'

'He's William, my cousin, William le Bret. William, this is Gwenn Herevi. We . . . we are to be married.'

'Prior Hubert told me we were having a wedding today,' William was all smiles, 'but I'd no notion it was to be yours.'

'Cousin? William le Bret?' Gwenn murmured. 'A relation of Alan le Bret's?'

'His brother.'

The resemblance was not clear to Gwenn. The pleasant but unremarkable features of this round, merry novice had none of Alan le Bret's distinctive chiselled lines, and his manner was humble, not proud.

William's rotund face had collapsed. 'Aye, mistress. Do I take it you have the misfortune to be acquainted with my brother?'

'Indeed. It was no misfortune. Your brother saved my life.'

The novice blinked, apparently startled. 'Alan saved you? From what? And how much did you have to pay him for that service, pray? A king's ransom?' Strange shadows chased across the young monk's face.

'I didn't pay him anything.'

Ned stepped in. 'William, no. Don't go raking up old coals.'

William laughed, unhappily. 'Depend upon it, mistress, Alan would have been after something.' He saw Gwenn glance at a wrapped bundle Ned had dropped on a pile of masonry. 'I've never known Alan lift a finger to help anyone unless he stood to gain by it.'

Feeling as though she had wandered into a quagmire, Gwenn held her peace.

'Enough, William, please,' Ned said. 'Alan never was the black sheep you would have painted him.'

'Was he not?' William shrugged. 'You always idolised him, Ned. You should never have chased after him when he left Richmond.' He hesitated, and his chubby cheeks reddened. 'I expect you've seen him more recently than I. I've not seen him since before he left.'

'William, I don't believe you're as set against Alan as you like to make out. You want to know how he is.' William scowled. With a gentle smile, Ned put him out of his misery. 'I last saw Alan roughly two years ago. He'd made it to captain and was off to find work with Duke Geoffrey. He's a fine soldier. When I was with him, none of our company could best him sword to sword. Your parents would have been proud of him.'

'My father, Ivon, might,' William acknowledged gruffly. A Breton sergeant, Ivon le Bret had retired from active soldiering, but he continued to work in the armoury at Richmond Castle in Yorkshire. 'My mother died the winter Alan ran off. She never was the same after he left.' William waved Ned's protestations of sympathy aside, and his tone grew sharp. 'Like you, Mother thought the world of him. I never did understand why she favoured him so. A worthless brawler who considered no one but himself.'

'William, that's not true.'

'Isn't it? We were happy till he left. Oh, I know Father always thought more of Alan because of his fascination with your brutal soldier's art. And because I was more interested in wielding a pen than a sword, I was overlooked.' William's stomach growled. He was on a strict fast since he was due to take his final vows the next day, and it was making him irritable.

'You're letting jealousy warp your memories, William,' Ned said. 'Ivon is proud to have a son who can read and write. I heard him tell my mother as much.'

William's nostrils flared. 'He had a strange way of showing it. It was always Alan he spent time with.' William looked down at his sandles and wriggled his toes. He shook his head at himself. 'My apologies, Ned. I don't often let demons run away with my tongue.'

'You blame him for your mother's death. My aunt, William's mother,' Ned explained to Gwenn, 'was a delicate woman. But her death and Alan's departure from Richmond might have been no more than an unhappy coincidence.'

William straightened his round shoulders. 'I'm happy Alan achieved his ambitions. Happy to hear that the devil might still be alive. I have often wondered. I did pray for him, despite my anger.'

'I'm sure you did.' Ned patted his cousin's arm, and wondered what hour it was. He felt exhausted. 'I thought, when you came to the cell window, that you were familiar, but when you informed me your name was Marzin I assumed it was some trick of the light. Why Marzin?'

William le Bret's round face lightened, and he indicated his fellow novice. 'Brother Dominig and I take our vows on the morrow. It's a custom of this house that new members of the order adopt a new name, as a token of our turning our back on the old way of life.' He threw an enquiring look at Ned. 'If you think it safe to stay till morning, I'd be glad if you and your lady would consent to witness my profession. We are allowed representatives from the outside world. I had no one coming, but now you are here, I'd be honoured if you'd stay.'

Ned glanced at Gwenn. He could not say whether it was safe to stay or not.

'I'm very tired, Ned,' Gwenn admitted. 'Perhaps we could sleep here.'

'We'll stay,' Ned decided, 'but I will keep watch.'

'No, Ned! You'll be worn out and not fit to travel.'

William concurred. 'Your lady is right. You're not built of iron. I'm fasting, and I have a vigil to keep in here with Dominig; but I can ask one of our brothers to keep watch.'

'We've imposed enough.'

'Nonsense! You are guests. And we are used to vigils, it is no trial to us monks to watch out for you.'

'My thanks,' Ned capitulated with a grin of relief. 'But I'll not be able to call you Marzin. You'll always be William to me. You look well. The monastic life suits you. They can't fast you too much.'

Ruefully, William put a hand to his extended belly. 'On the whole, they feed me well. When I explained to the prior that I couldn't paint on an empty stomach, he was very understanding,' his stomach growled again and he gave Ned a rueful glance, 'but because I'm being professed tomorrow, I must fast today. All day.' Sighing, he looked his cousin over. 'You look reasonably fit too, Ned, but what happened to your face? Someone should tend to that cut on your arm.'

'I'll do it,' Gwenn offered, 'when I've seen to the children.'

William shook his unshorn thatch of hair. 'You've enough to do taking care of the little ones, mistress. Brother Dominig will show you to the guesthouse. I'll see to Ned.'

Gwenn thanked him and followed Brother Dominig to the reed-thatched hut which served as guesthouse for the order.

When the cousins were alone, Ned succumbed to the

feeling of exhaustion which had been threatening to steal over him for some minutes, and sagged onto a chunk of masonry. 'What's the hour, William?'

'Mid-afternoon.'

'God's teeth, is that all? Why is my body telling me its midnight?'

'You look like death,' William said frankly. 'What happened, Ned?'

'We've been through the mill today, old friend.'

Making encouraging noises, William set about peeling aside the rags of what had once been a serviceable tunic from Ned's left arm, near the shoulder. He grimaced. 'A messy gash,' he muttered, 'but not deep. We'd best go to the water butt. I've ointments ready.'

Ned dragged himself to his feet. While William bathed and treated his injuries, Ned squatted on an upturned bucket by the water barrel and told his tale. William was pale when he had done.

'What about the law?' William asked. 'Will this enemy of St Clair's get away with this outrage, this murder?'

'Count François *is* the law around Vannes,' Ned answered dryly. 'The Duke is only interested in milking his Breton estates of their revenues.'

William let out a low whistle. 'You're up against Count François de Roncier? You pick a fine man to cross swords with, Ned.'

'I know. And I know the Count, William. Alan and I took our first commission with him, not knowing the man's true colours. And by the time we had found out, it was too late, for we were sworn to him.'

'Why didn't you leave?' William asked, working at Ned's shoulder.

'Leave? You ask me that? We were sworn to the man, William. A sacred oath.'

'Sacred? Honour among thieves, eh? A routier's oath is sacred, is it?'

Ned frowned. William would never understand. 'No one would take you on if they heard you broke your word. God may not smile on mercenaries, William, but even mercenaries have some honour.'

'I wrong you, Ned, I'm sorry. But to kill for pay . . .'

'Your bishops have been known to fight in holy wars,' Ned pointed out.

'A crusade. That's different,' William said stiffly.

'Is it? Oh hell, William. I've never been one for your nit-picking theology. Let's not argue. All I want is rest. When you've finished hacking at my arm, I'd like to go and find Gwenn.'

'Hacking, you call it?' William pretended to bridle. 'I'll have you know I'm counted the best healer in the monastery.'

'Then heaven preserve me from the worst!' Ned said lightly. He winced as William tied the linen bandage in place. 'My thanks.' He stood up, and yawned. 'I'll be glad when this day is done, William.'

The twinkle had leapt back into William's brown eyes. 'Naturally, for you'll be a married man by then, won't you, Ned?'

A crimson tide washed up Ned's cheekbones to the roots of his hair. 'I . . . I wasn't thinking of that.'

'Comely maid, I should think, when she's tidied up a bit,' William needled, an unholy gleam in his eyes.

'Aye.'

'She's your choice?' The bright colour flooded down Ned's throat. William chuckled. 'Your choice. I wish you luck, old friend.'

'My thanks, we shall need it,' Ned said, grappling for sanity while he tried to turn a deaf ear on the refrain which had begun piping in his head. One phrase was being repeated over and over again. Tonight, Gwenn Herevi will be your wife. Your wife. Your wife. Your wife.

Night was closing in. Prior Hubert had married them after Vespers. The children were asleep in the guest house, and Gwenn was preparing for bed.

In constructing their one-roomed guesthouse, the brethren had made use of the forest's most plentiful resource, wood; and though the cottage was a modest one, it was soundly built. Not only did it have a wooden frame, it had planked walls in place of the more usual wattle and daub. The monks slept communally, and their dormitory was built on the same lines. There were differences between the two buildings, however. For one thing, the monks' dormitory was double the size of the cottage; also the interior of the guesthouse was roughly plastered for insulation, as though the monks deemed that their feeble-minded lay visitors needed coddling, while they, bolstered by their faith, did not.

The plaster aside, there were no other refinements. The cottage had been built according to a design that was ages old when the Romans invaded Brittany. The fireplace was nothing more than a ring of stones in the centre of a pounded earth floor. There was no opening in the roof to let out the smoke, so it must rise up and billow in the crossbeams until it found its way out through the thick reed thatch. Four plain, wooden bedboxes were ranged round the fire and occupied almost all the space. The brothers' guesthouse was simply a place where travellers could put their heads down and rest.

Ned had collected kindling for a fire which now glowed softly in the centre of the room. The door of their lodgings was ajar, in a futile attempt to clear the room of some of the smoke, and Ned leaned thoughtfully on the door frame. He was wearing Sir Jean's fine woollen cloak which Gwenn had brought with her and given him, together with a bleached linen chainse and fresh tunic that his cousin had dug out of storage.

Gwenn held a reed taper to the tallow candle which Brother Dominig had jammed into a candlestand. The iron stand stood tall as a man, it was eaten with rust, and had a crick in its stem so it leaned at a drunken angle. There were no other furnishings. When Gwenn lit the candle, the smelly fat sputtered and splashed onto one of the mattresses. A moth fluttered through the doorway, and was drawn inevitably to the fire. 'Ned?'

He started. 'Mistress?'

'Please shut the door. It's not getting rid of the smoke, we'll be plagued with insects, and the draught is making this candle burn unevenly.' The door closed softly. 'Ned?'

'Yes?' Unbuckling his sword, Ned was wondering which mattress to sleep on. Carefully he placed his sword by the fire with its guard undone so he could draw it at a moment's notice. Whichever mattress he slept on, he'd want his sword close to hand. He picked the one nearest the door, in case the alarm bell rang in the night. He could not presume to lie with his wife after all she had suffered this day. It felt peculiar to regard her as his wife.

'You cannot call me Mistress Gwenn all our married life.'

'I know.' Ned smiled at her across the flames, thinking how pretty she was in the fireglow. The shadows masked the strain on her face, and the kindly light lent a faint flush to her pale cheeks. His wife. 'But habits cannot be changed overnight. Your father was insistent I kept my distance . . .' He broke off, cringing at his appalling tactlessness. 'Gwenn, forgive me, I did not mean to remind you . . .'

Her lips curved sadly. 'I don't need you to remind me, Ned. The memory of my father's last moments are seared indelibly in my mind. You do not wound me.' She sank down onto one of the mattresses. Ned stood by awkwardly, uncertain of his new role.

'At least the mattresses are dry,' she said.

Ned poked one with his foot. It rustled. 'Straw?'

'Either that or dried bracken. Lumpier than our old ones.' Abruptly, Gwenn ducked her head and began fumbling with her braids; but Ned had seen the sudden sheen in her eyes, and knew it indicated tears. Before he'd given it conscious thought, he found himself on his haunches at her side, hands on her shoulders.

'Gwenn, don't check your tears. Cry. It might ease the pain.'

Her eyes met his, dark and watery, but she shook her head. 'I . . . I mustn't. What if the children wake? If they saw me weeping, it would upset them even more.' She curled her fingers into fists, and her voice wobbled. 'I feel as though I'm in a dream, Ned. None of this seems real. I need to think, only there are so many worries eating away at me I don't know which to tackle first. Help me, Ned. Help me to think. I'm worried to death.'

Gwenn's appeal having neatly defined his role, Ned knew where he was. In a companionable manner, he settled himself at her side, put an arm about her shoulders, and hugged her to him. The most difficult part, for him, would be trying to put out of his mind how much he desired her. That insidious chanting began in his mind. She is your wife. Your wife.

'I've funds, you know,' Ned was determined to ignore the insistent chorus, 'so if that's a concern, dismiss it. Your uncle gave me this. It's yours. Give me your hand.' He dropped Waldin St Clair's purse into her palm.

'Waldin gave you this? Sweet Mother, it's heavy.' Gwenn untied the strings and gaped at an astonishing hoard which included small pennies from the Breton mints of Rennes and Nantes, some of the more valuable English silver pennies, deniers from Tours, and even gold bezants from the distant Byzantine capital of Constantinople. 'Waldin carried all this on his person?'

'Aye. It's the prize money of a champion. When Sir Waldin described the tournaments to me, he told me he reckoned it safer on his person than hidden elsewhere. He liked to know where it was. He threw it at me in the heat of the battle.'

'Guard it for me. It could see us to Jerusalem if need be.' Gwenn glanced at the bundle which contained her grandmother's statue. She might not have to sell the gemstone at once. 'Ned?'

'Mmm?' Gazing resolutely at the fire, Ned's response was muffled. She *is* your wife. She *is* . . .

'You could have run off with it,' Gwenn said in a low voice. 'You could have left us, and run off with a fortune.'

'And leave you to face de Roncier alone? How could you say such a thing?'

The hurt in Ned's eyes tugged Gwenn's heartstrings, and apologetically she lifted her fingers to touch his cheek. Her fingers lingered.

Ned held himself steady as a rock. He had to force himself to keep his eyes open, while concealing his feelings from her. He was certain she'd be frightened by them; the force of them frightened even him. He swallowed. Her fingers shifted, went to his hair; she was feeling the texture of it, stroking it, eyes shy, not driven by great emotion, he was well aware of that, but quietly, trustfully exploring. An ache started deep in Ned's belly. His breath was coming unevenly. He strove to moderate it.

'I count myself lucky to have so loyal a husband, Ned,' Gwenn said, unmindful of the disordering effect she was having on his senses. 'Not for one moment did I doubt you. You're a man in a thousand.'

'Gwenn,' Ned blurted, and could have cursed, for her hand fell away, 'I wish I had a ring for you.'

'I need no ring, Ned, to remind me to keep faith with you. I've sworn to keep myself for you, and I'll honour my vows.'

Ned's arm tightened, and he looked at Gwenn's mouth.

On her mattress three feet away, Katarin mumbled in her sleep. Gwenn's expression changed. 'Katarin's one of my main worries,' she announced abruptly. 'She's not uttered a word since we left Kermaria.'

'What?'

'Katarin won't talk.'

'She said something then.'

'In her sleep.' Gwenn got up and went to her sister's palliasse. She tenderly stroked an errant strand of hair from the little girl's face. 'When she's awake, I can't squeeze a word out of her.'

'She . . .' Ned hesitated, 'she wasn't struck in the fight?'

'No. She was with me all the time. No one laid a finger on her.' Katarin muttered and threw off her covering. Gwenn replaced it. 'I can't understand it.'

Leaning on his elbow, Ned asked, 'What's she saying?'

'I can't make it out. She's gabbling. Do you think she's all right?'

'If she can talk in her sleep, there can't be much wrong. She will be in shock, I should think. Give her a day or two to come round. Soon she'll be chattering away like a starling, and you'll be wishing for her silent for a space.'

'I hope so. Oh, Ned. It is good to have you to talk to. I'd be in a terrible state if I didn't have you.'

'The infant, is he all right?'

Gwenn nodded, and padded back over the mattresses to Ned. She kicked off her short kid boots. 'Philippe has the constitution of an ox. He doesn't seem to have noticed anything's amiss. He yells when he's angry, or when he's hungry, but he's soon soothed. He's an amazing child. If we can but get him away from here . . .'

'We will.'

Gwenn stood looking down at her husband. Dear Ned. He had been her only real friend for two years, and suddenly she found herself married to him. It was not easy to believe, but then nothing that had happened that day had been easy to believe. Her mind was too strained to think about the other, unacceptable events, it was best if she kept it fixed on her husband.

Ned smiled, took one of her hands and tugged. Gwenn's knees bent. Their eyes met, and Gwenn saw the flush on his cheeks. She lacked sexual experience, but she knew that the colour on his cheeks was not entirely due to the fire. Ned desired her.

'Gwenn,' Ned cleared his throat, but his voice remained husky, 'if it would help you to talk about your father . . .'

'No. Later, perhaps, not now.'

'Where do you want to sleep?'

She wrinkled her nose. 'I'll sleep with you, husband.'

Ned released his breath on a rush, pulled off his boots, and opened his arms. Gwenn went into them as eagerly as a pigeon coming home to roost after battling through a tempest. The heat of Ned's body was comforting, and at first she was content to be held, but every time she lowered her eyelids, images crowded in on her consciousness, violent, grisly, bloody images that made her eyes flick open and chased sleep away. She felt dislocated, out of herself, and if it wasn't for the feel of Ned's cradling arms, and the comforting smell of his body . . . She closed her eyes and burrowed deeper into his arms. A likeness of her father, lying in a dark pool on the rushes, flickered through her mind's eye. She shook it away, and wound her arm tight about Ned's waist. A heartbeat later, she felt the reassuring touch of Ned's hand on her hair. She tried to relax, and closed her eyes once more.

The fire burned down till it was only a dull cluster of stars winking gently in the centre of the floor. The candle hissed, and guttered. Time crawled by, and neither of them slept.

Ned was tussling with an altogether different vision, but it disturbed his rest as much as Gwenn's memories disturbed hers. He was imagining that Gwenn and he were naked. They lay pressed together, mouth on mouth. She loved him, and his hand was running down her smooth white skin from shoulder to thigh . . .

'Gwenn?' Ned whispered, unaware that the sound of his voice had banished yet another in a long line of ghastly horrors which were all Gwenn's battered mind seemed capable of producing. She raised her head from his chest, and her loose braids tickled his neck. 'Can't you sleep?'

'No. My mind's going round like a wheel on a cart.'

Rosemary, Ned could smell rosemary. His hand moved down Gwenn's cheek and came to rest on the small pulse in her neck. He could feel it beating, and slid his thumb across it in a delicate caress.

Gwenn enjoyed the sensation, and suddenly she realised she wanted Ned to kiss her. His kisses would heal her hurts. He would bring her back to herself. He would bring her down to earth. But Ned would not kiss her, despite his desire, unless she encouraged him. He would not have forgotten that she had once told him her liking did not match his.

Gwenn closed her eyes. 'I like that.'

'You do?' Ned repeated the gesture, with infinite care, holding her as though she were as fragile and as precious as glass from Araby.

'Mmm.' Reaching up to Ned's neck, Gwenn imitated his gesture. Ned groaned and, startled, she snatched her hand back. 'You don't like it?'

'Like it?' He caught her hand, kissed her fingertips and replaced them on his neck. 'I love it.'

Gwenn smiled. She had never seen a man look at a woman the way Ned was looking at her. All soft, and gentle, and so very open. Ned looked . . . vulnerable. It came to her that men did not always look at their wives in this manner. She was privileged to have Ned as her husband. The knowledge warmed her. A memory from happier times sprang to the forefront of her mind. She saw her uncle telling her she must take care with Ned Fletcher. She had needed his advice and had thought she understood what Waldin had been driving at, but even so she had not realised the extent of the power she had over Ned. His happiness rested entirely in her hands. It was a responsibility she was happy to shoulder, for Ned was kind. Ned cared for her. Ned would help look after the children. She would fight to keep him happy when he gave so generously to her. No harm would ever come to him from her, their need for each other was a mutual need.

Gwenn let her fingers wander over his neck, watching the play of expression on his face. He groaned again, shut his eyes, and when they reopened they were all but black. She felt a rush of tenderness for him. His love drove away the dark shadows. He healed her hurts. 'Always look at me like that, Ned,' she murmured.

'I always have,' he muttered, and pulled her close to his chest, 'only you were never allowed near enough to see.'

Gwenn untied the neck of his borrowed tunic and ran her fingertips over the sprinkling of fair hairs on his chest. Tentatively, feeling as though she were in a dream, She pressed her lips to his skin. Ned's breathing was becoming ragged.

'Gwenn don't.' He sounded so hoarse she hardly recognised his voice.

'Don't?' Gwenn rubbed her cheek against his chest, bemused at her own actions, but she could not stop. She had not realised how good it would be simply to cuddle Ned. He felt so nice, so warm and solid – so *alive*.

'Please, Gwenn, you're driving me to distraction!'

'In what way?'

Another row of explorative kisses burned Ned's throat. He took her wrist and tried, rather feebly, to push her away. 'I . . . I think you know in what way.'

'But Ned, I'm your wife.'

'I thought to spare you your wifely duties.'

'Honourable fool,' she said affectionately.

Ned groaned.

'You want me, don't you?'

'Want you? Sweet Christ!'

'Then make me Gwenn Fletcher in truth, Ned. Please. Help me.'

Ned swallowed.

'I need to forget Gwenn Herevi. Help me look forwards, because if I don't look forwards I will look back. And, if I look back, like Lot's wife, I'll turn into a pillar of salt. Help me, husband . . .'

Ned raised a trembling hand and stroked her cheek.

'Kiss me, Ned.' And, for modesty's sake, lest Katarin should awaken, Gwenn reached for her cloak and drew it over them. Trustfully she twined her arms about Ned's neck and waited for the touch of his lips. He was gentle, as she knew he would be, and his lips were soft. It was the second time Gwenn had been kissed, the last time had been with Ned's cousin and that had felt different – exciting and not a little frightening. Ned did not frighten her. He was all reassurance. After a moment, she made to draw back, and immediately he loosed his hold as though he feared she was rejecting him. 'I like kissing you, Ned.'

Ned's eyes shone. 'There are plenty more where that came from.'

They kissed again, and Ned's hand slid over the curve of Gwenn's hips and thighs, to the hem of her skirt. With his lips clinging to hers, he unclasped Gwenn's belt and drew her gown and underskirt up to her waist. One of his legs found its way between her thighs.

Gwenn shifted on the mattress. 'Show me what to do, Ned.'

Ned's hand moved lightly over her waist, and Gwenn gasped when he reached her breasts. He pushed her clothes higher, and Gwenn's mind clouded. It was bliss not to think. Blindly, she pressed closer to her husband and, in the absence of any direction from him, pushed one of her hands down the waist of his breeches and moved it gently over his buttocks. Ned groaned. Rightly taking this as encouragement, Gwenn pulled his hips to her, feeling the muscles cord and bunch under her fingers. He felt good, did Ned. Perhaps this marriage would work in more ways than one. Perhaps what she felt for Ned *could* turn to passion. . . .

As feeling took over, Gwenn's thoughts became more

tenuous. She was dimly aware that Ned was reaching for the ties of his trousers. Aware of a feverish impatience in him that she was beginning to understand, she assisted.

'Gwenn, I don't want to hurt you.' Ned leaned up on his elbows, and she saw he was gritting his teeth in an effort to control himself.

Gwenn arched up, and kissed his shoulder. 'Ned, you're too far away . . .' She tugged his shoulders, and that was that.

Ned fell into her.

'Oh, Ned.'

He pushed once, twice, and then it was over, almost before it had begun. 'Jesu, Gwenn, I'm sorry.' Shuddering, and obviously shamed to the point of tears, Ned buried his face in her neck.

'No need to apologise.' Gwenn stroked the flaxen hair back from his damp brow.

'I must have hurt you.'

'No.'

'It was too quick. You didn't . . . like it. Oh God, Gwenn, I wanted so much for you to like it.'

Cradling his head, Gwenn kissed a hot cheek. 'On my soul, it was fine, Ned.'

'I love you, Gwenn.'

'And I love you,' Gwenn responded, realising with a start that she did love Ned. Not in the way of the grand passions that the troubadours sang of, but she did, most definitely, love him. Who could know Ned and not love him?

She became aware of a sticky wetness seeping out of her. Ned's seed. It had been over more swiftly than she had thought it would, and the whole process was a thousand times more . . . animal than she had imagined, but whatever deficiencies there were in Ned's technique, his love more than made up for it. And as for her not liking his lovemaking, it had hurt a little, but Gwenn had expected that. She had been a virgin. She would grow to like it, in time.

Easing himself out of her body, and filled with self-loathing, Ned drew his wife's hand to rest on his shoulder. He avoided her eyes for fear of what he might read in them. Gwenn would despise him now, assuredly. Grimly, he hitched his trousers over his hips. He had spoilt it. His rushed, callow fumbling had left them both fully clothed, and he'd reached a climax the instant he had entered her. Last time Ned had had a woman – a whore in Vannes – he had gone on for an age. Why could it not have been like that with Gwenn, whom he loved? She must hate him . . . hate him . . .

Gwenn grasped his chin with cool fingers. 'Look at me, Ned.'

Ned braced himself to meet scorn and instead found himself basking in smiling warmth. Gwenn leaned forwards and pressed loving lips full on his. 'Good night, my husband,' she murmured, and nipped his lower lip between her teeth.

The relief was so intense it was almost his undoing. Swallowing down a rush of tears, he managed a smile and hugged his wife's slight body fiercely to his. 'Goodnight, Gwenn,' his voice was choked. 'God, how I love you. I'll never let you go.'

A few minutes later they were both asleep.

PART THREE

Demons and Devils

Remember Lot's wife.

Luke 17:32

Chapter Twenty-One

Hood up, Alan rode towards St Félix-in-the-Wood with the woodland chorus ringing in his ears. He had passed the night uncomfortably in a bed of leaves, and his muscles ached. He was profoundly worried about Kermaria. When he had reached St Clair's manor, he had found it crawling with de Roncier's company. It had been a shambles. The bodies of St Clair's men were laid out like so much meat in the courtyard, and a number of hard-faced de Roncier troopers were digging a grave-pit. The cookhouse had burned to the ground, and there were piles of arms everywhere. De Roncier's horses were being led into St Clair's stables.

With the Duke's sealed letter in his script, there was nothing to prevent Alan marching straight in with a stream of demands and enquiries, but if de Roncier was involved, he knew he would be spun a web of lies. A disloyal thought leapt into his head. De Roncier's intrigues against his family were as meticulously planned as his own Duke's intrigues against his father and brother Richard. All were petty family squabbles, the only difference was the scale. And the innocents always paid the price.

Alan had doubled back to the crossroads, illicitly tethering Firebrand and the palfrey in a nearby tithe barn where he hoped they would remain undiscovered. He had retraced his steps to Kermaria and spent an uncomfortable day crawling around the reed beds by the manor boundaries, trying to learn what he could about what had happened. His success had been limited. He had caught a peasant trapping a duck, and the peasant had been so relieved that Alan was not a de Roncier henchman that he had talked quite freely.

Jean St Clair was dead. The peasant was worried about who would become the next lord of the manor. François de Roncier's reputation had preceded him and understandably the poacher did not want him to be the lord. Alan had enquired after Ned, but the wellbeing of an English soldier was of no interest to a Breton peasant. He knew nothing. Alan had even asked about the concubine's daughter, but the poacher had no information about her either.

Hoping against hope that the brethren at St Félix-in-the-Wood would know more, Alan was now riding to the monastery. If he got no news out of the monks, he intended to pursue his enquiries at Kermaria in his official capacity.

He wondered how his brother would greet him. They had not parted on the best of terms. To his left, a wood pigeon cooed. Alan had the leading rein of the palfrey looped round his saddle horn; he intended to hand her over to the prior for safekeeping. Jean St Clair could no longer use her where he had gone and why should de Roncier be allowed to appropriate her for his Countess?

Alan had his cloak pinned tight, for it had rained in the night, and every now and then a gust of wind shook raindrops from the leaves and showered him. He rode easily. There were no hoofprints of footprints. No one had ridden this way since the rain. If by some mischance he was challenged by a de Roncier man, he trusted his position with the Duke would protect him.

A hundred yards down the track stood a broad oak whose deeply fissured bark betrayed its great age. On hearing the horses approach, a cowled figure who had been taking his ease in its roots uncurled and slipped behind it. The man was clothed in an unbleached habit of coarse homespun, and a wooden cross hung on a leather thong at his breast. His vigil being over, Brother

Marzin had taken Brother Jacob's place on watch. By his sandalled feet, a brass handbell lay ready to sound the warning. He picked up the bell. 'I'll see his face first,' he decided and, holding the clapper of the bell so it would not betray him, he sucked in a breath and waited.

When the sound of the hoofbeats had drawn level with his tree, he strode boldly into the horses' path. 'Good morrow, sir,' he said, happy there was only one man to contend with.

Reining in, Alan flung back his hood. 'Good morrow, Brother, I come in peace.' He frowned, and leaned forward to scrutinise the monk whose face had gone white as whey. He began to smile. 'Why, Will—'

'Peace? You?' William sent an incredulous laugh whirling round the clearing. 'When did you go anywhere in peace? I should have known it would be you. Like a buzzard, you're always on the look-out for a battlefield to pick over.'

So the monks *had* heard something. Alan swung from the courser, held out his arms, and hung onto his smile. 'I've come a long way to see you. Won't you embrace me, Will?' His smile wavered, for William had drawn back, as though Alan's touch would defile him.

'God has granted my prayer, I see,' William commented, tersely.

'Prayer? You wanted to see me?' Alan's smile hovered faintly about his lips, as though expecting to grow stronger at any moment. 'Let's bury the hatchet. Embrace me.'

William kept his brother at bay with a paint-dyed hand. 'I wanted to see you.' His voice was clipped, unfriendly. 'I wanted to see your face when you heard the news. I wanted to be the one to tell you what your leaving home did to Mother.'

Alan's smile died. 'What? What did my leaving do to Mother?'

'You know how she doted on you. You should have known what your going would do to her.'

In a stride, Alan had his brother by the shoulders. 'What happened, Will?' he demanded roughly.

'The winter after you ran off, Mother died,' William announced brutally. Alan whipped his hands away and backed off. Astonishingly, he looked as though he had been kicked in the teeth. Long ago, William assumed that his brother's profession had inured him to all feeling. Thank God, it appeared he was wrong. If Alan was capable of feeling, he was not quite the lost soul William had thought him. A reluctant sympathy began to grow in his breast.

'Died?' Alan repeated. 'Mother? No. You're lying, William. You seek to punish me for my sins. You hate me because I'm a mercenary and I've broken your most sacred laws. Tell me you're lying.' Alan had adored his mother. A loving woman, Mathilda le Bret's only fault was that she loved her menfolk too much. Alan had left England to make his own way in the world, in part because he resented the way his mother had taken it for granted that he would become his father's apprentice. She had tried to plan his life for him, but Alan had wanted to plan his own life. If ever he was apprenticed to his father, it would be his own decision, not his mother's. His leaving had been a statement of independence, but all the time he had been away he had reserved a space for her in his heart. Whenever he had been lonely, he had remembered her and been comforted by the thought that her uncritical love was always there for him. That could not be ended, surely? All gone. All gone, and he'd never even known . . .

William gulped. His elder brother had always kept his emotions buried, had always appeared invincible. A devil in William had wondered if his lawless brother was capable of suffering along with the rest of humanity. Apparently he was. But triumph, William discovered, had a bitter flavour. He did not like it. He had intended to blame their mother's death directly on Alan, but face to face with his brother's distress, the words stuck in his gullet. His expression must have done the accusing for him, however; Alan's alert grey eyes had become chinks.

'You blame me.' Alan sounded incredulous. 'I should have thought, Will, that a man of your calling ought to be giving thanks that God called her to Him.'

William fell to studying the oak's spreading roots. He heard Alan sigh and the chinking of harness, and glanced up. Alan had his back to him and was resting his forehead against the chestnut's neck, gripping the gelding's mane with tense white fingers. The gelding stamped a hoof. William's conscience and his sympathy were roused. In a rush of guilt, he struck at his chest with a clenched fist. '*Mea culpa,*' he said, like the penitent he was. And louder, 'Alan, Alan, forgive me for breaking it to you so bluntly. I've done you a great wrong.' He laid a contrite hand on his brother's shoulder. Alan caught his hand, turned, and the brothers embraced.

Fretful crying woke Gwenn soon after dawn. Disoriented, she wondered why Johanna had not run to attend to Philippe. Confident that the wet nurse would see to her brother in a moment, Gwenn lazed comfortably, until yesterday's events rushed into her consciousness accompanied by a lurching in the pit of her stomach.

Papa was dead, and Raymond, and Waldin, and many other brave souls. Shuddering, Gwenn nuzzled closer to the comforting warmth of Ned's long body. Johanna was at Kermaria, while she lay in the Benedictines' guesthouse. Outside, a mule was braying, on and on like a creaky saw. She was steeling herself to climb out of bed and look the ruins of her world in the face when Philippe fell silent.

Ned stirred, and opened an eye. 'Good morning, wife,' he mumbled, and smoothed her dishevelled hair.

'Good morning, Ned.' Recollecting what had happened between them, Gwenn blushed, and gave him a shy smile. She opened her mouth to say more but Philippe began to wail again, more demandingly this time. It was impossible to ignore him. Rubbing her eyes, she levered herself upright and saw they were no longer alone. The door of the guesthouse was open, and horizontal bars of grey dawn light streamed into the chamber. Another traveller's belongings were strewn over one of the palliasses. In normal times it would be quite unexceptional for a guest in a monastery lodge to awaken and find they were sharing lodgings with strangers. Monks' guesthouses were popular with travellers. But these were not normal times . . .

Elbowing Ned in the ribs, Gwenn indicated the figure seated cross-legged by the fire. A dark-haired man, in a short, serviceable green tunic, with a broad leather belt, he was not dressed for fighting and did not look like one of de Roncier's hounds. The newcomer had his back to them, and he had apparently been blowing on the fire to resurrect it, for he had small twigs and kindling in one hand. His other hand was raised to the baby, and long, nail-bitten fingers carefully stroked Philippe's cheek. Certainly not a de Roncier man. It was his touch, Gwenn realised, that had quieted her brother. Katarin was awake, thumb, as ever, jammed into her pink mouth. She was sitting on her mattress facing the newcomer, with her honey-brown hair spilling over her eyes. Unperturbed by the stranger, Katarin wore a dreamy look, as though she had not been awake long.

The man's sword was unbuckled and lay on top of a dark mantle, but Ned was not about to take any risks. Under cover of Gwenn's cloak, his fingers crept to his sword hilt. 'Good morning, sir,' he said. The newcomer turned, an amused smile lighting familiar grey eyes.

Gwenn gasped.

Ned let go of his sword hilt as though he'd grasped a bunch of nettles.

'So formal, Ned?' Alan rose to his feet and bowed in that mocking way of his.

'Alan! Jesu, what are you doing here?' Ned leapt up to embrace his cousin.

384

'I might ask the same of you,' Alan answered with an arch look at Gwenn who was painfully conscious that Alan must have watched them sleeping in each other's arms. 'You've changed, Ned. What are you up to? I would never have put you down as a despoiler of innocents.'

With an incoherent mutter Gwenn got up and went, hot-cheeked, to see to her brother's needs.

'Gwenn and I are married, Alan, if that's what you mean,' Ned said stiffly.

'Don't raise your hackles with me, Ned.' Alan smiled. 'The redoubtable prior told me you were wed. Congratulations.'

'And Alan, William is here, did you know? It's his profession today.'

The dark head nodded. 'I met him coming in. We've resolved our differences, and I'll stay to see him tonsured.'

Ned's lips curved. 'I'm glad of that. His grievances were eating away at him. Did he tell you they've made an artist of him?'

'So I understand. It would seem there's no stopping him. He tells me he's been invited to Mont St Michel to paint the cloisters once he's professed and has finished work here. It's a high honour. I'm glad he's found his true vocation.'

'Has he accepted ours?' Ned asked with a lopsided grin.

Alan laughed. 'I wouldn't say he accepts it, Ned. Tolerates it, perhaps.' He lowered his voice. 'I know what happened at Kermaria. It must have been hell on earth. Mistress, I'm sorry about your family, truly sorry. You have my deepest sympathies.'

'Th . . . thank you.' Philippe's mouth was gaping like a hungry fledgling's. The monks had provided Gwenn with a thin, milky gruel of soaked oats, and she tried to spoon it in, but she was unused to feeding her brother, and most of the gruel dripped down his chin. Johanna had made feeding him look so easy.

'What do you plan to do?'

385

Trusting a dribble had gone down her brother's throat, Gwenn answered, 'We're going north.'

'North? Why north?'

Ned explained. 'We go to Ploumanach. Gwenn has kinfolk there.'

Alan looked sceptically at the children. 'And you travel with these infants?'

'What do you expect us to do with them?' Gwenn glared indignantly at Alan. 'Leave them behind? We have to get my brother to safety. The Count will kill him if he can.'

Alan rubbed the bridge of his nose. 'Why should de Roncier hurt your brother, mistress?'

'My father married my mother, and Philippe was born after their marriage.' Her brown eyes were bright with defiance, as though she expected him to deride her own birth.

He caught her drift at once, and did not mock her. 'So the babe is St Clair's legitimate heir? Jesu. Poor sod. Poor, innocent, little sod.'

'Alan!' Ned said.

Placidly, Gwenn spooned more mess into her brother. After a pause, during which she shovelled with grim concentration, her head lifted. 'So you see, we must get them away. The Count will not rest until his position is secure.' Sensing he did not have all of his sister's attention, Philippe seized his chance, grabbed the spoon, and gruel slopped onto the floor. 'Hell's teeth, Philippe, why did you do that?'

Alan covered his mouth with his hand and couldn't bring himself to look at Ned. Gwenn mopped up the spill, recaptured the spoon, and continued her battle with the gruel.

'I thought one of the ports would be the best best, Alan,' Ned said. 'We've enough money to hire passage on a coastal trader. It's by far the swiftest route – we'll have them safe in a couple of days.'

'We?' Alan murmured, a slight frown nicking his brow.

'That's my plan. What do you think of it?'

Alan remembered the fleet of de Roncier ships jostling at their moorings on Vannes quayside. 'Not much.'

'What's wrong with it? You can't tell me it would be quicker to ride to Ploumanach?'

The fire had taken hold, and while he put his mind to his cousin's problem, Alan kicked more wood onto the flames. Sitting down, he crossed his legs, pulled his cloak from under his sword, and spread it out to dry.

'Alan?'

'Take your ease, cousin, while I mull this one over.' Ned sat down. 'Listen, Ned. If de Roncier is after the babe, the ports are the first place he will go. His men are crawling all over them – I know, I saw them in Vannes the day before yesterday.' Alan glanced at the plump bundle now dozing contented as a cat in Gwenn's arms. More by luck than good management, Philippe had eaten his fill. 'You are quite sure he's after the babe?'

'There's no doubt of it.'

'I advise you to go by land. Hire a guide with the money you would have spent on a ship. Inland Brittany is mostly forest, and if you find a guide with knowledge of the byways, you should be safe enough. It's wooded almost all the way, the trees will be your shield.'

Ned pursed his lips and looked at Gwenn to assess her reaction. 'It would take five days, maybe more, even with horses, which we haven't got.'

'We could buy mounts,' Gwenn put in. 'Do you think the good brothers would sell us that noisy old mule?'

Alan was not free to offer his services as their guide, being committed to the Duke, but he could help with horses. 'I've a mare I think might suit you,' he said.

'A mare?'

Alan picked his words carefully. 'I found her running loose on the road to Kermaria. She must have escaped her stall in the . . . confusion. Mistress, I think by rights she is yours anyway.'

'Where is she? Show me.' Gwenn thrust Philippe at Katarin. The instant she saw the brown palfrey tethered alongside Alan's courser, large tears glistened at the corners of her eyes. 'It's Dancer!' she cried. 'Oh, thank you, Alan! Thank you!' And, flinging her arms about Ned's bemused cousin, she planted a grateful kiss on his cheek and darted to the mare's head.

Alan rubbed the spot she had kissed, conscious that he was unshaven and bristly. Catching Ned's eyes on him, he felt impelled to speak. 'Your wife's not altered much, cousin. Impulsive as ever.'

Ned bent an adoring gaze to where Gwenn was whispering in Dancer's ear. 'I hope you are right, Alan. I don't want her to change, but I'm afraid that these blows must sour her sweet nature.'

'Sweet?' Alan raised a questioning brow. He remembered the doll-like creature the mob had chased in Vannes. That image had misled him, there had always been more to the concubine's daughter than that. 'Love blinds you, Ned. Gwenn Herevi was never sweet. Determined, aye. A little madam, aye, but sweet—'

'She's Gwenn Fletcher now,' Ned reminded him, without heat, 'and dear to my heart.'

'If you think your wife is sweet after you've been wed three months, I'll give you two fresh-minted marks, Ned. You always were besotted with the girl.' There was a desperate yearning in his cousin's face, as though he ached for something he could never have, which was odd in a man who had succeeded in marrying the woman of his dreams. However, the conversation was taking too emotional a turn for Alan's liking. 'And now you have wed her,' Alan grinned, 'you have what you desire.'

'Have I?' Ned muttered, so low Alan thought he must have misheard him. Ned lifted soulful blue eyes. 'Will you accompany us, Alan? You've learnt the lie of the land as well as any guide we could hire.'

'My apologies, cousin.' Alan shook his head. 'I'm

sworn to the Duke, and I've some business of his to conclude in the area.' No need, at this stage, to enlighten Ned as to the exact nature of his business at Kermaria.

'You won the post you wanted?'

'Aye. I'm Captain of Duke Geoffrey's personal guard—'

'You've done well, cousin. I knew you would. You must have worked hard.'

'I did. But luck played its part,' Alan admitted. 'I like His Grace and he—'

'He likes you,' Ned finished.

Alan gave one of his twisted, self-deprecating smiles. 'Aye. It would appear that he does. Strange, isn't it?'

'You know it is not,' Ned said shortly. 'Now, Alan, about your being our guide . . .'

'I've only been granted a few days' leave. Duke Geoffrey's expecting me back in Rennes, and I've a survey to conduct on some tenants of his.'

Ned bit his lip. 'Of course, we shall make our own way if we must. But you are the ideal man, Alan.'

Overhearing, Gwenn came back and, putting her hand on her husband's arm, added her plea. 'Do say you will help us, Alan. We can trust you.'

Alan laughed, to lighten the mood; for the pair of them looked very grave, and he didn't want them sinking their hooks into him. 'I never thought to hear you say that to me, Mistress Blanche.'

On hearing Alan's nickname for his wife, Ned looked sharply from one to the other.

'You're cruel to ridicule me,' Gwenn said. 'But I understand why you do it. You think to avoid helping us by rousing my pride. But what use is pride to me?'

'You *have* changed,' Alan conceded.

'Yesterday changed me for ever. Yesterday stripped me naked. My father was hacked down, and my brother, and a much-loved uncle. I have no home. Indeed, I had no future till Ned chose to give me one. I have nothing, only,' she pointed at the guesthouse, 'those children. And if I have any say in the matter, they will reach a safe port. So don't think that anger will lift me out of my supplicant's role, Alan le Bret, for I have been purged of pride, or anger, of . . . everything. All I have left is my love for those children, and Ned, of course. And if going down on my knees and begging to you might help them, then I'll do it, and not mind it. Help us. Please. We need you.'

'I've orders to be with the Duke in Rennes in five days' time,' Alan said, uncomfortably.

Ned put out a hand. 'You could spare us a week, Alan. Send one of the brothers with a message to Duke Geoffrey. Surely a week is no matter.'

'If it takes five days to reach Ploumanach with the children, it will take another three for me to get back. Add to that a couple of days for setbacks, and it would be more like two weeks.'

'Take two then,' Gwenn urged.

'No.'

'Alan, please.'

'No! I will not break faith with the Duke. You can look elsewhere for your guide.' And wishing he didn't feel like a snake, Alan turned on his heel and marched towards the monks' cookhouse from which was wafting the mouth-watering smell of Brother Peter's new batch of bread.

Even in broad daylight, when the door was bolted, the vault under the hall of Kermaria manor was as dark as the anchorite's cell. The only source of natural light was down the air vent; and as the light must squeeze past an army of weeds and a carpet of moss that had sprung up on the damp stones of the airway, the daylight was filtered almost to nothing.

The day before, when Nicholas Warr had locked the two women in the undercroft, he had provided them with a candle. This had burned out long ago, and although Johanna had scratted around and unearthed a stub in a wall sconce, that had not lasted long, and for several hours Johanna and Mary had been sitting in tomb-like darkness.

'This place is as black as night, but it must be tomorrow by now,' Mary whispered. 'I'm thirsty. Johanna, do you think they've forgotten we're here?'

'No.' The wet nurse was wondering how Ned Fletcher was faring. Had he got away? Was *she* still with him? And what of her baby?

'Then why don't they come?' Mary went on. 'They must be simple if they think they can starve us into submission. Why, one of those casks of salt beef would keep the two of us going for a year, and I know there were at least half a dozen at the last tally.'

'Hunger's not the weapon they are using,' Johanna said abstractedly. If the Viking had not returned, then he must be on Ned Fletcher's trail. Which must mean that her beloved was free . . . Johanna realised Mary was waiting for her to add more. 'They have another weapon up their sleeves, and they're waiting for it to bite.'

'Another weapon?' Mary shivered. 'What might that be, Johanna? I can't say I like it in the storeroom, the damp's making my muscles creak like a rusty gale, but we have everything we need: beef, cheeses, smoked fish, wine, ale.'

'No wine, and no ale,' Johanna reminded the maid. 'Don't you remember, they removed the casks they'd not drunk dry?'

'Aye, so they did. But we have everything else.'

'Everything save what we need most. We have no water. And already we are thirsty.'

Mary blinked into an infinity of blackness. Her sigh rustled like a breeze playing through dry, dead leaves. 'Water. I see. How long do you think they'll wait?'

'Who knows? But if I had any pennies to wager, I'd say that when they do come in, they'll be drinking themselves. They will want to torment us.' Johanna usually avoided contact with members of her own sex, but she found herself groping for Holy Mary's arm.

'Mary, I'm truly sorry they have you in here. I thought they'd release you with the others.'

'I'm glad to be here,' Mary lied stoically. 'I am glad to share in your courage, Johanna. You are a brave, loyal girl, and I'd not have you face them alone.'

'I'm not brave. And I'm certainly not the least bit loyal,' Johanna confessed. 'I only . . . only wanted the babe to be safe.' And Ned Fletcher, she added silently.

'You *are* brave, Johanna,' Mary insisted with the confident, ringing tones of a brimstone preacher. 'You can dress it how you will, but I know you are brave. And seeing you – the only one out of all of us with the faith to face that . . . that monster of a man – why, you inspired me.' Mary clasped Johanna's hand. 'We'll face them together.'

This was the first time that Johanna had drawn comfort from another woman's touch, used as she was to viewing all other females as potential rivals. She returned the pressure on her hand, answering huskily, 'Aye. We face them together.'

The scraping of the bolt made an end to conversation. Light angled into the vault. Two men entered, the Viking captain and Nicholas Warr, and as Johanna had predicted, Malait was clutching a waterskin.

Getting hastily to their feet, the two women exchanged glances. Mary licked parched lips. Johanna wondered about Ned Fletcher. Neither of them smiled.

'Good morning, my pretties.' Otto swaggered towards them, tantalisingly swinging the waterskin from a thong wrapped round his solid wrist. 'I thought it was time we had our little chat. Warr?'

'Captain?'

'Secure the door, and bring that lamp over. I want to mark their expressions.'

'Aye, sir.'

The Viking raised his water bottle and, removing the stopper, took a long pull. Water dribbled down his chin, and the rivulets were soaked up in his forest of a beard. Both women stared fixedly at the lamp the archer was carrying. 'Not thirsty, eh?' In the beard, the wide mouth curved. 'Pity. You won't want this, then.' Upending the container, Otto poured the contents onto the floor.

Mary shut her eyes and her dry throat tried in vain to swallow.

'You've a visitor, little spy,' the captain said, looking at Johanna.

Mary's hand jerked in Johanna's, and the wet nurse felt the other woman's eyes boring into her. 'A visitor?'

'Your brother. He's anxious for your welfare. Shall I send him in?'

'You've already decided what you will do,' Johanna said dully. 'Nothing I say will have any effect on your actions.'

Otto did not gainsay her.

Mary had withdrawn her hand from Johanna's and was regarding her suspiciously. 'What does he mean, Johanna? Little spy? You could not have been in this man's employ. Johanna?'

'Oh, be quiet, Mary,' Johanna snapped. 'Can't you see he seeks to break our amity?'

Otto's thick finger stabbed at Mary. 'You, get upstairs. I want you to show me where St Clair is supposed to have buried his brat. While you, little spy, can wait here. I'll send Conan down when we've found the grave.'

The faintest of sighs slid past Johanna's full lips. Ned Fletcher must have got the babe away. Both must be safe.

Holding up the lamp as he entered the cellar, Conan saw his sister was perched on a casket of salt beef, gently pressing her breasts. 'Missing the babe, Johanna?' he asked indifferently.

Johanna raised her head and looked at her brother. 'I only gave him suck in the evenings,' she answered. 'I was trying to wean him. It doesn't hurt much. My milk will soon dry up.' Johanna wondered if Conan had been sent to pronounce sentence on her. Mary must have shown Malait the grave of the peasant's baby by now. Had it convinced Malait that St Clair's heir was dead? Conan's face was impassive, it gave nothing away. Johanna wondered what her fate would be if Malait remained suspicious. Would he torture her, to make her talk? Vikings were renowned for violence and cruelty throughout Christendom.

'Well, Conan, what's to do?'

'You're free.'

'Free?'

'You're to come home with me. Here, you'll be thirsty.' Casually, the pedlar tossed a bulging waterskin onto her lap.

Johanna hid her astonishment behind as blank a front as she could summon. Ducking her head, she made a show of fumbling at the stopper. 'What happened to Mary?' she managed, and to give herself time to think, she put the bottle to her dry lips and drank.

'Not much. The maid pointed out the infant's grave to Malait, and now she's on her way to Huelgastel.'

'What . . . what made him believe us? I should have thought your captain would take some convincing.'

'He verified that what you said was the truth.'

'Verified? How?'

'Captain Malait had the grave dug over and found a baby boy.'

'No!'

Conan was amused by his sister's revulsion. 'Time we started back for Vannes, Johanna. Drink up.'

Johanna felt sick, with relief as well as revulsion. Thank Christ the grave had contained a boy. If it had been a girl, it would have been her death warrant.

Johanna kept her head down as she walked through the hall and into the courtyard. The yard was become a charnel house, with the bodies of the slain stacked under sheeting like logs ready for winter. Johanna averted her eyes, but not before she glimpsed a trousered leg sticking out from underneath the table linen. She had only lived at Kermaria for a few months, and never expected to feel sympathy for the people here, but now, seeing them laid out like so much dead wood, Johanna discovered she'd stayed long enough for fellow feeling to have grown.

Anxious to shake the dust of Kermaria from her shoes, Johanna turned her face to the bridge.

In the solar, conferring with Nicholas Warr, Otto watched from the high window. 'There she goes, Warr.'

Nicholas Warr stared at Johanna's retreating back. 'You say she refused to administer poppy juice to the child?'

'So her brother maintained.'

'And you suspect she's keeping something back?'

Otto bared discoloured teeth. 'I'm as sure of that as I'm sure the sun will rise at tomorrow's dawning.'

'Then why let her go, Captain?'

Otto's smile was tinged with triumph. 'Because, my dear fellow, she's as mutinous a wench as you could hope to meet, and now she's released, she will be off her guard. Her brother will be able to worm whatever it is out of her faster than I could if I had her flayed alive.'

'Do you trust the pedlar?'

Otto held up a chinking drawstring pouch. 'He's vermin. But as long as I hold this, I trust him. Conan will be back.'

'You've made me walk so far and so fast, Conan, my shoes are wearing out,' Johanna complained, stopping to sit on a milestone. A grey rat of a dog who had crawled out of the ground-elder by Kermaria crossroads and had been shadowing them squatted in the road by her shoes and scratched a ragged ear. Conan had not slackened his pace, but Johanna picked up her feet and examined them. Blisters were forming – she was not used to walking. The mongrel's stumpy tail gave a tentative wag. 'Why is this thing following us, Conan?'

With a sigh, Conan stopped and frowned over his shoulder. 'It's a pest, a stray.' Impatience was building up within him. They had not progressed above three miles; she walked painfully slowly, did his sister. 'You should have shown some restraint at table, Johanna,' he said maliciously. 'There's too much of you to carry about, that's why your feet ache. You're fatter than ever you were before you went to Kermaria.'

A shadow darkened Johanna's plump countenance. Ned had preferred Gwenn Herevi over her, and Gwenn Herevi was skinny as a rake. She did not like to think that there might be some truth in her brother's accusation. 'It's all very well for you to criticise, Conan, but how could I let all that food go to waste? They ate well at the manor. A saint on a Lenten fast would have been tempted. Besides, I was eating for two.'

'Three more like,' Conan responded sourly.

Johanna flexed her feet, counted another blister on one of her heels, and began massaging her toes.

'Come on, do,' Conan said, glancing at the sun. 'I want to be back in Vannes before they lock the gates.'

'Look, Conan, already there's a hole in this shoe.' Poking her finger through a rent in the leather where the upper had come away from the sole, Johanna waggled her shoe at him. The dog cocked its head on one side.

Conan prepared to walk on. 'You can buy more shoes in Vannes, I've lodgings directly over the cobbler's.'

'Buy more shoes? But Conan, I've no money.'

The pedlar stood still as a standing stone. 'What, none?'

Johanna should have been warned by the set of her brother's shoulders, but with her mind fixed on her feet, she did not notice. 'Not a penny,' she said cheerfully. 'I spent what I had on the material to make this dress.'

Conan turned. 'I'd hoped for help with the rent. I can't afford to keep you, Johanna. I don't need no bloody millstone.'

'I should have thought you'd have feathered your nest well enough on what I told you concerning Kermaria,' Johanna said sharply. 'You could at least help me out till I find . . . an alternative means of support.'

The pedlar gazed coldly at his sister. 'I found you that position at Kermaria,' he said as if he'd gone out of his way to find her the job. He had indeed done well out of placing her with St Clair, but it didn't suit him to admit that. 'I owe you nothing. Plums like that can't fall in your lap every day of the week.'

According to Otto Malait, the ungrateful wench was holding something back. Perhaps he could induce her to confide in him by trickery, or fear. Fear would have to be a last resort, it might turn her away from him. However, a pinch of it would not go amiss. If Johanna was worried he might not take her in, it might spur her to talk freely.

Not for a moment did it occur to Conan to play on his sister's affections. His life had never been enriched with family feeling, and he was Johanna's brother only when it suited him to be. In the inn all those months ago when he had overheard Ned Fletcher and Raymond Herevi mention a wet nurse, he had remembered the Count's interest in the St Clair family and had seen at once that there was gain for him in sending Johanna to Kermaria. His sister's needs had not weighed with him at all. If the opportunity had not presented itself, he would just as happily have seen her reduced to beggary.

Now, on the long road to Vannes, he was irritable. Johanna was too slow, but he could not abandon her till he had the information Malait wanted. He cast his eyes up the road and saw, balanced on the rim of the horizon, a building which to an innocent eye resembled a hundred other wayside taverns. Conan recognised it. It had an unsavoury reputation. Honest women shunned the place, for inside, women of another stamp took the drinks to the customers' trestles. And if, as often was the case, more intimate services were required of the women, they would lead their clients to an upstairs chamber where two rows of pallets were spread over the floorboards, each screened from the next by a series of dingy, moth-eaten curtains stretched out on poles. The tattered curtains made a mockery of privacy, but no one ever complained.

Following the direction of her brother's gaze, and not knowing the reputation of the inn, Johanna's eyes brightened. 'Is that a hostelry, Conan? I'm hungry, I've not broken my fast. And despite that water you gave me, I could drink a well dry.' Johanna was so invigorated by the sight of the inn that she jammed her shoes back on her swollen feet and hobbled towards him. The cur followed.

Conan opened his mouth to loose a scathing comment about gluttony, but inspiration struck and he held his peace. Perhaps if he indulged his sister and bought her wine, that would loosen her tongue. Maybe he should try persuasion on her instead of the threats he habitually used. Pinning a passable smile to his face, he held out his hand. 'Come on, Johanna. If you step out a little, I'll buy you some food when we reach the tavern.'

Johanna gave him a grateful smile and wondered silently what had suddenly persuaded him to offer her food instead of insults. She threaded her arm through his and limped steadily on.

Inside the hostelry, Johanna was at first too thirsty to take account of her surroundings, and when Conan ordered a full bottle of Gascon wine to be brought to their table – an expense she had never known him spare her before – it would have seemed churlish to have refused such untoward generosity and admit to a preference for a cool jug of freshly drawn water.

The wine was rich and heady, and made her head spin. ''Why, Conan!' she exclaimed when she had drained her cup. 'You are generous to me!'

Conan did not feel at all generous. Reluctantly, he topped up her cup. The mongrel who plagued him had slunk under the table; to relieve his feelings, Conan tried to kick it, but the dog, used to this treatment, nimbly evaded his boot. Indeed, the expenditure rankled to such an extent that when the whore who was serving them demanded instant payment, Conan fumbled the coins and dropped them on the floor. He picked them up, and the brainless creature under the trestle licked his hand. 'You've had a hard time of it lately, sister,' Conan said when the wench had disappeared with his money. And though the words stuck in his throat, he even managed to add, 'If your brother cannot buy you a drink at a time of trial, who can?'

If Conan's generosity was unexpected, his sympathy was doubly so, and the dim hostelry was lost in a sudden mist as Johanna counted her miseries and her eyes brimmed. Ned Fletcher's bright, Saxon features wavered in her mind's eye. Her feet throbbed. She had no money. She would never see the English captain again. Thrusting her nose into her cup, she emptied it like a trooper.

Trusting his money was well-spent, Conan had the bottle ready and poured bravely.

'I'm hungry, Conan,' Johanna said, wiping her nose with the back of her hand.

'I'll order in a minute, the servers are busy.' The servers were not busy, but Conan wanted his sister well-oiled before she ate. If she ate before she drank, it would cost twice as much in wine to make her talk. He regarded her impartially while he waited for the wine to take effect.

Johanna had rolled her wide sleeves up to her elbows and her plump arms rested on the table. Her cheeks were round, rosy and shiny as two apples, for the walk had made her hot, and her face and forehead bore a film of perspiration. Downy hairs covered her upper lip. The dress that she had so improvidently wasted her money on, was of good quality fabric, but it was now stained with the dust of the road and there were unsightly sweat marks under her arms.

Last winter, it had been the fashion among noble women to leave the side seams of their over-gown, or bliaud, open, lacing them at intervals so that the coloured undergown was revealed. Conan had seen Countess Eleanor de Roncier wear such a bliaud. His sister had clearly aped this fashion, but she had failed to take into account the fullness of her figure. Johanna's bliaud was in fact a replica of one of Gwenn Herevi's, and Johanna, no needlewoman, had cobbled it together in the hope of attracting Ned Fletcher's attention. But far from giving her the elegance that she was striving for, the effect was lumpy and messy. Conan grinned. Johanna bulged out of the sides of her gown like a sausage which was too fat for its casing. Controlling his expression, he replenished his sister's cup. He had lost count of how much she had drunk, but the bottle was down to three fingers, and he had barely sipped from his own cup.

Johanna lifted a hand to her head and rubbed it wearily. The wine had numbed the pain in her feet, but it was having a depressing effect on her senses. She wished Conan would hurry and order food. Wine had a strange effect on an empty stomach, and the one Conan had chosen seemed stronger than usual. Johanna felt listless and tired, and her eyes were having difficulty in focusing.

'It's a shame you never did as I asked about the poppy juice,' Conan opened, cautiously. Brown eyes blinked at him through plump fingers. 'The babe was obviously cursed, and you lost a chance to make a coin or two.' His sister removed her hand from her eyes and it flopped clumsily onto the table. Conan took this as a sign that the wine was doing its work.

'What do you mean, the babe was obviously cursed?' The whites of Johanna's eyes had gone pink, as though she had been weeping.

'He died, didn't he?' Conan said.

It was a struggle for Johanna to recollect the story she and Holy Mary had concocted between them. 'Oh, aye. The babe died of the marsh fever.'

'And as the infant's death was so obviously fated, I was thinking it a pity that you had not profited by it.

If you had given him the drug, you could have claimed the reward de Roncier offered.' He heaved a remorseful sigh. 'But as it is, the child is dead, and you have nothing.'

'I'm hungry.'

'In a minute, Johanna.'

Johanna raised the glass and summoned a shaky smile. 'I can wait. This wine takes the edge off my appetite.' And my grief, she thought. She wondered how much distance there was between her and Ned Fletcher and her babe. She hoped Malait had called off his dogs.

Conan smiled, and held out a fresh bottle. 'Have some more, sister.'

'I might have been rich, Conan,' Johanna announced confidingly, watching the red stream pour into her cup.

'Rich,' he agreed.

'Captain Malait did call his men off, didn't he?'

'Aye.'

Reassured that her captain was safely away, Johanna continued with her confession. It was wonderful to discover that she had a sympathetic brother. 'I might have had anything I wanted.' She paused to sip her wine; she had drunk too much to notice that this second bottle was a rougher, less dear, wine. Conan was not about to spend more than he had to.

'Not quite anything, sister, but certainly the Count's reward would have bought you a trinket or two.'

'No, Conan. You don't know . . . I could have had more than any poxy trinket if I'd set my mind to it. I saw where she hid it.' Conan's muscles clenched, but Johanna was too absorbed in her thoughts to notice. 'No one else knew. All I had to do was to reach out my hand and take it.'

Conan's breath was suspended. He did not have the faintest notion what his sister was babbling about, but it sounded as though they were coming to it. An encouraging noise was all the speech he dared make. 'Mmm?'

'I missed my chance, Conan. Because of Ned Fletcher. If it had not been for the English captain, I would have taken it months ago.'

'Taken what, Johanna?' Conan asked as casually as he could.

Unsteadily, Johanna set her cup down and stared at the table which was rocking slightly from side to side. 'Conan, I've been a fool.' She focused on him, and he was astonished to see disillusionment in her eyes. 'You'd kill me if you knew the chance I'd passed up.'

Conan reached for his sister's hand, and patted it awkwardly. 'Kill you? Never.'

'Oh, Conan,' to his horror her eyes began to fill, 'you are kind . . . Such a good brother . . .' She sobbed.

'There, there. Never mind, Johanna. Have another drink, and tell your brother all about it . . .'

Dusk was over in a matter of moments, for a dark blanket of clouds was draped low in the sky, hiding both evening star and moon. The blanket of grey seemed to absorb the last of the daylight rays, and all at once the western sky was no lighter than the eastern sky. Night settled over the forest.

Nose to the ground, a female wolf was beating the bounds of her territory. She was sleek and content, having gorged herself on a fox cub which had foolishly strayed too far from its lair. Her teats were full of milk, for she had cubs of her own. She would not leave them for long.

The wolf was unfettered by the lack of light. Here, where the trees grew at their thickest and wildest and a million leaves blocked out both sun and moon alike, even summer nights were of the darkest kind, but the wolf's lamp-like eyes had a feral glow to them which, though muted, was more than enough to light her path. She stalked boldly through the woody acres, for this was her domain, and there was little in it that she feared.

Her nostrils flared as she went, and she caught the interlopers' scent before she heard them. Holding her body as rigid as a century-old oak, she sniffed again. Here was a scent that lifted the fur on the back of her neck. Here was a scent that brought a low, rumbling growl to the base of her throat. Here was something the wolf *did* fear. Here was man.

The wolf had sense to keep her growl locked in her throat. Poised on her pads, ears pricked, she sniffed, judging the magnitude of the threat. She heard a cry, one of hunger, and when her teats ached in instant response, her instincts informed her that the men must have a baby with them. The wolf cocked her head to one side, wondering why the hateful yellow heat which men always placed beside them was not there now. There were other scents the wolf recognised; horse, and mule. The cry came again, her full teats burned, and lowering herself to her belly, she edged round the men's encampment to keep her own scent from reaching the horses. She crept closer. The smell of fear hung in the air.

Cloaks were spread out over the carpet of leaves and debris on the forest floor, like islands in a pool crowded with water weeds. A man and a woman were seated on one of the islands; they had a child and a baby with them, and the baby was quiet now, sucking milk from a cup held by the woman. On the other cloak, not two feet away from this group, another man sat alone.

'Katarin?' The woman whispered to the child. Her words meant nothing to the wolf. 'Would you like more bread?'

The child shook her head. It was this child, the wolf realised, who smelt most strongly of fear. The isolated man, whose gaze was abstracted, was staring fixedly at his knee-high boots.

'Katarin? Please try to answer me.' The woman's voice had a thread of desperation running through it, and the man with the boots looked across at her. 'Would you like more bread, Katarin? Or some milk?'

The child shook her head.

'It's no use badgering her,' the man seated next to

the woman said. His hair gleamed pale in the darkness.
'She'll answer you when she's ready.'

'Don't worry, mistress.' The man with the boots stirred. 'It's a temporary affliction. The child was hurt at Kermaria.'

'But, Alan, she bears no wound. I've examined every inch of her.'

'It's not her body that was wounded. I've seen similar illnesses before – in soldiers returning from battle. They escaped apparently unscathed, yet they too were struck dumb for a time. I have observed how it tends to afflict those with a more . . . delicate cast of mind. It passes.'

'But how long? How long till she heals?'

'I cannot say. Your sister seems strong in her body, but who can say what is going on in a child's mind – in anyone's mind? Give her time.' He stretched himself out on his cloak and dragged it over his shoulders. 'Get to sleep as soon as you can. We'll be on the move at first light.'

An owl hooted, and the she-wolf watched till the humans' stirrings ceased. The smell of fear thickened, and by it the wolf knew that the child was not asleep. Curious, and certain now that the interlopers intended her no harm, the wolf watched, and waited. The smell of another's fear was a potent attraction.

The little girl stirred, and sat up. Next to her, the woman sighed in her sleep, but she did not waken. The child got to her feet and began walking in a line that would lead her directly to the wolf. The wolf tensed, not to spring, for she was not hungry, but ready to fly for cover.

'Katarin,' the solitary man was awake, 'where are you going?'

The wind shook the leaves and there was silence.

The solitary man sighed, got up, and walked through the coal-black night to where the child hovered on the edge of the clearing. He stopped not three feet away from the wolf's twitching nose. Close up, the toes of his boots were shiny and polished. 'Can't you sleep, Katarin?' he asked gently.

Doubtfully, the girl shook her head.

The man lowered himself to the child's level and made his voice smile. 'Are you afraid?'

The shake was more positive.

'Not afraid, eh?' The man gave an amused snort. 'You're braver than I would be in your shoes, Katarin. Perhaps you are cold?'

The child considered this, and nodded.

'So am I, Katarin. And I'm lonely on my own. Come, you'll be warmer with me. Would you like to sleep with me?' He held his hand out towards her, and the child took it without hesitating.

'Sensible girl,' the man murmured, and picking her up he carried her back to his cloak.

The smell of fear was diffused now, broken up by the breeze; her milk-filled teats reminded the wolf of her young, and she crept soundlessly away. When she had put a good distance between her and the interlopers, she stood upright and raced off, a dark streak in a darker night, to see her cubs were safe.

Chapter Twenty-Two

It was cool under the heavy canopy of leaves, and as the bridleway was nothing more than a slender brown ribbon winding gently through a sea of foaming bracken, they had to ride in single file. Alan sat easily in his saddle; as guide he took the leader's place. Gwenn, riding Dancer, came second – she carried her brother before her; Ned brought up the rear with Katarin. The monks' best saddle had been put on Dancer, and Ned was left battling with a broken-down saddle he reckoned old enough to have seen service at Hastings. Its frame was cracked, and every time the mule put down a hoof, he felt the jarring right up his spine. It was uncomfortable for him, and no doubt for the mule too, which might explain the animal's reluctance to keep up with the others. The cantle of the saddle had had all the stuffing knocked out of it, and the skirt lay flat on the mule's back, but at the moment this was serving them well, for Katarin sat behind her brother-in-law, hands hooked round his belt.

'Ned, are you all right?' Gwenn reined in, and waited for her husband to catch up.

Jabbing in his heels, Ned tried to squeeze another few paces out of his reluctant steed. 'I'm beginning to wonder if I'd not do better to throw away this saddle altogether. I might make better progress bareback.'

'But what about Katarin?'

'That's a point,' Ned conceded. 'I doubt she'd stay on without one.' He twisted round to reassure himself that his silent companion was as comfortable as possible, and was rewarded with a vague smile. 'Good girl,' he murmured, 'you're doing well.'

Waiting till Ned's mule reached Dancer's hindquarters, Gwenn lowered her voice to a whisper. 'Ned, there's something I'd like you to keep from Alan.'

'Keep from Alan?' At this point the mule let out a bray of protest and, digging in its hoofs, refused to budge.

'I . . . I don't want him to know I've got the Stone Rose with me. You won't tell him, will you?'

Ned laboured away with his heels, with little effect on the recalcitrant mule. 'Why should I tell him? It's not the sort of thing it would occur to me to mention to Alan.'

'I know, Ned. But I . . . I don't want Alan discovering it's in your pack. You'll keep it from him, won't you?'

Ned threw her a puzzled glance, and tried shaking his mount's reins. 'Aye, but—'

'Ned, please.'

'I won't mention it if you don't want me to,' he promised, exasperated and panting with his effort on the mule. The animal was rolling its eyes and champing on its bit, and it would not take a step. 'Christ, this animal's got a hide of iron.' Ned swore and clambered from the saddle. 'I'll walk.'

Alan hailed them from the front. 'What's going on?'

Gwenn urged Dancer through plumes of green bracken towards Alan.

'It's Ned's mule,' she explained when she reached him. 'It won't keep up.'

'I'll take Katarin, if that helps.'

'You would?'

'You have kept your low opinion of me, I think,' Alan said in a soft, intimate voice.

Gwenn floundered under the cool, grey gaze, and the memory of the promise she had just extracted from Ned stung her to an instant denial that betrayed her true feelings better than she knew. 'No. No!'

'You always disliked me, didn't you, mistress?'

'Disliked you?' Gwenn looked nonplussed. 'I don't dislike you.' Her voice had a ring of truth to it, for though she did not trust Alan, there had always been a spark of something between them, which mistrust could not snuff out.

'But it galls you to accept my help.'

'No. Alan, I am grateful.' At that moment, a golden rod of light fell through the vaulting branches and bathed Alan's head with a halo of brightness. His hair assumed the blue-black sheen of a raven's wing, and for an instant the slate-coloured eyes sparkled with a brilliant clarity which more than equalled the brightness of the gem in the Stone Rose.

Startled, Gwenn found herself gazing into the depths of Alan's eyes. The effect of the shaft of sunlight on his countenance when all else was in shadow was extraordinary. It made her feel as though she could see to the heart of the man, even perhaps to his soul. As she gazed into eyes that were no longer unfathomable but clear as crystal, she became aware of a curling in her stomach, akin to embarrassment. It was as though she was seeing something very private, something which belonged to Alan alone and yet which attracted her very much. There was a part of Alan le Bret which she yearned to reach out for, which she yearned to cherish . . . Then Alan's horse took a step, the light shifted, the curtain dropped into place, and Alan's eyes looked the way they always did, remote and cloudy with shadows, and Gwenn was left struggling with a deep, inexplicable sense of loss.

'Mistress?'

'I . . . I beg your pardon?'

'I offered to lighten Ned's load and take Katarin.'

'My thanks, cousin.' Ned had caught up, mule and Katarin in tow. He rubbed the base of his spine and gave an expressive grimace. 'But I'm better walking.'

Alan frowned at the mule. 'I should never have allowed myself to be persuaded to act as your guide. I hope that monk gets my message to Duke Geoffrey. I risk losing the best place I ever had as it is, without that obstinate animal delaying me further.' He looked at Ned. It's a long way to Ploumanach, cousin. Can you keep pace all the way?'

'I'm not yet doddering, I can keep going for miles.' Ned grinned. 'Perhaps when I tire you can take my place.'

Alan favoured Gwenn with a slow, considering look which brought the hot blood rushing to her cheeks and sent sinful thoughts scurrying where they had no place to be. 'Take your place when you tire, Ned?' he mused, wickedly. 'I think I should enjoy that.'

Lifting her chin, and still trying to grasp exactly what it was she had seen in Alan's eyes, Gwenn clutched her brother to her breast. How was it that one moment the Duke's captain could rouse feelings of great tenderness in her and the next moment she could cheerfully strangle him? She wondered if Ned would react badly to Alan's provocative remark.

'My thanks, cousin, I knew I could rely on you.'

Ned's blinkered acceptance of anything Alan said or did irritated Gwenn further. She glared at Alan.

His wicked mouth edged up at the corners. Then, turning Firebrand's head in a northerly direction, he presented his back to his companions and spurred his mount down the track.

'Gwenn?'

'Yes, Ned.'

'Alan is not upsetting you, is he?'

'No. Alan is not upsetting me.'

'Because if he is, we could hire another guide.'

'No. We had better stick with Alan.' But despite her denials, she rode for the next hour in a fulminating silence as total as that her sister was keeping on the mule. Deep down, she realised that she was only angry because part of her had wanted to respond to Alan . . .

Conan had tracked Ned and Gwenn as far as St Félix-in-the-Wood. He was working on his own. He knew that when Otto Malait had stormed down on the prior like the Grim Reaper, he had failed to learn anything concerning Gwenn Herevi, but Conan had hopes that more cunning methods might bring success.

Blending into the shadows behind a hazel shrub, he watched as two of the brethren piled wood into two deep willow baskets with thick leather straps attached to the sides. As far as Conan could gather, the brothers were conferring about a mule, of all things, which did not sound promising. Nevertheless, he resolved to listen patiently.

'I would never have thought it possible, Brother Marzin, but I miss that mule.' The monk snapped an overlong branch into more manageable pieces. 'I regret Prior Hubert's selling of him.'

The other monk laughed and waved at the baskets. 'You miss the mule because he carried these, Dominig,' he said.

'No, Marzin, it's more than that. That mule belonged to my father, and I liked him. I shall miss him when I go to the river.' To Dominig's delight, Prior Hubert had given him permanent charge of the fish tanks and eel traps.

'That mule was an intractable beast.'

'I brought him from home. I liked him.'

'Theirs was the greater need, Brother Dominig,' came the pious answer.

Conan gave a silent, cavernous yawn.

'Aye, so it was. I cannot deny that. Poor girl. So young and left to shoulder so much responsibility.'

Mid-yawn, Conan stiffened and strained to hear. Girl? What girl? To his intense annoyance, he saw the dirty white cur creep into the corner of his vision. He had thought he had foisted the animal off on Johanna. Motioning the dog away, Conan prayed it would not betray him. His poorly stomach churned.

'True,' the monk named Marzin had a strong voice which was easy to hear despite its foreign lilt, 'but consider, Dominig, how God provided for her. He gave her Ned Fletcher to share her burden, and then my brother arrived.'

Wondering who the monk's brother was, and how he fitted into this, Conan listened for more. He remembered Ned Fletcher. Was this monk English like Ned Fletcher?

'I cannot help wondering,' Dominig mused, 'why God permitted the Count to destroy Mistress Gwenn's home in the first place. If He was so eager to provide for her, why did He allow such a howling injustice to take place?'

'Brother Dominig!' Marzin clucked disapproval.

Conan heard the reproof in the young monk's tone, but skulking behind the hazel, with a wary eye on the wretched dog and an obstructed view of the two monks, he was unable to discern the affectionate mockery lighting Brother Marzin's eyes.

'It's only a day since you took your vows, and already you are questioning His will.'

Another log thudded into a basket and, furtively parting the branches of the shrub, Conan saw that one of the monks, presumably Dominig, had his lips set in a straight line. 'Mock me if you will, Marzin,' he said miserably. 'But try as I might, I cannot understand how God can be so cruel.'

Marzin went over to his companion. 'It's man that is cruel, Dominig, not the Almighty,' he said gently.

Dominig gazed for a moment at Marzin's round, open countenance. 'You are blessed, Brother, you have such faith. Would that I had a tenth of your faith.'

Marzin's plump face was split by a smile. 'Faith upholds me when all else fails.'

'But, Marzin—'

Marzin shook his pale, newly tonsured crown. 'Not now, Dominig, the kindling is needed in the cookhouse.'

Obediently, Dominig scanned the clearing, his eyes chancing on a fallen branch in front of Conan's hazel

412

hide. Crossing to the shrub, the monk scooped up the bough. Conan's belly cramped with the fear of imminent discovery, but the monk merely straightened and reverted to his original theme. 'What do you think they will do with my mule when they reach their journey's end?'

'*Your* mule?' Marzin's voice stressed the possessive pronoun with definite reproof. 'We hold all our possessions in common, Dominig, have you forgot?'

'I haven't forgotten, Marzin,' Dominig's reply was almost sharp. 'But that animal did belong to my father. I brought him with me when I joined as a novice. I can't help it if I am attached to him.'

'Don't you think your attachment to that animal might in part be the reason Prior Hubert gave him up so easily?' Marzin asked astutely. 'In selling him, he broke your bondage to the past.'

'But it's a long way they're taking him.'

Where are they taking him? Behind his bush, Conan willed the dog to keep still. He willed the monks to supply him with the answer he needed. Where? Where were they going?

'No so far,' Marzin reassured his brother. 'Ploumanach is only five days away the way your mule plods.'

'Ploumanach,' Conan breathed, and a slow smile spread across his weathered face. 'Ploumanach.' In Breton, Ploumanach meant 'place of the monks', and that didn't tell Conan its location. He hadn't the foggiest idea where Ploumanach was, but he would find out.

'Five days away?' Brother Dominig's knowledge of distant places, like most people's, was limited to a ten-mile radius of his home, in his case the monastery. Anything outside that he knew about in only the most hazy terms.

'Relax, Ploumanach is in Brittany, Dominig,' Marzin replied with a laugh. 'Your mule is still in Christendom.'

Conan had the information he had come for. 'Ploumanach,' he muttered. 'Ploumanach.' And holding the branches aside with finger and thumb, the pedlar stole from the clearing.

If he did what was expected of him, he should hand this information on to Captain Malait together with what Johanna had told him about the jewel, but he was pulled two ways. Was it likely that the Viking's reward would come anywhere near the value of the gem? If it turned out to be half the size that Johanna had said, it would be worth a fortune.

The little white cur nudged his heels. About to lash out, it occurred to Conan that the mongrel, by not betraying his presence to the monks, was learning sense. He deserved a reward. Ferreting a heel of wheat loaf and a chunk of meat from his scrip, Conan threw them to the dog who devoured them in two famished bites.

Conan thought hard as he strode through the trees. Was this the moment to break away from de Roncier? He had been thinking that it was time he did something for himself, and this jewel of Gwenn Herevi's was a godsend – if it existed.

Conan understood that such a betrayal would mean exile from his home, for the Count had a long memory; but Conan was rootless. He did not feel bound to Vannes and southern Brittany, any more than he felt bound to his sister Johanna. He spared the sibling he had so casually abandoned in the disreputable hostelry no more than a passing thought. He was not his sister's keeper, and in any case the girl was no innocent – had she not already borne a child? Johanna could fend for herself.

The pedlar wavered, unable quite to take the final decision to strike out in a new direction. 'Ploumanach. Ploumanach,' he muttered, imprinting the name in his mind. 'Shall we go there, boy?' he asked the dog, whose canine eyes were riveted on his feeder. The stumpy tail wagged eagerly. Assuming the jewel existed, suppose it was lost or sold by the time he reached Ploumanach? He would have thrown away a spasmodic but fairly regular source of money by alienating Captain Malait. It was a risk. But on the other hand, if he got his hands on the gem, he would never have to worry about where the next crust was coming from.

Conan came to a decision.

It was the middle of the afternoon, and Philippe, who had spent the morning either dozing or gazing up at the nodding leaves, had tired of the novelty of the ride. His crying had at first been petulant and fretful, but now he was working himself up into a genuine rage, kicking his legs against the wrappings which held him immobile in his sister's arms.

Alan, coming at length to the conclusion that St Clair's heir was not going to cry himself to sleep, reined back. 'Do you want to stop?'

Gwenn flung him a grateful look, eyes harassed, hair in disarray, as she juggled with reins and infant's coverlet. 'Could we? Do you think it's safe?'

Alan dismounted. 'A few minutes won't hurt,' he said, stretching like a cat and coming towards her. 'We could all do with a break.'

'Philippe is not used to being confined. He doesn't normally cry like this, but he's learning to crawl, and he finds the restrictions irksome.'

Reaching Gwenn first, Ned took her reins from her and wound them round a branch before lifting Philippe from her lap. As soon as the baby was placed on the ground and his coverlet removed, the crying stopped.

'Knows his own mind, doesn't he?' Alan commented, and seeing Ned was intent on the baby, he offered Gwenn his hand with a gallant flourish. 'Lady Blanche?'

Gwenn slid to the ground in front of Alan and his hands went to her waist, steadying her. His lips were framing a light, flirtatious remark when something about the closeness of her, and the pink in her cheeks, gave him pause. For a moment he was whisked back two years to the time they had sheltered in the Locmariaquer dolmen and, as then, he felt faint stirrings of alarm. They had kissed then, they must not do so again. Carefully, Alan peeled his hands from her too-willowy waist where they seemed inclined to linger and stepped back.

Privately he agreed with Ned, Gwenn was pretty, but Alan had never found resisting prettiness difficult; looks did not count for much, and were not to be taken seriously. Prettiness, like flowers, soon faded. But this past day he had seen another side of Gwenn, a side he had always suspected was there. He had watched how she put her brother and sister's needs before her own, and he had seen the determination with which she battled on against the odds. He must repress his growing feeling for her. What would she think if she knew the way his thoughts were tending? Would she be shocked? Once or twice Alan had caught her eyes on him, and they had been glowing like dark amber. Unconsciously, he sighed. He must stop this, now, before it became too painful. He could not hurt Ned. Gwenn was Ned's wife.

Seeing the frown darkening his brow, Gwenn misinterpreted the reason for it. 'I'm sorry, Alan. We are making slower progress than you anticipated. It will be many days before you can rejoin your Duke.'

Gwenn's mouth . . . Her lips were rosy, and slightly parted. She was flushed from the ride, and looked very desirable. Though there were at least two paces between them now, Alan could feel the heat of her body. His scowl deepened while he tried to recall when he had last enjoyed a woman. It seemed an age ago. It was obviously time he found one, and the sooner the better. But would another woman's mouth look as tempting as Gwenn's?

'Alan?' Ned brought Alan back to earth with a thud.

'Aye?' Whatever was the matter with him? A harmless flirtation with Ned's wife was one thing, but adultery was out of the question. It had anyway never held any appeal for Alan, even before he had discovered the truth of his birth; learning that the man he had adored as his father was in fact his stepfather had only strengthened this conviction. Gwenn Herevi – no, that was wrong, she was Gwenn Fletcher now and he must strive to remember that – Gwenn Fletcher, tempting though she was, was not for him.

'Pass Katarin down, would you?'

Moving to the mule, Alan obliged, and the little girl gave him one of her rare smiles. Under the concerned gaze of the three adults, Katarin crossed to where her brother was crawling in the leaves.

Alan heard Gwenn's sigh, and Ned must have done too, for he put an arm round her and pulled her to his side. 'She'll heal, Gwenn,' Ned murmured, kissing her ear. Gwenn coloured, and threw a self-conscious glance at Alan; and Alan began loosening his horse's girth.

'Alan?'

'Yes, mistress?' Ned's arm was draped round her shoulders and it looked as though it belonged there.

'Is there a village nearby?'

'There's nothing for at least seven miles. Then we reach Pontivy. Why?'

Pontivy was a flourishing market town, and one of the larger settlements in the vicinity, complete with small military garrison under command of the Rohan family.

Gwenn's lips turned down at the edges. 'I . . . I'd hoped to persuade you to find a physician to examine Katarin.'

'I don't think that would be wise,' Ned objected swiftly. 'Malait might be hot on our trail. We should wait till we arrive at Ploumanach.'

Unhappily, Gwenn nodded. 'I expect you are right. But Alan could go to the town. They can't know Alan is with us. And won't sound silver buy us a healer we can trust to keep his mouth shut?'

'We should keep our eyes and ears open for the rest of the afternoon,' Alan said, remembering the Knights of St John had a hospital at Pontivy. 'If by the time we make camp we have not seen anything to alarm us, I think a visit to the town might be in order. We'll probably be out of food by then and will need more supplies, especially for the babe. I agree it has to be me who ventures into Pontivy.' It also occurred to Alan that he could find himself a woman. The presence of the Rohan garrison virtually guaranteed that there would be whores a-plenty. He saw nothing wrong with the trade they plied. In his mind, good, old-fashioned lust was perfectly natural, and no sin. Fornication between two consenting adults, where was the wrong in that? It was adultery that was fraught with perils, that and sex that took no heed of the consequences.

'Will we reach Pontivy by nightfall?' Gwenn asked.

'Unless that mule turns lame.'

'Perhaps . . . perhaps you could exchange Ned's mule in the town for something more comfortable?'

Alan looked consideringly at the mule. Without doubt the animal had seen better days. 'That will cost you too,' he said doubtfully, 'and a deal more than any physician. Do you have any idea how much a horse costs? Why, I've seen knights forced to ride around on mules that make a prince of Ned's beast.'

She lifted her chin. 'I told you. We have money.'

That mouth, even when she was angry . . .

'No, Gwenn!' Ned objected warmly. 'This mule does me very well.'

'Don't lie, Ned. It does not do well at all. It's a flea-bitten, crabby old thing, and I'd like you to have a horse like Alan's.'

Alan laughed to hear her assume that the courser belonged to him. 'This is not my horse, Gwenn. Fire-brand is on loan from Duke Geoffrey.'

Ned took Gwenn's chin and tipped her face to his. 'We're not wasting money on a horse for me.'

'Whose money is it?' she said, thrusting her bottom lip forwards.

'Why yours, you know that,' Ned answered equably.

'And we must save it, not waste it on a horse for me.'

Like St Jerome, Ned seemed to have a limitless supply of patience and his own brand of determination. When making her marriage vows Gwenn must have sworn to obey her husband, and if Alan were Ned, he'd not hesitate to command her obedience, and have done. But he was not Ned, and he was not married to Gwenn.

'I'm off to the stream to water Firebrand, lest Duke Geoffrey string me up for neglect,' he said abruptly and left the glade.

The great green forest which clothed inland Brittany was eaten into by rivers, and by the townships and settlements dotted at sparse intervals along the banks of the rivers. Alan's route had taken them to the River Blavet, and now they followed its tortuous course. They deviated from the Blavet only when it was necessary to avoid habitation. They had been slowed by these wide detours, as much as by the pace dictated by Ned's mule.

That night, the second of their journey, they made camp near a small tributary feeding the Blavet, in a section of the forest to the south of Pontivy. It was one of the larger settlements they must skirt, and the last for many a long mile where there would be a hospital. Alan was by no means sure that he could persuade a healer to leave the hospital and venture into the forest, but he resolved to try. The Knights of St John, he thought cynically, despite being primarily monks who followed the order of St Augustine, had a very worldly attitude to money, although that did mean there was a chance they might help him if he let them think a large donation to the hospital would be forthcoming. No one, not even hospitallers, did something for nothing.

Having agreed upon a suitable camp site, Alan left his companions and proceeded into the town. He headed for the bridge and the site of St Ivy's oratory.

He rode past a tavern, ringing with noise. The door

flew open and a bright javelin of light shot across the highway; for an instant it seemed that the road was the field of a knight's black shield with a golden band running diagonally across it. A wild, unkempt figure stared out of the tavern's signboard, sprouting leaves from fingers and feet and hair. This inn was known as the Green Man. The door slammed; the golden band was extinguished and the noise became muffled again.

Bats, hunting for moths, swooped low over Alan's head, while their prey beat desperate wings at the yellow crannies between the inn's closed shutters.

Behind the shutters of the quieter houses, the more god-fearing townsfolk slumbered.

It was not long before Alan picked out an elongated two-storey building which stood a little back from the other houses, at the river's edge. As it was stone, it had to be the hospital. A black arch in the perimeter wall marked the entrance, but at this time in the evening the vast, reinforced oak door was as firmly closed as the shutters against which the moths had been beating. St John's Hospital had shut for the night. A shifting light gleamed palely through a window slit to one side of the gate, so the porter was yet in his lodge. A distant bell tolled. The light in the chamber wavered and dimmed. Surmising correctly that the bell must have been the Compline bell, and that the porter was headed with his lantern for the chapel, Alan kneed Firebrand to the door, lifted a gloved fist, and struck at the wood.

'Open up, good brothers!' he called, loudly.

The door opened at once, but the response had been so swift it could not have been in answer to Alan's summons. A cloaked figure – a woman's – flew through the portal, almost under Firebrand's nose. The courser snorted and stamped his hoofs. Afraid the woman would be trampled, Alan hauled on his reins, and the horse backed, a trick the Duke himself had taught Firebrand. 'Take care,' Alan said. And he found himself looking down into huge dark eyes set in a washed-out oval face. The woman was young, but there was no time to make out more of her features, for she dragged her hood over her head.

'My thanks, Brother, for hearing my confession at this hour,' she murmured, in a low voice to the man standing in the doorway, and tried to press a coin into his palm.

The monk refused the woman's money. 'My best reward would be if you would follow Our Lord's words,' he said.

'Brother?'

'Go, and sin no more.'

The woman hung her head. 'You don't understand,' she said. 'But how could you?' Then she glanced at Alan, murmured what could have been an apology, and slipped into the thickening night.

Alan heard a sigh, and transferred his attention to the hospitaller.

'Good evening, my son.'

The monk was draped in the full black habit of the Augustinian order, and the white cross on his mantle seemed to glow in the jumping torchlight. Alan inclined his head, and dismounted. 'I've come on a mission of mercy, Brother. I'd like to buy food and—'

'This is a hospital, not a market,' the monk answered austerely. The door closed to a chink.

'I know, and my apologies for disturbing you at this hour. I would not do so if it were not urgent, but it is a matter of life and death, and I must be on the road at dawn.'

The hospitaller's thin, freckled nose appeared in the gap. 'Who are you? Are you a Rohan man?'

Alan hesitated, but found no reason to lie. 'I ride with the Duke.' He was not on the Duke's business this night, but he need not admit that.

The chink gaped wide. 'Come in then. You'd best bring your horse too. It wouldn't be safe out there.' The monk shook his head. 'These are terrible times, my son.'

'Aren't they always?' Alan responded lightly as he led Firebrand under the arch and into the torchlit courtyard.

Gwenn had wrapped her brother and sister in her cloak, and was telling Katarin a story to help send her to sleep. The arching branches crowded out moon and starlight, but St Félix's good monks had given them an aged horn lantern, and as its light was faint, Ned had thought it safe to use it.

Stretched out on his cloak a few feet away, Ned watched his wife in the dull glow. Half of his attention was on the tale she told, while the other half was greedily drinking in the regular features of the countenance he had loved for so long.

He had heard Gwenn's yarn many times before, but he always found it a delight. It was the story of a prince brought up among strangers because his family had enemies, and if those enemies found him, he would be in great danger. It was the story of King Arthur, and his upbringing with his stepbrother, Sir Kay. Ned was not certain of the effect that particular tale would have on the traumatised child. Gwenn reached the point when Arthur drew the sword from the stone. When he heard the child's sigh of pleasure, Ned relaxed.

With Alan gone to Pontivy, at last he and Gwenn were alone. Now she was his wife he could look at her without shame. He could watch the imperceptible movements of the muscles round her eyes and mouth, he could enjoy the curve of her lips. They were drawn down now, belying the lightness in her voice as she spun out the tale. Her shoulders drooped, betraying tiredness. Sorrow lingered heavily in Gwenn's heart.

After a few minutes, her melodious voice faltered and came to a halt. The story had played its part. Dark lashes fanned out across the child's pallid cheeks.

'She's asleep,' Ned said. Rising, he offered Gwenn his hand to draw her to her feet.

'Praise the Lord. I have a feeling that sleep might

do more than any potion to heal her.'

'You'll have to waken her if Alan brings a physician.'

Gwenn nodded and dropped his hand, moving away from him towards their pack. Ned knew she was fighting for control. 'Gwenn?'

'Yes?'

She turned stiffly, but as she was looking down and her face was in shadow, Ned couldn't read her expression. Guided by instinct, he murmured, 'Fears and sorrows grow large at night, my Gwenn. Sunrise will diminish them.' Hearing a choking sound, Ned moved closer, and reclaimed his wife's hand. Tentatively, he caressed her palm with his thumb. She stood like a creature of stone, staring at the ground. It seemed to Ned that she was waiting for something. He slid his arm round her waist and drew her, unresisting, towards him. 'Gwenn, I love you,' he said, unsteadily. 'I want to ease your hurts.'

She lifted her head and brushed fingers that were as cold as marble across his cheek. 'I know you do, Ned.' She smiled, and even in the twilight it looked forced. 'But you cannot.'

Ned made an inarticulate noise in his throat.

Her breast heaved. 'I'm sorry, Ned. I feel as if it was I that received a mortal blow at Kermaria, and however much I tell myself otherwise, I think no man can help me. Only God can help me. Do you think, Ned, that God has deserted me?'

Ned shook his head. He pulled her head onto his chest. Doll-like, she hung in the circle of his arms. He held his passion in check, determined that this night he would offer her only comfort. Tenderly he kissed the top of her head. But he had not armed himself against the effect her fragrance would have on him, and no sooner had he breathed in the scent of rosemary and Gwenn, than desire stirred. When her body had been forbidden to him, he had been able to control his longings; but she was no longer forbidden. Gwenn Herevi had miraculously become Gwenn Fletcher, and her body was temptation itself. Ned's loins ached, he was immediately aroused. He groaned. His wife's sweet body knocked all thoughts but one from his mind. How weak he was where she was concerned, how damnably weak. He wanted to make love to her, here and now, and if he did not release her immediately she would know it.

'Gwenn . . .' Confused by the force of his feelings for her, Ned put her at arm's length and regarded her with a kind of desperation. She had such power over him. It was wrong that a woman should have such a hold on a man, quite wrong. He wanted to fling her to the ground and take her regardless of her wishes, he who loved her above all things.

She stepped towards him. 'Ned.'

'Don't, Gwenn,' he blurted, tormented. 'I . . . I think you'd best stand back.'

Her lips curved in a sad, knowing smile, and she came a step closer. 'It's all right, Ned. I understand.'

Ned had a lump in his throat. He swallowed it down. 'You do?'

She nodded, and placed a hand over one of his grazed ones. 'Dear Ned,' she said, gently kissing his battle-scarred fingers. 'Dear, kind, considerate Ned.'

His fingers tingled. The tightness in his loins was unbearable. Manfully, he closed his eyes and tried not to moan. He heard her move, felt her take his hand and place it over one firm, sweet breast. His eyes snapped open. 'G . . . Gwenn?'

'Make love to me, Ned. Make me yours. Teach me to . . .' Gwenn hesitated, she had been going to say 'teach me to forget', but instead she said, 'Teach me to love you, like you love me. I need your love, Ned.'

'But . . . but . . . Alan? He might be back.'

'He won't return for an hour or so.' And remembering how swift their union had been on their wedding night, she added innocently, 'And it doesn't take long, does it?'

Ned winced.

'Ned? What's the matter?'

'N . . . nothing.'

She stood directly in front of him, rested her head against his chest and folded her slight arms about his waist. 'It's all right for you to love me, Ned. I'm your wife.'

'Aye. But you . . . you didn't . . . You disliked it.'

She looked up, and he saw with surprise that her cheeks were darkly flushed. 'Disliked it? No, Ned, I didn't dislike it. I liked you liking it.' And it took my mind off my hurts, she thought. 'Is there more to it than that?'

Again Ned winced. She was offering herself to him, unaware that she stabbed at his pride with almost every sentence she spoke. She felt no passion for him. One day, he vowed, one day, he would make her feel . . .

'Love me, Ned,' she said, and her delicate fingers slipped to his belt fastening.

Ned's hand rose to her neck. His fingers burrowed deep into the scented softness of her hair. Lowering his head, he murmured, 'God, Gwenn, I do love you. So very much.'

'Then love me now, Ned. Love me now.'

Their lips met. Ned's knees buckled, and they tumbled, a tangle of limbs, onto Jean St Clair's cloak. Gwenn gave a shaky laugh and planting a kiss on her husband's chin she pushed his tunic up so she could stroke his chest. Ned gave a shuddering gasp, and dragged Gwenn's mantle over them.

His mouth searched for hers, while his trembling hand ran down her hips to find her skirt-hem. 'Love you . . .'

Afterwards, Gwenn lay on her back, wide awake, listening to the sighing, whispering leaves that gave the forest its name, Bois de Soupirs. Ned's head was lost in the crook of her arm, and she assumed he had fallen asleep. Fondly, she stroked his light hair. This love-making was a mystifying business. Like the first time, it had not taken long; and, as before, Ned's cry of delight had been mixed with anguish. Gwenn's conscience smote her; Ned longed for her feelings to match his. She would have to have been fashioned from ice to remain unmoved by his undisguised need for her love. She felt profound affection for him, and it gave her pleasure to give him ease, but she knew that a deeper emotion eluded her. If only her mind was not misted with sorrow.

Absently twirling a strand of Ned's wavy hair round her forefinger, she sighed. She loved her husband, and was pleased her body gave him joy. She felt loving affection for him, but not passion. Would passion grow? Alan managed to wring responses from her simply by talking to her. He had kissed her once . . . No. No. That was wrong. She must not permit herself to consider how she would feel if Alan were her lover. She was married. Besides, how he would mock her if he knew. Firmly suppressing the thought that it was a shame she did not react to her husband's kisses as she did to Alan le Bret's taunts, Gwenn's mind came round to her husband again.

Dear Ned. Her dear, dear friend. In case he was awake, and because she did care for him and did not like to think of him hurting, she whispered, 'I love you, Ned.' His head moved under her hands, he murmured a response, and a warm kiss was pressed against his neck. He was awake. He lifted his head and his eyes glittered in the lamplight.

'Gwenn,' he said softly, and the despair in his voice caught at her heart, 'one day, you will love me.'

'But, Ned, I do.'

The flaxen head shifted in a negative gesture. 'I don't make your heart beat fast,' he said, sadly. 'The love you bear me is not enough. I fear . . .'

She smoothed a wrinkle from his brow. 'What do you fear?'

'One day you will meet someone who makes your heart knock against your breast and the blood sing in your veins, and I will have lost you.'

She laughed. His cousin had that effect on her, but she was not fond of Alan in the way that she was of Ned.

'I'm serious, Gwenn.' His voice was sober, thoughtful. 'You rouse me so that I can think of nothing but you. And when we make love, I want so much for you to be there with me.'

Another husky laugh. 'But I *am* with you.'

'No. No, my sweet Gwenn, you are not. My greatest fear is that one day you will meet someone who has the same effect on you as you do on me. And then you will forget Ned Fletcher, and you will leave.'

'No, Ned! Never!' She touched gentle fingers to his lips. 'I have promised to stand by you, and I will honour that promise. I do love you. I trust you more than anyone on earth. Trust is a great bond, Ned. Don't undervalue it.'

He looked doubtfully at her, misery in his every line, and she cast about for something that would prove how much she trusted him. Pushing down her skirts, she climbed from their makeshift couch and dragged Ned's saddlebag towards her. 'Look, Ned. I want to show you something before Alan gets back.'

Mystified, Ned rested up on one elbow and watched as she pulled out the bundle of wrappings that hid her statue.

'Do you remember my asking you not to mention to Alan that I had the Stone Rose with me?' He grunted assent, and shifted over on the cloak to make room for her as she came back with her effigy. 'Open the door of the lantern, will you? Look.' She made a slight twisting movement, and as the base fell away from the Virgin, a small pouch shot out. She picked it up, opened it, and held her bunched fist under Ned's nose.

Her fingers uncurled.

Ned's mouth fell open, and he reached for the gemstone. It was cold and hard, and heavier than it appeared, and it caught the feeble lantern light, transmitting it into the clear sparkle of a fall of water on a sunny day. 'Is it real?' he breathed. 'Did you have this all along?'

'It's real. It belonged to Grandmama. She gave it to me. The women of our family have held onto it for generations, as a secret security. To my knowledge you are the first of our menfolk ever to have been told about it.'

'A man could set himself up for life with this,' he said. Over the gem, their eyes met. Ned smiled, and dropped the jewel into his wife's palm. 'Your trust honours me.'

'Now I'm wed to you, Ned, everything I have is yours. In law, this gem belongs to you. You could buy yourself a warhorse, a farm, anything.'

'No. I . . . I couldn't. It's yours.'

'It's *ours*, Ned,' she answered softly, 'ours. We are going to share it.'

Ned leaped towards her and kissed her shoulder. 'My loyal Gwenn.'

'All I'm saying is that I won't desert you. I trust you. No woman in my family has ever trusted their man with this secret. You are the first, the very first. Ned?'

'Mmm?' Brow cleared of wrinkles, Ned idly weighed a dishevelled braid in his hand. His eyes lingered on the gentle swell of his wife's breasts.

'I'm telling you about the gem, but I don't want Alan to know.'

'Alan wouldn't steal your jewel,' Ned said as he put a hand round her neck and drew her towards him.

'You're too trusting,' Gwenn spoke into his mouth. Surprised by her husband's ardour, she allowed herself to be pushed back onto the cloak. She had not thought that Ned's need would return so soon, but she supposed she ought to feel glad that she had reassured him. While Ned's hand groped for her skirt, she tried not to sigh and fixed her unseeing gaze on the black, soughing canopy.

Chapter Twenty-Three

The hospital portal opened again after the tenth hour, and Alan led Firebrand out, laden with the goods he had bought. Brother Raoul, the hospitaller who had admitted him, had made it clear that he had been permitted entry at such a late hour purely on account of his connection with Duke Geoffrey. Brother Raoul had been happy to supply Alan with some foodstuffs, notably bread, cheese, apples, roast beef wrapped in muslin, and milk and oats for the infant; but more than this he would not do. There would be no physician to look at Katarin until they reached Gwenn's kin at Ploumanach. Gwenn would be disappointed, but God willing they would reach Ploumanach in a couple of days.

A stoneware bottle hanging from the saddlebow caught Alan's eyes. Brother Raoul had put it there for him; it contained the baby's milk, which Gwenn had insisted must be boiled, and it was swinging on a lengthy leather strap by his horse's neck. Concerned that Firebrand might be irritated by the bottle and that the milk might be churned to butter by the time he got back to camp – would boiled milk make butter? – Alan paused to rearrange his gear and packed the bottle more securely in the bag behind his saddle. It was difficult to credit that the Captain of the Duke's guard was worrying over a baby's milk . . .

Behind him, the iron bolt of the hospital grated home.

Tightening the strap of his saddlebag, Alan's ears

picked up a furtive movement in the shadows by the bridge, and every nerve pricked into alertness. The moon had risen, bleaching the stones of the wall and the bridge across the Blavet. The noise came from the midnight darkness under the bridge where the moonlight did not reach.

Alan's eyes skimmed road and riverbank. There was no one on the wide highway save himself, and he could see nothing in that dark place under the bridge. Thinking it must be a vole or a rat scuffling to its home in the bank, Alan had one foot in his stirrup when he heard the movement again. 'Who's there?' he called.

There was a splash, and someone caught their breath. Alan could not ignore it. It might be Malait, or another of de Roncier's company, and for his own peace of mind he must investigate. Swinging himself up into Duke Geoffrey's high knight's saddle, and feeling less vulnerable on horseback, Alan rode towards the bridge.

He drew rein by a clump of dock whose leaves gleamed like large white tongues in the moonlight, and listened. He could hear his own measured breathing; the creak of Firebrand's harness; the wind playing in the trees along the edge of the Blavet; and another barely perceptible flurry which brought the hairs on his neck standing to attention. Without doubt, someone was skulking under the bridge, and he could think of no good reason for them to be there.

Where road and bridge joined, a reed-lined path curled left along the riverbank. Alan urged Firebrand down the path. Slender rushes brushed his boots. In the shadowy coverts to the west, a fox barked. Fast on the heels of the bark, another stealthy scuffle came from the dark vault under the bridge, together with more flustered, frightened breathing. Whoever was down there, it was not the Viking. Otto Malait didn't have a timid bone in his body.

Easing his sword out, Alan dismounted. His sword flashed in the starlight. 'Who's there?' Someone whimpered. He moved closer. 'Who's there? Come out, damn you, and show me your face.'

Another whimper.

Alan moved his sword, and as the moonlight bounced off the steel, its reflection lit up an indistinct blur of a figure not three yards away. The figure was pressed against the moss-clad bulwarks of the bridge. 'If you don't come out, I'm coming in.'

The figure looked to left and right, as if to decide which way to fly. Alan lunged forward and the dark form was held at swordpoint. It had been so astonishingly easy that he suspected a trick. 'Come out slowly.' He made an impatient gesture with his sword, and obediently the figure, who was cloaked, shuffled from the refuge. Lifting the point of his sword, Alan flicked back the captive's hood, and gasped.

It was a woman. She was very young, and he had seen her pale oval face before. It was the girl who had emerged from the hospital. Alan lowered his sword and sheathed it. 'What are you doing here? Shouldn't you be abed?'

The woman bit her lip. 'I wasn't doing anything,' she blurted defensively. 'Honestly, sir, I was only . . .' a brief hesitation '. . . watching the river flow by.'

She was lying. She had something clutched in her hands; Alan saw her drop it behind her and kick it out of the way. 'What was that you threw down?'

'Threw down? Why, nothing, sir.' Straight dark brows defined shifting black eyes.

Encircling the woman's wrist with his fingers, Alan stooped to examine the ground behind her. He came up holding a scallop shell, such as were on sale to pilgrims at almost every shrine in Christendom, and a wilted bunch of flowers. The woman had probably stolen the shell from St Ivy's shrine. Alan glanced at the flaccid plant, and his brows snapped together. 'Spearwort, if I guess it aright,' he said. He felt absurdly relieved, for the plant and the scallop shell told him what the woman had been doing under the bridge in the dead of night. It was so far removed from the quarrel between Count François de Roncier and the late Jean St Clair that he would have laughed, had it not been so pitiful.

The woman had a consumptive's face; her cheeks were fleshless and wan, the bones beneath clearly visible even in the weak starlight. She looked emaciated. Alan regarded the limp plants and the shell for a moment, and then tossed them aside. Keeping a firm grasp of the skeletal arm, he pushed up the woman's sleeves and saw the telltale sores as dim blotches on her skin.

His prisoner made a moaning sound in her throat, and struggled weakly to free herself. 'I wasn't doing anything,' she wailed. 'I wasn't stealing, honestly, I wasn't.'

'I'm well aware of what you were doing,' Alan said quietly. 'Show me your legs.'

She went rigid. 'I will not! I'm not that sort of a woman.'

Deaf to his captive's protestations, Alan caught both her wrists in one hand and went down on his knees to examine legs that were as thin as lathes. There were sores there too, angry ones, that in the morning would be weeping and red. He climbed to his feet.

'Let me go!' The woman's voice trembled, for she understood that this stranger had seen through her deception. He knew that she had been scratching the acid juices from the plants into her skin with the scallop shell in order to raise ugly, blistering sores. She was a beggar and the trick with the spearwort, though painful, was her favourite stock-in-trade. She could attract more sympathy and consequently more alms from the passers-by if she was covered in sores. She usually began begging at the hospital gate after dawn. Brother Raoul knew her ploy, and named it a sin, but Brother Raoul did not betray her to the townsfolk. Would this stranger betray her?

'You fool,' Alan said. 'You could give yourself blood poisoning with that trick.'

'You . . . you won't cry it about the town?' the beggar-woman asked. When he shook his dark head, she breathed more easily. 'Thank you, sir,' she said, and her voice was not quite so defensive. 'You can let me go, if you've finished manhandling me.' She risked a direct glance, trying to make the stranger out. 'Who are you?'

'A traveller,' came the cryptic response. Her captor tugged at the frayed rope girdle which barely held her ragged clothing together and started hauling her towards the river.

'Hey! What are you doing?' Her tone sharpened as a different suspicion chilled her. She tried to fight him off, but in her feeble, half-starved state she was no match for him. 'I told you I'm not a wh—'

He whipped the girdle from her too-thin waist and a heartbeat later she was stripped of her shift. Naked and shivering, she crossed her arms in front of her under-sized breasts. So this was to be his price, was it? He wanted to use her. 'No! Please, sir. No!'

'Into the water,' Alan said harshly.

The woman stared in blank incomprehension.

'Into the water.' Alan nudged her shin with a booted foot, but gently. 'I want you to rinse that stuff off you.'

'You mean . . . you mean . . . you're not going to . . .'

'Rape you?' Cold, quicksilver eyes ran dismissively up and down the length of her body till the beggar-woman felt a blush cloak her throat and cheeks. 'No. I want you to wash that poison off your skin.'

She gaped, hugging her arms about her. 'Wash it off, sir?' She could not make him out at all.

Alan moved a step closer. The woman's body was ivory in the half-light. More fragile than Gwenn, and so thin as to be almost all bone, but she would be attractive if she carried more weight. Her eyes were sharp as daggers, and hostile. 'You want me to keep your secret?'

'Aye, sir.'

'Then scrub that poison off.'

433

The sharp eyes widened.

'Move, damn you! Else I'll do it for you.'

His tone was such that the woman believed him, and when he took a threatening pace towards her, she gave in to the inevitable and waded into the Blavet. 'It's cold,' she complained peevishly.

'If you hurry,' Alan offered gruffly, not knowing why he should care if this waif starved or not, 'I'll stand you a meal at the inn.' Her pale, too thin limbs gleaming in the starlight seemed to have uncovered a store of compassion in him.

The woman in the water shot him a look which was a heart-wrenching blend of hope and disbelief, and hurried.

The Green Man was all but closed when they got there, and the landlord, a pot-bellied, pigeon-toed fellow with a shiny bald pate, was clearing the boards with economical efficiency. To judge by the way the beggar-woman slunk in after Alan, she had never been allowed past the door before. The landlord threw her a disdainful look and half-raised a fist. The woman shrank closer to Alan, unable to prevent hungry eyes lingering on the cured hams which hung in the glow of a beaming fire.

Hands on his hips, Alan intercepted the landlord's sneer, and declared, 'She's with me.'

Noting the newcomer had a fine cloak, stout leather boots, and a good-quality sword, the landlord shrugged. He made it a rule never to query likely customers, however odd their companions. He motioned the newcomer and the beggar-woman to a table by the fire.

'Have you anyone to watch my horse?' Alan asked, noting with approval the military orderliness of the tavern. Serried ranks of hams and sausages dangled from the blackened beams close to the fire, being smoked. The beams away from the smoke and heat were in use too, hung with long pendants of shiny, golden onions, and bunches of dried herbs. Alan felt a sudden surge of longing to see his home, for his mother had always kept a good larder. He wondered how his father was faring without her. If it were not for his duty to the Duke, he would go and visit his father when he had Ned and Gwenn safe. But he was sworn to the Duke till after the tournament. After that, however, he should take the leave he was owed.

The landlord nodded. 'Mathieu!'

'Father?' A spindly weed of a lad popped up at the innkeeper's elbow.

'See to this man's mount, will you?'

'Aye, Father.' The boy slipped like an eel through the door.

While they ate, Alan studied the beggar-woman. The innkeeper knew her, and it was all too easy for Alan to conjure up a vision of her loitering by the tavern door, scavenging for discarded scraps like a stray. She would be pretty if she filled out a little, and now that her face was not twisted with that acute, feral mislike of all mankind that was common to most beggars, he glimpsed a hint of sweetness in the wasted features. Her injudicious use of the spearwort had not done much for her complexion, and her skin was marred with unsightly blotches. The lamplight revealed her to be even younger than Alan had thought, and he found himself wondering what had reduced her to beggary. Her eyes, like Gwenn's, were brown.

'Have you no family?' Gwenn had lost her family . . . Thank God for Cousin Ned.

The girl, for that was all she was, paused in the act of biting into a chicken leg, and as she lifted her head to look at Alan, her face took on a cunning, shiftless look. 'I'm a widow,' she said, employing the whine of the professional beggar. 'When my husband died, he left me destitute.'

Alan estimated her to be sixteen – about Gwenn's age. 'Isn't there something else you could do apart from begging?'

'Like what?' she asked, strong teeth worrying at her chicken bone.

His wave took in the orderly tavern. 'Work here, for instance?'

'Ha!' Hurling an acid glance at the landlord, the girl spoke through a mouthful of meat. 'Work for that mean old wind-bladder? You must be touched if you think he'd employ me.'

Alan dropped the subject. He had neither the time nor the inclination to root into her past, and he wondered at himself for showing even this much interest in her. It felt good to have seen her eat a decent meal, though. Thank God Gwenn had Ned.

While he waved for another pot of ale, it occurred to him that he had not purchased liquor from the hospital, and wine would be welcome on the road. 'Landlord?'

The man shuffled over, almost tripping over his feet. 'Sir?' The cloth he had tucked into his belt was snowy white and spotless.

'I'd like to buy some of your ale to take with me, and perhaps some wine. I've a couple of leather bottles you could fill. What have you got?'

While the landlord scratched his polished pate and began listing his stock, the girl studied her benefactor. This rare consideration from a complete stranger had won her interest. He was tall for a Breton and sounded vaguely foreign. Her guess was that he was a soldier, probably a footloose mercenary. She eyed his sword – he'd been quick to draw it when he'd prised her out from under the bridge. Black brows arched over alert, grey eyes. His nose was straight; his mouth full and sensuous. The man was handsome, if one went for those strong, dark, pirate looks. She knew his type; his creed would be love 'em and leave 'em, just like her Eujen's had been. And just like her Eujen, she found him dangerously, devilishly attractive.

While giving his order, Alan glanced briefly across at her; feeling her cheeks glow, the young woman dropped her eyes to her trencher in case he misunderstood her look, and thought she was making eyes at him. She never looked at men these days, not since Eujen had gone. She never looked at anyone, only glancing at people's purses to see how plump they were, or at their hands to see if they were giving her anything. The only face she had looked at properly in months was Brother Raoul's, and that was because he saw her fed, and asked how she was, and seemed to care.

She listened to her companion's deep voice asking the landlord how much he was owed, and wondered where he came from. She tore a chunk off her trencher. She could not for the life of her work out why a man like him should have taken it into his head to buy her a meal. If only she could find a man to protect her, and care for her, and not run off like Eujen had done when he had discovered she was pregnant. The girl sighed. It was easier to catch a rainbow than catch a man.

She cast her mind back to the unhappy time after Eujen had abandoned her and she had been forced to tell her parents that she was to have a child. Her parents, deeply religious, had been stunned by their daughter's pregnancy. They had thrown her out of her home in a nearby village, and she had trudged to Pontivy, thinking she could find work. But no one wanted to employ a pregnant girl who might become a burden on them, and she had soon been reduced to begging for scraps. Her baby had died, and the old crone who had helped her through the birth had told her that she was unlikely ever to bear a child again. She remembered weeping at the time, not only for the loss of her Eujen's child, but also because she was become barren. What man would take a barren woman to wife?

But the old woman had taken her by the shoulders and shaken her. 'You fool!' she had hissed. 'You should count it a blessing that you are barren!'

'A b . . . blessing?' Tears had streamed down her cheeks.

'Aye. For now you can follow the oldest profession in the world, but unlike most of the other poor sluts, *you* need never worry about the consequences. You need never beg.'

But she had not been able to bring herself to look at a man in that way, for none of them were Eujen. Unable to become a whore, in the end she had been driven back to begging.

And now, for the first time since Eujen had gone, she had stopped to look at a man, and her heart warned her that her benefactor was not the type who would let himself be pinned down by the likes of her. He was Eujen all over again. He had not told her his name when she had asked, only replying that he was a traveller. A traveller. What the foreigner meant was that, like Eujen, he had the wanderlust. He wanted no ties. But she warmed to him, nonetheless. He had made her wash the poison off. He had fed her. He had cared for her, if only for a few hours. Why was it that she was only attracted to men who'd run a thousand miles to escape commitment? This man's eyes were not green like Eujen's had been. This man had grey eyes which were as cold as a December frost, but by the saints, he was comely.

'There's no need to devour your trencher.' The foreigner sounded amused, and pulling her hand from her trencher he loosed a ripple of sensation up her arms such as she had not felt since Eujen.

Determined not to blush, the girl thrust her hands under the table. Her companion smiled at her with his mouth, but his eyes still carried December in their depths.

'You're not a beggar tonight. If you're hungry, I'll order more meat. Landlord!'

Half an hour later, they left the tavern. With her belly full for the first time in what seemed like a lifetime, the girl waited till they reached the stranger's princely horse. 'My thanks, sir, for your hospitality,' she said. 'I wish you God speed.' She wished he was not leaving. She wished he would stay.

Alan took Firebrand's bridle and pressed a gold bezant into the girl's palm.

'My thanks,' she acknowledged in a small voice, blinking at the bright disc. 'You are very generous, sir.' She wished she could give him something in return.

'No, I'm not.' He gathered his reins into his hands and swung up into the high saddle.

'A knight errant,' she murmured, head tilted to look at him.

He heard her, and his lips curled in amusement. 'I'm no knight,' he said, and raised his hand in a gesture of farewell, 'though there might be some truth in the errant part.'

'I know,' she said, wishing he would stay. A black brow lifted, he was waiting for her to continue. 'It doesn't matter,' she finished. He would be gone in a second or two. She drew as close to his horse as she dared, for she had no familiarity with horses and was a little afraid of them. She heard herself say, 'I . . . I'd like to repay your generosity.'

'Oh?'

Drawing in a breath, she nodded and, mimicking the women who hung about the Rohan garrison, the girl smoothed her shabby gown about her hips. She even moistened her lips and looked into his December eyes with the bold, direct stare she had seen those women use. 'I could give you my body.'

'No,' he said, curtly. Once he would have taken her up on her offer without hesitation, but not now, not any more. He could not so abuse her. He had put all thoughts of finding a bedfellow out of his mind when he had run across this half-starved waif. Her suggestion almost shocked him.

'You find me ugly,' she murmured, and her head dropped.

Alan's mind stirred with the memory of the beggar-girl's long, too slender limbs, gleaming white as a lily in the moonglow as she bathed in the river, and the dark curtain of her unbound hair. 'No,' he repeated, and then, guessing at her misery and what it had cost her to make her astounding offer, he lowered his voice and sought to soften his rejection of her. 'You are fair when you forget to hate the world.'

Now that she had taken her courage into her hands and offered herself to this foreign soldier, she discovered that she had not done so purely to repay a debt. She wanted some loving herself, and she did not think this man would use her roughly, as others might. This man would take his pleasure slow and gently . . .

She looked at the capable hands holding the horse's reins. She was a beggar and the town pariah, and she had not touched, or been touched by, anyone in a loving manner since Eujen. Apart from Brother Raoul's vague enquiries, all she ever got from anyone was a clout about the ears or a choice curse. Now, tonight, she yearned for closer contact. She wanted to kiss the stranger. She wanted to be held by him, even if just for one night, even if it was a lie and in the morning he would ride into the forest and forget he'd ever lain with her. 'Please, sir . . .' It was easy for a beggar to beg; any pride the girl had ever possessed had long been bludgeoned out of her.

'No, you told me yourself you were no whore.'

She tossed her head, dark hair rippling out over her threadbare cloak, and looked straight into his moon-silvered eyes. 'By St Ivy, I am no whore.'

'Then why?'

'I want some loving.'

Moved by the girl's simple admission, Alan made a strange noise in his throat. He spoke bluntly. 'We shared a meal, that's all. You can't offer yourself to a chance-met stranger and hope it will turn into love.'

'I know that. But I want . . . need . . .'

Alan dismounted and took her hand. He needed it too, but not if this girl-woman was to be left to pay the price. 'Look,' he said quietly, 'I am honoured by your offer, but I see you are not a harlot. You are forgetting the consequences.'

'Consequences?' The pale, oval face was strangely vacant. 'There can be no consequences. I'm barren.'

He searched her eyes. 'Barren? A young girl like you? How do you know?'

'I know it, sir. I'm a tree that will never bear fruit.'

She said it with such conviction that Alan believed her. He rested a hand on her shoulder. 'My thanks, but no,' he repeated, but in the manner of someone trying to convince himself.

The girl had glimpsed eagerness in the foreigner's eyes, swiftly banked down, and doubt in his expression, and knew he was tempted. Heartened, she pressed him. 'I won't try and make you stay, or say that you love me. There will be no commitment, beyond tonight.' He was listening to her.

'No commitment?'

'None.' She heard him swallow.

'And you swear you are safe? I don't want to think I'm leaving you behind with my babe in your belly.'

The girl's mouth curved, she was almost certain she was going to have her way. 'By St Ivy—'

'Very well.' A smile lightened the soldier's dark features, and his forefinger ran softly across her prominent cheekbones. 'Where do we go?'

'To the bridge. I sleep under it.'

'The bridge. Of course.'

The beggar-girl's assessment that her benefactor would take his pleasure slow and easy had been correct, and only when he had satisfied himself that she was enjoying it too had he let himself go and fallen with a convulsive sigh onto her breast. She stroked his thick hair, more relaxed and content than she had been for a year. Playfully, she nibbled his earlobe. He murmured and shifted, lifting his head so he blotted out the stars. 'No more,' he said with gentle but unyielding firmness.

'No more?' She did not want to believe him. He had been considerate, and she was hungry for more of the same. She ran a teasing hand down his leg and repeated huskily, 'No more?'

Alan felt wretched. Making love with this girl had not succeeded in stopping him thinking about Gwenn. He was in a miserable state of mind, and it was not one he would be in if he hadn't decided to do his cousin a good turn and see his family safe to Ploumanach. It is always good deeds, he reflected sourly, that get you into trouble. He eased himself away from his companion and sat up. 'No more. I have to go.'

'Daylight's hours away.'

'I have to go.' There was an ache in his belly, and activity would dissipate it. He reached for his hose and began dressing.

The beggar-girl watched the man who a few moments ago had been as considerate a lover as she could have wished for, and a dreadful feeling of inevitability fell over her. 'You hate me,' she murmured sadly. He was in a hurry, already he was clothed.

Alan glanced uneasily at the colourless oval face resting on its fern pillow. 'No, I don't hate you. It's me I hate.' He considered giving her more money, but did not wish to insult her. Instead he took her head between his hands and pressed his lips to her cold cheeks. 'Fare you well.'

'St Julian watch over you,' came the whispered response.

Firebrand was tethered to an overhanging alder; unhooking the reins, Alan led the Duke's courser onto Pontivy's main thoroughfare. He walked as far as the inn and, finding the shutters closed for the night, hammered until the landlord appeared.

'What is it?' Scrubbing sleep from his face, and none too pleased at being roused from his bed, the landlord scowled.

'I want a word about the girl.'

'What girl? We're closed. I gave you your wine—'

'I know that. But I'd like to ask you a favour.'

The landlord's scowl deepened and he did not reply. Favours usually cost money.

'That girl I was with.' Alan didn't know her name, hadn't wanted to know it.

'The beggar-maid?'

'That's the one. I was hoping,' Alan took a couple of coins from his pouch and juggled them in his palm, 'that you might see your way to employing her.'

'God's wounds! This is a reputable hostelry, I can't be employing poxy drabs.'

'I think she would work hard if you gave her the chance.'

The innkeeper swore. 'Nay. It's more likely she'd scare off my trade. Have you seen the state of her skin? She looks as though she's infected with the plague.'

Alan smiled crookedly. 'I think, if you employed her, you'd find her cured of that affliction.' He held out his palm, and the innkeeper's eyes did not shift from the coins.

'You're leaving the area?'

'Aye.'

'What's to stop me taking your money and not giving her work?'

Alan remembered the well-regimented inn, the neat lines of hams, the orderly onions, and the landlord's dazzling linen apron. He grinned. 'Nothing. I'm taking the chance that you're not a man to sweep things into the rushes. I shall trust to your honesty, landlord.'

The innkeeper's fingers closed round the money. 'I'll try her out,' he agreed reluctantly. 'But I give you notice, if I find her dishonest, I'll throw her back into the midden.'

'My thanks, landlord.'

It was rare for Alan to be moved to compassion, and it unsettled and disturbed him, but he could not have stalked off and dismissed that girl from his mind as once he might have done. He grimaced ruefully into the rustling night, conscious of a wave of regret at leaving her. Time was when he would not have spared her a moment's thought, but something had opened his eyes to her plight. It would have been easier if his eyes had remained closed. It would have been far simpler to ride off and forget her. Alan had another leave-taking preying on his mind. He was becoming as strongly attracted to Gwenn as his cousin was, and he would shortly have to say farewell to her. If he felt like this

443

over a girl he'd known for only one evening, how was he going to react when he parted from Gwenn? Briefly, he considered confessing his feelings to her, but he could not see what that would achieve. He could not bring himself to come between Ned and Gwenn, he had seen how they cared for each other, and even if his feelings were reciprocated, did he want to make an adulteress of Gwenn?

Fiercely, Alan dug in his heels and Firebrand surged through the waving bracken fronds. At least he was happier with himself having spoken to the landlord about the beggar-girl. It was best she remained nameless. Weren't beggars always nameless? Perhaps next time he passed this way he would visit the inn and see if she was there. Perhaps he might learn her name, next time.

Conan had stowed away among a merchant's bales of cloth in a trading vessel bound for the northern port of Lannion, before returning to its port of origin in Flanders. Lannion was half a day's walk from Ploumanach. Conan had tried to shake off the white mongrel, intending to abandon it on the quayside, but the animal had clung like a tick, and in the end Conan had taken it with him. If the dog threatened to give tongue and betray him, he could always slit its throat. But the animal had learnt that it paid to be silent, and while the merchantman skimmed homewards, the cur kept a cowed silence.

In Lannion, a fortuitous chance in la rue des Templiers had a donkey shedding its burden at the bottom of the hill. While the load was set to rights, the way was blocked to the church at the top, and in the muddle Conan cut the strings of the Flemish trader's elaborately tooled leather purse. As a result, he was in possession of enough minted silver to bide his time, and pick his moment.

He reached Ploumanach two days before Alan's party, hiring lodgings in a fisherman's cottage in one of the many fishing hamlets that had grown up in the surrounding inlets. While he and the dog waited, he set his mind to pondering on how he could get his hands on Gwenn Herevi's Virgin. His mind, undirected by any but himself for the first time in a decade, moved slowly.

The last leg of their journey to Ploumanach was without mishap, and Gwenn and her companions rode into the main village at sunset on a balmy evening; there was hardly a breath of wind in the air.

Alan and Ned had been talking tournaments for the last hour, and though Gwenn had paid attention at first, she had wearied of the topic and chose instead to take an interest in the changing countryside. Clumps of gorse flamed yellow in the evening light. Slender white ribbons of cloud trailed across a fading blue sky. The trees had thinned out some miles back and, though a few oaks grew here, by comparison with their proud brothers in the forest, these oaks were stunted, twisted dwarfs. There were tall pines though, and as they drew nearer the coast, the stunted oaks yielded to sprawling banks of bramble. The scent of pine lingered in the air, and in the distance, breaking up the skyline, the spiky spires of the trees formed a dark tracery screening off the distant heavens.

A seagull arrowed over their heads. They must be close to their destination. Gwenn dragged her attention from the terrain and focused it once more on the cousins' discussion.

'If you find you can't settle here, Ned,' Alan was saying, 'you could come to King Philip's August tournament. My Duke plans to go, and I shall be accompanying him. There are bound to be opportunities for a young man like yourself. You would love it.'

Philippe was asleep in Gwenn's lap, a contented little cherub, totally unaware of the dramatic train of events that had led to him being dragged to the other side of Brittany. What did the future hold for him? What did the future hold for any of them? Glancing at her husband, Gwenn felt a warm upsurge of emotion for him. Her future was with Ned. Holding her brother firmly, Gwenn steered Dancer towards him so they were riding with their arms just touching. Ned reached over and gave a plait a friendly tug. Smiling impishly at him, Gwenn faked a yawn. 'You're not still droning on about tourneys, are you? I should have thought you would have talked them to death.'

'Sorry, my sweet,' Ned's expression was wistful, 'they fascinate me. I would love to go to one.'

Gwenn bit her lip, recalling with a pang the times she had seen him hanging on her uncle's words as though they were his meat and drink. 'You could go, Ned. I see nothing to prevent you.'

Warm blue eyes met hers. Ned was trying, and failing, to hide his eagerness. 'But there's you, and the children. I have to consider you.'

'Poor Ned,' Alan teased, 'shackled to a wife and children at your tender age.'

Suddenly uncomfortable so close to Ned, Gwenn threw Alan a black look. 'Alan,' she urged Dancer level with Firebrand's glossy flanks, 'I'll have you know it won't be me who keeps Ned from attending the King's joust.'

Alan bowed his head. 'Very gracious of you, my lady.' He rolled audacious eyes at Ned, whose mule was dragging its heels. 'There you are, Ned, what more do you want? You have your wife's permission to go to King Philip's tournament.'

The irony in Alan's voice was wasted on Ned, busy belabouring his mule, but not on Gwenn. It was a rare man who heeded his wife's wishes when they conflicted with his own. A wife was a chattel. Gwenn was lucky with her Ned, he did not view her in that light. How did Alan le Bret view her? As a chattel of his cousin's?

'I'll look for you in August, Ned,' Alan said, and then he grinned at Gwenn, and she could not divine what he thought.

Lagging further behind, Ned's eyes shone with dreamy longing, but he refused to commit himself. 'I'll see.'

'Ned the noble,' Alan muttered, for Gwenn's ears alone.

Her eyes narrowed, for Alan had sounded almost savage. 'I'm blessed to have him,' she said, and braced herself for sarcasm.

But astonishingly, Alan did not mock her, he simply locked his cool gaze with hers and said with quiet emphasis, 'I know. He protects you from more than de Roncier.'

Unable at first to puzzle that one out, Gwenn was startled when Alan's eyes dropped to her mouth. She found herself looking at his, admiring the firm, clean curve of his upper lip, and the generous, sinful curve of the bottom one. When she had finished she realised that he was watching her and she understood what he had meant. Feeling like a guilty child who had been caught stealing a sweetmeat without asking, she jerked her gaze away from him and made a show of seeing to the baby dozing in the cradle of her arm. Then she pinned her eyes on the sandy road which was dyed sunset pink. She did not look at Alan again. This was a complication Gwenn could do without. For a second, she had caught herself thinking that she would like to kiss him. She had wanted to see if he tasted the same as he did two years ago. She must drive out such sinful thoughts. She had a husband for whom she felt a great affection, and she did not want to be drawn to Alan. Alan was not capable of loving in the way that Ned was; lust was what Alan le Bret was about. She had needed Alan to see the children safely to Ploumanach. For everyone's sake, the sooner he returned to his Duke now the job was done, the better.

They were entering a village. In one of the doorways sat an elderly matron, a spindle and distaff idle at her elbow while she warmed a wind-burned face in the gentle rays of the waning sun. With a lingering look at

447

Gwenn, which she ignored, Alan enquired the way of the woman.

She cupped a hand to her ear. 'You want Sir Gregor?' The aged voice was worn, and rusty as a rook's.

'Aye. Which way?'

A trembling talon pointed down the sand-strewn road which divided two rows of long, low cottages. Like a sponge, the street had soaked up the pink twilight; and not only the road, for the whitewashed cottages, too, glowed as rosy as the sky. 'Down there,' the old woman rasped. 'And when you reach the bay, skirt along the left hand path past Saint Guirec's shrine. You can't miss it. Sir Gregor's holding is built on the rocks on the peninsula.'

'My thanks,' Alan said, and clapping his spurs to his horse's sides, he cast his cousin's wife another pensive look.

Gwenn kept pace, but she avoided his eyes.

'We're nearly there, Gwenn,' he said. 'I'll wager you're glad to have made it before nightfall. You won't want another night in the open.'

'No.' Now they had actually arrived, she was nervous. Her throat was dry, and swallowing did not ease it. Up until this moment, her mind had been focused on getting her brother to Ploumanach alive. It had taxed her to keep going. She had not had the strength to think any further ahead than where they would be sleeping that night, and whether they were being followed by de Roncier's men and might be slaughtered in their sleep. She had not allowed herself the luxury of considering what sort of a reception she and her family might receive from her kin – her very distant kin.

What was Sir Gregor like? Was he married? Would he welcome an entire family turning up like beggars on his doorstep, with little more than the rags on their backs? Craning her neck to watch Ned and Katarin, Gwenn's eyes flitted briefly to her husband's saddlebags. Ned had managed to save the greater portion of Wald-

448

in's money, and they had the gemstone, of course. Perhaps she could use that to sweeten Sir Gregor if he looked disinclined to offer them aid.

She and Alan rode past the last of the cottages in silence. Their mounts' hoofs raised swirling pink clouds in the dusting of sand on the path, and the irregular clopping matched the pulse of Gwenn's heart. She could hear the sea now, another, more rhythmical beat, as waves broke gently on an unseen beach. They must come to it at any moment.

A brace of seagulls shot past them, dazzling flashes of pure white light; and a small bay opened out before them, entirely bathed in the warm, flaring beauty of the dying sun. It was a scene that was balm to the most wounded of souls, and for a few blissful moments Gwenn forgot her troubles and could only gaze in delight. The setting sun rested on the edge of the world, a few minutes later and it would sink from sight. It had all the colours of a ripe peach; and its rays tinted the western sky with the same rich hues. The sea was gold, and the sand and rocks were painted the palest, most subtle, sunset pink.

'It's beautiful,' Gwenn murmured and glanced across at Alan. He was not looking at the bay, his eyes were fixed on a modest stone structure which could only be the shrine the fisherman's widow mentioned.

Alan's chest ached. 'I'll miss you, my little sparring partner,' he admitted, so softly that his voice was almost lost in the gentle hushing of the sea. Ned had yet to breast the gorse bushes which fringed the beach.

'Miss me?' That she had not expected, though she knew she would miss him.

'If . . .' Alan did not shift his eyes from the shrine, and Gwenn noted his skin had darkened as though he were hiding some emotion. 'If anything ever happens to Ned, my Blanche, I want you to promise to call on me.'

Astounded by Alan's discomfiture, and by his unlooked for offer of assistance, Gwenn stared at him

449

for some seconds before she realised that her mouth hung open. Could it be that Alan actually *cared*? No, this was Alan le Bret, the Duke's cold captain . . . She snapped her mouth shut. 'Call on you? But I have relatives here.'

'They may not be . . .' Alan paused and turned to face her, giving her an inscrutable look which brought her out in goose-bumps, '. . . to your liking, and as Ned's cousin I am a relative of sorts.' The look faded and was replaced with a stiff smile.

He *was* embarrassed.

'Will you promise, Gwenn? I'll be leaving in the morning.'

'But why should anything happen to Ned? Have you stumbled across something you're not telling us?'

'No, nothing like that,' Alan said hastily, and shrugged, as though his offer was of no account. 'I merely wanted you to know you could turn to me, if you need me.'

'Thank you, Alan. I will remember.'

'I am,' Alan's mouth went up at the edges and as Ned rounded the corner, he gave Gwenn one of the mocking little bows which had become endearingly familiar, 'eternally your obedient servant, mistress.'

'My thanks, kind sir,' Gwenn replied in the same light tone. 'Where would I find you?'

'Ask for Duke Geoffrey.' He gave her one last, sinful smile and heeled Firebrand, urging him across glowing pink sands to St Guirec's shrine. The ache in his chest was not gone, but it had diminished.

Chapter Twenty-Four

'And so, Sir Gregor, that is our tale,' Gwenn finished, and spread her hands in the universal gesture of supplication. The interview she had dreaded ever since leaving Kermaria was proving to be as unpalatable as she had imagined. She loathed having to beg. If it were not for the innocents, poor, silent Katarin and dispossessed Philippe . . .

She gritted her teeth and pressed on. 'I know that we are only distantly related, but I implore you to have pity on us and take us in. If you don't, Lord knows what will become of the children. I am not penniless, but I cannot provide my brother and sister with the security they need.'

She alone of her party had been ushered into the solar, a fine, tall chamber with soaring beams which married in the lofty apex of a steeply slanted roof, and she was standing in front of a high, wood-panelled window seat. The window with its four narrow lights overlooked the ocean, a crow's nest of a window, for Sir Gregor's manor was built on a spit of land jutting into the sea. Its shutters were open to admit the warm, pink afterglow of the sinking sun. Two steps led from the solar floor to the window seat, which had been made comfortable and welcoming by two gorgeous silk cushions, upon which some wizard with a needle had emblazoned the most exquisite satin flowers. Ensconced on these cushions, opposite each other, sat Sir Gregor Wymark and his wife. As the apricot rays from the sunset spilled into the solar, they drew saintly haloes round the heads of the knight and his lady. Though Gwenn squinted, she was unable to make out her relatives' features, nor could she tell whether they regarded her with any sympathy.

Lord Gregor and Lady Wymark's solar was unlike any she had ever seen. Its walls were lined with richly coloured drapes. At the house in Vannes, Raymond had once recounted the *Romance of Tristan* to her, and Gwenn imagined King Mark's pavilion would resemble Lady Wymark's solar: all silk and satin and bright shimmery colours, with not a sharp corner in sight. It was warm too, for though a breeze floated gently through the seaward window and twitched the billowing wall-hangings the fire was piled high with blazing logs and the heavy scent of burning pine filled the room.

After the hardships and uncertainties of the flight from Kermaria, this solar seemed like heaven. The children would be safe in this womb of a place, for surely Lady Wymark was like her solar, warm and welcoming.

Gwenn's eyes could not linger on the furnishings, however exotic. She was waiting, with bated breath, for her relatives to reveal their hearts as well as their faces. She clasped her hands tightly to quell an almost irrepressible desire to play with her girdle.

'You poor child!' Lady Wymark murmured, half rising from her seat, but a sharp, chopping movement of her husband's blunt hand had her sinking back to her place.

'So you claim to be Izabel de Wirce's grandchild?' Sir Gregor said. He had a deep, gravelly voice.

'Aye, sir,' hope warmed Gwenn's breast, 'but when my grandmother married, her name became Herevi.'

The knight scratched an ear. 'Herevi . . . can't place it. Don't think I've heard that name before.'

'No, sir. There's no reason you should. Gwionn Herevi was only a squire when he married Grandmama.' There were a few moments' uncomfortable silence, enough to crush the faint hope which had stirred briefly in her breast.

'A squire?' Sir Gregor echoed, and though Gwenn did not know him, she did not miss the disbelief in his tone. 'You're telling me that Izabel de Wirce married a squire?'

Lady Wymark leaned forward, plump fingers twisting the hem of her veil. 'That is true, my love. I recall my mother telling me that story. I believe there was quite a scandal at the time. Why—'

'Peace, wife,' Sir Gregor rumbled, waving for silence. Gwenn was beginning to feel as though she were a plaintiff in court. She was on trial. 'And you maintain you are Izabel's grandchild?'

'I am.'

'Can you prove it?'

'P . . . prove it? Why, I . . . I don't know. I have nothing in writing, sir.'

Sir Gregor swung stiffly down from his perch and walked round her, and Gwenn had her first clear sight of him. He was squat and strong-thewed, a wall of a man a yard broad. He had the build of someone who relished exercise. Most of his might lay in his well-developed shoulders and arms, and it looked a solid, immovable kind of strength, with no give in it at all. Sir Gregor was in his early fifties; he had thinning grey hair, and a certain inflexibility in his gait warned of incipient rheumatism. Hairy eyebrows drooped over mud-coloured eyes, and though at the moment he was eyeing Gwenn narrowly, his eyes were deeply set in a face criss-crossed with laughter lines. He was not, Gwenn sensed, a harsh man, but his grating voice and that stolid toughness made him the type of man about whom she would think twice before crossing.

'My . . . my travelling companions will vouch for me,' she stammered.

'And who might they be that I should give them ear?' he fired back. 'A couple of mercenaries, and one of them, by your own admission, married to you. You wear no ring. You could be a group of travelling players out for an easy living for all I know. You'll have to do better than that.'

Gwenn was bone weary. Gazing straight ahead of her, she kept her head high and sucked in some air, and with it, hopefully, some endurance. 'As I explained, there was no opportunity to buy a ring.' She met the knight's eyes boldly. 'Sir, if you're not going to help us, please say so. I'll take my leave and not trouble you further. As I said, I have money. Look.' She drew out Waldin St Clair's purse which, foreseeing this very objection, she had taken from Ned. She tore it open, grabbed Sir Gregor's hand, and poured a cascade of coins into the wide palm. 'Take it. Take it all, sir, and put it towards the cost of our upkeep.'

Giving the money no more than a glance, Sir Gregor said gruffly, 'You could use this to bring up your brother and sister yourself.'

'Aye. But I couldn't guarantee my brother's safety in the same way that you could if you took us in. I have no way of knowing the Count's plans. I have been honest with you, sir. There may be danger in taking my brother in.'

'Has this de Roncier had you followed here?' the deep-timbred voice asked.

'I don't know. We've seen neither hide nor hair of him since leaving the monastery, but I cannot swear he's forgotten us. He's Herod reborn, and we might be bringing danger to your gates; but you have this fortified manor, and your men, and I could not provide all that.'

Lady Wymark stood up. She was dumpy, with a full figure. 'I believe she is telling the truth, Gregor,' she declared. 'I believe we should let her stay. Poor lamb.'

'Wait, Alis, you are always a mite hasty in your judgments.' The knight tipped Waldin's money into the wallet. 'Is there no way you can prove you are Gwenn Herevi?'

'Gwenn Fletcher. I am married to my father's Captain of the Guard.'

'Poor child,' Lady Wymark crooned with an expressive shudder. 'Forced to marry a mercenary!'

'No, my lady,' Gwenn said firmly. 'You mistake the matter. I was not forced. Ned is a good man.'

Lady Wymark could not have heard for she continued shaking her head. 'Poor child. A mercenary!'

Sighing, Gwenn caught Sir Gregor's muddy eyes on her. They were not unsympathetic. She turned to the table where she had placed her bundle, and unwrapped the Stone Rose. 'Sir, I am able to offer you more, if the money is not enough.' As she folded back the linen and lifted the Virgin out, she heard Sir Gregor's sharply indrawn breath. 'Sir?'

'Hand that over,' the crusty voice ordered.

The statue shrunk in his sinewy hands. After a lengthy examination, Sir Gregor lifted his head. 'This stone is local to these parts,' he said.

With a rustle of voluminous skirts, Lady Wymark approached her husband, and her pudgy, beringed fingers caressed the child sleeping in the Virgin's arms. 'I believe you're right, Gregor,' she said, stooping short-sightedly over the holy infant. She had brooding blue eyes, and when she bent her head, a double chin that her wimple could not contain. Wisps of light-brown hair escaped confinement, and baby-fine curls framed her face. Where her husband was solid and immoveable, she was all softness and give. 'There are rocks like this scattered all over the peninsula.'

'To whom does this statue belong?' the knight asked incisively.

'It was my grandmother's.'

'It was Izabel's!' Lady Wymark cried, dimpling sunnily at Gwenn. 'Gregor, if this icon belonged to Izabel de Wirce, then you have the proof you need. This girl is whom she claims.'

'Quiet, woman!' Sir Gregor growled. The untidy brows twitched upwards. '*Was* this Izabel's, Mistress Gwenn?'

'Aye, sir. I understand it was her mother's before that.'

The knight's face crumpled into a smile that was as

warm as his wife's. 'It would appear, Gwenn, my dear, that you have brought your proof with you. Welcome to Ploumanach.'

Overwhelmed with relief, though far from understanding what had brought about this sudden *volte-face*, Gwenn felt the tears rise. Lady Wymark opened well-covered arms and enveloped her in a perfumed embrace.

Sir Gregor's grating voice penetrated the swathes of scented linen that were all but suffocating Gwenn. 'It was your great-grandmother, my dear, who was a Wymark,' he said.

'Izabel's mother?' Gwenn emerged from his wife's stifling hug.

'Aye, Andaine Wymark. She was sent south to marry into the de Wirce family, a sound, political marriage, but it's possible she had no wish to leave Ploumanach, for she had this statue carved out of the local granite as a keepsake.'

'It is very beautiful here,' Lady Wymark declared. 'I can see why she might not have wanted to leave. *I* wouldn't want to leave, and I wasn't born here. It must have been very hard for your ancestor to be torn from her roots and sent south.'

'Enough, Alis. Curb your tongue, will you?' Sir Gregor said in his harsh voice, but Gwenn suspected that his harshness masked a deep and abiding affection for his wife. He went on, 'You have seen the rocks outside, my dear?'

'Rocks?'

His smile enlarged, and the wrinkles radiated from his eyes till his ruddy, sun-browned face came to resemble a withered pear taken out of winter storage. 'Aye. You can't miss them, gigantic boulders which God dropped on these northern shores when He created the world. The whole place is coloured by them, even the sand on the beach – all like your statue, all salmon pink.'

'Salmon pink? But, Sir Gregor, I thought . . .'

Gwenn knotted her brows. 'Do you mean that it wasn't the sunset that drenched the rocks with colour? Are you telling me that everything here is this colour naturally?' She indicated the Stone Rose which was, as Sir Gregor had said, that same rosy hue.

'Wait till tomorrow,' Lady Wymark told her. 'You'll see then.'

'You'll permit us to stay?'

Lady Wymark glanced longingly at her husband, and on receiving a confirmatory nod, she said 'You and the children must stay.'

Gwenn sagged with relief. 'My thanks. I can't tell you how much this means. You won't regret it, I'll see to that. I can sew, and make medicines, and help with the household. I'm not afraid of hard work, and Ned is a good soldier.' At mention of Ned, Lady Wymark frowned, but Gwenn was so content to have found a haven for Katarin and Philippe that she did not observe it. 'Shall I bring the children up, Lady Wymark, that you may meet them?'

The good lady beamed. 'Please do. I'm longing to meet *the children*,' she said with strange emphasis which again Gwenn missed. 'We've not been blessed with children of our own. Bring them up. I suspect you'd like a bath before we eat.'

'A bath?' Gwenn echoed, with a longing she could not hide. 'Oh, could we, my lady?'

Lady Wymark gave a blithe smile. 'I'll have the tubs filled. And Gwenn, call me Aunt Alis, will you?'

Gwenn smiled with her eyes. 'Of course . . . Aunt Alis.'

With a light step, Gwenn ran down the turning stairs to fetch her siblings. It had not been necessary to offer her relatives the gemstone, and while she would not have begrudged parting with it if it bought safety for Katarin and Philippe, she was glad the Stone Rose still housed its secret treasure.

Having seen Gwenn and the children accepted by Sir

Gregor and Lady Wymark, Alan put his personal feelings aside and confirmed his intention of leaving at daybreak the following morning. He found it more difficult than he had anticipated.

Initially, his host and hostess had been frosty in their manner towards Ned and himself, and Alan had deemed it politic to let fall that he was high in the service of the Duke of Brittany, and was expected by the Duke at Rennes. Thereafter, Sir Gregor and Lady Wymark had thawed, and Alan had been prettily thanked for his assistance. He had been well fed, and comfortably housed on a pallet in the hall, as was the custom. And Ned had received similar treatment, although by rights he should have been allocated a place in what served as married quarters.

Accommodation for married couples varied from establishment to establishment; at the Wymark manor the southern range of the hall had been set aside for their use. Curtains ran along that wall, and at first Alan had taken them for wall-hangings, for during supper they had been looped back behind great brass hooks. Once the board was cleared, however, the curtains were released, and with a few token gibes from the unattached members of the household, the married couples went into retreat behind them. There were no alcoves as such, but the curtains hid the modest from prying eyes and provided more privacy than Alan had seen in most halls.

Alan woke as the first fingers of light slid into the hall. 'I'm for stretching my legs before I spend another day in the saddle,' he told Ned who was yawning beside him. 'I'd like a word. Coming?'

Having left the manor, the cousins wandered in companionable silence along a slender path which snaked through vast boulders the wind had sculpted into nightmarish shapes. Ned looked at the twisted formations in awe. 'They have the shape of monsters, Alan,' he breathed.

The breeze threw Alan's hair into his eyes. Pushing it back, he agreed. 'Aye. You're happy to stay here, Cousin?'

'If Gwenn is.'

'Listen, little cousin' – Ned grinned; he topped Alan by a good two inches, and yet Alan insisted in calling him 'little' – 'Sir Gregor has a small force, but as his holding is built on a peninsula, it should be easy to defend if de Roncier renews his interest. But I am beginning to wonder whether he will. He would surely have struck before now if that was his intention. If his men had been tracking us, they would have found us. We left a trail a mile wide, and could have been attacked at any time – while we ate, while we slept. I don't know why de Roncier should decide to hold back now, but when I leave here, I'll go south and make enquiries at Kermaria.'

'Is that wise? I thought you were expected at Rennes?'

Alan had not told his cousin of Duke Geoffrey's commissioning of a survey of Kermaria, and he did not plan to tell him. 'I'm owed leave, and I'll be discreet. I'll see what I can dredge up concerning our old friend's activities, and if you can attend the King's tournament, I'll let you know what I discover. In the meantime, you should be safe here. God knows, it's a remote enough spot.'

Alan had some misgivings with regard to Sir Gregor and Lady Wymark, but they were minor ones and they concerned Ned, not Gwenn or the children, and he resolved to keep his counsel on that score. Sir Gregor and his wife would care for St Clair's children, and that was what mattered; there was no point in worrying Ned or raising doubts on the basis of a brief impression gained over one meal in Sir Gregor's hall. He might be making a mountain out of a molehill over the fact that Gwenn had been given different accommodation to that of her husband and had slept with the family and the unmarried women on the upper floor. Perhaps there had not been the time to find a space in the married quarters. Or perhaps Gwenn had elected to remain with the children on their first night here. Lady Wymark had been insistent the children were lodged upstairs, a sign to everyone, and a generous one, that she was accepting them as part of her family. But Alan had the impression that Lady Wymark looked down on Ned, and disapproved of him as Gwenn's husband.

He pushed his misgivings aside. It had been but one night, and everyone was in disarray. In any case, it was not his business to speculate on how Gwenn and Ned conducted their marriage. She was his cousin's wife, forbidden fruit to him. God, but it was not easy to go.

He shoved his hand at his cousin, and spoke more brusquely than he had intended. 'I'll bid you farewell, Ned. Will you say goodbye to your wife on my behalf?'

'Won't you say it to her in person, Alan? I'm sure she would like to thank you for escorting us here. We wouldn't have made it without you.'

'No,' Alan disclaimed all credit, 'I think that you would—'

'It would have taken us twice as long, and you know it. Gwenn will be disappointed to have missed you.'

Alan found himself looking at the sea. Whipped up by the morning wind, choppy, foam-crested waves lapped a distant islet and rode past the island as far as the horizon. With a sudden lurching of his senses that he put down to homesickness, Alan realised that on that horizon, just out of sight, lay England. Did the white-tipped waves touch England's shores? He focused on the rose-coloured rocks nearer to hand. It was beautiful, this rock-strewn shoreline. Gwenn would like it here. Would she like England, if ever she saw it? 'No fuss, cousin,' Alan said. His homesickness had put a catch in his throat. He was glad he'd never felt homesick before – he didn't much like it. 'Please bid her farewell for me.'

'I will. Alan, are you all right?'

'Aye. I suddenly missed England, that's all.'

'Did you?' Ned's eyes, blue as forget-me-nots in the morning light, were understanding. 'I miss home too, Alan. One day I shall take Gwenn to England.'

Alan stared at a boulder shaped like a rabbit.

'Farewell, cousin.' Ned gave Alan's shoulders an affectionate squeeze. 'God go with you.'

With an effort Alan roused himself. 'And with you. Don't forget the grand tournament. I might have dug up news concerning de Roncier, and I shall certainly make mention of his villainy to the Duke; but in any event, it would be good to see you there. I missed you these past two years.'

Ned was surprised and warmed by this admission, but knew better than to remark on it.

Alan continued, 'I've been thinking that after the summer joust I'll take my leave of the Duke and go home. I should visit my stepfather.'

Ned looked keenly at his cousin. 'That would be a good thing to do.'

'When we left England, I felt betrayed. All those years he had pretended to be my father, when all the time he had no claim on me. I told him as much. I told him I'd never be his apprentice, never follow in his footsteps, and how dare he and Mother expect it. Christ, I was cruel. Ivon cared for me better than most fathers, taught me all he knew, but Ned, it hurt.'

'Alan, you don't have to explain to me.'

'Be my confessor, Ned. God knows, I'm in need of one. The long and the short of it is, it's been too long since I saw him, and I'd hate him to have grown old in my absence.' Alan laughed, self-consciously. 'Seeing William seems to have wrung some sort of conscience out of me.'

'You always had a conscience, Alan, you don't deceive me.'

Alan's mouth curled into a rueful grin. 'There was a time you thought otherwise, Ned, old friend. Do you remember the incident with the concubine's daughter?'

'Concubine's daughter?' Ned lowered his brows in a

461

rare scowl. 'Do you continue to think of her in those terms, Alan? I never thought of her as that.'

'No, you fool, of course I don't. But I remember you hating me for getting her out of harm's way.'

Ned was as pink as the rocks. 'I didn't understand what you were trying to do. I should have trusted you.'

A lock of Alan's hair lifted in the wind. He stretched, and checked the position of the sun. 'Time I mounted up. I'll grab a crust and go.'

'God speed, Alan. If you do return to England, perchance we could go together.'

The sombre features lightened. 'England at harvest time,' he murmured dreamily. 'I should like that.'

'Aye. Though I doubt if Gwenn would leave the children.'

Alan's mouth edged up at one corner. 'And you wouldn't leave without her.'

'No.'

'You could, Ned. Come without her. You don't have to spend the rest of your life tied to her side. Scores of far prettier women trail after the knights and squires at the tourneys – just think what you're missing!'

'Alan!'

Alan shook his head, and sighed. 'I merely test your mettle, cousin. But there's no hope for you, is there? You're a lost cause.'

Ned's lips curved. 'Utterly. Ever since that first day.'

And all at once Alan was overcome with a surge of painful emotion so similar to the pang of homesickness that he had just experienced that it could not possibly be jealousy. 'I envy you your steadfast nature, Ned,' he muttered. And then, because he could not stand the shining happiness in his cousin's eyes a moment longer, he gave Ned a farewell wave and headed for the stables to find Duke Geoffrey's courser.

Conan had left the cur tethered at the fisherman's cot and was out in the open, crossing the beach, when he heard hoof beats. The drumming gave him ample warning of the rider leaving Sir Gregor's manor, and he was able to dash for the nearest cover, which happened to be St Guirec's shrine.

The wooden oratory was built below the high-water mark, and when the tide was in, as it was now, it lapped the rocky foundations upon which the saint's shrine was balanced. Conan had to wade thigh-high through shifting seawater and cling to the weathered eaves in order to keep himself from losing his footing. A seagull, put out at being dislodged from its watch on the roof of the shrine, spat a shriek of irritation at him and wheeled into the sky. A wavelet sprayed Conan's mouth with brine. His mouth puckered and he grimaced. This would put a flux in his belly if anything did. Conan hated water at the best of times; his clothes never seemed to stand up to it, and this icy swell held all of last night's chill and more besides. Silently he cursed the necessity for secrecy that had driven him into the water.

Last night he had seen who had ridden in with St Clair's bastard. Until then he had thought it was going to be easy. As well as the children, she had had two armed men with her. A stray thought surfaced, breaking the pedlar's tenuous hold on his ruminations; his sister, Johanna, would be pleased to know that the brat had survived. Irritably, Conan applied his mind to the problem in hand. He had recognised the two soldiers escorting the girl, and sight of them had doubt growing like weeds in his brain. As the doubts flourished, so Conan's confidence had withered.

The fair soldier, who had to be the Saxon that his soft-hearted sister was sweet on, would not pose a problem. The pedlar did not think that St Clair's captain would recognise him. But when Conan had looked at the other soldier, his hopes had dwindled to nothing. Dark of face, and dour, he used to head one of de Roncier's troops. He had been the one to shell out when Conan had first spied on St Clair's house in Vannes. Conan had never dealt directly with the Saxon, but this other – he did not think that this other mercenary would have forgotten him. Instantly recognisable himself, his cold, grey eyes were as calculating as ever. What was he doing here? He had left de Roncier's service with the Saxon, but he had not signed up with St Clair. Conan ransacked his mind for the man's name; but he had no memory for names, and it eluded him. He wondered if the dark one was aware of the Virgin's secret. If he was after its treasure, Conan might as well abandon all hope.

After a restless night spent pondering the various courses open to him, Conan was on the point of cutting his losses and returning to de Roncier's territory. He had the merchant's purse, and if he set a good pace, the Count need never know he had been toying with desertion.

Clinging to the shrine, listening to the horse ride towards the beach over the regular swish of the waves, Conan made up his mind. He would go back to Vannes. There was nothing for him here if that man was hanging around. The pedlar's teeth began to chatter. He willed the rider to hurry; he wanted to get out of the sea and get himself dry, and could not in case it was *him*.

At last, the horse must have reached the sand at the end of the peninsula path, for the hoofbeats changed, became muffled. And then there were more. Conan swore. Someone else was coming round the point. He'd be stuck in here for ever at this rate. Hearing a difference in the sound, his berry-brown face tipped to one side. These steps were lighter. This newcomer was not riding.

Cautiously Conan poked his head out. It was the concubine's daughter herself, flying along the cliff path with her veil streaming out behind her like a swallow's tail.

'Alan, wait! Alan!' she called.

'Alan le Bret!' Conran caught his breath as the full name came to him in a flash. 'That's it, Alan le Bret!'

And carefully, for he felt as though he were taking his life in his hands, he craned his neck to view the horseman. Sure enough, the rider was none other than the man whose presence in Ploumanach had robbed him of a night's sleep.

Conan watched as he reined in his horse, a magnificent chestnut, level with the shrine, and skewed round in his saddle to look at the concubine's daughter. Hastily, Conan shrank behind St Guirec. If he positioned himself carefully, he could peer past the saint's wooden feet and watch them safely.

'Alan, wait!' The girl ran up and caught hold of the animal's bridle. She was breathless. 'You weren't going without saying farewell, were you?'

Conan's ears sharpened. Alan le Bret was leaving, was he? Now there was stroke of good fortune.

The chestnut gelding, a mettlesome beast, sidled. 'I told Ned to say goodbye to you on my behalf.'

'I . . . I wanted . . .'

'Aye?'

Le Bret's voice was not encouraging, which confused Conan. Had he taken the gem already? And had the girl discovered its loss? She looked upset. Odd that. She should have learnt to guard her features in the years since Vannes.

Conan's instincts were blunted by years of hard living, and lack of exercise. He seldom employed them where other people were concerned; and because the Count de Roncier had done his thinking for him, his wits had dulled. But Conan's instincts had not completely atrophied, and dimly he perceived that if he were to work successfully on his own, he must allow for amendments to his plans. Most of his consciousness was focused on the numbing chill seeping through to his bones; but visions of a shining gemstone spurred him to great effort, and setting his discomfort aside he tried to peer into the workings of the girl's mind. It should be child's play, her face was so open. The wench was upset, any fool could see that. Concluding her expression was more wounded than condemnatory, Conan reasoned that Alan le Bret had not taken her treasure. His spirits lifted.

'I wanted to thank you for going out of your way for us, Alan,' the concubine's daughter said. 'You have been a true friend.'

'A friend,' the mercenary murmured, brows drawn. Those pewter eyes were as cold and aloof as they had been two years ago. No, that one will never change. The pedlar watched with interest the way the girl's fingers were twisting the courser's reins round and round her fingers, as though she did not want to release them. Alan le Bret must have seen it too, and apparently it vexed him, for he gave the reins a little shake and said in a dispassionate voice that lifted Conan back to Vannes, 'You've thanked me, mistress, so if you don't mind, I'll be on my way.'

St Clair's bastard dropped the reins as though they were red-hot, and thrust unsteady hands behind her back. 'Aye. I wish you well, Alan.'

He did not spur away immediately, though Conan's newly resurrected instincts told him that he wanted to. He sat, gazing down at the girl standing on the beach, and observed with apparent irrelevance, 'You came without your shoes.'

The girl looked away. 'Oh, yes. I had to run to catch you up. I didn't want you to go without seeing . . . thanking you . . .' Her voice died.

Alan le Bret continued to look down at the concubine's daughter, while she looked up at him. Conan saw the man's throat constrict, and noticed the sensuous lips were tightly compressed. With a sense of shock, he thought he understood. Could it be that he had misjudged this man? He had long thought that Alan le Bret was as cold a fish as one could hope to meet, but today, on this beach, Conan had an astonishing revelation. The coldness was a mask. The stillness which gripped the mercenary was not the stillness of a man who felt nothing, it was rather the stillness of a man who felt too much. The icy sea was forgotten. This man could not be in love with St Clair's bastard, surely? By her posture, the wench was not immune to him. So why was Alan le Bret leaving?

'Farewell, my Blanche,' the mercenary said softly, interrupting Conan's interesting but profitless speculations. He reached out a hand as though he would touch her. Conan found himself holding his breath, but the horseman checked himself, and took up his reins. 'Perhaps we will meet again, mistress, at the tournament?'

It had been a question, and the wench didn't answer in words. As her head was turned, Conan could not see her face, but he could imagine those luminous brown eyes were speaking for her.

With sudden viciousness, Alan le Bret dug in his heels. Sand swirled, and when it had settled, there was only the girl standing alone on the beach staring at the gorse bushes which marked the beginning of the Ploumanach road. The dust was slower to settle there, and the shrubs were moving in the draught made by the horse's swift passage.

The girl's head flopped forward, and for a long minute she stared at her toes which were lost in the rosy sand. Conan noticed the sea again, nipping relentlessly at his nerve endings. 'Hurry up, I'm freezing to death,' he muttered.

A silver tear-track trailed down the girl's cheek. He saw her raise a hand and wipe her lashes. Her sigh mingled with the swishing of the sea. Her head came up, and great, mournful eyes toured the beach. She looked puzzled, like someone on uncharted terrain with no familiar landmarks to guide her. Finally, when Conan was afraid the girl had grown roots, she swung about and retraced her steps.

'About time. Jesu, I'm numb right through, and soused as a herring,' Conan mumbled sourly when she was safely out of sight. Staggering ashore, he looked askance at his dripping clothing. A stabbing pain shot through his stomach. 'Christ aid.' Then he grinned. Why was he worrying about clothes and a griping belly? With what he had coming, he could happily spend the merchant's money. Resolving to buy clothes fit for a king and the best food to settle his stomach, Conan moved haltingly towards the village. He was shivering, he was in pain, but he was happy.

First he would see where a tailor could be found, and then he would hatch a plan or two. There was no doubt about it, the concubine's daughter yet guarded her gemstone, and but for the taking of it, it belonged to him.

Chapter Twenty-Five

Three days later, Gwenn had recovered from the ordeal of her journey and had begun to chafe at the lack of exercise. Alis Wymark had a sweet but indolent nature, and it took much cajolery on Gwenn's part before her aunt could be persuaded to accompany her and the children to one of the secluded coves which formed part of their peninsula. Apparently Alis was unused to putting a foot outside the manor proper without her tiring woman and at least one maidservant.

'But, Aunt,' Gwenn objected, laughing when she saw Alis piling cushions and blankets into the arms of her long-suffering tiring woman, 'there's no need to make a pack horse of poor Marzina! We're only going for a walk!'

'I know, dear,' Alis answered. 'But I like to be prepared. We shall need something to sit on, and we might decide to make a day of it. I've sent Felicia to the kitchen for a basket of provisions. It will save having to send back for them if we need them.'

Gwenn noted the innocently uttered and very revealing phrase 'send back for'. It would never occur to Alis to walk back herself for provisions if and when they were needed. As Sir Gregor's wife, she was used to being waited on hand and foot, and accepted it as her natural right that Marzina and Felicia should be dragged all the way to the beach with burdens which may or may not be used.

Alis finished stacking cushions on Marzina and heaved a sigh. She was out of condition, and sighed a lot. If she stopped asking others to do things for her and did them herself . . .

Gwenn mentally shook her head. Her aunt was loving and affectionate, and that mattered most. Philippe had blossomed under the lavish care bestowed on him by Alis and her women. Katarin, however, remained silent; Gwenn hoped that a peaceful walk to the beach might encourage her sister to come out of herself. Peaceful? With Marzina, and Felicia, and Lord knows who else?

There was something more important which Gwenn wanted to discuss with her aunt, preferably out of ear-shot of the other women. She and Ned had not been allocated the quarters their married status merited, and while Gwenn was happy to be near the children, she had duties to Ned, and she could see their separation was making him miserable.

On the beach, Marzina spread out the blankets, and Felicia set the basket to one side, next to a sea-smoothed boulder.

The wind whipped Gwenn's veil round her face and, ignoring her aunt's disapproving expression, she unpinned it and removed it. After a moment's contemplation, she divested Philippe of his tunic and linen swaddling bands. Gurgling with pleasure, her brother began to crawl across the gently sloping sands.

'Is it wise to remove all his clothes?' Alis panted as she sank onto the blankets and cushions amid a froth of silken skirts. She waved at the maidservant. 'Go after him, Felicia, there's a dear, and see he comes to no harm.'

Felicia kicked off her leather shoes, hitched up her skirts, and smilingly obeyed. Felicia could do worse than be maidservant to her aunt, Gwenn realised. 'It will do Philippe good to move about without restrictions,' she said. 'Besides, the June air is warm.'

'Won't the sand scratch his delicate skin?'

Gwenn smiled, and shook her head.

'You are sure, Gwenn? You have more experience

with babies than I do. I want to learn.'

'They are very resilient, Aunt. Philippe is tougher than he looks.'

'If you say so, dear.' Alis heaved another sigh and dabbed her sweat-damp brow delicately with the edge of her veil. 'It was further than I remembered from the manor.'

Gwenn concealed another smile, for the walk had been only a short one. Katarin trotted up, mutely asking for help in removing her belt. The little girl wanted to take her dress off to play in the sand with her brother and Felicia, and the belt buckle, a brass one which had been a gift from Alis, was too stiff for her growing fingers. Thinking to encourage her sister to use her tongue, Gwenn affected not to understand. Huge hazel eyes blinked, and the little girl nudged her on the shoulder, wrenching at the bright yellow buckle.

'Why, Katarin!' Gwenn feigned surprise. 'Do you want something?'

Another tug on the belt. Another appealing look.

'I'm afraid I don't understand you,' Gwenn said. 'Do you want something?'

Her sister nodded vigorously.

'Tell me, Katarin. Speak. What do you want me to do?'

Katarin pointed at her belt, caught Gwenn's hand and guided it to her waist.

'No. I won't do it. Not till you speak. You must *tell* me, Katarin. Use your tongue, I know you can.' Obdurately, Katarin shook her head. The child understood her, the shock of the killings at Kermaria had not damaged her sister's intelligence, thank the Lord, only her will to communicate.

'Try. Try, Katarin. Please, sweetheart.'

A sheen of tears coated the child's hazel eyes, but her tongue did not loosen. Backing away from Gwenn, she gave Alis, reclining on her silken cushions, a hopeful glance.

Gwenn surrendered and took off her sister's belt.

471

When Katarin's bliaud had been removed and she was clad only in her shift, the child gave Gwenn a shaky smile and scampered down the beach after her brother. Marzina, without being asked, followed Katarin.

Alis turned her soft blue eyes on Gwenn. 'Don't you think you make it worse when you try and force your sister to talk?' she asked gently. 'Perhaps you should let the sickness run its course?'

'She should have recovered already. We've been here three days, and you're kindness itself. She eats well, she sleeps well – she must know she is safe.'

'Your sister needs time.'

'Alan said that.'

'Alan?' Her aunt looked down her nose in a superior manner. 'Oh, you mean that other mercenary, Captain le Bret.'

Her aunt, though she possessed a heart of gold, appeared to have prejudices. Gwenn tossed back her plait. 'Aye, Alan,' she refused to refer to him as Captain le Bret, 'the man who guided us here. Our friend.' And one whom she missed every minute of the day . . .

Since Alan had gone, Gwenn had not felt at peace with herself. She had attributed her distress to continuing grief at the sudden loss of her family and her home. But if Alan's absence was not contributing to her unhappiness, why did she keep thinking of him? Why did she want to look into those cool grey eyes and touch that raven-dark hair?

Alis blanched. It was as though she had read her niece's thoughts. 'A friend? That man? Oh, my dear, no.'

'Why not? Why can't Alan be my friend?'

'But, my dear,' Alis waved her hands in delicate confusion, 'a mercenary . . . They can't be trusted.'

Ned, her husband, was a mercenary. So they were coming to it, though not in the manner that Gwenn had anticipated. Marzina and Felicia were out of earshot with the children, near the shoreline. Gwenn plunged in. 'Tell me, Aunt, what's the difference between my husband and his cousin, and the men who guard your manor?'

'My dear, the men who guard Ploumanach are bound to the land.'

'Slaves?'

'My dear! Indeed they are not! Their families have served the Wymark family for generations, and I would not dream of questioning *their* loyalty.'

Noticing that her fingers had curled into her palms, Gwenn deliberately uncurled them and made her hands rest loosely in her lap. She did not want to alienate this amiable woman who had put a roof over their heads, but she had to speak up for Ned, and for Alan. 'Aunt, I've learnt that mercenaries can be as loyal as men born to a place. Ned served my father honestly and diligently. He risked his life for mine, and—'

'And you should not have let him force you into marrying him.'

'Ned did not force me!' Her hands curled up again. She straightened them.

'My dear,' Alis went on, placid but immovable, 'I'm sure that Captain Fletcher is a nice enough lad, but can't you see he is not . . . er . . . quite suitable? I am glad that we are talking so freely about this, Gwenn, as it has been disturbing me. Things cannot remain as they are.'

'Things? What do you mean?'

'I'm talking about the so-called marriage between you and Captain Fletcher.'

'So-called? We *were* married. At St Félix-in-the-Wood. Prior Hubert married us himself, with the monks as our witnesses. There is no doubt about it, Aunt.'

'My poor girl,' Alis said, soothingly. 'All you have to do is say the word, and I'll ask our priest what can be done about getting you an annulment.'

'An . . . an annulment?'

'There's no need for you to worry, my dear. No one would contest the fact that your marriage should not have taken place. What with you in a state of shock . . .'

'But—'

'I don't suppose the marriage has been consummated, has it? You haven't let him . . . touch you, have you, Gwenn?'

For all that she gritted her teeth, Gwenn felt her colour rise.

'Oh dear,' Alis sighed, drawing her own conclusions. 'The beast. I had hoped he'd spared you that. It would have made matters easier if you were a virgin. However,' the soft voice brightened, 'all is not lost, I am sure. This very afternoon, I promise you I shall go and speak to Father Per—'

'Aunt! You will do no such thing!' Gwenn flamed. 'Ned and I were married in the sight of God! I have sworn to keep faith with my husband, and keep faith I will. If you cannot accept our marriage, then we shall leave Ploumanach.'

'My dear—'

'No! Hear me out. Ned loves me,' a look of distress marred the unruffled calm of Alis's face, 'and I have no doubt you think that terribly vulgar. But he does love me, and I am his lawful wife, and I am not going to let you or anyone else change that.'

'You could make a better alliance.'

'A *better* alliance?' Gwenn set her teeth. Darting a glance down the beach she saw the children and their companions were safely playing with a pile of shells, out of earshot. 'A *better* alliance? I doubt it. Ned deserves a loyal wife, and I . . . I am very fond of him. If you cannot see your way to providing for us in the same way that you provide for the other married couples working on your estate, then we shall leave.'

Alis goggled.

Gwenn forced a smile. 'I do not want to quarrel with you, Aunt, but I warn you it is no empty threat. If you cannot accept me *and* my husband, we shall have to go.'

'And the children, Gwenn? What of them?' Alis's gentle eyes strayed hungrily to Katarin and Philippe, and her undisguised longing squeezed Gwenn's heart.

'They would come with us, of course,' Gwenn declared, ruthlessly. She must suppress any sympathy she might feel for Sir Gregor's childless wife, because if she did not make her views felt now, at the beginning, matters would only deteriorate. 'I could not leave them. What would become of Katarin if I abandoned her?'

Alis had not removed her eyes from the children, and her hand had crept trembling to her generous breasts. 'No. Not the children. Please,' she whispered through lips that hardly moved. 'For years I have prayed for children, and though I came to accept that the good Lord decided I would not have little ones of my own, I thought . . . I thought . . .'

Weakening, Gwenn touched the older woman's hand and completed her sentence, 'You thought that He had sent you these.' She gestured at her siblings.

A small movement of Alis's veil indicated assent. 'I thought my prayers had been heeded. I thought my autumn years were to be brightened by their presence. I would cherish your brother and sister, Gwenn. I want to love them. But if you go,' the gentle blue eyes closed as if that thought was too horrible to contemplate, 'if you go, what a torment I will feel. Already I am fond of them, already I have become used to them. If you go, Gwenn, my life will seem more empty than ever it did before. I am an empty husk.'

'No, Aunt, don't say that. Oh, God, this is dreadful. I don't like using the children as a weapon, but you must understand my loyalty to Ned. Unless you accept him, unreservedly, I cannot stay. And how can I leave the children?'

Alis lifted swimming eyes to Gwenn's. 'You really feel loyalty to that . . . that . . . young man?'

Gwenn sensed that the older woman had been about to use a less favourable adjective to describe Ned, but let it pass. 'I am Ned's wife, and I intend to remain his wife.' Hard though it would be for her, maybe it would be best for the children if she left them here and went away with Ned to make a future elsewhere. They could go to the King's joust. Ned's experience as a soldier and his enthusiasm would ensure he found a patron and . . . and . . . they would see Alan, too. Not that that last must affect her decision. If she and Ned left the children in Alis's care, there would be no confusing conflict of interests, and they *would* be safe . . .

Alis's gaze was drawn to the group by the shoreline. She straightened her round shoulders and smiled resignedly, bringing dimples to either side of her mouth. 'You drive a hard bargain,' she observed, and Gwenn knew by her tone that she had won. They could stay, all of them. She would not have to abandon the children and Ned would be accepted.

'Will it be so hard, Aunt, to think the better of my husband?' Gwenn asked sadly.

'I . . . I . . . No, of course not.' Alis put a brave face on it. She may have been forced to bow to Gwenn's will, but she would try and like the mercenary who had married her niece. How else could she keep the children?

'It's not such a bad marriage, Aunt, when you look at it dispassionately.'

'You could have had a knight, or a merchant,' Alis said wistfully.

'Aunt, you're forgetting, I'm not legitimate. I am only a bast—'

'Hush, Gwenn!' Alis flung a shocked glance in the direction of the children. 'Katarin might hear you.'

'Oh, Aunt Alis,' Gwenn said, thanking God that her aunt had been blessed with a heart of gold, for she had a narrow bigot's mind, and it was only her warm heart that redeemed her, 'Katarin is a bastard too, and one day she is bound to discover it.'

'Not if I can help it,' Alis said stoutly.

Gwenn bit her tongue and held down a sigh. To her

mind such matters were best out in the open, but she did not think it was prudent to air that particular view today. She would have to proceed one step at a time. Today, she had made a stride, and she would save other strides for other days. 'Aunt?'

'Yes?' The smile Alis bent on Gwenn bore no trace of ill will. Not only was her aunt blessed with a loving heart, she had a generous nature too. Truly they had come to the right place.

'You will make arrangements for Ned and me to be housed together?'

'Everything shall be as you wish it, my dear,' Alis confirmed. 'Your Ned can shift his belongings to the family apartments.'

'Up to the solar?' Gwenn had not expected so complete a victory and knew how much it had cost Alis to suggest it. 'There's no need to go to such lengths. We shall be perfectly happy lodged in the hall with the other families.'

'But the children,' the older woman objected immediately. 'I do so love having them at hand.'

'The children may stay in the solar. Katarin has slept like a log every night since we arrived, and as long as she knows where I am, she will not fret. She likes you, Aunt Alis.'

'Oh, do you think so?'

'Indeed.' Gwenn heard a horse pounding along the shrub-lined path which wound from the manor to the tip of the peninsula. Glancing up the beach, she saw Ned charge out of the bushes, mounted on one of Sir Gregor's mares. His flaxen thatch was windswept, he had Dancer on a leading rein, and he had apparently been searching for Gwenn, for when he saw her, he was out of the saddle, slinging both horses' reins over a branch. Gwenn's heart twisted. Purposefully, Ned stalked towards them. 'It's N . . . my husband,' Gwenn announced, unnecessarily, for she could see that her aunt had seen him. Alis was watching Ned warily, as though he were a poisonous snake that might strike at any moment. If only she knew, Gwenn thought, he is softer than she is herself. Ned wouldn't hurt a soul.

'Good morning, Lady Wymark,' Ned said briskly, holding one of his solid, dependable hands out to Gwenn. Gwenn took an astonished look at the savage determination on her husband's face and without a word rose and placed her fingers in his. Ned did not look soft this morning. He looked as though he had come to the end of his tether; and his crushing grip told Gwenn that she had resolved the matter of her marriage not a moment too soon. 'I wondered if you could spare Gwenn for a couple of hours, Lady Wymark,' Ned went on, courteous but firm. 'Her mare needs exercising, and it's best if Gwenn rides her. She's a fine beast, and I'd not want her to lose her stamina.'

'N . . . no, I d . . . don't mind. The mare must be exercised,' Alis stammered, obviously alarmed by Ned's bearing. Gwenn could not bring herself to meet her eyes. Ned was unwittingly confirming her prejudices. Absurdly, a giggle rose in Gwenn's throat. Perhaps it would do no harm to let her aunt go on thinking that Ned was fierce – for a little while at least.

Concealing her amusement she asked, 'Are you content to stay with the children, Aunt?'

'What? Oh, yes, I'd be delighted to look after them.'

'Shall I send for one of the women?'

'N . . . no. No.' Her aunt was rallying. 'I can manage. You run along, my dear, and I'll bring them back to the solar when they've had their fill of the beach.'

'Thank you, Aunt.' Gwenn snatched up her veil, tucked it into her girdle, and let Ned lead her to Dancer. 'I'm glad you found me, Ned,' she opened, 'for I've been talking to my aunt . . .'

Conan was caught just when he was beginning to think that there might be a God in Heaven. He should have known better, he thought resentfully, when the pain had eased enough for him to think once more. He

478

should have known that life was not meant to be easy. If only he had not kept the merchant's wallet. But it had been too good to discard, and he had been fascinated by the outlandish design stamped on the leather. Fool. He was a fool. And to think that he had got so near . . .

He had marched up to the guard at Sir Gregor's gate, ready to offer himself up for work. He had demanded entry and was in the process of sweetening the man with one of his stolen coins when he heard a cavalcade of horses approaching the gate.

'Stand aside, man,' the guard admonished him. 'It's the merchant with my lady's cloth, and wine from the south.'

Meekly Conan stood aside, and as he lifted his eyes to the man at the head of the little procession, his skin chilled and he knew his luck had run out. For Lady Wymark's Flemish cloth merchant was the very man from whom he had lifted the scrip back in Lannion.

'Jesus God,' Conan said, whisking the incriminating object behind his back, for the merchant's eyes had been drawn to his lost scrip like a bee to the flowers on which it feeds.

Conan had taken to his heels, of course, but it had been all over for him the moment the merchant had set eyes on his wallet. The merchant's shriek was as piercing as a hawk's, and no sooner had he pointed his fat finger than half a dozen of Sir Gregor's burliest men went hurtling after Conan and pinned him to the ground.

Then came the accusations.

He denied it, naturally.

He said he had found the purse lying on the road and could not find its owner. And, naturally, no one believed him. Sir Gregor was the law in these parts, and they had him hauled up before the knight. He was tried; found guilty.

Then came the reckoning. Conan had always considered the loss of a hand was too great a penalty to pay for stealing. He had always vowed that he would never be caught. And if it had not been for the ill luck of having the same merchant come to visit Lady Wymark, he would have got away with it. It was too bad. The sentence was carried out at once. No one wanted the trouble and expense of keeping him locked up till the next quarter sessions. The merchant looked on, gloating and rubbing his hands together. His *two* hands.

Conan felt such agony that he did not even notice the added torture of the hot pitch being applied to his poor, bleeding stump. There was blood all over his new linen tunic. Kicked through the manor gate, he staggered back to the fisherman's cottage where he had taken up residence since coming to Ploumanach. The fisherman's wife was kind, in her way. She had bandaged his limb, and given him an evil-tasting draught which dulled the pain. If only, Conan thought, while he nursed his throbbing wrist, he had got rid of that sodding purse. If only he had not chosen that particular day to go the manor. They'd never take him on now, and he'd never get his hands – hand – on the wench's jewel. He'd lost that for ever. Branded as a thief in the eyes of the neighbourhood, Ploumanach had nothing to offer him. How would he live? What could he do with only his left hand? There was just one avenue open. Beggary.

In August, two months after Conan's sentence had been carried out, his arm was healing though it continued to ache. It was a dull, steady, throbbing ache, which plagued him day and night and was persistent enough to rob him of the will to look to his future. Begging, Conan discovered, was not as lucrative as peddling or spying. Soon, when he felt better, he would trudge back to Vannes and see if he could strike up again with Count François de Roncier. In the meantime his energy had drained away, and it was all he could do to sit and hold out the hand he had left, and beg for alms.

When he had first taken up begging, Conan had stationed himself by the inn, mongrel at his side; but as August arrived, he decided the village well would be a more fruitful location. It was hot, and sooner or later everyone must come to the well, whereas not everyone patronised the inn.

There was little shade by the well, and as the flies buzzed round him, Conan hoped that it would not be an August like last year. Even here, by the coast, the wind had dropped. Today, the sea shone smooth as polished metal. The fishermen grumbled and left their sails unhoisted. They took up oars instead. But it was almost too hot to row, and the fish seemed to sense this and swam provokingly near the surface, taunting the fishermen by dancing past their boats in their shoals – a million silvery darts which were always there when the nets lay heavy in the boats, and never there when they were lowered into the slow, shining, ceaseless swell. Conan gleaned all of this and more, from listening to his patrons as they drew fresh water. The habit of hoarding away all he heard had not deserted him.

Conan knew he was right to consider returning south where he could renew his association with Otto Malait and his lord. The beggar's life was not for him. It sapped a man's resources to have to rely on the charity of others.

Hearing hoofbeats on the road from Wymark manor, Conan sighed and eased himself into the best position, with his stump held out so passers-by would be treated to a full view of his loss. He bent his chin to his chest as though he were full of shame and had repented of his crime.

'Spare me a coin . . .' He had perfected the beggar's whine, pitching his voice high, so it carried far. Two riders, one male and one female, were approaching; and the man had a mule on a leading rein, packed for a long journey. 'Give a wretched man alms, I implore you. Give alms to the needy . . .'

'Ned, dig out a coin,' a soft voice said, and recognising it, Conan tensed. It was the concubine's daughter. Conan did not look at her, but instead lifted his eyes to her companion's face. The horseman was the Saxon mercenary, Ned Fletcher – apparently she'd married him. Swiftly Conan noted Ned Fletcher's bulging saddlebags, and his narrow, belted waist from which dangled a purse.

The Saxon delved in his scrip. 'Will this do?'

Conan caught the gleam of base metal and sighed. His dog, who sensed all his adopted master's moods, whimpered.

'Give the poor man more,' the soft voice pleaded. 'Look, he's lost a hand.'

'The man's no doubt a thief, and deserved his punishment,' came the unsympathetic response, and Conan held his breath to see if the Saxon would bend to his wife's will. Few men did.

'Nevertheless,' the soft voice insisted, 'I feel sorry for him.'

An English penny sparkled silver in the summer sun. 'Will this do?' The man's tone was tolerant, amused, the tone of a man head over heels in love.

'Aye.'

The coin twirled to the ground at Conan's feet, and the cur's tail thumped the dust. Gripped by fear that he might be recognised, Conan ducked his head and kept his gaze nailed to the ground by the horses' hoofs. 'May Christ Jesu bless you for your munificence, my lady,' he mumbled, left-handedly clawing in the grit for his coin.

'Poor man,' the concubine's daughter said. And then, in a lighter vein, 'Which way do we ride?'

'South. We ride south for half a day, and then we turn east.'

'I wonder whether we'll ever return,' she said wistfully.

Conan pricked his ears. Ever return? Were they going for good?

'Why shouldn't we return?' her husband answered.

'You'll need to see your family.'

'Yes. But if you go into service, we may not have any say in the matter.'

The Saxon reached out and squeezed his wife's arm. 'I'll not chain you, Gwenn. You're free to go where you will.'

'Oh, Ned.' The concubine's daughter drew in a breath and her voice became livelier. 'I've not been to the Île de France before.'

'Neither have I.' The Saxon clapped his heels to his gelding's mahogany flanks. 'Come on, my love.'

'You're not afraid my uncle will change his mind about lending you that horse, are you?' she asked him, teasingly.

Ears straining, Conan digested what he had heard. Would the girl leave without her statue? Would she leave her treasure behind her? Conan thought not. The blood began to rush along his veins, re-invigorating him. As the riders' voices faded, he raised his head and pushed himself to his feet, intent on branding the picture of them onto his brain. He'd not forget the girl's mare, an uncommonly pretty creature, with three white stockings. Unfortunately, the Englishman's mount was unremarkable, a large-boned dark brown gelding whose prints were twice the size of the dainty mare's. Eager to find some distinguishing trait about the routier's horse, something that would enable him to pick it out in a crowd, Conan squinted at the dusty tracks, scuffled by the mule, and discovered that Ned Fletcher's unremarkable gelding came down more heavily on his nearside.

A painful thudding filled Conan's head.

They must have the statue with them. He hadn't been able to get his hands on it before, what with it being in Sir Gregor's manor. But the Saxon was looking for a master. They were going without escort to the Île de France. And if they had the statue . . .

Conan's narrow lips spread into as broad a grin as he could muster. It had been a long time since he had smiled, and the muscles on the side of his face were tight with disuse. Workman-like, he flexed his legs. He may have a stump where his right hand should be, but thank Christ his legs were sound. Conan could walk. He'd always been able to walk.

With a bloodless smile splitting his pain-creased face, Conan the beggar shook himself like his dog. There'd be no more beggary for him. He'd use the silver penny to buy a loaf from the charitable fisherman's wife who continued to lend him her roof at nights. He'd buy meat and a skinful of ale, and then he'd be off. He'd trail the handsome young couple who were heading for the Île de France. And seeing as the little madam was riding a mare that a princess would covet, they'd be easy to track, not that Conan was unduly concerned about losing them when he knew their destination.

Excitement and anticipation lent wings to his feet. There was only one reason why Ned Fletcher and his wife should head for the Île de France in August, and that was King Philip's famous tournament, where the English captain apparently hoped to find a new master. At his well-side vigil, Conan had heard the gossips say that Lady Wymark had taken against her niece's husband because of his profession. That must be what had prompted them to leave.

Conan would follow the Fletchers to France.

Faithless as a whore, the fickle wind had changed, and, belatedly, his ship was coming in.

Chapter Twenty-Six

'How will we find him?' Gwenn asked, staring wide-eyed past the empty lists into a boiling crowd. 'There must be nigh on a thousand soldiers here.'

Close by, the heralds were overseeing repairs to some railings which marked the limit of the jousting field. Beside the railing, at one side of the lists, a raised platform had been built, and a ladder was propped precariously against its canopy. A carpenter was nailing swathes of rich blue silk to it, while his apprentice – who was meant to be steadying the ladder – was winking at a girl with breasts as round and cheeks as rosy as the apples she was offering for sale. The ladder slipped, only an inch, but the carpenter yelped and dropped his hammer to clutch at a crossbeam. The roll of cloth fell and a waterfall of blue silk poured over the dry earth. 'Jesu, Pierre!' The carpenter's furious shriek cut across the hubbub. 'Try to lift your mind above your belt! Hold the bloody ladder steady!'

Gwenn stifled a laugh. 'Ned, did you see that?'

Ned was not listening. He was sitting bolt upright in his saddle, blue eyes fever-bright and intent as he drank in the scene. It was exactly as Sir Waldin had described it, he was thinking, only Sir Waldin had failed to convey the grand scale of it all. There was so much of everything; so many people, so many horses, so much noise and bustle, and over such a large area. Dozens of multi-coloured pavilions were ranged round the fringe of the field like small jewels edging a bishop's ring. The lists themselves were empty, save for a scattering of swallows swooping low over the barriers. Ned's lips parted as he measured the length of the course, and ambitious dreams swirled in his mind's eye.

Ned was determined to do well here and make a name for himself. Gwenn came of knightly stock, and he wanted her to be proud of him. Sir Waldin had hinted that men could rise through the ranks here. And on the face of it, Ned was already well on the way. He had started life as a plain man-at-arms. He had been promoted to sergeant, and then to captain. He had married a knight's daughter, something which a year ago would have seemed inconceivable. If that could happen, why should he not become squire to some knight and thus earn his own knighthood? He'd *make* it happen. His cousin was the Duke of Brittany's captain, so he had the right connections.

'Ned?'

'Mmm? What is it?'

'How will we find Alan in all of this?' Gwenn gestured at the chaotic throng of pages and squires, of marshals and heralds, knights and nobles. Apart from the apple-seller and a couple of crimson-lipped prostitutes, there did not seem to be many women about. Gwenn felt a twinge of unease.

Ned smiled abstractedly. 'Oh, that's easy. We keep our eyes peeled for Brittany's pavilion. I can see the ermine from here.'

'You've seen the Duke's colours?' Waldin St Clair had seen to it that that particular gap in Gwenn's education had been filled. She knew the Duke of Brittany's shield bore ermine, represented by black dots on a white field.

'Aye. I see them. We can enquire of Alan's whereabouts from there.'

They ran Alan to earth later that afternoon, just beyond the King's cookhouse on the outskirts of the sprawling encampment which surrounded the central tourney field. He was stretched out on a wolf pelt, limbs loose, by a fire in front of a small, patched tent.

His hands pillowed his head, and he was watching the white clouds float by like thistledown on a sluggish summer wind. A smoky-blue plume rose vertically from his fire. He was cooking a fish, wrapped in leaves, on a makeshift spit. Idly, he reached out, and gave the skewer a turn.

When Ned's shadow fell over him, Alan smiled at his cousin quite unsurprised, as though he had seen him not half an hour before. 'You'll share this with me, I take it, Ned? It's trout. The King's still in Paris, and the official fare will be poisonous until his chef gets here.'

'It smells good. We'd love to share it,' Ned said equably.

'We?' Alan's gaze fell on Gwenn hovering uncertainly behind her husband, and a quiver ran through him.

'Well met, Alan,' Gwenn said. Alan's easy manner left him and Gwenn felt even more awkward. Half of her had been longing to see him again, counting the miles as they rode, but the other half had been dreading it. And here he was, scowling at her as though she was a woman who had walked uninvited into a man's world. And although it irritated her to admit it, she did indeed feel out of place. Ned should have come to the King's tourney on his own. She was no great dame to accompany her husband to the joust. Only great ladies and whores followed the circuit. But she was Ned's wife. At Ploumanach, there was little to hold Ned. Alis had tried to accept him, but she had never felt at ease with him. So with Philippe and Katarin safe and content at Wymark manor, he and Gwenn had decided to leave and fulfil Ned's long-cherished dream.

'Blanche.' Alan sat up and tossed a lock of dark hair out of his eyes. 'This an unlooked for pleasure. I dared not hope that you would come.' He was covering up his surprise by playing the gallant. Picking up his cloak, he threw it over a mossy tree stump that the King's men had failed to uproot, and indicated that Gwenn was to sit on it. It was a good couple of yards from his fire.

'My thanks.' Wishing she did not feel so defensive, Gwenn tried out a cheerful smile. 'Should I not be here?'

Alan was once more at his cooking, with his back to her. His voice was muffled. 'I thought you wouldn't want to leave the children.'

'It wasn't easy,' Gwenn confessed, and unconsciously her hand drifted to her stomach. 'But my aunt loves them dearly, and I know she will give them the care they need.'

'Gwenn is considering entering the Duchess's household,' Ned said. 'Why are you laughing, Alan?'

'I take it you want to see something of your wife?'

'Naturally. That's why we thought it best she—'

'Entered the Duchess's household?' Alan gave his head a firm shake. 'No, my innocent Ned. Duke Geoffrey and Duchess Constance are hardly ever together. If you put Gwenn in the Duchess's train and you enlist with the Duke's company, you won't see her more than about twice a year.'

There was a silence while Ned digested this. 'I assumed the Duke and Duchess met more frequently than that. The Duchess is coming to the tournament, isn't she? Or was I misinformed?'

'No, that information is correct. But it's a rare meeting, prompted by duty alone,' Alan said dryly. 'They took an instant dislike to one another, and so far have failed to produce a male heir. But Duke Geoffrey wants a son, and so . . .' Alan glanced at Gwenn who he saw was staring fixedly at the fire, 'so these occasional . . . er. . . . duty meetings take place. Rumour has it that the Duchess is pregnant already, but my guess is that His Grace wants to make sure.' Observing that Gwenn's hand had drifted protectively over her stomach, Alan brought his brows together. Was Gwenn pregnant? She noticed him staring and snatched her hand from her stomach, blushing red as a June rose. Her waist was slender as a wand, so if she was pregnant, it was early days. Alan wondered if his cousin knew. He had a

488

hollow feeling in the pit of his stomach. Jesu, but he was hungry.

Jabbing at his fish with a stick, Alan took up a ragged piece of cloth and lifted the spit from the fire. 'Done to a turn. Have you a tent with you?' he asked as he peeled the leaf wrappings from the trout. The skin was lightly browned, and the smell set his his mouth watering.

'We've no tent.'

'You're welcome to share mine. His Grace was generous, I've one to myself.'

Ned eyed Alan's cramped quarters with misgivings. Alan had washed his second tunic, and that and his chausses were hanging on the guy ropes to dry. 'We slept in taverns on the way here. I'd planned to sleep in the open.'

'That won't do. Why, even squires sleep in their master's tents. Besides, it wouldn't be safe for Gwenn.' Alan lowered his voice. 'Too many wolves on the prowl.'

'Wolves?' Gwenn demanded, staring at Alan's wolf pelt. Her veil danced as she squinted into the trees.

Offering her some fish on a fresh leaf, Alan smiled into her eyes. 'Only the human sort, my Blanche,' he murmured. 'Rest assured, that skin was not from these forests, it was a gift from my lord.' Their gazes joined, and for a moment Alan could not free his eyes. It had been two and a half months since he had seen her – a lifetime – and he had been thirsting for close sight of her. She looked tired, and though the sun had left a faint dusting of gold along her cheekbones, there were charcoal smudges under the deep brown eyes. Her lashes were thicker and longer than he had remembered, her nose prettier. Was her skin as soft as it looked?

Gwenn noticed that Alan's face had lost weight; the bones under his skin were more prominent. His hair was blacker and shinier than her memory had painted it, his eyes flecked with silver lights. Unusually, they were open as the day. Her stomach lurched. Her gaze slipped. His mouth was smiling, a gentle, resigned smile, with the merest hint of that sinful curve that had always made her cheeks burn. Hastily, Gwenn directed her eyes to the fish he was offering her. His fingernails were as bitten as ever.

Ned watched his wife and his cousin, and the play of expressions on their faces gave him a sudden sense of unease tinged with alarm.

Alan cleared his throat and addressed Ned over his shoulder. 'Your wife would be safer out of sight at night, cousin, lest the wolves mistake her for a woman of low virtue.'

Gwenn lowered her head over her portion of fish and wondered if she wanted to be safe. Alan le Bret had always been able to make her toes tingle. And Ned, well, she loved her husband, and she was carrying his child, but he never made her toes tingle. Oh, God. Life was growing more complicated by the day, and the more she thought about it, the worse the tangle became. At Wymark manor it had seemed obvious that they must make a life elsewhere. And where should they come but to the King's joust where Ned could ask Alan for help in finding a patron? And here was Alan, and Ned, and . . . Could a woman love *two* men? Dear God.

Ned was wrestling with a ghastly uncertainty. Could he trust his cousin with his wife? 'I think I will buy a tent, Alan. I thought I saw someone selling them, back by the river.'

'Don't think of it, Ned.' Alan shook his head. 'They're a bunch of thieves. They follow the tourney circuit, and double, even triple, the price. There are always dolts ready to pay through the nose in order to save a trip back to Paris. I've heard it said they remove tent pegs in the night in order to re-sell them at inflated prices to their original owners next day.'

Ned hesitated.

Alan sent his cousin a reassuring smile. 'Gwenn will

be quite safe in my tent, I assure you, Ned.'

Ned relaxed, and cursed himself for thinking ill of his cousin. 'My thanks, Alan.'

Less than a mile away, Count François de Roncier headed a small company of some twenty men bound for the King's joust. On his right hand rode a keen young knight of his household. This knight, a raw recruit, name of Walter Venner, was full of zeal. He was wearing his helmet, as were others in the Count's troop, but despite the heat, this knight had his visor down, and his features were completely obscured. It lent him a fearsome, mysterious air. François did not object, for he viewed the King's tournament as little more than an exercise in self-promotion, and Venner could only enhance his reputation by comporting himself in so bellicose a manner.

At his left hand Otto Malait sat astride the bony charger he favoured.

François was in a rare holiday mood, and he had been speaking in a jocular manner with his knight. He turned to include the Norseman in the conversation. 'Advise me, Malait. Where shall I pitch my tent? In the space reserved by King Philippe for the French, or in the section cordoned off by the Duke of Brittany?'

'A knotty problem, mon seigneur,' Otto responded, well aware that this must be some sort of test, for on the rare occasions the Count sought counsel, it was from the Dowager Countess, not his men. 'But as you are come at King Philip's invitation, I would suggest the French quarter. And you are French by blood, mon seigneur.'

François turned to Venner. 'What say you, Sir Walter?'

'I would think, mon seigneur, it would depend on which overlord you feel more bound to.' Venner's voice was muffled by his helm. 'Most of your lands are in Brittany, are they not?'

'They are.'

'I heard, mon seigneur, that you had family troubles with rival claimants to those lands. If I were you, I'd camp with Brittany. You've more at stake if you lost his favour.'

'What you say is true. But I've settled matters entirely to my satisfaction in Brittany.'

'You've . . .' the knight hesitated, 'eliminated your rival?'

'Just so.'

'Then, mon seigneur, I would say it mattered little where you strike camp.'

François beamed at his youngest knight, delighted to find the latest addition to his household had a modicum of intelligence. But he could not keep smiling at a man when all he could see of him was the glitter of his eyes through a slit in his visor. His smile died. 'I've an eye to advancing my interests in France,' François murmured under his breath. 'Captain?'

'Mon seigneur?'

'Find the French section. We'll camp there. And pitch my pavilion as close to King Philippe's as humanly possible.'

Two days before the jousting began, Conan limped into the enclosure.

He'd not had an easy journey, but in Paris he had begged passage for himself and the shabby grey mongrel on a carter's waggon. The carter was transporting hazel-wand cages bristling with hens, and it was agreed that Conan should keep an eye on them and make sure no one made off with them.

'These hens,' the burly Frenchman asserted proudly, 'are bound for the King's board. His chef would skin me alive if I lost any.'

Conan was set down on the outskirts of the teeming encampment, in the Breton section. Despite the rest his feet had had while riding in the cart, they remained sore. He'd walked his way through the soles of his boots, and though he'd spotted cobblers aplenty in Paris, he could not afford the city prices they'd been demanding. Consequently he was barefoot, a state of affairs that he was determined not to endure for much longer.

Hobbling out of the path of a mailed knight atop a mountain of a horse, Conan sat down to chafe his aching feet and consider where he'd be most likely to find the chicken *he* intended plucking. He deemed it wisest to begin immediately, before hunger and thirst took their toll, and he headed straight for the area that had been roped off for the Bretons' horses.

The girl's high-bred mare was easy to find. It was tethered not far from three young grooms with Brittany's livery splashed across their broad breasts. The lads were seated in a circle on upturned leather buckets, dicing on the base of a fourth bucket. They were meant to be on guard. The tallest of them was chewing a piece of straw. He looked enquiringly at Conan, while one of his fellows rolled the dice.

'Good day,' Conan said, ensuring his damaged arm was tucked well out of sight.

Lantern jaws masticating, the tall groom checked the fall of the dice and grimaced. 'God rot you, Samson,' he complained, good-naturedly, 'you've had the longest winning streak in history.'

Samson smiled and threw again.

'Pretty mare you have there,' Conan said, regarding Samson and his lucky dice.

The groom with the straw brought his overhanging brows down. 'What's that to you?'

Conan glanced meaningfully at the dice-thrower whose brown head was bent low over the makeshift table. 'If you'd permit a stranger to advise you . . .'

The straw was removed. 'Advise me?'

Conspiratorially, Conan lowered his voice and jerked his head at Samson who was intent on the dice. 'Aye. He bears watching, does that one.'

The Duke of Brittany's tall groom leaped the rope barrier and was at Conan's side in an instant. 'What do you mean?'

'Try turning out his sleeves. I think you'll discover

493

the reason for his good fortune.'

'Loaded dice?'

Conan nodded, and heard the hiss of the groom's indrawn breath.

'Jesus God! If you're right, that snake's filched a fortune.' He lifted his angry voice to a bellow. 'Samson! Freeze, you worm!'

'Le Bret,' Duke Geoffrey handed Alan a parchment upon which he had scrawled a few lines, 'see this message reaches my lady wife, will you?'

Alan bowed, and thrust the Duke's letter down the front of his tunic. 'I'll see to it myself, my lord.'

Duchess Constance of Brittany's white silk pavilion was pitched next to the Duke's. Having delivered the note, Alan stood in the shade under the Duchess's awning. He could see between the two rows of retainers' shelters to his own tent halfway down the line. It was easy to pick out because of the two triangular patches that were visible from this side. A hooded man was walking past it at that very moment.

With sudden insight, Alan stiffened, and turned all his attention on the cowled figure. A thick hood in August? The man was hiding his face. Now why should he do that if he were honest?

The figure paused outside Alan's tent and showed uncommon interest in the two triangular patches in the canvas.

Concluding that he had caught a sneak thief in the act of sizing up a likely place to rob, Alan started casually down the line of tents. Like most sensible people, Alan carried his valuables on his person. He hoped his cousin did the same. By the time he was two-thirds of the way down the line, the hooded figure had lifted the tent flap and ducked inside. Half expecting a shriek that would tell him that Gwenn was resting inside, Alan abandoned any pretence of indifference, snatched out his dagger and charged through the opening.

'Christ aid!' the fellow squealed.

Alan caught a glimpse of a taut, unshaven face and two terrified eyes, but the light was poor in his tent, and until he had the man outside . . .

The thief had disembowelled one of the saddlebags and Gwenn's spare bliaud was strewn over the groundsheet. Knife up, Alan lunged, delivering a cut to the thief's calf. The wretch yelped. Another knife gleamed dully in the shadows. His opponent was breathing hard, and he retaliated. It was a wild blow and easily deflected, and a certain awkwardness about it puzzled Alan; but in avoiding the blow in the restricted space, Alan's feet tangled in Gwenn's gown and some bedding. He kicked his feet free. A dog barked, and a ball of grey fur hurtled through the tent flap. Yellow teeth sank into one of Alan's boots. Alan couldn't shake it off. Seizing his chance, the thief slid past him. His breath was foul.

Determined to catch the intruder, Alan dived at him, caught an arm and held on. The man whimpered as though he'd severed a tendon. Steel streaked silver past Alan's eyes. To save his sight, Alan jerked back. The thief wriggled, kneed Alan in the groin, and fled. The mangy grey ball loosed hold of Alan's boot and shot out of the tent.

Doubled up in the entrance of his tent, and gasping with pain, Alan watched them go. There was something odd about that man. He had no shoes, but that in itself was not significant. Alan sharpened his gaze. The man's right hand was missing. So it was not the first time the knave had been a-thieving, but the punishment had obviously failed to reform him. Unsurprised, Alan sighed, and dusted himself down. There was no need to chase him. Thieves were usually cowards. Having burnt his fingers here, he'd not be back. 'Foiled you this time, my friend,' Alan murmured, and after stowing Gwenn's belongings in her bag, he returned to the Duke.

Alan did not mention the thief to Gwenn or Ned, but

while he arranged for his cousin's introduction to Duke Geoffrey, he advised Ned to stay close to his tent, saying that the summons to the Duke's presence might arrive at any moment.

While Gwenn sheltered from the afternoon sun in the relative cool of the tent, Ned had stationed himself outside, craning his neck to see past the other tents. His hungry blue eyes were trained on the distant lists where a handful of knights were practising, ready for the tourney which was set to begin in two days' time.

Gwenn wiped her damp brow with the back of her hand and sank languidly onto her bedroll. She could hear the clashing of swords, and wondered at the men who could don full armour in August and fight just for the glory of it. She was tired as well as hot.

Alan's tent was cramped, and she had not found it easy to sleep hemmed in on the one hand by her husband, and on the other by Alan. On the first night, she had been so worn out by travelling that she had dropped off almost at once, only to be shaken from her dreams minutes later by Ned. She had twisted round to peer at him. 'Ned?'

'If you want a cuddle,' Ned's voice was aggrieved, 'I think you should stick to your husband.'

With a rush of embarrassment, Gwenn realised it had been Alan's side she had been burrowing into.

'I . . . I'm sorry, Alan,' she mumbled, overcome with confusion as Ned dragged her proprietorially into his arms. And that had been that. Except that it hadn't been as simple as that, for afterwards Gwenn had felt afraid to close her eyes in case, in her sleep, she should roll over and find herself once more pressed against Alan's tense, muscled body.

Now it was day, and she could rest. 'I think I'll have a nap,' she said to Ned's back outside the tent flap. He turned, honest Saxon features registering anxiety. 'You're not sick, are you, Gwenn?'

'I'm not sick. Just hot and a little weary. Why don't you go and watch the knights?' This was not the time to tell him he was to be a father, not when he was distracted by the excitement of the coming tournament and his hopes that the Duke would employ him.

'Alan said to wait here. He might send for me.'

'If he does, I'll direct them to the field. Don't worry, if the Duke summons you, we'll find you.'

Ned glanced longingly over his shoulder, divided between what he saw as his duty to Gwenn and his desire to watch the activity at the lists.

'Go on, Ned. I'm poor company at the moment, and I just want to rest.'

'I won't be long,' he promised. Before Gwenn blinked he had gone.

Later that afternoon, the Duke's messenger, a well-favoured young Breton with a bushy thatch of curly brown hair and brilliant brown eyes, swaggered up to the tent asking for Ned Fletcher. He was wearing an antique, battered gambeson which Gwenn assumed to have been handed down to him from one of the Duke's knights. His trousers were filthy, and a large rent flapped open at his thigh. He had a cut on his hand, and both his face and hair were slick with sweat. He looked as though he'd galloped all the way from Jerusalem, and Gwenn was taken aback that the Duke should permit such ill-kempt men to assist him. The messenger seemed careless of his appearance, and on sighting Gwenn in Alan's quarters, an interested light sparked in the deep brown eyes. He produced a practised smile.

Gwenn ignored both the interested light and the too-charming smile, and waved in the direction of the lists. 'My *husband's* over there.'

A lanky lad, the messenger was standing too close, as though he thought he could dominate her with his imposing inches. 'You're married to the man who was foolish enough to get his master killed?'

Gwenn stiffened, discomposed for a moment as a spasm of real pain ran through her. Ned's former master and her father were one and the same, but the messenger was not to know that. She eyed him coolly. The Duke's messenger was insolent, and he had not yet controlled that irritating leer. In fact his grin was actually broadening. Arrogant young pup. 'Aye, I'm married,' she said icily.

'*Dommage*,' the young man murmured in French. Giving her a courtly bow, he took her hand, and before she realised what he was about, he lifted it to his lips and deposited a series of swift kisses on her knuckles. 'However,' he continued in a brighter tone, 'if you are the wife of this Ned Fletcher, I see I shall have to take him on.'

'Take him on? You?' She reclaimed her hand. 'What are you saying? It's not up to you, surely?'

The messenger bowed. His eyes were positively smouldering. 'Oh, but it is. My esquire is ailing, and' – ruefully Gwenn's courtier indicated his filthy, torn clothing – 'as you see, I am in dire need of another.'

'But . . . but . . . ?' Gwenn stuttered. She had been grossly mistaken as to this man's identity. This was no lackey. 'Wh. . . . who are you?'

'Raoul Martell, madame.'

'You . . . you're a knight?'

Another bow. Another assured, infuriating grin. 'Indeed, and at your service, madame.'

'Ned's used to a captain's position,' Gwenn blurted, and could have bitten her tongue out, for she did not want to stand in the way of Ned finding the work that he wanted.

Sir Raoul raised a brow. He was one of those rare people whose eyes could dance while he frowned. 'You think your husband unsuitable for me?'

'Unsuitable? No, of course not. It . . . it isn't that,' Gwenn backtracked hastily. This was Ned's chance to set his foot on the noble, knightly ladder. 'My husband's a hard worker. I'm sure you would find him very suitable.'

'You say he's watching at the lists, Madame Fletcher?'

Raoul Martell pronounced her name as though he

498

were caressing it, and his eyes were so dark they had no light in them at all. Gwenn shivered, and edged towards the tent flap. 'Aye. You'll find Ned at the lists.'

'How will I know him?'

'He's taller than most, with thick flaxen hair.' A reckless demon made her add, 'He's very handsome.'

Undaunted, Sir Raoul gave her a bow worthy of the Duchess Constance herself, and went jauntily towards the lists.

Though the post was temporary, Ned jumped at the chance Sir Raoul offered him. He was so keen to prove himself an able esquire that he did not leave Sir Raoul's side for the rest of that day. He carried the knight's lances, saw to his horses – a wealthy man, Sir Raoul had more than one mount. Ned cleaned and sharpened his master's sword, had Sir Raoul's second hauberk mended, and all the while he was hoping that his diligence would be rewarded by permission to assist the knight when it came to the grand tourney.

Ned apologised for his neglect of her, but Gwenn had not minded. She had been feeling queasy, and was only too glad to be left to her own devices. Besides, Alan seemed to have time on his hands, and he visited her more than once that afternoon. On the first occasion, he startled her by mentioning that he had informed the Duke of the murderous injustice visited on her family by François de Roncier. The Duke had promised he would look into the affair. Dryly, Alan had added that large wheels turned slowly. Gwenn sensed that he was unhappy at his Duke's lukewarm response. On his second visit to the tent – to fetch his spare dagger – he informed her that he planned taking a lengthy leave of absence from the Duke after the tourney, which strengthened her feeling that he was disillusioned with his carefree Duke. By the time Alan appeared for the third time, Gwenn was wondering if Ned had asked him to keep an eye on her. She did not wish to be an imposition.

That evening, at dusk, she lit their fire, and she and

Alan sat before it, staring into the crackling flames, waiting for Ned. 'There's no need for you to keep coming back to the tent tomorrow, Alan,' she said, hugging her knees. Like baleful yellow eyes, cooking fires and braziers winked into life all about them, and princes and paupers alike were reduced to mere black shadows drifting back and forth between flickering light. 'It must be irritating for you, having to see to me,' Gwenn pressed on, 'but I feel safe. I'm only a bowshot from the lists, all I have to do is call out and a dozen cavaliers would rush to assist me.'

Alan's head came up. He remembered the ragged thief he'd chased from the tent. It was more than likely the wretch had gone for good and would not harm a woman, but one never knew. Earlier, at the time of the evening Angelus, the heavy evening air had brought the echo of Paris's distant cathedral bells into the tilt-yard. While the bells were ringing, Alan had seen a cowled figure skulking behind the King's cookhouse. It seemed unlikely that his thief would risk capture by being caught in the same place twice, but he had a powerful suspicion it was the same man. Alan had managed to get a glimpse of the fellow's features the second time. It was Conan, the pedlar from Vannes. He was therefore not entirely sure that Gwenn was safe. If her husband could not be with her, then he must. But he did not want her alarmed.

'It's not an imposition,' Alan said, sincerely. 'My duties have been light of late, and I enjoy your company.'

Conscious of a tug in the region of her heart, Gwenn looked away. 'Why thank you, Alan,' she said huskily. 'I . . . I like your company also.' A black brow twitched upwards, and Gwenn was moved to enlarge. 'I never have to pretend with you. I can be myself. You make me feel at ease.'

'At ease,' Alan murmured softly.

Gwenn had the obscure feeling that her remark had displeased him.

'Like with Ned?' Alan forced the question through his lips not because he wanted to, but because he found he had to, though he knew he couldn't expect an honest answer. To his astonishment, she tried to give him one.

'N . . . no. Not at all like Ned. Ned's predictable, while you're . . .' she floundered. 'You're not predictable at all.'

He laughed. 'And this unpredictability puts you at ease?'

'No.' She hesitated. 'Some people can be predictable, but it's not at all reassuring. You're not inclined to judge, Alan, maybe it's that. No. It's not that. You're cold—'

'Cold?' He shot her a hooded look. If only she knew. He did not feel at all cold towards her. Ned's wife, he reminded himself. She is married to my cousin, she is my best friend's wife . . .

'Aye. You're detached, but I like that. You're careless of other people's views.'

'Careless?'

'If their ideas don't match yours, you don't seek to convert them. You let them be. You wouldn't impose your will on anyone.'

Smiling, Alan reached out, and though he knew he should not, he gently drew his fingers across the back of her hand. He felt absurdly like a poacher, and even more so when wine-dark colour ran into her cheeks. Gwenn bent her head over their water pot. Shamefully reassured, Alan said, 'So that's what you meant, my Blanche. For a moment there I was worried. I thought you were telling me you'd lost your liking for me.'

Her head jerked up, eyes flashing with a martial light. 'Liking for you? What are you talking about? I'm a married woman, Alan le Bret, and don't you forget it!'

The sinful mouth curved, transfixing her gaze. 'I don't forget it, not for one moment, I assure you, sweet Blanche. But sometimes I wish you might.'

Gwenn glared at him. Her feeling of warmth and

501

contentment had fled. 'Oh, don't you start, Alan,' she said wearily. 'I've had my fill with Sir Raoul.'

Instantly, Alan dropped his teasing mask. 'Martell's been pestering you?'

'Like the murrain. Sometimes I think that the only reason he agreed to take Ned on was because . . .' She hesitated; her suspicions made her sound arrogant in the extreme.

'No need for false modesty,' Alan said. 'He's one of the wolves I was telling you about.'

'He's a pain in the neck. He sends Ned off on some wild goose chase, and then comes here. I've made it plain I'm not interested.'

'I'll have words with him.'

'No, Alan! I'll deal with it myself. The grand tourney begins tomorrow, and Sir Raoul has promised that Ned will be his esquire. I'll . . . I'll not hazard that for the sake of one day. If he were to be angered, he might change his mind.'

Sober grey eyes captured hers. 'You swear you'll speak to me if he bullies you?'

Gwenn assented. She had not been able to mention this to Ned, but telling Alan had eased her mind. That was what she liked about Alan. He would flirt with her, but the moment he sensed she was uneasy, he would stop. Alan le Bret was sensitive. The discovery pleased her.

Ned crept late to bed that night; but before he fell asleep he told Gwenn that he had prevailed upon Sir Raoul to reserve her a place on the Duchess of Brittany's dais, near to her ladies-in-waiting. He seemed to regard this as something of a coup.

Gwenn was not at all sure she wanted to watch the tournament. She put her disquiet down to the fact that she did not want to watch any sort of a fight, even a regulated one. She had seen all the fighting she ever wanted to see at Kermaria.

'Ask for Lady Juliana,' Ned said, 'Sir Raoul's fiancée.'

'Sir Raoul has a fiancée?' Gwenn asked, momentarily startled out of her feeling of unease. Alan caught her eye, and winked. She hunched a shoulder on him and tried to ignore him.

'Oh, aye,' Ned gave a jaw-cracking yawn, 'a lovely, gracious lady – they're to be married at Christmas. God, but I'm tired.' Another yawn, and Ned slung a heavy arm over Gwenn's waist. 'Ask for Lady Juliana. She's been told to expect you. She will make sure you have a good view . . .'

Ned's voice trailed off, and Gwenn guessed he was already asleep. She wasn't sure she wanted a good view. A good view of what? Another bloodbath?

Chapter Twenty-Seven

A little before dawn, the cloudless sky was a speckled tapestry of pale, fragile stars. In the jousting field, the heralds were up before the birds, rubbing sleep-dazed eyes as they scurried to and fro across the arena. There was always another last-minute task to complete. It was still dark enough for them to need the torches set at intervals along the perimeter fence, and golden flames streamed from the iron stands like maidens' favours in a gentle, gusting wind which brought with it the fragrance of enough fresh-baked bread to feed an army.

Indeed an army was encamped round the field. Men had tramped from Gascony, there were knights from Aquitaine, knights from Toulouse, there was even a group of swarthy-complexioned young bloods from as far afield as Navarre. There were people from Brittany. Fortune-hunters had come in their droves from every corner of Christendom. There were duchesses, ladies, women and whores. There were princes, dukes and lords; there were beggars and pedlars, cutthroats and thieves – an ill-assorted army, whose aim was, since it was peacetime, to polish rusty war skills. And if it should chance that blood was let, then so much the better.

The Church might send its bishops to mouth the official line, which was to rail against the tourney as a terrible waste of life and limb. His Holiness the Pope might regret the loss of life, might worry that the tournament was used to settle ancient feuds, but these clerical, other-wordly opinions were ignored. In the main, the view was that a drop of judicious blood-letting never harmed any army. On the contrary, it made eyes all the keener, and hands took more care. In England, the Church's official line was heeded. Here in France it was disregarded. Besides, everyone knew that the Bishop of Paris had a place reserved for him on the royal stand.

The participants lived in the hope that they would be among the victors, for a tournament could be a lucrative source of income for a successful knight. It was designed to be similar to a war, in that a captured knight would have his harness and his horse taken by the victor. Since for many knights their warhorse represented all their wealth, this could be disastrous; and, as if the loss of their horse was not enough, the captured knight was also expected to negotiate a ransom to free himself. For the landless knight with no revenue, a tourney offered chances of riches, and at this one, the largest to be held in a decade, the pickings would be rich indeed. But it was not easy, the risk of great losses was high. Waldin St Clair had made a dazzling career at the jousts, but not many knights had his skill or stamina.

The sun climbed. Its long, bright rays tumbled over the fences and ran across the sand that, ominously, had been sprinkled on the jousting field. One by one, the stars winked out. The torches were doused. The rest of the army woke, crawled to their tent flaps, and squinted at the sky.

Swallows soared over the striped fields and verdant woods girdling Paris. As the shadows shortened on the river of primrose sand in the lists, the birds, unconscious that this was to be an arena of war, saw only a place where they could find food. By the time their flight carried them over the encampment, the city of tents was deserted, left to derelicts and strays who foraged silently among upturned cooking pots. Tent flaps and pennants trailed listlessly in a slack breeze. Having scooped some succulent insects from the encampment, the swallows flew hopefully on, over the lists. These, in stark contrast to the abandoned acres of canvas, fairly teemed with life.

The stands groaned under the largest crowd in Christendom. Those who had no place on the stands pressed up to the fence, got in the way of the horses, were shrieked at by red-cheeked heralds trying vainly to impose some sort of order on the proceedings. Beyond the lists, the paddocks were a confusion of stamping horses, jingling bits, and harassed grooms. Within hailing distance, the combatants waited, placed wagers while they pretended patience and a calm that no one could feel, for the air was crackling with excitement. Avoiding the noisy throng, the swallows swooped over the virgin sand in the lists.

Gwenn had found Duchess Constance's dais. From the outset, Lady Juliana had taken pains to welcome Gwenn. 'Your first tournament?' she had exclaimed. 'You must be very excited!'

Gwenn was not excited, she did not want to be here at all, but she held her peace. Perhaps it would not be as bad as she feared. The fighting was not real, after all; it would not be like Kermaria.

'Here, take this stool,' Lady Juliana went on, blithely unaware of Gwenn's doubts. 'My fiancé is to take the field at noon, and your husband's assisting.'

'Ned's not taking part?' Gwenn asked, going cold all over.

'Taking part? A squire? Heavens, no! But he'll have my husband's lances to hand and—'

'Don't you worry?' Gwenn blurted.

'Worry?' Lady Juliana put a tuck in her brow, in well-bred confusion. 'Why should I worry?'

'In case Sir Raoul is injured. It seems so dangerous, so pointless.'

Lady Juliana drew herself up, and fixed Gwenn with a disdainful look. 'Pointless? It's vital practice they are getting, Mistress Fletcher. If you are feeling faint-hearted, I think you should leave.'

507

'No.' Hastily Gwenn shook her head. Ned was proud to be involved in a tourney, and if he wanted her to watch, then watch she would. For a moment, she was tempted to reveal to Lady Juliana that she was niece to Sir Waldin St Clair, Champion of Champions. But she hastily dismissed the thought. She had not seen the Count François de Roncier at this tourney, but in this large crowd, that meant nothing. He or one of his spies might well be here, and it was best the St Clair name was never mentioned. 'It . . . I merely felt queasy for a moment. It has passed.'

Lady Juliana cast a knowledgeable eye over Gwenn's slim figure. 'You're breeding, aren't you, my dear?' Gwenn's jolt of surprise gave Lady Juliana her answer, and she lowered her voice, honouring Gwenn with a confidence: 'You and the Duchess alike, we pray. As that is the case, there is no shame if you have to leave the platform for a moment. The Duchess will understand. It is different when we women are carrying.'

Gwenn sat on her stool, knowing in her heart that the babe made no difference. She would feel distanced from the event even if she were not carrying Ned's child. The other women filling up the Duchess's stand were dressed in their brightest raiment and chattering like starlings. Sir Raoul, fully armoured, with his visor up, came to make his bow. As though someone had waved a fairy wand, the gossiping stopped. The knight drew all eyes. Gracefully acknowledging the Duchess, Sir Raoul bowed over Lady Juliana's fingertips.

'*Bon chance*, Sir Raoul,' his fiancée said formally, without a trace of emotion.

Sir Raoul inclined his head a fraction. He scanned the tongue-tied women, white teeth flashed, and then he loped towards his charger. The twittering began again.

And so it was whenever one of the combatants approached the stand. The chattering would cease, and the women would hold their breath while greetings were exchanged. Was the silence brought about because the women were wondering whether it was the last time they would see that particular combatant alive? How could they stand it? Gwenn wondered how many times Lady Juliana had sat through similar proceedings. Either the woman had nerves of steel, or no nerves at all. Perhaps it came to the same thing. It's all a show, she thought, but it is a deadly show. God guard them from hurt.

A brace of swallows was diving gracefully over the field. Gwenn watched them.

Sir Raoul was the first to ride out. Ned waited by the barrier, and if it had not been for him catching her eye, and gesticulating wildly, Gwenn would not have known it was Sir Raoul, for she had not marked his colours, and when he was sealed in his armour, with his pot pulled down over his face, there was no recognising him. Aware of Lady Juliana rigid at her elbow – so the woman *did* care – Gwenn was careful to maintain an expression of neutral interest. Sir Raoul's huge, brown warhorse thundered the length of the course, sending great clods of earth and clouds of sands flying in its wake. As soon as the knights clashed mid-field, the swallows vanished.

On his second charge, Sir Raoul's ash lance – Ned had told Gwenn it was ash – hit his challenger's shoulder with such force that the shaft gave way with a crack. Vicious fragments shot abroad. Gwenn held her breath while Sir Raoul's hapless opponent rocked sideways, desperately scrabbling to maintain his seat, but the blow had been too much, and slowly, almost gracefully, Sir Raoul's rival sank into the churned-up sand. It had been decreed that there would be no hand-to hand fighting until later in the day, at the mêlée. Then fortunes would change hands. At the moment the knights were merely flexing their muscles, sizing up the opposition, warming up. Sir Raoul's current foe was out of the competition, until later.

Gwenn watched the vanquished knight's squire catch the fleeing warhorse. The knight was hauled to his feet and surrounded by commiserating friends. He limped off to the tents, where refreshments awaited him.

The trumpets sounded.

The sand was raked.

A different squire ran onto the field, dragging another rack of bright-tipped lances up to the fence. Sir Raoul wheeled his charger about, lance in rest. A second challenger lined up, gonfalon aflutter. His mount was champing at the bit. This contestant had Sir Raoul unhorsed on the third charge. He was bruised, but not badly hurt. He followed the path of the other downed knight, towards the consolations offered in the King's refreshment pavilion.

And so it went on. Charge, miss. Charge, hit. Charge, crash, fall. Rake sand. Trumpets. Charge, crash. Charge . . .

Stifling a yawn, Gwenn longed for the evening to come and to bring with it a cooling wind. The bold August sun smote them all through the light white silk which shaded the Duchess of Brittany's stand. Gwenn glanced up at the fringe of the canopy. The ermine dots on the gonfalons undulated in a frustrating dream of a breeze, which was enough to make the pennants sway, ever so gently, but not enough to cool her. Gwenn was sticky. She was uncomfortable. The dais smelt unpleasantly of sweat. She wanted to go and lie down in the quiet of Alan's tent.

A glance at the Duchess showed her a lady enthroned in a high-backed cushioned chair which had sides like an abbot's stall. Duchess Constance's face showed polite interest, and it never wavered.

How did she do it? Gwenn had a cramp in her thigh. She longed to get up and stretch her legs. At least Duchess Constance can rest her back, Gwenn thought, with a rush of frustration. And the Duchess no doubt knows everyone here. It was difficult to feel involved when she did not know any of the combatants. Not that Gwenn wanted to feel involved, but it might have driven away the feeling that she wanted to get up and run till she had put as much distance between her and this stupid tournament as she possibly could. If her feelings had been engaged, she would no longer have been so horribly aware that, of all the crowd, she was an oddity, for she wanted it to be over and done with as quickly as possible.

A murmur of excitement ran through the ladies on the Duchess's dais, dragging Gwenn from her abstractions. Wearily, she looked at the field.

At the far end of the lists, the King had climbed onto a grey charger, richly caparisoned in azure and gold. A wooden replica of his shield had been set up on the central dividing barrier. After a token pass at his friend, Duke Geoffrey of Brittany, King Philip was to give the signal for the single combat to finish, and the day's mêlée would commence. Penned in like cattle behind the gates, the chivalry of Christendom waited for this charge to be done. When the King's baton fell, their turn would come. Dreaming of glittering prizes, and held back by a flimsy wooden bar, the knights were a mass of shifting helms.

Casually, smiling, King Philip of France tossed a jewel-encrusted gauntlet into the sand. The princes were to use spears. Confronting the King, at the near end of the field, was Duke Geoffrey. He was astride a fearsome charger, black as sin. Decked in the Duke's fluttering white and black colours, the warhorse looked brash and bold enough to terrify his royal opponent into submission. He twitched his flowing tail, and tossed his plaited mane. The beast's nostrils were flared and he was foaming at the bit. The sight unlocked a recollection of Waldin swearing to Ned that the horses loved tourneys as much as the men did. The black charger was slavering, just as the knights held in check behind the fence were. Gwenn's heart sat heavy in her breast.

Alan was at his Duke's side. Gwenn saw him lift the Duke's helm from his esquire and hand it to him. She saw the Duke smile, address Alan, and then Alan stood aside while the Duke prepared to gallop at the King of France. A shield bearing the arms of Brittany was set up at his end of the lists. Everyone fell quiet, waiting for the trumpets to blare.

A huge white bird chose that moment to pass overhead, and heads turned to the sky, for the flapping of the snowy wings came loudly through the expectant hush. The bird's bill was wicked as a knife, its tail a pointed diamond. Oblivious of its audience, the bird beat upwards through a cloudless sky and circled in the heights. The crowd turned their attention back to the two men in the arena. The bird began to lose height.

The prince's charge was more of a show than the previous ones. A bond of friendship tied Brittany and France, and it was a mark of their trust for one another that they consented to take to the field. Not a drop of royal blood was to be shed, and to this end they must hold a spear, not a lance, and aim for their opponent's shield on the fence.

The huge white bird dropped out of the sky and landed on the central fence, on Brittany's shield. On the Duchess's dais, a waiting-woman gasped, 'It's a raven, my lady! On your lord's shield! Christ save him!' Ravens were associated with death.

The Duchess looked on, impassively. 'It's a *white* raven,' she said sedately, 'Only black ones are evil.'

The trumpets sounded. Spurs flashed. Hoofs ripped through the sand.

The Duchess of Brittany's waiting-woman gulped. 'If you say so, my lady.'

'I do.' With inflexible calm, the Duchess shifted her eyes to where her husband was thundering full tilt across the lists.

The two warhorses were closing on each other. It would have been all too easy for one of the princes to break his word and aim for the heart, but as they had arranged, they turned their spears aside at the last moment and hurled them into the wooden shields marked with their arms. Brittany's spear hung, quivering in France's colours. The crowd shrieked their appreciation. France's spear thudded into the sand, the great white raven impaled on its point. Blood and feathers were everywhere. A wing flapped, once. There was a second's silence, before the crowd went wild. Gwenn felt sick.

The trumpets let out a clarion blast, one of the King's heralds ran onto the field with the baton. The King threw it down. The gates opened at either end of the field and, pennants flying, the army of knights roared onto the sand.

The mêlée had begun.

Swirls of dust and sand lifted into the hot air, and at first the spectators had to view the mêlée as if through a sandstorm. There were so many twisting, fighting men, so many screaming, biting horses, that it was well nigh impossible to tell one combatant from another. But at length the crowd of booty-hungry knights thinned as they spread over the field. Some were down, and as the sandy fog cleared, Gwenn was able to distinguish individuals.

There was Sir Raoul, she knew his colours now. Not content with losing one horse to his opponent at the jousting earlier, he was trying his arm in the mêlée. Gwenn did not think that his luck had changed, for his elaborate green and white caparison had been slashed to tatters and hung raggedly from his steed's back. Sir Raoul kicked his mount into the press, and Gwenn lost sight of him. The King of France had judiciously left the field, no doubt holding the view that an army's commander should never be put at risk. A dark flash caught Gwenn's eyes. Following it, she saw the ermine, saw a warhorse's wide nostrils, and an ebony tail streaming like a banner. Duke Geoffrey was in the thick of it – not for him the strategic withdrawal. She watched as he unhorsed a man, and crimson blood mingled with the sand. The ducal sword waved in triumph and, with either supreme arrogance or supreme folly, Duke Geoffrey lifted his helmet in the air and grinned at his Duchess seated primly on her dais. The Duchess inclined her head. The Duke jammed his helm back on his head, dug his spurs in his mount's flanks, and was off again.

Ned had gone from his place on the sidelines, but Gwenn picked out Alan. He was stationed by the palisade where the Duke's arms were laid out. As the two cousins were not of the knightly class, they were forbidden to venture onto the field of combat. Alan was intent on the conflict, dark brows frowning with concentration, and knowing that he had to stay on the boundary, Gwenn was surprised when she saw him take a step forwards as though he would enter the fray. Where was Ned?

Suddenly, gripped by a hideous premonition, Gwenn forgot about the heat. She forgot about the cramp in her thigh, and got up, slowly. Alan's dark complexion was paler than the field of the Duke's shield. He was tugging his sword out. She saw him shout. He ran between two mounted knights who were battling it out centre field. He was swallowed up by thrashing limbs. Where *was* Ned?

'Sit down, Mistress Fletcher!' Lady Juliana hissed. 'You mar the view.'

But Gwenn could not sit down. She stood, with her heart in her mouth, staring at the spot where Alan had been. 'No, no,' she muttered, in a daze. 'Something . . . something dreadful is happening.'

'Mistress Fletcher,' the Lady Juliana addressed her sharply, 'if you are ailing, you may withdraw.'

'No. I'm not ailing. It's . . .' Gwenn gasped, for there was Alan, in the middle of the action. He had sheathed his sword and was crouching down, dragging the body of a man by the belt. The man's flaxen hair was uncovered, and mired with sand and dust. There was blood on his chest. As Alan neared the northern gate, the gate nearest Gwenn, he bellowed. A marshal raced to assist him.

It was no knight that Alan was succouring.

Impossibly, it was Ned.

Lady Juliana had seen what was happening. She rose gracefully. 'Come, Mistress Fletcher,' she said with the unruffled assurance of a woman who had tended men's hurts on such occasions a thousand times before. When Gwenn made no move, she gently took her arm. 'We'll go to my fiancé's pavilion and see what needs to be done.'

Alan had barely had time to lay Ned down on the pallet when Duchess Constance's messenger arrived, chest heaving, at Sir Raoul's pavilion. 'Lady Juliana!' the messenger panted, shoving his head unceremoniously through the tent flap. 'The Duchess is calling for you! There's been another accident!'

'Another?' Lady Juliana lifted her eyes from the bloody mess that had been Ned Fletcher's chest and avoided looking at Gwenn.

'My lady, you're to come at once!'

Lady Juliana rocked back on her heels, secretly relieved at her timely reprieve. As God was her witness, she didn't mind helping when a man had a chance. But Ned Fletcher was a doomed man and she did not want to be the one to tell his young, pregnant wife. 'One moment, my man.' She stared at Gwenn's jawline. 'Can you cope, my dear?'

'I . . . I think so.' Trembling fingers reached for Ned's slashed gambeson. 'But there's not much we can do, is there?'

Lady Juliana squirmed, unable to avoid such a direct question. 'My dear, I'm afraid it's only a matter of time. It's tragic, such an unlucky blow. Both lungs are affected.'

'*Both?*' This from Alan.

'Aye. With lungs, if one only is damaged, it is not necessarily a mortal blow. But two . . . It's tragic. And when the bubbles of blood come to the mouth, you know the end is near.' Lady Juliana pressed a linen cloth to Ned's mouth and displayed the stained cloth to the injured man's wife and cousin.

Gwenn fixed her with agonised dark eyes. 'You're saying he's going? That it's only a matter of time?'

'Yes.'

'But there must be something we can do! We'll try anything, won't we, Alan?'

'Anything. My lady, are you certain we can do nothing?' Iron fingers sank into Lady Juliana's arms.

'I'm sorry, Captain. He's drowning—'

His wife stirred. 'Ned's drowning in his own blood. Oh, sweet Jesus. Ned. *Ned*.'

Gwenn felt Ned's pain as if it were her own. If only there was something she could do to help him. She would sell her soul if it kept Ned alive. That morning he had been so happy, so excited because he was participating in the day's events. He had been so vital. Ned was young. Ned was strong. He should not be dying. How could God destroy someone as kind and selfless as Ned? Where was the divine purpose in Ned's death? And why had it been Ned who had stopped that lance? It might just as easily have been someone else. Why Ned? Why?

The ducal messenger was wringing his hands. 'My lady, you *must* come,' he said. 'The Duchess has need of you.'

'Yes, you're needed elsewhere,' Gwenn said dully. 'Thank you, Lady Juliana. We'll manage.'

'Good girl,' Lady Juliana approved, briskly. She shook herself free of Alan's grip, faltering only when she saw the impotent rage in his eyes. 'I . . . I'll see a priest is sent, so he doesn't die unshriven.' Lady Juliana picked up her skirts and fled.

She kept her word, and soon one of Duke Geoffrey's chaplains arrived at Sir Raoul's pavilion. He took one look at Ned and efficiently administered the last rites. This done, he hovered near the entrance, unwilling to leave till Sir Raoul's squire had gone to God.

The pain in Ned's chest had expanded and taken over the whole of his body. He couldn't move. He could barely see for the black shapes which floated like dark wraiths across his sight. But he could hear. He could hear a sawing noise. It was very loud. He could also hear voices, Gwenn's, and Alan's, and one other.

Ned wanted to speak to his wife. The sawing noise faded. Ned managed a pathetic gasp. 'Gwenn?' Was that him? He tried again. 'Gwenn?' When he had done, he was desperate for air, and as he laboured to drag in a breath, the sawing noise recommenced, and he made the chilling discovery that the sawing noise wasn't sawing at all, but his lungs fighting for air.

'Hush, Ned.' Gwenn's voice that, with a break in it, as though she were forcing back tears. 'Try to rest. Try to regain your strength.'

Something light brushed across Ned's brow. Her hand? A cloth? His senses were disordered, and it was difficult to make the distinction. He couldn't even tell whether it was a palliasse upon which he lay, or the bare earth.

'Gwenn?' He coughed, and pain shrieked along every nerve. Immediately that soft something feathered across his lips. He heard a sob, a smothered gasp, and dimly made out what she said.

'Look, Alan, more blood. Oh, Ned, don't leave me.' Her voice dropped. 'You're all I've got. Without you . . .'

Ned tried to sit up, but his limbs were sleeping. He tried to make his lips give Gwenn the reassurance that she pleaded for, but they would not work either. He gave up the struggle, resolving to rest, as Gwenn had suggested, for then he would be able to tell her. In a moment he would have conserved the strength to remind her that he would never leave her. Never. Had he not sworn it?

The only sound in the tent was the harsh rasping of Ned's breathing.

'I don't understand it,' the priest murmured in an undertone to Alan, whom he recognised. 'By rights your countryman should be dead already. He's suffering greatly. If only we could ease his passage.'

Numb with grief, Alan watched Gwenn kneeling by his cousin's bed, grasping those solid, waxen hands. He knew what was holding Ned back from the brink of death. Gwenn was, with the tears in her eyes, and the catch in her voice, and the loving touch of her hand. It was Gwenn who was making Ned cling to life, and in so doing she was prolonging his agony, for Ned would never leave this earth while she was at his side, pleading for him to stay. Ned's face had been blue when they had brought him here. Now it was like a death-mask, and yet he lived. It was cruel that his last moments should be tortured ones. Ned had never in all his young life tormented anyone. Alan thought he knew how he could ease his cousin's passage to death. Yet he hesitated. 'You swear there's no hope?' he whispered to the cleric.

'None. God is waiting for him. Your friend is a dead man clinging to this world like a miser to his money.'

Alan nodded. He walked to the bed and held out his hand. 'Gwenn? Come with me.'

Gwenn looked at him from a world of sorrow, eyelids swollen and red.

A cold stone lay in Alan's belly. 'Come, Gwenn.' He bent, and taking her hand from Ned's nerveless one, enfolded it in his own. Ruthlessly, ignoring her reluctance, he drew her into dazzling sunlight. 'We'll walk awhile.'

'But, Alan, I want to be with him.'

'No. It's better for Ned if you come with me.'

In the shadowy pavilion, Ned stirred, and stretched his hand after his wife, while sooty flakes swirled in his vision. Weakly, his hand sank back. The pain was unendurable. God help me, Ned thought. Where's Gwenn? He strained to see her, but impenetrable grey veils screened her from his sight. Ned's search was not completely fruitless, for in a small recess of his fragmented consciousness he found a space, a heavenly space, that was not all pain.

Gwenn? Gwenn?

The space was dark, but welcoming, because it contained no pain. Ned reached towards it, but his body and the pain he was enduring were weighing him down. Tentatively, he pushed his pain aside.

The Duke's chaplain had taken Gwenn's place at Ned's bedside. Scenting release, he made the sign of the cross, and smiled.

Gwenn? Where was Gwenn? Lurching back into himself, Ned discovered there was nothing where Gwenn had been except unendurable agony. Floundering, he sought that blissful, pain-free space. It had grown larger. It was almost big enough for him to walk into, and it was expanding. Soon it would be large enough to swallow up the whole of the earth, the sky, and all of God's creation. But there was one thing missing, one vital thing. It did not hold Gwenn. Ned jerked himself back, back towards pain . . . His hand lifted, stretching to the afternoon sunlight pouring through the door slit. The chaplain caught his hand. Ned focused on him. The chaplain had brown eyes, like Gwenn's, and in them, Ned discovered warm and abiding love, and great understanding. It occurred to him that if he died, he would be leaving Gwenn with his cousin. Simultaneous with that thought, came a crucifying convulsion. 'Gwenn . . .' he moaned.

'Relax, my son,' the priest murmured. 'You cannot fight the inevitable. Relax, and trust to God that your souls will meet in the eternal. Let go.'

'But Gwenn . . .'

His groan was weak, but the priest heard. 'Your friend will care for her.'

Ned tried to shake his head. Tried to say that that would not do, but he had no power to explain to a priest, even one with compassionate eyes.

'Put yourself, and Gwenn, into God's hands, my son. Trust in His infinite wisdom.'

Ned's mouth wouldn't move. He wanted to confess that he did not think he could do that. What if he let go, and Gwenn never came? An eternity without her was unthinkable, but he was bone-tired. 'Tell Alan . . . tell my cousin . . .'

'Aye?'

'. . . Tell him to see her safe to Plou—' he coughed, 'Ploumanach.'

'I will.'

Ned drew a rattling, agonised breath. 'Father?'

'My son?'

'Ask him—' choke '— ask Alan to tell my mother . . . to give her my love, and . . .' Ned was unable to finish. He was past talking. He was past worrying. His eyes closed. The great darkness was in front of him; the darkness where there was no pain. It seemed to beckon him. Slowly, Ned let go, and left his broken body behind him. He was not confident he would see Gwenn again, and could only hope that perhaps, out there, in those vast unchartered reaches, that would not matter. Bathed in peace, Ned breathed a blissful sigh. His last.

'*Requiescat in pace*,' the Duke's chaplain muttered, and solemnly he reached out and folded Ned's capable, farmer's hands over the wound in the shattered, bloody chest.

Having escaped one death-bed scene, Lady Juliana had found herself plunged into another, for minutes after the accident in which her fiancé's esquire had been hurt, the Duke of Brittany had fallen.

Head bowed, Lady Juliana left the ermine pavilion. Her proud features wore a stunned, incredulous look.

Sir Raoul was waiting for her. He pushed past the guards. 'What news?' he demanded, eyeing the closed tent flap.

Lady Juliana shook her head. It was a struggle to find any words. 'He's gone, Raoul,' she said. 'The Duke is gone . . .'

Sir Raoul crossed himself. 'Mother of God, not Brittany too! He was twenty-eight, only a year older than

I. How did he die? One reckless gesture too many, I suppose. He was ever a showman.'

'He was crushed, and . . . Please, Raoul, I don't want to talk about it.'

'My apologies, my dear. And Duchess Constance? How is she taking it?'

'Composedly. She's not shed a tear. But King Philip's weeping would cause the Seine to burst its banks.'

Sir Raoul jerked his head at the white silk pavilion. 'His Grace the King is inside?'

'Aye. And crying like a babe. The Duchess is comforting him.'

'It's a bad business.'

'Aye.' Lady Juliana had only come out for a breath of clean, untainted air. The heat and the smell of death in the tent was suffocating. When the King left, she would have to see to her Duchess.

'All in all three men have died this day,' Sir Raoul informed her. 'Our Duke, Fletcher, and a knight from Gascony whom I do not know. Two more men have been sorely wounded, and are fighting for their lives. Oh, aye, and apparently there's a dead beggar.'

'Beggar? What beggar?' Lady Juliana seized on the diversion, for beggars did not count.

'Christ knows. He only had one hand, so the man was probably a convicted thief. One of the King's guards heard a stray dog barking in the forest. When the barking didn't let up, he investigated and found the body. The guard knew him for a beggar because he had seen the same man hanging around for scraps by the cookhouse. His throat had been cut, and he'd been mutilated. Hacked about.'

A look of distaste flickered across Lady Juliana's features. 'No grisly details, Raoul. I've had my fill for today.'

'Sorry, my dear. But what in blazes could anyone gain by torturing a lousy beggar.'

'Raoul, please.'

'My apologies. Dear God, it's been a bad day. The

521

rest of the tournament will probably be cancelled.'

'I should think so.'

'A bad business,' the knight muttered glumly, 'a bad business.'

'You will have to do something about the young man's widow, Raoul. She's pregnant.'

'Oh, hell, is she?' Raoul Martell sighed. 'Then I suppose I will, especially as Fletcher was trying to warn me.'

'Warn you?' Lady Juliana looked a question.

Flushing, Sir Raoul fixed his eyes on a tent peg. 'Aye, he was warning me. Some Frenchman took it into his head that I caused him to lose a favourite hawk.'

'And did you?'

'What, lose the wretched man his sparrowhawk? Jesu, no. It was not my fault if his falconer trained the bird ill. A tourney's no place for a half-trained bird. It happened yesterday. All I did was ride past his hawk; it took a dislike to my horse, bated, snapped its leash, and was into the blue before you could bat an eye. The Frenchman took it into his head I was to blame. At any rate, he banded together with some other French knights and they chose me as their target. Fletcher ran onto the field to warn me.'

'By now he will be dead,' Lady Juliana whispered. The guy ropes of the ducal pavilion creaked. The tent flap was folded back, and Philip of France strode past them. His eyelids were swollen, his cheeks mottled and his lips compressed, but he was every inch a king. Lady Juliana curtsied deeply, and the knights bowed; but they were too slow, and their obeisances were directed at the King's back.

'I'd best go in, Raoul.'

'Aye. You attend your Duchess, and I'll attend Ned Fletcher's widow. Adieu till later, my dear.' And bending over his fiancée's hand, Sir Raoul pressed his lips to her fingers and turned on his heel.

It was past the ninth hour and the light was fading.

Ned had been laid to rest under newly cut turves that afternoon, less than an hour after he had died. Alan and Gwenn had been his only mourners, Sir Raoul being too taken up with the Duke's death. It had been a hasty, improvised burial on hallowed ground in a nearby village churchyard. For Alan it had been heartbreaking; it had been too quick, and too impersonal. He had seen many such funerals, funerals of hired men whose masters hardly knew them. But it was no stranger Alan was bidding farewell today. This was his childhood playmate and cousin. For Gwenn it must have been hell. She seemed to have gone into deep shock.

On their return from the burial, she had disappeared into the tent. She had been alone there for three hours, and Alan hadn't heard so much as a whisper from her. It was unnatural. He had spent most of those three hours gazing sightlessly into his tent-side fire, straining his ears in case she broke down. It was the loneliest, most miserable guard duty that he had ever undertaken. He couldn't believe Ned was dead. His cousin had been the happiest, most contented, *accepting* man Alan had ever known. And Ned was no more. Alan couldn't believe Duke Geoffrey had gone either, but at least the Duke's death could be thought of calmly, without emotion. Alan wondered how the Duchess was reacting to her husband's death.

Alan's stomach felt empty. How could he feel hunger at a time like this? He drank a skinful of wine; but his hunger was unabated, a gnawing ache, deep in his guts. He had no food with him. He did not want to leave Gwenn to go to the cookhouse, not even for half an hour. And from his tent? Nothing. No sobbing, no weeping. Nothing.

Gwenn had taken the purse that a heavy-browed Sir Raoul had offered her by way of compensation for a lost husband. She had nodded when the knight said that he had arranged for Ned's burial, and she seemed to accept, for the time being at least, Alan's guardianship for her. But not a solitary tear had she shed. It was as if this latest tragedy had turned her to stone.

When Alan had told Sir Raoul that Ned's last wishes had been that he should take care of Gwenn, the knight's brow had cleared – what with the Duke of Brittany's death, the nobles had politics on their minds, and no doubt the future of an untried squire's widow did not loom large. No one had objected to her spending the night in Alan's tent. Had she been a lady of high estate, matters would have been arranged very differently. Not that Alan was complaining. If anyone was indelicate enough to imply that he would lay a hand on her while she grieved for her husband, he'd split their slanderous tongues for them.

He had heard the rumours concerning Ned's foray into the lists. He scowled an accusation at the fading glow in the western sky. 'Ned, you were a fool, a chivalrous fool. See where your folly has left us.' But it was no use blaming the dead. Ned could not help his nature any more than he could his. He would miss his vital young cousin.

Marshalling his emotions, Alan eyed the closed flap with misgivings. She had gone into his tent meekly as a lamb, asking if she could be left alone. Assuming she wished to grieve in private, Alan had withdrawn. But she was not grieving. What was she doing? Could he disturb her? Should he disturb her? His stomach growled, and thus prompted, Alan rose to his feet. There was bread and water in his tent.

She was sitting cross-legged exactly as he had left her, on the thin mattress she had shared with Ned. Sir Raoul's drawstring purse was in front of her. It was unopened. Great eyes lifted briefly to Alan as he came in, then fell to the ground.

'I came for water,' Alan said, unhooking the flask from a knob on a tent pole.

Silence.

'Are you thirsty?'

Silence.

'Gwenn . . .' Helplessly, Alan watched her downcast

head. With a jerky movement he slung the waterskin onto his pallet and tried again. 'Gwenn? Oh, Jesu, Gwenn, *say* something.'

Silence.

He knelt in front of her and reached for her hands. She shuddered, which was not the reaction that he looked for but it was a reaction of sorts, which was a beginning. He picked them up. 'Gwenn, please. You can't cut yourself off like this.'

'Why not?' Her voice was harsh, not her voice at all.

'It . . . it's not healthy.'

'My sister cut herself off when life became unbearable.'

'Katarin is sick, shocked. She had suffered much.'

'Am I not sick and shocked? Have I not suffered much? I vow I will suffer no more, Alan. If I have to cut myself off to ensure that, then so be it.' And, as if to underline her words, she jerked free of his hold and hunched away from him.

At least she was talking. Alan's aim was to goad her into relieving her feelings. 'Katarin's a child, Gwenn. You cannot retreat like she did.'

'For God's sake, Alan!' Her mouth was angry. 'My husband has died! You don't get over something like that in a few minutes, you know.'

'You loved him.'

She swallowed, and her answer was husky. 'Aye. Ned is . . . was very lovable.'

Alan could only agree.

'Why did Ned have to die, Alan?'

She sounded like a child, crying at the night, and Alan had no comfort to offer her.

'I should have been there. I should have been with him.'

He made a swift, negative gesture. 'No.'

'I should. It's your fault I wasn't with him. If you hadn't taken me outside . . .'

Her voice cracked, and brown, melancholy eyes met his directly. She *was* grieving, inwardly and in silence;

525

and her grief hit him like a blow in his empty stomach. To think that he had once wished her and Ned unmarried. They were unmarried now, and just look at her. It wasn't Ned who was the fool, Alan reflected sourly, but himself. He was a selfish, simple, bloody fool. If he were granted one boon now, it would be that he could master time and turn it back for her. He would do anything to lift that bleak misery from her eyes.

'Oh, Alan, why did Ned have to die!' Her iron control slipped for an instant, and Alan heard a small sob. 'He swore he'd never leave me! He promised, Alan! And now he's broken his word! It's your fault—'

'No!'

'It is! I've no one now! No one!'

'You have me,' Alan said, taking her hands again. They were cold as blocks of ice.

'You!' she exclaimed, derisively to Alan's ears.

He bit his lip and told himself that it was her grief that made her cruel. 'And there's Katarin, and Philippe,' he continued. 'You are not alone. You have your relatives in north Brittany. They'll take responsibility for you. Ned wanted me to take you to them. I'll happily oblige.'

'I don't want anyone to take responsibility for me,' Gwenn muttered, with a flash of her old waywardness. 'I want to take responsibility for myself. I want to be independent.'

Alan shook his head. Women never took responsibility for themselves, and with the world structured as it was, how could they? Her grief was unhinging her. 'Take responsibility for yourself? You're not serious, Gwenn. It is your loss talking. You cannot be independent, it's impossible.'

Her eyes glittered. 'Impossible? Why? You're independent.'

'It's different for me. I'm a man. I can fight my own battles.'

'You're not taking me seriously.'

'How can I? Such a notion is ridiculous.'

'Why? Why is it ridiculous? All I want is to be an island, like you.'

'An island?' Was that how she saw him?

'I like you, Alan. I admit that I don't know you well, but I probably know you as well as anyone. I've watched you. You have no ties. You're careful to keep your friends at a distance. And I've noticed that whatever happens, Alan le Bret never gets hurt. And that is because his feelings are never engaged. I have decided to become like you. I am going to be independent. I have been hurt enough, and Ned's death is the last blow I shall take. From now on,' she spoke as solemnly as a nun making her holy vows, 'I shall be an island. I take responsibility for myself, and myself alone.'

Alan could tell her that that way led to damnation and misery, and he should know, he had trod the solitary path for years. To think that she, in her grief, was taking him for her model . . . But he had changed. He had rejoined the human race, and was allowing himself to feel. As ever, they were out of step. Would they ever be in step? 'I think,' he said slowly, 'you need to rest. I think we should discuss this in the morning.'

'Don't patronise me! We'll discuss it now!'

'You're overwrought.'

'I won't deny that. But I tell you this, I won't let you cart me back to Ploumanach. Lady Wymark did not approve of Ned, but she would offer false sympathy, and I do not think that I could stand it. She will be glad I am no longer married to a mercenary, and after a respectable time has elapsed, she and my uncle will honour me by finding me another husband. Only this new husband will be respectable – a pot-bellied merchant or some such – because they want someone they can have at their board who will not embarrass them.'

Alan grimaced. 'You paint a vivid image. But I trust Lady Wymark would not force you to marry against your will.'

'Force? What is force? I agree that she would probably not drag me kicking and screaming to the church gate. No, she would not do that. But there are other, more subtler persuasions. As her guest, I would feel bound to repay her for her generosity to me and my family. In the end I would surrender, and I would marry the pot-bellied merchant, and I would have to spend my days breeding pot-bellied children, and . . .' her voice was almost audible '. . . I do not want that. So my thanks, Alan, for offering to escort me to Ploumanach, but I do not wish to go.'

Deciding his best course was to go along with her and hope that by morning she would see reason, Alan said, 'You will need money.'

Gwenn pointed at Sir Raoul's purse. 'Money I have.'

Alan picked up the purse. The knight's conscience had obviously pricked him, for it was heavy. 'It won't last for ever.'

'It will last long enough,' Gwenn answered shortly. She had the contents of the Stone Rose and what remained in Waldin St Clair's wallet, but she did not trust this rootless mercenary as she had trusted her husband, and she would not tell him about *that*.

'You'll need protection.'

She smiled sweetly at Sir Raoul's purse. 'I can buy it.'

'And what will you do, Gwenn, with this independence of yours?'

'I have a desire to go to England.'

'To England?'

'Aye.' Her hand fluttered delicately to her stomach. 'I would like to meet Ned's mother, and tell her what a good man her son was. I want to tell her how brave he was, and that his last thoughts were of her and—'

'There's no need for you to go to England,' Alan interrupted curtly. 'I'm homeward bound myself, and, with Duke Geoffrey dead, there is no reason for me to delay.'

'Alan,' gentle brown eyes regarded him, 'I'm sorry your Duke is dead. I am not the only one to have suffered this day. Ned was your cousin, and you have also lost your Duke. Do you have work, now Duke Geoffrey is gone?'

'I can always find work. As I was trying to tell you, Gwenn, after meeting my brother I vowed to visit my father. I shall call on my aunt, Ned's mother, and I can give her your messages. There's no need for you to make the journey.'

Gwenn caressed her flat stomach and a secretive smile softened the contours of her mouth. 'You are very kind, Alan, but I have a message that only I can deliver.'

He raised a brow.

'I am carrying Ned's child. And I think that Ned's mother would like to see her grandchild in the flesh, don't you?'

'You *are* pregnant? God's blood, woman! If you're pregnant, you're insane to consider such a journey!'

'The Duchess travels when she's pregnant.'

'Aye! And the Duchess has a litter, and waiting women, and scores of soldiers to protect her. But you, alone,' Alan spluttered, 'why you'd be a sitting duck for every renegade and outlaw between here and Richmond!'

'No I won't. I told you, Alan, I'll hire good protection.'

'And how will you judge if you can trust your protector, Gwenn? Jesu!' Alan let fly a string of oaths. 'You think you know the world, but you don't. You're still an innocent. Like as not you'll hire the first unprincipled thief you run across, and he'll take one look at this fat little purse of yours and relieve you of it, and you'll be abandoned in the middle of Christ knows where.'

'I'll hire *you*.'

For a moment he thought he had misheard her. 'What?'

'I'll hire you. We'll be travelling the same road anyway. Will you take my purse and run off with it, Alan?' she asked in honeyed tones.

'You know I would not!'

'Well,' she said calmly, 'I'm willing to risk it. I'll trust you to take me to Ned's mother.' She drew a deep breath. 'Tell me, Alan le Bret, will you accept my commission, or do I look elsewhere for my protector?'

Chapter Twenty-Eight

Blade honed to shining, deadly perfection, Otto Malait
slammed his cleaned sword back into his sheath with a
satisfied grin and flexed his brawny arms. Now for the
girl. He had waited two days for the storm caused by
the Duke of Brittany's death to blow over, and he did
not intend waiting a moment longer.

Yesterday, the area cordoned off by the Bretons had
been crawling with messengers and solemn-faced
guards, and he'd not had a chance to locate her tent,
but at last the traffic had thinned. Otto tugged his
trailing yellow beard while he brought to mind Conan's
last words. With his last breath, the pedlar had babbled
about the girl's tent and that of the Captain of the
Guard's, and Otto could only assume that the Fletchers
were billeted with the Duke's personal bodyguard.

Sentries were positioned by the late Duke's white silk
pavilion. Otto walked openly up to them. The points of
their spears shifted to rest on his chest. 'Good day,'
Otto opened, and he made his lips smile.

'Good day,' one of the guards responded. He had a
shock of unruly grizzled hair which stuck out of the
bottom of his helmet like a dirty wad of sheep's wool,
and his nose was the colour of old claret.

'I'm looking for your captain,' Otto went on.

The guard exchanged glances with his companion, a
thin, weasel-faced man with light brown hair as fine as
his comrade's was thick. 'If it's work you're looking
for,' the first guard grounded his spear, 'you're out of
luck. I don't know where you can have been hiding,

but in case you haven't heard, our Duke—'

'I know about that. I'm not looking for work.'

'Oh?' The guard's eyes narrowed while he eyed the burly Viking up and down, dwelling on the heavy sword and the axe that these savage Norsemen favoured. 'What are you after?'

'I'm catching up with an old friend,' Otto thought another smile wouldn't go amiss, 'name of Fletcher. Mistress Gwenn Fletcher. I heard she was lodged near your captain.'

'Fl . . . Fletcher?' The guard, a Breton born and bred, had difficulty with the foreign name. 'Never heard of her, but the captain was lodged—'

'*Was?*'

Muscles tensed in the thick column of Otto's neck.

The guard grinned. 'Didn't I say? Our captain's resigned. Left yesterday evening with the funeral procession. Bound for Paris. He wasn't planning on returning.'

'Shit.' Otto was hard put to restrain himself from grabbing the man by the throat in order to shake the information out of him. 'And Mistress Fletcher?'

'Like I told you. I don't know any Mistress Fletcher.'

Stubbornly, Otto held on to the last thing Conan had said. 'I was told she was lodged near your captain.'

'It's important you find her?'

Otto clenched his jaw and his fists, a gesture that did not escape the guards. It was very difficult to keep smiling. 'You might put it like that.'

The guard pointed his spear down the avenue between two rows of canvas. 'See that large waggon – the cook's, with the pots hanging off the side?'

'Aye.'

'Try over there. Our captain set up his tent past that. Your Mistress Fletcher might yet be there.'

Otto grunted and swung round, and under the curious gaze of the guards stalked in the direction indicated.

'Love,' the weasel-faced guard with the thinning hair pronounced knowingly, 'enough to drive a man mad.'

Alan's last duty to his master, Geoffrey, Duke of Brittany, was a doleful one. He attended his funeral. The Duke was buried in the choir of Nôtre Dame in Paris, and Alan could not but notice that while the late Duke's wife was dry-eyed, his friend the King of France wept openly. Alan regretted Duke Geoffrey's death himself. He had been a skilled swordsman and an excellent horseman, and, though Henry of England's third son had undoubtedly been arrogant and spoilt, he had possessed a lively sense of humour. He had neglected his wife, but Alan had never found any deliberate malice in him. After being employed by Count François de Roncier, it had been refreshing to stumble on an easy-going master like the Duke of Brittany. While Alan had been signed with him, he had come to the conclusion that the Plantagenet princes' constant feuding was similar in nature to François de Roncier's feud with Jean St Clair. At bottom, both feuds were based on a greedy desire for power. Both de Roncier and the Duke had been shamelessly out for themselves. Alan nourished a hearty contempt for de Roncier, but he had liked Duke Geoffrey, something he had never been able to rationalise. Neither man cared much for anyone but himself. What was it then that the Duke had that de Roncier had not? The Duke was a good loser, de Roncier was not. The Duke had charm, and a roguish sense of humour.

Duke Geoffrey had been twenty-eight years old when the life had been crushed out of him, and he had left no male heir to inherit his vast estates. Eyeing the widowed Duchess's ceremonial ermine bliaud closely, Alan wondered if the rumours concerning her condition were true. Duchess Constance did not look pregnant, but then neither did Gwenn, and Gwenn was confident that if all went well she would bear Ned's child next spring.

Where would Gwenn be by then? The monks' mournful dirge rose to fill the cavernous space above the cathedral choir. Would she be in England, with Ned's mother? Or back with Sir Gregor and Lady Wymark in Ploumanach? She had set her heart on England, and no amount of argument had persuaded her to change this foolhardy plan. She would, she had informed him coldly, get there with or without his help.

Alan looked at the delicate patterns of Nôtre Dame's soaring tracery, but was unmoved by their beauty. He looked at the caricatured faces of the people of Paris as they had been immortalised on the monks' misericordes – works of genius, each of them – but today he could not appreciate them. He looked at the cathedral's lofty coloured glass windows. Light was pouring through them; it tumbled onto the patterned tiles, painting them with God's brightest hues. Alan was looking at some of the finest of man's works, but today he could not find it in him to admire any of it.

He would have to go with Gwenn to Richmond, though he was not looking forward to travelling in her company. It would be nothing less than purgatory. He wanted Gwenn, and though he could not have explained why, Ned's death had made this possibility even more remote, and not only because she seemed dead to feeling. Her heart had grown hard with this last bereavement, and Alan did not think that anyone would storm it again.

Alan sighed. No, he was not looking forward to the journey north, but he could no more abandon Gwenn to her folly than he could murder her. He would just have to grit his teeth and conceal his feelings.

He watched a mitred bishop lift a clod of earth on a silver trowel, and cast it onto the lid of the Duke's elaborately painted coffin. Thud. The Duchess's long white hand reached for the trowel. Thud. And King Philip's. Thud. Alan's throat ached. This funeral was a far cry from the humble ceremony provided for Ned, but it was no less poignant.

Alan's feet had gone to sleep. He shuffled them, and wished the interminable service at an end. He hated funerals, and the wearisome thoughts they fostered. He wanted to get back to the inn where he had found lodgings. He wanted to see Gwenn had everything she needed. And then, he supposed, he would have to make preparations for their journey to Richmond.

The evening shadows ran along the hoof-scarred surface of the empty tiltyard. The sand had not been raked, and rust-coloured stains marked the places where blood had been spilled. The white raven had been discreetly removed. On the fencing, knights' bright flags fluttered forlornly, with no one to see them. The swallows had returned. With a clear field, the birds assiduously worked the length of the lists as if they feared the crowds might return and they would be driven away.

The tourney field might be deserted, but the camp site was not. It had taken Otto most of the afternoon to verify that Gwenn was not lodged in one of the tents in the Breton section. He had combed the entire encampment, and when he was stopped and challenged as to his business there, he answered with questions of his own. Finally, when he had eliminated the last possible tent from his enquiries, he was forced to conclude that she had gone. And if what he had learned was correct, the concubine's daughter was proving to be just as much the whore as her mother had been. Ned Fletcher – this had been easy to discover – had been killed. A young woman had been sighted riding off in the company of the Duke's captain. She had been riding at the back of the ducal funeral train, heading for Paris.

Paris. With a face as black as Death himself, Otto threw his saddle on his horse, secured the girth and vaulted up. The man from whom he had squeezed that little gem had been short-sighted, and he had been unable to describe accurately either the young woman or her mount.

Otto cantered towards Paris, but he could not be positive that he was following the right trail. At present, it was the only trail he had.

Back at Kermaria, Otto had been surprised that Conan had not returned for his purse but, supposing that the pedlar had come to a grisly end wrangling over a bottle of wine, he had kept the money and forgotten him. He had had a fine few days spending what the pedlar had earned. When he spotted Conan hanging around the cookhouse, Otto had kept his distance, his curiosity aroused. He noticed that the pedlar had lost a hand, but that alone would not have prevented him from doing trade with de Roncier, and it seemed hardly likely that he had found a new master. The only circumstance that might prevent the pedlar from working for the Count, Otto reasoned, was if he was after larger game . . .

Initially, Conan had been stubbornly reluctant to share his good fortune with his old friend. But Otto had dragged him into the forest and had loosened the pedlar's tongue. And then he had talked too much; screaming, begging, pleading. Otto did not like men who squealed like pigs. He had learned that the pedlar was not the only old acquaintance attending this tourney. Ned Fletcher was here, with the concubine's daughter, who was now the Saxon's wife. And Conan said that she had in her possession a pink stone statue of the Virgin Mary – a statue Otto knew existed, for he had held it in his own hands. Conan swore the statue had a heart that was worth a king's ransom.

Otto had long brooded on the incident when Gwenn had helped Alan make him a laughing-stock. At the time, he had accepted that the Dowager Countess had been mistaken concerning the existence of a gemstone; like Count François, Otto had dismissed the tale as nothing more than the embroidered ramblings of a toothless crone. But now, having heard the pedlar's garbled testimony, Otto was a wiser man. Johanna had spent several months with the St Clair brat, time

536

enough to stumble across the truth. If the pedlar's grubby sister swore the gemstone existed, the gemstone existed. Otto's fingers itched to claim it for his own. This time, he vowed, it would not be him who was crowned with asses' ears.

His blood tingled with excitement. Otto wanted to be free from the tyrant work. He wanted to be free from worrying about money. He wanted to be free from Count François. In short, he wanted to be his own man. It was not that he minded fighting, he loved it; but he longed to pick his fights when he wanted, and not at another's bidding. Digging his spurs into his mount's flanks so sharply that they drew blood, he urged his horse to a gallop.

If he hurried, he would make the city gates by nightfall.

The Duchess of Brittany was most generous with Alan when he came to take his leave of her.

'So you are Alan le Bret,' the Duchess said, looking at him thoughtfully. 'A Breton captain for the Duke of Brittany. I must say, though you are dark, you don't have the Breton look. You're too tall.'

'I was born in England, Your Grace, near Richmond, and I took my name from the man who brought me up, not knowing my real father. My stepfather was the Breton, my mother is of the old Saxon blood.'

'Le Bret,' the Duchess murmured, frowning. She gave him a keen look. 'You say you hail from Richmond?'

'Aye.'

'Your stepfather could not by chance be Ivon le Bret, the armourer?'

'The same.'

'I remember Ivon. A good craftsman.' The Duchess gave him a pale smile. 'My husband spoke well of you, Alan le Bret.'

'You are kind, Your Grace.'

'No. I merely speak the truth. I am sorry you feel

you must resign now he is gone. Is it that you do not relish having a woman as your commander?'

'Your Grace—'

'I would never turn off a good man, Captain le Bret.'

'Madame, I know that. But I have sworn to visit my father. He is old now, and—'

'I understand. He's still at Richmond?'

'Aye.'

'I wish you God speed. You have your arrears of pay?'

'Thank you, Your Grace, I have. And I have returned my horse to your stablemaster.'

The Duchess Constance arched a slim, charcoal-darkened brow. 'Which of my husband's horses did you ride?'

'Firebrand, Your Grace.'

'And did you find him to your liking?'

'Very much so—'

An elegant white hand waved. 'Keep him, Alan le Bret.'

Alan blinked. 'K . . . keep Firebrand, Your Grace?'

Another airy gesture dismissed any protestations. 'It will save you hiring one for your ride home, though you'll have to pay to ship him to England.'

Alan was overwhelmed. The gift of the courser was largesse he had not looked for. 'You are very generous, Your Grace.'

Duchess Constance stooped her head to examine the stamped terracotta tiles at her feet. 'No. My husband would have wished it, I am sure,' she said softly. When she lifted her eyes, Alan saw they were moist. She cleared her throat, 'You may go now.'

'Duchess.' Alan bent his knee, and walked to the door.

'Captain?'

'Madame?'

'When you decide you are ready to work again, remember that I need good men at my castle in Richmond, but because of the edict banning mercenaries, it would have to be on a different basis.'

'Madame, I am very grateful.'

'Get you gone, Alan le Bret. And send my love to
Yorkshire, will you? Wild as it is, I love that place,
and count it my true home.'

Gwenn was uncommunicative as they rode to the
Norman coast.

They had sold the gelding Sir Gregor loaned to Ned,
but kept the mule. Alan drove their horses as hard as
he could, for it kept his mind off worrying about her.
They were on the road to Dieppe where he could book
passage on a trader. Riding hard would also serve to
keep his mind off the other, less altruistic thoughts
which leaped into his head every time he looked at her.

The countryside rolled past him unobserved. The
shape of Gwenn's lips made his own feel dry. The
shining tendrils of hair which escaped from her veil
and played about her cheeks made him long to reach
across and twine them round his fingers. Irritated with
himself, he would drag his eyes from her and attempt
to rivet them to the horizon ahead. But not long would
pass before he would realise his gaze was lingering on
the curve of her hip and thigh. Angrily, hating himself,
he would pin his eyes on that distant horizon. Another
moment would pass, and before he knew it he would
be admiring the way she rode, head high, veil billowing
behind her. He had not felt so intensely while Ned had
been alive. It was as though Ned had been a living
shield, and the strength of his cousin's love had not
only kept Alan at a distance, it had protected him,
keeping him unaware of the depth of his feelings for
Gwenn. The journey to the Norman port was far more
painful than when he had escorted them from Vannes
to Ploumanach.

Alan kept up such a hard pace that by sunrise on
the fourth day after the Duke's interment, they clattered onto the quayside at Dieppe. They hoped to sail
with the morning tide. It had been a beautiful dawning,

with the sun rising in unclouded splendour and the sea reflecting the blue calm of the skies. Alan slid from Firebrand, and stretched his legs. His thighs were aching; they had ridden roughly thirty miles a day with hardly a pause.

'Gwenn, will you hold the horses?' he asked, flinging her his reins and trying not to look at her. She was still mounted, and he wondered whether her legs were aching as much as his were. His conscience stirred. Perhaps, given her condition, he should have set a more sedate pace. Perhaps he should link his hands and squire her down from Dancer. But he couldn't trust himself to touch her. Nodding brusquely at her, he made for the gangplank of the nearest vessel, where a couple of loud-mouthed sailors were soliciting custom by proclaiming they had space on the deck of their ship.

Gwenn watched Alan march off with dull eyes, vaguely aware through her misery that something was upsetting him. He had been off-hand ever since they had left Paris. Wincing, Gwenn tumbled from the saddle.

A flock of black-backed gulls was bobbing up and down on the swell in the harbour, waiting for scraps of gutted fish to be thrown back to the sea; while above them a handful more wheeled and circled, buttercup-coloured legs trailing, bills ajar. Their cries hung thin and plaintive on the warming air. Gwenn's legs were so fatigued they were shaking, and she had pins and needles in her feet.

She was missing Ned. She felt the lack of him as a dull, persistent ache which sat in her belly alongside his child. Dear, kind, sweet Ned, who always had time for a quick smile and a loving glance. She bitterly regretted not telling him she loved him more often. She wished she had told him how much she appreciated his steady affection and his constancy. Poor Ned. She had known that he adored her, and she had meanly with-held the full measure of her love from him, holding out for . . . For what? Something better? There was nothing better than what Ned had to offer, and now that it was too late, now that Ned was gone, she could see that. She had been his world. He had put her first, and would always have done so, and that made his love the purest, cleanest love there was. She was no soothsayer, but she knew that whatever God planned for her future, no man would ever love her as Ned had done, wholeheartedly and unreservedly. He had made her feel safe, and she, ungrateful wench that she was, had begun to chafe at his love, to feel bound by it. Well, God had snatched Ned from her. She was on her own.

Gwenn turned her face into Dancer's warm shoulder and stifled a groan. Why was it that she had had to lose Ned before she had learnt to appreciate him?

Dancer whickered softly at her.

'No doubt you are as relieved as I that we've stopped, Dancer,' Gwenn murmured, patting the proud arch of the mare's neck. 'Alan has been a slave driver, hasn't he? Do you think he grieves for Duke Geoffrey as well as Ned, Dancer? Do you think that's what ails him?'

One of the sailors had taken Alan onto the deck of the merchantman. He had his back to her and was talking to someone, no doubt the ship's captain. Wearily, Gwenn shook her numbed feet in turn, and while she waited for the blood to flow, she rested against the satin coat of her mother's mare, and considered Alan. In his cold, efficient way, he was her rock in this latest tragedy. Gwenn didn't know why she had gone through that pretence of hiring him, for it had been a pretence, and they both had known it. Had Alan been Ned, she would have been able to ask him outright for help. But Alan was not Ned, and blurred with grief as her thoughts had been, she had been desperately afraid that Alan might refuse her request. She could not have withstood his rejection. Her feelings for Alan had never been the least like her feelings for Ned. The first shock of her grief was fading, and she realised that her relationship with Ned would always have remained platonic if it had not been for the extreme circumstances into which they had been flung. But Alan was different. Alan had always been different.

On the ship, Alan turned, and seeing her watching, half-lifted his hand in acknowledgement.

'Handsome devil, isn't he?' Gwenn murmured. 'I have always been attracted to him. At first I didn't even like him, but I have always been attracted to him. Why, oh why could I not have been attracted to Ned in the same way? Alan can be vile. And at the moment, he's . . .' She broke off, for Alan had concluded his business with the captain and was striding towards her, an odd, tight smile on his lips.

'Unless the winds change we'll be in England this evening,' he announced, with a touch of triumph in his voice. 'The captain isn't carrying a full cargo, and he is glad to have us aboard.'

'Good,' she said. 'And the horses?'

'I've reserved a bay on the uncovered section of the deck. Shall we go and inspect it?'

'Lead on.'

The first night in England, they secured places in a Benedictine guesthouse. Their cells were in different parts of the monastery, for the monks did not permit married men and women to sleep under the same roof, let alone unmarried ones. That night Gwenn chanced to be the only female guest, and there was nothing for it but that she must spend the night on her own.

'You'll be all right here, Gwenn?' Alan asked, depositing her saddlebag onto the pallet.

'I'm sure I will.'

They were standing close in the doorway, almost touching; the cell was barely large enough to contain the mattress, and there was nowhere else to be. It could hardly be plainer, with its peeling limewashed walls and stone floor. An unvarnished wooden cross hung crookedly under the single window slit. Under her summer tan, Gwenn was drawn and her mouth turned down. Alan felt uneasy about leaving her. 'I don't know what you've got in your bag, Gwenn, but it's heavy.' Alan's innocuous comment brought a rich blush into Gwenn's cheeks.

Her eyes slid away and fastened on the window slit. 'Oh. Th . . . there's n . . . nothing much in it,' she stammered. 'Only some of Ned's belongings which I imagine his mother might like.'

Alan grunted, and kicked the pallet with his boot. It rustled, being no more than two sacks stuffed with straw and sewn together. 'I hope you sleep well, Gwenn. The mattress looks lumpy.'

Gwenn almost groaned aloud. She had said much the same thing to Ned in the Bois de Soupirs on their wedding night. The rush of misery which accompanied this thought had her wrapping her arms about her middle. The coldness in her belly that was associated with the loss of Ned seemed to have grown larger and more solid with the passage of time. Would she have to carry this burden around with her for ever?

She forced her lips to move. 'My thanks, Alan. I'm sure it will be fine.'

'Good night,' Alan said, but he did not go, and Gwenn felt his eyes on her as she turned and began to fumble with the catches on her pack.

Head bowed, she answered without turning round, 'Good night, Alan.' Quietly, Alan closed the cell door.

Gwenn sank onto the palliasse and put her head in her hands. She had decided on impulse to come to England. Had she done the right thing? She felt so lonely, so alone. She wanted to talk to Alan, but he was making a point of keeping his distance, and she was afraid of confiding in him.

What would Ned's mother be like? She must be a kind woman to have borne a son like Ned, but would she welcome a foreign daughter-in-law? Perhaps it would have been better to have returned to Ploumanach. Gwenn was not concerned about her siblings' physical welfare, for she did not doubt that Alis would lavish every care on her orphaned brother and sister, but Katarin might be missing her. She resolved to beg some parchment from the monks in the morning. She must write to her aunt, and explain what had happened. She would confess that she had sold Ned's gelding, and she would promise to visit them as soon as she could. She must give Sir Gregor the money his horse had brought.

With this decision made, Gwenn trusted that the cold, hard, miserable core within her would melt somewhat. It did not. When her mother had died, her father had fallen to pieces. Gwenn was beginning to understand how he must have felt. People had tried to comfort her father by assuring him that time would ease his pain, but her father had been killed before that time had come. How long would it be for her? How long must she endure this?

Pulling the parcel that was the Stone Rose out of her saddlebag, she removed the wrappings and stared at it. 'Why? Why did Ned have to die?' Staring at the statue brought Gwenn no comfort; indeed, it seemed to unleash a rush of memories, none of them happy. The Stone Rose had belonged to Izabel, and she had died violently. Her mother had had a shelf put up for it at Kermaria, and she was dead. Her father was dead, and Raymond. And now Ned, who had carried the statue all the way from Vannes to Ploumanach and thence into France. It was beginning to look as though the Virgin, or what it contained, was cursed. It was certainly no blessing. With a start, Gwenn realised that she was in sole possession of it. Would the curse affect her too?

Misliking the morbid trend of her thoughts, she bundled the Stone Rose into its shroud and thrust it to the bottom of her pack. Let it lie there.

Sitting lonely as a nun in her cell, she thought about the moment when she had sat with Alan in his tent and it had suddenly seemed so very important that she accompany him. Overwhelmed with the brutal and sudden nature of Ned's death, she had looked across at Alan, and known she could not be parted from him.

She wondered whether he was glad to be back in his own country. England was unlike Brittany. The people were taller, more prosperous-looking. To Gwenn's eyes they seemed sharper, more . . . worldly. Their voices were alien. French did not sing on an English tongue; and as for their common language, she wished now that she had troubled to learn more than the few phrases she had picked up from Ned. He had always taken pains to speak slowly and clearly so she understood his English, but these folk gabbled nineteen to the dozen, and she could hardly catch one word in twenty.

Pushing her bag onto the floor, Gwenn unpinned her veil, removed her outer garments, and stretched full-length on the pallet. Alan was right, it was lumpy. Sighing, she pummelled the worst of the lumps to oblivion, pulled the homespun blanket the monks had provided over herself, and closed her eyes. Alan had said it would take a few days to reach Yorkshire, he could teach her some English on the way. That way the journey would pass more swiftly.

Having missed the morning tide, Otto Malait was approximately twelve hours behind his quarry. He slept wrapped in his cloak on the rocking deck of his ship, and hoped the soldier-guide whom Gwenn Fletcher had apparently hired was not an early riser. When Otto had set out after her, he had not bargained on the trail leading him to England. It had cost him to buy passage across the Channel, and he was determined to snare Mistress Fletcher before it cost him much more. As Otto shifted angrily on his hard board bed and waited for sleep, he ground his stained teeth and hoped the damned gemstone would be worth it.

After another day riding the horses into the ground, Alan pulled up at dusk outside an inn whose creaking board depicted a lanky bird, proclaiming it to be The Crane.

'I'm sorry, Gwenn,' Alan apologised, 'there's a Gilbertine nunnery a few miles ahead, and I hoped we would reach it by nightfall. We could have stayed there, but I misjudged the distance, and we must stop here or sleep by the road.' He dismounted, went to Dancer's head, and stroked the mare's nose.

'What's wrong with this place?' Gwenn asked. Despite the hard pace they had kept up, she had enjoyed their ride. Against all expectation, it seemed she had shed some of her burden of grief at the Benedictine monastery. A casual glance did not reveal anything alarming about the roadside tavern. True, the sign could have done with repainting, but the doorstep had been swept clean, and someone had planted a profusion of marigolds in pots along the wall. 'It doesn't look any worse than the others we have passed, in fact it's pretty.'

'It's no worse than the others, but I fear we shall have to sleep in the common room, for I doubt there's a private chamber.'

Gwenn thought she understood Alan's hesitation. Members of the knightly classes usually stayed in the monasteries, as they had done the previous night, while the lower orders confined themselves to the inns and taverns dotted across the countryside. It was the same in Brittany. 'I'm not proud, Alan,' she said. 'I'll take my chance with the fleas in the common chamber. To tell you the truth, last night was the first night I have ever slept on my own; before I always slept with Katarin, and Philippe, and—'

'And Ned,' Alan supplied, rather sharply Gwenn thought.

'And Ned, aye. And I must confess I didn't like it much last night. I felt lonely.' Heaving herself out of the saddle, she grabbed Alan's arm for support. 'Holy Mother, I'm stiff,' she admitted, and then she became aware that Alan stood like a menhir. She frowned, and released him. He was staring at her face.

'It's good to see you looking better, Gwenn,' he said, at last. 'I'll see if they have a private chamber.'

'But Alan, I just told you . . .' But Alan was already striding through the inn door and she was objecting to thin air. Throwing the animals' reins loosely round a bramble, Gwenn followed him into the inn.

'I'm sorry, sir,' the landlord was saying, in English that was as clear as Ned's had been. 'We've only the one chamber up top. Your lady will have to sleep along with the rest of us.'

'Damn!' As Gwenn moved into Alan's line of vision, his cheeks darkened.

'I don't mind where I sleep, landlord,' Gwenn smiled. 'Your common chamber will suit me very well.'

'Very good, mistress. Would you care for some supper? We have the usual joints of ham, but as it's getting late in the year it's on the dry side. You might find the fish more to your taste. My wife has baked a fine perch tonight and we've a thick vegetable broth; or if you'd rather, we've salted eels and shellfish . . .'

Gwenn and another woman, a merchant's wife, were the first to join the landlord's three children in the upper chamber. A large room, it was reached by a stepladder from the tavern below. The common bed-chamber was more of a loft than a room, and the only place where an adult could stand unstooped was in its centre, on account of the angle of the rafters. A lantern dangled from a hook in the central beam.

Notwithstanding the lack of headspace, Gwenn claimed a spot at the edge of the chamber where rafters met floor. She dug Ned's cloak, the one that had been her father's, out of her saddlebag, and spread it out on the rough-hewn boards. There were no palliasses here. Carefully placing her bag where she could use it as a pillow, she doused her candle, cocooned herself in her mantle, and set about courting sleep. Would Alan lie beside her when he came up? She hoped so. The thought had her stomach fluttering. She did not relish the thought of wakening with a complete stranger beside her and, more than that, she wanted Alan beside her, to have him close. She could never love Alan as she had loved Ned, but she desired him, there was no point in pretending otherwise to herself. She wanted him to come and lie beside her. She would like it if he kissed her, she knew she would. Lying on the boards, she tried to imagine him kissing her, and then, abruptly, she stopped herself. What was she doing? He had been very aloof of late. What did he think of her?

The merchant's wife began to snore. Mice scratched in the rafters. The landlord's children shuffled and groaned in their sleep. Gwenn lay awake, listening to the noises, comfortable noises, such as she had heard all her life, and she wondered why she was not falling asleep. After she and Alan had finished their meal, she had been yawning over her wine, which was why she had come up. But now . . .

She wished Alan would hurry. She would feel better when he was here.

She must have drowsed, because when she next opened her eyes, he was squatting on his haunches beside her, the dangling lantern making a silhouette of him. He was looking at her, and she had the impression he had been there for some time. 'Alan?' His saddlebag lay some feet away from her. Gwenn held out a hand and, after a momentary hesitation, he took it. His thumb moved slowly across her knuckles, and Gwenn felt the beginnings of a response deep inside her, in the tightening of her stomach muscles. He was close enough for her to smell sweet wine on his breath. 'Stay close by me, will you, Alan? I'm happier with you near.'

'How close?'

She could tell from his tone that he was smiling, and her heart rose to hear the old, teasing note was back in his voice. Since Ned's death, it had been missing. It's the wine, she thought, the wine has relaxed him. 'So no one can get between us. Please, Alan, I want you next to me.'

Abruptly, he shook his head and dropped her hand. And then the scales dropped from her eyes and Gwenn understood. Her unhappiness had blinded her to why Alan had been so remote. He had not taken a dislike to her. It was not that. It was not that at all, in fact it was quite the reverse. Alan desired her, and he was trying not to take advantage of her. Something clicked into place inside her, and she became aware of an overwhelming sense of justice, an overwhelming sense of rightness. It felt extraordinarily joyous. Yes. This was meant to be. This would slowly right the wrong in her life. Still uncertain as to whether what she felt for Alan was love or lust, Gwenn's revelation had her sitting bolt upright, and she cracked her head on the rafters.

'Jesu, Gwenn, be careful,' Alan muttered, and he put a hand on her hair and rubbed her smarting skull. His hand lingered, and she wanted it to, for she had been missing human contact lately.

'It's all right, Alan,' she caught his hand. 'It's all right. I understand—'

'Shut up, will you,' an irascible voice cut in. 'Some of us are trying to sleep.'

'Alan—'

He placed a gentle finger on her lips. 'Hush, Blanche. I'll fetch my things.' Alan dragged his pack over and prepared for sleep.

She waited till he was stretched out at her side, and timidly touched his shoulder. His fingers covered hers.

'Go to sleep, Gwen.'

'But, Alan . . . It's all right. I understand, and I . . . I don't mind.'

He rolled over, and their faces were less than a foot apart. 'Hush. You don't know what you are saying. It's your grief that speaks for you.'

'That's not true!' she mouthed back at him, happier than she had been in months. She loved Ned, and his death was a tragedy, but Waldin had seen they were unsuited. Would Waldin have considered Alan her match? 'I know you want me, Alan. We . . . we could comfort each other, and I'm perfectly safe, in case you've forgotten.'

He was slow to catch her meaning. 'Safe?'

'No harm could come of any . . . union. I can't have your baby because . . . because I'm already carrying Ned's. So you needn't worry about having to commit yourself to me, Alan. I know you would hate that. We could comfort each other. Just a little comfort, Alan. I . . . I would like that. Alan . . .'

'Comfort,' Alan muttered, and then his voice went hard, and she knew that he would refuse her. 'No, Gwenn. I can't.'

The need to be held made her bold. 'Why?' she demanded, as the tight knot twisted in her belly. 'Why?'

He smoothed back her hair. 'Because, sweet Blanche,' he was gentle again, as though he understood she hurt inside, 'if we ever make love, it will not be in the common bedchamber of a common inn with a dozen strangers as our witnesses. If we ever make love . . .'

'Aye?' The knot in her belly dissolved. This was not outright rejection. Alan's head was a dark shape against the lamplit rafters. He shook it, and she imagined him smiling.

'It will not be like that.' He sighed deeply, and she felt his breath as a warm caress on her cheek. 'We must sleep now, Gwenn. We've a long ride in the morning. Good night.'

Someone turned down the lamp. Alan settled into his cloak and, rolling onto her back, Gwenn gazed up at the ceiling. Half of her was astounded and shocked that she, a widow of barely a week, had offered herself on a trencher to Alan le Bret, but the other half knew it felt right. They were lying so close she could feel the heat of his body. It was reassuring. She heard him shift, and angled her head towards him. The lamp flickered, and it was hard to see, but she thought that he was watching her. She closed her eyes, and surreptitiously, shamelessly, edged closer, till her forehead was lightly pressed against his arm. She heard a break in the regular rhythm of his breathing and froze, vowing not to move again in case he pushed her away. After she had been lying still for what seemed like an eternity, she felt a light pressure on her head. She dared not move, and kept her own breathing light and even, in the hope he would think she had fallen asleep.

'Gwenn?'

She did not respnd.

'Gwenn, I know you're awake.'

She hardly breathed at all.

'Gwen?'

His hand slid down, and his fingers caressed the skin under the neck of her gown. Gwenn kept her eyes clamped shut. Alan gave another sigh, and then he rolled slowly towards her and eased her into his arms.

Gwenn decided she could allow herself the smallest sigh of pleasure.

'Sorceress,' his voice, amused, murmured in her ear. 'I knew you were awake.'

'I didn't think you'd mind. I . . . I only wanted to be held. I thought I'd feel better if you held me.'

'And do you?'

She felt her colour rise and was thankful the lamplight was weak. 'Aye. You don't find sin in that?'

'No. There's no sin in that.' He added something under his breath which sounded like, 'More's the pity.'

Gwenn wound an arm about Alan's waist. 'Good night, Alan, and God bless.'

'Good night.'

Comforted, Gwenn dropped easily into sleep, but Alan lay awake turning their conversation over in his mind. He had been startled by her reaction when she had realised that he desired her, but not displeased. He kept remembering what she had said, about it being safe. And being pregnant with Ned's child, she was right. She had said that she did not mind their coupling. Alan's pride wanted more than that. Alan's pride demanded that Gwenn should desire him too. It was not clear in his mind whether good women felt desire in quite the same way that bad women did. He saw Gwenn as a good woman, but . . . His thoughts trailed off, he was not in the mood for philosophising. At least it appeared that Gwenn thought she might be comforted by the act of love . . .

He rested his cheek against the softness of her hair, and breathed in the sweet, fresh smell of it. His loins ached. It was almost too much temptation. Briefly, he wondered whether any harm could come to her baby, and instantly there flashed into his mind the memory of his mother and stepfather making love in the room the family shared above the forge. His mother had been pregnant then, with Will, and she would not have consented if lovemaking threatened her unborn child; Alan's mother had always been the best of mothers. No harm then would come to Gwenn's babe if they did make love. He suppressed a groan. It was like a gift from God, every man's dream. The woman who was the sum of his desires was safe, and willing.

If Gwenn had not consented, he would have kept his distance till she was safely at Sword Point, but her consent made that impossible. He would go mad if he didn't have her. He was barely managing to keep his hands off her tonight, and that was only because they were not alone. Odd that, he had never felt the need for privacy before. Privacy was such a luxury that most men took their pleasures where and when they could.

Gwenn gave a moan of distress in her sleep, and involuntarily Alan's arms tightened round her. She was so slight, just a wand of a girl, with too-small breasts rather like the beggar, not at all the sort of woman he usually took to his bed.

Alan calculated that if they rode between thirty and forty miles a day, it would take them a week to reach Richmond. He had kept the patched tent that the Duke, God rest him, had issued him with. He had avoided pitching it for fear of what he might do, but now . . . They could make love in glorious privacy in the tent.

Chapter Twenty-Nine

It was harvest-time, and the peasants of England laboured in the fields on their lords' behalf.

Often they would turn anxious eyes to the heavens, hoping and praying that the weather would hold fair until the harvest was gathered and they would be released from their duty. All over the realm, peasants were united in a single desire: that they should be free to give their womenfolk a hand with the crops they had planted on their own narrow strips. Their strips were what counted; the crops that grew on them would ensure their families were well fed in the coming winter. Every day the farmers worked for their lords was a day lost, for they would not gain so much as a mouthful of the bread milled from the lords' grain. That disappeared into the storehouses of the manors and castles of England. An early storm, coming while the peasants were bound to the lords' fields, could wreck the fruits of a year's work. If their lord was generous, their families might not starve in the winter months, but an early storm would certainly cause belts to be tightened and faces to grow pinched. It demeaned a man to go begging to his lord, especially when he had slaved all year, and it was not his fault if God sent foul weather. It made him beholden. But then, despite what it said in the Gospels, everyone knew that God usually came down on the side of the rich and the powerful.

The old Roman road Gwenn and Alan rode along was covered in a fine, dry dust; their horses' hoofs kicked it into drifting swirls which hung in their wake, ready to choke anyone travelling behind them. The air was hot and windless. There was nothing to be gained by cantering, though they tried it from time to time; the air that rushed at their faces was no cooler, and cantering only made the poor, toiling beasts beneath them hotter than ever, and in the end the horses transferred their heat to their riders.

No, Alan decided, it was better to proceed slowly. Better to walk north as it was so warm. He didn't want a horse to founder. Even Firebrand was drooping. In any case, he found he was no longer inclined to gallop home.

Scarlet poppies studded the hedgerows and strips. The wheat wilted in the heat, its ears fat and heavy, ripe for the reaper. God's gold. The sky was a glorious, even blue.

They stopped at a village for an evening meal, bought freshly picked apples, bread, and mead from the tavern while the sun was yet up. Everything was tinged with rich, vibrant, harvest colours that seemed ready to sing.

'You'll want beds, I expect?' the alewife asked, eyeing Alan's purse and indicating the stairs at the back of the inn. 'We've proper mattresses,' she went on with a touch of pride, 'stuffed with fresh grasses.'

'My thanks, but no,' Alan said quickly. 'We must press on.' Gwenn blushed.

Outside, he squired her onto Dancer, and she gave him a smile of thanks so warm he felt it in his toes. Marvelling at the power this slip of a girl had over him, he mounted Firebrand and they trotted onto the sun-warmed road.

He chose a sheltered spot between some bramble bushes and a stream, and when they had seen their horses were content, Gwenn walked upstream to see to her toilet, while Alan pitched the tent. He spread his cloak over the meadow grasses and reached into Gwenn's saddlebag, which she had left open after removing her comb and her soap, to draw out her cloak. There was a thud, and a bundle fell out. Alan picked it up; his hand was already moving to return the bundle unopened to Gwenn's pack when something about the size of it struck a faint chord. Heart pounding, Alan unwrapped it.

The statue was cold to his touch and looked much the same as he remembered. He puzzled over the walnut plinth but then, recalling how Otto Malait had smashed the original, his brow cleared. Did this base have a secret compartment too? Idly, Alan gave it a gentle twist . . .

Gwenn took a long time; when Alan had bathed himself further downstream so as not to disturb her, she had not returned. He built a fire between the tent and the muttering stream, but still she did not come. Hoping she had not gone coy on him, he went to look for her.

He found her sitting behind a ripening blackberry bush in one of the last patches of sunlight, a cloth round her shoulders while she combed out her hair. Rooted to the spot, he watched her. He'd never seen her with it loose before, and it hung about her like a dark cloak, shining in the waning sunlight. It was even longer and more luxuriant than he had imagined.

He must have moved, for she glanced up and berry-bright colour stained her cheeks. 'I'm sorry, Alan, if I've kept you waiting. But I felt so dusty, I had to wash all of me, and my hair gets very tangled.'

'Here, let me.' Kneeling on the grass at her side, he relieved her of the comb.

'You start at the ends and work up,' Gwenn began to instruct him, but she broke off when she saw that he was as competent as any lady's maid. Her flush deepened. 'You've done this before, I see.'

'No . . .'

She shot him a look of disbelief.

Alan grinned, and deftly finishing one section of her hair, began on another. 'I had a mother, once, and when I was a boy, I used to watch her.'

Gwenn tried to imagine Alan as a little boy. 'Tell me about your mother, Alan.'

He shrugged, and spoke in a distant voice. 'There's not much to tell. She was tall, and when she was young she had dark hair like yours, but it faded to grey. She married the Breton sergeant at Richmond Castle, and for years she let me think that he was my father . . .' Alan moved behind her, working on her hair. The sun sank below the top of the brambles; and as dusk gathered in the valley of the river, the fire that Alan had lit began to glow. The evening stars dotted the heavens.

After a space, Gwenn concluded softly, 'So Alan le Bret is not a Breton after all.'

'No.' He gave a strained laugh. 'Christ knows what I am. A mongrel, by all accounts.'

'It only matters if you let it. You kept the sergeant's name, so you must love and respect him as your true father.'

Alan gave her a sharp look, and silently went on with his combing. Now that the sun had gone, he could no longer see very well, and he was finding the tangles by touch. Somehow she had managed to rinse her hair with rosemary. He wondered if her skin was scented too.

'Does your father – your stepfather – live at Richmond?' She tilted her head to look at him, and her hair rippled out over Alan's hands. As his fingers fumbled with the comb, he rested them for a moment on the nape of her neck.

'Will I . . .' Gwenn went very still for the touch of Alan's fingers disturbed her in a way that Ned's had never done. She swallowed. 'Will I meet him?'

'Gwenn . . .' Alan muttered, in a suffocated voice, and she half-turned towards him. Slowly, he lifted a heavy swathe of hair aside and pressed his lips to her neck. 'Gwenn.' He kissed her again, and when he realised that her breathing was as ragged as his, his hands were on her shoulders, impatiently turning her towards him. The comb fell into the grass. 'Gwenn . . .'

And then they were kneeling breast to breast, while the stream chuckled over the stones. His arms went round her, and he was holding her as close as he could, and though he pressed his head into her neck and she pressed hers into his, it seemed they could not get close enough. He heard a groan, his own, and gave a shaky laugh. 'I think that I had better finish your hair later, don't you?'

She answered with a nod. He drew her to her feet and somehow they reached the tent, and stumbled inside.

He released her hand while he wrenched off his belt and shrugged himself out of his tunic. Gwenn sat on her cloak, biting her lips. He dropped down beside her. 'You're not afraid, my Blanche?' Forcing the wild passion inside him to subside, Alan cupped her face with his hands and placed a brotherly kiss on her brow. She was wearing her green bliaud, the one with laces at the sides, and while he wanted to tear it from her and push her onto her mantle, he told himself to go gently. She would be used to gentleness having had Ned as her husband.

'Afraid? Why should I be afraid? Are you so terrible a lover, Alan le Bret, that I should quake before you?' She answered with bold words, but her eyes gave a different reply. She *was* afraid.

He smiled, attempting lightness. 'Aye, you should tremble indeed. Look,' he displayed his own shaking hands, 'look what you do to me. Are you so terrible a lover, sweet Blanche?'

'I . . . I do that to you?' Her hands embraced his, holding them firmly between them so the trembling stopped. It was a tender, innocent gesture that managed to fuel the fire in his loins.

Her eyes were dark as sloes. They were inviting. He let her keep his hands, and cautiously dipped his head, so his mouth found hers. It was the first time they had kissed as lovers, and it was very sweet. Her lips were warm. They trembled beneath his, and while she did not fling herself at him, she did not draw back either.

Her eyes were huge, watching him, and something in them made his insides melt. And then because the sight of her was threatening to make him lose control, Alan shut his eyes, fought down the desire to snatch her into his arms, and made his mouth explore hers slowly.

Her fingers tightened on his. She leaned towards him.

Alan's tongue traced the contours of her lips. She released his hands, and he tensed, half expecting this to be the moment when she would pull away and announce that she had changed her mind. But her fingers slid up his face and into his hair, and her other arm curled round his waist.

He groaned, and raising his head, opened his eyes. Gwenn lay relaxed against his chest, dark lashes fanned out across glowing cheeks. She gave an inarticulate murmur, and pressed closer. Then she was kissing him, raining hot, blind kisses against his throat. His breathing was uneven. So was hers. She pulled at the opening of his chainse and pressed more wild kisses to his neck, which burned at the contact. Her dark head was moving feverishly across his chest. Alan rested his hand on her rosemary-scented hair. Astonishingly, his palm tingled. Everywhere her lips went, he tingled. When she kissed him through the stuff of his shirt, he tingled. Helpless, he marvelled at the depths of emotion Gwenn stirred in him.

This was not the seduction he had planned. He had thought to lead her gently. He should be in control, but he was beginning to realise that he was in her hands as much as she was in his, and he was not sure he liked it. He wanted to be able to crush her to him, he wanted to stay in command of his senses, he wanted . . .

Gwenn's lips found his, and clung.

I must remain detached, Alan told himself, I must . . . But she opened her mouth to give entry to his tongue, and then he was drowning in need. Her hands were lifting the hem of his shirt, sliding up his

560

chest, disturbing his pulses. Clumsy with lust, he tried to caress her breasts, but her bliaud was between them.

'Oh, the devil with this gown,' he gasped, tearing his mouth from hers and scarcely able to draw breath. 'Gwenn?' He pushed her onto her back.

'Mmm?'

Her sloe-dark eyes looked drugged. Her hair was spread over their cloaks like a fan of black silk. She was adorable, she twisted his heart. He kissed her freckled nose, and tugged at the complicated lacings. 'This has to come off . . .' he kissed her shoulder '. . . Gwenn, help me. Show me how this blasted ribbon unfastens . . .' He was not so far gone that he did not notice that his request seemed to have startled her, for her eyes opened wide, and the wanton woman that a moment ago had heated his blood seemed suddenly to have reverted into an innocent, blushing child.

'You . . . you want my dress off?'

'Damn right I do.'

She looked away at that, cheekbones bright with colour, but she gave a curt little nod, and Alan decided that he must have been mistaken about her confusion for her fingers went to the bows and she unfastened her bliaud. She sat up and pulled it over her head, leaving her clad in a light undergown. Alan stripped off his shirt. She averted her eyes from his naked chest. He frowned. 'Gwenn?'

She swallowed, and forced her eyes to meet his. Half naked, Alan looked frighteningly . . . male. She was no virgin, but Ned had never lain naked with her, and the thought that Alan might want her naked had only just occurred to her. She found it disturbing. A covert glance informed her that a light sprinkling of dark hair covered his chest and arrowed into his breeches. Her mouth was dry, and suddenly fearful of what she might have unleashed in her companion, she tried not to moisten her lips, sensing he would take it as an invitation.

'Don't look at me as though you fear I'll eat you.'

561

Alan's sinful mouth curved.

'W . . . won't you?'

'Not unless you want me to.' His hand reached across to feel the texture of a long tress. 'Black silk,' he murmured.

Gwenn's scalp warmed. Alan's thumb found an earlobe. He caressed it. That warmed to. She leaned towards him, wanting him to hold her tightly but too shy to look at him, too shy to tell him with words. Her hand crept to his chest and ran over the dark hairs, reached for his neck, pulled his head towards her . . .

'Do you insist on keeping this on?' he muttered, plucking the neck of her undergown.

She managed to look at him. 'N . . . not if you don't want me to . . .'

Alan smiled with his eyes and cleared his throat to make his voice soft. 'No, I don't. But never mind.' He brought his lips closer. 'Come here, my Blanche.'

She wound slight arms round his rib-cage. Their lips joined, and their tongues tangled. He heard her moan of pleasure, and slid a hand over the thin linen of her gown to capture one of her breasts. Her body's instant response fired his senses, and sliding his hand to her other breast, Alan repeated the movement. The response was equally delightful, and he heard her catch her breath. Feeling as though his loins were on fire, he shifted his hand from one breast to the other, and buried his head in her neck. The scent of rosemary enveloped him. His mouth searched for the small patch of skin he could reach through the neck of her shift. She groaned, and shifted against him.

'Hold me, Alan.' Her voice, broken and husky as he had never heard it, disordered his senses further. 'Hold me tight.'

He moved his lips down, over the bodice of her gown to her breasts, and experimentally, tenderly, he bit the soft flesh through the fabric. She gasped, and lifting his head, he saw she was regarding him through dazed brown eyes.

562

He stroked the length of her body, and admitted, somewhat wryly, 'I would far rather eat you than your gown, Gwenn . . .'

She bit her lip.

He lowered his head and, keeping his gaze on her, nuzzled a breast through the linen. Her nipple tightened. Her eyes were cloudy. With desire? 'Take this off, my Blanche. Let me love you properly.' And without breaking eye contact, his fingers caught the hem of her undergown. He pulled it up, and with cheeks as bright as the poppies in the fields, she lifted her hips to assist.

Her skin gleamed pearly pink in the glow from the fire opposite the tent flap. Naked, and with as yet no outward sign of her pregnancy other than an attractive darkening of her nipples, she was more slender and delicate than he had imagined, and more beautiful by far. Defensively, she had crossed her arms in front of her, hiding herself. 'Oh no, sweet love,' he said. 'I want to see you.' Relentlessly, he peeled her hands away and pressed a kiss between her breasts. Her heart was racing, and her breathing ragged. He heard himself say, 'You're lovely . . .'

'Alan . . .' There was a catch in her voice, and definite need.

He stretched out beside her and drew her into his arms, and the feel of her breasts sliding warm against his chest wrenched a groan from him. It would have to be soon . . .

'Gwenn . . .' His lips travelled down, found a taut nipple, and he circled it with his tongue in a leisurely manner, giving her time to grow used to him while he tried to dampen his ardour for her. But it was difficult, the way she twisted, and turned, and clung to him.

Hands twining possessively in Alan's thick hair, Gwenn found she was losing herself in a mass of sensations that she had never known existed. The breast that he was devoting himself to was aching, wanting more of these incredible caresses. What was he doing?

It was so intimate, this kissing that was like, and not like, a baby's suckling. She had a tightness in her belly which, while it was a pleasure, felt almost like pain. Whatever it was, she welcomed it, for it made her forget other, deeper pains. Her neglected breast was aching for similar treatment from Alan's clever lips. Mindlessly, she guided his head towards it.

As Alan's mouth closed obediently over her other breast, he smiled. His Blanche was ready for him.

His hand traced the slight curve of her hips and, tentatively, he let his fingers drift across her pubic bone. She tugged his hair, pulled his head towards her mouth. Alan kissed her, fingers drifting lower. Gwenn squirmed like a siren against him, and he pressed himself against her, letting her feel how much he desired her. She groaned, and bit his bottom lip. Her nails were cutting into his flesh, as though she was afraid to let go of him in case he should vanish. She was moist inside, ready for him. Alan wondered why she was so shy about caressing him, surely no married woman could be as innocent of a man's needs as Gwenn seemed to be? But the hot blood was beating in his brain, and the last rational thought that he had was that if there was any doubt about Gwenn's sexual experience, there was no question about her response. He desired her, and she wanted him, and if all she wanted to do to him was to hold him, then that was enough.

He slid his breeches over his hips and eased her legs apart, moving the hardness of his thighs between her softer ones. Her eyes were shut. He wanted them open. He levered himself onto his elbows. 'Gwenn . . .' He stroked her cheek with the backs of his fingers. 'Gwenn . . .' Brown, loving eyes opened, and turned his limbs to water. 'Now?'

'Now,' she agreed. 'Only, please, hold me . . .' And putting her hands to his hips, she pulled him towards her.

His body joined hers as though they had been made for one another, and he smothered her gasp of surprise

with his mouth. She fitted him like a glove. He kissed
her with rough passion, and when her hands slid up
his back, they loosed a shudder of delight that shook
his whole frame. Alan began to move inside her, and
heard his voice, hoarse, call her name.

'Love me, Alan . . .' Dimly he made out her words.
Each thrust brought him nearer the edge. 'Love
me . . . as hard . . . as you can. Oh, Alan . . . Alan.
Hold me . . . tight . . .'

This last was unnecessary, for he was already holding
her more tightly than he had held any woman. He
wanted to be closer, to merge with her. 'Gwenn.' He
gasped his delight in her ear. She was kissing his neck
in glorious abandon, licking him, biting his skin. Her
hips arched to his, she twined her feet round his calves,
and pushed and pushed and pushed towards his every
thrust.

'Alan. Oh, Alan.'

Her soft, delirious cries filled the tent, the most
potent aphrodisiac on earth. He wanted it to last for
ever. What a transformation, he thought in wonder,
from the shy creature he had held in his arms a moment
ago. He felt his climax approaching. 'No . . . no. Not
yet,' he almost screamed in frustration. 'Tell me you
hate it.'

He was astonished to hear a throaty giggle. 'I hate
it.'

Startled, and put off his stride, he lifted his head
and looked into brown eyes that were as soft and welcoming as a man could wish. He was deep in passion's
thrall, but despite this, an answering smile tugged his
lips. He moved inside her.

Gwenn let out a gratifying groan of shameless
pleasure. 'I hate it, Alan,' she gasped, pushing at his
hips when he stopped moving. Insides dissolving, Alan
managed another thrust. 'I hate it.' He rewarded her
with another. 'I hate it.' One more. 'I hate it. I . . .
Oh!'

He was witness to the wonder which flared into her

eyes, and for one glorious moment she looked at him as though he were a god. Then, shuddering and pulsing all over, she closed her eyes and hid her face in his chest. Her delight was too much for him, and a couple of thrusts later, it was over for him too.

Berthe, the middle-aged alewife at the Sun Inn, stood by her cooking fire with her arms akimbo and, with eyes that had seen it all before, regarded the blond foreigner who had drunk her out of mead.

The last of her customers to leave, he was a large lad – a Norseman most likely – and currently he looked harmless enough with his helmet at his feet and his corn-coloured head slumped over her trestle. The discarded remnants of a meal sat at his elbow. Berthe knew appearances could be deceptive. She reached for a broom, and thus armed, approached him. Prodding him roughly on the shoulder, she did not wait for him to stir, but asked, 'You sleeping here, laddie, or will you be leaving?'

She didn't see him move, not so much as a flutter of the heavy eyelids, but suddenly one ham of a hand whipped out, caught hold of the broom handle, and before Berthe had time to drop it she was hauled towards two red-rimmed blue eyes and an untidy beard.

The eyes blinked. 'I don't like your tone, mistress,' the stranger said.

Berthe didn't like his, but prudently decided not to tell him. 'Sir?' She was not alarmed, all she had to do was give a shriek and her Alfred would charge in from the storeroom. It gave a woman confidence to have a husband like her Alfred. Simple, but strong, and completely devoted to her. What woman wanted more from a man?

The Viking released the broom and Berthe took a couple of precautionary steps backwards. 'What did you want, woman?' He scowled into his empty cup.

'I'm locking up,' she told him bluntly. 'And if you want to stop here, there'll be the price of a bed to pay

566

for. In advance.' Berthe had learnt the hard way, and people with infinitely more charm than this character had slept in her beds and blithely skipped off before sunrise without settling their debts. She was wise to that trick and was not about to let this one try it on her. The Norseman's bloodshot eyes were sharp and cunning, and cold as a wolf's, so cold they made Berthe want to shiver. He smiled, and Berthe did not like his smile any more than his eyes. He slapped a coin on the table and Berthe's heart sank. She did not want this one to stop here. Like as not he'd slit their throats in the night and skip off with the takings.

'I won't be staying,' he declared, and relief flooded through the alewife. 'I want information. I'm looking for a young woman, name of Gwenn Her . . . Fletcher. She's Breton; small, very dark, and travelling with an armed soldier. They were last seen riding north along this road. Have you seen them?'

Berthe remembered the couple who had eaten at the alehouse earlier and gone on. A nice-looking couple, obviously recently wed, and very much in love. She recalled the man calling the girl Gwenn. 'Friends of yours?' Berthe queried.

The stranger gave Berthe another spine-chilling smile. 'Oh aye. We go way back.'

The alewife didn't like the foreigner, and neither did she believe him. 'I've not seen them,' she said firmly.

The dead eyes narrowed to slits. 'They were riding this way.'

His gaze was boring holes in her, but Berthe was determined not to flinch. 'I've not seen them,' she repeated, and scooping up his coin, she tossed it back to him. 'Here, take this and be on your way.'

'They were seen this morning.'

'They may well have been on this road, sir.' Berthe made her voice as casual and convincing as she could, for though she had Alfred dozing in the back, this man had succeeded in frightening her. 'But they could have turned off, or they might have ridden past without stopping. Whatever, I've not seen them.' She made as if to turn back to the fire.

Pouching his coin, the Norseman stood up and his stool toppled to the floor with a crack that made Berthe wince. He was a tower of a man, no question of that. He caught her wrist and leaned towards her. 'If I find you've lied to me, woman, I'll come back and flay you alive.'

'I'm not lying,' Berthe said steadily.

Walking to the door, the stranger paused and threw her a final, terrible smile. 'I hope for your sake you're not.'

Gwenn woke at dawn to a chorus of birdsong and a luxurious feeling of warmth and contentment. She had slept properly for the first time in over a week. She was lying on her side, and one of Alan's arms was draped round her shoulders. His hand rested lightly, protectively, on her breast. She didn't move for fear of waking him and breaking the spell of the moment. She breathed in his fragrance, happy to drowse, happy to remember the joy of giving herself to him. She had not known, had had no idea, that making love could be so astoundingly beautiful.

How was it that Alan who had not said a word about love had managed to loose a storm of sensation in her, while Ned who confessed his love daily had left her almost unmoved? Gwenn was beginning to accept that Alan found her as attractive as she found him. Was he beginning to care for her? Did Alan need her as much as she suspected she needed him? He was certainly looking after her. But no, she must not get carried away because he happened to be a good lover. Alan had wanted to come to England anyway, he was not here for her sake. She must remember who she was dealing with. This was Alan le Bret, a man who prided himself on his independence, a man totally unlike his cousin.

As Gwenn thought of Ned, the miserable knot in her

stomach made itself felt once more. Her sense of well-being diminished. Making love with Alan had banished her unhappiness, but only for a time. She supposed she ought to be grateful for little blessings.

'Gwenn?'

She turned and, gazing into dove-grey eyes that were sleepy and smiling, and soft as the dawn, was attacked by a painful rush of longing. If only he would always look at her like that; as though he did love her, as though he did need her. Hastily, Gwenn pulled herself together. That tender look would vanish when he was fully awake. It was only there because they had been lovers last night. Besides, love brought pain. Alan had learnt that years ago. What would it take to teach her the lesson?

'Good morning.' She smiled shyly, and flushed, suddenly conscious of her lack of clothes and of their intimacy.

Reading her blush as shame, the grey eyes cooled.

Gwenn had known that soft look wouldn't last.

'Regretting it already?' he asked quietly.

'N . . . no.'

'You liked it.'

It was a statement, but she took it as a question. 'Aye. And so, I think, did you.'

He did not deny it, and with a sad ghost of a smile he let his fingers wander through the silky strands of her hair. Her mouth had a bruised look to it. Alan was tempted to kiss it and take the taste of her onto his tongue again. His loins throbbed, and inwardly he cursed. He had hoped to be free of the demon desire this morning. He stretched his arms above his head. They should be getting up, but he felt very lazy, very comfortable where he was. Forcing himself upright, he noticed Gwenn's saddlebag lay where he had left it by the entrance. That had been careless, in view of what it contained, but fortunately it didn't look as though it had been rifled while they slept. Perhaps a discussion about the contents would quell his ardour.

He told himself that he was not picking this topic because he wanted her to trust him, far from it; he was trying to distract himself from the feel of the warm, relaxed thigh pressed against his. He was trying to prove that he didn't want to roll over with her in his arms and make love to her just one more time . . .

Her eyes were on his mouth, and he wished they weren't. It was very distracting. 'Ned wasn't carrying anything valuable in his pack, was he?' he opened, cautiously.

Gwenn jerked, and turned her eyes away. 'V . . . valuable? No, I don't think so. Like you, he took to carrying our money on his person. Why?'

Smiling, he pressed on. 'And you? Do you keep things of worth in your bag?'

She sat up, cloak clutched to her breasts, and he couldn't miss the apprehensive look she shot at the saddlebag, nor the lines of tension which appeared round her mouth. 'Anything of worth? Whatever are you talking about?'

Alan's smile died. She would not trust him. She was not going to confide in him. Doggedly, he continued, praying she would change her mind. 'In France, at the tourney, I caught someone sneaking into the tent.'

'You never told us.'

'I saw no point. I thought I'd routed a thief.' Alan patted the purse which hung round his neck. 'You know I carry my valuables on me. I wondered if the man was after something that you or Ned were carrying.'

Her cheeks emptied of colour. 'No,' she said, very curt, and hunched her shoulder on him in that dismissive way of hers. 'Cutpurses aren't selective. They go for anything they can lay their hands on, don't they? There's no reason to assume your thief was after something in particular.'

'That was what I thought, the first time. But when I saw him hanging around the second time—'

'Second time?'

Alan wouldn't have thought it possible, but Gwenn had gone a shade whiter. Trust me, Gwenn. Please trust me. 'Yes, he was lurking by the King's cookhouse, eyeing my tent as if waiting his chance. I concluded he must be after something special.'

'I can't think what.'

'Can't you?' Gently, Alan reached for her chin, and brought it round. Her eyes were hooded. Crushing an overpowering feeling of disappointment, Alan added, 'I recognised the thief, the second time.'

'Re . . . recognised him?' She had forgotten to hold the cloak over her breasts and was twisting the material into a ball.

Fighting a yearning to slide his hands about her face and kiss her till she was senseless, Alan peeled his hand from her chin. Her lack of trust betrayed her lack of feeling for him, but the knowledge did not douse the fire she had lit in his veins. Where was his pride?

'I'd seen him before, in Vannes.' Alan gave her time to digest his announcement. 'Our sneak thief was a pedlar who went by the name of Conan.'

Frantic fingers clutched his forearm. 'Did you say Conan? From Vannes? Johanna, Philippe's nurse, had a brother called Conan, a pedlar. Oh, God. I don't understand.' She shoved her hair over her shoulders.

Alan threw what pride he had left to the wind. A few, simple words, but it was the hardest thing he had ever done. 'Gwenn, trust me. I'd like to help.'

The eyes that stared out of the pale, discomposed face were distraught, but this did not hide their astonishment. 'Help? You can't help.' Reaching for her undergown, Gwenn dragged it over her head, murmuring distractedly, 'I must think. Pass me my gown, Alan, I'm going to wash.'

Complying with her request, Alan held down a sigh and grabbed his breeches and chainse.

They were proceeding along another dusty English highway; Gwenn had been lost in gloomy reverie for hours. The sun was sinking towards the west, and Alan had not decided where they would stop that night. He saw her launch a furtive glance over her shoulder, not her first by any means. She had been doing that at intervals all day. Sometimes she turned her face towards him, but he knew she hardly saw him. She was riding in another world, and it wasn't one he inhabited.

'Gwenn, don't be afraid.' On impulse, Alan reached for her hand. 'What is it? If it's the pedlar, forget him. He can't trouble us.'

'How so?'

'He was murdered the same day that Ned . . .' A shadow crossed her face, and Alan cursed himself.

Gwenn glanced at the hand clasping hers, admitting she warmed to his touch. All day she had studiously avoided contact with him, half afraid that if she touched him, it would spark off the extraordinary passion they had shared the night before. Alan made her feel, and she was not sure she could cope with it. She did not want to become dependent on him. What would happen when they reached Sword Point and had to part? Gwenn could not bear any more losses. Gently, she withdrew her hand. 'Why do the good have to die, Alan?'

'The good? I doubt that the pedlar—'

'Oh, I'm not referring to him. I've been thinking about my family, and Ned, all of them good people in their way. I'm not saying that they were perfect, no one is. But they didn't deserve to die, Alan. I feel betrayed, not by them, they couldn't fight fortune. But I loved them all. God has betrayed me.' Her smile was crooked. 'My grandmother would have been very shocked to hear me say that. Is it blasphemy, Alan?'

Alan regarded her helplessly and wished he had a gift with words. An impassable gulf yawned between them. Gwenn was educated. From an early age she had sat with her brother and pored over his books. She could read *and* write. Her education enabled her to puzzle out the finer nuances of her feelings, and come to some understanding of herself. But while Alan spoke three languages passably well, he could neither read nor write. He had no mastery of words, and no glib answers. How did you counter grief such as hers? Biting his lip, it occurred to Alan that the most learned, silver-tongued churchman in Christendom probably had nothing to offer Gwenn.

She may not trust him, not yet, but Alan knew one way to take her mind off her hurts. He brightened and, quite forgetting that he was supposed to have worked her out of his blood, he offered her his hand again.

Gwenn's heart lifted at Alan's gesture and, reading the question in his eyes, she gave him a smile. Perhaps the carnal comfort Alan offered, however short-lived, was better than nothing. Blushing, she let his warm fingers close tightly over hers.

The trail having gone cold on him, Otto was seething when he rode into the village. Village? It wasn't so much a village as a stretch of common land enclosed along its length by two tracks edged with an assortment of shabby farmsteads. Empty stocks stood in the centre of the green. Pigs, hobbled by their hindlegs to stakes, were rooting around the common; and the village children were in the bushes, guzzling ripe blackberries, screeching and squabbling over the juicy fruit like a flock of unruly starlings.

Otto had been racking his brains ever since he had realised that he had lost Gwenn Fletcher and her escort, trying to guess where she was likely to be headed. Ned Fletcher had gone to Brittany from England with his cousin Alan le Bret. Was the concubine's daughter going to Fletcher's family? He could think of no other reason for her to be in England. Where was it the two English cousins had hailed from? Somewhere in the north, Otto thought. The word Richmond sprang into his mind. Wasn't Richmond connected in some way with the Dukedom of Brittany?

Otto wasn't about to travel that far, not unless he

was positive he would catch her. He drew rein by the brambles, near the children, while he mulled over his strategy, examining the cottages to discover an inn. A drink would slide down beautifully.

No inn. Otto swore, and the children nearest him turned purple, juice-stained faces towards him. The youngest – it might have been a girl, Otto was unsure whether the darned sack the child wore was a long tunic or a short gown – stuck its thumb in its black-berry-dyed mouth and stared.

'I'm lost,' impatiently, he addressed the children. They took a step back, blinking like wary owls. Select-ing his softest, gentlest voice, he went on, 'I'm looking for an inn. Where will I find one?'

'No inn here,' the elder of the children spoke. This one was definitely a boy, in chausses and bare-chested; he had freckled skin and a mop of badly cut brown hair which refused to lie flat. Some bramble leaves had stuck in it.

'Where can I buy food?'

Shrugging, the boy wiped blackberry juice from his cheeks and pointed a dirty finger at the nearest cottage. 'Try Henry Smith's. The others went there. His wife sold them bread and cheese.'

'Others?'

'Strangers, like you. A man and a woman. They had *two* horses *and* a mule,' the boy said, clearly awed by such riches.

'Two horses, eh?' Otto looked suitably impressed and not, he hoped, too eager. It had to be them. He beamed at the children. 'You like horses, do you, lad? Good ones, were they?'

Vigorously, the boy nodded. 'The man's was a wonder, a glossy chestnut racer.' He paused, adding fairly, 'The woman's wasn't bad either; a pretty brown mare with three white stockings on her feet.'

'How extraordinary! An acquaintance of mine has just such a mare. You don't by any chance happen to know if the woman was called Gwenn Fletcher, do you?'

The untidy head shook, and a bramble leaf fluttered to the ground. 'Didn't get close enough to hear her name. But I think the woman called the man Alan.'

'Alan, you say?' His tone had the children backing into the bushes. 'Not Alan le Bret?' Surely the concubine's daughter would never hire Alan le Bret as her guide and protector? It couldn't be him. On the other hand, Alan le Bret had been in service with Duke Geoffrey, and he was Ned Fletcher's cousin. It was possible . . .

'Don't know,' the boy responded. 'But Mistress Smith might.'

'Aye, that she might. My thanks, boy.' And Otto smiled.

Chapter Thirty

Sword Point Farm, so named because it was perched on the southern edge of a sword-shaped spit of land, was owned by the Duchess Constance. Agnes Fletcher and her late husband had been her tenants. Agnes, Ned's mother, suffered a great shock when her nephew carried the sad tidings to the farm. She had last seen Alan riding off in the company of her son, but instead of bringing her Edward back to her, he had brought the news of his death.

Accompanying Alan was a Breton lass, dark and pretty, with sympathetic brown eyes which were crowded with secrets. Agnes saw the girl's wedding ring, and something in her manner had led Agnes to believe that she was attached to Alan; but Alan had introduced her as Ned's widow; her name was Gwenn, and she had shyly announced that she was bearing Ned's child. Her grandchild.

'I've brought you the money Ned earned,' Gwenn added with a sweet smile. 'I know he would wish you to have it.'

Agnes realised that Ned's wife must stay awhile, so they could get to know each other.

Alan did not stop long at Sword Point; no blame to him, for he had reconciliations to make with his stepfather in Richmond, and was anxious to be on his way. Filled with grief as Agnes was at the tidings, she yet thought it odd that Alan should ride off without so much as a wave or a smile to the girl with whom he had travelled so many long miles. But her nephew had been a cold fish when he had left England, and Agnes had no reason to suppose that he had changed.

After five days Agnes felt she had known Gwenn for years, and she had to shake herself and pinch her arm to remind herself that a week ago she had not even met her. It was not hard for her to see why her son had loved her. Gwenn was kind, and patient, and suffered Agnes's many questions concerning her son with a tolerance unusual in one so young. When her need to know all that had happened to Ned was satisfied, Agnes started enquiring into Gwenn's life. Gwenn was hesitant at first, not wanting to reopen old wounds, but Agnes sensed she needed to talk and persisted, and after a few days it all tumbled out, and Gwenn told Agnes the whole, not withholding anything, not even the fact that she and Alan had become lovers on the way to Sword Point.

Gwenn had given Agnes a straight look and said with disarming frankness, 'I won't apologise, Agnes, for it did not affect my relationship with Ned. I never betrayed Ned. It was a comfort. But I do hope you don't hate me for it.'

'Hate you?' Agnes had taken her hand. 'I couldn't hate you. My son chose you, and you kept faith with him and have brought me his child.' Agnes guessed then that Gwenn loved Alan, and had loved him for a long time. She looked closely at her daughter-in-law, and wondered if she knew it, and then Agnes remembered how Gwenn's brown eyes had stared hungrily after him till he had ridden out of sight round the bend in the road. She knew.

'Does Alan know? That you love him, I mean.'

Gwenn gave her a startled look, and a faint flush stained her cheek. She shook her head. 'No, he doesn't know.'

Agnes tried to analyse what it had been about the two of them when they had first ridden up and she had seen the ring that made her assume Gwenn was married to her nephew. She recalled Alan taking the Richmond road, riding stiffly in the saddle, carefully, oh so carefully, not looking back. 'Why don't you tell him?'

'No.' Gwenn was adamant. 'He doesn't want to know. He doesn't need it. And I'm not sure I do. It will only lead to more pain.'

'But Gwenn,' Agnes began to protest, but Gwenn was having none of it, and changed the subject to the Stone Rose, and how she had come to fear it. When she had done, Agnes examined the statue Gwenn had placed on the scrubbed oak table, and the gemstone lying in her hand, and for a moment Gwenn's fear infected her.

'I have decided it must be evil,' Gwenn whispered. 'Everyone who keeps the Stone Rose comes to grief. What do you think will happen to me if I keep it?'

Throwing off her fear, Agnes ladled out some common-sense advice. She told Gwenn she was being over-imaginative. She was suffering from delayed reaction to the crises she had gone through. 'The Stone Rose is only a statue,' Agnes said firmly, 'and a statue – especially one which represents the Mother of Our Lord – could not possibly be evil.'

It was Holy Rood Day, and roughly a month since Ned had been killed. Gwenn had been at Sword Point for almost a week. Dancer needed exercising, and Gwenn had fallen easily into her old habit of riding at dawn. Ned had always ridden out with her at Kermaria, and she found herself thinking of him, but as the days passed, the pain of his loss, though still keen, grew less piercing.

The upper road from Richmond to St Agatha's was lightly wooded, and Gwenn liked to ride that way, for at that time of day she usually had the road to herself. Agnes had reassured her she was perfectly safe on that path, for it snaked round the White Canons' monastery at Easby – the nearest village to Sword Point – and no outlaw in his right mind ever attacked anyone so close to habitation. From the road, Gwenn could not see the abbey or St Agatha's Church which the White Canons attended, for their pale stone walls lay beyond a shifting screen of beech, hazel and oak. The trees were trying on their September colours, and ambers and golds were beginning to blend with the green. They would soon lose their leaves, but for another week or so, the abbey remained concealed. Squirrels leapt and darted among the trees and dropped cob-nut husks onto the road. Pigeons clattered in and out of elders, gorging themselves on the dark, shiny berries. Rooks cawed, and the wind carried the rich, damp scents of autumn.

That Holy Rood Day, Gwen came upon a White Canon from Easby Abbey. He was a garrulous Englishman, with a sun-burned face and an unmonkish pride in his French which bordered on boasting. On discovering Gwenn's fluency in that tongue, the canon eagerly displayed his erudition and spoke at length about his business in Richmond.

Gwenn gave him half an ear, for she was wondering what Alan had been doing this past week. The love-making had enchanted her, it had been more sweet and tender than she could ever have imagined. And on their way north, they had made love often after that first, glorious time. Each time it had been different, each time Gwenn had been more and more certain of her feelings for Alan. She loved him. Not as a friend, not in the gentle, platonic way that she had loved Ned, but deeply, fiercely, passionately. She loved Alan as a woman loves her man. Alan had had as much pleasure out of their union as she had done, she knew he had. She prayed that he reciprocated her feelings and that in time, he would reveal his love for her. But a week had dragged by. What was he doing? Had she misread him?

The canon, Stephen by name, rattled on. 'It is no private matter, as everyone knows. Sadly, we are in dispute with the castle over milling rights, and I have here,' Canon Stephen patted his chest, 'a letter from the steward. We are to discuss his answer in chapter, but I fear the matter is far from resolved. If the villagers at Easby prefer the convenience of our mill to that at the castle, I fail to see why they should not use it.'

Gwenn made sympathetic noises, though she understood that the castle miller would not want to lose the revenues gained from grinding the villagers' meal, any more than the canons would. Whatever this canon professed, the row concerned tithes, not the villagers' convenience.

Canon Stephen seemed to come to the conclusion that he ought not to be discussing the abbey's business so freely, for he changed the subject. 'You speak French well, my child.'

'So I should. My father was French.'

'And you are newly come from there?'

'Aye, though I count myself Breton, not French. I lived in Brittany.'

It was then that the canon loosed his thunderbolt.

'There's much traffic these days between Richmond and the Continent,' he observed. 'People arrive almost every day. Yesterday, while I was consulting with the steward, a horseman rode in. He'd ridden across England, having caught ship in Dieppe.'

Gwenn felt a frisson of fear. She hoped the monk was referring to Alan. 'Wh . . . what was he like, this horseman? Was he a little above medium height, with striking dark features, the son of the castle armourer?'

'You mean Alan le Bret, Ivon's lad? I remember Alan. He's back, is he?'

'He rode in last week.'

'No, I wasn't talking about Alan,' the canon said, blithely unaware of the effect his words were having on the girl keeping pace alongside. 'But this fellow must be a friend of his, because he came up to me and asked me if I'd seen him. I'm afraid I misled him – I didn't know Alan was back.'

'What . . . what did the horseman look like?'

'Oh, fair as an angel, and fierce as St Michael.'

'Not . . . not like a Viking?'

'Very like. Pardon me, are you feeling all right, my child? You're white as milk.'

Murmuring disjointedly, Gwenn took abrupt leave of the astonished canon and galloped back to Sword Point.

Agnes was still abed. Shutters darkened the one, large, ground-floor room of the farm cottage.

When Gwenn tore in, out of breath and with her hair hanging in a tangle about her cheeks, for her braid had worked loose, Agnes sat up in alarm. 'What's amiss, Gwenn? You're pale as marble.'

'A horseman rode into the castle last night,' Gwenn blurted, voice trembling. 'He's come straight from Normandy.'

Heaving up on her pillow, Agnes squinted through the gloom at her daughter-in-law. 'He's come, no doubt, with a letter from Duchess Constance.'

Agnes had been maid to Duchess Constance before she wedded the King's son, and now she was her pensioner.

Gwenn drew near to the bed and put both hands to her forehead, clenching her fists so the white bones in her knuckles showed. 'No. No. I think not. He sounds like a mercenary I knew in Vannes. He must have heard about the statue. He must be looking for the statue and the gem within it.' Perspiration dampened her temples. 'And to think I thought it was over. Oh, Agnes, I prayed we'd left all that behind us. I thought a new land would mean a fresh start. That statue will be our deaths, I know it will.'

Gwenn was only sixteen, but at that moment she looked sixty. She was Ned's wife, and petite though she was, she was carrying his child. In Ned's absence, it was Agnes's place to offer her advice. Agnes thought quickly. 'You could get rid of it.'

'Rid of it?' The great, brown eyes were blank.

'Yes.'

'But that would be . . .' Gwenn trailed of, chewing

a nail with desperate savagery.

'Sacrilege?' Agnes could see that her daughter-in-law was terrified, there were fine lines around her eyes and mouth that had not been there yesterday. Agnes pulled Gwenn's finger from her mouth. 'Don't do that, Gwenn.'

Gwenn started, jumpy as a hare, and curled her fingers into a fist. 'Sorry. But would getting rid of the Stone Rose really help? You said yourself – it's only a statue. Can a statue of the Blessed Virgin harm anyone?'

'Gwenn, in your heart you know the statue is not the problem. It's the gemstone that's attracting trouble.'

'I've come to loathe the Stone Rose.'

'I can see that. It's associated with past miseries. But don't let a lump of pink granite,' Agnes allowed a sneer to enter her voice, for it would do Gwenn no harm to realise her icon could be mocked, 'colour your life. It has become an obsession with you, and is blinding you to the real problem, which is the diamond.' Agnes could not accept that in itself the Stone Rose was evil. But it was Gwenn's belief that counted, and if Gwenn believed in evil, the statue had best be destroyed.

Gwenn went cold as she thought about it, as she numbered her sorrows. Her eyes skated over the beaten earth floor, and her mind sought for another way out. She had no option but to hide the gem and get rid of the statue, for while she kept it she was a marked woman, potential prey for every mercenary who had ever heard about the Stone Rose and what it was meant to contain.

She gripped Agnes's arm. 'And what about Alan? What do I tell him when he discovers a horseman has been creeping around, asking questions? Do I tell him about the gem? Dare I put it in Alan's keeping? What if he—?'

'I think, Gwenn, you should trust Alan.'

Gwenn's laugh was wild and bitter. 'Trust Alan? Are your wits addled?'

583

'I am his aunt, Gwenn. Never forget that,' Agnes said. Alan was due a measure of loyalty. And while Agnes knew her nephew had done more than his share of evil, she could not help loving him. And so, she believed, did Gwenn. This would be a test for Gwenn as much as for Alan, but Gwenn was yet to realise this.

Agnes was wrong. Gwenn had realised. Dropping her eyes, she murmured, 'My apologies.' She sat silently for a space, thinking. She wanted to trust Alan. She wanted him to love her. But she had never been able to put out of her mind the fact that he had once attempted to take the diamond. If he knew she had it, would he still covet it? Would he affect to love her for it? Did she love Alan enough to trust him, unreservedly? She sucked in a breath, opened her eyes fully, and gave Agnes a direct look. 'I'll hide the gem and take the statue to the river.'

'Aye.'

'And I'll take the gamble with Alan. Win all, or lose all.'

Agnes thought it a shame that Gwenn realised how much hung in the balance, for her decision was difficult enough without concerning herself over Alan. Agnes could not help her there. Gwenn had put her finger on it. It *was* a risk. But if her gamble paid off . . .

'At least I'll know where his loyalties lie,' Gwenn said, steadily. She squared her shoulders. 'The waiting will be over. I'll get rid of it, Agnes, and tell Alan everything. It's the only thing to do. Then there will be no more wondering. It might even be a relief.' Gwenn moved swiftly to the door.

'God speed.' Agnes blessed her with the sign of the cross.

The latch clicked. Light streamed briefly into the room and then all was plunged into dimness as the door closed.

Agnes sat, patiently waiting for Gwenn to return. She thought about her daughter-in-law.

Agnes no longer had the vigour of youth, and until Gwenn had arrived at Sword Point, she had been lonely. She thought she was dying. Unlike Gwenn, who had her life in front of her, she was not afraid of death. But Gwenn's arrival had given her something to live for. She liked Gwenn; Ned had proved himself a good judge of character when he chose her to be his wife. Agnes looked forward to meeting her grandchild. The Grim Reaper would come for her soon, but in the meantime she could fill her last days cobbling together some baby linen. Agnes had once sewed court dresses for a duchess, but this simple task was all her weakened eyes could manage now. While she waited for the final sleep to claim her, she would watch her grandchild grow, and die content.

In the night, the Yorkshire dale had been refreshed with rain. Now the sun was rising and the meadow grasses shone lush and green. Sheep ambled across the pastures below Sword Point, fluffy white blobs grazing on the rich grasses like slow-moving clouds drifting across a rain-washed sky. While the landscape was beautiful, the farm's buildings and outhouses were not. They had not been maintained since Ned's father had died, and a mournful air of neglect hung over the place.

Having decided to rid herself of the statue and the evil that seemed to be dogging her, Gwenn hooked up her skirts and dashed along the pathway which ran between two wooden farm buildings. She stopped at the tall oak whose foreshortened shadow pointed up the hill, pausing only to twist the walnut base from the statue and thrust the pouch deep within the fork of the oak's spreading roots. She had been quick to learn her way about Sword Point, and headed straight for the River Swale. As she passed the outhouse where Dancer had been hastily stabled, her horse greeted her with a friendly whinny, and such was Gwenn's state of mind that the familiar sound set her heart thudding. Clutching the statue, she pressed on, working her way round the worm-eaten farm buildings and onto the track. Her mind was a confusion of fears and wishes.

Panting, she checked the path which cut across the dale to the river. It was empty. High in the blue heavens, so high she could not see them, skylarks sang. Closer to earth, a flock of lapwings tumbled into view, vying with each other in athletic, aerobatic displays. Gwenn hurried on, keeping the Stone Rose close to her breast. The mysterious horseman who had ridden in from Brittany could be a messenger from the Duchess as Agnes had suggested, but Gwenn did not think so. If the horseman was fair as an angel and fierce as St Michael, he sounded very like de Roncier's Viking captain.

Was he after the gem? Did all of Brittany know her secret? When Alan had grilled her about the Stone Rose, Gwenn suspected he knew. But he had left her with Agnes and the gemstone had remained in her keeping, and Gwenn had concluded that he knew nothing.

If only he had come back to visit her lately, she could have had it out with him. But she had not set eyes on him since he left for Richmond. His neglect was a clear signal of his lack of feeling for her. Agnes believed she should trust him. But Agnes was Alan's aunt, and she looked to see the best in her sister's son. Gwenn stumbled towards the river. If only Alan was more like Ned, who was, even without the dubbing ceremony, more the perfect knight than any man she'd known.

A couple of bow shots ahead, Gwenn could see beeches and ashtrees stretching over the Swale. She could hear the water brawling over the rocky bed as it surged through the dale towards the gully where the waterfall bubbled and frothed like so much brown ale.

Someone gave a shout, and Gwenn whirled round. A lone horseman on a great grey was cutting across the pasture; the horse's hoofs were gouging scoops of emerald turf and throwing them high in the air.

Her mouth went dry. It was not Firebrand, but at

586

this distance Gwenn was unable to make out whether the horseman was fair or dark. Sunlight sparkled on a shiny horned helmet. Her heart dropped to her belly. The horseman was fair, like an angel, and a long beard tumbled across a wide, mail-clad chest.

Stricken with panic, Gwenn whirled towards the river, desperate for somewhere to hide, but she would never reach the beech trees in time. She could not outrun that brute of a horse. She halted, turned, and stood her ground. The worst the Viking could do was kill her, and death no longer frightened her, for out of her spinning thoughts one single strand stood stark and clear. The worst had already happened . . .

Since Gwenn's arrival, Agnes had expressed a desire to live out the first few days of her grief quietly. Apart from Gwenn's lonely dawn rides, they had only left the farm to go to Easby village where they had conversed with the White Canons, no one else. To Gwenn's knowledge, the only person in Richmond to know she was lodged at Sword Point was Alan; and the only way the Norseman could have found her so quickly after seeing the White Canon was if Alan had betrayed her. Alan must have betrayed her. Set against this, nothing was important; not her life, not even – may God forgive her – the life of the babe in her belly. Gwenn had wanted to trust Alan, had wanted him to be an honourable man. So much for her dreams. She loved a ruthless bastard of a man, and he had betrayed her.

Would the Norseman torture her to find out where she had put the gemstone? Would he share the proceeds with Alan?

The horse, a stallion, thundered up to her. The Viking hauled on his reins, and the beast came to a shuddering halt. Hot, horsey breath fanned her face.

'Well met, Mistress Fletcher.' Otto Malait flung himself to the ground and dived at her throat. 'I've been scouring all England for you.'

Outside Sword Point Farm, Alan dismounted gingerly, groaning in relief when his feet touched firm ground.

He had a hangover; and every step of the road from Richmond had set a hammer beating on the anvil of his brain.

He tethered Firebrand to a bay tree in his aunt's overgrown herb garden. The door was ajar. He rapped his knuckles on it, and the noise made him flinch. His nerves were shredded that morning, and he only had himself to blame. He had run into old drinking companions the evening before and had been drawn into lengthy reminiscences around the forge with his friends and his stepfather. He and Ivon were fully reconciled, and during the course of the evening, much ale had been drunk, and much wine. 'It's the combination that's the killer,' Alan muttered to himself, angry at his own stupidity.

There was no response from the farmhouse. Agnes was growing deaf. Wincing, Alan knocked once more, and raised his voice. 'Agnes? Gwenn?' His throat was as gritty as a mason's file.

'In here, Alan. Come straight in.'

Agnes was climbing painstakingly down the stairs from the loft. Alan helped her down the last few rungs. 'I thought you moved your bed downstairs because you find the stairs a trial.'

Agnes smiled. 'I do find them a trial.'

Alan led his aunt to the trestle and pulled out a bench for her. 'You should ask Gwenn if you need something down from the loft. Where is she?'

'Gone to the river. Didn't you spot her from the road?'

'No.' Alan rubbed sore eyes. 'I can hardly see out this morning.'

'Good night, was it, nephew?'

Alan groaned, sank onto the bench, and closed his eyes.

'Alan, I think you should go and see if Gwenn is safe.'

Weary grey eyes peered past hooded lids. 'Why shouldn't Gwenn be safe? She's only gone to the river.'

'No, Alan. I think you should go. Something has happened. It's connected with that blessed statue. She rushed in here talking about messengers from Normandy.'

Her nephew's head shot up. 'Messengers from Normandy? Who?'

'I've no idea.'

Alan caught her wrist. 'Think, Aunt. Exactly what did she say?'

'A White Canon told her a horseman rode in from Dieppe, someone she knew in Vannes. He has been asking questions. Gwenn took the figurine to the river and . . . Alan?'

The door cracked against its frame, and seeing that she was speaking to an empty room, Agnes shook her head and smiled.

Charging into the yard, Alan remembered his sword. In his befuddled state that morning, he had jammed it under his pack at the back of the saddle. Cursing the few seconds' delay, he dragged it out, buckled it into place, and flung himself on Firebrand. The farmhouse was surrounded with a split-rail fence to keep the White Canons' sheep from the cottage garden, and though it was down in places, his route was barred by a gate. Alan dug in his spurs. The courser cleared the gate with ease, and then they were galloping over Swaledale's springy turf, noses pointed to the river.

The greensward sloped gently away from them. At the bottom, in front of the trees which shielded the river from view, two figures were struggling. A hulking great warhorse with its reins slack about its head placidly cropped the grass. It was the horse that betrayed to Alan the identity of the mysterious visitor from Normandy. The animal was past its best, a lanky grey, long in the bone, and it was favoured by an old colleague.

Alan spurred Firebrand and was carried down the hill faster than the wind. Of all people, he wished it were not Otto Malait.

He was almost there, and not a heartbeat too soon,

589

for the Viking's fingers were a vice round Gwenn's throat. Her face was puce. She must have knocked Malait's helmet off, for it lay on the turf, next to the Stone Rose which had been separated from its stand. The wooden shards lay in the grass at Gwenn's feet, and the drawstring pouch was not in sight.

'Where is it, girl?' Otto shook her, easing his grip on her throat enough to let her speak if she would. She hung like a child's rag doll from his giant's hands, and let out a feeble groan. Otto renewed his grip, and weakly she tried to free herself.

Alan wanted to cry out, to shriek at Malait to release her, but he urged Firebrand on and bit on his tongue. Malait had his back to him and did not appear to have heard his careering approach. The Norseman was wearing a mail tunic, but his arms were unprotected. Alan had the element of surprise on his side, and he must make the most of it, for if he did not, Malait would not scruple at holding Gwenn as a hostage against him.

Thanking God that all his wits did not appear to have been drowned in last night's ale, Alan gripped his sword and bent low over his saddle. If he could charge past the Norseman and make a pass as he did so . . . It was a coward's strike. It was not the sort of blow that an honourable man would make, but what choice did he have?

He was almost on them, and with a sick sense of dread saw Gwenn's hands go slack and her arms swing loose at her sides. Gwenn had lost consciousness. Legs hugging Firebrand's barrel chest, Alan pointed his sword. A dozen yards to go . . . nine . . . six . . . three . . .

At the last moment, Otto started, and swung round. The pale eyes bulged. He dropped Gwenn and leaped sideways; but he was not fleet enough, and Alan's sword caught him a glancing blow on his unmailed arm. Wheeling Firebrand round, Alan did not pause to let him recover, but charged again. Otto snatched out his sword and backed to where Gwenn lay senseless on the grass.

Terror tugged Alan's entrails. 'No! Leave her!'

Otto's grin was lost in his beard. 'Come off your high horse and fight me on equal terms, le Bret.' Standing over the unconscious girl, Otto delivered a bruising kick to her buttocks. She made a choking sound in her throat. 'Oh, listen, le Bret,' he declared in tones of amazement, 'she's breathing. But not, I think, for much longer.' He bent over her.

'You bastard!' Alan swung his leg over Firebrand's neck so as to avoid making his opponent a present of his back, and jumped. His insides were liquid with fear for Gwenn. 'I'm down! Let her alone. Has she told you where it is?'

Otto straightened, and the look on his face told Alan she had not.

'If you kill her, you'll never find it,' Alan warned him, urgently.

'She's not told you?'

'Me?' Alan could not keep the bitterness from his tone. 'When I've already tried to steal it? Do you really think she'd trust a mercenary?'

The two men circled each other. 'Never thought I'd see you lose colour over a wench, le Bret,' Otto taunted. 'Or is it the thought of losing her riches?'

On the grass, Gwenn coughed, and her limbs made a tentative movement. She would have to recover unaided, for Alan's hands were fully occupied with the Norseman. Praying that Malait's mount would not trample her, Alan tried to clear his wine-fuddled mind. Firebrand could be relied on never to step on a human body; an intelligent horse would not harm anyone without good reason. But Malait's horse? Alan could not say what it would do.

Alan tried to focus his blurred thoughts. Gwenn must have removed the gem from the statue before Malait had found her. If Alan could distract him while she came to her senses, she might be able to mount Firebrand and ride to the White Canons for help.

Otto's sword sparked in the sun. Alan warded it off, mechanically. The blow jarred his arm and set off ringing noises in his head; but his fighting reflexes took over and his blood surged through his veins. Despite the ringing noises, he was still in command of himself. He could fight.

Otto skipped back and thrust almost at once. Again, Alan parried the blow, but this thrust when he met it sent him reeling; the Norseman's greater bulk gave tremendous force to his blows.

Alan's sword flashed, Otto bounced backwards, grinning, and the stroke went wide. Otto lunged, Alan's wine-soused feet were slow to respond, and Viking steel streaked silver fire across Alan's chest.

'Shit!' There was a diagonal slash across his tunic. His skin stung, but the wound was not serious. An inch closer, however . . . If he got out of this in one piece, he'd never drink again.

Warily, he edged round, trying to keep Gwenn at his back and Otto before him. He heard her moan, and closed his ears to her distress. He must keep his mind on his opponent.

'What's amiss, le Bret, afraid I'll disembowel your wench?' Otto made a half-hearted pass which Alan deflected with ease. The Norseman struck again, with more determination. Steel crashed, and a moment later Alan's sword flew out and nicked a lock from the Norseman's straggling beard.

Dancing backwards, the pale eyes fired. 'Waking up at last? Good. You were fighting like a woman.' Otto began his attack in earnest, and Alan had no thought for anything but his own survival.

Consciousness came back to Gwenn in uneasy stages. Her first thought was that the Viking had screwed her head from her shoulders. Her next was that her neck must be black with bruises, for the air burned hot as molten lead as it flowed past her crushed throat membranes. Her starved lungs ached; and though she was greedy for air, pain dictated that she must ration it, and breathe slowly. She was lying on dew-damp grass. As her battered senses rallied, her ears sharpened, and she was able to interpret the significance of the noises close at hand. Someone was panting. There was a crash, a grunt. More hard breathing. A groan.

Gwenn lifted leaden eyelids and pushed herself to her elbows. Dizzyingly, the meadow rolled and dipped, a great green sea of grass. A wave of nausea rushed to meet her. Pushing it aside, she saw two men. The blond one made her heart sink, but on seeing the dark, slighter form, it bounded in her breast. Alan! Her voice was disconnected, which was a blessing, she might have distracted him, and she could see he was fighting for his life. She tried to sit up. The meadow heaved and rocked. She didn't want to watch, but her eyes were drawn as though by a string to the deadly duel. They had sprung apart for a few moments to draw breath. Alan looked like death. His face had a bruised, exhausted look to it, his eyes were strained, his skin drawn tight across his cheekbones. He looked . . . ill. Sweat was pouring down his forehead and gathered on his brows. Impatiently, he lifted his arm and sleeved it. Gwenn wondered where Alan's gambeson was, he was not dressed for combat, being clad in a simple blue tunic she had not seen before.

The Viking, though breathing hard, was flushed with the thrill of the fight. His eyes looked ready to pop from their sockets. His chest was protected with a sleeveless mail tunic. He was ready for battle, and relishing every moment. Alan was neither ready nor relishing it.

While she steadied her rocking senses, Gwenn wondered what Alan was fighting for. For her? Or was he risking himself for the diamond? Alan's woollen tunic had a slash across it, and the sight of the red tinge on the cut edges made her blood run cold. Either way, it made no difference, she wanted him to live. 'God protect him,' she murmured, climbing shakily to her knees. With no conscious stratagem in mind, she hauled herself upright and staggered towards the horses.

'Yes, Gwenn!' Alan wasted precious time to shout at her. 'Ride! Ride! Ride for the abbey!'

Seeing his opponent momentarily diverted, Otto closed in, slashing wildly. The two combatants fell together. Swords cut and hacked. One of them cried out. Gwenn's breath froze, but it was the Viking who broke away, blood streaking from under his arm. She breathed again.

'The horses, Gwenn! Move!'

Alan's shriek of desperation set her legs moving like a puppet's. She reached the Norseman's bony stallion first. Grazing, with his head down, the horse had lost the power to terrify. Taking the reins, she looked up at the high warrior's saddle. The Viking's dreadful axe hung on a thong from the pommel. Gwenn hesitated. Alan had his back to her. He was keeping the Viking from reaching her, hair tumbled about his head and dark with sweat. She set her foot in the stirrup. She took it out again. She couldn't go. It wasn't possible.

'Go!'

He wasn't looking at her, but she shook her head. It was no good. She couldn't leave him facing that brute.

'For God's sake, Gwenn! I can't . . . hold him . . . much longer . . .'

And then the worst happened. While sending her an anguished look, Alan's feet slipped on the lush meadow grass and he went down at her feet. His skull hit the ground with a sickening thud. After a moment when time seemed to stand still, he opened his eyes and looked an unmistakable apology at her. Gwenn's heart turned over. Blindly she moved towards him. His lips framed one word. 'Gwenn.' And then his eyes closed and his head lolled to one side.

The Viking hugged his wounded arm close to his chest. Blood dripped down his sleeve to the stocky wrist. Glancing disinterestedly at Gwenn, he kicked Alan's sword well out of his reach. He stooped over his motionless adversary. His sword lifted . . .

Helplessly, Gwenn retreated, backing up against the

stallion. Sliding her fingers along the saddle horn, she grabbed the chased handle of the barbaric axe. With her breath coming in short, jerky gasps, she wrenched it towards her. The thong snapped. She had to act quickly. She needed two hands to lift the axe, but lift it she did, raising it above her head. A strand of fine blond hair waved in the breeze as the Viking bowed over Alan, and she wished she had not noticed it. It made the monster human, made it impossible for her to kill him. But she must kill him, she must, and swiftly. The axe-head glinted in the sunlight. Gwenn quivered to her core. She had never killed a man, she couldn't kill a man, but she had to kill this one, because if she didn't he would butcher Alan, and then he would turn on her, though that last scarcely mattered.

The Norseman's neck was white, and glistening with sweat. She raised the axe. She sent it chopping down, with a disgusted moan she twisted it at the last second, so the flat of the blade, not the edge, cracked against his skull. He grunted softly and dropped like a stone, right over Alan.

The axe fell from Gwenn's nerveless fingers. She hadn't been able to bring herself to kill him, but God grant she had knocked him into the next century. She had bought a little time.

Her knees softened. She fell to the ground and feverishly rolled the solid body off Alan. 'Alan?' She shook him. Alan's head rolled. Keeping it steady, she gripped his arm. 'Alan? Wake up!' His cheeks were grey, and his lips pale. 'Alan.' Not a movement. She shook him less gently. 'Alan! Oh, God, not Alan too. Please, God, not Alan too.'

She drew his head onto her knees. Blood. Her pulse pounded. His blood was everywhere. Tenderly parting the sweat-streaked hair, she found its source, a great gash in his skull. He had cracked his head on a stone when he fell. Glancing at the rich turf, her eyes fell at once on the culprit. The Stone Rose smiled innocently up at her from the spot where a moment ago Alan's head had lain. The pink granite bore telltale traces of blood.

Cold as ice, she scrabbled for his pulse and failed to find it. She was seized with the most hideous conviction. The statue had killed Alan, as it killed everyone she ever loved. The Stone Rose had killed Alan. In a moment she became a madwoman. 'No! No! You shall not have him! You shall not. Oh, God. Wake up, Alan. I need you! You can't die, you're a devil, and devils don't die!'

Frenzied, raging, she pushed him off her knees, pressing her head to the torn tunic to hear his heartbeat. But her ears were filled with the frantic drumming of her own racing heart. Wildly, she clutched his shoulders, but he lay on the meadow like a corpse. 'Alan? Alan?' She pressed her face against the bloody tunic. 'Alan,' she murmured into the warmth of his chest, 'I need you. Don't leave me.'

Alan coughed, and drew in a convulsive lungful of air.

Gwenn flew upright. The grey eyes were open and focused on her. Shuddering, she touched his cheek. His sinful mouth drew up at one side. He started, shot up, glanced at the prone figure and groped for his sword. 'Malait?'

'Out cold,' Gwenn said, lips curving with joy. He was alive. Whole, and alive.

Alan nudged the motionless body, relaxed, and sat back on his haunches. He rubbed the back of his head. 'I'm either dreaming, or dead. You'd never look at me like that if I were alive. Isn't that a look a knight's daughter ought to reserve for her Perfect Knight? I must be dead.'

'No,' Gwenn bit her lip to dim her smile, she knew it was brilliant, 'you're not dead. Though for a moment I feared you were.'

A dark brow arched. 'Feared?'

'Aye. I thought the statue had claimed you, as it claims everyone I love.'

'Love?' Alan's strong voice was heartrendingly uncertain. He caught her chin in a fierce grip. 'You love me?'

She had no words, but she nodded. His eyes were that beautiful dove-grey, as they had been that morning after they had first made love.

'Me? A landless mercenary? A bastard?'

'That last is my title too,' she reminded him shakily.

He gave Gwenn another of those dear, crooked smiles, and drew her to him. 'Oh, God.' He grimaced. 'My head.'

Gwenn drew back. He had her hand in a bruising grip, but she made no complaint.

'What hit me?' he said.

'Our Lady.'

'Our Lady?' It was a moment before he caught up with her. 'Oh, you mean that cursed statue.'

'Cursed is the right word. It *is* cursed. She has killed so many, and I thought she'd done for you too. I was going to hurl it into the river when he,' she indicated Otto, 'came upon me.'

Alan grunted, and released her. Turning the Viking onto his back, he examined him. 'Did you hit him?'

'Aye, with the flat of his axe.'

Alan frowned, and regarded her sombrely. 'He's dead.'

'Dead? Merciful Heaven, you mean I—?'

'I doubt it was your blow. That could only have stunned him. It was this.' He pointed at the sticky bloodstain darkening the Norseman's left sleeve. 'I must have hit an artery. He bled to death.'

Staggering to his feet, Alan wiped his sword on the Viking's trousers. Catching Gwenn's gaze on him and reading censure in it, he caught his bottom lip. 'You think me callous? You mustn't delude yourself about me. I'm not like your Ned.'

Gwenn smiled. 'I know.' Then, seeing Alan was white as whey and swaying on his feet, she took his arm. 'What do we do about him?' She pointed at Otto's body.

'Ride to the abbey and inform the White Canons what has happened on their land. They'll help us deal with it.'

'Come on, then. To the abbey it is. Let me help you mount up.'

Alan's hand went round her waist. 'Ride with me? Please?'

'Yes.'

The sun was at its height by the time Alan and Gwenn had finished with their explanations and the body had been brought from the riverbank. For the time being they were free to return to Sword Point, though they had both sworn to attend the next court session at the castle, where they would have to repeat their explanations at a formal enquiry held by the sheriff.

Alan held Gwenn firmly in one hand, the other was hooked round Firebrand's reins. On foot, they walked under the arch in the porter's lodge and started up the hill.

'That's over, for a while anyway,' Alan said.

'Yes.'

'I don't think we need concern ourselves with the inquest. Malait's a stranger here, and though I've been away, the people here trust me.' Alan shot Gwenn a sideways glance. 'I expect it surprises you to hear that people trust me.'

'It doesn't surprise me.' And it didn't, not any more. That morning, in a moment of blind panic, when Gwenn had seen Malait charging towards her and hadn't time to think, she had mistrusted him. But now she was calm and could see clearly. She could trust Alan.

'No? Gwenn,' Alan swallowed and, keeping his gaze on the road, spoke in a rapid undertone, 'you saw me at my lowest at Locmariaquer. I'd never tried to steal anything before, or since.'

'Alan, you don't have to tell me that. I know that, now.'

Alan's head came up and he looked at Gwenn, and his eyes lit up. 'You do?'

Gwenn nodded, conscious of a warm upsurge of happiness. 'I love you, Alan.'

His hand gripped hers like a vice. 'Can you see yourself living above the forge in Richmond?'

'I can, if you are there.'

'I'll never be one of your chivalrous knights.'

'I know. You don't have a chivalrous bone in your body,' Gwenn laughed, on a note of pure delight, and flung her arms about his waist to hug him. 'But you are alive, Alan, and I love you. And that is what counts.'

Alan pushed her back against the whorled bark of an oak, threw Firebrand's reins over a branch, and pressed his body to hers. He put his hands either side of her face. In expectation of his kiss, Gwenn closed her eyes.

He kept her waiting. 'I've no land,' he said, lips so near Gwenn's she could feel the heat of them. 'I work to live. If we stay in England, it will be hard. I cannot be a mercenary in England. I've a mind to apprentice myself to my stepfather and learn a different trade.'

She opened her eyes and smiled. 'You'll make the most ancient and unlikely apprentice in Christendom.'

'Ivon taught me much as a lad. I'll learn the rest quickly.'

'I'm sure of it.' His lips moved to hers.

She held him off. 'Wait, Alan. It's best if you know everything. My grandmother did have a gemstone, and I have it.' Gwenn explained it all, and when she had done, Alan's breath had stopped. He stroked back a strand of her hair. 'Did you hear me, Alan? I've money and the gem—'

She got no further. With an inarticulate murmur, Alan buried his face in her hair. 'Thank God,' he said, in a muffled voice. 'At last I believe you do trust me.'

'You knew it all?'

'Not Waldin's booty. I knew about the gem.'

'Since when?'

'Since that day our bodies first joined.'

'Alan,' she looked into dove-grey eyes, and felt his body one long caress against hers, 'I love you.'

Tightening his hold, Alan smiled down at her. 'Marry me, my Blanche,' he murmured unsteadily, 'for I love you.'